Case Studies in Contemporary Criticism

NATHANIEL HAWTHORNE

The Scarlet Letter

Case Studies in Contemporary Criticism

SERIES EDITOR: Ross C Murfin

Jane Austen, *Emma*
EDITED BY Alistair M. Duckworth, University of Florida

Charlotte Brontë, *Jane Eyre*
EDITED BY Beth Newman, Southern Methodist University

Emily Brontë, *Wuthering Heights*,
Second Edition, EDITED BY Linda H. Peterson, Yale University

Geoffrey Chaucer, *The Wife of Bath*
EDITED BY Peter G. Beidler, Lehigh University

Kate Chopin, *The Awakening*,
Second Edition, EDITED BY Nancy A. Walker, Vanderbilt University

Samuel Taylor Coleridge, *The Rime of the Ancient Mariner*
EDITED BY Paul H. Fry, Yale University

Joseph Conrad, *Heart of Darkness*,
Second Edition, EDITED BY Ross C Murfin, Southern Methodist University

Joseph Conrad, *The Secret Sharer*
EDITED BY Daniel R. Schwarz, Cornell University

Charles Dickens, *Great Expectations*
EDITED BY Janice Carlisle, Tulane University

E. M. Forster, *Howards End*
EDITED BY Alistair M. Duckworth, University of Florida

Thomas Hardy, *Tess of the d'Urbervilles*
EDITED BY John Paul Riquelme, Boston University

Nathaniel Hawthorne, *The Scarlet Letter*,
Second Edition, EDITED BY Ross C Murfin, Southern Methodist University

Henry James, *The Turn of the Screw*,
Second Edition, EDITED BY Peter G. Beidler, Lehigh University

James Joyce, *The Dead*
EDITED BY Daniel R. Schwarz, Cornell University

James Joyce, *A Portrait of the Artist as a Young Man*,
Second Edition, EDITED BY R. Brandon Kershner, University of Florida

A Companion to James Joyce's Ulysses
EDITED BY Margot Norris, University of California, Irvine

Thomas Mann, *Death in Venice*
EDITED BY Naomi Ritter, University of Missouri

William Shakespeare, *Hamlet*
EDITED BY Susanne L. Wofford, University of Wisconsin–Madison

Mary Shelley, *Frankenstein*,
Second Edition, EDITED BY Johanna M. Smith, University of Texas at Arlington

Bram Stoker, *Dracula*
EDITED BY John Paul Riquelme, Boston University

Jonathan Swift, *Gulliver's Travels*
EDITED BY Christopher Fox, University of Notre Dame

Edith Wharton, *The House of Mirth*
EDITED BY Shari Benstock, University of Miami

Case Studies in Contemporary Criticism

SERIES EDITOR: Ross C Murfin, *Southern Methodist University*

NATHANIEL HAWTHORNE
The Scarlet Letter

Complete, Authoritative Text with Biographical, Historical, and Cultural Contexts, Critical History, and Essays from Contemporary Critical Perspectives

SECOND EDITION

EDITED BY

Ross C Murfin

Southern Methodist University

Bedford/St. Martin's

BOSTON ♦ NEW YORK

For Bedford / St. Martin's

Executive Editor: Stephen A. Scipione
Associate Editor: Amy Hurd Gershman
Senior Production Supervisor: Nancy J. Myers
Senior Marketing Manager: Jenna Bookin Barry
Project Management: DeMasi Design and Publishing Services
Cover Design: Donna L. Dennison
Cover Art: William Jennys (American, 1774–1858), *Mrs. Cephas Smith (Mary Gove) and Child* (Detail), about 1803. Oil on Canvas. 41¾ × 31⅝". Museum of Fine Arts, Boston. Emily L. Ainsley Fund, M. Theresa B. Hopkins Fund, A. Shuman Collection, and Lucy Dalbiac Luard Fund. 1974.136. Photograph © 2004 Museum of Fine Arts, Boston.
Composition: Stratford Publishing Services, Inc.
Printing and Binding: Haddon Craftsmen, an RR Donnelley & Sons Company

President: Joan E. Feinberg
Editorial Director: Denise B. Wydra
Editor in Chief: Karen S. Henry
Director of Marketing: Karen Melton Soeltz
Director of Editing, Design, and Production: Marcia Cohen
Manager, Publishing Services: Emily Berleth

Library of Congress Control Number: 2005928461

Manufactured in the United States of America.

1 0 9 8
f e d c b

For information, write: Bedford / St. Martin's,
75 Arlington Street, Boston, MA 02116 (617-399-4000)

ISBN-10: 0-312-25693-0
ISBN-13: 978-0-312-25693-7

Published and distributed outside North America by:
PALGRAVE MACMILLAN
Houndmills, Basingstoke, Hampshire RG21 2XS and London
Companies and representatives throughout the world.
ISBN: 1-4039-4632-9
A catalogue record for this book is available from the British Library.

Acknowledgments

Acknowledgments and copyrights are continued at the back of the book on page 507, which constitutes an extension of the copyright page.

About the Series

Volumes in the *Case Studies in Contemporary Criticism* series introduce college students to the current critical and theoretical ferment in literary studies. Each volume reprints the complete text of a significant literary work, together with critical essays that approach the work from different theoretical perspectives and editorial matter that introduces both the literary work and the critics' theoretical perspectives.

The volume editor of each *Case Study* has selected and prepared an authoritative text of a classic work, written introductions (sometimes supplemented by cultural documents) that place the work in biographical and historical context, and surveyed the critical responses to the work since its original publication. Thus situated biographically, historically, and critically, the work is subsequently examined in several critical essays that have been prepared especially for students. The essays show theory in practice; whether written by established scholars or exceptional young critics, they demonstrate how current theoretical approaches can generate compelling readings of great literature.

As series editor, I have prepared introductions to the critical essays and to the theoretical approaches they entail. The introductions, accompanied by bibliographies, explain and historicize the principal concepts, major figures, and key works of particular theoretical approaches as a prelude to discussing how they pertain to the critical essays that follow. It is my hope that the introductions will reveal to students that effective criticism — including their own — is informed by a set of coherent assumptions that can be not only articulated but also modified and extended through comparison of different theoretical approaches. Finally, I have included a glossary of key terms that recur in these volumes and in the discourse of contemporary theory and criticism.

I hope that the *Case Studies in Contemporary Criticism* series will reaffirm the richness of its literary works, even as it presents invigorating new ways to mine their apparently inexhaustible wealth.

I would like to thank Supryia M. Ray, with whom I wrote *The Bedford Glossary of Critical and Literary Terms,* for her invaluable help in revising introductions to the critical approaches represented in this volume.

Ross C Murfin
Southern Methodist University
Series Editor

About This Volume

Part One reprints the Centenary Edition of *The Scarlet Letter,* a critical, unmodernized reconstruction of Hawthorne's 1850 text established by the Ohio State University Center for Textual Studies and the Ohio State University Press. This authoritative text has been certified as approved by the Center for Editions of American Authors and the Modern Language Association. Part Two includes exemplary critical essays from psychoanalytic, reader-response, feminist, and new historicist perspectives. Each of these essays is preceded by an introduction to its critical approach and a bibliography of further readings about the approach. A fifth essay demonstrates how several critical perspectives can be drawn on and combined. Part One opens with an introduction to Hawthorne's life and work, and Part Two begins with a critical history of *The Scarlet Letter* since its initial publication. Finally, a glossary presents succinct definitions and discussions of key critical and theoretical terms.

New to the Second Edition

In response to the comments of instructors who assigned the first edition, new essays by Stephen Railton, Brook Thomas, and Lora Romero have been included in the second edition. In Part One, following the text of *The Scarlet Letter,* a gathering of documents and illustrations presents some of Hawthorne's cultural and historical influences. All the introductions (to Parts One and Two, and to the critical essays) and the glossary have been revised and brought up to date.

Acknowledgments

At Bedford/St. Martin's I thank once again Charles Christensen, Joan Feinberg, and Steve Scipione, and thank for the first time Emily Berleth, Anne Noyes, and Amy Hurd Gershman for their work on the second edition. I remain grateful to reviewers of the first edition — William Cain, John Limon, and Charles N. Watson — and would like to express my appreciation to the reviewers who shaped the second edition, Kevin Chambers, Gonzaga University; Robert Coleman, University of South Alabama; Gregory Eiselein, Kansas State University; Russell Greer, Texas Woman's University; Susan K. Hagen, Birmingham-Southern College; Karen Hollinger, Armstrong Atlantic State University; Mark A. Johnson, Central Missouri State University; Keith Kroll, Kalamazoo Valley Community College; Robert S. Levine, University of Maryland; James L. Machor, Kansas State University; Vicki Lynn Samson, Mesa College; Roberta Rosenberg, Christopher Newport University; F. S. Schwarzbach, Kent State University; Greta Corinne Skogseth, Montcalm Community College; Gustavus T. Stadler, Haverford College; and Jim Wohlpart, Florida Gulf Coast University.

I am greatly indebted to all of the contributors to this volume. I'm especially grateful to Stephen Railton and Brook Thomas for helping me secure permission to reprint their essays, and again to Brook Thomas for allowing me to cut his magisterial essay down to a size that can be accommodated in this *Case Studies* format.

I would also like to express my appreciation to Mariella Kruger, whose informed and probing questions regarding the contents of this second edition were timely and helpful; to Katelyn Ellison, who, as part of a directed studies on Hawthorne, proposed a set of materials for the "Contextual Documents and Illustrations" section; and to my longtime friend and collaborator, Supryia Ray. She not only greatly expanded and shaped this section (which did not appear in the first edition) but also introduced it via a marvelously helpful and insightful narrative. Finally, I would like to express my appreciation to two wonderful assistants without whom this book could not have been completed: Carolyn Jeter and Linda May of Southern Methodist University's Office of the Provost. They have been ready with wit and wisdom — as well as assistance — at times when there simply weren't enough hours in the day.

Ross C Murfin
Southern Methodist University

Contents

PART TWO

The Scarlet Letter: A Case Study in Contemporary Criticism

Case Studies in Contemporary Criticism

NATHANIEL HAWTHORNE

The Scarlet Letter

PART ONE

The Scarlet Letter: The Complete Text in Cultural Context

Introduction: Biographical and Historical Contexts

Nathaniel Hawthorne, born Nathaniel Hathorne, Jr., was the son of Elizabeth Manning Hathorne of Salem, Massachusetts, and a man he hardly ever saw: Nathaniel Hathorne, also of Salem.

The senior Nathaniel, a sea captain, had no sooner married than he headed off to sea, leaving a pregnant young bride of twenty-one behind in the house he and his brother shared with their rigidly puritanical mother and three equally sharp and stern unmarried sisters. When the baby, christened Elizabeth but to be known all her life as "Ebe," was born seven months after the wedding, Nathaniel Hathorne, Sr., was off at sea.

As Nina Baym has suggested in an article entitled "Nathaniel Hawthorne and His Mother" (1982), life with four pious, stern, and eccentric women must not have been very pleasant for Elizabeth Hathorne, a young woman who had become pregnant before getting married. And yet Elizabeth was to stay with the Hathornes for seven years, a period in which she bore two more children, both of them conceived during her husband's brief shore leaves. The first of these was Nathaniel Jr., later to become the author of *The Scarlet Letter;* the second was Maria Louisa, known simply as Louisa.

Nathaniel Sr. was, as usual, at sea when his only son was born, and he set forth on what was to be his final voyage just two weeks before the birth of his second daughter. Not long after sailing, he became ill with a fever and died, in Surinam in South America, far from the Salem where he had rarely lived — and from the wife and children he had hardly known.

Nina Baym succinctly characterizes a man, a marriage that was hardly a marriage, and, consequently, a young mother's predicament: "He left Elizabeth a widow at the age of twenty-eight, with children aged six and four and an infant of a few months. In seven years of married life he had spent little more than seven months in Salem, and had been absent from home at the births of all his children" (Baym 9). It is little wonder that Elizabeth, given what we know about her in-laws, returned to her own family, the Mannings, shortly after learning of her husband's death.

The Mannings were prosperous, middle-class people who had established and developed a stagecoach line connecting Marblehead, Newbury, and Boston. The family was a large and seemingly affectionate one; certainly, we know that Nathaniel and his two sisters were doted on, especially by their numerous unmarried aunts and uncles.

Thanks to the Mannings, young Nathaniel received a solid education. When he seriously injured his foot while playing ball, the head of his school in Salem — the famous lexicographer J. E. Worcester — continued to provide the injured student with his lessons at home. This long period of confinement proved critically important to the development of Hawthorne as a writer; while recuperating, he read not only allegories like Spenser's *The Faerie Queene* and Bunyan's *The Pilgrim's Progress* but also plays by Shakespeare, historical novels by Sir Walter Scott, and popular Gothic romances. Allegorical, dramatic, historical, and supernatural, or Gothic, elements can be found in abundance throughout *The Scarlet Letter.*

When he was about thirteen years old, Hawthorne was to receive an education different from the kind available from schoolmasters and books. His mother took an opportunity to move herself and her children out of the busy family compound in Salem and into a house adjacent to the one where her brother Richard lived, near Sebago Lake in Raymond, Maine. Although Hawthorne was only in Raymond sporadically over the next two years and consistently for two years after that, his time there was as important to his development as the period of convalescence in Salem.

In rural Maine, Hawthorne developed a deep appreciation of nature. He became enamored of hunting and fishing, of walking and skating, of paths leading deep into forests. Because of this experience, the world of the woods held a powerful fascination for Hawthorne that resurfaced within the characters he created in his fiction. In *The Scarlet Letter,* Hester Prynne and Arthur Dimmesdale hope to find in a forest beyond the outskirts of Boston some chance for freedom or, at least, relief from their tragic predicament.

The Maine years drew to an inevitable end; in 1819, the day after his fifteenth birthday, Nathaniel was sent back to Salem. There, as a student in Mr. Archer's "New School," he prepared for entrance into college. There, too, he began to prepare for a career beyond his college career by beginning to work at the craft of writing. He wrote mainly satiric, parodic pieces, interspersed with similarly disrespectful poetical compositions. His models were *The Spectator* papers of Addison and Steele; his audience was at first composed only of his family.

Hawthorne continued to write during his years at Bowdoin College, back in Maine, but he also developed new interests. He had met Franklin Pierce, later to become the fourteenth American president, on his first trip by coach to Bowdoin, and, during his undergraduate years, he came to share Pierce's enthusiasm for Democratic party politics. Like Pierce, he was also active in the Athenean Literary Society. And, like Pierce, he was known for enjoying other activities that were less sanctioned by college officials.

The president of Bowdoin, who took an active interest in students' behavior, fined Hawthorne several times during his student days for gambling at cards, among other things. "When the President asked what we played for," Hawthorne wrote home during his freshman year, "I thought it proper to inform him it was 50 cts. although it happened to be a Quart of Wine, but if I had told him of that he would probably have fined me for having a blow." Those critics who find in *The Scarlet Letter* more approval than disapproval for the deeply conservative ways of seventeenth-century Puritan society might do well to reread this frank communication between a twenty-year-old Hawthorne and his mother.

Following college, Hawthorne returned to Salem, to which his family had gone to live several years earlier. The next twelve years, spent mainly with his family, were among the worst of his life. His letters to Sophia Peabody, the woman who was to become his wife, refer to his mother's house as "Castle Dismal" and himself as a "prisoner" in a "lonely chamber." A notebook that came to light in the 1970s suggests that these letters accurately represent Hawthorne's state of mind at the time. Before the notebook's rediscovery, biographers had speculated that the letters were highly imaginative and even literary in character — that they greatly exaggerated, in other words, the gloom and depression the writer felt.

After all, Hawthorne was writing Gothic fiction during these years back at home, as well as reading histories, especially of New England. Along with *Fanshawe* (1828), a novel with strong Gothic elements that he published anonymously and tried to suppress, Hawthorne wrote tales for magazines using pen names such as "Oberon," "Ashley Allan Royce," or "The Reverend A. A. Royce." He set many of these stories and sketches in the historical past that he found so fascinating. Literature, he once explained, "is a plant which thrives best in spots where blood has been spilt long ago."

Eventually, Hawthorne began publishing sketches and stories in his own name, some of them powerful works that were to be collected in a successful volume entitled *Twice-Told Tales*. Henry Wadsworth Longfellow, a former Bowdoin classmate whose reputation as a writer had developed more quickly than Hawthorne's, wrote a favorable review imploring Hawthorne to "tell us more." Even good press, though, failed to make writing profitable as an occupation, so Hawthorne decided, after becoming secretly engaged to Sophia in 1838, to accept a political appointment in 1839 as Measurer of Coal and Salt in the Boston Custom-House.

Hawthorne wrote relatively little during the years he spent in the dusty hulls of ships. For that reason and others he eventually resigned and moved, on New Year's Day, 1841, to Brook Farm, an experimental Utopian community. Technically an Institute of Agriculture and Education, Brook Farm was in fact designed as a haven for intellectuals. The short-range goal of its founder, George Ripley, was to provide its residents with a place to think and write while they worked only to supply life's basic necessities. But the ultimate philosophical goal of the place was that of most, if not all, Utopian communities: the regeneration of society.

Hawthorne had moved to Brook Farm thinking that, after a few years of living, working, and writing, he would marry Sophia and have her join him there. Unfortunately, the Farm proved a disappointment. Hawthorne rather quickly decided it was no place for Sophia. He didn't care for the work and found himself suddenly unable to write. Hawthorne was also less than impressed with the idealists who lived and visited at the Farm. From the Brook Farm days on, he was skeptical of people who believe that all social ills are ultimately curable. In his later *Life of Franklin Pierce*, he wrote that "there is no instance, in all history, of the human will and intellect having perfected any great moral reform by methods which it adapted to that end" (113–14).

In "The Custom-House," his preface to *The Scarlet Letter,* he refers to the "impracticable schemes" of "the dreamy brethren of Brook Farm" (p. 38 in this volume). And in the novel that follows, an essentially skeptical attitude toward the possibility of moral or social perfectibility is everywhere implicit. Puritan society, for all its efforts, has been unable to prevent the Reverend Arthur Dimmesdale from "sinning." The most good is done by his partner, Hester, who finally lives alone at the edge of the city and accomplishes what she does slowly, painfully, partly by talking, but mainly by listening, to the people who "brought all their sorrows and perplexities" to her, "as one who had herself gone through a mighty trouble" (p. 201).

Hawthorne married in 1842, the year after his sojourn at Brook Farm. His new residence was the Old Manse in Concord, where he and Sophia were to live for several years. Originally a parsonage, the Old Manse had been home to several writers before Hawthorne. The late Dr. Ezra Ripley had written over 3,000 sermons in the house, and more recently Ralph Waldo Emerson had composed "Nature" there, an essay that had helped galvanize the American Transcendental movement.

In general, Hawthorne remained unconvinced by the views of the Transcendentalists, whose writings were regularly published by Margaret Fuller, first editor of *The Dial,* a Transcendentalist organ. Their vision was far too hopeful, even idealistic, to satisfy a skeptic holding an essentially tragic view of the human condition. But, perhaps because Sophia and her sister were sympathetic to the movement, Hawthorne was cordial with his Transcendentalist neighbors when they called at his house to visit. He was especially friendly with Emerson and Thoreau, with whom he took long walks and conversed.

The years at the Old Manse were productive ones for Hawthorne: he published *Grandfather's Chair,* a child's history of New England; a second edition of *Twice-Told Tales;* and a new volume of stories, entitled *Mosses from an Old Manse,* that was favorably reviewed by Herman Melville. And these were pleasant domestic years for Hawthorne as well: he and Sophia were happy together and their happiness was compounded, in 1843, by the birth of their first child, Una. But, pleasant and productive as the times were, they certainly were not prosperous; the family became so poor, in fact, that at one point in 1844 Sophia and Una had to go and live with the Peabodys while Hawthorne returned, briefly, to live with his mother — just to enable him to pay the bills.

In his biography *Nathaniel Hawthorne in His Times* (1980), James R. Mellow relates that "for months, Hawthorne's friends had been making a concerted effort to get him a political appointment" (255). John L. O'Sullivan, the editor of the *Democratic Review,* put pressure on President Polk's Democratic administration, as did Franklin Pierce, a former U.S. senator who within half a dozen years would be running for president. (Pierce made Hawthorne's case to the historian George Bancroft, an old Bowdoin classmate, who happened to be Secretary of the Navy at the time.) As a result of his friends' efforts, Hawthorne found himself offered a job as Inspector of the Revenue for the Port of Salem in April of 1846. It was a position he could hardly turn down, since he was supporting not only a wife and child but also his mother and his sisters, who had by this point moved in with him.

For the second time in a decade, Hawthorne found himself working in a Custom-House. At first, he found the job "beneficially distracting," and it allowed him time for consorting with his fellow-writers as well as for staying close to his family, which grew by one when a son, Julian, was born. Finally, though, the business of managing subordinates — of collecting imposts, signing documents, and confirming that his name was stamped on paid-up cargo — became more than a little tedious. "The Custom-House," which follows this introduction and precedes the text of *The Scarlet Letter,* describes Hawthorne's boredom and frustration with the job. It also tells how he unexpectedly lost the position in 1849, after the Whigs had come to power in 1848 and General Zachary Taylor had succeeded Polk as president.

The loss of his post, combined with the death of his mother, was devastating for Hawthorne, but ultimately liberating as well. He plunged into writing with almost maniacal dedication. Had Hawthorne stayed on, year after year, as Surveyor of the Salem Custom-House, he probably never would have written *The Scarlet Letter.* With this novel, he not only earned for himself and for his family the comfortable living as a writer that had eluded him for decades, but he also established himself as one of America's foremost literary talents.

"The Custom-House," of course, does more than merely recount Hawthorne's job as Surveyor and how he lost it. It also tells us about his relation to that same Puritan past that he presents in *The Scarlet Letter.* Like Hester, Hawthorne feels somewhat alienated from and intimidated by "stern and black-browed Puritans" (p. 27). And yet they are his very own ancestors — the progenitors of the pious eccentrics his mother had had to endure for seven years. "What is he?" Hawthorne imagines one of his forefathers murmuring to another from a shadow world beyond the grave. "A writer of story-books! What kind of a business in life, — what mode of glorifying God, or being serviceable to mankind in his day and generation, — may that be? Why, the degenerate fellow might as well have been a fiddler!" (p. 27). Hawthorne, we realize, took on the Surveyor's job not only to alleviate his financial burdens but also to prove himself to his forebears — or, at least, to that conservative and old-fashioned side of himself that he allows to speak through imagined ancestral voices.

"The Custom-House" makes us realize that Hawthorne was descended from New England Puritans not unlike those he describes in the first pages of *The Scarlet Letter.* In the novel's first chapter, he speaks of "bearded men, in sad-colored garments and gray, steeple-crowned hats, intermixed with women, some wearing hoods" (p. 53), and a chapter later he says that these early Boston settlers were "people amongst whom religion and law were almost identical" (p. 55). In "The Custom-House," he speaks of his own "first ancestor," who came to Massachusetts from England as a "grave, bearded, sable-cloaked, and steeple-crowned progenitor" (p. 26).

This ancestor, William Hathorne — "who came so early [in 1630], with his Bible and his sword" — is presented as a man for whom "religion and law" must have been "almost identical":

> He was a soldier, legislator, judge; he was a ruler in the Church; he had all the Puritanic traits, both good and evil. He was likewise a bitter persecutor; as witness the Quakers, who have remembered him in their histories, and relate an incident of his hard severity towards a woman of their sect. (27)

For those who have read *The Scarlet Letter,* it is difficult not to wonder if Hawthorne had that woman in mind when he created his heroine, Hester Prynne. No Quaker, she is nonetheless the victim of Puritan judges who have acted toward her with "hard severity" at best.

Next in line among Hawthorne's ancestors stood another Puritan judge. This one, John Hathorne, was involved in the now-infamous Salem witch trials of 1692. According to "the histories that Nathaniel Hawthorne read" as a young man, John Hathorne was a "stern, relentless prosecutor" who believed that "Satan enticed followers into his service and used them in his special warfare against New England." Thus, as Arlin Turner explains in *Nathaniel Hawthorne: A Biography* (1980),

John Hathorne "saw it his duty to discover any who had joined the devil's band and to extract a confession, . . . evidence that could be introduced at the [witchcraft] trials later" (64). Unlike one of the other two judges, Samuel Sewall, John Hathorne never repented of his part in one of the worst atrocities committed by an early North American colonist.

As readers of *The Scarlet Letter,* we may be tempted once again to make connections among history, Hawthorne's family history, and his most famous work of fiction. We may be tempted as well to wonder if the novel itself is not some belated act of repentance, an expression of regret by Nathaniel Hawthorne for the sins of an ancestor. To be sure, Hester Prynne has not been accused of witchcraft; rather, she has borne a child fathered by someone other than her elderly — and long-absent — husband. But the sympathetically portrayed heroine of *The Scarlet Letter* is the victim of magistrates who act with "hard severity," even when they believe that they are acting mercifully.

That severity is evident even from the words of a minor character in the novel who, a Puritan himself, does not see the magistrates' judgment as harsh. "Now, good Sir," a "townsman" explains to the "stranger," who turns out to be Hester's long-lost husband:

> "Our Massachusetts magistracy, bethinking themselves that this woman is youthful and fair, and doubtless was strongly tempted to her fall; — and that, moreover, as is most likely, her husband may be at the bottom of the sea; — they have not been bold to put in force the extremity of our righteous law against her. The penalty thereof is death. But, in their great mercy and tenderness of heart, they have doomed Mistress Prynne to stand only a space of three hours on the platform of the pillory, and then and thereafter, for the remainder of her natural life, to wear a mark of shame upon her bosom." (p. 64)

Hester, unlike alleged witches judged in the Salem witchcraft trials, utters no curse against her judges while standing on the pillory platform, wearing her mark of shame. In fact, she speaks only the following words — "I will not speak!" (p. 68) — when exhorted to confess the name of her sexual partner before Governor Bellingham and the assembled multitude. But her silence itself is an indication of her tragic alienation from a harsh society whose religion and law are almost identical. And so, too, is the scarlet *A* on her breast: "It had the effect of a spell, taking her out of the ordinary relations with humanity, and inclosing her in a sphere by herself" (p. 58). She is no less isolated than an accused witch — or a Quaker among Puritans.

Of course, in the "Custom-House," several pages after that on which we read about Hawthorne's stern first American ancestor, we are told that the source, or historical prototype, for Hester Prynne was neither a Quaker woman harshly dealt with by William Hathorne nor a woman prosecuted as a witch by his son John. We are told, rather, that the source for Hester Prynne was Hester Prynne herself. Hawthorne writes that "one idle and rainy day," while he was "poking and burrowing into the heaped-up rubbish in the corner" of the Salem Custom-House, where he served as Surveyor, he came upon "a small package, carefully done up in a piece of ancient yellow parchment" (p. 41) containing the papers of a long-dead predecessor, an "ancient Surveyor" named Jonathan Pue.

> But the object that most drew my attention, in the mysterious package, was a certain affair of fine red cloth, much worn and faded. There were traces about it of gold embroidery, which, however, was greatly frayed and defaced. . . . This rag of scarlet cloth, — for time, and wear, and a sacrilegious moth, had reduced it to little other than a rag, — on careful examination, assumed the shape of a letter. It was the capital letter A. By an accurate measurement, each limb proved to be precisely three inches and a quarter in length. (p. 43)

Shortly after discovering the letter, Hawthorne claims, he learned the story behind the letter by reading the papers of Surveyor Pue.

In these "foolscap sheets, containing many particulars respecting the life and conversation of one Hester Prynne" (p. 43), Hawthorne claims that he

> found the record of [the] doings and sufferings of this singular woman, for most of which the reader is referred to the story entitled "THE SCARLET LETTER"; and it should be borne carefully in mind, that the main facts of that story are authorized and authenticated by the document of Mr. Surveyor Pue. The original papers, together with the scarlet letter itself, — a most curious relic, — are still in my possession, and shall be freely exhibited to whomsoever . . . may desire a sight of them. (p. 44)

Much of what Hawthorne has to tell us in "The Custom-House" is undeniably true. "The election of General Taylor to the Presidency" (p. 50), like Hawthorne's subsequent dismissal from his position as

Surveyor, is historical fact. Even Hawthorne's depiction of a fellow Custom-House worker, the "permanent Inspector" (p. 32) who "possessed no higher attribute" than the "ability to recollect the good dinners" he had enjoyed (p. 33), must have seemed realistic to Hawthorne's contemporaries. Indeed, it prompted a cry of foul from the editor of the Salem *Register*, who wrote that the "chapter" about the "venerable gentleman" whose "chief crime seems to be that he loves a good dinner" managed to "obliterate . . . whatever sympathy was felt for Hawthorne's removal from office."

But the business about finding the "package, carefully done up in . . . ancient yellow parchment" is altogether a different story. It is, we may assume, just that: a fictional story with the semblance of biographical and historical truth. Hawthorne's mid-nineteenth-century audience was a practical one not entirely accustomed to the "imaginings" of a "romance-writer," yet even among these early readers there must have been those who saw through Hawthorne's account of finding the scarlet letter and the story of the "real" Hester Prynne. In "The Custom-House," Hawthorne describes the half-real, half-unreal world of a familiar room lit by moonlight: "the floor of our familiar room," he points out, "become[s] a neutral territory, somewhere between the real world and fairy-land, where the Actual and the Imaginary may meet, and each imbue itself with the nature of the other" (p. 46). The story of finding Surveyor Pue's package is a kind of frame story that brings about that meeting, bridging the gap between fact and fiction by imbuing a biographical introduction with a touch of fantasy — and the fiction that follows with the air of fact.

This is not to say that Hawthorne entirely made up the idea of a woman sentenced to wear a scarlet letter, only that he didn't find such a letter in the Custom-House where he worked nor did he come upon any historical account of a real woman named Hester Prynne. Instead, what he may well have discovered, either while working at the Custom-House or earlier, in the solitary decade following his graduation from college, was Joseph B. Felt's 1827 volume *The Annals of Salem*. There he would have read that, in 1694, a law was passed requiring adulterers to wear a two-inch-high capital *A*, colored to stand out against the background of the wearer's clothes.

As Charles Boewe and Murray G. Murphey point out in their essay "Hester Prynne in History" (1960), Hawthorne may also have read the story of Goodwife Mendame of Duxbury in old historical annals of the region (Goodwife Mendame was found guilty of adultery, whipped, and forced "to weare a badge with the capital letters *AD* cut in the cloth upon her left sleeve"). Finally, he may even have come across the following entry in the records of the Salem Quarterly Court for November 1688: "Hester Craford, for fornication with John Wedg, as she confessed, was ordered to be severely whipped and that security be given to save the town from the charge of keeping the child" (Boewe and Murphey, 202–03). There would seem to be, then, no end of sources for Hester Prynne in the annals of the period of Hawthorne's first (and second) ancestor.

Among those historical models not yet discussed and deserving of particular attention is the famous seventeenth-century antinomian Anne Hutchinson. Antinomians rejected the Puritan concept of religion as the observance of institutionalized precepts; rather than stressing God's will as something taught and enforced by a church, they believed that God reveals Himself through the inner experience of the individual. Instead of believing that good actions prove the doer to be predestined for salvation, antinomians argued that faith alone is necessary. Anne Hutchinson argued that she did not need Puritan elders to teach her true from false and right from wrong, because divine guidance and inspiration could be attained through intuition and faith. Nor did she accept the authority of the Puritan elders. As Michael Colacurcio puts it in his ground-breaking article, "Footsteps of Ann Hutchinson" (1972), her "proclamation — variously worded at various times . . . — that 'the chosen of man' are not necessarily 'the sealed of heaven,'" brought about "a state of near civil war in Boston" (471).

In the opening scene of *The Scarlet Letter* Hawthorne describes, next to the prison door from which Hester Prynne steps with her three-month-old baby, "a wild rose-bush" contrasting sharply with the "beetle-browed and gloomy front" of the prison and the rusty "ponderous iron-work" of its door. "Whether it had merely survived out of the stern old wilderness, . . . or whether . . . it had sprung up under the footsteps of the sainted Ann Hutchinson, as she entered the prison-door, — we shall not take upon us to determine" (p. 54), the narrator adds. What Hawthorne *has* determined through these remarks about the rose bush and the imprisoned (but saintly) Anne Hutchinson is that we regard Anne Hutchinson and Hester Prynne in the same light.

Hester's "crime" against society is sexual, not theological as was Mrs. Hutchinson's. And yet, on a deeper level, the two women are much the same. In her thinking, Hester, like Anne Hutchinson, questions the authority and desirability of her Puritan society, wondering at one point whether "the whole system of society" (p. 135) shouldn't be torn down and rebuilt, and deciding at another that "in Heaven's own time, a new truth would be revealed, in order to establish the whole relation between man and woman on a surer ground" (p. 201). And, of course, by her one antisocial act, Hester, like Anne Hutchinson, has disregarded, and implicitly denied the authority of, the Puritan moral law. "The world's law was no law for her mind," we read of Hester (p. 134). What the narrator gives us in those nine words is a short definition of antinomianism.

Using essays Hawthorne himself wrote about Anne Hutchinson's life and times, Colacurcio draws still more parallels between the literary character and the historical figure. He points out, for instance, that although Hutchinson's transgression was not sexual, it was often spoken of in such terms: her influence was seen as "seductive," her ideas as illegitimate children and even monstrous births. Colacurcio also suggests an interesting link between Hester's secret accomplice, Arthur Dimmesdale, and John Cotton, the great Boston minister and scholar. As Hawthorne himself points out in his own historical sketches, Cotton ultimately sat in judgment of Anne Hutchinson, even though she, who had been his parishioner both in England and in New England, always believed him to be a partner in, and to some extent even a source for, her alleged heresies. (And yet "Cotton alone, Hawthorne reports, is excepted from her final denunciations.") Cotton was historically the theological partner of John Wilson; together those two are known to have urged public confessions not unlike the one Wilson and Dimmesdale try to pry from Hester Prynne. "Like Ann Hutchinson," Colacurcio observes, "Hester Prynne is an extraordinary woman who falls afoul of a theocratic and male-dominated society; and the problems which cause them to be singled out for exemplary punishment both begin in a special sort of relationship with a pastor who is one of the acknowledged intellectual and spiritual leaders of that society" (461).

Hawthorne obviously absorbed a great deal of history during his years of reading in his "Castle Dismal," and he reworked that history into his novels and tales. In an essay entitled "The New England Sources of *The Scarlet Letter*" (1959), Charles Ryskamp goes far beyond indicating the possible historical sources for Prynne, Dimmesdale, and Wilson. He shows that particular histories of New England, especially Caleb Snow's *A History of Boston,* the best available in Hawthorne's day, were followed closely by the novelist as he fashioned the world of his most famous novel.

Snow's *History* provided a precise description of the houses and streets of Boston as they existed in the mid-seventeenth century; Hawthorne follows these descriptions in detail in setting his own story. He has placed the homes of the Governor and of the Reverend John Wilson in the proper locations, and he even uses historical names for persons who are not central characters in his story. It is also Snow's *History* that Hawthorne usually relies on when there is any doubt about the facts. Snow is the only historian Hawthorne could have read who says that the Boston jailer of the period was named Brackett; every other historian mentions a jailer named Parker. Hawthorne, however, follows Snow's lead, referring, in Chapter 4 of *The Scarlet Letter*, to "Master Brackett, the jailer" (p. 69).

Even some of the bizarre events in the novel are grounded in Snow's *History*. The great letter *A* that appears in the sky on the night of John Winthrop's death is based loosely on Snow's account of the night after John Cotton died, a night when "Strange and alarming signs appeared in the heavens." As for the more ordinary details of Hawthorne's story, many are even more closely based on the *History*.

Perhaps the most impressive example Ryskamp gives of Hawthorne's attention to historical detail and reliance on Snow is the comparison he makes between Snow's description of a great, early Boston house and Hawthorne's description of Governor Bellingham's mansion, to which, in the seventh chapter, Hester takes a pair of gloves she has fringed and embroidered. To indicate "what was considered elegance of architecture . . . a century and a half ago," Snow refers to a "wooden building," the outside "covered with plastering" in which the "broken glass" of "common junk bottles" had been used to "make a hard surface on the mortar. . . . This surface was also variegated with ornamental squares, diamonds, and flowers-de-luce" (Ryskamp 264–65). And how does Hawthorne describe the Governor's house? As a "large wooden house, . . . the walls being overspread with a kind of stucco, in which fragments of broken glass were plentifully intermixed. . . . It was further decorated with strange and seemingly cabalistic figures and diagrams" (p. 91).

What is most interesting about Ryskamp's article, though, is that, in addition to showing how often Hawthorne tells the historian's version of the truth in writing *The Scarlet Letter*, it also recounts how often Hawthorne distorts the truth as represented by Snow, Cotton Mather, and others. Governor Winthrop actually died in March 1649; Hawthorne's novel says he died in May. Governor Bellingham would not have been governor at the novel's opening — not, that is, if seven years were to pass between Hester's day and Dimmesdale's night on the scaffold, as the novel indicates. Mistress Ann Hibbins, the self-styled witch of the novel, is a historical figure Hawthorne would have read about in Snow. (She was condemned and executed for witchcraft in 1655.) But she was *not,* according to Snow, Governor Bellingham's sister. As for the Reverend John Wilson, in some ways accurately described by Hawthorne, he would not have been an old man with "a border of grizzled locks beneath his skull-cap" (p. 66).

Why would Hawthorne so carefully follow history in some instances only to violate it in others? Because, as Ryskamp reminds us, the novel is a place where — to use the language of "The Custom-House" — "the Actual and the Imaginary . . . meet." By having Winthrop die in March, not May, Hawthorne makes his novel more effective by compressing its action. By putting Dimmesdale on a balcony with "the eldest clergyman of Boston" (p. 65), a balcony from which the two men will attempt to pry a confession from a determinedly taciturn young woman, Hawthorne highlights the youthful confusion of Dimmesdale and darkly underscores the inappropriateness of his position.

As a work of fiction, then, *The Scarlet Letter* has its *own* reality, and that reality has a special form; like all historical novels and romances, it is itself an artifact of history, the history of a complex nineteenth-century culture, as well as a representation of the history of a previous culture. The very truths of the novel are sometimes conveyed by what are historical inaccuracies. By making Bellingham governor at the book's beginning, when Hester stands on the scaffold, and by transforming Mistress Hibbins into Bellingham's sister, Hawthorne forges connections that throw into question his own, perhaps our own, distinctions between legitimate and illegitimate, good and bad.

Finally, *The Scarlet Letter* is a composite. The story it tells of seventeenth-century New England is a mixture of fact and fancy, of history and imagination. As we have seen, the novel's main character is a blend of the "sainted Ann Hutchinson," adulteress Hester Craford, Goodwife Mendame of Duxbury, as well as the Quaker woman harshly judged by William Hathorne and the accused witches prosecuted by John. She is also, of course, as Nina Baym suggests, Hawthorne's own mother, who became pregnant out of wedlock, who suffered the stern disapproval of the puritanical Hathornes, and whose first child, Ebe, according to Baym, "grew up into a strikingly independent, only partially socialized woman, much as though she had been exempted from normal social expectations by those entrusted with rearing her" (9).

But to some extent, Hester is also Margaret Fuller, the feminist founder of *The Dial,* toward whom Hawthorne had always had mixed feelings. As critics have long pointed out, she is partially Hawthorne himself. Like Hester, Hawthorne was an artist who felt significantly alienated from a family and a society of sober pragmatists. A history embroidered by fancy, *The Scarlet Letter* outraged Puritanical readers of Hawthorne's day because of its treatment of adultery, much as Hester's act of adultery had outraged *her* society. As for Pearl, she is as much Hawthorne's daughter, Una, as she is his sister, Ebe; this much we know from Hawthorne's notebooks, in which Una is described in words later used to describe Pearl.

Similarly, the period of history Hawthorne represents in the novel is as much his own period as it is any earlier one, as Larry J. Reynolds points out in "*The Scarlet Letter* and Revolutions Abroad" (1985). Eighteen hundred forty-eight, the year before Hawthorne began his novel, was a year of revolutions in Europe, revolutions that had been applauded by intellectuals of Hawthorne's day, including Margaret Fuller. Even Hawthorne's wife, an admirer of Fuller's, had thought the 1848 French revolution "good news" (Reynolds 47). Hawthorne himself, however, was skeptical. Like many Americans, he viewed the victory of Taylor and his Whig party as an American manifestation of the spirit of 1848. But that Whig revolution cost him his job. By the time he started working on the novel, which he, being jobless, now had time to write, it had become clear that revolutionary efforts in Europe were doomed to failure.

So, in *The Scarlet Letter*, Hawthorne quietly and indirectly cautions against revolutionary fervor by writing the novel the way he does — and by setting it where and when he does. "The opening scenes . . . take place in May 1642 and the closing ones in May 1649," Reynolds explains in his essay. "These dates coincide almost exactly with those of the English Civil war fought between King Charles I and his Puritan Parliament. . . . By the final scenes of the novel, when Arthur is deciding to die as a martyr, Charles I has just been beheaded" (52–53). Additionally, the scaffold so prominently featured in the novel's opening is, according to Reynolds, a "historical inaccuracy intentionally used by Hawthorne to develop the theme of revolution. . . . With increasing frequency during the first French Revolution," the word scaffold had "served as a synecdoche for a public beheading — by the executioner's axe or the guillotine" (51). (Note that Hawthorne, in "The Custom-House," connects his own mistreatment by the victorious Whigs with French revolutionary activity, referring to himself as "A DECAPITATED SURVEYOR," p. 52.)

Reynolds suggests that Hawthorne, because of his distrust of revolution, presents Hester and Arthur sympathetically as long as they are trying to "regain their rightful place in the social or spiritual order," but unsympathetically "when they become revolutionary instead and attempt to overthrow an established order" (58). As Reynolds describes, at the beginning of the novel Hester is the almost regal-seeming martyr, a martyr antagonized by the Puritan mob. Later, she becomes the revolutionary, thinking thoughts about the overturning of society and dreaming dreams of "a revolution in the sphere of thought and feeling." At this point Hawthorne's narrator becomes less sympathetic. Still later, when Dimmesdale conforms to the social order by repenting of his sin, that act is viewed by the narrator with approval. The narrator equally approves Hester's final return to New England, where she reattaches the scarlet letter to her breast and counsels wretched people in her cottage. It is better to accept than to revolt, the ending of the novel suggests, delivering a mid-nineteenth-century message to a mid-nineteenth-century audience, while seeming to be about the mid-seventeenth century.

In the pages that follow, you will find historical documents that further conceptualize *The Scarlet Letter.* You will also find interpretations of the novel written since Baym wrote "Nathaniel Hawthorne and His Mother," Colacurcio wrote "Footsteps of Ann Hutchinson," Ryskamp wrote "The New England Sources of *The Scarlet Letter,*" and Reynolds wrote "*The Scarlet Letter* and Revolutions Abroad."

Some of these essayists go further than Reynolds in suggesting that *The Scarlet Letter* was a reflection by Hawthorne on the history of his own day. Others would have it that, when we read *The Scarlet Letter,* our own historical period and its concerns become implicated as well, turning the text into one in which we end up reading about our own times as well as those of Hawthorne and Hester, of Polk and the Puritans.

But before that composite of contextual and critical material comes the text itself, a complicated mix of biography and history, of seventeenth- and nineteenth-century history, and, most important, of history and the imagination that brings it to life. It is to that text that you should now turn.

WORKS CITED

Baym, Nina. "Nathaniel Hawthorne and His Mother: A Biographical Speculation." *American Literature* 54 (1982): 1–27.

Boewe, Charles, and Murray G. Murphey. "Hester Prynne in History." *American Literature* 32 (1960): 202–04.

Colacurcio, Michael. "Footsteps of Ann Hutchinson: The Context of *The Scarlet Letter.*" *ELH* 39 (1972): 459–94.

Hawthorne, Nathaniel. *Life of Franklin Pierce.* Boston: Ticknor, Reed, and Fields, 1852.

Mellow, James R. *Nathaniel Hawthorne in His Times.* Boston: Houghton, 1980. One of the two standard biographies of Hawthorne.

Reynolds, Larry J. "*The Scarlet Letter* and Revolutions Abroad." *American Literature* 57 (1985): 44–67.

Ryskamp, Charles. "The New England Sources of *The Scarlet Letter.*" *American Literature* 31 (1959): 257–72.

Turner, Arlin. *Nathaniel Hawthorne: A Biography.* New York: Oxford UP, 1980. One of the two standard biographies of Hawthorne.

The Scarlet Letter

PREFACE

To the Second Edition

Much to the author's surprise, and (if he may say so without additional offence) considerably to his amusement, he finds that his sketch of official life, introductory to THE SCARLET LETTER, has created an unprecedented excitement in the respectable community immediately around him. It could hardly have been more violent, indeed, had he burned down the Custom-House, and quenched its last smoking ember in the blood of a certain venerable personage, against whom he is supposed to cherish a peculiar malevolence. As the public disapprobation would weigh very heavily on him, were he conscious of deserving it, the author begs leave to say, that he has carefully read over the introductory pages, with a purpose to alter or expunge whatever might be found amiss, and to make the best reparation in his power for the atrocities of which he has been adjudged guilty. But it appears to him, that the only remarkable features of the sketch are its frank and genuine good-humor, and the general accuracy with which he has conveyed his sincere impressions of the characters therein described. As to enmity, or ill-feeling of any kind, personal or political, he utterly disclaims such motives. The sketch might, perhaps, have been wholly omitted, without loss to the public, or detriment to the book; but, having undertaken to write it, he conceives that it could not have been done in a better or kindlier spirit, nor, so far as his abilities availed, with a livelier effect of truth.

The author is constrained, therefore, to republish his introductory sketch without the change of a word.

SALEM, *March* 30, 1850.

THE CUSTOM-HOUSE

Introductory to "The Scarlet Letter"

It is a little remarkable, that — though disinclined to talk overmuch of myself and my affairs at the fireside, and to my personal friends — an autobiographical impulse should twice in my life have taken possession of me, in addressing the public. The first time was three or four years since, when I favored the reader — inexcusably, and for no early reason, that either the indulgent reader or the intrusive author could imagine — with a description of my way of life in the deep quietude of an Old Manse. And now — because, beyond my deserts, I was happy enough to find a listener or two on the former occasion — I again seize the public by the button, and talk of my three years' experience in a Custom-House. The example of the famous "P. P., Clerk of this Parish,"[1] was never more faithfully followed. The truth seems to be, however, that, when he casts his leaves forth upon the wind, the author addresses, not the many who will fling aside his volume, or never take it up, but the few who will understand him, better than most of his schoolmates and lifemates. Some authors, indeed, do far more than this, and indulge themselves in such confidential depths of revelation as could fittingly be addressed, only and exclusively, to the one heart and mind of perfect sympathy; as if the printed book, thrown at large on the wide world, were certain to find out the divided segment of the writer's own nature, and complete his circle of existence by bringing him into communion with it. It is scarcely decorous, however, to speak all, even where we speak impersonally. But — as thoughts are frozen and utterance benumbed, unless the speaker stand in some true relation with his audience — it may be pardonable to imagine that a friend, a kind and apprehensive, though not the closest friend, is listening to our talk; and then, a native reserve being thawed by this genial consciousness, we

[1] P.P., who in 1715 parodied an autobiography by Bishop Gilbert Burnet, was in fact British satirists John Gay and Alexander Pope.

may prate of the circumstances that lie around us, and even of ourself, but still keep the inmost Me behind its veil. To this extent and within these limits, an author, methinks, may be autobiographical, without violating either the reader's rights or his own.

It will be seen, likewise, that this Custom-House sketch has a certain propriety, of a kind always recognized in literature, as explaining how a large portion of the following pages came into my possession, and as offering proofs of the authenticity of a narrative therein contained. This, in fact, — a desire to put myself in my true position as editor, or very little more, of the most prolix among the tales that make up my volume, — this, and no other, is my true reason for assuming a personal relation with the public. In accomplishing the main purpose, it has appeared allowable, by a few extra touches, to give a faint representation of a mode of life not heretofore described, together with some of the characters that move in it, among whom the author happened to make one.

In my native town of Salem, at the head of what, half a century ago, in the days of old King Derby, was a bustling wharf, — but which is now burdened with decayed wooden warehouses, and exhibits few or no symptoms of commercial life; except, perhaps, a bark or brig, halfway down its melancholy length, discharging hides; or, nearer at hand, a Nova Scotia schooner, pitching out her cargo of firewood, — at the head, I say, of this dilapidated wharf, which the tide often overflows, and along which, at the base and in the rear of the row of buildings, the track of many languid years is seen in a border of unthrifty grass, — here, with a view from its front windows adown this not very enlivening prospect, and thence across the harbour, stands a spacious edifice of brick. From the loftiest point of its roof, during precisely three and a half hours of each forenoon, floats or droops, in breeze or calm, the banner of the republic; but with the thirteen stripes turned vertically, instead of horizontally, and thus indicating that a civil, and not a military post of Uncle Sam's government, is here established. Its front is ornamented with a portico of half a dozen wooden pillars, supporting a balcony, beneath which a flight of wide granite steps descends towards the street. Over the entrance hovers an enormous specimen of the American eagle, with outspread wings, a shield before her breast, and, if I recollect aright, a bunch of intermingled thunderbolts and barbed arrows in each claw. With the customary infirmity of temper that characterizes this unhappy fowl, she appears, by the fierceness of her beak and eye and the general truculency of her attitude, to threaten mischief to the inoffensive community; and especially to warn all citizens, careful of their safety, against intruding on the premises which she overshadows with her wings. Nevertheless, vixenly as she looks, many people are seeking, at this very moment, to shelter themselves under the wing of the federal eagle; imagining, I presume, that her bosom has all the softness and snugness of an eider-down pillow. But she has no great tenderness, even in her best of moods, and, sooner or later, — oftener soon than late, — is apt to fling off her nestlings with a scratch of her claw, a dab of her beak, or a rangling wound from her barbed arrows.

The pavement round about the above-described edifice — which we may as well name at once as the Custom-House of the port — has grass enough growing in its chinks to show that it has not, of late days, been worn by any multitudinous resort of business. In some months of the year, however, there often chances a forenoon when affairs move onward with a livelier tread. Such occasions might remind the elderly citizen of that period, before the last war with England, when Salem was a port by itself; not scorned, as she is now, by her own merchants and ship-owners, who permit her wharves to crumble to ruin, while their ventures go to swell, needlessly and imperceptibly, the mighty flood of commerce at New York or Boston. On some such morning, when three or four vessels happen to have arrived at once, — usually from Africa or South America, — or to be on the verge of their departure thitherward, there is a sound of frequent feet, passing briskly up and down the granite steps. Here, before his own wife has greeted him, you may greet the sea-flushed ship-master, just in port, with his vessel's papers under his arm in a tarnished tin box. Here, too, comes his owner, cheerful or sombre, gracious or in the sulks, accordingly as his scheme of the now accomplished voyage has been realized in merchandise that will readily be turned to gold, or has buried him under a bulk of incommodities, such as nobody will care to rid him of. Here, likewise, — the germ of the wrinkle-browed, grizzly-bearded, careworn merchant, — we have the smart young clerk, who gets the taste of traffic as a wolf-cub does of blood, and already sends adventures in his master's ships, when he had better be sailing mimic boats upon a mill-pond. Another figure in the scene is the outward-bound sailor, in quest of a protection; or the recently arrived one, pale and feeble, seeking a passport to the hospital. Nor must we forget the captains of the rusty little schooners that bring firewood from the British provinces; a rough-looking set of tarpaulins, without the alertness of the Yankee aspect, but contributing an item of no slight importance to our decaying trade.

Cluster all these individuals together, as they sometimes were, with other miscellaneous ones to diversify the group, and, for the time being, it made the Custom-House a stirring scene. More frequently, however, on ascending the steps, you would discern — in the entry, if it were summer time, or in their appropriate rooms, if wintry or inclement weather — a row of venerable figures, sitting in old-fashioned chairs, which were tipped on their hind legs back against the wall. Oftentimes they were asleep, but occasionally might be heard talking together, in voices between speech and a snore, and with that lack of energy that distinguishes the occupants of alms-houses, and all other human beings who depend for subsistence on charity, on monopolized labor, or any thing else but their own independent exertions. These old gentlemen — seated, like Matthew, at the receipt of custom, but not very liable to be summoned thence, like him, for apostolic errands — were Custom-House officers.

Furthermore, on the left hand as you enter the front door, is a certain room or office, about fifteen feet square, and of a lofty height; with two of its arched windows commanding a view of the aforesaid dilapidated wharf, and the third looking across a narrow lane, and along a portion of Derby Street. All three give glimpses of the shops of grocers, block-makers, slop-sellers, and ship-chandlers; around the doors of which are generally to be seen, laughing and gossiping, clusters of old salts, and such other wharf-rats as haunt the Wapping of a seaport.[2] The room itself is cobwebbed, and dingy with old paint; its floor is strewn with gray sand, in a fashion that has elsewhere fallen into long disuse; and it is easy to conclude, from the general slovenliness of the place, that this is a sanctuary into which womankind, with her tools of magic, the broom and mop, has very infrequent access. In the way of furniture, there is a stove with a voluminous funnel; an old pine desk, with a three-legged stool beside it; two or three wooden-bottom chairs, exceedingly decrepit and infirm; and, — not to forget the library, — on some shelves, a score or two of volumes of the Acts of Congress, and a bulky Digest of the Revenue Laws. A tin pipe ascends through the ceiling, and forms a medium of vocal communication with other parts of the edifice. And here, some six months ago, — pacing from corner to corner, or lounging on the long-legged stool, with his elbow on the desk, and his eyes wandering up and down the columns of the morning newspaper, — you might have recognized, honored reader, the same

[2] Here Hawthorne draws an uncomplimentary comparison between Salem and a London slum on the Thames River.

individual who welcomed you into his cheery little study, where the sunshine glimmered so pleasantly through the willow branches, on the western side of the Old Manse. But now, should you go thither to seek him, you would inquire in vain for the Loco-foco Surveyor. The besom° of reform has swept him out of office; and a worthier successor wears his dignity and pockets his emoluments.°

This old town of Salem — my native place, though I have dwelt much away from it, both in boyhood and maturer years — possesses, or did possess, a hold on my affections, the force of which I have never realized during my seasons of actual residence here. Indeed, so far as its physical aspect is concerned, with its flat, unvaried surface, covered chiefly with wooden houses, few or none of which pretend to architectural beauty, — its irregularity, which is neither picturesque nor quaint, but only tame, — its long and lazy street, lounging wearisomely through the whole extent of the peninsula, with Gallows Hill and New Guinea at one end, and a view of the alms-house at the other, — such being the features of my native town, it would be quite as reasonable to form a sentimental attachment to a disarranged checkerboard. And yet, though invariably happiest elsewhere, there is within me a feeling for old Salem, which, in lack of a better phrase, I must be content to call affection. The sentiment is probably assignable to the deep and aged roots which my family has struck into the soil. It is now nearly two centuries and a quarter since the original Briton, the earliest emigrant of my name, made his appearance in the wild and forest-bordered settlement, which has since become a city. And here his descendants have been born and died, and have mingled their earthy substance with the soil; until no small portion of it must necessarily be akin to the mortal frame wherewith, for a little while, I walk the streets. In part, therefore, the attachment which I speak of is the mere sensuous sympathy of dust for dust. Few of my countrymen can know what it is; nor, as frequent transplantation is perhaps better for the stock, need they consider it desirable to know.

But the sentiment has likewise its moral quality. The figure of that first ancestor, invested by family tradition with a dim and dusky grandeur, was present to my boyish imagination, as far back as I can remember. It still haunts me, and induces a sort of home-feeling with the past, which I scarcely claim in reference to the present phase of the town. I seem to have a stronger claim to a residence here on account of this grave, bearded, sable-cloaked, and steeple-crowned progenitor, — who came

besom: Broom. ***emoluments:*** Earnings.

so early, with his Bible and his sword, and trode the unworn street with such a stately port, and made so large a figure, as a man of war and peace, — a stronger claim than for myself, whose name is seldom heard and my face hardly known. He was a soldier, legislator, judge; he was a ruler in the Church; he had all the Puritanic traits, both good and evil. He was likewise a bitter persecutor; as witness the Quakers, who have remembered him in their histories, and relate an incident of his hard severity towards a woman of their sect, which will last longer, it is to be feared, than any record of his better deeds, although these were many. His son, too, inherited the persecuting spirit, and made himself so conspicuous in the martyrdom of the witches, that their blood may fairly be said to have left a stain upon him. So deep a stain, indeed, that his old dry bones, in the Charter Street burial-ground, must still retain it, if they have not crumbled utterly to dust! I know not whether these ancestors of mine bethought themselves to repent, and ask pardon of Heaven for their cruelties; or whether they are now groaning under the heavy consequences of them, in another state of being. At all events, I, the present writer, as their representative, hereby take shame upon myself for their sakes, and pray that any curse incurred by them — as I have heard, and as the dreary and unprosperous condition of the race, for many a long year back, would argue to exist — may be now and henceforth removed.

Doubtless, however, either of these stern and black-browed Puritans would have thought it quite a sufficient retribution for his sins, that, after so long a lapse of years, the old trunk of the family tree, with so much venerable moss upon it, should have borne, as its topmost bough, an idler like myself. No aim, that I have ever cherished, would they recognize as laudable; no success of mine — if my life, beyond its domestic scope, had ever been brightened by success — would they deem otherwise than worthless, if not positively disgraceful. "What is he?" murmurs one gray shadow of my forefathers to the other. "A writer of story-books! What kind of a business in life, — what mode of glorifying God, or being serviceable to mankind in his day and generation, — may that be? Why, the degenerate fellow might as well have been a fiddler!" Such are the compliments bandied between my great-grandsires and myself, across the gulf of time! And yet, let them scorn me as they will, strong traits of their nature have intertwined themselves with mine.

Planted deep, in the town's earliest infancy and childhood, by these two earnest and energetic men, the race has ever since subsisted here; always, too, in respectability; never, so far as I have known, disgraced by a single unworthy member; but seldom or never, on the other hand, after the first two generations, performing any memorable deed, or so much as putting forward a claim to public notice. Gradually, they have sunk almost out of sight; as old houses, here and there about the streets, get covered half-way to the eaves by the accumulation of new soil. From father to son, for above a hundred years, they followed the sea; a gray-headed shipmaster, in each generation, retiring from the quarter-deck to the homestead, while a boy of fourteen took the hereditary place before the mast, confronting the salt spray and the gale, which had blustered against his sire and grandsire. The boy, also, in due time, passed from the forecastle to the cabin, spent a tempestuous manhood, and returned from his world-wanderings, to grow old, and die, and mingle his dust with the natal earth. This long connection of a family with one spot, as its place of birth and burial, creates a kindred between the human being and the locality, quite independent of any charm in the scenery or moral circumstances that surround him. It is not love, but instinct. The new inhabitant — who came himself from a foreign land, or whose father or grandfather came — has little claim to be called a Salemite; he has no conception of the oyster-like tenacity with which an old settler, over whom his third century is creeping, clings to the spot where his successive generations have been embedded. It is no matter that the place is joyless for him; that he is weary of the old wooden houses, the mud and dust, the dead level of site and sentiment, the chill east wind, and the chillest of social atmospheres; — all these, and whatever faults besides he may see or imagine, are nothing to the purpose. The spell survives, and just as powerfully as if the natal spot were an earthly paradise. So has it been in my case. I felt it almost as a destiny to make Salem my home; so that the mould of features and cast of character which had all along been familiar here — ever, as one representative of the race lay down in his grave, another assuming, as it were, his sentry-march along the Main Street — might still in my little day be seen and recognized in the old town. Nevertheless, this very sentiment is an evidence that the connection, which has become an unhealthy one, should at last be severed. Human nature will not flourish, any more than a potato, if it be planted and replanted, for too long a series of generations, in the same worn-out soil. My children have had other birthplaces, and, so far as their fortunes may be within my control, shall strike their roots into unaccustomed earth.

On emerging from the Old Manse, it was chiefly this strange, indolent, unjoyous attachment for my native town, that brought me to fill a place in Uncle Sam's brick edifice, when I might as well, or better, have gone somewhere else. My doom was on me. It was not the first time, nor the second, that I had gone away, — as it seemed, permanently, — but yet returned, like the bad half-penny; or as if Salem were for me the inevitable centre of the universe. So, one fine morning, I ascended the flight of granite steps, with the President's commission in my pocket, and was introduced to the corps of gentlemen who were to aid me in my weighty responsibility, as chief executive officer of the Custom-House.

I doubt greatly — or rather, I do not doubt at all — whether any public functionary of the United States, either in the civil or military line, has ever had such a patriarchal body of veterans under his orders as myself. The whereabouts of the Oldest Inhabitants was at once settled, when I looked at them. For upwards of twenty years before this epoch, the independent position of the Collector had kept the Salem Custom-House out of the whirlpool of political vicissitude, which makes the tenure of office generally so fragile. A soldier, — New England's most distinguished soldier, — he stood firmly on the pedestal of his gallant services; and, himself secure in the wise liberality of the successive administrations through which he had held office, he had been the safety of his subordinates in many an hour of danger and heart-quake. General Miller was radically conservative; a man over whose kindly nature habit had no slight influence; attaching himself strongly to familiar faces, and with difficulty moved to change, even when change might have brought unquestionable improvement. Thus, on taking charge of my department, I found few but aged men. They were ancient sea-captains, for the most part, who, after being tost on every sea, and standing up sturdily against life's tempestuous blast, had finally drifted into this quiet nook; where, with little to disturb them, except the periodical terrors of a Presidential election, they one and all acquired a new lease of existence. Though by no means less liable than their fellow-men to age and infirmity, they had evidently some talisman or other that kept death at bay. Two or three of their number, as I was assured, being gouty and rheumatic, or perhaps bed-ridden, never dreamed of making their appearance at the Custom-House, during a large part of the year; but, after a torpid winter, would creep out into the warm sunshine of May or June, go lazily about what they termed duty, and, at their own leisure and convenience, betake themselves to bed again. I must plead guilty to the charge of abbreviating the official breath of more than one of these venerable servants of the republic. They were allowed, on my representation, to rest from their arduous labors, and soon afterwards — as if their sole principle of life had been zeal for their country's service; as I verily believe it was — withdrew to a better world. It is a pious consolation to me, that, through my interference, a sufficient space was allowed them for repentance of the evil and corrupt practices, into which, as a matter of course, every Custom-House officer must be supposed to fall. Neither the front nor the back entrance of the Custom-House opens on the road to Paradise.

The greater part of my officers were Whigs. It was well for their venerable brotherhood, that the new Surveyor was not a politician, and, though a faithful Democrat in principle, neither received nor held his office with any reference to political services. Had it been otherwise, — had an active politician been put into this influential post, to assume the easy task of making head against a Whig Collector, whose infirmities withheld him from the personal administration of his office, — hardly a man of the old corps would have drawn the breath of official life, within a month after the exterminating angel had come up the Custom-House steps. According to the received code in such matters, it would have been nothing short of duty, in a politician, to bring every one of those white heads under the axe of the guillotine. It was plain enough to discern, that the old fellows dreaded some such discourtesy at my hands. It pained, and at the same time amused me, to behold the terrors that attended my advent; to see a furrowed cheek, weather-beaten by half a century of storm, turn ashy pale at the glance of so harmless an individual as myself; to detect, as one or another addressed me, the tremor of a voice, which, in long-past days, had been wont to bellow through a speaking-trumpet, hoarsely enough to frighten Boreas himself to silence. They knew, these excellent old persons, that, by all established rule, — and, as regarded some of them, weighed by their own lack of efficiency for business, — they ought to have given place to younger men, more orthodox in politics, and altogether fitter than themselves to serve our common Uncle. I knew it too, but could never quite find in my heart to act upon the knowledge. Much and deservedly to my own discredit, therefore, and considerably to the detriment of my official conscience, they continued, during my incumbency, to creep about the wharves, and loiter up and down the Custom-House steps. They spent a good deal of time, also, asleep in their accustomed corners, with their chairs tilted back against the wall; awaking, however, once or twice in a forenoon, to bore one another with the several thousandth repetition of old sea-stories, and mouldy jokes, that had grown to be pass-words and countersigns among them.

The discovery was soon made, I imagine, that the new Surveyor had no great harm in him. So, with lightsome hearts, and the happy consciousness of being usefully employed, — in their own behalf, at least, if not for our beloved country, — these good old gentlemen went through the various formalities of office. Sagaciously, under their spectacles, did they peep into the holds of vessels! Mighty was their fuss about little matters, and marvellous, sometimes, the obtuseness that allowed greater ones to slip between their fingers! Whenever such a mischance occurred, — when a wagon-load of valuable merchandise had been smuggled ashore, at noonday, perhaps, and directly beneath their unsuspicious noses, — nothing could exceed the vigilance and alacrity with which they proceeded to lock, and double-lock, and secure with tape and sealing-wax, all the avenues of the delinquent vessel. Instead of a reprimand for their previous negligence, the case seemed rather to require an eulogium on their praiseworthy caution, after the mischief had happened; a grateful recognition of the promptitude of their zeal, the moment that there was no longer any remedy!

Unless people are more than commonly disagreeable, it is my foolish habit to contract a kindness for them. The better part of my companion's character, if it have a better part, is that which usually comes uppermost in my regard, and forms the type whereby I recognize the man. As most of these old Custom-House officers had good traits, and as my position in reference to them, being paternal and protective, was favorable to the growth of friendly sentiments, I soon grew to like them all. It was pleasant, in the summer forenoons, — when the fervent heat, that almost liquefied the rest of the human family, merely communicated a genial warmth to their half-torpid systems, — it was pleasant to hear them chatting in the back entry, a row of them all tipped against the wall, as usual; while the frozen witticisms of past generations were thawed out, and came bubbling with laughter from their lips. Externally, the jollity of aged men has much in common with the mirth of children; the intellect, any more than a deep sense of humor, has little to do with the matter; it is, with both, a gleam that plays upon the surface, and imparts a sunny and cheery aspect alike to the green branch, and gray, mouldering trunk. In one case, however, it is real sunshine; in the other, it more resembles the phosphorescent glow of decaying wood.

It would be sad injustice, the reader must understand, to represent all my excellent old friends as in their dotage. In the first place, my coadjutors were not invariably old; there were men among them in their strength and prime, of marked ability and energy, and altogether superior to the sluggish and dependent mode of life on which their evil stars had cast them. Then, moreover, the white locks of age were sometimes found to be the thatch of an intellectual tenement in good repair. But, as respects the majority of my corps of veterans, there will be no wrong done, if I characterize them generally as a set of wearisome old souls, who had gathered nothing worth preservation from their varied experience of life. They seemed to have flung away all the golden grain of practical wisdom, which they had enjoyed so many opportunities of harvesting, and most carefully to have stored their memories with the husks. They spoke with far more interest and unction of their morning's breakfast, or yesterday's, to-day's, or to-morrow's dinner, than of the shipwreck of forty or fifty years ago, and all the world's wonders which they had witnessed with their youthful eyes.

The father of the Custom-House — the patriarch, not only of this little squad of officials, but, I am bold to say, of the respectable body of tide-waiters all over the United States — was a certain permanent Inspector. He might truly be termed a legitimate son of the revenue system, dyed in the wool, or rather, born in the purple; since his sire, a Revolutionary colonel, and formerly collector of the port, had created an office for him, and appointed him to fill it, at a period of the early ages which few living men can now remember. This Inspector, when I first knew him, was a man of fourscore years, or thereabouts, and certainly one of the most wonderful specimens of winter-green that you would be likely to discover in a lifetime's search. With his florid cheek, his compact figure, smartly arrayed in a bright-buttoned blue coat, his brisk and vigorous step, and his hale and hearty aspect, altogether, he seemed — not young, indeed — but a kind of new contrivance of Mother Nature in the shape of man, whom age and infirmity had no business to touch. His voice and laugh, which perpetually reëchoed through the Custom-House, had nothing of the tremulous quaver and cackle of an old man's utterance; they came strutting out of his lungs, like the crow of a cock, or the blast of a clarion. Looking at him merely as an animal, — and there was very little else to look at, — he was a most satisfactory object, from the thorough healthfulness and wholesomeness of his system, and his capacity, at that extreme age, to enjoy all, or nearly all, the delights which he had ever aimed at, or conceived of. The careless security of his life in the Custom-House, on a regular income, and with but slight and infrequent apprehensions of removal, had no doubt contributed to make time pass lightly over him. The original and more potent causes, however, lay in the rare perfection of his animal nature, the moderate proportion of intellect, and the very trifling admixture of moral and spiritual ingredients; these latter qualities, indeed, being in barely enough measure to keep the old gentleman from walking on all-fours. He possessed no power of thought, no depth of feeling, no troublesome sensibilities; nothing, in short, but a few commonplace instincts, which, aided by the cheerful temper that grew inevitably out of his physical well-being, did duty very respectably, and to general acceptance, in lieu of a heart. He had been the husband of three wives, all long since dead; the father of twenty children, most of whom, at every age of childhood or maturity, had likewise returned to dust. Here, one would suppose, might have been sorrow enough to imbue the sunniest disposition, through and through, with a sable tinge. Not so with our old Inspector! One brief sigh sufficed to carry off the entire burden of these dismal reminiscences. The next moment, he was as ready for sport as any unbreeched infant; far readier than the Collector's junior clerk, who, at nineteen years, was much the elder and graver man of the two.

I used to watch and study this patriarchal personage with, I think, livelier curiosity than any other form of humanity there presented to my notice. He was, in truth, a rare phenomenon; so perfect in one point of view; so shallow, so delusive, so impalpable, such an absolute nonentity, in every other. My conclusion was that he had no soul, no heart, no mind; nothing, as I have already said, but instincts; and yet, withal so cunningly had the few materials of his character been put together, that there was no painful perception of deficiency, but, on my part, an entire contentment with what I found in him. It might be difficult — and it was so — to conceive how he should exist hereafter, so earthy and sensuous did he seem; but surely his existence here, admitting that it was to terminate with his last breath, had been not unkindly given; with no higher moral responsibilities than the beasts of the field, but with a larger scope of enjoyment than theirs, and with all their blessed immunity from the dreariness and duskiness of age.

One point, in which he had vastly the advantage over his four-footed brethren, was his ability to recollect the good dinners which it had made no small portion of the happiness of his life to eat. His gourmandism was a highly agreeable trait; and to hear him talk of roast-meat was as appetizing as a pickle or an oyster. As he possessed no higher attribute, and neither sacrificed nor vitiated any spiritual endowment by devoting all his energies and ingenuities to subserve the delight and profit of his maw, it always pleased and satisfied me to hear him expatiate on fish, poultry, and butcher's meat, and the most eligible methods of preparing them for the table. His reminiscences of good cheer, however ancient the date of the actual banquet, seemed to bring the savor of pig or turkey under one's very nostrils. There were flavors on his palate, that had lingered there not less than sixty or seventy years, and were still apparently as fresh as that of the muttonchop which he had just devoured for his breakfast. I have heard him smack his lips over dinners, every guest at which, except himself, had long been food for worms. It was marvellous to observe how the ghosts of bygone meals were continually rising up before him; not in anger or retribution, but as if grateful for his former appreciation, and seeking to reduplicate an endless series of enjoyment, at once shadowy and sensual. A tenderloin of beef, a hind-quarter of veal, a spare-rib of pork, a particular chicken, or a remarkably praiseworthy turkey, which had perhaps adorned his board in the days of the elder Adams, would be remembered; while all the subsequent experience of our race, and all the events that brightened or darkened his individual career, had gone over him with as little permanent effect as the passing breeze. The chief tragic event of the old man's life, so far as I could judge, was his mishap with a certain goose, which lived and died some twenty or forty years ago; a goose of most promising figure, but which, at table, proved so inveterately tough that the carving-knife would make no impression on its carcass; and it could only be divided with an axe and handsaw.

But it is time to quit this sketch; on which, however, I should be glad to dwell at considerably more length, because, of all men whom I have ever known, this individual was fittest to be a Custom-House officer. Most persons, owing to causes which I may not have space to hint at, suffer moral detriment from this peculiar mode of life. The old Inspector was incapable of it, and, were he to continue in office to the end of time, would be just as good as he was then, and sit down to dinner with just as good an appetite.

There is one likeness, without which my gallery of Custom-House portraits would be strangely incomplete; but which my comparatively few opportunities for observation enable me to sketch only in the merest outline. It is that of the Collector, our gallant old General, who, after his brilliant military service, subsequently to which he had ruled over a wild Western territory, had come hither, twenty years before, to spend the decline of his varied and honorable life. The brave soldier had already numbered, nearly or quite, his threescore years and ten, and was pursuing the remainder of his earthly march, burdened with infirmities which even the martial music of his own spirit-stirring recollections could do little towards lightening. The step was palsied now, that had been foremost in the charge. It was only with the assistance of a servant, and by leaning his hand heavily on the iron balustrade, that he could slowly and painfully ascend the Custom-House steps, and, with a toilsome progress across the floor, attain his customary chair beside the fireplace. There he used to sit, gazing with a somewhat dim serenity of aspect at the figures that came and went; amid the rustle of papers, the administering of oaths, the discussion of business, and the casual talk of the office; all which sounds and circumstances seemed but indistinctly to impress his senses, and hardly to make their way into his inner sphere of contemplation. His countenance, in this repose, was mild and kindly. If his notice was sought, an expression of courtesy and interest gleamed out upon his features; proving that there was light within him, and that it was only the outward medium of the intellectual lamp that obstructed the rays in their passage. The closer you penetrated to the substance of his mind, the sounder it appeared. When no longer called upon to speak, or listen, either of which operations cost him an evident effort, his face would briefly subside into its former not uncheerful quietude. It was not painful to behold this look; for, though dim, it had not the imbecility of decaying age. The framework of his nature, originally strong and massive, was not yet crumbled into ruin.

To observe and define his character, however, under such disadvantages, was as difficult a task as to trace out and build up anew, in imagination, an old fortress, like Ticonderoga,[3] from a view of its gray and broken ruins. Here and there, perchance, the walls may remain almost complete; but elsewhere may be only a shapeless mound, cumbrous with its very strength, and overgrown, through long years of peace and neglect, with grass and alien weeds.

Nevertheless, looking at the old warrior with affection, — for, slight as was the communication between us, my feeling towards him, like that of all bipeds and quadrupeds who knew him, might not improperly be termed so, — I could discern the main points of his portrait. It was marked with the noble and heroic qualities which showed it to be not by a mere accident, but of good right, that he had won a distinguished name. His spirit could never, I conceive, have been characterized by an uneasy activity; it must, at any period of his life, have required an impulse to set him in motion; but, once stirred up, with obstacles to overcome, and an adequate object to be attained, it was not in the man to give out or fail. The heat that had formerly pervaded his nature, and which was not yet extinct, was never of the kind that flashes and flickers in a blaze, but, rather, a deep, red glow, as of iron in a furnace. Weight, solidity, firmness; this was the expression of his repose, even in such

[3] Eighteenth-century fort in upstate New York.

decay as had crept untimely over him, at the period of which I speak. But I could imagine, even then, that, under some excitement which should go deeply into his consciousness, — roused by a trumpet-peal, loud enough to awaken all of his energies that were not dead, but only slumbering, — he was yet capable of flinging off his infirmities like a sick man's gown, dropping the staff of age to seize a battle-sword, and starting up once more a warrior. And, in so intense a moment, his demeanour would have still been calm. Such an exhibition, however, was but to be pictured in fancy; not to be anticipated, nor desired. What I saw in him — as evidently as the indestructible ramparts of Old Ticonderoga, already cited as the most appropriate simile — were the features of stubborn and ponderous endurance, which might well have amounted to obstinacy in his earlier days; of integrity, that, like most of his other endowments, lay in a somewhat heavy mass, and was just as unmalleable and unmanageable as a ton of iron ore; and of benevolence, which, fiercely as he led the bayonets on at Chippewa or Fort Erie, I take to be of quite as genuine a stamp as what actuates any or all the polemical philanthropists of the age. He had slain men with his own hand, for aught I know; — certainly, they had fallen, like blades of grass at the sweep of the scythe, before the charge to which his spirit imparted its triumphant energy; — but, be that as it might, there was never in his heart so much cruelty as would have brushed the down off a butterfly's wing. I have not known the man, to whose innate kindliness I would more confidently make an appeal.

Many characteristics — and those, too, which contribute not the least forcibly to impart resemblance in a sketch — must have vanished, or been obscured, before I met the General. All merely graceful attributes are usually the most evanescent; nor does Nature adorn the human ruin with blossoms of new beauty, that have their roots and proper nutriment only in the chinks and crevices of decay, as she sows wall-flowers over the ruined fortress of Ticonderoga. Still, even in respect of grace and beauty, there were points well worth noting. A ray of humor, now and then, would make its way through the veil of dim obstruction, and glimmer pleasantly upon our faces. A trait of native elegance, seldom seen in the masculine character after childhood or early youth, was shown in the General's fondness for the sight and fragrance of flowers. An old soldier might be supposed to prize only the bloody laurel on his brow; but here was one, who seemed to have a young girl's appreciation of the floral tribe.

There, beside the fireplace, the brave old General used to sit; while the Surveyor — though seldom, when it could be avoided, taking upon himself the difficult task of engaging him in conversation — was fond of standing at a distance, and watching his quiet and almost slumberous countenance. He seemed away from us, although we saw him but a few yards off; remote, though we passed close beside his chair; unattainable, though we might have stretched forth our hands and touched his own. It might be, that he lived a more real life within his thoughts, than amid the unappropriate environment of the Collector's office. The evolutions of the parade; the tumult of the battle; the flourish of old, heroic music, heard thirty years before; — such scenes and sounds, perhaps, were all alive before his intellectual sense. Meanwhile, the merchants and shipmasters, the spruce clerks, and uncouth sailors, entered and departed; the bustle of this commercial and Custom-House life kept up its little murmur roundabout him; and neither with the men nor their affairs did the General appear to sustain the most distant relation. He was as much out of place as an old sword — now rusty, but which had flashed once in the battle's front, and showed still a bright gleam along its blade — would have been, among the inkstands, paper-folders, and mahogany rulers, on the Deputy Collector's desk.

There was one thing that much aided me in renewing and recreating the stalwart soldier of the Niagara frontier, — the man of true and simple energy. It was the recollection of those memorable words of his, — "I'll try, Sir!" — spoken on the very verge of a desperate and heroic enterprise, and breathing the soul and spirit of New England hardihood, comprehending all perils, and encountering all. If, in our country, valor were rewarded by heraldic honor, this phrase — which it seems so easy to speak, but which only he, with such a task of danger and glory before him, has ever spoken — would be the best and fittest of all mottoes for the General's shield of arms.

It contributes greatly towards a man's moral and intellectual health, to be brought into habits of companionship with individuals unlike himself, who care little for his pursuits, and whose sphere and abilities he must go out of himself to appreciate. The accidents of my life have often afforded me this advantage, but never with more fulness and variety than during my continuance in office. There was one man, especially, the observation of whose character gave me a new idea of talent. His gifts were emphatically those of a man of business; prompt, acute, clear-minded; with an eye that saw through all perplexities, and a faculty of arrangement that made them vanish, as by the waving of an enchanter's wand. Bred up from boyhood in the Custom-House, it was his proper field of activity; and the many intricacies of business, so harassing to the interloper, presented themselves before him with the regularity of a perfectly comprehended system. In my contemplation, he stood as the ideal of his class. He was, indeed, the Custom-House in himself; or, at all events, the main-spring that kept its variously revolving wheels in motion; for, in an institution like this, where its officers are appointed to subserve their own profit and convenience, and seldom with a leading reference to their fitness for the duty to be performed, they must perforce seek elsewhere the dexterity which is not in them. Thus, by an inevitable necessity, as a magnet attracts steel-filings, so did our man of business draw to himself the difficulties which everybody met with. With an easy condescension, and kind forbearance towards our stupidity, — which, to his order of mind, must have seemed little short of crime, — would he forthwith, by the merest touch of his finger, make the incomprehensible as clear as daylight. The merchants valued him not less than we, his esoteric friends. His integrity was perfect; it was a law of nature with him, rather than a choice or a principle; nor can it be otherwise than the main condition of an intellect so remarkably clear and accurate as his, to be honest and regular in the administration of affairs. A stain on his conscience, as to any thing that came within the range of his vocation, would trouble such a man very much in the same way, though to a far greater degree, than an error in the balance of an account, or an ink-blot on the fair page of a book of record. Here, in a word, — and it is a rare instance in my life, — I had met with a person thoroughly adapted to the situation which he held.

Such were some of the people with whom I now found myself connected. I took it in good part at the hands of Providence, that I was thrown into a position so little akin to my past habits; and set myself seriously to gather from it whatever profit was to be had. After my fellowship of toil and impracticable schemes, with the dreamy brethren of Brook Farm; after living for three years within the subtile influence of an intellect like Emerson's; after those wild, free days on the Assabeth, indulging fantastic speculations beside our fire of fallen boughs, with Ellery Channing; after talking with Thoreau about pine-trees and Indian relics, in his hermitage at Walden; after growing fastidious by sympathy with the classic refinement of Hillard's culture; after becoming imbued with poetic sentiment at Longfellow's hearth-stone; — it was time, at length, that I should exercise other faculties of my nature, and nourish myself with food for which I had hitherto had little appetite.[4] Even the

[4] In addition to Ralph Waldo Emerson, Henry David Thoreau, and Henry Wadsworth Longfellow, Hawthorne here refers to William Ellery Channing — Emerson's friend and a religious and social reformer — and his close friend George Stillman Hillard, a Boston attorney.

old Inspector was desirable, as a change of diet, to a man who had known Alcott. I looked upon it as an evidence, in some measure, of a system naturally well balanced, and lacking no essential part of a thorough organization, that, with such associates to remember, I could mingle at once with men of altogether different qualities, and never murmur at the change.

Literature, its exertions and objects, were now of little moment in my regard. I cared not, at this period, for books; they were apart from me. Nature, — except it were human nature, — the nature that is developed in earth and sky, was, in one sense, hidden from me; and all the imaginative delight, wherewith it had been spiritualized, passed away out of my mind. A gift, a faculty, if it had not departed, was suspended and inanimate within me. There would have been something sad, unutterably dreary in all this, had I not been conscious that it lay at my own option to recall whatever was valuable in the past. It might be true, indeed, that this was a life which could not, with impunity, be lived too long; else, it might make me permanently other than I had been, without transforming me into any shape which it would be worth my while to take. But I never considered it as other than a transitory life. There was always a prophetic instinct, a low whisper in my ear, that, within no long period, and whenever a new change of custom should be essential to my good, a change would come.

Meanwhile, there I was, a Surveyor of the Revenue, and, so far as I have been able to understand, as good a Surveyor as need be. A man of thought, fancy, and sensibility, (had he ten times the Surveyor's proportion of those qualities,) may, at any time, be a man of affairs, if he will only choose to give himself the trouble. My fellow-officers and the merchants and sea-captains with whom my official duties brought me into any manner of connection, viewed me in no other light, and probably knew me in no other character. None of them, I presume, had ever read a page of my inditing, or would have cared a fig the more for me, if they had read them all; nor would it have mended the matter, in the least, had those same unprofitable pages been written with a pen like that of Burns or of Chaucer, each of whom was a Custom-House officer in his day, as well as I. It is a good lesson — though it may often be a hard one — for a man who has dreamed of literary fame, and of making for himself a rank among the world's dignitaries by such means, to step aside out of the narrow circle in which his claims are recognized, and to find how utterly devoid of significance, beyond that circle, is all that he achieves, and all he aims at. I know not that I especially needed the lesson, either in the way of warning or rebuke; but, at any rate, I learned it thoroughly; nor, it gives me pleasure to reflect, did the truth, as it came home to my perception, ever cost me a pang, or require to be thrown off in a sigh. In the way of literary talk, it is true, the Naval Officer — an excellent fellow, who came into office with me, and went out only a little later — would often engage me in a discussion about one or the other of his favorite topics, Napoleon or Shakespeare. The Collector's junior clerk, too, — a young gentleman who, it was whispered, occasionally covered a sheet of Uncle Sam's letter-paper with what, (at the distance of a few yards,) looked very much like poetry, — used now and then to speak to me of books, as matters with which I might possibly be conversant. This was my all of lettered intercourse; and it was quite sufficient for my necessities.

No longer seeking nor caring that my name should be blazoned abroad on title-pages, I smiled to think that it had now another kind of vogue. The Custom-House marker imprinted it, with a stencil and black paint, on pepper-bags, and baskets of anatto, and cigar-boxes, and bales of all kinds of dutiable merchandise, in testimony that these commodities had paid the impost, and gone regularly through the office. Borne on such queer vehicle of fame, a knowledge of my existence, so far as a name conveys it, was carried where it had never been before, and, I hope, will never go again.

But the past was not dead. Once in a great while, the thoughts, that had seemed so vital and so active, yet had been put to rest so quietly, revived again. One of the most remarkable occasions, when the habit of bygone days awoke in me, was that which brings it within the law of literary propriety to offer the public the sketch which I am now writing.

In the second story of the Custom-House, there is a large room, in which the brick-work and naked rafters have never been covered with panelling and plaster. The edifice — originally projected on a scale adapted to the old commercial enterprise of the port, and with an idea of subsequent prosperity destined never to be realized — contains far more space than its occupants know what to do with. This airy hall, therefore, over the Collector's apartments, remains unfinished to this day, and, in spite of the aged cobwebs that festoon its dusky beams, appears still to await the labor of the carpenter and mason. At one end of the room, in a recess, were a number of barrels, piled one upon another, containing bundles of official documents. Large quantities of similar rubbish lay lumbering the floor. It was sorrowful to think how many days, and weeks, and months, and years of toil, had been wasted on these musty papers, which were now only an encumbrance on earth, and were hidden away in this forgotten corner, never more to be glanced at by human eyes. But, then, what reams of other manuscripts — filled, not with the dulness of official formalities, but with the thought of inventive brains and the rich effusion of deep hearts — had gone equally to oblivion; and that, moreover, without serving a purpose in their days, as these heaped-up papers had, and — saddest of all — without purchasing for their writers the comfortable livelihood which the clerks of the Custom-House had gained by these worthless scratchings of the pen! Yet not altogether worthless, perhaps, as materials of local history. Here, no doubt, statistics of the former commerce of Salem might be discovered, and memorials of her princely merchants, — old King Derby, — old Billy Gray, — old Simon Forrester, — and many another magnate in his day; whose powdered head, however, was scarcely in the tomb, before his mountain-pile of wealth began to dwindle. The founders of the greater part of the families which now compose the aristocracy of Salem might here be traced, from the petty and obscure beginnings of their traffic, at periods generally much posterior to the Revolution, upward to what their children look upon as long-established rank.

Prior to the Revolution, there is a dearth of records; the earlier documents and archives of the Custom-House having, probably, been carried off to Halifax, when all the King's officials accompanied the British army in its flight from Boston. It has often been a matter of regret with me; for, going back, perhaps, to the days of the Protectorate, those papers must have contained many references to forgotten or remembered men, and to antique customs, which would have affected me with the same pleasure as when I used to pick up Indian arrow-heads in the field near the Old Manse.

But, one idle and rainy day, it was my fortune to make a discovery of some little interest. Poking and burrowing into the heaped-up rubbish in the corner; unfolding one and another document, and reading the names of vessels that had long ago foundered at sea or rotted at the wharves, and those of merchants, never heard of now on 'Change,° nor very readily decipherable on their mossy tombstones; glancing at such matters with the saddened, weary, half-reluctant interest which we bestow on the corpse of dead activity, — and exerting my fancy, sluggish with little use, to raise up from these dry bones an image of the old town's brighter aspect, when India was a new region, and only Salem knew the way thither, — I chanced to lay my hand on a small package, carefully done up in a piece of ancient yellow parchment. This envelope

'Change: Boston Merchant Exchange.

had the air of an official record of some period long past, when clerks engrossed their stiff and formal chirography° on more substantial materials than at present. There was something about it that quickened an instinctive curiosity, and made me undo the faded red tape, that tied up the package, with the sense that a treasure would here be brought to light. Unbending the rigid folds of the parchment cover, I found it to be a commission, under the hand and seal of Governor Shirley, in favor of one Jonathan Pue, as Surveyor of his Majesty's Customs for the port of Salem, in the Province of Massachusetts Bay. I remembered to have read (probably in Felt's Annals) a notice of the decease of Mr. Surveyor Pue, about fourscore years ago; and likewise, in a newspaper of recent times, an account of the digging up of his remains in the little graveyard of St. Peter's Church, during the renewal of that edifice. Nothing, if I rightly call to mind, was left of my respected predecessor, save an imperfect skeleton, and some fragments of apparel and a wig of majestic frizzle; which, unlike the head that it once adorned, was in very satisfactory preservation. But, on examining the papers which the parchment commission served to envelop, I found more traces of Mr. Pue's mental part, and the internal operations of his head, than the frizzled wig had contained of the venerable skull itself.

They were documents, in short, not official, but of a private nature, or, at least, written in his private capacity, and apparently with his own hand. I could account for their being included in the heap of Custom-House lumber only by the fact, that Mr. Pue's death had happened suddenly; and that these papers, which he probably kept in his official desk, had never come to the knowledge of his heirs, or were supposed to relate to the business of the revenue. On the transfer of the archives to Halifax, this package, proving to be of no public concern, was left behind, and had remained ever since unopened.

The ancient Surveyor — being little molested, I suppose, at that early day, with business pertaining to his office — seems to have devoted some of his many leisure hours to researches as a local antiquarian, and other inquisitions of a similar nature. These supplied material for petty activity to a mind that would otherwise have been eaten up with rust. A portion of his facts, by the by, did me good service in the preparation of the article entitled "MAIN STREET," included in the present volume. The remainder may perhaps be applied to purposes equally valuable, hereafter; or not impossibly may be worked up, so far as they

chirography: Handwriting.

go, into a regular history of Salem, should my veneration for the natal soil ever impel me to so pious a task. Meanwhile, they shall be at the command of any gentleman, inclined, and competent, to take the unprofitable labor off my hands. As a final disposition, I contemplate depositing them with the Essex Historical Society.

But the object that most drew my attention, in the mysterious package, was a certain affair of fine red cloth, much worn and faded. There were traces about it of gold embroidery, which, however, was greatly frayed and defaced; so that none, or very little, of the glitter was left. It had been wrought, as was easy to perceive, with wonderful skill of needlework; and the stitch (as I am assured by ladies conversant with such mysteries) gives evidence of a now forgotten art, not to be recovered even by the process of picking out the threads. This rag of scarlet cloth, — for time, and wear, and a sacrilegious moth, had reduced it to little other than a rag, — on careful examination, assumed the shape of a letter. It was the capital letter A. By an accurate measurement, each limb proved to be precisely three inches and a quarter in length. It had been intended, there could be no doubt, as an ornamental article of dress; but how it was to be worn, or what rank, honor, and dignity, in by-past times, were signified by it, was a riddle which (so evanescent are the fashions of the world in these particulars) I saw little hope of solving. And yet it strangely interested me. My eyes fastened themselves upon the old scarlet letter, and would not be turned aside. Certainly, there was some deep meaning in it, most worthy of interpretation, and which, as it were, streamed forth from the mystic symbol, subtly communicating itself to my sensibilities, but evading the analysis of my mind.

While thus perplexed, — and cogitating, among other hypotheses, whether the letter might not have been one of those decorations which the white men used to contrive, in order to take the eyes of Indians, — I happened to place it on my breast. It seemed to me, — the reader may smile, but must not doubt my word, — it seemed to me, then, that I experienced a sensation not altogether physical, yet almost so, as of burning heat; and as if the letter were not of red cloth, but red-hot iron. I shuddered, and involuntarily let it fall upon the floor.

In the absorbing contemplation of the scarlet letter, I had hitherto neglected to examine a small roll of dingy paper, around which it had been twisted. This I now opened, and had the satisfaction to find, recorded by the old Surveyor's pen, a reasonably complete explanation of the whole affair. There were several foolscap sheets, containing many particulars respecting the life and conversation of one Hester Prynne, who appeared to have been rather a noteworthy personage in the view of our ancestors. She had flourished during a period between the early days of Massachusetts and the close of the seventeenth century. Aged persons, alive in the time of Mr. Surveyor Pue, and from whose oral testimony he had made up his narrative, remembered her, in their youth, as a very old, but not decrepit woman, of a stately and solemn aspect. It had been her habit, from an almost immemorial date, to go about the country as a kind of voluntary nurse, and doing whatever miscellaneous good she might; taking upon herself, likewise, to give advice in all matters, especially those of the heart; by which means, as a person of such propensities inevitably must, she gained from many people the reverence due to an angel, but, I should imagine, was looked upon by others as an intruder and a nuisance. Prying farther into the manuscript, I found the record of other doings and sufferings of this singular woman, for most of which the reader is referred to the story entitled "THE SCARLET LETTER"; and it should be borne carefully in mind, that the main facts of that story are authorized and authenticated by the document of Mr. Surveyor Pue. The original papers, together with the scarlet letter itself, — a most curious relic, — are still in my possession, and shall be freely exhibited to whomsoever, induced by the great interest of the narrative, may desire a sight of them. I must not be understood as affirming, that, in the dressing up of the tale, and imagining the motives and modes of passion that influenced the characters who figure in it, I have invariably confined myself within the limits of the old Surveyor's half a dozen sheets of foolscap. On the contrary, I have allowed myself, as to such points, nearly or altogether as much license as if the facts had been entirely of my own invention. What I contend for is the authenticity of the outline.

This incident recalled my mind, in some degree, to its old track. There seemed to be here the groundwork of a tale. It impressed me as if the ancient Surveyor, in his garb of a hundred years gone by, and wearing his immortal wig, — which was buried with him, but did not perish in the grave, — had met me in the deserted chamber of the Custom-House. In his port was the dignity of one who had borne his Majesty's commission, and who was therefore illuminated by a ray of the splendor that shone so dazzlingly about the throne. How unlike, alas! the hangdog look of a republican official, who, as the servant of the people, feels himself less than the least, and below the lowest, of his masters. With his own ghostly hand, the obscurely seen, but majestic, figure had imparted to me the scarlet symbol, and the little roll of explanatory manuscript. With his own ghostly voice, he had exhorted me, on the sacred consideration of my filial duty and reverence towards him, — who might reasonably regard himself as my official ancestor, — to bring his mouldy and moth-eaten lucubrations° before the public. "Do this," said the ghost of Mr. Surveyor Pue, emphatically nodding the head that looked so imposing within its memorable wig, "do this, and the profit shall be all your own! You will shortly need it; for it is not in your days as it was in mine, when a man's office was a life-lease, and oftentimes an heir-loom. But, I charge you, in this matter of old Mistress Prynne, give to your predecessor's memory the credit which will be rightfully its due!" And I said to the ghost of Mr. Surveyor Pue, — "I will!"

On Hester Prynne's story, therefore, I bestowed much thought. It was the subject of my meditations for many an hour, while pacing to and fro across my room, or traversing, with a hundredfold repetition, the long extent from the front-door of the Custom-House to the side-entrance, and back again. Great were the weariness and annoyance of the old Inspector and the Weighers and Gaugers, whose slumbers were disturbed by the unmercifully lengthened tramp of my passing and returning footsteps. Remembering their own former habits, they used to say that the Surveyor was walking the quarter-deck. They probably fancied that my sole object — and, indeed, the sole object for which a sane man could ever put himself into voluntary motion — was, to get an appetite for dinner. And to say the truth, an appetite, sharpened by the east-wind that generally blew along the passage, was the only valuable result of so much indefatigable exercise. So little adapted is the atmosphere of a Custom-House to the delicate harvest of fancy and sensibility, that, had I remained there through ten Presidencies yet to come, I doubt whether the tale of "The Scarlet Letter" would ever have been brought before the public eye. My imagination was a tarnished mirror. It would not reflect, or only with miserable dimness, the figures with which I did my best to people it. The characters of the narrative would not be warmed and rendered malleable, by any heat that I could kindle at my intellectual forge. They would take neither the glow of passion nor the tenderness of sentiment, but retained all the rigidity of dead corpses, and stared me in the face with a fixed and ghastly grin of contemptuous defiance. "What have you to do with us?" that expression seemed to say. "The little power you might once have possessed over the tribe of unrealities is gone! You have bartered it for a pittance of the public gold. Go, then, and earn your wages!" In short, the

lucubrations: Studies.

almost torpid creatures of my own fancy twitted me with imbecility, and not without fair occasion.

It was not merely during the three hours and a half which Uncle Sam claimed as his share of my daily life, that this wretched numbness held possession of me. It went with me on my sea-shore walks and rambles into the country, whenever — which was seldom and reluctantly — I bestirred myself to seek that invigorating charm of Nature, which used to give me such freshness and activity of thought, the moment that I stepped across the threshold of the Old Manse. The same torpor, as regarded the capacity for intellectual effort, accompanied me home, and weighed upon me in the chamber which I most absurdly termed my study. Nor did it quit me, when, late at night, I sat in the deserted parlour, lighted only by the glimmering coal-fire and the moon, striving to picture forth imaginary scenes, which, the next day, might flow out on the brightening page in many-hued description.

If the imaginative faculty refused to act at such an hour, it might well be deemed a hopeless case. Moonlight, in a familiar room, falling so white upon the carpet, and showing all its figures so distinctly, — making every object so minutely visible, yet so unlike a morning or noontide visibility, — is a medium the most suitable for a romance-writer to get acquainted with his illusive guests. There is the little domestic scenery of the well-known apartment; the chairs, with each its separate individuality; the centre-table, sustaining a work-basket, a volume or two, and an extinguished lamp; the sofa; the book-case; the picture on the wall; — all these details, so completely seen, are so spiritualized by the unusual light, that they seem to lose their actual substance, and become things of intellect. Nothing is too small or too trifling to undergo this change, and acquire dignity thereby. A child's shoe; the doll, seated in her little wicker carriage; the hobby-horse; — whatever, in a word, has been used or played with, during the day, is now invested with a quality of strangeness and remoteness, though still almost as vividly present as by daylight. Thus, therefore, the floor of our familiar room has become a neutral territory, somewhere between the real world and fairy-land, where the Actual and the Imaginary may meet, and each imbue itself with the nature of the other. Ghosts might enter here, without affrighting us. It would be too much in keeping with the scene to excite surprise, were we to look about us and discover a form, beloved, but gone hence, now sitting quietly in a streak of this magic moonshine, with an aspect that would make us doubt whether it had returned from afar, or had never once stirred from our fireside.

The somewhat dim coal-fire has an essential influence in producing the effect which I would describe. It throws its unobtrusive tinge throughout the room, with a faint ruddiness upon the walls and ceiling, and a reflected gleam from the polish of the furniture. This warmer light mingles itself with the cold spirituality of the moonbeams, and communicates, as it were, a heart and sensibilities of human tenderness to the forms which fancy summons up. It converts them from snow-images into men and women. Glancing at the looking-glass, we behold — deep within its haunted verge — the smouldering glow of the half-extinguished anthracite, the white moonbeams on the floor, and a repetition of all the gleam and shadow of the picture, with one remove farther from the actual, and nearer to the imaginative. Then, at such an hour, and with this scene before him, if a man, sitting all alone, cannot dream strange things, and make them look like truth, he need never try to write romances.

But, for myself, during the whole of my Custom-House experience, moonlight and sunshine, and the glow of firelight, were just alike in my regard; and neither of them was of one whit more avail than the twinkle of a tallow-candle. An entire class of susceptibilities, and a gift connected with them, — of no great richness or value, but the best I had, — was gone from me.

It is my belief, however, that, had I attempted a different order of composition, my faculties would not have been found so pointless and inefficacious. I might, for instance, have contented myself with writing out the narratives of a veteran shipmaster, one of the Inspectors, whom I should be most ungrateful not to mention; since scarcely a day passed that he did not stir me to laughter and admiration by his marvellous gifts as a story-teller. Could I have preserved the picturesque force of his style, and the humorous coloring which nature taught him how to throw over his descriptions, the result, I honestly believe, would have been something new in literature. Or I might readily have found a more serious task. It was a folly, with the materiality of this daily life pressing so intrusively upon me, to attempt to fling myself back into another age; or to insist on creating the semblance of a world out of airy matter, when, at every moment, the impalpable beauty of my soap-bubble was broken by the rude contact of some actual circumstance. The wiser effort would have been, to diffuse thought and imagination through the opaque substance of to-day, and thus to make it a bright transparency; to spiritualize the burden that began to weigh so heavily; to seek, resolutely, the true and indestructible value that lay hidden in the petty and wearisome incidents, and ordinary characters, with which I was now conversant. The fault was mine. The page of life that was spread out before me seemed dull and commonplace, only because I had not fathomed its deeper import. A better book than I shall ever write was there; leaf after leaf presenting itself to me, just as it was written out by the reality of the flitting hour, and vanishing as fast as written, only because my brain wanted the insight and my hand the cunning to transcribe it. At some future day, it may be, I shall remember a few scattered fragments and broken paragraphs, and write them down, and find the letters turn to gold upon the page.

These perceptions have come too late. At the instant, I was only conscious that what would have been a pleasure once was now a hopeless toil. There was no occasion to make much moan about this state of affairs. I had ceased to be a writer of tolerably poor tales and essays, and had become a tolerably good Surveyor of the Customs. That was all. But, nevertheless, it is any thing but agreeable to be haunted by a suspicion that one's intellect is dwindling away; or exhaling, without your consciousness, like ether out of a phial; so that, at every glance, you find a smaller and less volatile residuum. Of the fact, there could be no doubt; and, examining myself and others, I was led to conclusions in reference to the effect of public office on the character, not very favorable to the mode of life in question. In some other form, perhaps, I may hereafter develop these effects. Suffice it here to say, that a Custom-House officer, of long continuance, can hardly be a very praiseworthy or respectable personage, for many reasons; one of them, the tenure by which he holds his situation, and another, the very nature of his business, which — though, I trust, an honest one — is of such a sort that he does not share in the united effort of mankind.

An effect — which I believe to be observable, more or less, in every individual who has occupied the position — is, that, while he leans on the mighty arm of the Republic, his own proper strength departs from him. He loses, in an extent proportioned to the weakness or force of his original nature, the capability of self-support. If he possess an unusual share of native energy, or the enervating magic of place do not operate too long upon him, his forfeited powers may be redeemable. The ejected officer — fortunate in the unkindly shove that sends him forth betimes, to struggle amid a struggling world — may return to himself, and become all that he has ever been. But this seldom happens. He usually keeps his ground just long enough for his own ruin, and is then thrust out, with sinews all unstrung, to totter along the difficult footpath of life as he best may. Conscious of his own infirmity, — that his tempered steel and elasticity are lost, — he for ever afterwards looks wistfully about him in quest of support external to himself. His pervading and continual hope — a hallucination, which, in the face of all discouragement, and making light of impossibilities, haunts him while he lives, and, I fancy, like the convulsive throes of the cholera, torments him for a brief space after death — is, that, finally, and in no long time, by some happy coincidence of circumstances, he shall be restored to office. This faith, more than any thing else, steals the pith and availability out of whatever enterprise he may dream of undertaking. Why should he toil and moil, and be at so much trouble to pick himself up out of the mud, when, in a little while hence, the strong arm of his Uncle will raise and support him? Why should he work for his living here, or go to dig gold in California, when he is so soon to be made happy, at monthly intervals, with a little pile of glittering coin out of his Uncle's pocket? It is sadly curious to observe how slight a taste of office suffices to infect a poor fellow with this singular disease. Uncle Sam's gold — meaning no disrespect to the worthy old gentleman — has, in this respect, a quality of enchantment like that of the Devil's wages. Whoever touches it should look well to himself, or he may find the bargain to go hard against him, involving, if not his soul, yet many of its better attributes; its sturdy force, its courage and constancy, its truth, its self-reliance, and all that gives the emphasis to manly character.

Here was a fine prospect in the distance! Not that the Surveyor brought the lesson home to himself, or admitted that he could be so utterly undone, either by continuance in office, or ejectment. Yet my reflections were not the most comfortable. I began to grow melancholy and restless; continually prying into my mind, to discover which of its poor properties were gone, and what degree of detriment had already accrued to the remainder. I endeavoured to calculate how much longer I could stay in the Custom-House, and yet go forth a man. To confess the truth, it was my greatest apprehension, — as it would never be a measure of policy to turn out so quiet an individual as myself, and it being hardly in the nature of a public officer to resign, — it was my chief trouble, therefore, that I was likely to grow gray and decrepit in the Surveyorship, and become much such another animal as the old Inspector. Might it not, in the tedious lapse of official life that lay before me, finally be with me as it was with this venerable friend, — to make the dinner-hour the nucleus of the day, and to spend the rest of it, as an old dog spends it, asleep in the sunshine or the shade? A dreary look-forward this, for a man who felt it to be the best definition of happiness to live throughout the whole range of his faculties and sensibilities! But, all this while, I was giving myself very unnecessary alarm. Providence had meditated better things for me than I could possibly imagine for myself.

A remarkable event of the third year of my Surveyorship — to adopt the tone of "P.P." — was the election of General Taylor to the Presidency. It is essential in order to form a complete estimate of the advantages of official life, to view the incumbent at the in-coming of a hostile administration. His position is then one of the most singularly irksome, and, in every contingency, disagreeable, that a wretched mortal can possibly occupy; with seldom an alternative of good, on either hand, although what presents itself to him as the worst event may very probably be the best. But it is a strange experience, to a man of pride and sensibility, to know that his interests are within the control of individuals who neither love nor understand him, and by whom, since one or the other must needs happen, he would rather be injured than obliged. Strange, too, for one who has kept his calmness throughout the contest, to observe the bloodthirstiness that is developed in the hour of triumph, and to be conscious that he is himself among its objects! There are few uglier traits of human nature than this tendency — which I now witnessed in men no worse than their neighbours — to grow cruel, merely because they possessed the power of inflicting harm. If the guillotine, as applied to office-holders, were a literal fact, instead of one of the most apt of metaphors, it is my sincere belief, that the active members of the victorious party were sufficiently excited to have chopped off all our heads, and have thanked Heaven for the opportunity! It appears to me — who have been a calm and curious observer, as well in victory as defeat — that this fierce and bitter spirit of malice and revenge has never distinguished the many triumphs of my own party as it now did that of the Whigs. The Democrats take the offices, as a general rule, because they need them, and because the practice of many years has made it the law of political warfare, which, unless a different system be proclaimed, it were weakness and cowardice to murmur at. But the long habit of victory has made them generous. They know how to spare, when they see occasion; and when they strike, the axe may be sharp, indeed, but its edge is seldom poisoned with ill-will; nor is it their custom ignominiously to kick the head which they have just struck off.

In short, unpleasant as was my predicament, at best, I saw much reason to congratulate myself that I was on the losing side, rather than the triumphant one. If, heretofore, I had been none of the warmest of partisans, I began now, at this season of peril and adversity, to be pretty acutely sensible with which party my predilections lay; nor was it without something like regret and shame, that, according to a reasonable calculation of chances, I saw my own prospect of retaining office to be better than those of my Democratic brethren. But who can see an inch into futurity, beyond his nose? My own head was the first that fell!

The moment when a man's head drops off is seldom or never, I am inclined to think, precisely the most agreeable of his life. Nevertheless, like the greater part of our misfortunes, even so serious a contingency brings its remedy and consolation with it, if the sufferer will but make the best, rather than the worst, of the accident which has befallen him. In my particular case, the consolatory topics were close at hand, and, indeed, had suggested themselves to my meditations a considerable time before it was requisite to use them. In view of my previous weariness of office, and vague thoughts of resignation, my fortune somewhat resembled that of a person who should entertain an idea of committing suicide, and, altogether beyond his hopes, meet with the good hap to be murdered. In the Custom-House, as before in the Old Manse, I had spent three years; a term long enough to rest a weary brain; long enough to break off old intellectual habits, and make room for new ones; long enough, and too long, to have lived in an unnatural state, doing what was really of no advantage nor delight to any human being, and withholding myself from toil that would, at least, have stilled an unquiet impulse in me. Then, moreover, as regarded his unceremonious ejectment, the late Surveyor was not altogether ill-pleased to be recognized by the Whigs as an enemy; since his inactivity in political affairs, — his tendency to roam, at will, in that broad and quiet field where all mankind may meet, rather than confine himself to those narrow paths where brethren of the same household must diverge from one another, — had sometimes made it questionable with his brother Democrats whether he was a friend. Now, after he had won the crown of martyrdom, (though with no longer a head to wear it on,) the point might be looked upon as settled. Finally, little heroic as he was, it seemed more decorous to be overthrown in the downfall of the party with which he had been content to stand, than to remain a forlorn survivor, when so many worthier men were falling; and, at last, after subsisting for four years on the mercy of a hostile administration, to be compelled then to define his position anew, and claim the yet more humiliating mercy of a friendly one.

Meanwhile, the press had taken up my affair, and kept me, for a week or two, careering through the public prints, in my decapitated state, like Irving's Headless Horseman; ghastly and grim, and longing to be buried, as a politically dead man ought. So much for my figurative self. The real human being, all this time, with his head safely on his shoulders, had brought himself to the comfortable conclusion, that every thing was for the best; and, making an investment in ink, paper, and steel-pens, had opened his long-disused writing-desk, and was again a literary man.

Now it was, that the lucubrations of my ancient predecessor, Mr. Surveyor Pue, came into play. Rusty through long idleness, some little space was requisite before my intellectual machinery could be brought to work upon the tale, with an effect in any degree satisfactory. Even yet, though my thoughts were ultimately much absorbed in the task, it wears, to my eye, a stern and sombre aspect; too much ungladdened by genial sunshine; too little relieved by the tender and familiar influences which soften almost every scene of nature and real life, and, undoubtedly, should soften every picture of them. This uncaptivating effect is perhaps due to the period of hardly accomplished revolution, and still seething turmoil, in which the story shaped itself. It is no indication, however, of a lack of cheerfulness in the writer's mind; for he was happier, while straying through the gloom of these sunless fantasies, than at any time since he had quitted the Old Manse. Some of the briefer articles, which contribute to make up the volume, have likewise been written since my involuntary withdrawal from the toils and honors of public life, and the remainder are gleaned from annuals and magazines, of such antique date that they have gone round the circle, and come back to novelty again.[5] Keeping up the metaphor of the political guillotine, the whole may be considered as the POSTHUMOUS PAPERS OF A DECAPITATED SURVEYOR; and the sketch which I am now bringing to a close, if too autobiographical for a modest person to publish in his lifetime, will readily be excused in a gentleman who writes from beyond the grave. Peace be with all the world! My blessing on my friends! My forgiveness to my enemies! For I am in the realm of quiet!

The life of the Custom-House lies like a dream behind me. The old Inspector, — who, by the by, I regret to say, was overthrown and killed by a horse, some time ago; else he would certainly have lived for ever, — he, and all those other venerable personages who sat with him at the receipt of custom, are but shadows in my view; white-headed and wrinkled images, which my fancy used to sport with, and has now flung aside for ever. The merchants, — Pingree, Phillips, Shepard, Upton, Kimball, Bertram, Hunt, — these, and many other names, which had

[5] At the time of writing this article, the author intended to publish, along with "The Scarlet Letter," several shorter tales and sketches. These it has been thought advisable to defer. (Hawthorne's note.)

such a classic familiarity for my ear six months ago, — these men of traffic, who seemed to occupy so important a position in the world, — how little time has it required to disconnect me from them all, not merely in act, but recollection! It is with an effort that I recall the figures and appellations of these few. Soon, likewise, my old native town will loom upon me through the haze of memory, a mist brooding over and around it; as if it were no portion of the real earth, but an overgrown village in cloud-land, with only imaginary inhabitants to people its wooden houses, and walk its homely lanes, and the unpicturesque prolixity of its main street. Henceforth, it ceases to be a reality of my life. I am a citizen of somewhere else. My good townspeople will not much regret me; for — though it has been as dear an object as any, in my literary efforts, to be of some importance in their eyes, and to win myself a pleasant memory in this abode and burial-place of so many of my forefathers — there has never been, for me, the genial atmosphere which a literary man requires, in order to ripen the best harvest of his mind. I shall do better amongst other faces; and these familiar ones, it need hardly be said, will do just as well without me.

It may be, however, — O, transporting and triumphant thought! — that the great-grandchildren of the present race may sometimes think kindly of the scribbler of bygone days, when the antiquary of days to come, among the sites memorable in the town's history, shall point out the locality of THE TOWN-PUMP!

THE SCARLET LETTER

I. The Prison-Door

A throng of bearded men, in sad-colored garments and gray, steeple-crowned hats, intermixed with women, some wearing hoods, and others bareheaded, was assembled in front of a wooden edifice, the door of which was heavily timbered with oak, and studded with iron spikes.

The founders of a new colony, whatever Utopia of human virtue and happiness they might originally project, have invariably recognized it among their earliest practical necessities to allot a portion of the virgin soil as a cemetery, and another portion as the site of a prison. In accordance with this rule, it may safely be assumed that the forefathers of Boston had built the first prison-house, somewhere in the vicinity of Cornhill, almost as seasonably as they marked out the first burial-ground, on Isaac Johnson's lot, and round about his grave, which subsequently became the nucleus of all the congregated sepulchres in the old churchyard of King's Chapel. Certain it is, that, some fifteen or twenty years after the settlement of the town, the wooden jail was already marked with weather-stains and other indications of age, which gave a yet darker aspect to its beetle-browed and gloomy front. The rust on the ponderous iron-work of its oaken door looked more antique than any thing else in the new world. Like all that pertains to crime, it seemed never to have known a youthful era. Before this ugly edifice, and between it and the wheel-track of the street, was a grass-plot, much overgrown with burdock, pig-weed, apple-peru, and such unsightly vegetation, which evidently found something congenial in the soil that had so early borne the black flower of civilized society, a prison. But, on one side of the portal, and rooted almost at the threshold, was a wild rose-bush, covered, in this month of June, with its delicate gems, which might be imagined to offer their fragrance and fragile beauty to the prisoner as he went in, and to the condemned criminal as he came forth to his doom, in token that the deep heart of Nature could pity and be kind to him.

This rose-bush, by a strange chance, has been kept alive in history; but whether it had merely survived out of the stern old wilderness, so long after the fall of the gigantic pines and oaks that originally overshadowed it, — or whether, as there is fair authority for believing, it had sprung up under the footsteps of the sainted Ann Hutchinson,[6] as she entered the prison-door, — we shall not take upon us to determine. Finding it so directly on the threshold of our narrative, which is now about to issue from that inauspicious portal, we could hardly do otherwise than pluck one of its flowers and present it to the reader. It may serve, let us hope, to symbolize some sweet moral blossom, that may be found along the track, or relieve the darkening close of a tale of human frailty and sorrow.

II. The Market-Place

The grass-plot before the jail, in Prison Lane, on a certain summer morning, not less than two centuries ago, was occupied by a pretty large number of the inhabitants of Boston; all with their eyes intently fastened on the iron-clamped oaken door. Amongst any other population, or at a later period in the history of New England, the grim rigid-

[6] Anne Hutchinson (1591–1643) preached the Antinomian doctrine that salvation derives from God's grace, not from good works. She was banished to Rhode Island for her beliefs.

ity that petrified the bearded physiognomies of these good people would have augured some awful business in hand. It could have betokened nothing short of the anticipated execution of some noted culprit, on whom the sentence of a legal tribunal had but confirmed the verdict of public sentiment. But, in that early severity of the Puritan character, an inference of this kind could not so indubitably be drawn. It might be that a sluggish bond-servant, or an undutiful child, whom his parents had given over to the civil authority, was to be corrected at the whipping-post. It might be, that an Antinomian, a Quaker, or other heterodox religionist, was to be scourged out of the town, or an idle and vagrant Indian, whom the white man's fire-water had made riotous about the streets, was to be driven with stripes into the shadow of the forest. It might be, too, that a witch, like old Mistress Hibbins, the bitter-tempered widow of the magistrate, was to die upon the gallows. In either case, there was very much the same solemnity of demeanour on the part of the spectators; as befitted a people amongst whom religion and law were almost identical, and in whose character both were so thoroughly interfused, that the mildest and the severest acts of public discipline were alike made venerable and awful. Meagre, indeed, and cold, was the sympathy that a transgressor might look for, from such bystanders at the scaffold. On the other hand, a penalty which, in our days, would infer a degree of mocking infamy and ridicule, might then be invested with almost as stern a dignity as the punishment of death itself.

It was a circumstance to be noted, on the summer morning when our story begins its course, that the women, of whom there were several in the crowd, appeared to take a peculiar interest in whatever penal infliction might be expected to ensue. The age had not so much refinement, that any sense of impropriety restrained the wearers of petticoat and farthingale from stepping forth into the public ways, and wedging their not unsubstantial persons, if occasion were, into the throng nearest to the scaffold at an execution. Morally, as well as materially, there was a coarser fibre in those wives and maidens of old English birth and breeding, than in their fair descendants, separated from them by a series of six or seven generations; for, throughout that chain of ancestry, every successive mother has transmitted to her child a fainter bloom, a more delicate and briefer beauty, and a slighter physical frame, if not a character of less force and solidity, than her own. The women, who were now standing about the prison-door, stood within less than half a century of the period when the man-like Elizabeth had been the not altogether unsuitable representative of the sex. They were her countrywomen; and the beef and ale of their native land, with a moral diet not a whit more refined, entered largely into their composition. The bright morning sun, therefore, shone on broad shoulders and well-developed busts, and on round and ruddy cheeks, that had ripened in the far-off island, and had hardly yet grown paler or thinner in the atmosphere of New England. There was, moreover, a boldness and rotundity of speech among these matrons, as most of them seemed to be, that would startle us at the present day, whether in respect to its purport or its volume of tone.

"Goodwives," said a hard-featured dame of fifty, "I'll tell ye a piece of my mind. It would be greatly for the public behoof, if we women, being of mature age and church-members in good repute, should have the handling of such malefactresses as this Hester Prynne. What think ye, gossips? If the hussy stood up for judgment before us five, that are now here in a knot together, would she come off with such a sentence as the worshipful magistrates have awarded? Marry, I trow not!"

"People say," said another, "that the Reverend Master Dimmesdale, her godly pastor, takes it very grievously to heart that such a scandal should have come upon his congregation."

"The magistrates are God-fearing gentlemen, but merciful overmuch, — that is a truth," added a third autumnal matron. "At the very least, they should have put the brand of a hot iron on Hester Prynne's forehead. Madam Hester would have winced at that, I warrant me. But she, — the naughty baggage, — little will she care what they put upon the bodice of her gown! Why, look you, she may cover it with a brooch, or such like heathenish adornment, and so walk the streets as brave as ever!"

"Ah, but," interposed, more softly, a young wife, holding a child by the hand, "let her cover the mark as she will, the pang of it will be always in her heart."

"What do we talk of marks and brands, whether on the bodice of her gown, or the flesh of her forehead?" cried another female, the ugliest as well as the most pitiless of these self-constituted judges. "This woman has brought shame upon us all, and ought to die. Is there not law for it? Truly there is, both in the Scripture and the statute-book. Then let the magistrates, who have made it of no effect, thank themselves if their own wives and daughters go astray!"

"Mercy on us, goodwife," exclaimed a man in the crowd, "is there no virtue in woman, save what springs from a wholesome fear of the gallows? That is the hardest word yet! Hush, now, gossips; for the lock is turning in the prison-door, and here comes Mistress Prynne herself."

The door of the jail being flung open from within, there appeared, in the first place, like a black shadow emerging into the sunshine, the grim and grisly presence of the town-beadle,[7] with a sword by his side and his staff of office in his hand. This personage prefigured and represented in his aspect the whole dismal severity of the Puritanic code of law, which it was his business to administer in its final and closest application to the offender. Stretching forth the official staff in his left hand, he laid his right upon the shoulder of a young woman, whom he thus drew forward; until, on the threshold of the prison-door, she repelled him, by an action marked with natural dignity and force of character, and stepped into the open air, as if by her own free-will. She bore in her arms a child, a baby of some three months old, who winked and turned aside its little face from the too vivid light of day; because its existence, heretofore, had brought it acquainted only with the gray twilight of a dungeon, or other darksome apartment of the prison.

When the young woman — the mother of this child — stood fully revealed before the crowd, it seemed to be her first impulse to clasp the infant closely to her bosom; not so much by an impulse of motherly affection, as that she might thereby conceal a certain token, which was wrought or fastened into her dress. In a moment, however, wisely judging that one token of her shame would but poorly serve to hide another, she took the baby on her arm, and, with a burning blush, and yet a haughty smile, and a glance that would not be abashed, looked around at her townspeople and neighbours. On the breast of her gown, in fine red cloth, surrounded with an elaborate embroidery and fantastic flourishes of gold thread, appeared the letter A. It was so artistically done, and with so much fertility and gorgeous luxuriance of fancy, that it had all the effect of a last and fitting decoration to the apparel which she wore; and which was of a splendor in accordance with the taste of the age, but greatly beyond what was allowed by the sumptuary regulations of the colony.

The young woman was tall, with a figure of perfect elegance, on a large scale. She had dark and abundant hair, so glossy that it threw off the sunshine with a gleam, and a face which, besides being beautiful from regularity of feature and richness of complexion, had the impressiveness belonging to a marked brow and deep black eyes. She was lady-like, too, after the manner of the feminine gentility of those days;

[7] In this context, a church officer responsible for keeping order in a town/congregation.

characterized by a certain state and dignity, rather than by the delicate, evanescent, and indescribable grace, which is now recognized as its indication. And never had Hester Prynne appeared more lady-like, in the antique interpretation of the term, than as she issued from the prison. Those who had before known her, and had expected to behold her dimmed and obscured by a disastrous cloud, were astonished, and even startled, to perceive how her beauty shone out, and made a halo of the misfortune and ignominy in which she was enveloped. It may be true, that, to a sensitive observer, there was something exquisitely painful in it. Her attire, which, indeed, she had wrought for the occasion, in prison, and had modelled much after her own fancy, seemed to express the attitude of her spirit, the desperate recklessness of her mood, by its wild and picturesque peculiarity. But the point which drew all eyes, and, as it were, transfigured the wearer, — so that both men and women, who had been familiarly acquainted with Hester Prynne, were now impressed as if they beheld her for the first time, — was that SCARLET LETTER, so fantastically embroidered and illuminated upon her bosom. It had the effect of a spell, taking her out of the ordinary relations with humanity, and inclosing her in a sphere by herself.

"She hath good skill at her needle, that's certain," remarked one of the female spectators; "but did ever a woman, before this brazen hussy, contrive such a way of showing it! Why, gossips, what is it but to laugh in the faces of our godly magistrates, and make a pride out of what they, worthy gentlemen, meant for a punishment?"

"It were well," muttered the most iron-visaged of the old dames, "if we stripped Madam Hester's rich gown off her dainty shoulders; and as for the red letter, which she hath stitched so curiously, I'll bestow a rag of mine own rheumatic flannel, to make a fitter one!"

"O, peace, neighbours, peace!" whispered their youngest companion. "Do not let her hear you! Not a stitch in that embroidered letter, but she has felt it in her heart."

The grim beadle now made a gesture with his staff.

"Make way, good people, make way, in the King's name," cried he. "Open a passage; and, I promise ye, Mistress Prynne shall be set where man, woman, and child may have a fair sight of her brave apparel, from this time till an hour past meridian.° A blessing on the righteous Colony of the Massachusetts, where iniquity is dragged out into the sunshine! Come along, Madam Hester, and show your scarlet letter in the market-place!"

meridian: Noon.

A lane was forthwith opened through the crowd of spectators. Preceded by the beadle, and attended by an irregular procession of stern-browed men and unkindly-visaged women, Hester Prynne set forth towards the place appointed for her punishment. A crowd of eager and curious schoolboys, understanding little of the matter in hand, except that it gave them a half-holiday, ran before her progress, turning their heads continually to stare into her face, and at the winking baby in her arms, and at the ignominious letter on her breast. It was no great distance, in those days, from the prison-door to the market-place. Measured by the prisoner's experience, however, it might be reckoned a journey of some length; for, haughty as her demeanour was, she perchance underwent an agony from every footstep of those that thronged to see her, as if her heart had been flung into the street for them all to spurn and trample upon. In our nature, however, there is a provision, alike marvellous and merciful, that the sufferer should never know the intensity of what he endures by its present torture, but chiefly by the pang that rankles after it. With almost a serene deportment, therefore, Hester Prynne passed through this portion of her ordeal, and came to a sort of scaffold, at the western extremity of the market-place. It stood nearly beneath the eaves of Boston's earliest church, and appeared to be a fixture there.

In fact, this scaffold constituted a portion of a penal machine, which now, for two or three generations past, has been merely historical and traditionary among us, but was held, in the old time, to be as effectual an agent in the promotion of good citizenship, as ever was the guillotine among the terrorists of France. It was, in short, the platform of the pillory; and above it rose the framework of that instrument of discipline, so fashioned as to confine the human head in its tight grasp, and thus hold it up to the public gaze. The very ideal of ignominy was embodied and made manifest in this contrivance of wood and iron. There can be no outrage, methinks, against our common nature, — whatever be the delinquencies of the individual, — no outrage more flagrant than to forbid the culprit to hide his face for shame; as it was the essence of this punishment to do. In Hester Prynne's instance, however, as not unfrequently in other cases, her sentence bore, that she should stand a certain time upon the platform, but without undergoing that gripe about the neck and confinement of the head, the proneness to which was the most devilish characteristic of this ugly engine. Knowing well her part, she ascended a flight of wooden steps, and was thus displayed to the surrounding multitude, at about the height of a man's shoulders above the street.

Had there been a Papist among the crowd of Puritans, he might have seen in this beautiful woman, so picturesque in her attire and mien, and with the infant at her bosom, an object to remind him of the image of Divine Maternity, which so many illustrious painters have vied with one another to represent; something which should remind him, indeed, but only by contrast, of that sacred image of sinless motherhood whose infant was to redeem the world. Here, there was the taint of deepest sin in the most sacred quality of human life, working such effect, that the world was only the darker for this woman's beauty, and the more lost for the infant that she had borne.

The scene was not without a mixture of awe, such as must always invest the spectacle of guilt and shame in a fellow-creature, before society shall have grown corrupt enough to smile, instead of shuddering, at it. The witnesses of Hester Prynne's disgrace had not yet passed beyond their simplicity. They were stern enough to look upon her death, had that been the sentence, without a murmur at its severity, but had none of the heartlessness of another social state, which would find only a theme for jest in an exhibition like the present. Even had there been a disposition to turn the matter into ridicule, it must have been repressed and overpowered by the solemn presence of men no less dignified than the Governor, and several of his counsellors, a judge, a general, and the ministers of the town; all of whom sat or stood in a balcony of the meeting-house, looking down upon the platform. When such personages could constitute a part of the spectacle, without risking the majesty or reverence of rank and office, it was safely to be inferred that the infliction of a legal sentence would have an earnest and effectual meaning. Accordingly, the crowd was sombre and grave. The unhappy culprit sustained herself as best a woman might, under the heavy weight of a thousand unrelenting eyes, all fastened upon her, and concentred at her bosom. It was almost intolerable to be borne. Of an impulsive and passionate nature, she had fortified herself to encounter the stings and venomous stabs of public contumely, wreaking itself in every variety of insult; but there was a quality so much more terrible in the solemn mood of the popular mind, that she longed rather to behold all those rigid countenances contorted with scornful merriment, and herself the object. Had a roar of laughter burst from the multitude, — each man, each woman, each little shrill-voiced child, contributing their individual parts, — Hester Prynne might have repaid them all with a bitter and disdainful smile. But, under the leaden infliction which it was her doom to endure, she felt, at moments, as if she must needs shriek out with the full power of her lungs, and cast herself from the scaffold down upon the ground, or else go mad at once.

Yet there were intervals when the whole scene, in which she was the most conspicuous object, seemed to vanish from her eyes, or, at least, glimmered indistinctly before them, like a mass of imperfectly shaped and spectral images. Her mind, and especially her memory, was preternaturally active, and kept bringing up other scenes than this roughly hewn street of a little town, on the edge of the Western wilderness; other faces than were lowering upon her from beneath the brims of those steeple-crowned hats. Reminiscences, the most trifling and immaterial, passages of infancy and school-days, sports, childish quarrels, and the little domestic traits of her maiden years, came swarming back upon her, intermingled with recollections of whatever was gravest in her subsequent life; one picture precisely as vivid as another; as if all were of similar importance, or all alike a play. Possibly, it was an instinctive device of her spirit, to relieve itself, by the exhibition of these phantasmagoric forms, from the cruel weight and hardness of the reality.

Be that as it might, the scaffold of the pillory was a point of view that revealed to Hester Prynne the entire track along which she had been treading, since her happy infancy. Standing on that miserable eminence, she saw again her native village, in Old England, and her paternal home; a decayed house of gray stone, with a poverty-stricken aspect, but retaining a half-obliterated shield of arms over the portal, in token of antique gentility. She saw her father's face, with its bald brow, and reverend white beard, that flowed over the old-fashioned Elizabethan ruff; her mother's, too, with the look of heedful and anxious love which it always wore in her remembrance, and which, even since her death, had so often laid the impediment of a gentle remonstrance in her daughter's pathway. She saw her own face, glowing with girlish beauty, and illuminating all the interior of the dusky mirror in which she had been wont to gaze at it. There she beheld another countenance, of a man well stricken in years, a pale, thin, scholar-like visage, with eyes dim and bleared by the lamp-light that had served them to pore over many ponderous books. Yet those same bleared optics had a strange, penetrating power, when it was their owner's purpose to read the human soul. This figure of the study and the cloister, as Hester Prynne's womanly fancy failed not to recall, was slightly deformed, with the left shoulder a trifle higher than the right. Next rose before her, in memory's picture-gallery, the intricate and narrow thoroughfares, the tall, gray houses, the huge cathedrals, and the public edifices, ancient in date and quaint in architecture, of a Continental city; where a new life had awaited her, still in connection with the misshapen scholar; a new life, but feeding itself on time-worn materials, like a tuft of green moss on a crumbling wall. Lastly, in lieu of these shifting scenes, came back the rude market-place of the Puritan settlement, with all the townspeople assembled and levelling their stern regards at Hester Prynne, — yes, at herself, — who stood on the scaffold of the pillory, an infant on her arm, and the letter A, in scarlet, fantastically embroidered with gold thread, upon her bosom!

Could it be true? She clutched the child so fiercely to her breast, that it sent forth a cry; she turned her eyes downward at the scarlet letter, and even touched it with her finger, to assure herself that the infant and the shame were real. Yes! — these were her realities, — all else had vanished!

III. The Recognition

From this intense consciousness of being the object of severe and universal observation, the wearer of the scarlet letter was at length relieved by discerning, on the outskirts of the crowd, a figure which irresistibly took possession of her thoughts. An Indian, in his native garb, was standing there; but the red men were not so infrequent visitors of the English settlements, that one of them would have attracted any notice from Hester Prynne, at such a time; much less would he have excluded all other objects and ideas from her mind. By the Indian's side, and evidently sustaining a companionship with him, stood a white man, clad in a strange disarray of civilized and savage costume.

He was small in stature, with a furrowed visage, which, as yet, could hardly be termed aged. There was a remarkable intelligence in his features, as of a person who had so cultivated his mental part that it could not fail to mould the physical to itself, and become manifest by unmistakable tokens. Although, by a seemingly careless arrangement of his heterogeneous garb, he had endeavoured to conceal or abate the peculiarity, it was sufficiently evident to Hester Prynne, that one of this man's shoulders rose higher than the other. Again, at the first instant of perceiving that thin visage, and the slight deformity of the figure, she pressed her infant to her bosom, with so convulsive a force that the poor babe uttered another cry of pain. But the mother did not seem to hear it.

At his arrival in the market-place, and some time before she saw him, the stranger had bent his eyes on Hester Prynne. It was carelessly, at first, like a man chiefly accustomed to look inward, and to whom external matters are of little value and import, unless they bear relation to something within his mind. Very soon, however, his look became keen and penetrative. A writhing horror twisted itself across his features, like a snake gliding swiftly over them, and making one little pause, with all its wreathed intervolutions in open sight. His face darkened with some powerful emotion, which, nevertheless, he so instantaneously controlled by an effort of his will, that, save at a single moment, its expression might have passed for calmness. After a brief space, the convulsion grew almost imperceptible, and finally subsided into the depths of his nature. When he found the eyes of Hester Prynne fastened on his own, and saw that she appeared to recognize him, he slowly and calmly raised his finger, made a gesture with it in the air, and laid it on his lips.

Then, touching the shoulder of a townsman who stood next to him, he addressed him in a formal and courteous manner.

"I pray you, good Sir," said he, who is this woman? — and wherefore is she here set up to public shame?"

"You must needs be a stranger in this region, friend," answered the townsman, looking curiously at the questioner and his savage companion; "else you would surely have heard of Mistress Hester Prynne, and her evil doings. She hath raised a great scandal, I promise you, in godly Master Dimmesdale's church."

"You say truly," replied the other. "I am a stranger, and have been a wanderer, sorely against my will. I have met with grievous mishaps by sea and land, and have been long held in bonds among the heathen-folk, to the southward; and am now brought hither by this Indian, to be redeemed out of my captivity. Will it please you, therefore, to tell me of Hester Prynne's, — have I her name rightly? — of this woman's offences, and what has brought her to yonder scaffold?"

"Truly, friend, and methinks it must gladden your heart, after your troubles and sojourn in the wilderness," said the townsman, "to find yourself, at length, in a land where iniquity is searched out, and punished in the sight of rulers and people; as here in our godly New England. Yonder woman, Sir, you must know, was the wife of a certain learned man, English by birth, but who had long dwelt in Amsterdam, whence, some good time agone, he was minded to cross over and cast in his lot with us of the Massachusetts. To this purpose, he sent his wife before him, remaining himself to look after some necessary affairs. Marry, good Sir, in some two years, or less, that the woman has been a dweller here in Boston, no tidings have come of this learned gentleman, Master Prynne; and his young wife, look you, being left to her own misguidance ———"

"Ah! — aha! — I conceive you," said the stranger, with a bitter smile. "So learned a man as you speak of should have learned this too in his books. And who, by your favor, Sir, may be the father of yonder babe — it is some three or four months old, I should judge — which Mistress Prynne is holding in her arms?"

"Of a truth, friend, that matter remaineth a riddle; and the Daniel who shall expound it is yet a-wanting," answered the townsman. "Madam Hester absolutely refuseth to speak, and the magistrates have laid their heads together in vain. Peradventure the guilty one stands looking on at this sad spectacle, unknown of man, and forgetting that God sees him."

"The learned man," observed the stranger, with another smile, "should come himself to look into the mystery."

"It behooves him well, if he be still in life," responded the townsman. "Now, good Sir, our Massachusetts magistracy, bethinking themselves that this woman is youthful and fair, and doubtless was strongly tempted to her fall; — and that, moreover, as is most likely, her husband may be at the bottom of the sea; — they have not been bold to put in force the extremity of our righteous law against her. The penalty thereof is death. But, in their great mercy and tenderness of heart, they have doomed Mistress Prynne to stand only a space of three hours on the platform of the pillory, and then and thereafter, for the remainder of her natural life, to wear a mark of shame upon her bosom."

"A wise sentence!" remarked the stranger, gravely bowing his head. "Thus she will be a living sermon against sin, until the ignominious letter be engraved upon her tombstone. It irks me, nevertheless, that the partner of her iniquity should not, at least, stand on the scaffold by her side. But he will be known! — he will be known! — he will be known!"

He bowed courteously to the communicative townsman, and, whispering a few words to his Indian attendant, they both made their way through the crowd.

While this passed, Hester Prynne had been standing on her pedestal, still with a fixed gaze towards the stranger; so fixed a gaze, that, at moments of intense absorption, all other objects in the visible world seemed to vanish, leaving only him and her. Such an interview, perhaps, would have been more terrible than even to meet him as she now did, with the hot, midday sun burning down upon her face, and lighting up its shame; with the scarlet token of infamy on her breast; with the sin-born infant in her arms; with a whole people, drawn forth as to a festival, staring at the features that should have been seen only in the quiet gleam of the fireside, in the happy shadow of a home, or beneath a matronly veil, at church. Dreadful as it was, she was conscious of a shelter in the presence of these thousand witnesses. It was better to stand thus, with so many betwixt him and her, than to greet him, face to face, they two alone. She fled for refuge, as it were, to the public exposure, and dreaded the moment when its protection should be withdrawn from her. Involved in these thoughts, she scarcely heard a voice behind her, until it had repeated her name more than once, in a loud and solemn tone, audible to the whole multitude.

"Hearken unto me, Hester Prynne!" said the voice.

It has already been noticed, that directly over the platform on which Hester Prynne stood was a kind of balcony, or open gallery, appended to the meeting-house. It was the place whence proclamations were wont to be made, amidst an assemblage of the magistracy, with all the ceremonial that attended such public observances in those days. Here, to witness the scene which we are describing, sat Governor Bellingham himself, with four sergeants about his chair, bearing halberds,[8] as a guard of honor. He wore a dark feather in his hat, a border of embroidery on his cloak, and a black velvet tunic beneath; a gentleman advanced in years, and with a hard experience written in his wrinkles. He was not ill fitted to be the head and representative of a community, which owed its origin and progress, and its present state of development, not to the impulses of youth, but to the stern and tempered energies of manhood, and the sombre sagacity of age; accomplishing so much, precisely because it imagined and hoped so little. The other eminent characters, by whom the chief ruler was surrounded, were distinguished by a dignity of mien, belonging to a period when the forms of authority were felt to possess the sacredness of divine institutions. They were, doubtless, good men, just, and sage. But, out of the whole human family, it would not have been easy to select the same number of wise and virtuous persons, who should be less capable of sitting in judgment on an erring woman's heart, and disentangling its mesh of good and evil, than the sages of rigid aspect towards whom Hester Prynne now turned her face. She seemed conscious, indeed, that whatever sympathy she might expect lay in the larger and warmer heart of the multitude; for, as she lifted her eyes towards the balcony, the unhappy woman grew pale and trembled.

The voice which had called her attention was that of the reverend and famous John Wilson, the eldest clergyman of Boston, a great scholar, like most of his contemporaries in the profession, and withal a

[8] A weapon dating from the fifteenth century consisting of an axe-spear combination mounted on the end of a long handle.

man of kind and genial spirit. This last attribute, however, had been less carefully developed than his intellectual gifts, and was, in truth, rather a matter of shame than self-congratulation with him. There he stood, with a border of grizzled locks beneath his skull-cap; while his gray eyes, accustomed to the shaded light of his study, were winking, like those of Hester's infant in the unadulterated sunshine. He looked like the darkly engraved portraits which we see prefixed to old volumes of sermons; and had no more right than one of those portraits would have, to step forth, as he now did, and meddle with a question of human guilt, passion, and anguish.

"Hester Prynne," said the clergyman, "I have striven with my young brother here, under whose preaching of the word you have been privileged to sit," — here Mr. Wilson laid his hand on the shoulder of a pale young man beside him, — "I have sought, I say, to persuade this godly youth, that he should deal with you, here in the face of Heaven, and before these wise and upright rulers, and in hearing of all the people, as touching the vileness and blackness of your sin. Knowing your natural temper better than I, he could the better judge what arguments to use, whether of tenderness or terror, such as might prevail over your hardness and obstinacy; insomuch that you should no longer hide the name of him who tempted you to this grievous fall. But he opposes to me, (with a young man's oversoftness, albeit wise beyond his years,) that it were wronging the very nature of woman to force her to lay open her heart's secrets in such broad daylight, and in presence of so great a multitude. Truly, as I sought to convince him, the shame lay in the commission of the sin, and not in the showing of it forth. What say you to it, once again, brother Dimmesdale? Must it be thou or I that shall deal with this poor sinner's soul?"

There was a murmur among the dignified and reverend occupants of the balcony; and Governor Bellingham gave expression to its purport, speaking in an authoritative voice, although tempered with respect towards the youthful clergyman whom he addressed.

"Good Master Dimmesdale," said he, "the responsibility of this woman's soul lies greatly with you. It behooves you, therefore, to exhort her to repentance, and to confession, as a proof and consequence thereof."

The directness of this appeal drew the eyes of the whole crowd upon the Reverend Mr. Dimmesdale; a young clergyman, who had come from one of the great English universities, bringing all the learning of the age into our wild forestland. His eloquence and religious fervor had already given the earnest of high eminence in his profession.

He was a person of very striking aspect, with a white, lofty, and impending brow, large, brown, melancholy eyes, and a mouth which, unless when he forcibly compressed it, was apt to be tremulous, expressing both nervous sensibility and a vast power of self-restraint. Notwithstanding his high native gifts and scholar-like attainments, there was an air about this young minister, — an apprehensive, a startled, a half-frightened look, — as of a being who felt himself quite astray and at a loss in the pathway of human existence, and could only be at ease in some seclusion of his own. Therefore, so far as his duties would permit, he trode in the shadowy by-paths, and thus kept himself simple and childlike; coming forth, when occasion was, with a freshness, and fragrance, and dewy purity of thought, which, as many people said, affected them like the speech of an angel.

Such was the young man whom the Reverend Mr. Wilson and the Governor had introduced so openly to the public notice, bidding him speak, in the hearing of all men, to that mystery of a woman's soul, so sacred even in its pollution. The trying nature of his position drove the blood from his cheek, and made his lips tremulous.

"Speak to the woman, my brother," said Mr. Wilson. "It is of moment to her soul, and therefore, as the worshipful Governor says, momentous to thine own, in whose charge hers is. Exhort her to confess the truth!"

The Reverend Mr. Dimmesdale bent his head, in silent prayer, as it seemed, and then came forward.

"Hester Prynne," said he, leaning over the balcony, and looking down stedfastly into her eyes, "thou hearest what this good man says, and seest the accountability under which I labor. If thou feelest it to be for thy soul's peace, and that thy earthly punishment will thereby be made more effectual to salvation, I charge thee to speak out the name of thy fellow-sinner and fellow-sufferer! Be not silent from any mistaken pity and tenderness for him; for, believe me, Hester, though he were to step down from a high place, and stand there beside thee, on thy pedestal of shame, yet better were it so, than to hide a guilty heart through life. What can thy silence do for him, except it tempt him — yea, compel him, as it were — to add hypocrisy to sin? Heaven hath granted thee an open ignominy, that thereby thou mayest work out an open triumph over the evil within thee, and the sorrow without. Take heed how thou deniest to him — who, perchance, hath not the courage to grasp it for himself — the bitter, but wholesome, cup that is now presented to thy lips!"

The young pastor's voice was tremulously sweet, rich, deep, and broken. The feeling that it so evidently manifested, rather than the direct purport of the words, caused it to vibrate within all hearts, and brought the listeners into one accord of sympathy. Even the poor baby, at Hester's bosom, was affected by the same influence; for it directed its hitherto vacant gaze towards Mr. Dimmesdale, and held up its little arms, with a half pleased, half plaintive murmur. So powerful seemed the minister's appeal, that the people could not believe but that Hester Prynne would speak out the guilty name; or else that the guilty one himself, in whatever high or lowly place he stood, would be drawn forth by an inward and inevitable necessity, and compelled to ascend the scaffold.

Hester shook her head.

"Woman, transgress not beyond the limits of Heaven's mercy!" cried the Reverend Mr. Wilson, more harshly than before. "That little babe hath been gifted with a voice, to second and confirm the counsel which thou hast heard. Speak out the name! That, and thy repentance, may avail to take the scarlet letter off thy breast."

"Never!" replied Hester Prynne, looking, not at Mr. Wilson, but into the deep and troubled eyes of the younger clergyman. "It is too deeply branded. Ye cannot take it off. And would that I might endure his agony, as well as mine!"

"Speak, woman!" said another voice, coldly and sternly, proceeding from the crowd about the scaffold. "Speak; and give your child a father!"

"I will not speak!" answered Hester, turning pale as death, but responding to this voice, which she too surely recognized. "And my child must seek a heavenly Father; she shall never know an earthly one!"

"She will not speak!" murmured Mr. Dimmesdale, who, leaning over the balcony, with his hand upon his heart, had awaited the result of his appeal. He now drew back, with a long respiration. "Wondrous strength and generosity of a woman's heart! She will not speak!"

Discerning the impracticable state of the poor culprit's mind, the elder clergyman, who had carefully prepared himself for the occasion, addressed to the multitude a discourse on sin, in all its branches, but with continual reference to the ignominious letter. So forcibly did he dwell upon this symbol, for the hour or more during which his periods were rolling over the people's heads, that it assumed new terrors in their imagination, and seemed to derive its scarlet hue from the flames of the infernal pit. Hester Prynne, meanwhile, kept her place upon the pedestal of shame, with glazed eyes, and an air of weary indifference. She had borne, that morning, all that nature could endure; and as her temperament was not of the order that escapes from too intense suffering by a swoon, her spirit could only shelter itself beneath a stony crust of insensibility, while the faculties of animal life remained entire. In this state, the voice of the preacher thundered remorselessly, but unavailingly, upon her ears. The infant, during the latter portion of her ordeal, pierced the air with its wailings and screams; she strove to hush it, mechanically, but seemed scarcely to sympathize with its trouble. With the same hard demeanour, she was led back to prison, and vanished from the public gaze within its iron-clamped portal. It was whispered, by those who peered after her, that the scarlet letter threw a lurid gleam along the dark passage-way of the interior.

IV. The Interview

After her return to the prison, Hester Prynne was found to be in a state of nervous excitement that demanded constant watchfulness, lest she should perpetrate violence on herself, or do some half-frenzied mischief to the poor babe. As night approached, it proving impossible to quell her insubordination by rebuke or threats of punishment, Master Brackett, the jailer, thought fit to introduce a physician. He described him as a man of skill in all Christian modes of physical science, and likewise familiar with whatever the savage people could teach, in respect to medicinal herbs and roots that grew in the forest. To say the truth, there was much need of professional assistance, not merely for Hester herself, but still more urgently for the child; who, drawing its sustenance from the maternal bosom, seemed to have drank in with it all the turmoil, the anguish, and despair, which pervaded the mother's system. It now writhed in convulsions of pain, and was a forcible type, in its little frame, of the moral agony which Hester Prynne had borne throughout the day.

Closely following the jailer into the dismal apartment, appeared that individual, of singular aspect, whose presence in the crowd had been of such deep interest to the wearer of the scarlet letter. He was lodged in the prison, not as suspected of any offence, but as the most convenient and suitable mode of disposing of him, until the magistrates should have conferred with the Indian sagamores° respecting his ransom. His name was announced as Roger Chillingworth. The jailer, after ushering him into the room, remained a moment, marvelling at the comparative quiet that followed his entrance; for Hester Prynne had immediately become as still as death, although the child continued to moan.

"Prithee, friend, leave me alone with my patient," said the practitioner. "Trust me, good jailer, you shall briefly have peace in your house;

sagamores: Leaders.

and, I promise you, Mistress Prynne shall hereafter be more amenable to just authority than you may have found her heretofore."

"Nay, if your worship can accomplish that," answered Master Brackett, "I shall own you for a man of skill indeed! Verily, the woman hath been like a possessed one; and there lacks little, that I should take in hand to drive Satan out of her with stripes."

The stranger had entered the room with the characteristic quietude of the profession to which he announced himself as belonging. Nor did his demeanour change, when the withdrawal of the prison-keeper left him face to face with the woman, whose absorbed notice of him, in the crowd, had intimated so close a relation between himself and her. His first care was given to the child; whose cries, indeed, as she lay writhing on the trundle-bed, made it of peremptory necessity to postpone all other business to the task of soothing her. He examined the infant carefully, and then proceeded to unclasp a leathern case, which he took from beneath his dress. It appeared to contain certain medical preparations, one of which he mingled with a cup of water.

"My old studies in alchemy," observed he, "and my sojourn, for above a year past, among a people well versed in the kindly properties of simples, have made a better physician of me than many that claim the medical degree. Here, woman! The child is yours, — she is none of mine, — neither will she recognize my voice or aspect as a father's. Administer this draught, therefore, with thine own hand."

Hester repelled the offered medicine, at the same time gazing with strongly marked apprehension into his face.

"Wouldst thou avenge thyself on the innocent babe?" whispered she.

"Foolish woman!" responded the physician, half coldly, half soothingly. "What should ail me to harm this misbegotten and miserable babe? The medicine is potent for good; and were it my child, — yea, mine own, as well as thine! — I could do no better for it."

As she still hesitated, being, in fact, in no reasonable state of mind, he took the infant in his arms, and himself administered the draught. It soon proved its efficacy, and redeemed the leech's pledge. The moans of the little patient subsided; its convulsive tossings gradually ceased; and in a few moments, as is the custom of young children after relief from pain, it sank into a profound and dewy slumber. The physician, as he had a fair right to be termed, next bestowed his attention on the mother. With calm and intent scrutiny, he felt her pulse, looked into her eyes, — a gaze that made her heart shrink and shudder, because so familiar, and yet so strange and cold, — and, finally, satisfied with his investigation proceeded to mingle another draught.

"I know not Lethe or Nepenthe," remarked he; "but I have learned many new secrets in the wilderness, and here is one of them, — a recipe that an Indian taught me, in requital of some lessons of my own, that were as old as Paracelsus.[9] Drink it! It may be less soothing than a sinless conscience. That I cannot give thee. But it will calm the swell and heaving of thy passion, like oil thrown on the waves of a tempestuous sea."

He presented the cup to Hester, who received it with a slow, earnest look into his face; not precisely a look of fear, yet full of doubt and questioning, as to what his purposes might be. She looked also at her slumbering child.

"I have thought of death," said she, — "have wished for it, — would even have prayed for it, were it fit that such as I should pray for any thing. Yet, if death be in this cup, I bid thee think again, ere thou beholdest me quaff it. See! It is even now at my lips."

"Drink, then," replied he, still with the same cold composure. "Dost thou know me so little, Hester Prynne? Are my purposes wont to be so shallow? Even if I imagine a scheme of vengeance, what could I do better for my object than to let thee live, — than to give thee medicines against all harm and peril of life, — so that this burning shame may still blaze upon thy bosom?" — As he spoke, he laid his long forefinger on the scarlet letter, which forthwith seemed to scorch into Hester's breast, as if it had been red-hot. He noticed her involuntary gesture, and smiled. — "Live, therefore, and bear about thy doom with thee, in the eyes of men and women,— in the eyes of him whom thou didst call thy husband, — in the eyes of yonder child! And, that thou mayest live, take off this draught."

Without further expostulation or delay, Hester Prynne drained the cup, and, at the motion of the man of skill, seated herself on the bed where the child was sleeping; while he drew the only chair which the room afforded, and took his own seat beside her. She could not but tremble at these preparations; for she felt that — having now done all that humanity, or principle, or, if so it were, a refined cruelty, impelled him to do, for the relief of physical suffering — he was next to treat with her as the man whom she had most deeply and irreparably injured.

"Hester," said he, "I ask not wherefore, nor how, thou hast fallen into the pit, or say rather, thou hast ascended to the pedestal of infamy, on which I found thee. The reason is not far to seek. It was my folly, and thy weakness. I, — a man of thought, — the book-worm of great

[9] In Greek mythology, Lethe was the River of Forgetfulness; Nepenthe was an Egyptian drug allowing users to forget their sorrows. Paracelsus was a famous sixteenth-century alchemist.

libraries, — a man already in decay, having given my best years to feed the hungry dream of knowledge, — what had I to do with youth and beauty like thine own! Misshapen from my birth-hour, how could I delude myself with the idea that intellectual gifts might veil physical deformity in a young girl's fantasy! Men call me wise. If sages were ever wise in their own behoof, I might have foreseen all this. I might have known that, as I came out of the vast and dismal forest, and entered this settlement of Christian men, the very first object to meet my eyes would be thyself, Hester Prynne, standing up, a statue of ignominy, before the people. Nay, from the moment when we came down the old church-steps together, a married pair, I might have beheld the bale-fire of that scarlet letter blazing at the end of our path!"

"Thou knowest," said Hester, — for, depressed as she was, she could not endure this last quiet stab at the token of her shame, — "thou knowest that I was frank with thee. I felt no love, nor feigned any."

"True!" replied he. "It was my folly! I have said it. But, up to that epoch of my life, I had lived in vain. The world had been so cheerless! My heart was a habitation large enough for many guests, but lonely and chill, and without a household fire. I longed to kindle one! It seemed not so wild a dream, — old as I was, and sombre as I was, and misshapen as I was, — that the simple bliss, which is scattered far and wide, for all mankind to gather up, might yet be mine. And so, Hester, I drew thee into my heart, into its innermost chamber, and sought to warm thee by the warmth which thy presence made there!"

"I have greatly wronged thee," murmured Hester.

"We have wronged each other," answered he. "Mine was the first wrong, when I betrayed thy budding youth into a false and unnatural relation with my decay. Therefore, as a man who has not thought and philosophized in vain, I seek no vengeance, plot no evil against thee. Between thee and me, the scale hangs fairly balanced. But, Hester, the man lives who has wronged us both! Who is he?"

"Ask me not!" replied Hester Prynne, looking firmly into his face. "That thou shalt never know!"

"Never, sayest thou?" rejoined he, with a smile of dark and self-relying intelligence. "Never know him! Believe me, Hester, there are few things, — whether in the outward world, or, to a certain depth, in the invisible sphere of thought, — few things hidden from the man, who devotes himself earnestly and unreservedly to the solution of a mystery. Thou mayest cover up thy secret from the prying multitude. Thou mayest conceal it, too, from the ministers and magistrates, even as thou didst this day, when they sought to wrench the name out of thy heart, and give thee a partner on thy pedestal. But, as for me, I come to the inquest with other senses than they possess. I shall seek this man, as I have sought truth in books; as I have sought gold in alchemy. There is a sympathy that will make me conscious of him. I shall see him tremble. I shall feel myself shudder, suddenly and unawares. Sooner or later, he must needs be mine!"

The eyes of the wrinkled scholar glowed so intensely upon her, that Hester Prynne clasped her hands over her heart, dreading lest he should read the secret there at once.

"Thou wilt not reveal his name? Not the less he is mine," resumed he, with a look of confidence, as if destiny were at one with him. "He bears no letter of infamy wrought into his garment, as thou dost; but I shall read it on his heart. Yet fear not for him! Think not that I shall interfere with Heaven's own method of retribution, or, to my own loss, betray him to the gripe of human law. Neither do thou imagine that I shall contrive aught against his life; no, nor against his fame, if, as I judge, he be a man of fair repute. Let him live! Let him hide himself in outward honor, if he may! Not the less he shall be mine!"

"Thy acts are like mercy," said Hester, bewildered and appalled. "But thy words interpret thee as a terror!"

"One thing, thou that wast my wife, I would enjoin upon thee," continued the scholar. "Thou hast kept the secret of thy paramour. Keep, likewise, mine! There are none in this land that know me. Breathe not, to any human soul, that thou didst ever call me husband! Here, on this wild outskirt of the earth, I shall pitch my tent; for, elsewhere a wanderer, and isolated from human interests, I find here a woman, a man, a child, amongst whom and myself there exist the closest ligaments. No matter whether of love or hate; no matter whether of right or wrong! Thou and thine, Hester Prynne, belong to me. My home is where thou art, and where he is. But betray me not!"

"Wherefore dost thou desire it?" inquired Hester, shrinking, she hardly knew why, from this secret bond. "Why not announce thyself openly, and cast me off at once?"

"It may be," he replied, "because I will not encounter the dishonor that besmirches the husband of a faithless woman. It may be for other reasons. Enough, it is my purpose to live and die unknown. Let, therefore, thy husband be to the world as one already dead, and of whom no tidings shall ever come. Recognize me not, by word, by sign, by look! Breathe not the secret, above all, to the man thou wottest of. Shouldst thou fail me in this, beware! His fame, his position, his life, will be in my hands. Beware!"

"I will keep thy secret, as I have his," said Hester.

"Swear it!" rejoined he.

And she took the oath.

"And now, Mistress Prynne," said old Roger Chillingworth, as he was hereafter to be named, "I leave thee alone; alone with thy infant, and the scarlet letter! How is it, Hester? Doth thy sentence bind thee to wear the token in thy sleep? Art thou not afraid of nightmares and hideous dreams?"

"Why dost thou smile so at me?" inquired Hester, troubled at the expression of his eyes. "Art thou like the Black Man[10] that haunts the forest round about us? Hast thou enticed me into a bond that will prove the ruin of my soul?"

"Not thy soul," he answered, with another smile. "No, not thine!"

V. Hester at Her Needle

Hester Prynne's term of confinement was now at an end. Her prison-door was thrown open, and she came forth into the sunshine, which, falling on all alike, seemed, to her sick and morbid heart, as if meant for no other purpose than to reveal the scarlet letter on her breast. Perhaps there was a more real torture in her first unattended footsteps from the threshold of the prison, than even in the procession and spectacle that have been described, where she was made the common infamy, at which all mankind was summoned to point its finger. Then, she was supported by an unnatural tension of the nerves, and by all the combative energy of her character, which enabled her to convert the scene into a kind of lurid triumph. It was, moreover, a separate and insulated event, to occur but once in her lifetime, and to meet which, therefore, reckless of economy, she might call up the vital strength that would have sufficed for many quiet years. The very law that condemned her — a giant of stern features, but with vigor to support, as well as to annihilate, in his iron arm — had held her up, through the terrible ordeal of her ignominy. But now, with this unattended walk from her prison-door, began the daily custom, and she must either sustain and carry it forward by the ordinary resources of her nature, or sink beneath it. She could no longer borrow from the future, to help her through the present grief. To-morrow would bring its own trial with it; so would the next day, and so would the next; each its own trial, and yet the very

[10] Term used by New England Puritans to refer to the devil or a subordinate devil or demon.

same that was now so unutterably grievous to be borne. The days of the far-off future would toil onward, still with the same burden for her to take up, and bear along with her, but never to fling down; for the accumulating days, and added years, would pile up their misery upon the heap of shame. Throughout them all, giving up her individuality, she would become the general symbol at which the preacher and moralist might point, and in which they might vivify and embody their images of woman's frailty and sinful passion. Thus the young and pure would be taught to look at her, with the scarlet letter flaming on her breast, — at her, the child of honorable parents, — at her, the mother of a babe, that would hereafter be a woman, — at her, who had once been innocent, — as the figure, the body, the reality of sin. And over her grave, the infamy that she must carry thither would be her only monument.

It may seem marvellous, that, with the world before her, — kept by no restrictive clause of her condemnation within the limits of the Puritan settlement, so remote and so obscure, — free to return to her birthplace, or to any other European land, and there hide her character and identity under a new exterior, as completely as if emerging into another state of being, — and having also the passes of the dark, inscrutable forest open to her, where the wildness of her nature might assimilate itself with a people whose customs and life were alien from the law that had condemned her, — it may seem marvellous, that this woman should still call that place her home, where, and where only, she must needs be the type of shame. But there is a fatality, a feeling so irresistible and inevitable that it has the force of doom, which almost invariably compels human beings to linger around and haunt, ghost-like, the spot where some great and marked event has given the color to their lifetime; and still the more irresistibly, the darker the tinge that saddens it. Her sin, her ignominy, were the roots which she had struck into the soil. It was as if a new birth, with stronger assimilations than the first, had converted the forest-land, still so uncongenial to every other pilgrim and wanderer, into Hester Prynne's wild and dreary, but life-long home. All other scenes of earth — even that village of rural England, where happy infancy and stainless maidenhood seemed yet to be in her mother's keeping, like garments put off long ago — were foreign to her, in comparison. The chain that bound her here was of iron links, and galling to her inmost soul, but never could be broken.

It might be, too, — doubtless it was so, although she hid the secret from herself, and grew pale whenever it struggled out of her heart, like a serpent from its hole, — it might be that another feeling kept her within the scene and pathway that had been so fatal. There dwelt, there trode the feet of one with whom she deemed herself connected in a union, that, unrecognized on earth, would bring them together before the bar of final judgment, and make that their marriage-altar, for a joint futurity of endless retribution. Over and over again, the tempter of souls had thrust this idea upon Hester's contemplation, and laughed at the passionate and desperate joy with which she seized, and then strove to cast it from her. She barely looked the idea in the face, and hastened to bar it in its dungeon. What she compelled herself to believe, — what, finally, she reasoned upon, as her motive for continuing a resident of New England, — was half a truth, and half a self-delusion. Here, she said to herself, had been the scene of her guilt, and here should be the scene of her earthly punishment; and so, perchance, the torture of her daily shame would at length purge her soul, and work out another purity than that which she had lost; more saint-like, because the result of martyrdom.

Hester Prynne, therefore, did not flee. On the outskirts of the town, within the verge of the peninsula, but not in close vicinity to any other habitation, there was a small thatched cottage. It had been built by an earlier settler, and abandoned, because the soil about it was too sterile for cultivation, while its comparative remoteness put it out of the sphere of that social activity which already marked the habits of the emigrants. It stood on the shore, looking across a basin of the sea at the forest-covered hills, towards the west. A clump of scrubby trees, such as alone grew on the peninsula, did not so much conceal the cottage from view, as seem to denote that here was some object which would fain have been, or at least ought to be, concealed. In this little, lonesome dwelling, with some slender means that she possessed, and by the license of the magistrates, who still kept an inquisitorial watch over her, Hester established herself, with her infant child. A mystic shadow of suspicion immediately attached itself to the spot. Children, too young to comprehend wherefore this woman should be shut out from the sphere of human charities, would creep nigh enough to behold her plying her needle at the cottage-window, or standing in the door-way, or laboring in her little garden, or coming forth along he pathway that led townward; and, discerning the scarlet letter on her breast, would scamper off, with a strange, contagious fear.

Lonely as was Hester's situation, and without a friend on earth who dared to show himself, she, however, incurred no risk of want. She possessed an art that sufficed, even in a land that afforded comparatively little scope for its exercise, to supply food for her thriving infant and herself. It was the art — then, as now, almost the only one within a woman's grasp — of needle-work. She bore on her breast, in the curiously embroidered letter, a specimen of her delicate and imaginative skill, of which the dames of a court might gladly have availed themselves, to add the richer and more spiritual adornment of human ingenuity to their fabrics of silk and gold. Here, indeed, in the sable simplicity that generally characterized the Puritanic modes of dress, there might be an infrequent call for the finer productions of her handiwork. Yet the taste of the age, demanding whatever was elaborate in compositions of this kind, did not fail to extend its influence over our stern progenitors, who had cast behind them so many fashions which it might seem harder to dispense with. Public ceremonies, such as ordinations, the installation of magistrates, and all that could give majesty to the forms in which a new government manifested itself to the people, were, as a matter of policy, marked by a stately and well-conducted ceremonial, and a sombre, but yet a studied magnificence. Deep ruffs, painfully wrought bands, and gorgeously embroidered gloves, were all deemed necessary to the official state of men assuming the reins of power; and were readily allowed to individuals dignified by rank or wealth, even while sumptuary laws forbade these and similar extravagances to the plebeian order. In the array of funerals, too, — whether for the apparel of the dead body, or to typify, by manifold emblematic devices of sable cloth and snowy lawn, the sorrow of the survivors — there was a frequent and characteristic demand for such labor as Hester Prynne could supply. Baby-linen — for babies then wore robes of state — afforded still another possibility of toil and emolument.

By degrees, nor very slowly, her handiwork became what would now be termed the fashion. Whether from commiseration for a woman of so miserable a destiny; or from the morbid curiosity that gives a fictitious value even to common or worthless things; or by whatever other intangible circumstance was then, as now, sufficient to bestow, on some persons, what others might seek in vain; or because Hester really filled a gap which must otherwise have remained vacant; it is certain that she had ready and fairly requited employment for as many hours as she saw fit to occupy with her needle. Vanity, it may be, chose to mortify itself, by putting on, for ceremonials of pomp and state, the garments that had been wrought by her sinful hands. Her needle-work was seen on the ruff of the Governor; military men wore it on their scarfs, and the minister on his band; it decked the baby's little cap; it was shut up, to be mildewed and moulder away, in the coffins of the dead. But it is not recorded that, in a single instance, her skill was called in aid to embroider the white veil which was to cover the pure blushes of a bride. The exception indicated the ever relentless vigor with which society frowned upon her sin.

Hester sought not to acquire any thing beyond a subsistence, of the plainest and most ascetic description, for herself, and a simple abundance for her child. Her own dress was of the coarsest materials and the most sombre hue; with only that one ornament, — the scarlet letter, — which it was her doom to wear. The child's attire, on the other hand, was distinguished by a fanciful, or, we might rather say, a fantastic ingenuity, which served, indeed, to heighten the airy charm that early began to develop itself in the little girl, but which appeared to have also a deeper meaning. We may speak further of it hereafter. Except for that small expenditure in the decoration of her infant, Hester bestowed all her superfluous means in charity, on wretches less miserable than herself, and who not unfrequently insulted the hand that fed them. Much of the time, which she might readily have applied to the better efforts of her art, she employed in making coarse garments for the poor. It is probable that there was an idea of penance in this mode of occupation, and that she offered up a real sacrifice of enjoyment, in devoting so many hours to such rude handiwork. She had in her nature a rich, voluptuous, Oriental characteristic, — a taste for the gorgeously beautiful, which, save in the exquisite productions of her needle, found nothing else, in all the possibilities of her life, to exercise itself upon. Women derive a pleasure, incomprehensible to the other sex, from the delicate toil of the needle. To Hester Prynne it might have been a mode of expressing, and therefore soothing, the passion of her life. Like all other joys, she rejected it as sin. This morbid meddling of conscience with an immaterial matter betokened, it is to be feared, no genuine and stedfast penitence, but something doubtful, something that might be deeply wrong, beneath.

In this manner, Hester Prynne came to have a part to perform in the world. With her native energy of character, and rare capacity, it could not entirely cast her off, although it had set a mark upon her, more intolerable to a woman's heart than that which branded the brow of Cain. In all her intercourse with society, however, there was nothing that made her feel as if she belonged to it. Every gesture, every word, and even the silence of those with whom she came in contact, implied, and often expressed, that she was banished, and as much alone as if she inhabited another sphere, or communicated with the common nature by other organs and senses than the rest of human kind. She stood apart from mortal interests, yet close beside them, like a ghost that revisits the familiar fireside, and can no longer make itself seen or felt; no more smile with the household joy, nor mourn with the kindred sorrow; or, should it succeed in manifesting its forbidden sympathy, awakening only terror and horrible repugnance. These emotions, in fact, and its bitterest scorn besides, seemed to be the sole portion that she retained in the universal heart. It was not an age of delicacy; and her position, although she understood it well, and was in little danger of forgetting it, was often brought before her vivid self-perception, like a new anguish, by the rudest touch upon the tenderest spot. The poor, as we have already said, whom she sought out to be the objects of her bounty, often reviled the hand that was stretched forth to succor them. Dames of elevated rank, likewise, whose doors she entered in the way of her occupation, were accustomed to distil drops of bitterness into her heart; sometimes through that alchemy of quiet malice, by which women can concoct a subtile poison from ordinary trifles; and sometimes, also, by a coarser expression, that fell upon the sufferer's defenceless breast like a rough blow upon an ulcerated wound. Hester had schooled herself long and well; she never responded to these attacks, save by a flush of crimson that rose irrepressibly over her pale cheek, and again subsided into the depths of her bosom. She was patient, — a martyr, indeed, — but she forbore to pray for her enemies; lest, in spite of her forgiving aspirations, the words of the blessing should stubbornly twist themselves into a curse.

Continually, and in a thousand other ways, did she feel the innumerable throbs of anguish that had been so cunningly contrived for her by the undying, the ever-active sentence of the Puritan tribunal. Clergymen paused in the street to address words of exhortation, that brought a crowd, with its mingled grin and frown, around the poor, sinful woman. If she entered a church, trusting to share the Sabbath smile of the Universal Father, it was often her mishap to find herself the text of the discourse. She grew to have a dread of children; for they had imbibed from their parents a vague idea of something horrible in this dreary woman, gliding silently through the town, with never any companion but one only child. Therefore, first allowing her to pass, they pursued her at a distance with shrill cries, and the utterance of a word that had no distinct purport to their own minds, but was none the less terrible to her, as proceeding from lips that babbled it unconsciously. It seemed to argue so wide a diffusion of her shame, that all nature knew of it; it could have caused her no deeper pang, had the leaves of the trees whispered the dark story among themselves, — had the summer breeze murmured about it, — had the wintry blast shrieked it aloud! Another peculiar torture was felt in the gaze of a new eye. When strangers looked curiously at the scarlet letter, — and none ever failed to do so, — they branded it afresh into Hester's soul; so that, oftentimes, she could scarcely refrain, yet always did refrain, from covering the symbol with her hand. But then, again, an accustomed eye had likewise its own anguish to inflict. Its cool stare of familiarity was intolerable. From first to last, in short, Hester Prynne had always this dreadful agony in feeling a human eye upon the token; the spot never grew callous; it seemed, on the contrary, to grow more sensitive with daily torture.

But sometimes, once in many days, or perchance in many months, she felt an eye — a human eye — upon the ignominious brand, that seemed to give a momentary relief, as if half of her agony were shared. The next instant, back it all rushed again, with still a deeper throb of pain; for, in that brief interval, she had sinned anew. Had Hester sinned alone?

Her imagination was somewhat affected, and, had she been of a softer moral and intellectual fibre, would have been still more so, by the strange and solitary anguish of her life. Walking to and fro, with those lonely footsteps, in the little world with which she was outwardly connected, it now and then appeared to Hester, — if altogether fancy, it was nevertheless too potent to be resisted, — she felt or fancied, then, that the scarlet letter had endowed her with a new sense. She shuddered to believe, yet could not help believing, that it gave her a sympathetic knowledge of the hidden sin in other hearts. She was terror-stricken by the revelations that were thus made. What were they? Could they be other than the insidious whispers of the bad angel, who would fain have persuaded the struggling woman, as yet only half his victim, that the outward guise of purity was but a lie, and that, if truth were everywhere to be shown, a scarlet letter would blaze forth on many a bosom besides Hester Prynne's? Or, must she receive those intimations — so obscure, yet so distinct — as truth? In all her miserable experience, there was nothing else so awful and so loathsome as this sense. It perplexed, as well as shocked her, by the irreverent inopportuneness of the occasions that brought it into vivid action. Sometimes, the red infamy upon her breast would give a sympathetic throb, as she passed near a venerable minister or magistrate, the model of piety and justice, to whom that age of antique reverence looked up, as to a mortal man in fellowship with angels. "What evil thing is at hand?" would Hester say to herself. Lifting her reluctant eyes, there would be nothing human within the scope of view, save the form of this earthly saint! Again, a mystic sisterhood would contumaciously assert itself, as she met the sanctified frown of some matron, who, according to the rumor of all tongues, had kept cold snow within her bosom throughout life. That unsunned snow in the matron's bosom, and the burning shame on Hester Prynne's, — what had the two in common? Or, once more, the electric thrill would give her warning, — "Behold, Hester, here is a companion!" — and, looking up, she would detect the eyes of a young maiden glancing at the scarlet letter, shyly and aside, and quickly averted, with a faint, chill crimson in her cheeks; as if her purity were somewhat sullied by that momentary glance. O Fiend, whose talisman was that fatal symbol, wouldst thou leave nothing, whether in youth or age, for this poor sinner to revere? — Such loss of faith is ever one of the saddest results of sin. Be it accepted as a proof that all was not corrupt in this poor victim of her own frailty, and man's hard law, that Hester Prynne yet struggled to believe that no fellow-mortal was guilty like herself.

The vulgar, who, in those dreary old times, were always contributing a grotesque horror to what interested their imaginations, had a story about the scarlet letter which we might readily work up into a terrific legend. They averred, that the symbol was not mere scarlet cloth, tinged in an early dye-pot, but was red-hot with infernal fire, and could be seen glowing all alight, whenever Hester Prynne walked abroad in the night-time. And we must needs say, it seared Hester's bosom so deeply, that perhaps there was more truth in the rumor than our modern incredulity may be inclined to admit.

VI. Pearl

We have as yet hardly spoken of the infant; that little creature, whose innocent life had sprung, by the inscrutable decree of Providence, a lovely and immortal flower, out of the rank luxuriance of a guilty passion. How strange it seemed to the sad woman, as she watched the growth, and the beauty that became every day more brilliant, and the intelligence that threw its quivering sunshine over the tiny features of this child! Her Pearl! — For so had Hester called her; not as a name expressive of her aspect, which had nothing of the calm, white, unimpassioned lustre that would be indicated by the comparison. But she named the infant "Pearl," as being of great price, — purchased with all she had, — her mother's only treasure! How strange, indeed! Man had marked this woman's sin by a scarlet letter, which had such potent and disastrous efficacy that no human sympathy could reach her, save it were sinful like herself. God, as a direct consequence of the sin which man thus punished, had given her a lovely child, whose place was on that same dishonored bosom, to connect her parent for ever with the race and descent of mortals, and to be finally a blessed soul in heaven! Yet these thoughts affected Hester Prynne less with hope than apprehension. She knew that her deed had been evil; she could have no faith, therefore, that its result would be for good. Day after day, she looked fearfully into the child's expanding nature; ever dreading to detect some dark and wild peculiarity, that should correspond with the guiltiness to which she owed her being.

Certainly, there was no physical defect. By its perfect shape, its vigor, and its natural dexterity in the use of all its untried limbs, the infant was worthy to have been brought forth in Eden; worthy to have been left there, to be the plaything of the angels, after the world's first parents were driven out. The child had a native grace which does not invariably coexist with faultless beauty; its attire, however simple, always impressed the beholder as if it were the very garb that precisely became it best. But little Pearl was not clad in rustic weeds. Her mother, with a morbid purpose that may be better understood hereafter, had bought the richest tissues that could be procured, and allowed her imaginative faculty its full play in the arrangement and decoration of the dresses which the child wore, before the public eye. So magnificent was the small figure, when thus arrayed, and such was the splendor of Pearl's own proper beauty, shining through the gorgeous robes which might have extinguished a paler loveliness, that there was an absolute circle of radiance around her, on the darksome cottage-floor. And yet a russet gown, torn and soiled with the child's rude play, made a picture of her just as perfect. Pearl's aspect was imbued with a spell of infinite variety; in this one child there were many children, comprehending the full scope between the wild-flower prettiness of a peasant-baby, and the pomp, in little, of an infant princess. Throughout all, however, there was a trait of passion, a certain depth of hue, which she never lost; and if, in any of her changes, she had grown fainter or paler, she would have ceased to be herself; — it would have been no longer Pearl!

This outward mutability indicated, and did not more than fairly express, the various properties of her inner life. Her nature appeared to possess depth, too, as well as variety; but — or else Hester's fears deceived her — it lacked reference and adaptation to the world into which she was born. The child could not be made amenable to rules. In giving her existence, a great law had been broken; and the result was a being, whose elements were perhaps beautiful and brilliant, but all in disorder; or with an order peculiar to themselves, amidst which the point of variety and arrangement was difficult or impossible to be discovered. Hester could only account for the child's character — and even then, most vaguely and imperfectly — by recalling what she herself had been, during that momentous period while Pearl was imbibing her soul from the spiritual world, and her bodily frame from its material of earth. The mother's impassioned state had been the medium through which were transmitted to the unborn infant the rays of its moral life; and, however white and clear originally, they had taken the deep stains of crimson and gold, the fiery lustre, the black shadow, and the untempered light, of the intervening substance. Above all, the warfare of Hester's spirit, at that epoch, was perpetuated in Pearl. She could recognize her wild, desperate, defiant mood, the flightiness of her temper, and even some of the very cloud-shapes of gloom and despondency that had brooded in her heart. They were now illuminated by the morning radiance of a young child's disposition, but, later in the day of earthly existence, might be prolific of the storm and whirlwind.

The discipline of the family, in those days, was of a far more rigid kind than now. The frown, the harsh rebuke, the frequent application of the rod, enjoined by Scriptural authority, were used, not merely in the way of punishment for actual offences, but as a wholesome regimen for the growth and promotion of all childish virtues. Hester Prynne, nevertheless, the lonely mother of this one child, ran little risk of erring on the side of undue severity. Mindful, however, of her own errors and misfortunes, she early sought to impose a tender, but strict, control over the infant immortality that was committed to her charge. But the task was beyond her skill. After testing both smiles and frowns, and proving that neither mode of treatment possessed any calculable influence, Hester was ultimately compelled to stand aside, and permit the child to be swayed by her own impulses. Physical compulsion or restraint was effectual, of course, while it lasted. As to any other kind of discipline, whether addressed to her mind or heart, little Pearl might or might not be within its reach, in accordance with the caprice that ruled the moment. Her mother, while Pearl was yet an infant, grew acquainted with a certain peculiar look, that warned her when it would be labor thrown away to insist, persuade, or plead. It was a look so intelligent, yet inexplicable, so perverse, sometimes so malicious, but generally accompanied by a wild flow of spirits, that Hester could not help questioning, at such moments, whether Pearl was a human child. She seemed rather an airy sprite, which, after playing its fantastic sports for a little while upon the cottage-floor, would flit away with a mocking smile. Whenever that look appeared in her wild, bright, deeply black eyes, it invested her with a strange remoteness and intangibility; it was as if she were hovering in the air and might vanish, like a glimmering light that comes we know not whence, and goes we know not whither. Beholding it, Hester was constrained to rush towards the child, — to pursue the little elf in the flight which she invariably began, — to snatch her to her bosom, with a close pressure and earnest kisses, — not so much from overflowing love, as to assure herself that Pearl was flesh and blood, and not utterly delusive. But Pearl's laugh, when she was caught, though full of merriment and music, made her mother more doubtful than before.

Heart-smitten at this bewildering and baffling spell, that so often came between herself and her sole treasure, whom she had bought so dear, and who was all her world, Hester sometimes burst into passionate tears. Then, perhaps, — for there was no foreseeing how it might affect her, — Pearl would frown, and clench her little fist, and harden her small features into a stern, unsympathizing look of discontent. Not seldom, she would laugh anew, and louder than before, like a thing incapable and unintelligent of human sorrow. Or — but this more rarely happened — she would be convulsed with a rage of grief, and sob out her love for her mother, in broken words, and seem intent on proving that she had a heart, by breaking it. Yet Hester was hardly safe in confiding herself to that gusty tenderness; it passed, as suddenly as it came. Brooding over all these matters, the mother felt like one who has evoked a spirit, but, by some irregularity in the process of conjuration, has failed to win the master-word that should control this new and incomprehensible intelligence. Her only real comfort was when the child lay in the placidity of sleep. Then she was sure of her, and tasted hours of quiet, sad, delicious happiness; until — perhaps with that perverse expression glimmering from beneath her opening lids — little Pearl awoke!

How soon — with what strange rapidity, indeed! — did Pearl arrive at an age that was capable of social intercourse, beyond the mother's ever-ready smile and nonsense-words! And then what a happiness would it have been, could Hester Prynne have heard her clear, birdlike voice mingling with the uproar of other childish voices, and have distinguished and unravelled her own darling's tones, amid all the entangled outcry of a group of sportive children! But this could never be. Pearl was a born outcast of the infantile world. An imp of evil, emblem and product of sin, she had no right among christened infants. Nothing was more remarkable than the instinct, as it seemed, with which the child comprehended her loneliness; the destiny that had drawn an inviolable circle round about her; the whole peculiarity, in short, of her position in respect to other children. Never, since her release from prison, had

Hester met the public gaze without her. In all her walks about the town, Pearl, too, was there; first as the babe in arms, and afterwards as the little girl, small companion of her mother, holding a forefinger with her whole grasp, and tripping along at the rate of three or four footsteps to one of Hester's. She saw the children of the settlement, on the grassy margin of the street, or at the domestic thresholds, disporting themselves in such grim fashion as the Puritanic nurture would permit; playing at going to church, perchance; or at scourging Quakers; or taking scalps in a sham-fight with the Indians; or scaring one another with freaks of imitative witchcraft. Pearl saw, and gazed intently, but never sought to make acquaintance. If spoken to, she would not speak again. If the children gathered about her, as they sometimes did, Pearl would grow positively terrible in her puny wrath, snatching up stones to fling at them, with shrill, incoherent exclamations that made her mother tremble, because they had so much the sound of a witch's anathemas in some unknown tongue.

The truth was, that the little Puritans, being of the most intolerant brood that ever lived, had got a vague idea of something outlandish, unearthly, or at variance with ordinary fashions, in the mother and child; and therefore scorned them in their hearts, and not unfrequently reviled them with their tongues. Pearl felt the sentiment, and requited it with the bitterest hatred that can be supposed to rankle in a childish bosom. These outbreaks of a fierce temper had a kind of value, and even comfort, for her mother; because there was at least an intelligible earnestness in the mood, instead of the fitful caprice that so often thwarted her in the child's manifestations. It appalled her, nevertheless, to discern here, again, a shadowy reflection of the evil that had existed in herself. All this enmity and passion had Pearl inherited, by inalienable right, out of Hester's heart. Mother and daughter stood together in the same circle of seclusion from human society; and in the nature of the child seemed to be perpetuated those unquiet elements that had distracted Hester Prynne before Pearl's birth, but had since begun to be soothed away by the softening influences of maternity.

At home, within and around her mother's cottage, Pearl wanted not a wide and various circle of acquaintance. The spell of life went forth from her ever creative spirit, and communicated itself to a thousand objects, as a torch kindles a flame wherever it may be applied. The unlikeliest materials, a stick, a bunch of rags, a flower, were the puppets of Pearl's witchcraft, and, without undergoing any outward change, became spiritually adapted to whatever drama occupied the stage of her inner world. Her one baby-voice served a multitude of imaginary personages, old and young, to talk withal. The pine-trees, aged, black, and solemn, and flinging groans and other melancholy utterances on the breeze, needed little transformation to figure as Puritan elders; the ugliest weeds of the garden were their children, whom Pearl smote down and uprooted, most unmercifully. It was wonderful, the vast variety of forms into which she threw her intellect, with no continuity, indeed, but darting up and dancing, always in a state of preternatural activity, — soon sinking down, as if exhausted by so rapid and feverish a tide of life, — and succeeded by other shapes of a similar wild energy. It was like nothing so much as the phantasmagoric play of the northern lights. In the mere exercise of the fancy, however, and the sportiveness of a growing mind, there might be little more than was observable in other children of bright faculties; except as Pearl, in the dearth of human playmates, was thrown more upon the visionary throng which she created. The singularity lay in the hostile feelings with which the child regarded all these offspring of her own heart and mind. She never created a friend, but seemed always to be sowing broadcast the dragon's teeth whence sprung a harvest of armed enemies, against whom she rushed to battle. It was inexpressibly sad — then what depth of sorrow to a mother, who felt in her own heart the cause! — to observe, in one so young, this constant recognition of an adverse world, and so fierce a training of the energies that were to make good her cause, in the contest that must ensue.

Gazing at Pearl, Hester Prynne often dropped her work upon her knees, and cried out, with an agony which she would fain have hidden, but which made utterance for itself, betwixt speech and a groan, — "O Father in Heaven, — if Thou art still my Father, — what is this being which I have brought into the world!" And Pearl, overhearing the ejaculation, or aware, through some more subtile channel, of those throbs of anguish, would turn her vivid and beautiful little face upon her mother, smile with sprite-like intelligence, and resume her play.

One peculiarity of the child's deportment remains yet to be told. The very first thing which she had noticed, in her life was — what? — not the mother's smile, responding to it, as other babies do, by that faint, embryo smile of the little mouth, remembered so doubtfully afterwards, and with such fond discussion whether it were indeed a smile. By no means! But that first object of which Pearl seemed to become aware was — shall we say it? — the scarlet letter on Hester's bosom! One day, as her mother stooped over the cradle, the infant's eyes had been caught by the glimmering of the gold embroidery about the letter; and, putting up her little hand, she grasped at it, smiling, not doubtfully, but with a decided gleam that gave her face the look of a much older child. Then, gasping for breath, did Hester Prynne clutch the fatal token, instinctively endeavouring to tear it away; so infinite was the torture inflicted by the intelligent touch of Pearl's baby-hand. Again, as if her mother's agonized gesture were meant only to make sport for her, did little Pearl look into her eyes, and smile! From that epoch, except when the child was asleep, Hester had never felt a moment's safety; not a moment's calm enjoyment of her. Weeks, it is true, would sometimes elapse, during which Pearl's gaze might never once be fixed upon the scarlet letter; but then, again, it would come at unawares, like the stroke of sudden death, and always with that peculiar smile, and odd expression of the eyes.

Once, this freakish, elfish cast came into the child's eyes, while Hester was looking at her own image in them, as mothers are fond of doing; and, suddenly, — for women in solitude, and with troubled hearts, are pestered with unaccountable delusions, — she fancied that she beheld, not her own miniature portrait, but another face in the small black mirror of Pearl's eye. It was a face, fiend-like, full of smiling malice, yet bearing the semblance of features that she had known full well, though seldom with a smile, and never with malice, in them. It was as if an evil spirit possessed the child, and had just then peeped forth in mockery. Many a time afterwards had Hester been tortured, though less vividly, by the same illusion.

In the afternoon of a certain summer's day, after Pearl grew big enough to run about, she amused herself with gathering handfuls of wild-flowers, and flinging them, one by one, at her mother's bosom; dancing up and down, like a little elf, whenever she hit the scarlet letter. Hester's first motion had been to cover her bosom with her clasped hands. But, whether from pride or resignation, or a feeling that her penance might best be wrought out by this unutterable pain, she resisted the impulse, and sat erect, pale as death, looking sadly into little Pearl's wild eyes. Still came the battery of flowers, almost invariably hitting the mark, and covering the mother's breast with hurts for which she could find no balm in this world, nor knew how to seek it in another. At last, her shot being all expended, the child stood still and gazed at Hester, with that little, laughing image of a fiend peeping out — or, whether it peeped or no, her mother so imagined it — from the unsearchable abyss of her black eyes.

"Child, what art thou? cried the mother.

"O, I am your little Pearl!" answered the child.

But, while she said it, Pearl laughed and began to dance up and down, with the humorsome gesticulation of a little imp, whose next freak might be to fly up the chimney.

"Art thou my child, in very truth?" asked Hester.

Nor did she put the question altogether idly, but, for the moment, with a portion of genuine earnestness; for, such was Pearl's wonderful intelligence, that her mother half doubted whether she were not acquainted with the secret spell of her existence, and might not now reveal herself.

"Yes; I am little Pearl!" repeated the child, continuing her antics.

"Thou art not my child! Thou art no Pearl of mine!" said the mother, half playfully; for it was often the case that a sportive impulse came over her, in the midst of her deepest suffering. "Tell me, then, what thou art, and who sent thee hither?"

"Tell me, mother!" said the child, seriously, coming up to Hester, and pressing herself close to her knees. "Do thou tell me!"

"Thy Heavenly Father sent thee!" answered Hester Prynne.

But she said it with a hesitation that did not escape the acuteness of the child. Whether moved only by her ordinary freakishness, or because an evil spirit prompted her, she put up her small forefinger, and touched the scarlet letter.

"He did not send me!" cried she, positively. "I have no Heavenly Father!"

"Hush, Pearl, hush! Thou must not talk so!" answered the mother, suppressing a groan. "He sent us all into this world. He sent even me, thy mother. Then, much more, thee! Or, if not, thou strange and elfish child, whence didst thou come?"

"Tell me! Tell me!" repeated Pearl, no longer seriously, but laughing, and capering about the floor. "It is thou that must tell me!"

But Hester could not resolve the query, being herself in a dismal labyrinth of doubt. She remembered — betwixt a smile and a shudder — the talk of the neighbouring townspeople; who, seeking vainly elsewhere for the child's paternity, and observing some of her odd attributes, had given out that poor little Pearl was a demon offspring; such as, ever since old Catholic times, had occasionally been seen on earth, through the agency of their mothers' sin, and to promote some foul and wicked purpose. Luther, according to the scandal of his monkish enemies, was a brat of that hellish breed; nor was Pearl the only child to whom this inauspicious origin was assigned, among the New England Puritans.

VII. The Governor's Hall

Hester Prynne went, one day, to the mansion of Governor Bellingham, with a pair of gloves, which she had fringed and embroidered to his order, and which were to be worn on some great occasion of state; for, though the chances of a popular election had caused this former ruler to descend a step or two from the highest rank, he still held an honorable and influential place among the colonial magistracy.

Another and far more important reason than the delivery of a pair of embroidered gloves impelled Hester, at this time, to seek an interview with a personage of so much power and activity in the affairs of the settlement. It had reached her ears, that there was a design on the part of some of the leading inhabitants, cherishing the more rigid order of principles in religion and government, to deprive her of her child. On the supposition that Pearl, as already hinted, was of demon origin, these good people not unreasonably argued that a Christian interest in the mother's soul required them to remove such a stumbling-block from her path. If the child, on the other hand, were really capable of moral and religious growth, and possessed the elements of ultimate salvation, then, surely, it would enjoy all the fairer prospect of these advantages by being transferred to wiser and better guardianship than Hester Prynne's. Among those who promoted the design, Governor Bellingham was said to be one of the most busy. It may appear singular, and, indeed, not a little ludicrous, that an affair of this kind, which, in later days, would have been referred to no higher jurisdiction than that of the selectmen of the town, should then have been a question publicly discussed, and on which statesmen of eminence took sides. At that epoch of pristine simplicity, however, matters of even slighter public interest, and of far less intrinsic weight than the welfare of Hester and her child, were strangely mixed up with the deliberations of legislators and acts of state. The period was hardly, if at all, earlier than that of our story, when a dispute concerning the right of property in a pig, not only caused a fierce and bitter contest in the legislative body of the colony, but resulted in an important modification of the framework itself of the legislature.

Full of concern, therefore, — but so conscious of her own right, that it seemed scarcely an unequal match between the public, on the one side, and a lonely woman, backed by the sympathies of nature, on the other, — Hester Prynne set forth from her solitary cottage. Little Pearl, of course, was her companion. She was now of an age to run lightly along by her mother's side, and, constantly in motion from morn till sunset, could have accomplished a much longer journey than that before her. Often, nevertheless, more from caprice than necessity, she demanded to be taken up in arms, but was soon as imperious to be set down again, and frisked onward before Hester on the grassy path-way, with many a harmless trip and tumble. We have spoken of Pearl's rich and luxuriant beauty; a beauty that shone with deep and vivid tints; a bright complexion, eyes possessing intensity both of depth and glow, and hair already of a deep, glossy brown, and which, in after years, would be nearly akin to black. There was fire in her and throughout her; she seemed the unpremeditated offshoot of a passionate moment. Her mother, in contriving the child's garb, had allowed the gorgeous tendencies of her imagination their full play; arraying her in a crimson velvet tunic, of a peculiar cut, abundantly embroidered with fantasies and flourishes of gold thread. So much strength of coloring, which must have given a wan and pallid aspect to cheeks of a fainter bloom, was admirably adapted to Pearl's beauty, and made her the very brightest little jet of flame that ever danced upon the earth.

But it was a remarkable attribute of this garb, and, indeed, of the child's whole appearance, that it irresistibly and inevitably reminded the beholder of the token which Hester Prynne was doomed to wear upon her bosom. It was the scarlet letter in another form; the scarlet letter endowed with life! The mother herself — as if the red ignominy were so deeply scorched into her brain, that all her conceptions assumed its form — had carefully wrought out the similitude; lavishing many hours of morbid ingenuity, to create an analogy between the object of her affection, and the emblem of her guilt and torture. But, in truth, Pearl was the one, as well as the other; and only in consequence of that identity had Hester contrived so perfectly to represent the scarlet letter in her appearance.

As the two wayfarers came within the precincts of the town, the children of the Puritans looked up from their play, — or what passed for play with those sombre little urchins, — and spake gravely one to another: —

"Behold, verily, there is the woman of the scarlet letter; and, of a truth, moreover, there is the likeness of the scarlet letter running along by her side! Come, therefore, and let us fling mud at them!"

But Pearl, who was a dauntless child, after frowning, stamping her foot, and shaking her little hand with a variety of threatening gestures, suddenly made a rush at the knot of her enemies, and put them all to flight. She resembled, in her fierce pursuit of them, an infant pestilence, — the scarlet fever, or some such half-fledged angel of judgment, — whose mission was to punish the sins of the rising generation. She screamed and shouted, too, with a terrific volume of sound, which doubtless caused the hearts of the fugitives to quake within them. The victory accomplished, Pearl returned quietly to her mother, and looked up smiling into her face.

Without further adventure, they reached the dwelling of Governor Bellingham. This was a large wooden house, built in a fashion of which there are specimens still extant in the streets of our elder towns; now moss-grown, crumbling to decay, and melancholy at heart with the many sorrowful or joyful occurrences, remembered or forgotten, that have happened, and passed away, within their dusky chambers. Then, however, there was the freshness of the passing year on its exterior, and the cheerfulness, gleaming forth from the sunny windows, of a human habitation into which death had never entered. It had indeed a very cheery aspect; the walls being overspread with a kind of stucco, in which fragments of broken glass were plentifully intermixed; so that, when the sunshine fell aslant-wise over the front of the edifice, it glittered and sparkled as if diamonds had been flung against it by the double handful. The brilliancy might have befitted Aladdin's palace, rather than the mansion of a grave old Puritan ruler. It was further decorated with strange and seemingly cabalistic figures and diagrams, suitable to the quaint taste of the age, which had been drawn in the stucco when newly laid on, and had now grown hard and durable, for the admiration of after times.

Pearl, looking at this bright wonder of a house, began to caper and dance, and imperatively required that the whole breadth of sunshine should be stripped off its front, and given her to play with.

"No, my little Pearl!" said her mother. "Thou must gather thine own sunshine. I have none to give thee!"

They approached the door; which was of an arched form, and flanked on each side by a narrow tower or projection of the edifice, in both of which were lattice-windows, with wooden shutters to close over them at need. Lifting the iron hammer that hung at the portal, Hester Prynne gave a summons, which was answered by one of the Governor's bond-servants; a free-born Englishman, but now a seven years' slave. During that term he was to be the property of his master, and as much a commodity of bargain and sale as an ox, or a joint-stool. The serf wore the blue coat, which was the customary garb of serving-men at that period, and long before, in the old hereditary halls of England.

"Is the worshipful Governor Bellingham within?" inquired Hester.

"Yea, forsooth," replied the bond-servant, staring with wide-open eyes at the scarlet letter, which, being a new-comer in the country, he had never before seen. "Yea, his honorable worship is within. But he hath a godly minister or two with him, and likewise a leech. Ye may not see his worship now."

"Nevertheless, I will enter," answered Hester Prynne; and the bond-servant, perhaps judging from the decision of her air and the glittering symbol in her bosom, that she was a great lady in the land, offered no opposition.

So the mother and little Pearl were admitted into the hall of entrance. With many variations, suggested by the nature of his building-materials, diversity of climate, and a different mode of social life, Governor Bellingham had planned his new habitation after the residences of gentlemen of fair estate in his native land. Here, then, was a wide and reasonably lofty hall, extending through the whole depth of the house, and forming a medium of general communication, more or less directly, with all the other apartments. At one extremity, this spacious room was lighted by the windows of the two towers, which formed a small recess on either side of the portal. At the other end, though partly muffled by a curtain, it was more powerfully illuminated by one of those embowed hall-windows which we read of in old books, and which was provided with a deep and cushioned seat. Here, on the cushion, lay a folio tome, probably of the Chronicles of England, or other such substantial literature; even as, in our own days, we scatter gilded volumes on the centre-table, to be turned over by the casual guest. The furniture of the hall consisted of some ponderous chairs, the backs of which were elaborately carved with wreaths of oaken flowers; and likewise a table in the same taste; the whole being of the Elizabethan age, or perhaps earlier, and heirlooms, transferred hither from the Governor's paternal home. On the table — in token that the sentiment of old English hospitality had not been left behind — stood a large pewter tankard, at the bottom of which, had Hester or Pearl peeped into it, they might have seen the frothy remnant of a recent draught of ale.

On the wall hung a row of portraits, representing the forefathers of the Bellingham lineage, some with armour on their breasts, and others with stately ruffs and robes of peace. All were characterized by the sternness and severity which old portraits so invariably put on; as if they were the ghosts, rather than the pictures, of departed worthies, and were gazing with harsh and intolerant criticism at the pursuits and enjoyments of living men.

At about the centre of the oaken panels, that lined the hall, was suspended a suit of mail, not, like the pictures, an ancestral relic, but of the most modern date; for it had been manufactured by a skilful armorer in London, the same year in which Governor Bellingham came over to New England. There was a steel head-piece, a cuirass, a gorget, and greaves, with a pair of gauntlets° and a sword hanging beneath; all, and especially the helmet and breastplate, so highly burnished as to glow with white radiance, and scatter an illumination everywhere about upon the floor. This bright panoply was not meant for mere idle show, but had been worn by the Governor on many a solemn muster and training field, and had glittered, moreover, at the head of a regiment in the Pequod war. For, though bred a lawyer, and accustomed to speak of Bacon, Coke, Noye, and Finch,[11] as his professional associates, the exigencies of this new country had transformed Governor Bellingham into a soldier, as well as a statesman and ruler.

Little Pearl — who was as greatly pleased with the gleaming armour as she had been with the glittering frontispiece of the house — spent some time looking into the polished mirror of the breastplate.

"Mother," cried she, "I see you here. Look! Look!"

Hester looked, by way of humoring the child; and she saw that, owing to the peculiar effect of this convex mirror, the scarlet letter was represented in exaggerated and gigantic proportions, so as to be greatly the most prominent feature of her appearance. In truth, she seemed absolutely hidden behind it. Pearl pointed upward, also, at a similar picture in the headpiece; smiling at her mother, with the elfish intelligence that was so familiar an expression on her small physiognomy. That look of naughty merriment was likewise reflected in the mirror, with so much breadth and intensity of effect, that it made Hester Prynne feel as if it could not be the image of her own child, but of an imp who was seeking to mould itself into Pearl's shape.

"Come along, Pearl!" said she, drawing her away. "Come and look into this fair garden. It may be, we shall see flowers there; more beautiful ones than we find in the woods."

Pearl, accordingly, ran to the bow-window, at the farther end of the

cuirass . . . gorget . . . greaves . . . gauntlets: Protective gear for the upper body, throat, legs, and hands.

[11] Sir Francis Bacon (1561–1626), Sir Edward Coke (1552–1634), William Noye (1577–1634), and Sir John Finch (1584–1660) were all experts on English Common Law.

hall, and looked along the vista of a garden-walk, carpeted with closely shaven grass, and bordered with some rude and immature attempt at shrubbery. But the proprietor appeared already to have relinquished, as hopeless, the effort to perpetuate on this side of the Atlantic, in a hard soil and amid the close struggle for subsistence, the native English taste for ornamental gardening. Cabbages grew in plain sight; and a pumpkin vine, rooted at some distance, had run across the intervening space, and deposited one of its gigantic products directly beneath the hall-window; as if to warn the Governor that this great lump of vegetable gold was as rich an ornament as New England earth would offer him. There were a few rose-bushes, however, and a number of apple-trees, probably the descendants of those planted by the Reverend Mr. Blackstone, the first settler of the peninsula; that half mythological personage who rides through our early annals, seated on the back of a bull.

Pearl, seeing the rose-bushes, began to cry for a red rose, and would not be pacified.

"Hush, child, hush!" said her mother earnestly. "Do not cry, dear little Pearl! I hear voices in the garden. The Governor is coming, and gentlemen along with him!"

In fact, adown the vista of the garden-avenue, a number of persons were seen approaching towards the house. Pearl, in utter scorn of her mother's attempt to quiet her, gave an eldritch° scream, and then became silent; not from any notion of obedience, but because the quick and mobile curiosity of her disposition was excited by the appearance of these new personages.

VIII. The Elf-Child and the Minister

Governor Bellingham, in a loose gown and easy cap, — such as elderly gentlemen loved to indue themselves with, in their domestic privacy, — walked foremost, and appeared to be showing off his estate, and expatiating on his projected improvements. The wide circumference of an elaborate ruff, beneath his gray beard in the antiquated fashion of King James's reign, caused his head to look not a little like that of John the Baptist in a charger.° The impression made by his aspect, so rigid and severe, and frost-bitten with more than autumnal age, was hardly in keeping with the appliances of worldly enjoyment wherewith he had evidently done his utmost to surround himself. But it is an error to

eldritch: Unearthly. ***charger:*** Plate.

suppose that our grave forefathers — though accustomed to speak and think of human existence as a state merely of trial and warfare, and though unfeignedly prepared to sacrifice goods and life at the behest of duty — made it a matter of conscience to reject such means of comfort, or even luxury, as lay fairly within their grasp. This creed was never taught, for instance, by the venerable pastor, John Wilson, whose beard, white as a snow-drift, was seen over Governor Bellingham's shoulder; while its wearer suggested that pears and peaches might yet be naturalized in the New England climate, and that purple grapes might possibly be compelled to flourish, against the sunny garden-wall. The old clergyman, nurtured at the rich bosom of the English Church, had a long established and legitimate taste for all good and comfortable things; and however stern he might show himself in the pulpit, or in his public reproof of such transgressions as that of Hester Prynne, still, the genial benevolence of his private life had won him warmer affection than was accorded to any of his professional contemporaries.

Behind the Governor and Mr. Wilson came two other guests; one, the Reverend Arthur Dimmesdale, whom the reader may remember, as having taken a brief and reluctant part in the scene of Hester Prynne's disgrace; and, in close companionship with him, old Roger Chillingworth, a person of great skill in physic, who, for two or three years past, had been settled in the town. It was understood that this learned man was the physician as well as friend of the young minister, whose health had severely suffered, of late, by his too unreserved self-sacrifice to the labors and duties of the pastoral relation.

The Governor, in advance of his visitors, ascended one or two steps, and, throwing open the leaves of the great hall window, found himself close to little Pearl. The shadow of the curtain fell on Hester Prynne, and partially concealed her.

"What have we here?" said Governor Bellingham, looking with surprise at the scarlet little figure before him. "I profess, I have never seen the like, since my days of vanity, in old King James's time, when I was wont to esteem it a high favor to be admitted to a court mask! There used to be a swarm of these small apparitions, in holiday-time; and we called them children of the Lord of Misrule. But how gat such a guest into my hall?"

"Ay, indeed!" cried good old Mr. Wilson. "What little bird of scarlet plumage may this be? Methinks I have seen just such figures, when the sun has been shining through a richly painted window, and tracing out the golden and crimson images across the floor. But that was in the old land. Prithee, young one, who art thou, and what has ailed thy mother to bedizen° thee in this strange fashion? Art thou a Christian child, — ha? Dost know thy catechism? Or art thou one of those naughty elfs or fairies, whom we thought to have left behind us, with other relics of Papistry, in merry old England?"

"I am mother's child," answered the scarlet vision, "and my name is Pearl!"

"Pearl? — Ruby, rather! — or Coral! — or Red Rose, at the very least, judging from thy hue!" responded the old minister, putting forth his hand in a vain attempt to pat little Pearl on the cheek. "But where is this mother of thine? Ah! I see," he added; and, turning to Governor Bellingham, whispered, — "This is the selfsame child of whom we have held speech together; and behold here the unhappy woman, Hester Prynne, her mother!"

"Sayest thou so?" cried the Governor. "Nay, we might have judged that such a child's mother must needs be a scarlet woman, and a worthy type of her of Babylon! But she comes at a good time; and we will look into this matter forthwith."

Governor Bellingham stepped through the window into the hall, followed by his three guests.

"Hester Prynne," said he, fixing his naturally stern regard on the wearer of the scarlet letter, "there hath been much question concerning thee, of late. The point hath been weightily discussed, whether we, that are of authority and influence, do well discharge our consciences by trusting an immortal soul, such as there is in yonder child, to the guidance of one who hath stumbled and fallen, amid the pitfalls of this world. Speak thou, the child's own mother! Were it not, thinkest thou, for thy little one's temporal and eternal welfare, that she be taken out of thy charge, and clad soberly, and disciplined strictly, and instructed in the truths of heaven and earth? What canst thou do for the child, in this kind?"

"I can teach my little Pearl what I have learned from this!" answered Hester Prynne, laying her finger on the red token.

"Woman, it is thy badge of shame!" replied the stern magistrate. "It is because of the stain which that letter indicates, that we would transfer thy child to other hands."

"Nevertheless," said the mother calmly, though growing more pale, "this badge hath taught me, — it daily teaches me, — it is teaching me at this moment, — lessons whereof my child may be the wiser and better, albeit they can profit nothing to myself."

bedizen: Make gaudy.

"We will judge warily," said Bellingham, "and look well what we are about to do. Good Master Wilson, I pray you, examine this Pearl, — since that is her name, — and see whether she hath had such Christian nurture as befits a child of her age."

The old minister seated himself in an arm-chair, and made an effort to draw Pearl betwixt his knees. But the child, unaccustomed to the touch or familiarity of any but her mother, escaped through the open window and stood on the upper step, looking like a wild, tropical bird, of rich plumage, ready to take flight into the upper air. Mr. Wilson, not a little astonished at this outbreak, — for he was a grandfatherly sort of personage, and usually a vast favorite with children, — essayed, however, to proceed with the examination.

"Pearl," said he, with great solemnity, "thou must take heed to instruction, that so, in due season, thou mayest wear in thy bosom the pearl of great price. Canst thou tell me, my child, who made thee?"

Now Pearl knew well enough who made her; for Hester Prynne, the daughter of a pious home, very soon after her talk with the child about her Heavenly Father, had begun to inform her of those truths which the human spirit, at whatever stage of immaturity, imbibes with such eager interest. Pearl, therefore, so large were the attainments of her three years' lifetime, could have borne a fair examination in the New England Primer, or the first column of the Westminster Catechism, although unacquainted with the outward form of either of those celebrated works. But that perversity, which all children have more or less of, and of which little Pearl had a tenfold portion, now, at the most inopportune moment, took thorough possession of her, and closed her lips, or impelled her to speak words amiss. After putting her finger in her mouth, with many ungracious refusals to answer good Mr. Wilson's question, the child finally announced that she had not been made at all, but had been plucked by her mother off the bush of wild roses, that grew by the prison-door.

This fantasy was probably suggested by the near proximity of the Governor's red roses, as Pearl stood outside of the window; together with her recollection of the prison rose-bush, which she had passed in coming hither.

Old Roger Chillingworth, with a smile on his face, whispered something in the young clergyman's ear. Hester Prynne looked at the man of skill, and even then, with her fate hanging in the balance, was startled to perceive what a change had come over his features, — how much uglier they were, — how his dark complexion seemed to have grown duskier, and his figure more misshapen, — since the days when she had familiarly known him. She met his eyes for an instant, but was immediately constrained to give all her attention to the scene now going forward.

"This is awful!" cried the Governor, slowly recovering from the astonishment into which Pearl's response had thrown him. "Here is a child of three years old, and she cannot tell who made her! Without question, she is equally in the dark as to her soul, its present depravity, and future destiny! Methinks, gentlemen, we need inquire no further."

Hester caught hold of Pearl, and drew her forcibly into her arms, confronting the old Puritan magistrate with almost a fierce expression. Alone in the world, cast off by it, and with this sole treasure to keep her heart alive, she felt that she possessed indefeasible rights against the world, and was ready to defend them to the death.

"God gave me the child!" cried she. "He gave her, in requital of all things else, which ye had taken from me. She is my happiness! — she is my torture, none the less! Pearl keeps me here in life! Pearl punishes me too! See ye not, she is the scarlet letter, only capable of being loved, and so endowed with a million-fold the power of retribution for my sin? Ye shall not take her! I will die first!"

"My poor woman," said the not unkind old minister, "the child shall be well cared for! — far better than thou canst do it."

"God gave her into my keeping," repeated Hester Prynne, raising her voice almost to a shriek. "I will not give her up!" — And here, by a sudden impulse, she turned to the young clergyman, Mr. Dimmesdale, at whom, up to this moment, she had seemed hardly so much as once to direct her eyes. — "Speak thou for me!" cried she. "Thou wast my pastor, and hadst charge of my soul, and knowest me better than these men can. I will not lose the child! Speak for me! Thou knowest, — for thou hast sympathies which these men lack! — thou knowest what is in my heart, and what are a mother's rights, and how much the stronger they are, when that mother has but her child and the scarlet letter! Look thou to it! I will not lose the child! Look to it!"

At this wild and singular appeal, which indicated that Hester Prynne's situation had provoked her to little less than madness, the young minister at once came forward, pale, and holding his hand over his heart, as was his custom whenever his peculiarly nervous temperament was thrown into agitation. He looked now more careworn and emaciated than as we described him at the scene of Hester's public ignominy; and whether it were his failing health, or whatever the cause might be, his large dark eyes had a world of pain in their troubled and melancholy depth.

"There is truth in what she says," began the minister, with a voice sweet, tremulous, but powerful, insomuch that the hall reëchoed, and the hollow armour rang with it, — "truth in what Hester says, and in the feeling which inspires her! God gave her the child, and gave her, too, an instinctive knowledge of its nature and requirements, — both seemingly so peculiar, — which no other mortal being can possess. And, moreover, is there not a quality of awful sacredness in the relation between this mother and this child?"

"Ay! — how is that, good Master Dimmesdale?" interrupted the Governor. "Make that plain, I pray you!"

"It must be even so," resumed the minister. "For, if we deem it otherwise, do we not thereby say that the Heavenly Father, the Creator of all flesh, hath lightly recognized a deed of sin, and made of no account the distinction between unhallowed lust and holy love? This child of its father's guilt and its mother's shame hath come from the hand of God, to work in many ways upon her heart, who pleads so earnestly, and with such bitterness of spirit, the right to keep her. It was meant for a blessing; for the one blessing of her life! It was meant, doubtless, as the mother herself hath told us, for a retribution too; a torture, to be felt at many an unthought of moment; a pang, a sting, an ever-recurring agony, in the midst of a troubled joy! Hath she not expressed this thought in the garb of the poor child, so forcibly reminding us of that red symbol which sears her bosom?"

"Well said, again!" cried good Mr. Wilson. "I feared the woman had no better thought than to make a mountebank of her child!"

"O, not so! — not so!" continued Mr. Dimmesdale. "She recognizes, believe me, the solemn miracle which God hath wrought, in the existence of that child. And may she feel, too, — what, methinks, is the very truth, — that this boon was meant, above all things else, to keep the mother's soul alive, and to preserve her from blacker depths of sin into which Satan might else have sought to plunge her! Therefore it is good for this poor, sinful woman that she hath an infant immortality, a being capable of eternal joy or sorrow, confided to her care, — to be trained up by her to righteousness, — to remind her, at every moment, of her fall — but yet to teach her, as it were by the Creator's sacred pledge, that, if she bring the child to heaven, the child also will bring its parent thither! Herein is the sinful mother happier than the sinful father. For Hester Prynne's sake, then, and no less for the poor child's sake, let us leave them as Providence hath seen fit to place them!"

"You speak, my friend, with a strange earnestness," said old Roger Chillingworth, smiling at him.

"And there is weighty import in what my young brother hath spoken," added the Reverend Mr. Wilson. "What say you, worshipful Master Bellingham? Hath he not pleaded well for the poor woman?"

"Indeed hath he," answered the magistrate, "and hath adduced such arguments, that we will even leave the matter as it now stands; so long, at least, as there shall be no further scandal in the woman. Care must be had, nevertheless, to put the child to due and stated examination in the catechism at thy hands or Master Dimmesdale's. Moreover, at a proper season, the tithing-men must take heed that she go both to school and to meeting."

The young minister, on ceasing to speak, had withdrawn a few steps from the group, and stood with his face partially concealed in the heavy folds of the window-curtain; while the shadow of his figure, which the sunlight cast upon the floor, was tremulous with the vehemence of his appeal. Pearl, that wild and flighty little elf, stole softly towards him, and, taking his hand in the grasp of both her own, laid her cheek against it; a caress so tender, and withal so unobtrusive, that her mother, who was looking on, asked herself, — "Is that my Pearl?" Yet she knew that there was love in the child's heart, although it mostly revealed itself in passion, and hardly twice in her lifetime had been softened by such gentleness as now. The minister, — for, save the long-sought regards of woman, nothing is sweeter than these marks of childish preference, accorded spontaneously by a spiritual instinct, and therefore seeming to imply in us something truly worthy to be loved, — the minister looked round, laid his hand on the child's head, hesitated an instant, and then kissed her brow. Little Pearl's unwonted mood of sentiment lasted no longer; she laughed, and went capering down the hall, so airily, that old Mr. Wilson raised a question whether even her tiptoes touched the floor.

"The little baggage hath witchcraft in her, I profess," said he to Mr. Dimmesdale. "She needs no old woman's broomstick to fly withal!"

"A strange child!" remarked old Roger Chillingworth. "It is easy to see the mother's part in her. Would it be beyond a philosopher's research, think ye, gentlemen, to analyze that child's nature, and, from its make and mould, to give a shrewd guess at the father?"

"Nay; it would be sinful, in such a question, to follow the clew of profane philosophy," said Mr. Wilson. "Better to fast and pray upon it; and still better, it may be, to leave the mystery as we find it, unless Providence reveal it of its own accord. Thereby, every good Christian man hath a title to show a father's kindness towards the poor, deserted babe."

The affair being so satisfactorily concluded, Hester Prynne, with Pearl, departed from the house. As they descended the steps, it is averred that the lattice of a chamber-window was thrown open, and forth into the sunny day was thrust the face of Mistress Hibbins, Governor Bellingham's bitter-tempered sister, and the same who, a few years later, was executed as a witch.

"Hist, hist!" said she, while her ill-omened physiognomy seemed to cast a shadow over the cheerful newness of the house. "Wilt thou go with us to-night? There will be a merry company in the forest; and I wellnigh promised the Black Man that comely Hester Prynne should make one."

"Make my excuse to him, so please you!" answered Hester, with a triumphant smile. "I must tarry at home, and keep watch over my little Pearl. Had they taken her from me, I would willingly have gone with thee into the forest, and signed my name in the Black Man's book too, and that with mine own blood!"

"We shall have thee there anon!" said the witch-lady, frowning, as she drew back her head.

But here — if we suppose this interview betwixt Mistress Hibbins and Hester Prynne to be authentic, and not a parable — was already an illustration of the young minister's argument against sundering the relation of a fallen mother to the offspring of her frailty. Even thus early had the child saved her from Satan's snare.

IX. The Leech

Under the appellation of Roger Chillingworth, the reader will remember, was hidden another name, which its former wearer had resolved should never more be spoken. It has been related, how, in the crowd that witnessed Hester Prynne's ignominious exposure, stood a man, elderly, travel-worn, who, just emerging from the perilous wilderness, beheld the woman, in whom he hoped to find embodied the warmth and cheerfulness of home, set up as a type of sin before the people. Her matronly fame was trodden under all men's feet. Infamy was babbling around her in the public market-place. For her kindred, should the tidings ever reach them, and for the companions of her unspotted life, there remained nothing but the contagion of her dishonor; which would not fail to be distributed in strict accordance and proportion with the intimacy and sacredness of their previous relationship. Then why — since the choice was with himself — should the individual, whose connection with the fallen woman had been the most intimate and sacred of them all, come forward to vindicate his claim to an inheritance so little desirable? He resolved not to be pilloried beside her on her pedestal of shame. Unknown to all but Hester Prynne, and possessing the lock and key of her silence, he chose to withdraw his name from the roll of mankind, and, as regarded his former ties and interests, to vanish out of life as completely as if he indeed lay at the bottom of the ocean, whither rumor had long ago consigned him. This purpose once effected, new interests would immediately spring up, and likewise a new purpose; dark, it is true, if not guilty, but of force enough to engage the full strength of his faculties.

In pursuance of this resolve, he took up his residence in the Puritan town, as Roger Chillingworth, without other introduction than the learning and intelligence of which he possessed more than a common measure. As his studies, at a previous period of his life, had made him extensively acquainted with the medical science of the day, it was as a physician that he presented himself, and as such was cordially received. Skilful men, of the medical and chirurgical profession, were of rare occurrence in the colony. They seldom, it would appear, partook of the religious zeal that brought other emigrants across the Atlantic. In their researches into the human frame, it may be that the higher and more subtile faculties of such men were materialized, and that they lost the spiritual view of existence amid the intricacies of that wondrous mechanism, which seemed to involve art enough to comprise all of life within itself. At all events, the health of the good town of Boston, so far as medicine had aught to do with it, had hitherto lain in the guardianship of an aged deacon and apothecary, whose piety and godly deportment were stronger testimonials in his favor, than any that he could have produced in the shape of a diploma. The only surgeon was one who combined the occasional exercise of that noble art with the daily and habitual flourish of a razor. To such a professional body Roger Chillingworth was a brilliant acquisition. He soon manifested his familiarity with the ponderous and imposing machinery of antique physic; in which every remedy contained a multitude of far-fetched and heterogeneous ingredients, as elaborately compounded as if the proposed result had been the Elixir of Life. In his Indian captivity, moreover, he had gained much knowledge of the properties of native herbs and roots; nor did he conceal from his patients, that these simple medicines, Nature's boon to the untutored savage, had quite as large a share of his own confidence as the European pharmacopœia, which so many learned doctors had spent centuries in elaborating.

This learned stranger was exemplary, as regarded at least the outward forms of a religious life, and, early after his arrival, had chosen for his spiritual guide the Reverend Mr. Dimmesdale. The young divine, whose scholar-like renown still lived in Oxford, was considered by his more fervent admirers as little less than a heaven-ordained apostle, destined, should he live and labor for the ordinary term of life, to do as great deeds for the now feeble New England Church, as the early Fathers had achieved for the infancy of the Christian faith. About this period, however, the health of Mr. Dimmesdale had evidently begun to fail. By those best acquainted with his habits, the paleness of the young minister's cheek was accounted for by his too earnest devotion to study, his scrupulous fulfilment of parochial duty, and, more than all, by the fasts and vigils of which he made a frequent practice, in order to keep the grossness of this earthly state from clogging and obscuring his spiritual lamp. Some declared, that, if Mr. Dimmesdale were really going to die, it was cause enough, that the world was not worthy to be any longer trodden by his feet. He himself, on the other hand, with characteristic humility, avowed his belief, that, if Providence should see fit to remove him, it would be because of his own unworthiness to perform its humblest mission here on earth. With all this difference of opinion as to the cause of his decline, there could be no question of the fact. His form grew emaciated; his voice, though still rich and sweet, had a certain melancholy prophecy of decay in it; he was often observed, on any slight alarm or other sudden accident, to put his hand over his heart, with first a flush and then a paleness, indicative of pain.

Such was the young clergyman's condition, and so imminent the prospect that his dawning light would be extinguished, all untimely, when Roger Chillingworth made his advent to the town. His first entry on the scene, few people could tell whence, dropping down, as it were, out of the sky, or starting from the nether earth, had an aspect of mystery, which was easily heightened to the miraculous. He was now known to be a man of skill; it was observed that he gathered herbs, and the blossoms of wild-flowers, and dug up roots and plucked off twigs from the forest-trees, like one acquainted with hidden virtues in what was valueless to common eyes. He was heard to speak of Sir Kenelm Digby,[12] and other famous men, — whose scientific attainments were esteemed hardly less than supernatural, — as having been his correspondents or associates. Why, with such rank in the learned world, had he come hither? What could he, whose sphere was in great cities, be seeking

[12] An English politician and diplomat, Sir Kenelm Digby (1603–1665), was best known for his scientific experiments and dabblings in black magic.

in the wilderness? In answer to this query, a rumor gained ground, — and, however absurd, was entertained by some very sensible people, — that Heaven had wrought an absolute miracle, by transporting an eminent Doctor of Physic, from a German university, bodily through the air, and setting him down at the door of Mr. Dimmesdale's study! Individuals of wiser faith, indeed, who knew that Heaven promotes its purposes without aiming at the stage-effect of what is called miraculous interposition, were inclined to see a providential hand in Roger Chillingworth's so opportune arrival.

This idea was countenanced by the strong interest which the physician ever manifested in the young clergyman; he attached himself to him as a parishioner, and sought to win a friendly regard and confidence from his naturally reserved sensibility. He expressed great alarm at his pastor's state of health, but was anxious to attempt the cure, and, if early undertaken, seemed not despondent of a favorable result. The elders, the deacons, the motherly dames, and the young and fair maidens, of Mr. Dimmesdale's flock, were alike importunate that he should make trial of the physician's frankly offered skill. Mr. Dimmesdale gently repelled their entreaties.

"I need no medicine," said he.

But how could the young minister say so, when, with every successive Sabbath, his cheek was paler and thinner, and his voice more tremulous than before, — when it had now become a constant habit, rather than a casual gesture, to press his hand over his heart? Was he weary of his labors? Did he wish to die? These questions were solemnly propounded to Mr. Dimmesdale by the elder ministers of Boston and the deacons of his church, who, to use their own phrase, "dealt with him" on the sin of rejecting the aid which Providence so manifestly held out. He listened in silence, and finally promised to confer with the physician.

"Were it God's will," said the Reverend Mr. Dimmesdale, when, in fulfilment of this pledge, he requested old Roger Chillingworth's professional advice, "I could be well content, that my labors, and my sorrows, and my sins, and my pains, should shortly end with me, and what is earthly of them be buried in my grave, and the spiritual go with me to my eternal state, rather than that you should put your skill to the proof in my behalf."

"Ah," replied Roger Chillingworth, with that quietness which, whether imposed or natural, marked all his deportment, "it is thus that a young clergyman is apt to speak. Youthful men, not having taken a deep root, give up their hold of life so easily! And saintly men, who walk with God on earth, would fain be away, to walk with him on the golden pavements of the New Jerusalem."

"Nay," rejoined the young minister, putting his hand to his heart, with a flush of pain flitting over his brow, "were I worthier to walk there, I could be better content to toil here."

"Good men ever interpret themselves too meanly," said the physician.

In this manner, the mysterious old Roger Chillingworth became the medical adviser of the Reverend Mr. Dimmesdale. As not only the disease interested the physician, but he was strongly moved to look into the character and qualities of the patient, these two men, so different in age, came gradually to spend much time together. For the sake of the minister's health, and to enable the leech to gather plants with healing balm in them, they took long walks on the sea-shore, or in the forest; mingling various talk with the plash and murmur of the waves, and the solemn wind-anthem among the tree-tops. Often, likewise, one was the guest of the other, in his place of study and retirement. There was a fascination for the minister in the company of the man of science, in whom he recognized an intellectual cultivation of no moderate depth or scope; together with a range and freedom of ideas, that he would have vainly looked for among the members of his own profession. In truth, he was startled, if not shocked, to find this attribute in the physician. Mr. Dimmesdale was a true priest, a true religionist, with the reverential sentiment largely developed, and an order of mind that impelled itself powerfully along the track of a creed, and wore its passage continually deeper with the lapse of time. In no state of society would he have been what is called a man of liberal views; it would always be essential to his peace to feel the pressure of a faith about him, supporting, while it confined him within its iron framework. Not the less, however, though with a tremulous enjoyment, did he feel the occasional relief of looking at the universe through the medium of another kind of intellect than those with which he habitually held converse. It was as if a window were thrown open, admitting a freer atmosphere into the close and stifled study, where his life was wasting itself away, amid lamp-light, or obstructed day-beams, and the musty fragrance, be it sensual or moral, that exhales from books. But the air was too fresh and chill to be long breathed, with comfort. So the minister, and the physician with him, withdrew again within the limits of what their church defined as orthodox.

Thus Roger Chillingworth scrutinized his patient carefully, both as he saw him in his ordinary life, keeping an accustomed pathway in the range of thoughts familiar to him, and as he appeared when thrown amidst other moral scenery, the novelty of which might call out something new to the surface of his character. He deemed it essential, it would seem, to know the man, before attempting to do him good. Wherever there is a heart and an intellect, the diseases of the physical frame are tinged with the peculiarities of these. In Arthur Dimmesdale, thought and imagination were so active, and sensibility so intense, that the bodily infirmity would be likely to have its groundwork there. So Roger Chillingworth — the man of skill, the kind and friendly physician — strove to go deep into his patient's bosom, delving among his principles, prying into his recollections, and probing every thing with a cautious touch, like a treasure-seeker in a dark cavern. Few secrets can escape an investigator, who has opportunity and license to undertake such a quest, and skill to follow it up. A man burdened with a secret should especially avoid the intimacy of his physician. If the latter possess native sagacity, and a nameless something more, — let us call it intuition; if he show no intrusive egotism, nor disagreeably prominent characteristics of his own; if he have the power, which must be born with him, to bring his mind into such affinity with his patient's, that this last shall unawares have spoken what he imagines himself only to have thought; if such revelations be received without tumult, and acknowledged not so often by an uttered sympathy, as by silence, an inarticulate breath, and here and there a word, to indicate that all is understood; if, to these qualifications of a confidant be joined the advantages afforded by his recognized character as a physician; — then, at some inevitable moment, will the soul of the sufferer be dissolved, and flow forth in a dark, but transparent stream, bringing all its mysteries into the daylight.

Roger Chillingworth possessed all, or most, of the attributes above enumerated. Nevertheless, time went on; a kind of intimacy, as we have said, grew up between these two cultivated minds, which had as wide a field as the whole sphere of human thought and study, to meet upon; they discussed every topic of ethics and religion, of public affairs, and private character; they talked much, on both sides, of matters that seemed personal to themselves; and yet no secret, such as the physician fancied must exist there, ever stole out of the minister's consciousness into his companion's ear. The latter had his suspicions, indeed, that even the nature of Mr. Dimmesdale's bodily disease had never fairly been revealed to him. It was a strange reserve!

After a time, at a hint from Roger Chillingworth, the friends of Mr. Dimmesdale effected an arrangement by which the two were lodged in the same house; so that every ebb and flow of the minister's life-tide might pass under the eye of his anxious and attached physician. There was much joy throughout the town, when this greatly desirable object was attained. It was held to be the best possible measure for the young clergyman's welfare; unless, indeed, as often urged by such as felt authorized to do so, he had selected some one of the many blooming damsels, spiritually devoted to him, to become his devoted wife. This latter step, however, there was no present prospect that Arthur Dimmesdale would be prevailed upon to take; he rejected all suggestions of the kind, as if priestly celibacy were one of his articles of church-discipline. Doomed by his own choice, therefore, as Mr. Dimmesdale so evidently was, to eat his unsavory morsel always at another's board, and endure the life-long chill which must be his lot who seeks to warm himself only at another's fireside, it truly seemed that this sagacious, experienced, benevolent, old physician, with his concord of paternal and reverential love for the young pastor, was the very man, of all mankind, to be constantly within reach of his voice.

The new abode of the two friends was with a pious widow, of good social rank, who dwelt in a house covering pretty nearly the site on which the venerable structure of King's Chapel has since been built. It had the grave-yard, originally Isaac Johnson's home-field, on one side, and so was well adapted to call up serious reflections, suited to their respective employments, in both minister and man of physic. The motherly care of the good widow assigned to Mr. Dimmesdale a front apartment, with a sunny exposure, and heavy window-curtains to create a noontide shadow, when desirable. The walls were hung round with tapestry, said to be from the Gobelin looms,[13] and, at all events, representing the Scriptural story of David and Bathsheba, and Nathan the Prophet, in colors still unfaded, but which made the fair woman of the scene almost as grimly picturesque as the woe-denouncing seer. Here, the pale clergyman piled up his library, rich with parchment-bound folios of the Fathers, and the lore of Rabbis, and monkish erudition, of which the Protestant divines, even while they vilified and decried that class of writers, were yet constrained often to avail themselves. On the other side of the house, old Roger Chillingworth arranged his study and laboratory; not such as a modern man of science would reckon even tolerably complete, but provided with a distilling apparatus, and the means of compounding drugs and chemicals, which the practised alchemist knew well how to turn to purpose. With such commodiousness

[13] The looms of the Parisian Gobelin family, on which were produced famous tapestries representing biblical and other stories.

of situation, these two learned persons sat themselves down, each in his own domain, yet familiarly passing from one apartment to the other, and bestowing a mutual and not incurious inspection into one another's business.

And the Reverend Arthur Dimmesdale's best discerning friends, as we have intimated, very reasonably imagined that the hand of Providence had done all this, for the purpose — besought in so many public, and domestic, and secret prayers — of restoring the young minister to health. But — it must now be said — another portion of the community had latterly begun to take its own view of the relation betwixt Mr. Dimmesdale and the mysterious old physician. When an uninstructed multitude attempts to see with its eyes, it is exceedingly apt to be deceived. When, however, it forms its judgment, as it usually does, on the intuitions of its great and warm heart, the conclusions thus attained are often so profound and so unerring, as to possess the character of truths supernaturally revealed. The people, in the case of which we speak, could justify its prejudice against Roger Chillingworth by no fact or argument worthy of serious refutation. There was an aged handicraftsman, it is true, who had been a citizen of London at the period of Sir Thomas Overbury's[14] murder, now some thirty years agone; he testified to having seen the physician, under some other name, which the narrator of the story had now forgotten, in company with Doctor Forman, the famous old conjurer, who was implicated in the affair of Overbury. Two or three individuals hinted, that the man of skill, during his Indian captivity, had enlarged his medical attainments by joining in the incantations of the savage priests; who were universally acknowledged to be powerful enchanters, often performing seemingly miraculous cures by their skill in the black art. A large number — and many of these were persons of such sober sense and practical observation, that their opinions would have been valuable, in other matters — affirmed that Roger Chillingworth's aspect had undergone a remarkable change while he had dwelt in town, and especially since his abode with Mr. Dimmesdale. At first, his expression had been calm, meditative, scholarlike. Now, there was something ugly and evil in his face, which they had not previously noticed, and which grew still the more obvious to sight, the oftener they looked upon him. According to the vulgar idea, the fire in his laboratory had been brought from the lower regions, and was fed with infernal fuel; and so, as might be expected, his visage was getting sooty with the smoke.

[14] Sir Thomas Overbury (1581–1613), was killed at the behest of the countess of Essex because he opposed her marriage to his patron, Viscount Rochester.

To sum up the matter, it grew to be a widely diffused opinion, that the Reverend Arthur Dimmesdale, like many other personages of especial sanctity, in all ages of the Christian world, was haunted either by Satan himself, or Satan's emissary, in the guise of old Roger Chillingworth. This diabolical agent had the Divine permission, for a season, to burrow into the clergyman's intimacy, and plot against his soul. No sensible man, it was confessed, could doubt on which side the victory would turn. The people looked, with an unshaken hope, to see the minister come forth out of the conflict, transfigured with the glory which he would unquestionably win. Meanwhile, nevertheless, it was sad to think of the perchance mortal agony through which he must struggle towards his triumph.

Alas, to judge from the gloom and terror in the depths of the poor minister's eyes, the battle was a sore one, and the victory any thing but secure!

X. The Leech and His Patient

Old Roger Chillingworth, throughout life, had been calm in temperament, kindly, though not of warm affections, but ever, and in all his relations with the world, a pure and upright man. He had begun an investigation, as he imagined, with the severe and equal integrity of a judge, desirous only of truth, even as if the question involved no more than the air-drawn lines and figures of a geometrical problem, instead of human passions, and wrongs inflicted on himself. But, as he proceeded, a terrible fascination, a kind of fierce, though still calm, necessity seized the old man within its gripe, and never set him free again, until he had done all its bidding. He now dug into the poor clergyman's heart, like a miner searching for gold; or, rather, like a sexton delving into a grave, possibly in quest of a jewel that had been buried on the dead man's bosom, but likely to find nothing save mortality and corruption. Alas for his own soul, if these were what he sought!

Sometimes, a light glimmered out of the physician's eyes, burning blue and ominous, like the reflection of a furnace, or, let us say, like one of those gleams of ghastly fire that darted from Bunyan's awful doorway in the hill-side, and quivered on the pilgrim's[15] face. The soil where this dark miner was working had perchance shown indications that encouraged him.

[15] The protagonist of John Bunyan's (1628–1688), *Pilgrim's Progress* goes through Hell's gates enroute to the Celestial City.

"This man," said he, at one such moment, to himself, "pure as they deem him, — all spiritual as he seems, — hath inherited a strong animal nature from his father or his mother. Let us dig a little farther in the direction of this vein!"

Then, after long search into the minister's dim interior, and turning over many precious materials, in the shape of high aspirations for the welfare of his race, warm love of souls, pure sentiments, natural piety, strengthened by thought and study, and illuminated by revelation, — all of which invaluable gold was perhaps no better than rubbish to the seeker — he would turn back, discouraged, and begin his quest towards another point. He groped along as stealthily, with as cautious a tread, and as wary an outlook, as a thief entering a chamber where a man lies only half asleep, — or, it may be broad awake, — with purpose to steal the very treasure which this man guards as the apple of his eye. In spite of his premeditated carefulness, the floor would now and then creak; his garments would rustle; the shadow of his presence, in a forbidden proximity, would be thrown across his victim. In other words, Mr. Dimmesdale, whose sensibility of nerve often produced the effect of spiritual intuition, would become vaguely aware that something inimical to his peace had thrust itself into relation with him. But old Roger Chillingworth, too, had perceptions that were almost intuitive; and when the minister threw his startled eyes towards him, there the physician sat; his kind, watchful, sympathizing, but never intrusive friend.

Yet Mr. Dimmesdale would perhaps have seen this individual's character more perfectly, if a certain morbidness, to which sick hearts are liable, had not rendered him suspicious of all mankind. Trusting no man as his friend, he could not recognize his enemy when the latter actually appeared. He therefore still kept up a familiar intercourse with him, daily receiving the old physician in his study; or visiting the laboratory, and, for recreation's sake, watching the processes by which weeds were converted into drugs of potency.

One day, leaning his forehead on his hand, and his elbow on the sill of the open window, that looked towards the grave-yard, he talked with Roger Chillingworth, while the old man was examining a bundle of unsightly plants.

"Where," asked he, with a look askance at them, — for it was the clergyman's peculiarity that he seldom, now-a-days, looked straightforth at any object, whether human or inanimate, — "where, my kind doctor, did you gather those herbs, with such a dark, flabby leaf?"

"Even in the grave-yard, here at hand," answered the physician, continuing his employment. "They are new to me. I found them growing on a grave, which bore no tombstone, nor other memorial of the dead man, save these ugly weeds that have taken upon themselves to keep him in remembrance. They grew out of his heart, and typify, it may be, some hideous secret that was buried with him, and which he had done better to confess during his lifetime."

"Perchance," said Mr. Dimmesdale, "he earnestly desired it, but could not."

"And wherefore?" rejoined the physician. "Wherefore not; since all the powers of nature call so earnestly for the confession of sin, that these black weeds have sprung up out of a buried heart, to make manifest an unspoken crime?"

"That, good Sir, is but a fantasy of yours," replied the minister. "There can be, if I forebode aright, no power, short of the Divine mercy, to disclose, whether by uttered words, or by type or emblem, the secrets that may be buried with a human heart. The heart, making itself guilty of such secrets, must perforce hold them, until the day when all hidden things shall be revealed. Nor have I so read or interpreted Holy Writ, as to understand that the disclosure of human thoughts and deeds, then to be made, is intended as a part of the retribution. That, surely, were a shallow view of it. No; these revelations, unless I greatly err, are meant merely to promote the intellectual satisfaction of all intelligent beings, who will stand waiting, on that day, to see the dark problem of this life made plain. A knowledge of men's hearts will be needful to the completest solution of that problem. And I conceive, moreover, that the hearts holding such miserable secrets as you speak of will yield them up, at that last day, not with reluctance, but with a joy unutterable."

"Then why not reveal them here?" asked Roger Chillingworth, glancing quietly aside at the minister. "Why should not the guilty ones sooner avail themselves of this unutterable solace?"

"They mostly do," said the clergyman, gripping hard at his breast, as if afflicted with an importunate throb of pain. "Many, many a poor soul hath given its confidence to me, not only on the death-bed, but while strong in life, and fair in reputation. And ever, after such an outpouring, O, what a relief have I witnessed in those sinful brethren! even as in one who at last draws free air, after long stifling with his own polluted breath. How can it be otherwise? Why should a wretched man, guilty, we will say, of murder, prefer to keep the dead corpse buried in his own heart, rather than fling it forth at once, and let the universe take care of it!"

"Yet some men bury their secrets thus," observed the calm physician.

"True; there are such men," answered Mr. Dimmesdale. "But, not to suggest more obvious reasons, it may be that they are kept silent by the very constitution of their nature. Or, — can we not suppose it? — guilty as they may be, retaining, nevertheless, a zeal for God's glory and man's welfare, they shrink from displaying themselves black and filthy in the view of men; because, thenceforward, no good can be achieved by them; no evil of the past be redeemed by better service. So, to their own unutterable torment, they go about among their fellow-creatures, looking pure as new-fallen snow; while their hearts are all speckled and spotted with iniquity of which they cannot rid themselves."

"These men deceive themselves," said Roger Chillingworth, with somewhat more emphasis than usual, and making a slight gesture with his forefinger. "They fear to take up the shame that rightfully belongs to them. Their love for man, their zeal for God's service, — these holy impulses may or may not coexist in their hearts with the evil inmates to which their guilt has unbarred the door, and which must needs propagate a hellish breed within them. But, if they seek to glorify God, let them not lift heavenward their unclean hands! If they would serve their fellow-men, let them do it by making manifest the power and reality of conscience, in constraining them to penitential self-abasement! Wouldst thou have me to believe, O wise and pious friend, that a false show can be better — can be more for God's glory, or man's welfare — than God's own truth? Trust me, such men deceive themselves!"

"It may be so," said the young clergyman indifferently, as waiving a discussion that he considered irrelevant or unseasonable. He had a ready faculty, indeed, of escaping from any topic that agitated his too sensitive and nervous temperament. — "But, now, I would ask of my well-skilled physician, whether, in good sooth, he deems me to have profited by his kindly care of this weak frame of mine?"

Before Roger Chillingworth could answer, they heard the clear, wild laughter of a young child's voice, proceeding from the adjacent burial-ground. Looking instinctively from the open window, — for it was summer-time, — the minister beheld Hester Prynne and little Pearl passing along the footpath that traversed the inclosure. Pearl looked as beautiful as the day, but was in one of those moods of perverse merriment which, whenever they occurred, seemed to remove her entirely out of the sphere of sympathy or human contact. She now skipped irreverently from one grave to another; until, coming to the broad, flat, armorial tombstone of a departed worthy, — perhaps of Isaac Johnson himself, — she began to dance upon it. In reply to her mother's command and entreaty that she would behave more decorously, little Pearl paused to gather the prickly burrs from a tall burdock, which grew beside the tomb. Taking a handful of these, she arranged them along the lines of the scarlet letter that decorated the maternal bosom, to which the burrs, as their nature was, tenaciously adhered. Hester did not pluck them off.

Roger Chillingworth had by this time approached the window, and smiled grimly down.

"There is no law, nor reverence for authority, no regard for human ordinances or opinions, right or wrong, mixed up with that child's composition," remarked he, as much to himself as to his companion. "I saw her, the other day, bespatter the Governor himself with water, at the cattle-trough in Spring Lane. What, in Heaven's name, is she? Is the imp altogether evil? Hath she affections? Hath she any discoverable principle of being?"

"None, — save the freedom of a broken law," answered Mr. Dimmesdale, in a quiet way, as if he had been discussing the point within himself. "Whether capable of good, I know not."

The child probably overheard their voices; for, looking up to the window, with a bright, but naughty smile of mirth and intelligence, she threw one of the prickly burrs at the Reverend Mr. Dimmesdale. The sensitive clergyman shrunk, with nervous dread, from the light missile. Detecting his emotion, Pearl clapped her little hands in the most extravagant ecstasy. Hester Prynne, likewise, had involuntarily looked up; and all these four persons, old and young, regarded one another in silence, till the child laughed aloud, and shouted, — "Come away, mother! Come away, or yonder old Black Man will catch you! He hath got hold of the minister already. Come away, mother, or he will catch you! But he cannot catch little Pearl!"

So she drew her mother away, skipping, dancing, and frisking fantastically among the hillocks of the dead people, like a creature that had nothing in common with a bygone and buried generation, nor owned herself akin to it. It was as if she had been made afresh, out of new elements, and must perforce be permitted to live her own life, and be a law unto herself, without her eccentricities being reckoned to her for a crime.

"There goes a woman," resumed Roger Chillingworth, after a pause, "who, be her demerits what they may, hath none of that mystery of hidden sinfulness which you deem so grievous to be borne. Is Hester Prynne the less miserable, think you, for that scarlet letter on her breast?"

"I do verily believe it," answered the clergyman. "Nevertheless, I cannot answer for her. There was a look of pain in her face, which I would gladly have been spared the sight of. But still, methinks, it must needs be better for the sufferer to be free to show his pain, as this poor woman Hester is, than to cover it all up in his heart."

There was another pause; and the physician began anew to examine and arrange the plants which he had gathered.

"You inquired of me, a little time agone," said he, at length, "my judgment as touching your health."

"I did," answered the clergyman, "and would gladly learn it. Speak frankly, I pray you, be it for life or death."

"Freely, then, and plainly," said the physician, still busy with his plants, but keeping a wary eye on Mr. Dimmesdale, "the disorder is a strange one; not so much in itself, nor as outwardly manifested, — in so far, at least, as the symptoms have been laid open to my observation. Looking daily at you, my good Sir, and watching the tokens of your aspect, now for months gone by, I should deem you a man sore sick, it may be, yet not so sick but that an instructed and watchful physician might well hope to cure you. But — I know not what to say — the disease is what I seem to know, yet know it not."

"You speak in riddles, learned Sir," said the pale minister, glancing aside out of the window.

"Then, to speak more plainly," continued the physician, "and I crave pardon, Sir, — should it seem to require pardon, — for this needful plainness of my speech. Let me ask, — as your friend, — as one having charge, under Providence, of your life and physical well-being, — hath all the operation of this disorder been fairly laid open and recounted to me?"

"How can you question it?" asked the minister. "Surely, it were child's play to call in a physician, and then hide the sore!"

"You would tell me, then, that I know all?" said Roger Chillingworth, deliberately, and fixing an eye, bright with intense and concentrated intelligence, on the minister's face. "Be it so! But, again! He to whom only the outward and physical evil is laid open knoweth, oftentimes, but half the evil which he is called upon to cure. A bodily disease, which we look upon as whole and entire within itself, may, after all, be but a symptom of some ailment in the spiritual part. Your pardon, once again, good Sir, if my speech give the shadow of offence. You, Sir, of all men whom I have known, are he whose body is the closest conjoined, and imbued, and identified, so to speak, with the spirit whereof it is the instrument."

"Then I need ask no further," said the clergyman, somewhat hastily rising from his chair. "You deal not, I take it, in medicine for the soul!"

"Thus, a sickness," continued Roger Chillingworth, going on, in an unaltered tone, without heeding the interruption, — but standing up, and confronting the emaciated and white-cheeked minister with his low, dark, and misshapen figure, — "a sickness, a sore place, if we may so call it, in your spirit, hath immediately its appropriate manifestation in your bodily frame. Would you, therefore, that your physician heal the bodily evil? How may this be, unless you first lay open to him the wound or trouble in your soul?"

"No! — not to thee! — not to an earthly physician!" cried Mr. Dimmesdale, passionately, and turning his eyes, full and bright, and with a kind of fierceness, on old Roger Chillingworth. "Not to thee! But, if it be the soul's disease, then do I commit myself to the one Physician of the soul! He, if it stand with his good pleasure, can cure; or he can kill! Let him do with me as, in his justice and wisdom, he shall see good. But who art thou, that meddlest in this matter? — that dares thrust himself between the sufferer and his God?"

With a frantic gesture, he rushed out of the room.

"It is as well to have made this step," said Roger Chillingworth to himself, looking after the minister with a grave smile. "There is nothing lost. We shall be friends again anon. But see, now, how passion takes hold upon this man, and hurrieth him out of himself? As with one passion, so with another! He hath done a wild thing ere now, this pious Master Dimmesdale, in the hot passion of his heart!"

It proved not difficult to reëstablish the intimacy of the two companions, on the same footing and in the same degree as heretofore. The young clergyman, after a few hours of privacy, was sensible that the disorder of his nerves had hurried him into an unseemly outbreak of temper, which there had been nothing in the physician's words to excuse or palliate. He marvelled, indeed, at the violence with which he had thrust back the kind old man, when merely proffering the advice which it was his duty to bestow, and which the minister himself had expressly sought. With these remorseful feelings, he lost no time in making the amplest apologies, and besought his friend still to continue the care, which, if not successful in restoring him to health, had, in all probability, been the means of prolonging his feeble existence to that hour. Roger Chillingworth readily assented, and went on with his medical supervision of the minister; doing his best for him, in all good faith, but always quitting the patient's apartment, at the close of a professional interview, with a mysterious and puzzled smile upon his lips. This expression was invisible in Mr. Dimmesdale's presence, but grew strongly evident as the physician crossed the threshold.

"A rare case!" he muttered. "I must needs look deeper into it. A strange sympathy betwixt soul and body! Were it only for the art's sake, I must search this matter to the bottom!"

It came to pass, not long after the scene above recorded, that the Reverend Mr. Dimmesdale, at noonday, and entirely unawares, fell into a deep, deep slumber, sitting in his chair, with a large black-letter volume open before him on the table. It must have been a work of vast ability in the somniferous school of literature. The profound depth of the minister's repose was the more remarkable; inasmuch as he was one of those persons whose sleep, ordinarily, is as light, as fitful, and as easily scared away, as a small bird hopping on a twig. To such an unwonted remoteness, however, had his spirit now withdrawn into itself, that he stirred not in his chair, when old Roger Chillingworth, without any extraordinary precaution, came into the room. The physician advanced directly in front of his patient, laid his hand upon his bosom, and thrust aside the vestment, that, hitherto, had always covered it even from the professional eye.

Then, indeed, Mr. Dimmesdale shuddered, and slightly stirred.

After a brief pause, the physician turned away.

But with what a wild look of wonder, joy, and horror! With what a ghastly rapture, as it were, too mighty to be expressed only by the eye and features, and therefore bursting forth through the whole ugliness of his figure, and making itself even riotously manifest by the extravagant gestures with which he threw up his arms towards the ceiling, and stamped his foot upon the floor! Had a man seen old Roger Chillingworth, at that moment of his ecstasy, he would have had no need to ask how Satan comports himself, when a precious human soul is lost to heaven, and won into his kingdom.

But what distinguished the physician's ecstasy from Satan's was the trait of wonder in it!

XI. The Interior of a Heart

After the incident last described, the intercourse between the clergyman and the physician, though externally the same, was really of another character than it had previously been. The intellect of Roger Chillingworth had now a sufficiently plain path before it. It was not, indeed, precisely that which he had laid out for himself to tread. Calm, gentle, passionless, as he appeared, there was yet, we fear, a quiet depth of malice, hitherto latent, but active now, in this unfortunate old man, which led him to imagine a more intimate revenge than any mortal had ever wreaked upon an enemy. To make himself the one trusted friend, to whom should be confided all the fear, the remorse, the agony, the ineffectual repentance, the backward rush of sinful thoughts, expelled in vain! All that guilty sorrow, hidden from the world, whose great heart would have pitied and forgiven, to be revealed to him, the Pitiless, to him, the Unforgiving! All that dark treasure to be lavished on the very man, to whom nothing else could so adequately pay the debt of vengeance!

The clergyman's shy and sensitive reserve had balked this scheme. Roger Chillingworth, however, was inclined to be hardly, if at all, less satisfied with the aspect of affairs, which Providence — using the avenger and his victim for its own purposes, and, perchance, pardoning, where it seemed most to punish — had substituted for his black devices. A revelation, he could almost say, had been granted to him. It mattered little, for his object, whether celestial, or from what other region. By its aid, in all the subsequent relations betwixt him and Mr. Dimmesdale, not merely the external presence, but the very inmost soul of the latter seemed to be brought out before his eyes, so that he could see and comprehend its every movement. He became, thenceforth, not a spectator only, but a chief actor, in the poor minister's interior world. He could play upon him as he chose. Would he arouse him with a throb of agony? The victim was for ever on the rack; it needed only to know the spring that controlled the engine; — and the physician knew it well! Would he startle him with sudden fear? As at the waving of a magician's wand, uprose a grisly phantom, — uprose a thousand phantoms, — in many shapes, of death, or more awful shame, all flocking roundabout the clergyman, and pointing with their fingers at his breast!

All this was accomplished with a subtlety so perfect, that the minister, though he had constantly a dim perception of some evil influence watching over him, could never gain a knowledge of its actual nature. True, he looked doubtfully, fearfully, — even, at times, with horror and the bitterness of hatred, — at the deformed figure of the old physician. His gestures, his gait, his grizzled beard, his slightest and most indifferent acts, the very fashion of his garments, were odious in the clergyman's sight; a token, implicitly to be relied on, of a deeper antipathy in the breast of the latter than he was willing to acknowledge to himself. For, as it was impossible to assign a reason for such distrust and abhorrence, so Mr. Dimmesdale, conscious that the poison of one morbid spot was infecting his heart's entire substance, attributed all his presentiments to no other cause. He took himself to task for his bad sympathies in reference to Roger Chillingworth, disregarded the lesson that he should have drawn from them, and did his best to root them out. Unable to accomplish this, he nevertheless, as a matter of principle, continued his habits of social familiarity with the old man, and thus gave him constant opportunities for perfecting the purpose to which — poor, forlorn creature that he was, and more wretched than his victim — the avenger had devoted himself.

While thus suffering under bodily disease, and gnawed and tortured by some black trouble of the soul, and given over to the machinations of his deadliest enemy, the Reverend Mr. Dimmesdale had achieved a brilliant popularity in his sacred office. He won it, indeed, in great part, by his sorrows. His intellectual gifts, his moral perceptions, his power of experiencing and communicating emotion, were kept in a state of preternatural activity by the prick and anguish of his daily life. His fame, though still on its upward slope, already overshadowed the soberer reputations of his fellow-clergymen, eminent as several of them were. There were scholars among them, who had spent more years in acquiring abstruse lore, connected with the divine profession, than Mr. Dimmesdale had lived; and who might well, therefore, be more profoundly versed in such solid and valuable attainments than their youthful brother. There were men, too, of a sturdier texture of mind than his, and endowed with a far greater share of the shrewd, hard, iron or granite understanding; which, duly mingled with a fair proportion of doctrinal ingredient, constitutes a highly respectable, efficacious, and unamiable variety of the clerical species. There were others, again, true saintly fathers, whose faculties had been elaborated by weary toil among their books, and by patient thought, and etherealized, moreover, by spiritual communications with the better world, into which their purity of life had almost introduced these holy personages, with their garments of mortality still clinging to them. All that they lacked was the gift that descended upon the chosen disciples, at Pentecost, in tongues of flame; symbolizing, it would seem, not the power of speech in foreign and unknown languages, but that of addressing the whole human brotherhood in the heart's native language. These fathers, otherwise so apostolic, lacked Heaven's last and rarest attestation of their office, the Tongue of Flame. They would have vainly sought — had they ever dreamed of seeking — to express the highest truths through the humblest medium of familiar words and images. Their voices came down, afar and indistinctly, from the upper heights where they habitually dwelt.

Not improbably, it was to this latter class of men that Mr. Dimmesdale, by many of his traits of character, naturally belonged. To their high mountain-peaks of faith and sanctity he would have climbed, had not the tendency been thwarted by the burden, whatever it might be, of crime or anguish, beneath which it was his doom to totter. It kept him down, on a level with the lowest; him, the man of ethereal attributes, whose voice the angels might else have listened to and answered! But this very burden it was, that gave him sympathies so intimate with the sinful brotherhood of mankind; so that his heart vibrated in unison with theirs, and received their pain into itself, and sent its own throb of pain through a thousand other hearts, in gushes of sad, persuasive eloquence. Oftenest persuasive, but sometimes terrible! The people knew not the power that moved them thus. They deemed the young clergyman a miracle of holiness. They fancied him the mouth-piece of Heaven's messages of wisdom, and rebuke, and love. In their eyes, the very ground on which he trod was sanctified. The virgins of his church grew pale around him, victims of a passion so imbued with religious sentiment that they imagined it to be all religion, and brought it openly, in their white bosoms, as their most acceptable sacrifice before the altar. The aged members of his flock, beholding Mr. Dimmesdale's frame so feeble, while they were themselves so rugged in their infirmity, believed that he would go heavenward before them, and enjoined it upon their children, that their old bones should be buried close to their young pastor's holy grave. And, all this time, perchance, when poor Mr. Dimmesdale was thinking of his grave, he questioned with himself whether the grass would ever grow on it, because an accursed thing must there be buried!

It is inconceivable, the agony with which this public veneration tortured him! It was his genuine impulse to adore the truth, and to reckon all things shadow-like, and utterly devoid of weight or value, that had not its divine essence as the life within their life. Then, what was he? — a substance? — or the dimmest of all shadows? He longed to speak out, from his own pulpit, at the full height of his voice, and tell the people what he was. "I, whom you behold in these black garments of the priesthood, — I, who ascend the sacred desk, and turn my pale face heavenward, taking upon myself to hold communion, in your behalf, with the Most High Omniscience, — I, in whose daily life you discern the sanctity of Enoch,[16] — I, whose footsteps, as you suppose, leave a gleam along my earthly track, whereby the pilgrims that shall come

[16] The biblical Enoch was such a good man that he went to Heaven without dying first (Genesis 5:21–22; Hebrews 11:5).

after me may be guided to the regions of the blest, — I, who have laid the hand of baptism upon your children, — I, who have breathed the parting prayer over your dying friends, to whom the Amen sounded faintly from a world which they had quitted, — I, your pastor, whom you so reverence and trust, am utterly a pollution and a lie!"

More than once, Mr. Dimmesdale had gone into the pulpit, with a purpose never to come down its steps, until he should have spoken words like the above. More than once, he had cleared his throat, and drawn in the long, deep, and tremulous breath, which, when sent forth again, would come burdened with the black secret of his soul. More than once — nay, more than a hundred times — he had actually spoken! Spoken! But how? He had told his hearers that he was altogether vile, a viler companion of the vilest, the worst of sinners, an abomination, a thing of unimaginable iniquity; and that the only wonder was, that they did not see his wretched body shrivelled up before their eyes, by the burning wrath of the Almighty! Could there be plainer speech than this? Would not the people start up in their seats, by a simultaneous impulse, and tear him down out of the pulpit which he defiled? Not so, indeed! They heard it all, and did but reverence him the more. They little guessed what deadly purport lurked in those self-condemning words. "The godly youth!" said they among themselves. "The saint on earth! Alas, if he discern such sinfulness in his own white soul, what horrid spectacle would he behold in thine or mine!" The minister well knew — subtle, but remorseful hypocrite that he was! — the light in which his vague confession would be viewed. He had striven to put a cheat upon himself by making the avowal of a guilty conscience, but had gained only one other sin, and a self-acknowledged shame, without the momentary relief of being self-deceived. He had spoken the very truth, and transformed it into the veriest falsehood. And yet, by the constitution of his nature, he loved the truth, and loathed the lie, as few men ever did. Therefore, above all things else, he loathed his miserable self!

His inward trouble drove him to practices, more in accordance with the old, corrupted faith of Rome, than with the better light of the church in which he had been born and bred. In Mr. Dimmesdale's secret closet, under lock and key, there was a bloody scourge. Oftentimes, this Protestant and Puritan divine had plied it on his own shoulders; laughing bitterly at himself the while, and smiting so much the more pitilessly, because of that bitter laugh. It was his custom, too, as it has been that of many other pious Puritans, to fast, — not, however, like them, in order to purify the body and render it the fitter medium of celestial illumination, — but rigorously, and until his knees trembled beneath him, as an act of penance. He kept vigils, likewise, night after night, sometimes in utter darkness; sometimes with a glimmering lamp; and sometimes, viewing his own face in a looking-glass, by the most powerful light which he could throw upon it. He thus typified the constant introspection wherewith he tortured, but could not purify, himself. In these lengthened vigils, his brain often reeled, and visions seemed to flit before him; perhaps seen doubtfully, and by a faint light of their own, in the remote dimness of the chamber, or more vividly, and close beside him, within the looking-glass. Now it was a herd of diabolic shapes, that grinned and mocked at the pale minister, and beckoned him away with them; now a group of shining angels, who flew upward heavily, as sorrow-laden, but grew more ethereal as they rose. Now came the dead friends of his youth, and his white-bearded father, with a saint-like frown, and his mother, turning her face away as she passed by. Ghost of a mother, — thinnest fantasy of a mother, — methinks she might yet have thrown a pitying glance towards her son! And now, through the chamber which these spectral thoughts had made so ghastly, glided Hester Prynne, leading along little Pearl, in her scarlet garb, and pointing her forefinger, first, at the scarlet letter on her bosom, and then at the clergyman's own breast.

None of these visions ever quite deluded him. At any moment, by an effort of his will, he could discern substances through their misty lack of substance, and convince himself that they were not solid in their nature, like yonder table of carved oak, or that big, square, leathern-bound and brazen-clasped volume of divinity. But, for all that, they were, in one sense, the truest and most substantial things which the poor minister now dealt with. It is the unspeakable misery of a life so false as his, that it steals the pith and substance out of whatever realities there are around us, and which were meant by Heaven to be the spirit's joy and nutriment. To the untrue man, the whole universe is false, — it is impalpable, — it shrinks to nothing within his grasp. And he himself, in so far as he shows himself in a false light, becomes a shadow, or, indeed, ceases to exist. The only truth, that continued to give Mr. Dimmesdale a real existence on this earth, was the anguish in his inmost soul, and the undissembled expression of it in his aspect. Had he once found power to smile, and wear a face of gayety, there would have been no such man!

On one of those ugly nights, which we have faintly hinted at, but forborne to picture forth, the minister started from his chair. A new thought had struck him. There might be a moment's peace in it. Attiring himself with as much care as if it had been for public worship, and precisely in the same manner, he stole softly down the staircase, undid the door, and issued forth.

XII. The Minister's Vigil

Walking in the shadow of a dream, as it were, and perhaps actually under the influence of a species of somnambulism, Mr. Dimmesdale reached the spot, where, now so long since, Hester Prynne had lived through her first hour of public ignominy. The same platform or scaffold, black and weather-stained with the storm or sunshine of seven long years, and foot-worn, too, with the tread of many culprits who had since ascended it, remained standing beneath the balcony of the meeting-house. The minister went up the steps.

It was an obscure night of early May. An unvaried pall of cloud muffled the whole expanse of sky from zenith to horizon. If the same multitude which had stood as eyewitnesses while Hester Prynne sustained her punishment could now have been summoned forth, they would have discerned no face above the platform, nor hardly the outline of a human shape, in the dark gray of the midnight. But the town was all asleep. There was no peril of discovery. The minister might stand there, if it so pleased him, until morning should redden in the east, without other risk than that the dank and chill night-air would creep into his frame, and stiffen his joints with rheumatism, and clog his throat with catarrh and cough; thereby defrauding the expectant audience of tomorrow's prayer and sermon. No eye could see him, save that ever-wakeful one which had seen him in his closet, wielding the bloody scourge. Why, then, had he come hither? Was it but the mockery of penitence? A mockery, indeed, but in which his soul trifled with itself! A mockery at which angels blushed and wept, while fiends rejoiced, with jeering laughter! He had been driven hither by the impulse of that Remorse which dogged him everywhere, and whose own sister and closely linked companion was that Cowardice which invariably drew him back, with her tremulous gripe, just when the other impulse had hurried him to the verge of a disclosure. Poor, miserable man! what right had infirmity like his to burden itself with crime? Crime is for the iron-nerved, who have their choice either to endure it, or, if it press too hard, to exert their fierce and savage strength for a good purpose, and fling it off at once! This feeble and most sensitive of spirits could do neither, yet continually did one thing or another, which intertwined, in the same inextricable knot, the agony of heaven-defying guilt and vain repentance.

And thus, while standing on the scaffold, in this vain show of expiation, Mr. Dimmesdale was overcome with a great horror of mind, as if the universe were gazing at a scarlet token on his naked breast, right over his heart. On that spot, in very truth, there was, and there had long been, the gnawing and poisonous tooth of bodily pain. Without any effort of his will, or power to restrain himself, he shrieked aloud; an outcry that went pealing through the night, and was beaten back from one house to another, and reverberated from the hills in the background; as if a company of devils, detecting so much misery and terror in it, had made a plaything of the sound, and were bandying it to and fro.

"It is done!" muttered the minister, covering his face with his hands. "The whole town will awake, and hurry forth, and find me here!"

But it was not so. The shriek had perhaps sounded with a far greater power, to his own startled ears, than it actually possessed. The town did not awake; or, if it did, the drowsy slumberers mistook the cry either for something frightful in a dream, or for the noise of witches; whose voices, at that period, were often heard to pass over the settlements or lonely cottages, as they rode with Satan through the air. The clergyman, therefore, hearing no symptoms of disturbance, uncovered his eyes and looked about him. At one of the chamber-windows of Governor Bellingham's mansion, which stood at some distance, on the line of another street, he beheld the appearance of the old magistrate himself, with a lamp in his hand, a white night-cap on his head, and a long white gown enveloping his figure. He looked like a ghost, evoked unseasonably from the grave. The cry had evidently startled him. At another window of the same house, moreover, appeared old Mistress Hibbins, the Governor's sister, also with a lamp, which, even thus far off, revealed the expression of her sour and discontented face. She thrust forth her head from the lattice, and looked anxiously upward. Beyond the shadow of a doubt, this venerable witch-lady had heard Mr. Dimmesdale's outcry, and interpreted it, with its multitudinous echoes and reverberations, as the clamor of the fiends and night-hags, with whom she was well known to make excursions into the forest.

Detecting the gleam of Governor Bellingham's lamp, the old lady quickly extinguished her own, and vanished. Possibly, she went up among the clouds. The minister saw nothing further of her motions. The magistrate, after a wary observation of the darkness — into which, nevertheless, he could see but little farther than he might into a millstone — retired from the window.

The minister grew comparatively calm. His eyes, however, were soon greeted by a little, glimmering light, which, at first a long way off, was approaching up the street. It threw a gleam of recognition on here a post, and there a garden-fence, and here a latticed window-pane, and there a pump, with its full trough of water, and here, again, an arched door of oak, with an iron knocker, and a rough log for the door-step. The Reverend Mr. Dimmesdale noted all these minute particulars, even while firmly convinced that the doom of his existence was stealing onward, in the footsteps which he now heard; and that the gleam of the lantern would fall upon him, in a few moments more, and reveal his long-hidden secret. As the light drew nearer, he beheld, within its illuminated circle, his brother clergyman, — or, to speak more accurately, his professional father, as well as highly valued friend, — the Reverend Mr. Wilson; who, as Mr. Dimmesdale now conjectured, had been praying at the bedside of some dying man. And so he had. The good old minister came freshly from the death-chamber of Governor Winthrop,[17] who had passed from earth to heaven within that very hour. And now, surrounded, like the saint-like personages of olden times, with a radiant halo, that glorified him amid this gloomy night of sin, — as if the departed Governor had left him an inheritance of his glory, or as if he had caught upon himself the distant shine of the celestial city, while looking thitherward to see the triumphant pilgrim pass within its gates, — now, in short, good Father Wilson was moving homeward, aiding his footsteps with a lighted lantern! The glimmer of this luminary suggested the above conceits to Mr. Dimmesdale, who smiled, — nay, almost laughed at them, — and then wondered if he were going mad.

As the Reverend Mr. Wilson passed beside the scaffold, closely muffling his Geneva cloak about him with one arm, and holding the lantern before his breast with the other, the minister could hardly restrain himself from speaking.

"A good evening to you, venerable Father Wilson! Come up hither, I pray you, and pass a pleasant hour with me!"

Good heavens! Had Mr. Dimmesdale actually spoken? For one instant, he believed that these words had passed his lips. But they were uttered only within his imagination. The venerable Father Wilson continued to step slowly onward, looking carefully at the muddy pathway before his feet, and never once turning his head towards the guilty platform. When the light of the glimmering lantern had faded quite away,

[17] John Winthrop (1588–1649), who helped found the Massachusetts Bay Colony in 1630, served as its first governor.

the minister discovered, by the faintness which came over him, that the last few moments had been a crisis of terrible anxiety; although his mind had made an involuntary effort to relieve itself by a kind of lurid playfulness.

Shortly afterwards, the like grisly sense of the humorous again stole in among the solemn phantoms of his thought. He felt his limbs growing stiff with the unaccustomed chilliness of the night, and doubted whether he should be able to descend the steps of the scaffold. Morning would break, and find him there. The neighbourhood would begin to rouse itself. The earliest riser, coming forth in the dim twilight, would perceive a vaguely defined figure aloft on the place of shame; and, half crazed betwixt alarm and curiosity, would go, knocking from door to door, summoning all the people to behold the ghost — as he needs must think it — of some defunct transgressor. A dusky tumult would flap its wings from one house to another. Then — the morning light still waxing stronger — old patriarchs would rise up in great haste, each in his flannel gown, and matronly dames, without pausing to put off their night-gear. The whole tribe of decorous personages, who had never heretofore been seen with a single hair of their heads awry, would start into public view, with the disorder of a nightmare in their aspects. Old Governor Bellingham would come grimly forth, with his King James's ruff fastened askew; and Mistress Hibbins, with some twigs of the forest clinging to her skirts, and looking sourer than ever, as having hardly got a wink of sleep after her night ride; and good Father Wilson, too, after spending half the night at a death-bed, and liking ill to be disturbed, thus early, out of his dreams about the glorified saints. Hither, likewise, would come the elders and deacons of Mr. Dimmesdale's church, and the young virgins who so idolized their minister, and had made a shrine for him in their white bosoms; which, now, by the by, in their hurry and confusion, they would scantly have given themselves time to cover with their kerchiefs. All people, in a word, would come stumbling over their thresholds, and turning up their amazed and horror-stricken visages around the scaffold. Whom would they discern there, with the red eastern light upon his brow? Whom, but the Reverend Arthur Dimmesdale, half frozen to death, overwhelmed with shame, and standing where Hester Prynne had stood!

Carried away by the grotesque horror of this picture, the minister, unawares, and to his own infinite alarm, burst into a great peal of laughter. It was immediately responded to by a light, airy, childish laugh, in which, with a thrill of the heart, — but he knew not whether of exquisite pain, or pleasure as acute, — he recognized the tones of little Pearl.

"Pearl! Little Pearl!" cried he, after a moment's pause; then, suppressing his voice, — "Hester! Hester Prynne! Are you there?"

"Yes, it is Hester Prynne!" she replied, in a tone of surprise; and the minister heard her footsteps approaching from the sidewalk, along which she had been passing. — "It is I, and my little Pearl."

"Whence come you, Hester?" asked the minister. "What sent you hither?"

"I have been watching at a death-bed," answered Hester Prynne; — "at Governor Winthrop's death-bed, and have taken his measure for a robe, and am now going homeward to my dwelling."

"Come up hither, Hester, thou and little Pearl," said the Reverend Mr. Dimmesdale. "Ye have both been here before, but I was not with you. Come up hither once again, and we will stand all three together!"

She silently ascended the steps, and stood on the platform, holding little Pearl by the hand. The minister felt for the child's other hand, and took it. The moment that he did so, there came what seemed a tumultuous rush of new life, other life than his own, pouring like a torrent into his heart, and hurrying through all his veins, as if the mother and the child were communicating their vital warmth to his half-torpid system. The three formed an electric chain.

"Minister!" whispered little Pearl.

"What wouldst thou say, child?" asked Mr. Dimmesdale.

"Wilt thou stand here with mother and me, to-morrow noontide?" inquired Pearl.

"Nay; not so, my little Pearl!" answered the minister; for, with the new energy of the moment, all the dread of public exposure, that had so long been the anguish of his life, had returned upon him; and he was already trembling at the conjunction in which — with a strange joy, nevertheless — he now found himself. "Not so, my child. I shall, indeed, stand with thy mother and thee one other day, but not to-morrow!"

Pearl laughed, and attempted to pull away her hand. But the minister held it fast.

"A moment longer, my child!" said he.

"But wilt thou promise," asked Pearl, "to take my hand, and mother's hand, to-morrow noontide?"

"Not then, Pearl" said the minister, "but another time!"

"And what other time?" persisted the child.

"At the great judgment day!" whispered the minister, — and, strangely enough, the sense that he was a professional teacher of the truth impelled him to answer the child so. "Then, and there, before the judgment-seat, thy mother, and thou, and I, must stand together! But the day-light of this world shall not see our meeting!"

Pearl laughed again.

But, before Mr. Dimmesdale had done speaking, a light gleamed far and wide over all the muffled sky. It was doubtless caused by one of those meteors, which the night-watcher may so often observe burning out to waste, in the vacant regions of the atmosphere. So powerful was its radiance, that it thoroughly illuminated the dense medium of cloud betwixt the sky and earth. The great vault brightened, like the dome of an immense lamp. It showed the familiar scene of the street, with the distinctness of mid-day, but also with the awfulness that is always imparted to familiar objects by an unaccustomed light. The wooden houses, with their jutting stories and quaint gable-peaks; the doorsteps and thresholds, with the early grass springing up about them; the garden-plots, black with freshly turned earth; the wheel-track, little worn, and, even in the market-place, margined with green on either side; — all were visible, but with a singularity of aspect that seemed to give another moral interpretation to the things of this world than they had ever borne before. And there stood the minister, with his hand over his heart; and Hester Prynne, with the embroidered letter glimmering on her bosom; and little Pearl, herself a symbol, and the connecting link between those two. They stood in the noon of that strange and solemn splendor, as if it were the light that is to reveal all secrets, and the day-break that shall unite all who belong to one another.

There was witchcraft in little Pearl's eyes; and her face, as she glanced upward at the minister, wore that naughty smile which made its expression frequently so elfish. She withdrew her hand from Mr. Dimmesdale's, and pointed across the street. But he clasped both his hands over his breast, and cast his eyes towards the zenith.

Nothing was more common, in those days, than to interpret all meteoric appearances, and other natural phenomena, that occurred with less regularity than the rise and set of sun and moon, as so many revelations from a supernatural source. Thus, a blazing spear, a sword of flame, a bow, or a sheaf of arrows, seen in the midnight sky, prefigured Indian warfare. Pestilence was known to have been foreboded by a shower of crimson light. We doubt whether any marked event, for good or evil, ever befell New England, from its settlement down to Revolutionary times, of which the inhabitants had not been previously warned by some spectacle of this nature. Not seldom, it had been seen by multitudes. Oftener, however, its credibility rested on the faith of some lonely eyewitness, who beheld the wonder through the colored, magnifying, and distorting medium of his imagination, and shaped it more distinctly in his after-thought. It was, indeed, a majestic idea, that the destiny of nations should be revealed, in these awful hieroglyphics, on the cope of heaven. A scroll so wide might not be deemed too expansive for Providence to write a people's doom upon. The belief was a favorite one with our fore-fathers, as betokening that their infant commonwealth was under a celestial guardianship of peculiar intimacy and strictness. But what shall we say, when an individual discovers a revelation, addressed to himself alone, on the same vast sheet of record! In such a case, it could only be the symptom of a highly disordered mental state, when a man, rendered morbidly self-contemplative by long, intense, and secret pain, had extended his egotism over the whole expanse of nature, until the firmament itself should appear no more than a fitting page for his soul's history and fate.

We impute it, therefore, solely to the disease in his own eye and heart, that the minister, looking upward to the zenith, beheld there the appearance of an immense letter, — the letter A, — marked out in lines of dull red light. Not but the meteor may have shown itself at that point, burning duskily through a veil of cloud; but with no such shape as his guilty imagination gave it; or, at least, with so little definiteness, that another's guilt might have seen another symbol in it.

There was a singular circumstance that characterized Mr. Dimmesdale's psychological state, at this moment. All the time that he gazed upward to the zenith, he was, nevertheless, perfectly aware that little Pearl was pointing her finger towards old Roger Chillingworth, who stood at no great distance from the scaffold. The minister appeared to see him, with the same glance that discerned the miraculous letter. To his features, as to all other objects, the meteoric light imparted a new expression; or it might well be that the physician was not careful then, as at all other times, to hide the malevolence with which he looked upon his victim. Certainly, if the meteor kindled up the sky, and disclosed the earth, with an awfulness that admonished Hester Prynne and the clergyman of the day of judgment, then might Roger Chillingworth have passed with them for the arch-fiend, standing there, with a smile and scowl, to claim his own. So vivid was the expression, or so intense the minister's perception of it, that it seemed still to remain painted on the darkness, after the meteor had vanished, with an effect as if the street and all things else were at once annihilated.

"Who is that man, Hester?" gasped Mr. Dimmesdale, overcome with terror. "I shiver at him! Dost thou know the man? I hate him, Hester!"

She remembered her oath, and was silent.

"I tell thee, my soul shivers at him," muttered the minister again. "Who is he? Who is he? Canst thou do nothing for me? I have a nameless horror of the man."

"Minister," said little Pearl, "I can tell thee who he is!"

"Quickly, then, child!" said the minister, bending his ear close to her lips. "Quickly! — and as low as thou canst whisper."

Pearl mumbled something into his ear, that sounded, indeed, like human language, but was only such gibberish as children may be heard amusing themselves with, by the hour together. At all events, if it involved any secret information in regard to old Roger Chillingworth, it was in a tongue unknown to the erudite clergyman, and did but increase the bewilderment of his mind. The elfish child then laughed aloud.

"Dost thou mock me now?" said the minister.

"Thou wast not bold! — thou wast not true!" answered the child. "Thou wouldst not promise to take my hand, and mother's hand, tomorrow noontide!"

"Worthy Sir," said the physician, who had now advanced to the foot of the platform. "Pious Master Dimmesdale! can this be you? Well, well, indeed! We men of study, whose heads are in our books, have need to be straitly looked after! We dream in our waking moments, and walk in our sleep. Come, good Sir, and my dear friend, I pray you, let me lead you home!"

"How knewest thou that I was here?" asked the minister, fearfully.

"Verily, and in good faith," answered Roger Chillingworth, "I knew nothing of the matter. I had spent the better part of the night at the bedside of the worshipful Governor Winthrop, doing what my poor skill might to give him ease. He going home to a better world, I, likewise, was on my way homeward, when this strange light shone out. Come with me, I beseech you, Reverend Sir; else you will be poorly able to do Sabbath duty to-morrow. Aha! see now, how they trouble the brain, — these books! — these books! You should study less, good Sir, and take a little pastime; or these night-whimseys will grow upon you!"

"I will go home with you," said Mr. Dimmesdale.

With a chill despondency, like one awaking, all nerveless, from an ugly dream, he yielded himself to the physician, and was led away.

The next day, however, being the Sabbath, he preached a discourse which was held to be the richest and most powerful, and the most replete with heavenly influences, that had ever proceeded from his lips. Souls, it is said, more souls than one, were brought to the truth by the efficacy of that sermon, and vowed within themselves to cherish a holy gratitude towards Mr. Dimmesdale throughout the long hereafter. But, as he came down the pulpit-steps, the gray-bearded sexton met him, holding up a black glove, which the minister recognized as his own.

"It was found," said the sexton, "this morning, on the scaffold, where evil-doers are set up to public shame. Satan dropped it there, I take it, intending a scurrilous jest against your reverence. But, indeed, he was blind and foolish, as he ever and always is. A pure hand needs no glove to cover it!"

"Thank you, my good friend," said the minister gravely, but startled at heart; for, so confused was this remembrance, that he had almost brought himself to look at the events of the past night as visionary. "Yes, it seems to be my glove indeed!"

"And, since Satan saw fit to steal it, your reverence must needs handle him without gloves, henceforward," remarked the old sexton, grimly smiling. "But did your reverence hear of the portent that was seen last night? A great red letter in the sky, — the letter A, — which we interpret to stand for Angel. For, as our good Governor Winthrop was made an angel this past night, it was doubtless held fit that there should be some notice thereof!"

"No," answered the minister. "I had not heard of it."

XIII. Another View of Hester

In her late singular interview with Mr. Dimmesdale, Hester Prynne was shocked at the condition to which she found the clergyman reduced. His nerve seemed absolutely destroyed. His moral force was abased into more than childish weakness. It grovelled helpless on the ground, even while his intellectual faculties retained their pristine strength, or had perhaps acquired a morbid energy, which disease only could have given them. With her knowledge of a train of circumstances hidden from all others, she could readily infer, that, besides the legitimate action of his own conscience, a terrible machinery had been brought to bear, and was still operating, on Mr. Dimmesdale's well-being and repose. Knowing what this poor, fallen man had once been, her whole soul was moved by the shuddering terror with which he had appealed to her, — the outcast woman, — for support against his instinctively discovered enemy. She decided, moreover, that he had a right to her utmost aid. Little accustomed, in her long seclusion from society, to measure her ideas of right and wrong by any standard external to herself, Hester saw — or seemed to see — that there lay a responsibility upon her, in reference to the clergyman, which she owed to no other, nor to the whole world besides. The links that united her to the rest of human kind — links of flowers, or silk, or gold, or whatever the material — had all been broken. Here was the iron link of mutual crime, which neither he nor she could break. Like all other ties, it brought along with it its obligations.

Hester Prynne did not now occupy precisely the same position in which we beheld her during the earlier periods of her ignominy. Years had come, and gone. Pearl was now seven years old. Her mother, with the scarlet letter on her breast, glittering in its fantastic embroidery, had long been a familiar object to the townspeople. As is apt to be the case when a person stands out in any prominence before the community, and, at the same time, interferes neither with public nor individual interests and convenience, a species of general regard had ultimately grown up in reference to Hester Prynne. It is to the credit of human nature, that, except where its selfishness is brought into play, it loves more readily than it hates. Hatred, by a gradual and quiet process, will even be transformed to love, unless the change be impeded by a continually new irritation of the original feeling of hostility. In this matter of Hester Prynne, there was neither irritation nor irksomeness. She never battled with the public, but submitted uncomplainingly to its worst usage; she made no claim upon it, in requital for what she suffered; she did not weigh upon its sympathies. Then, also, the blameless purity of her life, during all these years in which she had been set apart to infamy, was reckoned largely in her favor. With nothing now to lose, in the sight of mankind, and with no hope, and seemingly no wish, of gaining any thing, it could only be a genuine regard for virtue that had brought back the poor wanderer to its paths.

It was perceived, too, that, while Hester never put forward even the humblest title to share in the world's privileges, — farther than to breathe the common air, and earn daily bread for little Pearl and herself by the faithful labor of her hands, — she was quick to acknowledge her sisterhood with the race of man, whenever benefits were to be conferred. None so ready as she to give of her little substance to every demand of poverty; even though the bitter-hearted pauper threw back a gibe in requital of the food brought regularly to his door, or the garments wrought for him by the fingers that could have embroidered a monarch's robe. None so self-devoted as Hester, when pestilence stalled through the town. In all seasons of calamity, indeed, whether general or of individuals, the outcast of society at once found her place. She came, not as a guest, but as a rightful inmate, into the household that was darkened by trouble; as if its gloomy twilight were a medium in which she was entitled to hold intercourse with her fellow-creatures. There glimmered the embroidered letter, with comfort in its unearthly ray. Elsewhere the token of sin, it was the taper of the sick-chamber. It had even thrown its gleam, in the sufferer's hard extremity, across the verge of time. It had shown him where to set his foot, while the light of earth was fast becoming dim, and ere the light of futurity could reach him. In such emergencies, Hester's nature showed itself warm and rich; a well-spring of human tenderness, unfailing to every real demand, and inexhaustible by the largest. Her breast, with its badge of shame, was but the softer pillow for the head that needed one. She was self-ordained a Sister of Mercy; or, we may rather say, the world's heavy hand had so ordained her, when neither the world nor she looked forward to this result. The letter was the symbol of her calling. Such helpfulness was found in her, — so much power to do, and power to sympathize, — that many people refused to interpret the scarlet A by its original signification. They said that it meant Able; so strong was Hester Prynne, with a woman's strength.

It was only the darkened house that could contain her. When sunshine came again, she was not there. Her shadow had faded across the threshold. The helpful inmate had departed, without one backward glance to gather up the meed of gratitude, if any were in the hearts of those whom she had served so zealously. Meeting them in the street, she never raised her head to receive their greeting. If they were resolute to accost her, she laid her finger on the scarlet letter, and passed on. This might be pride, but was so like humility, that it produced all the softening influence of the latter quality on the public mind. The public is despotic in its temper; it is capable of denying common justice, when too strenuously demanded as a right; but quite as frequently it awards more than justice, when the appeal is made, as despots love to have it made, entirely to its generosity. Interpreting Hester Prynne's deportment as an appeal of this nature, society was inclined to show its former victim a more benign countenance than she cared to be favored with, or, perchance, than she deserved.

The rulers, and the wise and learned men of the community, were longer in acknowledging the influence of Hester's good qualities than the people. The prejudices which they shared in common with the latter were fortified in themselves by an iron framework of reasoning, that made it a far tougher labor to expel them. Day by day, nevertheless, their sour and rigid wrinkles were relaxing into something which, in the due course of years, might grow to be an expression of almost benevolence. Thus it was with the men of rank, on whom their eminent position imposed the guardianship of the public morals. Individuals in private life, meanwhile, had quite forgiven Hester Prynne for her frailty; nay, more, they had begun to look upon the scarlet letter as the token, not of that one sin, for which she had borne so long and dreary a penance, but of her many good deeds since. "Do you see that woman with the embroidered badge?" they would say to strangers. "It is our Hester, — the town's own Hester, — who is so kind to the poor, so helpful to the sick, so comfortable to the afflicted!" Then, it is true, the propensity of human nature to tell the very worst of itself, when embodied in the person of another, would constrain them to whisper the black scandal of bygone years. It was none the less a fact, however, that, in the eyes of the very men who spoke thus, the scarlet letter had the effect of the cross on a nun's bosom. It imparted to the wearer a kind of sacredness, which enabled her to walk securely amid all peril. Had she fallen among thieves, it would have kept her safe. It was reported, and believed by many, that an Indian had drawn his arrow against the badge, and that the missile struck it, but fell harmless to the ground.

The effect of the symbol — or rather, of the position in respect to society that was indicated by it — on the mind of Hester Prynne herself, was powerful and peculiar. All the light and graceful foliage of her character had been withered up by this red-hot brand, and had long ago fallen away, leaving a bare and harsh outline, which might have been repulsive, had she possessed friends or companions to be repelled by it. Even the attractiveness of her person had undergone a similar change. It might be partly owing to the studied austerity of her dress, and partly to the lack of demonstration in her manners. It was a sad transformation, too, that her rich and luxuriant hair had either been cut off, or was so completely hidden by a cap, that not a shining lock of it ever once gushed into the sunshine. It was due in part to all these causes, but still more to something else, that there seemed to be no longer any thing in Hester's face for Love to dwell upon; nothing in Hester's form, though majestic and statue-like, that Passion would ever dream of clasping in its embrace; nothing in Hester's bosom, to make it ever again the pillow of Affection. Some attribute had departed from her, the permanence of which had been essential to keep her a woman. Such is frequently the fate, and such the stern development, of the feminine character and person, when the woman has encountered, and lived through, an experience of peculiar severity. If she be all tenderness, she will die. If she survive, the tenderness will either be crushed out of her, or — and the outward semblance is the same — crushed so deeply into her heart that it can never show itself more. The latter is perhaps the truest theory. She who has once been woman, and ceased to be so, might at any moment become a woman again, if there were only the magic touch to effect the transfiguration. We shall see whether Hester Prynne were ever afterwards so touched, and so transfigured.

Much of the marble coldness of Hester's impression was to be attributed to the circumstance that her life had turned, in a great measure, from passion and feeling, to thought. Standing alone in the world, — alone, as to any dependence on society, and with little Pearl to be guided and protected, — alone, and hopeless of retrieving her position, even had she not scorned to consider it desirable, — she cast away the fragments of a broken chain. The world's law was no law for her mind. It was an age in which the human intellect, newly emancipated, had taken a more active and a wider range than for many centuries before. Men of the sword had overthrown nobles and kings. Men bolder than these had overthrown and rearranged — not actually, but within the sphere of theory, which was their most real abode — the whole system of ancient prejudice, wherewith was linked much of ancient principle. Hester Prynne imbibed this spirit. She assumed a freedom of speculation, then common enough on the other side of the Atlantic, but which our forefathers, had they known of it, would have held to be a deadlier crime than that stigmatized by the scarlet letter. In her lonesome cottage, by the sea-shore, thoughts visited her, such as dared to enter no other dwelling in New England; shadowy guests, that would have been as perilous as demons to their entertainer, could they have been seen so much as knocking at her door.

It is remarkable, that persons who speculate the most boldly often conform with the most perfect quietude to the external regulations of society. The thought suffices them, without investing itself in the flesh and blood of action. So it seemed to be with Hester. Yet, had little Pearl never come to her from the spiritual world, it might have been far otherwise. Then, she might have come down to us in history, hand in hand with Ann Hutchinson, as the foundress of a religious sect. She might, in one of her phases, have been a prophetess. She might, and not improbably would, have suffered death from the stern tribunals of the period, for attempting to undermine the foundations of the Puritan establishment. But, in the education of her child, the mother's enthusiasm of thought had something to wreak itself upon. Providence, in the person of this little girl, had assigned to Hester's charge the germ and blossom of womanhood, to be cherished and developed amid a host of difficulties. Every thing was against her. The world was hostile. The child's own nature had something wrong in it, which continually betokened that she had been born amiss, — the effluence of her mother's lawless passion, — and often impelled Hester to ask, in bitterness of heart, whether it were for ill or good that the poor little creature had been born at all.

Indeed, the same dark question often rose into her mind, with reference to the whole race of womanhood. Was existence worth accepting, even to the happiest among them? As concerned her own individual existence, she had long ago decided in the negative, and dismissed the point as settled. A tendency to speculation, though it may keep woman quiet, as it does man, yet makes her sad. She discerns, it may be, such a hopeless task before her. As a first step, the whole system of society is to be torn down, and built up anew. Then, the very nature of the opposite sex, or its long hereditary habit, which has become like nature, is to be essentially modified, before woman can be allowed to assume what seems a fair and suitable position. Finally, all other difficulties being obviated, woman cannot take advantage of these preliminary reforms, until she herself shall have undergone a still mightier change; in which, perhaps, the ethereal essence, wherein she has her truest life, will be found to have evaporated. A woman never overcomes these problems by any exercise of thought. They are not to be solved, or only in one way. If her heart chance to come uppermost, they vanish. Thus, Hester Prynne, whose heart had lost its regular and healthy throb, wandered without a clew in the dark labyrinth of mind; now turned aside by an insurmountable precipice; now starting back from a deep chasm. There was wild and ghastly scenery all around her, and a home and comfort nowhere. At times, a fearful doubt strove to possess her soul, whether it were not better to send Pearl at once to heaven, and go herself to such futurity as Eternal Justice should provide.

The scarlet letter had not done its office.

Now, however, her interview with the Reverend Mr. Dimmesdale, on the night of his vigil, had given her a new theme of reflection, and held up to her an object that appeared worthy of any exertion and sacrifice for its attainment. She had witnessed the intense misery beneath which the minister struggled, or, to speak more accurately, had ceased to struggle. She saw that he stood on the verge of lunacy, if he had not already stepped across it. It was impossible to doubt, that, whatever painful efficacy there might be in the secret sting of remorse, a deadlier venom had been infused into it by the hand that proffered relief. A secret enemy had been continually by his side, under the semblance of a friend and helper, and had availed himself of the opportunities thus afforded for tampering with the delicate springs of Mr. Dimmesdale's nature. Hester could not but ask herself, whether there had not originally been a defect of truth, courage, and loyalty, on her own part, in allowing the minister to be thrown into a position where so much evil was to be foreboded, and nothing auspicious to be hoped. Her only justification lay in the fact, that she had been able to discern no method of rescuing him from a blacker ruin than had overwhelmed herself, except by acquiescing in Roger Chillingworth's scheme of disguise. Under that impulse, she had made her choice, and had chosen, as it now appeared, the more wretched alternative of the two. She determined to redeem her error, so far as it might yet be possible. Strengthened by years of hard and solemn trial, she felt herself no longer so inadequate to cope with Roger Chillingworth as on that night, abased by sin, and half maddened by the ignominy that was still new, when they had talked together in the prison-chamber. She had climbed her way, since then, to a higher point. The old man, on the other hand, had brought himself nearer to her level, or perhaps below it, by the revenge which he had stooped for.

In fine, Hester Prynne resolved to meet her former husband, and do what might be in her power for the rescue of the victim on whom he had so evidently set his gripe. The occasion was not long to seek. One afternoon, walking with Pearl in a retired part of the peninsula, she beheld the old physician, with a basket on one arm, and a staff in the other hand, stooping along the ground, in quest of roots and herbs to concoct his medicines withal.

XIV. Hester and the Physician

Hester bade little Pearl run down to the margin of the water, and play with the shells and tangled sea-weed, until she should have talked awhile with yonder gatherer of herbs. So the child flew away like a bird, and, making bare her small white feet, went pattering along the moist margin of the sea. Here and there, she came to a full stop, and peeped curiously into a pool, left by the retiring tide as a mirror for Pearl to see her face in. Forth peeped at her, out of the pool, with dark, glistening curls around her head, and an elf-smile in her eyes, the image of a little maid, whom Pearl, having no other playmate, invited to take her hand and run a race with her. But the visionary little maid, on her part, beckoned likewise, as if to say, — "This is a better place! Come thou into the pool!" And Pearl, stepping in, mid-leg deep, beheld her own white feet at the bottom; while, out of a still lower depth, came the gleam of a kind of fragmentary smile, floating to and fro in the agitated water.

Meanwhile, her mother had accosted the physician.

"I would speak a word with you," said she, — "a word that concerns us much."

"Aha! And is it Mistress Hester that has a word for old Roger Chillingworth?" answered he, raising himself from his stooping posture. "With all my heart! Why, Mistress, I hear good tidings of you on all hands! No longer ago than yester-eve, a magistrate, a wise and godly man, was discoursing of your affairs, Mistress Hester, and whispered me that there had been question concerning you in the council. It was debated whether or no, with safety to the common weal, yonder scarlet letter might be taken off your bosom. On my life, Hester, I made my entreaty to the worshipful magistrate that it might be done forthwith!"

"It lies not in the pleasure of the magistrates to take off this badge," calmly replied Hester. "Were I worthy to be quit of it, it would fall away of its own nature, or be transformed into something that should speak a different purport."

"Nay, then, wear it, if it suit you better," rejoined he. "A woman must needs follow her own fancy, touching the adornment of her person. The letter is gayly embroidered, and shows right bravely on your bosom!"

All this while, Hester had been looking steadily at the old man, and was shocked, as well as wonder-smitten, to discern what a change had been wrought upon him within the past seven years. It was not so much that he had grown older; for though the traces of advancing life were visible, he bore his age well, and seemed to retain a wiry vigor and alertness. But the former aspect of an intellectual and studious man, calm and quiet, which was what she best remembered in him, had altogether vanished, and been succeeded by an eager, searching, almost fierce, yet carefully guarded look. It seemed to be his wish and purpose to mask this expression with a smile; but the latter played him false, and flickered over his visage so derisively, that the spectator could see his blackness all the better for it. Ever and anon, too, there came a glare of red light out of his eyes; as if the old man's soul were on fire, and kept on smouldering duskily within his breast, until, by some casual puff of passion, it was blown into a momentary flame. This he repressed as speedily as possible, and strove to look as if nothing of the kind had happened.

In a word, old Roger Chillingworth was a striking evidence of man's faculty of transforming himself into a devil, if he will only, for a reasonable space of time, undertake a devil's office. This unhappy person had effected such a transformation by devoting himself, for seven years, to the constant analysis of a heart full of torture, and deriving his enjoyment thence, and adding fuel to those fiery tortures which he analyzed and gloated over.

The scarlet letter burned on Hester Prynne's bosom. Here was another ruin, the responsibility of which came partly home to her.

"What see you in my face," asked the physician, "that you look at it so earnestly?"

"Something that would make me weep, if there were any tears bitter enough for it," answered she. "But let it pass! It is of yonder miserable man that I would speak."

"And what of him?" cried Roger Chillingworth eagerly, as if he loved the topic, and were glad of an opportunity to discuss it with the only person of whom he could make a confidant. "Not to hide the truth, Mistress Hester, my thoughts happen just now to be busy with the gentleman. So speak freely; and I will make an answer."

"When we last spake together," said Hester, "now seven years ago, it was your pleasure to extort a promise of secrecy, as touching the former relation betwixt yourself and me. As the life and good fame of yonder man were in your hands, there seemed no choice to me, save to be silent, in accordance with your behest. Yet it was not without heavy misgivings that I thus bound myself; for, having cast off all duty towards other human beings, there remained a duty towards him; and something whispered me that I was betraying it, in pledging myself to keep your counsel. Since that day, no man is so near to him as you. You tread behind his every footstep. You are beside him, sleeping and waking. You search his thoughts. You burrow and rankle in his heart! Your clutch is on his life, and you cause him to die daily a living death; and still he knows you not. In permitting this, I have surely acted a false part by the only man to whom the power was left me to be true!"

"What choice had you?" asked Roger Chillingworth. "My finger, pointed at this man, would have hurled him from his pulpit into a dungeon, — thence, peradventure, to the gallows!"

"It had been better so!" said Hester Prynne.

"What evil have I done the man?" asked Roger Chillingworth again. "I tell thee, Hester Prynne, the richest fee that ever physician earned from monarch could not have bought such care as I have wasted on this miserable priest! But for my aid, his life would have burned away in torments, within the first two years after the perpetration of his crime and thine. For, Hester, his spirit lacked the strength that could have borne up, as thine has, beneath a burden like thy scarlet letter. O, I could reveal a goodly secret! But enough! What art can do, I have exhausted on him. That he now breathes, and creeps about on earth, is owing all to me!"

"Better he had died at once!" said Hester Prynne.

"Yea, woman, thou sayest truly!" cried old Roger Chillingworth, letting the lurid fire of his heart blaze out before her eyes. "Better had he died at once! Never did mortal suffer what this man has suffered. And all, all, in the sight of his worst enemy! He has been conscious of me. He has felt an influence dwelling always upon him like a curse. He knew, by some spiritual sense, — for the Creator never made another being so sensitive as this, — he knew that no friendly hand was pulling at his heart-strings, and that an eye was looking curiously into him, which sought only evil, and found it. But he knew not that the eye and hand were mine! With the superstition common to his brotherhood, he fancied himself given over to a fiend, to be tortured with frightful dreams, and desperate thoughts, the sting of remorse, and despair of pardon; as a foretaste of what awaits him beyond the grave. But it was the constant shadow of my presence! — the closest propinquity of the man whom he had most vilely wronged! — and who had grown to exist only by this perpetual poison of the direst revenge! Yea, indeed! — he did not err! — there was a fiend at his elbow! A mortal man, with once a human heart, has become a fiend for his especial torment!"

The unfortunate physician, while uttering these words, lifted his hands with a look of horror, as if he had beheld some frightful shape, which he could not recognize, usurping the place of his own image in a glass. It was one of those moments — which sometimes occur only at the interval of years — when a man's moral aspect is faithfully revealed to his mind's eye. Not improbably, he had never before viewed himself as he did now.

"Hast thou not tortured him enough?" said Hester, noticing the old man's look. "Has he not paid thee all?"

"No! — no! — He has but increased the debt!" answered the physician; and, as he proceeded, his manner lost its fiercer characteristics, and subsided into the gloom. "Dost thou remember me, Hester, as I was nine years agone? Even then, I was in the autumn of my days, nor was it the early autumn. But all my life had been made up of earnest, studious, thoughtful, quiet years, bestowed faithfully for the increase of mine own knowledge, and faithfully, too, though this latter object was but casual to the other, — faithfully for the advancement of human welfare. No life had been more peaceful and innocent than mine; few lives so rich with benefits conferred. Dost thou remember me? Was I not, though you might deem me cold, nevertheless a man thoughtful for others, craving little for himself, — kind, true, just, and of constant, if not warm affections? Was I not all this?"

"All this, and more," said Hester.

"And what am I now?" demanded he, looking into her face, and permitting the whole evil within him to be written on his features. "I have already told thee what I am! A fiend! Who made me so?"

"It was myself!" cried Hester, shuddering. "It was I, not less than he. Why hast thou not avenged thyself on me?"

"I have left thee to the scarlet letter," replied Roger Chillingworth. "If that have not avenged me, I can do no more!"

He laid his finger on it, with a smile.

"It has avenged thee!" answered Hester Prynne.

"I judged no less," said the physician. "And now, what wouldst thou with me touching this man?"

"I must reveal the secret," answered Hester, firmly. "He must discern thee in thy true character. What may be the result, I know not. But this long debt of confidence, due from me to him, whose bane and ruin I have been, shall at length be paid. So far as concerns the overthrow or preservation of his fair fame and his earthly state, and perchance his life, he is in thy hands. Nor do I, — whom the scarlet letter has disciplined to truth, though it be the truth of red-hot iron, entering into the soul, — nor do I perceive such advantage in his living any longer a life of ghastly emptiness, that I shall stoop to implore thy mercy. Do with him as thou wilt! There is no good for him, — no good for me, — no good for thee! There is no good for little Pearl! There is no path to guide us out of this dismal maze!"

"Woman, I could wellnigh pity thee!" said Roger Chillingworth, unable to restrain a thrill of admiration too; for there was a quality almost majestic in the despair which she expressed. "Thou hadst great elements. Peradventure, hadst thou met earlier with a better love than mine, this evil had not been. I pity thee, for the good that has been wasted in thy nature!"

"And I thee," answered Hester Prynne, "for the hatred that has transformed a wise and just man to a fiend! Wilt thou yet purge it out of thee, and be once more human? If not for his sake, then doubly for thine own! Forgive, and leave his further retribution to the Power that claims it! I said, but now, that there could be no good event for him, or thee, or me, who are here wandering together in this gloomy maze of evil, and stumbling, at every step, over the guilt wherewith we have strewn our path. It is not so! There might be good for thee, and thee alone, since thou hast been deeply wronged, and hast it at thy will to pardon. Wilt thou give up that only privilege? Wilt thou reject that priceless benefit?"

"Peace, Hester, peace!" replied the old man, with gloomy sternness. "It is not granted me to pardon. I have no such power as thou tellest me of. My old faith, long forgotten, comes back to me, and explains all that we do, and all we suffer. By thy first step awry, thou didst plant the germ of evil; but, since that moment, it has all been a dark necessity. Ye that have wronged me are not sinful, save in a kind of typical illusion; neither am I fiend-like, who have snatched a fiend's office from his hands. It is our fate. Let the black flower blossom as it may! Now go thy ways, and deal as thou wilt with yonder man."

He waved his hand, and betook himself again to his employment of gathering herbs.

XV. Hester and Pearl

So Roger Chillingworth — a deformed old figure, with a face that haunted men's memories longer than they liked — took leave of Hester Prynne, and went stooping away along the earth. He gathered here and there an herb, or grubbed up a root, and put it into the basket on his arm. His gray beard almost touched the ground, as he crept onward. Hester gazed after him a little while, looking with a half-fantastic curiosity to see whether the tender grass of early spring would not be blighted beneath him, and show the wavering track of his footsteps, sere and brown, across its cheerful verdure. She wondered what sort of herbs they were, which the old man was so sedulous to gather. Would not the earth, quickened to an evil purpose by the sympathy of his eye, greet him with poisonous shrubs, of species hitherto unknown, that would start up under his fingers? Or might it suffice him, that every wholesome growth should be converted into something deleterious and malignant at his touch? Did the sun, which shone so brightly everywhere else, really fall upon him? Or was there, as it rather seemed, a circle of ominous shadow moving along with his deformity, whichever way he turned himself? And whither was he now going? Would he not suddenly sink into the earth, leaving a barren and blasted spot, where, in due course of time, would be seen deadly nightshade, dogwood, henbane, and whatever else of vegetable wickedness the climate could produce, all flourishing with hideous luxuriance? Or would he spread bat's wings and flee away, looking so much the uglier, the higher he rose towards heaven?

"Be it sin or no," said Hester Prynne bitterly, as she still gazed after him, "I hate the man!"

She upbraided herself for the sentiment, but could not overcome or lessen it. Attempting to do so, she thought of those long-past days, in a distant land, when he used to emerge at eventide from the seclusion of his study, and sit down in the fire-light of their home, and in the light of her nuptial smile. He needed to bask himself in that smile, he said, in order that the chill of so many lonely hours among his books might be taken off the scholar's heart. Such scenes had once appeared not otherwise than happy, but now, as viewed through the dismal medium of her subsequent life, they classed themselves among her ugliest remembrances. She marvelled how such scenes could have been! She marvelled how she could ever have been wrought upon to marry him! She deemed it her crime most to be repented of, that she had ever endured, and reciprocated, the lukewarm grasp of his hand, and had suffered the smile of her lips and eyes to mingle and melt into his own. And it seemed a fouler offence committed by Roger Chillingworth, than any which had since been done him, that, in the time when her heart knew no better, he had persuaded her to fancy herself happy by his side.

"Yes, I hate him!" repeated Hester, more bitterly than before. "He betrayed me! He has done me worse wrong than I did him!"

Let men tremble to win the hand of woman, unless they win along with it the utmost passion of her heart! Else it may be their miserable fortune, as it was Roger Chillingworth's, when some mightier touch than their own may have awakened all her sensibilities, to be reproached even for the calm content, the marble image of happiness, which they will have imposed upon her as the warm reality. But Hester ought long ago to have done with this injustice. What did it betoken? Had seven long years, under the torture of the scarlet letter, inflicted so much of misery, and wrought out no repentance?

The emotions of that brief space, while she stood gazing after the crooked figure of old Roger Chillingworth, threw a dark light on Hester's state of mind, revealing much that she might not otherwise have acknowledged to herself.

He being gone, she summoned back her child.

"Pearl! Little Pearl! Where are you?"

Pearl, whose activity of spirit never flagged, had been at no loss for amusement while her mother talked with the old gatherer of herbs. At first, as already told, she had flirted fancifully with her own image in a pool of water, beckoning the phantom forth, and — as it declined to venture — seeking a passage for herself into its sphere of impalpable earth and unattainable sky. Soon finding, however, that either she or the image was unreal, she turned elsewhere for better pastime. She made little boats out of birch-bark, and freighted them with snail-shells, and sent out more ventures on the mighty deep than any merchant in New England; but the larger part of them foundered near the shore. She seized a live horse-shoe by the tail, and made prize of several five-fingers, and laid out a jelly-fish to melt in the warm sun. Then she took up the white foam, that streaked the line of the advancing tide, and threw it upon the breeze, scampering after it with winged footsteps, to catch the great snow-flakes ere they fell. Perceiving a flock of beach-birds, that fed and fluttered along the shore, the naughty child picked up her apron full of pebbles, and, creeping from rock to rock after these small sea-fowl, displayed remarkable dexterity in pelting them. One little gray bird, with a white breast, Pearl was almost sure, had been hit by a pebble, and fluttered away with a broken wing. But then the elf-child sighed, and gave up her sport; because it grieved her to have done harm to a little being that was as wild as the sea-breeze, or as wild as Pearl herself.

Her final employment was to gather sea-weed, of various kinds, and make herself a scarf, or mantle, and a head-dress, and thus assume the aspect of a little mermaid. She inherited her mother's gift for devising drapery and costume. As the last touch to her mermaid's garb, Pearl took some eel-grass, and imitated, as best she could, on her own bosom, the decoration with which she was so familiar on her mother's. A letter, — the letter A, — but freshly green, instead of scarlet! The child bent her chin upon her breast, and contemplated this device with strange interest; even as if the only thing for which she had been sent into the world was to make out its hidden import.

"I wonder if mother will ask me what it means!" thought Pearl.

Just then, she heard her mother's voice, and, flitting along as lightly as one of the little sea-birds, appeared before Hester Prynne, dancing, laughing, and pointing her finger to the ornament upon her bosom.

"My little Pearl," said Hester, after a moment's silence, "the green letter, and on thy childish bosom, has no purport. But dost thou know, my child, what this letter means which thy mother is doomed to wear?"

"Yes, mother," said the child. "It is the great letter A. Thou hast taught it me in the horn-book."

Hester looked steadily into her little face; but, though there was that singular expression which she had so often remarked in her black eyes, she could not satisfy herself whether Pearl really attached any meaning to the symbol. She felt a morbid desire to ascertain the point.

"Dost thou know, child, wherefore thy mother wears this letter?"

"Truly do I!" answered Pearl, looking brightly into her mother's face. "It is for the same reason that the minister keeps his hand over his heart!"

"And what reason is that?" asked Hester, half smiling at the absurd incongruity of the child's observation; but, on second thoughts, turning pale. "What has the letter to do with any heart, save mine?"

"Nay, mother, I have told all I know," said Pearl, more seriously than she was wont to speak. "Ask yonder old man whom thou hast been talking with! It may be he can tell. But in good earnest now, mother dear, what does this scarlet letter mean? — and why dost thou wear it on thy bosom? — and why does the minister keep his hand over his heart?"

She took her mother's hand in both her own, and gazed into her eyes with an earnestness that was seldom seen in her wild and capricious character. The thought occurred to Hester, that the child might really be seeking to approach her with childlike confidence, and doing what she could, and as intelligently as she knew how, to establish a meeting-point of sympathy. It showed Pearl in an unwonted aspect. Heretofore, the mother, while loving her child with the intensity of a sole affection, had schooled herself to hope for little other return than the waywardness of an April breeze; which spends its time in airy sport, and has its gusts of inexplicable passion, and is petulant in its best of moods, and chills oftener than caresses you, when you take it to your bosom; in requital of which misdemeanours, it will sometimes, of its own vague purpose, kiss your cheek with a kind of doubtful tenderness, and play gently with your hair, and then begone about its other idle business, leaving a dreamy pleasure at your heart. And this, moreover, was a mother's estimate of the child's disposition. Any other observer might have seen few but unamiable traits, and have given them a far darker coloring. But now the idea came strongly into Hester's mind, that Pearl, with her remarkable precocity and acuteness, might already have approached the age when she could be made a friend, and intrusted with as much of her mother's sorrows as could be imparted, without irreverence either to the parent or the child. In the little chaos of Pearl's character, there might be seen emerging — and could have been, from the very first — the stedfast principles of an unflinching courage, — an uncontrollable will, — a sturdy pride, which might be disciplined into self-respect, — and a bitter scorn of many things, which, when examined, might be found to have the taint of falsehood in them. She possessed affections, too, though hitherto acrid and disagreeable, as are the richest flavors of unripe fruit. With all these sterling attributes, thought Hester, the evil which she inherited from her mother must be great indeed, if a noble woman do not grow out of this elfish child.

Pearl's inevitable tendency to hover about the enigma of the scarlet letter seemed an innate quality of her being. From the earliest epoch of her conscious life, she had entered upon this as her appointed mission. Hester had often fancied that Providence had a design of justice and retribution, in endowing the child with this marked propensity; but never, until now, had she bethought herself to ask, whether, linked with that design, there might not likewise be a purpose of mercy and beneficence. If little Pearl were entertained with faith and trust, as a spirit-messenger no less than an early child, might it not be her errand to soothe away the sorrow that lay cold in her mother's heart, and converted it into a tomb? — and to help her to overcome the passion, once so wild, and even yet neither dead nor asleep, but only imprisoned within the same tomb-like heart?

Such were some of the thoughts that now stirred in Hester's mind, with as much vivacity of impression as if they had actually been whispered into her ear. And there was little Pearl, all this while, holding her mother's hand in both her own, and turning her face upward, while she put these searching questions, once, and again, and still a third time.

"What does the letter mean, mother? — and why dost thou wear it? — and why does the minister keep his hand over his heart?"

"What shall I say?" thought Hester to herself. — "No! If this be the price of the child's sympathy, I cannot pay it!"

Then she spoke aloud.

"Silly Pearl," said she, "what questions are these? There are many things in this world that a child must not ask about. What know I of the minister's heart? And as for the scarlet letter, I wear it for the sake of its gold thread!"

In all the seven bygone years, Hester Prynne had never before been false to the symbol on her bosom. It may be that it was the talisman of a stern and severe, but yet a guardian spirit, who now forsook her; as recognizing that, in spite of his strict watch over her heart, some new evil had crept into it, or some old one had never been expelled. As for little Pearl, the earnestness soon passed out of her face.

But the child did not see fit to let the matter drop. Two or three times, as her mother and she went homeward, and as often at supper-time, and while Hester was putting her to bed, and once after she seemed to be fairly asleep, Pearl looked up, with mischief gleaming in her black eyes.

"Mother," said she, "what does the scarlet letter mean?"

And the next morning, the first indication the child gave of being awake was by popping up her head from the pillow, and making that other inquiry, which she had so unaccountably connected with her investigations about the scarlet letter: —

"Mother! — Mother! — Why does the minister keep his hand over his heart?"

"Hold thy tongue, naughty child!" answered her mother, with an asperity that she had never permitted to herself before. "Do not tease me; else I shall shut thee into the dark closet!"

XVI. A Forest Walk

Hester Prynne remained constant in her resolve to make known to Mr. Dimmesdale, at whatever risk of present pain or ulterior consequences, the true character of the man who had crept into his intimacy. For several days, however, she vainly sought an opportunity of addressing him in some of the meditative walks which she knew him to be in the habit of taking, along the shores of the peninsula, or on the wooded hills of the neighbouring country. There would have been no scandal, indeed, nor peril to the holy whiteness of the clergyman's good fame, had she visited him in his own study; where many a penitent, ere now, had confessed sins of perhaps as deep a dye as the one betokened by the scarlet letter. But, partly that she dreaded the secret or undisguised interference of old Roger Chillingworth, and partly that her conscious heart imputed suspicion where none could have been felt, and partly that both the minister and she would need the whole wide world to breathe in, while they talked together, — for all these reasons, Hester never thought of meeting him in any narrower privacy than beneath the open sky.

At last, while attending in a sick-chamber, whither the Reverend Mr. Dimmesdale had been summoned to make a prayer, she learnt that he had gone, the day before, to visit the Apostle Eliot, among his Indian converts. He would probably return, by a certain hour, in the afternoon of the morrow. Betimes, therefore, the next day, Hester took little Pearl, — who was necessarily the companion of all her mother's expeditions, however inconvenient her presence, — and set forth.

The road, after the two wayfarers had crossed from the peninsula to the mainland, was no other than a footpath. It straggled onward into the mystery of the primeval forest. This hemmed it in so narrowly, and stood so black and dense on either side, and disclosed such imperfect glimpses of the sky above, that, to Hester's mind, it imaged not amiss the moral wilderness in which she had so long been wandering. The day was chill and sombre. Overhead was a gray expanse of cloud, slightly stirred, however, by a breeze; so that a gleam of flickering sunshine might now and then be seen at its solitary play along the path. This flitting cheerfulness was always at the farther extremity of some long vista through the forest. The sportive sunlight — feebly sportive, at best, in the predominant pensiveness of the day and scene — withdrew itself as they came nigh, and left the spots where it had danced the drearier, because they had hoped to find them bright.

"Mother," said little Pearl, "the sunshine does not love you. It runs away and hides itself, because it is afraid of something on your bosom. Now, see! There it is, playing, a good way off. Stand you here, and let me run and catch it. I am but a child. It will not flee from me; for I wear nothing on my bosom yet!"

"Nor ever will, my child, I hope," said Hester.

"And why not, mother?" asked Pearl, stopping short, just at the beginning of her race. "Will not it come of its own accord, when I am a woman grown?"

"Run away, child," answered her mother, "and catch the sunshine! It will soon be gone."

Pearl set forth, at a great pace, and, as Hester smiled to perceive, did actually catch the sunshine, and stood laughing in the midst of it, all brightened by its splendor, and scintillating with the vivacity excited by rapid motion. The light lingered about the lonely child, as if glad of such a playmate, until her mother had drawn almost nigh enough to step into the magic circle too.

"It will go now!" said Pearl shaking her head.

"See!" answered Hester, smiling. "Now I can stretch out my hand, and grasp some of it."

As she attempted to do so, the sunshine vanished; or, to judge from the bright expression that was dancing on Pearl's features, her mother could have fancied that the child had absorbed it into herself, and would give it forth again, with a gleam about her path, as they should plunge into some gloomier shade. There was no other attribute that so much impressed her with a sense of new and untransmitted vigor in Pearl's nature, as this never-failing vivacity of spirits; she had not the disease of sadness, which almost all children, in these latter days, inherit, with the scrofula,[18] from the troubles of their ancestors. Perhaps this too was a disease, and but the reflex of the wild energy with which Hester had fought against her sorrows, before Pearl's birth. It was certainly a doubtful charm, imparting a hard, metallic lustre to the child's character. She wanted — what some people want throughout life — a grief that should deeply touch her, and thus humanize and make her capable of sympathy. But there was time enough yet for little Pearl!

"Come, my child!" said Hester, looking about her, from the spot where Pearl had stood still in the sunshine. "We will sit down a little way within the wood, and rest ourselves."

"I am not aweary, mother," replied the little girl. "But you may sit down, if you will tell me a story meanwhile."

"A story, child!" said Hester. "And about what?"

"O, a story about the Black Man!" answered Pearl, taking hold of her mother's gown, and looking up, half earnestly, half mischievously, into her face. "How he haunts this forest, and carries a book with him, — a big, heavy book, with iron clasps; and how this ugly Black Man offers his book and an iron pen to every body that meets him here among the trees; and they are to write their names with their own blood. And then he sets his mark on their bosoms! Didst thou ever meet the Black Man, mother?"

"And who told you this story, Pearl?" asked her mother, recognizing a common superstition of the period.

"It was the old dame in the chimney-corner, at the house where you watched last night," said the child. "But she fancied me asleep while she was talking of it. She said that a thousand and a thousand people had met him here, and had written in his book, and have his mark on them. And that ugly-tempered lady, old Mistress Hibbins, was one. And, mother, the old dame said that this scarlet letter was the Black Man's mark on thee, and that it glows like a red flame when thou meetest him at midnight, here in the dark wood. Is it true, mother? And dost thou go to meet him in the night-time?"

"Didst thou ever awake, and find thy mother gone?" asked Hester.

"Not that I remember," said the child. "If thou fearest to leave me in our cottage, thou mightest take me along with thee. I would very gladly go! But, mother, tell me now! Is there such a Black Man? And didst thou ever meet him? And is this his mark?"

[18] A tubercular swelling of lymph nodes (commonly in the neck), this condition was in fact not hereditary.

"Wilt thou let me be at peace, if I once tell thee?" asked her mother.

"Yes, if thou tellest me all," answered Pearl.

"Once in my life I met the Black Man!" said her mother. "This scarlet letter is his mark!"

Thus conversing, they entered sufficiently deep into the wood to secure themselves from the observation of any casual passenger along the forest-track. Here they sat down on a luxuriant heap of moss; which, at some epoch of the preceding century, had been a gigantic pine, with its roots and trunk in the darksome shade, and its head aloft in the upper atmosphere. It was a little dell where they had seated themselves, with a leaf-strewn bank rising gently on either side, and a brook flowing through the midst, over a bed of fallen and drowned leaves. The trees impending over it had flung down great branches, from time to time, which choked up the current, and compelled it to form eddies and black depths at some points; while, in its swifter and livelier passages, there appeared a channel-way of pebbles, and brown, sparkling sand. Letting the eyes follow along the course of the stream, they could catch the reflected light from its water, at some short distance within the forest, but soon lost all traces of it amid the bewilderment of tree-trunks and underbrush, and here and there a huge rock, covered over with gray lichens. All these giant trees and boulders of granite seemed intent on making a mystery of the course of this small brook; fearing, perhaps, that, with its never-ceasing loquacity, it should whisper tales out of the heart of the old forest whence it flowed, or mirror its revelations on the smooth surface of a pool. Continually, indeed, as it stole onward, the streamlet kept up a babble, kind, quiet, soothing, but melancholy, like the voice of a young child that was spending its infancy without playfulness, and knew not how to be merry among sad acquaintance and events of sombre hue.

"O brook! O foolish and tiresome little brook!" cried Pearl, after listening awhile to its talk. "Why art thou so sad? Pluck up a spirit, and do not be all the time sighing and murmuring!"

But the brook, in the course of its little lifetime among the forest-trees, had gone through so solemn an experience that it could not help talking about it, and seemed to have nothing else to say. Pearl resembled the brook, inasmuch as the current of her life gushed from a well-spring as mysterious, and had flowed through scenes shadowed as heavily with gloom. But, unlike the little stream, she danced and sparkled, and prattled airily along her course.

"What does this sad little brook say, mother?" inquired she.

"If thou hadst a sorrow of thine own, the brook might tell thee of it," answered her mother, "even as it is telling me of mine! But now, Pearl, I hear a footstep along the path, and the noise of one putting aside the branches. I would have thee betake thyself to play, and leave me to speak with him that comes yonder."

"Is it the Black Man?" asked Pearl.

"Wilt thou go and play, child?" repeated her mother. "But do not stray far into the wood. And take heed that thou come at my first call."

"Yes, mother," answered Pearl. "But, if it be the Black Man, wilt thou not let me stay a moment, and look at him, with his big book under his arm?"

"Go, silly child!" said her mother, impatiently. "It is no Black Man! Thou canst see him now through the trees. It is the minister!"

"And so it is!" said the child. "And, mother, he has his hand over his heart! Is it because, when the minister wrote his name in the book, the Black Man set his mark in that place? But why does he not wear it outside his bosom, as thou dost, mother?"

"Go now, child, and thou shalt tease me as thou wilt another time!" cried Hester Prynne. "But do not stray far. Keep where thou canst hear the babble of the brook."

The child went singing away, following up the current of the brook, and striving to mingle a more lightsome cadence with its melancholy voice. But the little stream would not be comforted, and still kept telling its unintelligible secret of some very mournful mystery that had happened — or making a prophetic lamentation about something that was yet to happen — within the verge of the dismal forest. So Pearl, who had enough of shadow in her own little life, chose to break off all acquaintance with this repining brook. She set herself, therefore, to gathering violets and wood-anemones, and some scarlet columbines that she found growing in the crevices of a high rock.

When her elf-child had departed, Hester Prynne made a step or two towards the track that led through the forest, but still remained under the deep shadow of the trees. She beheld the minister advancing along the path, entirely alone, and leaning on a staff which he had cut by the way-side. He looked haggard and feeble, and betrayed a nerveless despondency in his air, which had never so remarkably characterized him in his walks about the settlement, nor in any other situation where he deemed himself liable to notice. Here it was wofully visible, in this intense seclusion of the forest, which of itself would have been a heavy trial to the spirits. There was a listlessness in his gait; as if he saw no reason for taking one step farther, nor felt any desire to do so, but would have been glad, could he be glad of any thing, to fling himself down at the root of the nearest tree, and lie there passive for evermore. The leaves might bestrew him, and the soil gradually accumulate and form a little hillock over his frame, no matter whether there were life in it or no. Death was too definite an object to be wished for, or avoided.

To Hester's eye, the Reverend Mr. Dimmesdale exhibited no symptom of positive and vivacious suffering, except that, as little Pearl had remarked, he kept his hand over his heart.

XVII. The Pastor and His Parishioner

Slowly as the minister walked, he had almost gone by, before Hester Prynne could gather voice enough to attract his observation. At length, she succeeded.

"Arthur Dimmesdale!" she said, faintly at first; then louder, but hoarsely. "Arthur Dimmesdale!"

"Who speaks?" answered the minister.

Gathering himself quickly up, he stood more erect, like a man taken by surprise in a mood to which he was reluctant to have witnesses. Throwing his eyes anxiously in the direction of the voice, he indistinctly beheld a form under the trees, clad in garments so sombre, and so little relieved from the gray twilight into which the clouded sky and the heavy foliage had darkened the noontide, that he knew not whether it were a woman or a shadow. It may be, that his pathway through life was haunted thus, by a spectre that had stolen out from among his thoughts.

He made a step nigher, and discovered the scarlet letter.

"Hester! Hester Prynne!" said he. "Is it thou? Art thou in life?"

"Even so!" she answered. "In such life as has been mine these seven years past! And thou, Arthur Dimmesdale, dost thou yet live?"

It was no wonder that they thus questioned one another's actual and bodily existence, and even doubted of their own. So strangely did they meet, in the dim wood, that it was like the first encounter, in the world beyond the grave, of two spirits who had been intimately connected in their former life, but now stood coldly shuddering, in mutual dread; as not yet familiar with their state, nor wonted to the companionship of disembodied beings. Each a ghost, and awe-stricken at the other ghost! They were awe-stricken likewise at themselves; because the crisis flung back to them their consciousness, and revealed to each heart its history and experience, as life never does, except at such breathless epochs. The soul beheld its features in the mirror of the passing moment. It was with fear, and tremulously, and, as it were, by a slow, reluctant necessity, that Arthur Dimmesdale put forth his hand, chill as death, and touched the chill hand of Hester Prynne. The grasp, cold as it was, took away what was dreariest in the interview. They now felt themselves, at least, inhabitants of the same sphere.

Without a word more spoken, — neither he nor she assuming the guidance, but with an unexpressed consent, — they glided back into the shadow of the woods, whence Hester had emerged, and sat down on the heap of moss where she and Pearl had before been sitting. When they found voice to speak, it was, at first, only to utter remarks and inquiries such as any two acquaintances might have made, about the gloomy sky, the threatening storm, and, next, the health of each. Thus they went onward, not boldly, but step by step, into the themes that were brooding deepest in their hearts. So long estranged by fate and circumstances, they needed something slight and casual to run before, and throw open the doors of intercourse, so that their real thoughts might be led across the threshold.

After a while, the minister fixed his eyes on Hester Prynne's.

"Hester," said he, "hast thou found peace?"

She smiled drearily, looking down upon her bosom.

"Hast thou?" she asked.

"None! — nothing but despair!" he answered. "What else could I look for, being what I am, and leading such a life as mine? Were I an atheist, — a man devoid of conscience, — a wretch with coarse and brutal instincts, — I might have found peace, long ere now. Nay, I never should have lost it! But, as matters stand with my soul, whatever of good capacity there originally was in me, all of God's gifts that were the choicest have become the ministers of spiritual torment. Hester, I am most miserable!"

"The people reverence thee," said Hester. "And surely thou workest good among them! Doth this bring thee no comfort?"

"More misery, Hester! — only the more misery!" answered the clergyman, with a bitter smile. "As concerns the good which I may appear to do, I have no faith in it. It must needs be a delusion. What can a ruined soul, like mine, effect towards the redemption of other souls? — or a polluted soul, towards their purification? And as for the people's reverence, would that it were turned to scorn and hatred! Canst thou deem it, Hester, a consolation, that I must stand up in my pulpit, and meet so many eyes turned upward to my face, as if the light of heaven were beaming from it! — must see my flock hungry for the truth, and listening to my words as if a tongue of Pentecost were speaking! — and then look inward, and discern the black reality of what they idolize? I have laughed, in bitterness and agony of heart, at the contrast between what I seem and what I am! And Satan laughs at it!"

"You wrong yourself in this," said Hester, gently. "You have deeply and sorely repented. Your sin is left behind you, in the days long past. Your present life is not less holy, in very truth, than it seems in people's eyes. Is there no reality in the penitence thus sealed and witnessed by good works? And wherefore should it not bring you peace?"

"No, Hester, no!" replied the clergyman. "There is no substance in it! It is cold and dead, and can do nothing for me! Of penance I have had enough! Of penitence there has been none! Else, I should long ago have thrown off these garments of mock holiness, and have shown myself to mankind as they will see me at the judgment-seat. Happy are you, Hester, that wear the scarlet letter openly upon your bosom! Mine burns in secret! Thou little knowest what a relief it is, after the torment of a seven years' cheat, to look into an eye that recognizes me for what I am! Had I one friend, — or were it my worst enemy! — to whom, when sickened with the praises of all other men, I could daily betake myself, and be known as the vilest of all sinners, methinks my soul might keep itself alive thereby. Even thus much of truth would save me! But, now, it is all falsehood! — all emptiness! — all death!"

Hester Prynne looked into his face, but hesitated to speak. Yet, uttering his long-restrained emotions so vehemently as he did, his words here offered her the very point of circumstances in which to interpose what she came to say. She conquered her fears, and spoke.

"Such a friend as thou hast even now wished for," said she, "with whom to weep over thy sin, thou hast in me, the partner of it!" — Again she hesitated, but brought out the words with an effort. — "Thou hast long had such an enemy, and dwellest with him under the same roof!"

The minister started to his feet, gasping for breath, and clutching at his heart as if he would have torn it out of his bosom.

"Ha! What sayest thou?" cried he. "An enemy! And under mine own roof! What mean you?"

Hester Prynne was now fully sensible of the deep injury for which she was responsible to this unhappy man, in permitting him to lie for so many years, or, indeed, for a single moment, at the mercy of one, whose purposes could not be other than malevolent. The very contiguity of his enemy, beneath whatever mask the latter might conceal himself, was enough to disturb the magnetic sphere of a being so sensitive as Arthur Dimmesdale. There had been a period when Hester was less alive to this consideration; or, perhaps, in the misanthropy of her own trouble, she left the minister to bear what she might picture to herself as a more tolerable doom. But of late, since the night of his vigil, all her sympathies towards him had been both softened and invigorated. She now read his heart more accurately. She doubted not, that the continual presence of Roger Chillingworth, — the secret poison of his malignity, infecting all the air about him, — and his authorized interference, as a physician, with the minister's physical and spiritual infirmities, — that these bad opportunities had been turned to a cruel purpose. By means of them, the sufferer's conscience had been kept in an irritated state, the tendency of which was, not to cure by wholesome pain, but to disorganize and corrupt his spiritual being. Its result, on earth, could hardly fail to be insanity, and hereafter, that eternal alienation from the Good and True, of which madness is perhaps the earthly type.

Such was the ruin to which she had brought the man, once, — nay, why should we not speak it? — still so passionately loved! Hester felt that the sacrifice of the clergyman's good name, and death itself, as she had already told Roger Chillingworth, would have been infinitely preferable to the alternative which she had taken upon herself to choose. And now, rather than have had this grievous wrong to confess, she would gladly have lain down on the forest-leaves, and died there, at Arthur Dimmesdale's feet.

"O Arthur," cried she, "forgive me! In all things else, I have striven to be true! Truth was the one virtue which I might have held fast, and did hold fast through all extremity; save when thy good, — thy life, — thy fame, — were put in question! Then I consented to a deception. But a lie is never good, even though death threaten on the other side! Dost thou not see what I would say? That old man! — the physician! — he whom they call Roger Chillingworth! — he was my husband!"

The minister looked at her, for an instant, with all that violence of passion, which — intermixed, in more shapes than one, with his higher, purer, softer qualities — was, in fact, the portion of him which the Devil claimed, and through which he sought to win the rest. Never was there a blacker or a fiercer frown, than Hester now encountered. For the brief space that it lasted, it was a dark transfiguration. But his character had been so much enfeebled by suffering, that even its lower energies were incapable of more than a temporary struggle. He sank down on the ground, and buried his face in his hands.

"I might have known it!" murmured he. "I did know it! Was not the secret told me in the natural recoil of my heart, at the first sight of him, and as often as I have seen him since? Why did I not understand?

O Hester Prynne, thou little, little knowest all the horror of this thing! And the shame! — the indelicacy! — the horrible ugliness of this exposure of a sick and guilty heart to the very eye that would gloat over it! Woman, woman, thou art accountable for this! I cannot forgive thee!"

"Thou shalt forgive me!" cried Hester, flinging herself on the fallen leaves beside him. "Let God punish! Thou shalt forgive!"

With sudden and desperate tenderness, she threw her arms around him, and pressed his head against her bosom; little caring though his cheek rested on the scarlet letter. He would have released himself, but strove in vain to do so. Hester would not set him free, lest he should look her sternly in the face. All the world had frowned on her, — for seven long years had it frowned upon this lonely woman, — and still she bore it all, nor ever once turned away her firm, sad eyes. Heaven, likewise, had frowned upon her, and she had not died. But the frown of this pale, weak, sinful, and sorrow-stricken man was what Hester could not bear, and live!

"Wilt thou yet forgive me?" she repeated, over and over again. "Wilt thou not frown? Wilt thou forgive?"

"I do forgive you, Hester," replied the minister, at length, with a deep utterance out of an abyss of sadness, but no anger. "I freely forgive you now. May God forgive us both! We are not, Hester, the worst sinners in the world. There is one worse than even the polluted priest! That old man's revenge has been blacker than my sin. He has violated, in cold blood, the sanctity of a human heart. Thou and I, Hester, never did so!"

"Never, never!" whispered she. "What we did had a consecration of its own. We felt it so! We said so to each other! Hast thou forgotten it?"

"Hush, Hester!" said Arthur Dimmesdale, rising from the ground. "No; I have not forgotten!"

They sat down again, side by side, and hand clasped in hand, on the mossy trunk of the fallen tree. Life had never brought them a gloomier hour; it was the point whither their pathway had so long been tending, and darkening ever, as it stole along; — and yet it inclosed a charm that made them linger upon it, and claim another, and another, and, after all, another moment. The forest was obscure around them, and creaked with a blast that was passing through it. The boughs were tossing heavily above their heads; while one solemn old tree groaned dolefully to another, as if telling the sad story of the pair that sat beneath, or constrained to forebode evil to come.

And yet they lingered. How dreary looked the forest-track that led backward to the settlement, where Hester Prynne must take up again the burden of her ignominy, and the minister the hollow mockery of his good name! So they lingered an instant longer. No golden light had ever been so precious as the gloom of this dark forest. Here, seen only by his eyes, the scarlet letter need not burn into the bosom of the fallen woman! Here, seen only by her eyes, Arthur Dimmesdale, false to God and man, might be, for one moment, true!

He started at a thought that suddenly occurred to him.

"Hester," cried he, "here is a new horror! Roger Chillingworth knows your purpose to reveal his true character. Will he continue, then, to keep our secret? What will now be the course of his revenge?"

"There is a strange secrecy in his nature," replied Hester, thoughtfully; "and it has grown upon him by the hidden practices of his revenge. I deem it not likely that he will betray the secret. He will doubtless seek other means of satiating his dark passion."

"And I! — how am I to live longer, breathing the same air with this deadly enemy?" exclaimed Arthur Dimmesdale, shrinking within himself, and pressing his hand nervously against his heart, — a gesture that had grown involuntary with him. "Think for me, Hester! Thou art strong. Resolve for me!"

"Thou must dwell no longer with this man," said Hester, slowly and firmly. "Thy heart must be no longer under his evil eye!"

"It were far worse than death!" replied the minister. "But how to avoid it? What choice remains to me? Shall I lie down again on these withered leaves, where I cast myself when thou didst tell me what he was? Must I sink down there, and die at once?"

"Alas, what a ruin has befallen thee!" said Hester, with the tears gushing into her eyes. "Wilt thou die for very weakness? There is no other cause!"

"The judgment of God is on me," answered the conscience-stricken priest. "It is too mighty for me to struggle with!"

"Heaven would show mercy," rejoined Hester, "hadst thou but the strength to take advantage of it."

"Be thou strong for me!" answered he. "Advise me what to do."

"Is the world then so narrow?" exclaimed Hester Prynne, fixing her deep eyes on the minister's, and instinctively exercising a magnetic power over a spirit so shattered and subdued, that it could hardly hold itself erect. "Doth the universe lie within the compass of yonder town, which only a little time ago was but a leaf-strewn desert, as lonely as this around us? Whither leads yonder forest-track? Backward to the settlement, thou sayest! Yes; but onward, too! Deeper it goes, and deeper, into the wilderness, less plainly to be seen at every step; until, some few miles hence, the yellow leaves will show no vestige of the white man's tread. There thou art free! So brief a journey would bring thee from a world where thou hast been most wretched, to one where thou mayest still be happy! Is there not shade enough in all this boundless forest to hide thy heart from the gaze of Roger Chillingworth?"

"Yes, Hester; but only under the fallen leaves!" replied the minister, with a sad smile.

"Then there is the broad pathway of the sea!" continued Hester. "It brought thee hither. If thou so choose, it will bear thee back again. In our native land, whether in some remote rural village or in vast London, — or, surely, in Germany, in France, in pleasant Italy, — thou wouldst be beyond his power and knowledge! And what hast thou to do with all these iron men, and their opinions? They have kept thy better part in bondage too long already!"

"It cannot be!" answered the minister, listening as if he were called upon to realize a dream. "I am powerless to go. Wretched and sinful as I am, I have had no other thought than to drag on my earthly existence in the sphere where Providence hath placed me. Lost as my own soul is, I would still do what I may for other human souls! I dare not quit my post, though an unfaithful sentinel, whose sure reward is death and dishonor, when his dreary watch shall come to an end!"

"Thou art crushed under this seven years' weight of misery," replied Hester, fervently resolved to buoy him up with her own energy. "But thou shalt leave it all behind thee! It shall not cumber thy steps, as thou treadest along the forest-path; neither shalt thou freight the ship with it, if thou prefer to cross the sea. Leave this wreck and ruin here where it hath happened! Meddle no more with it! Begin all anew! Hast thou exhausted possibility in the failure of this one trial? Not so! The future is yet full of trial and success. There is happiness to be enjoyed! There is good to be done! Exchange this false life of thine for a true one. Be, if thy spirit summon thee to such a mission, the teacher and apostle of the red men. Or, — as is more thy nature, — be a scholar and a sage among the wisest and the most renowned of the cultivated world. Preach! Write! Act! Do any thing, save to lie down and die! Give up this name of Arthur Dimmesdale, and make thyself another, and a high one, such as thou canst wear without fear or shame. Why shouldst thou tarry so much as one other day in the torments that have so gnawed into thy life! — that have made thee feeble to will and to do! — that will leave thee powerless even to repent! Up, and away!"

"O Hester!" cried Arthur Dimmesdale, in whose eyes a fitful light, kindled by her enthusiasm, flashed up and died away, "thou tellest of running a race to a man whose knees are tottering beneath him! I must die here. There is not the strength or courage left me to venture into the wide, strange, difficult world, alone!"

It was the last expression of the despondency of a broken spirit. He lacked energy to grasp the better fortune that seemed within his reach.

He repeated the word.

"Alone, Hester!"

"Thou shalt not go alone!" answered she, in a deep whisper.

Then, all was spoken!

XVIII. A Flood of Sunshine

Arthur Dimmesdale gazed into Hester's face with a look in which hope and joy shone out, indeed, but with fear betwixt them, and a kind of horror at her boldness, who had spoken what he vaguely hinted at, but dared not speak.

But Hester Prynne, with a mind of native courage and activity, and for so long a period not merely estranged, but outlawed, from society, had habituated herself to such latitude of speculation as was altogether foreign to the clergyman. She had wandered, without rule or guidance, in a moral wilderness; as vast, as intricate and shadowy, as the untamed forest, amid the gloom of which they were now holding a colloquy that was to decide their fate. Her intellect and heart had their home, as it were, in desert places, where she roamed as freely as the wild Indian in his woods. For years past she had looked from this estranged point of view at human institutions, and whatever priests or legislators had established; criticizing all with hardly more reverence than the Indian would feel for the clerical band, the judicial robe, the pillory, the gallows, the fireside, or the church. The tendency of her fate and fortunes had been to set her free. The scarlet letter was her passport into regions where other women dared not tread. Shame, Despair, Solitude! These had been her teachers, — stern and wild ones, — and they had made her strong, but taught her much amiss.

The minister, on the other hand, had never gone through an experience calculated to lead him beyond the scope of generally received laws; although, in a single instance, he had so fearfully transgressed one of the most sacred of them. But this had been a sin of passion, not of principle, nor even purpose. Since that wretched epoch, he had watched, with morbid zeal and minuteness, not his acts, — for those it was easy to arrange, — but each breath of emotion, and his every thought. At the head of the social system, as the clergymen of that day stood, he was only the more trammelled by its regulations, its principles, and even its prejudices. As a priest, the framework of his order inevitably hemmed him in. As a man who had once sinned, but who kept his conscience all alive and painfully sensitive by the fretting of an unhealed wound, he might have been supposed safer within the line of virtue, than if he had never sinned at all.

Thus, we seem to see that, as regarded Hester Prynne, the whole seven years of outlaw and ignominy had been little other than a preparation for this very hour. But Arthur Dimmesdale! Were such a man once more to fall, what plea could be urged in extenuation of his crime? None; unless it avail him somewhat, that he was broken down by long and exquisite suffering; that his mind was darkened and confused by the very remorse which harrowed it; that, between fleeing as an avowed criminal, and remaining as a hypocrite, conscience might find it hard to strike the balance; that it was human to avoid the peril of death and infamy, and the inscrutable machinations of an enemy; that, finally, to this poor pilgrim, on his dreary and desert path, faint, sick, miserable, there appeared a glimpse of human affection and sympathy, a new life, and a true one, in exchange for the heavy doom which he was now expiating. And be the stern and sad truth spoken, that the breach which guilt has once made into the human soul is never, in this mortal state, repaired. It may be watched and guarded; so that the enemy shall not force his way again into the citadel, and might even, in his subsequent assaults, select some other avenue, in preference to that where he had formerly succeeded. But there is still the ruined wall, and, near it, the stealthy tread of the foe that would win over again his unforgotten triumph.

The struggle, if there were one, need not be described. Let it suffice, that the clergyman resolved to flee, and not alone.

"If, in all these past seven years," thought he, "I could recall one instant of peace or hope, I would yet endure, for the sake of that earnest of Heaven's mercy. But now, — since I am irrevocably doomed, — wherefore should I not snatch the solace allowed to the condemned culprit before his execution? Or, if this be the path to a better life, as Hester would persuade me, I surely give up no fairer prospect by pursuing it! Neither can I any longer live without her companionship; so powerful is she to sustain, — so tender to soothe! O Thou to whom I dare not lift mine eyes, wilt Thou yet pardon me!"

"Thou wilt go!" said Hester calmly, as he met her glance.

The decision once made, a glow of strange enjoyment threw its flickering brightness over the trouble of his breast. It was the exhilarating effect — upon a prisoner just escaped from the dungeon of his own heart — of breathing the wild, free atmosphere of an unredeemed, unchristianized, lawless region. His spirit rose, as it were, with a bound, and attained a nearer prospect of the sky, than throughout all the misery which had kept him grovelling on the earth. Of a deeply religious temperament, there was inevitably a tinge of the devotional in his mood.

"Do I feel joy again?" cried he, wondering at himself. "Methought the germ of it was dead in me! O Hester, thou art my better angel! I seem to have flung myself — sick, sin-stained, and sorrow-blackened — down upon these forest-leaves, and to have risen up all made anew, and with new powers to glorify Him that hath been merciful! This is already the better life! Why did we not find it sooner?"

"Let us not look back," answered Hester Prynne. "The past is gone! Wherefore should we linger upon it now? See! With this symbol, I undo it all, and make it as it had never been!"

So speaking, she undid the clasp that fastened the scarlet letter, and, taking it from her bosom, threw it to a distance among the withered leaves. The mystic token alighted on the hither verge of the stream. With a hand's breadth farther flight it would have fallen into the water, and have given the little brook another woe to carry onward, besides the unintelligible tale which it still kept murmuring about. But there lay the embroidered letter, glittering like a lost jewel, which some ill-fated wanderer might pick up, and thenceforth be haunted by strange phantoms of guilt, sinkings of the heart, and unaccountable misfortune.

The stigma gone, Hester heaved a long, deep sigh, in which the burden of shame and anguish departed from her spirit. O exquisite relief! She had not known the weight, until she felt the freedom! By another impulse, she took off the formal cap that confined her hair; and down it fell upon her shoulders, dark and rich, with at once a shadow and a light in its abundance, and imparting the charm of softness to her features. There played around her mouth, and beamed out of her eyes, a radiant and tender smile, that seemed gushing from the very heart of womanhood. A crimson flush was glowing on her cheek, that had been long so pale. Her sex, her youth, and the whole richness of her beauty, came back from what men call the irrevocable past, and clustered themselves, with her maiden hope, and a happiness before unknown, within the magic circle of this hour. And, as if the gloom of the earth and sky had been but the effluence of these two mortal hearts, it vanished with their sorrow. All at once, as with a sudden smile of heaven, forth burst the sunshine, pouring a very flood into the obscure forest, gladdening each green leaf, transmuting the yellow fallen ones to gold, and gleaming adown the gray trunks of the solemn trees. The objects that had made a shadow hitherto, embodied the brightness now. The course of the little brook might be traced by its merry gleam afar into the wood's heart of mystery, which had become a mystery of joy.

Such was the sympathy of Nature — that wild, heathen Nature of the forest, never subjugated by human law, nor illumined by higher truth — with the bliss of these two spirits! Love, whether newly born, or aroused from a deathlike slumber, must always create a sunshine, filling the heart so full of radiance, that it overflows upon the outward world. Had the forest still kept its gloom, it would have been bright in Hester's eyes, and bright in Arthur Dimmesdale's!

Hester looked at him with the thrill of another joy.

"Thou must know Pearl!" said she. "Our little Pearl! Thou hast seen her, — yes, I know it! — but thou wilt see her now with other eyes. She is a strange child! I hardly comprehend her! But thou wilt love her dearly, as I do, and wilt advise me how to deal with her."

"Dost thou think the child will be glad to know me?" asked the minister, somewhat uneasily. "I have long shrunk from children, because they often show a distrust, — a backwardness to be familiar with me. I have even been afraid of little Pearl!"

"Ah, that was sad!" answered the mother. "But she will love thee dearly, and thou her. She is not far off. I will call her! Pearl! Pearl!"

"I see the child," observed the minister. "Yonder she is, standing in a streak of sunshine, a good way off, on the other side of the brook. So thou thinkest the child will love me?"

Hester smiled, and again called to Pearl, who was visible, at some distance, as the minister had described her, like a bright-apparelled vision, in a sunbeam, which fell down upon her through an arch of boughs. The ray quivered to and fro, making her figure dim or distinct, — now like a real child, now like a child's spirit, — as the splendor went and came again. She heard her mother's voice, and approached slowly through the forest.

Pearl had not found the hour pass wearisomely, while her mother sat talking with the clergyman. The great black forest — stern as it showed itself to those who brought the guilt and troubles of the world into its bosom — became the playmate of the lonely infant, as well as it knew how. Sombre as it was, it put on the kindest of its moods to welcome her. It offered her the partridge-berries, the growth of the preceding autumn, but ripening only in the spring, and now red as drops of blood upon the withered leaves. These Pearl gathered, and was pleased with their wild flavor. The small denizens of the wilderness hardly took pains to move out of her path. A partridge, indeed, with a brood of ten behind her, ran forward threateningly, but soon repented of her fierceness, and clucked to her young ones not to be afraid. A pigeon, alone on a low branch, allowed Pearl to come beneath, and uttered a sound as much of greeting as alarm. A squirrel, from the lofty depths of his domestic tree, chattered either in anger or merriment, — for a squirrel is such a choleric and humorous little personage that it is hard to distinguish between his moods, — so he chattered at the child, and flung down a nut upon her head. It was a last year's nut, and already gnawed by his sharp tooth. A fox, startled from his sleep by her light footstep on the leaves, looked inquisitively at Pearl, as doubting whether it were better to steal off, or renew his nap on the same spot. A wolf, it is said, — but here the tale has surely lapsed into the improbable, — came up, and smelt of Pearl's robe, and offered his savage head to be patted by her hand. The truth seems to be, however, that the mother-forest, and these wild things which it nourished, all recognized a kindred wildness in the human child.

And she was gentler here than in the grassy-margined streets of the settlement, or in her mother's cottage. The flowers appeared to know it; and one and another whispered, as she passed, "Adorn thyself with me, thou beautiful child, adorn thyself with me!" — and, to please them, Pearl gathered the violets, and anemones, and columbines, and some twigs of the freshest green, which the old trees held down before her eyes. With these she decorated her hair, and her young waist, and became a nymph-child, or an infant dryad, or whatever else was in closest sympathy with the antique wood. In such guise had Pearl adorned herself, when she heard her mother's voice, and came slowly back.

Slowly; for she saw the clergyman!

XIX. The Child at the Brook-Side

"Thou wilt love her dearly," repeated Hester Prynne, as she and the minister sat watching little Pearl. "Dost thou not think her beautiful? And see with what natural skill she has made those simple flowers adorn her! Had she gathered pearls, and diamonds, and rubies, in the wood, they could not have become her better. She is a splendid child! But I know whose brow she has!"

"Dost thou know, Hester," said Arthur Dimmesdale, with an unquiet smile, "that this dear child, tripping about always at thy side, hath caused me many an alarm? Methought — O Hester, what a thought is that, and how terrible to dread it! — that my own features were partly repeated in her face, and so strikingly that the world might see them! But she is mostly thine!"

"No, no! Not mostly!" answered the mother with a tender smile. "A little longer, and thou needest not to be afraid to trace whose child she is. But how strangely beautiful she looks, with those wild flowers in her hair! It is as if one of the fairies, whom we left in our dear old England, had decked her out to meet us."

It was with a feeling which neither of them had ever before experienced, that they sat and watched Pearl's slow advance. In her was visible the tie that united them. She had been offered to the world, these seven years past, as the living hieroglyphic, in which was revealed the secret they so darkly sought to hide, — all written in this symbol, — all plainly manifest, — had there been a prophet or magician skilled to read the character of flame! And Pearl was the oneness of their being. Be the foregone evil what it might, how could they doubt that their earthly lives and future destinies were conjoined, when they beheld at once the material union, and the spiritual idea, in whom they met, and were to dwell immortally together? Thoughts like these — and perhaps other thoughts, which they did not acknowledge or define — threw an awe about the child, as she came onward.

"Let her see nothing strange — no passion nor eagerness — in thy way of accosting her," whispered Hester. "Our Pearl is a fitful and fantastic little elf, sometimes. Especially, she is seldom tolerant of emotion, when she does not fully comprehend the why and wherefore. But the child hath strong affections! She loves me, and will love thee!"

"Thou canst not think," said the minister, glancing aside at Hester Prynne, "how my heart dreads this interview, and yearns for it! But, in truth, as I already told thee, children are not readily won to be familiar with me. They will not climb my knee, nor prattle in my ear, nor answer to my smile; but stand apart, and eye me strangely. Even little babes, when I take them in my arms, weep bitterly. Yet Pearl, twice in her little lifetime, hath been kind to me! The first time, — thou knowest it well! The last was when thou ledst her with thee to the house of yonder stern old Governor."

"And thou didst plead so bravely in her behalf and mine!" answered the mother. "I remember it; and so shall little Pearl. Fear nothing! She may be strange and shy at first, but will soon learn to love thee!"

By this time Pearl had reached the margin of the brook, and stood on the farther side, gazing silently at Hester and the clergyman, who still sat together on the mossy tree-trunk, waiting to receive her. Just where she had paused the brook chanced to form a pool, so smooth and quiet that it reflected a perfect image of her little figure, with all the brilliant picturesqueness of her beauty, in its adornment of flowers and wreathed foliage, but more refined and spiritualized than the reality. This image, so nearly identical with the living Pearl, seemed to communicate somewhat of its own shadowy and intangible quality to the child herself. It was strange, the way in which Pearl stood, looking so stedfastly at them through the dim medium of the forest-gloom; herself, meanwhile, all glorified with a ray of sunshine, that was attracted thitherward as by a certain sympathy. In the brook beneath stood another child, — another and the same, — with likewise its ray of golden light. Hester felt herself, in some indistinct and tantalizing manner, estranged from Pearl; as if the child, in her lonely ramble through the forest, had strayed out of the sphere in which she and her mother dwelt together, and was now vainly seeking to return to it.

There was both truth and error in the impression; the child and mother were estranged, but through Hester's fault, not Pearl's. Since the latter rambled from her side, another inmate had been admitted within the circle of the mother's feelings, and so modified the aspect of them all, that Pearl, the returning wanderer, could not find her wonted place, and hardly knew where she was.

"I have a strange fancy," observed the sensitive minister, "that this brook is the boundary between two worlds, and that thou canst never meet thy Pearl again. Or is she an elfish spirit, who, as the legends of our childhood taught us, is forbidden to cross a running stream? Pray hasten her; for this delay has already imparted a tremor to my nerves."

"Come, dearest child!" said Hester encouragingly, and stretching out both her arms. "How slow thou art! When hast thou been so sluggish before now? Here is a friend of mine, who must be thy friend also. Thou wilt have twice as much love, henceforward, as thy mother alone could give thee! Leap across the brook and come to us. Thou canst leap like a young deer!"

Pearl, without responding in any manner to these honey-sweet expressions, remained on the other side of the brook. Now she fixed her bright, wild eyes on her mother, now on the minister, and now included them both in the same glance; as if to detect and explain to herself the relation which they bore to one another. For some unaccountable reason, as Arthur Dimmesdale felt the child's eyes upon himself, his hand — with that gesture so habitual as to have become involuntary — stole over his heart. At length, assuming a singular air of authority, Pearl stretched out her hand, with the small forefinger extended, and pointing evidently towards her mother's breast. And beneath, in the mirror of the brook, there was the flower-girdled and sunny image of little Pearl, pointing her small forefinger too.

"Thou strange child, why dost thou not come to me?" exclaimed Hester.

Pearl still pointed with her forefinger; and a frown gathered on her brow; the more impressive from the childish, the almost baby-like aspect of the features that conveyed it. As her mother still kept beckoning to her, and arraying her face in a holiday suit of unaccustomed smiles, the child stamped her foot with a yet more imperious look and gesture. In the brook, again, was the fantastic beauty of the image, with its reflected frown, its pointed finger, and imperious gesture, giving emphasis to the aspect of little Pearl.

"Hasten, Pearl; or I shall be angry with thee!" cried Hester Prynne, who, however inured to such behaviour on the elf-child's part at other seasons, was naturally anxious for a more seemly deportment now. "Leap across the brook, naughty child, and run hither! Else I must come to thee!"

But Pearl, not a whit startled at her mother's threats, any more than mollified by her entreaties, now suddenly burst into a fit of passion, gesticulating violently, and throwing her small figure into the most extravagant contortions. She accompanied this wild outbreak with piercing shrieks, which the woods reverberated on all sides; so that, alone as she was in her childish and unreasonable wrath, it seemed as if a hidden multitude were lending her their sympathy and encouragement. Seen in the brook, once more, was the shadowy wrath of Pearl's image, crowned and girdled with flowers, but stamping its foot, wildly gesticulating, and, in the midst of all, still pointing its small forefinger at Hester's bosom!

"I see what ails the child," whispered Hester to the clergyman, and turning pale in spite of a strong effort to conceal her trouble and annoyance. "Children will not abide any, the slightest, change in the accustomed aspect of things that are daily before their eyes. Pearl misses something which she has always seen me wear!"

"I pray you," answered the minister, "if thou hast any means of pacifying the child, do it forthwith! Save it were the cankered wrath of an old witch, like Mistress Hibbins," added he, attempting to smile, "I know nothing that I would not sooner encounter than this passion in a child. In Pearl's young beauty, as in the wrinkled witch, it has a preternatural effect. Pacify her, if thou lovest me!"

Hester turned again towards Pearl, with a crimson blush upon her cheek, a conscious glance aside at the clergyman, and then a heavy sigh;

while, even before she had time to speak, the blush yielded to a deadly pallor.

"Pearl," said she, sadly, "look down at thy feet! There! — before thee! — on the hither side of the brook!"

The child turned her eyes to the point indicated; and there lay the scarlet letter, so close upon the margin of the stream, that the gold embroidery was reflected in it.

"Bring it hither!" said Hester.

"Come thou and take it up!" answered Pearl.

"Was ever such a child!" observed Hester aside to the minister. "O, I have much to tell thee about her. But, in very truth, she is right as regards this hateful token. I must bear its torture yet a little longer, — only a few days longer, — until we shall have left this region, and look back hither as to a land which we have dreamed of. The forest cannot hide it! The mid-ocean shall take it from my hand, and swallow it up for ever!"

With these words, she advanced to the margin of the brook, took up the scarlet letter, and fastened it again into her bosom. Hopefully, but a moment ago, as Hester had spoken of drowning it in the deep sea, there was a sense of inevitable doom upon her, as she thus received back this deadly symbol from the hand of fate. She had flung it into infinite space! — she had drawn an hour's free breath! — and here again was the scarlet misery, glittering on the old spot! So it ever is, whether thus typified or no, that an evil deed invests itself with the character of doom. Hester next gathered up the heavy tresses of her hair, and confined them beneath her cap. As if there were a withering spell in the sad letter, her beauty, the warmth and richness of her womanhood, departed, like fading sunshine; and a gray shadow seemed to fall across her.

When the dreary change was wrought, she extended her hand to Pearl.

"Dost thou know thy mother now, child?" asked she, reproachfully, but with a subdued tone. "Wilt thou come across the brook, and own thy mother, now that she has her shame upon her, — now that she is sad?"

"Yes; now I will!" answered the child, bounding across the brook, and clasping Hester in her arms. "Now thou art my mother indeed! And I am thy little Pearl!"

In a mood of tenderness that was not usual with her, she drew down her mother's head, and kissed her brow and both her cheeks. But then — by a kind of necessity that always impelled this child to alloy whatever comfort she might chance to give with a throb of anguish — Pearl put up her mouth, and kissed the scarlet letter too!

"That was not kind!" said Hester. "When thou hast shown me a little love, thou mockest me!"

"Why doth the minister sit yonder?" asked Pearl.

"He waits to welcome thee," replied her mother. "Come thou, and entreat his blessing! He loves thee, my little Pearl, and loves thy mother too. Wilt thou not love him? Come! he longs to greet thee!"

"Doth he love us?" said Pearl, looking up with acute intelligence into her mother's face. "Will he go back with us, hand in hand, we three together, into the town?"

"Not now, dear child," answered Hester. "But in days to come he will walk hand in hand with us. We will have a home and fireside of our own; and thou shalt sit upon his knee; and he will teach thee many things, and love thee dearly. Thou wilt love him; wilt thou not?"

"And will he always keep his hand over his heart?" inquired Pearl.

"Foolish child, what a question is that!" exclaimed her mother. "Come and ask his blessing!"

But, whether influenced by the jealousy that seems instinctive with every petted child towards a dangerous rival, or from whatever caprice of her freakish nature, Pearl would show no favor to the clergyman. It was only by an exertion of force that her mother brought her up to him, hanging back, and manifesting her reluctance by odd grimaces; of which, ever since her babyhood, she had possessed a singular variety, and could transform her mobile physiognomy into a series of different aspects, with a new mischief in them, each and all. The minister — painfully embarrassed, but hoping that a kiss might prove a talisman to admit him into the child's kindlier regards — bent forward, and impressed one on her brow. Hereupon, Pearl broke away from her mother, and, running to the brook, stooped over it, and bathed her forehead, until the unwelcome kiss was quite washed off, and diffused through a long lapse of the gliding water. She then remained apart, silently watching Hester and the clergyman; while they talked together, and made such arrangements as were suggested by their new position, and the purposes soon to be fulfilled.

And now this fateful interview had come to a close. The dell was to be left a solitude among its dark, old trees, which, with their multitudinous tongues, would whisper long of what had passed there, and no mortal be the wiser. And the melancholy brook would add this other tale to the mystery with which its little heart was already overburdened, and whereof it still kept up a murmuring babble, with not a whit more cheerfulness of tone than for ages heretofore.

XX. The Minister in a Maze

As the minister departed, in advance of Hester Prynne and little Pearl, he threw a backward glance; half expecting that he should discover only some faintly traced features or outline of the mother and the child, slowly fading into the twilight of the woods. So great a vicissitude in his life could not at once be received as real. But there was Hester, clad in her gray robe, still standing beside the tree-trunk, which some blast had overthrown a long antiquity ago, and which time had ever since been covering with moss, so that these two fated ones, with earth's heaviest burden on them, might there sit down together, and find a single hour's rest and solace. And there was Pearl, too, lightly dancing from the margin of the brook, — now that the intrusive third person was gone, — and taking her old place by her mother's side. So the minister had not fallen asleep, and dreamed!

In order to free his mind from this indistinctness and duplicity of impression, which vexed it with a strange disquietude, he recalled and more thoroughly defined the plans which Hester and himself had sketched for their departure. It had been determined between them, that the Old World, with its crowds and cities, offered them a more eligible shelter and concealment than the wilds of New England, or all America, with its alternatives of an Indian wigwam, or the few settlements of Europeans, scattered thinly along the seaboard. Not to speak of the clergyman's health, so inadequate to sustain the hardships of a forest life, his native gifts, his culture, and his entire development would secure him a home only in the midst of civilization and refinement; the higher the state, the more delicately adapted to it the man. In furtherance of this choice, it so happened that a ship lay in the harbour; one of those questionable cruisers, frequent at that day, which, without being absolutely outlaws of the deep, yet roamed over its surface with a remarkable irresponsibility of character. This vessel had recently arrived from the Spanish Main, and, within three days' time, would sail for Bristol. Hester Prynne — whose vocation, as a self-enlisted Sister of Charity, had brought her acquainted with the captain and crew — could take upon herself to secure the passage of two individuals and a child, with all the secrecy which circumstances rendered more than desirable.

The minister had inquired of Hester, with no little interest, the precise time at which the vessel might be expected to depart. It would probably be on the fourth day from the present. "That is most fortunate!" he had then said to himself. Now, why the Reverend Mr. Dimmesdale considered it so very fortunate, we hesitate to reveal. Nevertheless, — to hold nothing back from the reader, — it was because, on the third day from the present, he was to preach the Election Sermon; and, as such an occasion formed an honorable epoch in the life of a New England clergyman, he could not have chanced upon a more suitable mode and time of terminating his professional career. "At least, they shall say of me," thought this exemplary man, "that I leave no public duty unperformed, nor ill performed!" Sad, indeed, that an introspection so profound and acute as this poor minister's should be so miserably deceived! We have had, and may still have, worse things to tell of him; but none, we apprehend, so pitiably weak; no evidence, at once so slight and irrefragable, of a subtle disease, that had long since begun to eat into the real substance of his character. No man, for any considerable period, can wear one face to himself, and another to the multitude, without finally getting bewildered as to which may be the true.

The excitement of Mr. Dimmesdale's feelings, as he returned from his interview with Hester, lent him unaccustomed physical energy, and hurried him townward at a rapid pace. The pathway among the woods seemed wilder, more uncouth with its rude natural obstacles, and less trodden by the foot of man, than he remembered it on his outward journey. But he leaped across the plashy places, thrust himself through the clinging underbrush, climbed the ascent, plunged into the hollow, and overcame, in short, all the difficulties of the track, with an unwearable activity that astonished him. He could not but recall how feebly, and with what frequent pauses for breath, he had toiled over the same ground only two days before. As he drew near the town, he took an impression of change from the series of familiar objects that presented themselves. It seemed not yesterday, not one, nor two, but many days, or even years ago, since he had quitted them. There, indeed, was each former trace of the street, as he remembered it, and all the peculiarities of the houses, with the due multitude of gable-peaks, and a weathercock at every point where his memory suggested one. Not the less, however, came this importunately obtrusive sense of change. The same was true as regarded the acquaintances whom he met, and all the well-known shapes of human life, about the little town. They looked neither older nor younger, now; the beards of the aged were no whiter, nor could the creeping babe of yesterday walk on his feet to-day; it was impossible to describe in what respect they differed from the individuals on whom he had so recently bestowed a parting glance; and yet the minister's deepest sense seemed to inform him of their mutability. A similar impression struck him most remarkably, as he passed under the walls of his own church. The edifice had so very strange, and yet so familiar, an aspect, that Mr. Dimmesdale's mind vibrated between two ideas; either that he had seen it only in a dream hitherto, or that he was merely dreaming about it now.

This phenomenon, in the various shapes which it assumed, indicated no external change, but so sudden and important a change in the spectator of the familiar scene, that the intervening space of a single day had operated on his consciousness like the lapse of years. The minister's own will, and Hester's will, and the fate that grew between them, had wrought this transformation. It was the same town as heretofore; but the same minister returned not from the forest. He might have said to the friends who greeted him, — "I am not the man for whom you take me! I left him yonder in the forest, withdrawn into a secret dell, by a mossy tree-trunk, and near a melancholy brook! Go, seek your minister, and see if his emaciated figure, his thin cheek, his white, heavy, pain-wrinkled brow, be not flung down there like a cast-off garment!" His friends, no doubt, would still have insisted with him, — "Thou art thyself the man!" — but the error would have been their own, not his.

Before Mr. Dimmesdale reached home, his inner man gave him other evidences of a revolution in the sphere of thought and feeling. In truth, nothing short of a total change of dynasty and moral code, in that interior kingdom, was adequate to account for the impulses now communicated to the unfortunate and startled minister. At every step he was incited to do some strange, wild, wicked thing or other, with a sense that it would be at once involuntary and intentional; in spite of himself, yet growing out of a profounder self than that which opposed the impulse. For instance, he met one of his own deacons. The good old man addressed him with the paternal affection and patriarchal privilege, which his venerable age, his upright and holy character, and his station in the Church, entitled him to use; and, conjoined with this, the deep, almost worshipping respect, which the minister's professional and private claims alike demanded. Never was there a more beautiful example of how the majesty of age and wisdom may comport with the obeisance and respect enjoined upon it, as from a lower social rank and inferior order of endowment, towards a higher. Now, during a conversation of some two or three moments between the Reverend Mr. Dimmesdale and this excellent and hoary-bearded deacon, it was only by the most careful self-control that the former could refrain from uttering certain blasphemous suggestions that rose into his mind, respecting the communion-supper. He absolutely trembled and turned pale as ashes, lest his tongue should wag itself, in utterance of these horrible matters, and plead his own consent for so doing, without his having fairly given it. And, even with this terror in his heart, he could hardly avoid laughing to imagine how the sanctified old patriarchal deacon would have been petrified by his minister's impiety!

Again, another incident of the same nature. Hurrying along the street, the Reverend Mr. Dimmesdale encountered the eldest female member of his church; a most pious and exemplary old dame; poor, widowed, lonely, and with a heart as full of reminiscences about her dead husband and children, and her dead friends of long ago, as a burial-ground is full of storied grave-stones. Yet all this, which would else have been such heavy sorrow, was made almost a solemn joy to her devout old soul by religious consolations and the truths of Scripture, wherewith she had fed herself continually for more than thirty years. And, since Mr. Dimmesdale had taken her in charge, the good grandam's chief earthly comfort — which, unless it had been likewise a heavenly comfort, could have been none at all — was to meet her pastor, whether casually, or of set purpose, and be refreshed with a word of warm, fragrant, heaven-breathing Gospel truth from his beloved lips into her dulled, but rapturously attentive ear. But, on this occasion, up to the moment of putting his lips to the old woman's ear, Mr. Dimmesdale, as the great enemy of souls would have it, could recall no text of Scripture, nor aught else, except a brief, pithy, and, as it then appeared to him, unanswerable argument against the immortality of the human soul. The instilment thereof into her mind would probably have caused this aged sister to drop down dead, at once, as by the effect of an intensely poisonous infusion. What he really did whisper, the minister could never afterwards recollect. There was, perhaps, a fortunate disorder in his utterance, which failed to impart any distinct idea to the good widow's comprehension, or which Providence interpreted after a method of its own. Assuredly, as the minister looked back, he beheld an expression of divine gratitude and ecstasy that seemed like the shine of the celestial city on her face, so wrinkled and ashy pale.

Again, a third instance. After parting from the old church-member, he met the youngest sister of them all. It was a maiden newly won — and won by the Reverend Mr. Dimmesdale's own sermon, on the Sabbath after his vigil — to barter the transitory pleasures of the world for the heavenly hope, that was to assume brighter substance as life grew dark around her, and which would gild the utter gloom with final glory. She was fair and pure as a lily that had bloomed in Paradise. The minister knew well that he was himself enshrined within the stainless sanctity of her heart, which hung its snowy curtains about his image, imparting to religion the warmth of love, and to love a religious purity. Satan, that afternoon, had surely led the poor young girl away from her mother's side, and thrown her into the pathway of this sorely tempted, or — shall we not rather say? — this lost and desperate man. As she drew nigh, the arch-fiend whispered him to condense into small compass and drop into her tender bosom a germ of evil that would be sure to blossom darkly soon, and bear black fruit betimes. Such was his sense of power over this virgin soul, trusting him as she did, that the minister felt potent to blight all the field of innocence with but one wicked look, and develop all its opposite with but a word. So — with a mightier struggle than he had yet sustained — he held his Geneva cloak before his face, and hurried onward, making no sign of recognition, and leaving the young sister to digest his rudeness as she might. She ransacked her conscience, — which was full of harmless little matters, like her pocket or her work-bag, — and took herself to task, poor thing, for a thousand imaginary faults; and went about her household duties with swollen eyelids the next morning.

Before the minister had time to celebrate his victory over this last temptation, he was conscious of another impulse, more ludicrous, and almost as horrible. It was, — we blush to tell it, — it was to stop short in the road, and teach some very wicked words to a knot of little Puritan children who were playing there, and had but just begun to talk. Denying himself this freak, as unworthy of his cloth, he met a drunken seaman, one of the ship's crew from the Spanish Main. And, here, since he had so valiantly forborne all other wickedness, poor Mr. Dimmesdale longed, at least, to shake hands with the tarry blackguard, and recreate himself with a few improper jests, such as dissolute sailors so abound with, and a volley of good, round, solid, satisfactory, and heaven-defying oaths! It was not so much a better principle, as partly his natural good taste, and still more his buckramed° habit of clerical decorum, that carried him safely through the latter crisis.

"What is it that haunts and tempts me thus?" cried the minister to himself, at length, pausing in the street, and striking his hand against his forehead. "Am I mad? or am I given over utterly to the fiend? Did I make a contract with him in the forest, and sign it with my blood? And does

buckramed: Stiff.

he now summon me to its fulfilment, by suggesting the performance of every wickedness which his most foul imagination can conceive?"

At the moment when the Reverend Mr. Dimmesdale thus communed with himself, and struck his forehead with his hand, old Mistress Hibbins, the reputed witch-lady, is said to have been passing by. She made a very grand appearance; having on a high head-dress, a rich gown of velvet, and a ruff done up with the famous yellow starch, of which Ann Turner, her especial friend, had taught her the secret, before this last good lady had been hanged for Sir Thomas Overbury's murder. Whether the witch had read the minister's thoughts, or no, she came to a full stop, looked shrewdly into his face, smiled craftily, and — though little given to converse with clergymen — began a conversation.

"So, reverend Sir, you have made a visit into the forest," observed the witch-lady, nodding her high head-dress at him. "The next time, I pray you to allow me only a fair warning, and I shall be proud to bear you company. Without taking overmuch upon myself, my good word will go far towards gaining any strange gentleman a fair reception from yonder potentate you wot of!"

"I profess, madam," answered the clergyman, with a grave obeisance, such as the lady's rank demanded, and his own good-breeding made imperative, — "I profess, on my conscience and character, that I am utterly bewildered as touching the purport of your words! I went not into the forest to seek a potentate; neither do I, at any future time, design a visit thither, with a view to gaining the favor of such personage. My one sufficient object was to greet that pious friend of mine, the Apostle Eliot, and rejoice with him over the many precious souls he hath won from heathendom!"

"Ha, ha, ha!" cackled the old witch-lady, still nodding her high head-dress at the minister. "Well, well, we must needs talk thus in the daytime! You carry it off like an old hand! But at midnight, and in the forest, we shall have other talk together!"

She passed on with her aged stateliness, but often turning back her head and smiling at him, like one willing to recognize a secret intimacy of connection.

"Have I then sold myself," thought the minister, "to the fiend whom, if men say true, this yellow-starched and velveted old hag has chosen for her prince and master!"

The wretched minister! He had made a bargain very like it! Tempted by a dream of happiness, he had yielded himself with deliberate choice, as he had never done before, to what he knew was deadly sin. And the infectious poison of that sin had been thus rapidly diffused throughout his moral system. It had stupefied all blessed impulses, and awakened into vivid life the whole brotherhood of bad ones. Scorn, bitterness, unprovoked malignity, gratuitous desire of ill, ridicule of whatever was good and holy, all awoke, to tempt, even while they frightened him. And his encounter with old Mistress Hibbins, if it were a real incident, did but show his sympathy and fellowship with wicked mortals and the world of perverted spirits.

He had by this time reached his dwelling, on the edge of the burial-ground, and, hastening up the stairs, took refuge in his study. The minister was glad to have reached this shelter, without first betraying himself to the world by any of those strange and wicked eccentricities to which he had been continually impelled while passing through the streets. He entered the accustomed room, and looked around him on its books, its windows, its fireplace, and the tapestried comfort of the walls, with the same perception of strangeness that had haunted him throughout his walk from the forest-dell into the town, and thitherward. Here he had studied and written; here, gone through fast and vigil, and come forth half alive; here, striven to pray; here, borne a hundred thousand agonies! There was the Bible, in its rich old Hebrew, with Moses and the Prophets speaking to him, and God's voice through all! There, on the table, with the inky pen beside it, was an unfinished sermon, with a sentence broken in the midst, where his thoughts had ceased to gush out upon the page two days before. He knew that it was himself, the thin and white-cheeked minister, who had done and suffered these things, and written thus far into the Election Sermon! But he seemed to stand apart, and eye this former self with scornful, pitying, but half-envious curiosity. That self was gone! Another man had returned out of the forest; a wiser one; with a knowledge of hidden mysteries which the simplicity of the former never could have reached. A bitter kind of knowledge that!

While occupied with these reflections, a knock came at the door of the study, and the minister said, "Come in!" — not wholly devoid of an idea that he might behold an evil spirit. And so he did! It was old Roger Chillingworth that entered. The minister stood, white and speechless, with one hand on the Hebrew Scriptures, and the other spread upon his breast.

"Welcome home, reverend Sir!" said the physician. "And how found you that godly man, the Apostle Eliot? But methinks, dear Sir, you look pale; as if the travel through the wilderness had been too sore for you. Will not my aid be requisite to put you in heart and strength to preach your Election Sermon?"

"Nay, I think not so," rejoined the Reverend Mr. Dimmesdale. "My journey, and the sight of the holy Apostle yonder, and the free air which I have breathed, have done me good, after so long confinement in my study. I think to need no more of your drugs, my kind physician, good though they be, and administered by a friendly hand."

All this time, Roger Chillingworth was looking at the minister with the grave and intent regard of a physician towards his patient. But, in spite of this outward show, the latter was almost convinced of the old man's knowledge, or, at least, his confident suspicion, with respect to his own interview with Hester Prynne. The physician knew, then, that, in the minister's regard, he was no longer a trusted friend, but his bitterest enemy. So much being known, it would appear natural that a part of it should be expressed. It is singular, however, how long a time often passes before words embody things; and with what security two persons, who choose to avoid a certain subject, may approach its very verge, and retire without disturbing it. Thus, the minister felt no apprehension that Roger Chillingworth would touch, in express words, upon the real position which they sustained towards one another. Yet did the physician, in his dark way, creep frightfully near the secret.

"Were it not better," said he, "that you use my poor skill to-night? Verily, dear Sir, we must take pains to make you strong and vigorous for this occasion of the Election discourse. The people look for great things from you; apprehending that another year may come about, and find their pastor gone."

"Yea, to another world," replied the minister, with pious resignation. "Heaven grant it be a better one; for, in good sooth, I hardly think to tarry with my flock through the flitting seasons of another year! But, touching your medicine, kind Sir, in my present frame of body I need it not."

"I joy to hear it," answered the physician. "It may be that my remedies, so long administered in vain, begin now to take due effect. Happy man were I, and well deserving of New England's gratitude, could I achieve this cure!"

"I thank you from my heart, most watchful friend," said the Reverend Mr. Dimmesdale, with a solemn smile. "I thank you, and can but requite your good deeds with my prayers."

"A good man's prayers are golden recompense!" rejoined old Roger Chillingworth, as he took his leave. "Yea, they are the current gold coin of the New Jerusalem, with the King's own mint-mark on them!"

Left alone, the minister summoned a servant of the house, and requested food, which, being set before him, he ate with ravenous appetite. Then, flinging the already written pages of the Election Sermon into the fire, he forthwith began another, which he wrote with such an impulsive flow of thought and emotion, that he fancied himself inspired; and only wondered that Heaven should see fit to transmit the grand and solemn music of its oracles through so foul an organ-pipe as he. However, leaving that mystery to solve itself, or go unsolved for ever, he drove his task onward, with earnest haste and ecstasy. Thus the night fled away, as if it were a winged steed, and he careering on it; morning came, and peeped blushing through the curtains; and at last sunrise threw a golden beam into the study, and laid it right across the minister's bedazzled eyes. There he was, with the pen still between his fingers, and a vast, immeasurable tract of written space behind him!

XXI. The New England Holiday

Betimes in the morning of the day on which the new Governor was to receive his office at the hands of the people, Hester Prynne and little Pearl came into the market-place. It was already thronged with the craftsmen and other plebeian inhabitants of the town, in considerable numbers; among whom, likewise, were many rough figures, whose attire of deer-skins marked them as belonging to some of the forest settlements, which surrounded the little metropolis of the colony.

On this public holiday, as on all other occasions, for seven years past, Hester was clad in a garment of coarse gray cloth. Not more by its hue than by some indescribable peculiarity in its fashion, it had the effect of making her fade personally out of sight and outline; while, again, the scarlet letter brought her back from this twilight indistinctness, and revealed her under the moral aspect of its own illumination. Her face, so long familiar to the townspeople, showed the marble quietude which they were accustomed to behold there. It was like a mask; or rather, like the frozen calmness of a dead woman's features; owing this dreary resemblance to the fact that Hester was actually dead, in respect to any claim of sympathy, and had departed out of the world with which she still seemed to mingle.

It might be, on this one day, that there was an expression unseen before, nor, indeed, vivid enough to be detected now; unless some preternaturally gifted observer should have first read the heart, and have afterwards sought a corresponding development in the countenance and mien. Such a spiritual seer might have conceived, that, after sustaining the gaze of the multitude through seven miserable years as a necessity, a penance, and something which it was a stern religion to endure, she now, for one last time more, encountered it freely and voluntarily, in order to convert what had so long been agony into a kind of triumph. "Look your last on the scarlet letter and its wearer!" — the people's victim and life-long bond-slave, as they fancied her, might say to them. "Yet a little while, and she will be beyond your reach! A few hours longer, and the deep, mysterious ocean will quench and hide for ever the symbol which ye have caused to burn upon her bosom!" Nor were it an inconsistency too improbable to be assigned to human nature, should we suppose a feeling of regret in Hester's mind, at the moment when she was about to win her freedom from the pain which had been thus deeply incorporated with her being. Might there not be an irresistible desire to quaff a last, long, breathless draught of the cup of wormwood and aloes, with which nearly all her years of womanhood had been perpetually flavored? The wine of life, henceforth to be presented to her lips, must be indeed rich, delicious, and exhilarating, in its chased and golden beaker; or else leave an inevitable and weary languor, after the lees of bitterness wherewith she had been drugged, as with a cordial of intensest potency.

Pearl was decked out with airy gayety. It would have been impossible to guess that this bright and sunny apparition owed its existence to the shape of gloomy gray; or that a fancy, at once so gorgeous and so delicate as must have been requisite to contrive the child's apparel, was the same that had achieved a task perhaps more difficult, in imparting so distinct a peculiarity to Hester's simple robe. The dress, so proper was it to little Pearl, seemed an effluence, or inevitable development and outward manifestation of her character, no more to be separated from her than the many-hued brilliancy from a butterfly's wing, or the painted glory from the leaf of a bright flower. As with these, so with the child; her garb was all of one idea with her nature. On this eventful day, moreover, there was a certain singular inquietude and excitement in her mood, resembling nothing so much as the shimmer of a diamond, that sparkles and flashes with the varied throbbings of the breast on which it is displayed. Children have always a sympathy in the agitations of those connected with them; always, especially, a sense of any trouble or impending revolution, of whatever kind, in domestic circumstances; and therefore Pearl, who was the gem on her mother's unquiet bosom, betrayed, by the very dance of her spirits, the emotions which none could detect in the marble passiveness of Hester's brow.

This effervescence made her flit with a bird-like movement, rather than walk by her mother's side. She broke continually into shouts of a wild, inarticulate, and sometimes piercing music. When they reached the market-place, she became still more restless, on perceiving the stir and bustle that enlivened the spot; for it was usually more like the broad and lonesome green before a village meeting-house, than the centre of a town's business.

"Why, what is this, mother?" cried she. "Wherefore have all the people left their work to-day? Is it a play-day for the whole world? See, there is the blacksmith! He has washed his sooty face, and put on his Sabbath-day clothes, and looks as if he would gladly be merry, if any kind body would only teach him how! And there is Master Brackett, the old jailer, nodding and smiling at me. Why does he do so, mother?"

"He remembers thee a little babe, my child," answered Hester.

"He should not nod and smile at me, for all that, — the black, grim, ugly-eyed old man!" said Pearl. "He may nod at thee if he will; for thou art clad in gray, and wearest the scarlet letter. But, see, mother, how many faces of strange people, and Indians among them, and sailors! What have they all come to do here in the market-place?"

"They wait to see the procession pass," said Hester. "For the Governor and the magistrates are to go by, and the ministers, and all the great people and good people, with the music, and the soldiers marching before them."

"And will the minister be there?" asked Pearl. "And will he hold out both his hands to me, as when thou ledst me to him from the brook-side?"

"He will be there, child," answered her mother. "But he will not greet thee to-day; nor must thou greet him."

"What a strange, sad man is he!" said the child, as if speaking partly to herself. "In the dark night-time, he calls us to him, and holds thy hand and mine, as when we stood with him on the scaffold yonder! And in the deep forest, where only the old trees can hear, and the strip of sky see it, he talks with thee, sitting on a heap of moss! And he kisses my forehead, too, so that the little brook would hardly wash it off! But here in the sunny day, and among all the people, he knows us not; nor must we know him! A strange, sad man is he, with his hand always over his heart!"

"Be quiet, Pearl! Thou understandest not these things," said her mother. "Think not now of the minister, but look about thee, and see how cheery is every body's face to-day. The children have come from their schools, and the grown people from their workshops and their fields, on purpose to be happy. For, to-day, a new man is beginning to rule over them; and so — as has been the custom of mankind ever since a nation was first gathered — they make merry and rejoice; as if a good and golden year were at length to pass over the poor old world!"

It was as Hester said, in regard to the unwonted jollity that brightened the faces of the people. Into this festal season of the year — as it already was, and continued to be during the greater part of two centuries — the Puritans compressed whatever mirth and public joy they deemed allowable to human infirmity; thereby so far dispelling the customary cloud, that, for the space of a single holiday, they appeared scarcely more grave than most other communities at a period of general affliction.

But we perhaps exaggerate the gray or sable tinge, which undoubtedly characterized the mood and manners of the age. The persons now in the market-place of Boston had not been born to an inheritance of Puritanic gloom. They were native Englishmen, whose fathers had lived in the sunny richness of the Elizabethan epoch; a time when the life of England, viewed as one great mass, would appear to have been as stately, magnificent, and joyous, as the world has ever witnessed. Had they followed their hereditary taste, the New England settlers would have illustrated all events of public importance by bonfires, banquets, pageantries, and processions. Nor would it have been impracticable, in the observance of majestic ceremonies, to combine mirthful recreation with solemnity, and give, as it were, a grotesque and brilliant embroidery to the great robe of state, which a nation, at such festivals, puts on. There was some shadow of an attempt of this kind in the mode of celebrating the day on which the political year of the colony commenced. The dim reflection of a remembered splendor, a colorless and manifold diluted repetition of what they had beheld in proud old London, — we will not say at a royal coronation, but at a Lord Mayor's show, — might be traced in the customs which our forefathers instituted, with reference to the annual installation of magistrates. The fathers and founders of the commonwealth — the statesman, the priest, and the soldier — deemed it a duty then to assume the outward state and majesty, which, in accordance with antique style, was looked upon as the proper garb of public or social eminence. All came forth, to move in procession before the people's eye, and thus impart a needed dignity to the simple framework of a government so newly constructed.

Then, too, the people were countenanced, if not encouraged, in relaxing the severe and close application to their various modes of rugged industry, which, at all other times, seemed of the same piece and material with their religion. Here, it is true, were none of the appliances which popular merriment would so readily have found in the England of Elizabeth's time, or that of James; — no rude shows of a theatrical kind; no minstrel with his harp and legendary ballad, nor gleeman, with an ape dancing to his music; no juggler, with his tricks of mimic witchcraft; no Merry Andrew, to stir up the multitude with jests, perhaps hundreds of years old, but still effective, by their appeals to the very broadest sources of mirthful sympathy. All such professors of the several branches of jocularity would have been sternly repressed, not only by the rigid discipline of law, but by the general sentiment which gives law its vitality. Not the less, however, the great, honest face of the people smiled, grimly, perhaps, but widely too. Nor were sports wanting, such as the colonists had witnessed, and shared in, long ago, at the country fairs and on the village-greens of England; and which it was thought well to keep alive on this new soil, for the sake of the courage and manliness that were essential in them. Wrestling-matches, in the differing fashions of Cornwall and Devonshire, were seen here and there about the market-place; in one corner, there was a friendly bout at quarterstaff; and — what attracted most interest of all — on the platform of the pillory, already so noted in our pages, two masters of defence were commencing an exhibition with the buckler and broadsword. But, much to the disappointment of the crowd, this latter business was broken off by the interposition of the town beadle, who had no idea of permitting the majesty of the law to be violated by such an abuse of one of its consecrated places.

It may not be too much to affirm, on the whole, (the people being then in the first stages of joyless deportment, and the offspring of sires who had known how to be merry, in their day,) that they would compare favorably, in point of holiday keeping, with their descendants, even at so long an interval as ourselves. Their immediate posterity, the generation next to the early emigrants, wore the blackest shade of Puritanism, and so darkened the national visage with it, that all the subsequent years have not sufficed to clear it up. We have yet to learn again the forgotten art of gayety.

The picture of human life in the market-place, though its general tint was the sad gray, brown, or black of the English emigrants, was yet enlivened by some diversity of hue. A party of Indians — in their savage finery of curiously embroidered deer-skin robes, wampum-belts, red and yellow ochre, and feathers, and armed with the bow and arrow and stone-headed spear — stood apart, with countenances of inflexible gravity, beyond what even the Puritan aspect could attain. Nor, wild as were these painted barbarians, were they the wildest feature of the scene.

This distinction could more justly be claimed by some mariners, — a part of the crew of the vessel from the Spanish Main, — who had come ashore to see the humors of Election Day. They were rough-looking desperadoes, with sun-blackened faces, and an immensity of beard; their wide, short trousers were confined about the waist by belts, often clasped with a rough plate of gold, and sustaining always a long knife, and, in some instances, a sword. From beneath their broad-brimmed hats of palm-leaf, gleamed eyes which, even in good nature and merriment, had a kind of animal ferocity. They transgressed, without fear or scruple, the rules of behaviour that were binding on all others; smoking tobacco under the beadle's very nose, although each whiff would have cost a townsman a shilling; and quaffing, at their pleasure, draughts of wine or aqua-vitae from pocket-flasks, which they freely tendered to the gaping crowd around them. It remarkably characterized the incomplete morality of the age, rigid as we call it, that a license was allowed the seafaring class, not merely for their freaks on shore, but for far more desperate deeds on their proper element. The sailor of that day would go near to be arraigned as a pirate in our own. There could be little doubt, for instance, that this very ship's crew, though no unfavorable specimens of the nautical brotherhood, had been guilty, as we should phrase it, of depredations on the Spanish commerce, such as would have perilled all their necks in a modern court of justice.

But the sea, in those old times, heaved, swelled, and foamed very much at its own will, or subject only to the tempestuous wind, with hardly any attempts at regulation by human law. The buccaneer on the wave might relinquish his calling, and become at once, if he chose, a man of probity and piety on land; nor, even in the full career of his reckless life, was he regarded as a personage with whom it was disreputable to traffic, or casually associate. Thus, the Puritan elders, in their black cloaks, starched bands, and steeple-crowned hats, smiled not unbenignantly at the clamor and rude deportment of these jolly seafaring men; and it excited neither surprise nor animadversion° when so reputable a citizen as old Roger Chillingworth, the physician, was seen to enter the market-place, in close and familiar talk with the commander of the questionable vessel.

The latter was by far the most showy and gallant figure, so far as apparel went, anywhere to be seen among the multitude. He wore a profusion of ribbons on his garment, and gold lace on his hat, which was

animadversion: Critical, censurious comment.

also encircled by a gold chain, and surmounted with a feather. There was a sword at his side, and a sword-cut on his forehead, which, by the arrangement of his hair, he seemed anxious rather to display than hide. A landsman could hardly have worn this garb and shown his face, and worn and shown them both with such a galliard air, without undergoing stern question before a magistrate, and probably incurring fine or imprisonment, or perhaps an exhibition in the stocks. As regarded the shipmaster, however, all was looked upon as pertaining to the character, as to a fish his glistening scales.

After parting from the physician, the commander of the Bristol ship strolled idly through the market-place; until, happening to approach the spot where Hester Prynne was standing, he appeared to recognize, and did not hesitate to address her. As was usually the case wherever Hester stood, a small, vacant area — a sort of magic circle — had formed itself about her, into which, though the people were elbowing one another at a little distance, none ventured, or felt disposed to intrude. It was a forcible type of the moral solitude in which the scarlet letter enveloped its fated wearer; partly by her own reserve, and partly by the instinctive, though no longer so unkindly, withdrawal of her fellow-creatures. Now, if never before, it answered a good purpose, by enabling Hester and the seaman to speak together without risk of being overheard; and so changed was Hester Prynne's repute before the public, that the matron in town most eminent for rigid morality could not have held such intercourse with less result of scandal than herself.

"So, mistress," said the mariner, "I must bid the steward make ready one more berth than you bargained for! No fear of scurvy or ship-fever, this voyage! What with the ship's surgeon and this other doctor, our only danger will be from drug or pill; more by token, as there is a lot of apothecary's stuff aboard, which I traded for with a Spanish vessel."

"What mean you?" inquired Hester, startled more than she permitted to appear. "Have you another passenger?"

"Why, know you not," cried the shipmaster, "that this physician here — Chillingworth, he calls himself — is minded to try my cabin-fare with you? Ay, ay, you must have known it; for he tells me he is of your party, and a close friend to the gentleman you spoke of, — he that is in peril from these sour old Puritan rulers!"

"They know each other well, indeed," replied Hester, with a mien of calmness, though in the utmost consternation. "They have long dwelt together."

Nothing further passed between the mariner and Hester Prynne.

But, at that instant, she beheld old Roger Chillingworth himself, standing in the remotest corner of the market-place, and smiling on her; a smile which — across the wide and bustling square, and through all the talk and laughter, and various thoughts, moods, and interests of the crowd — conveyed secret and fearful meaning.

XXII. The Procession

Before Hester Prynne could call together her thoughts, and consider what was practicable to be done in this new and startling aspect of affairs, the sound of military music was heard approaching along a contiguous street. It denoted the advance of the procession of magistrates and citizens, on its way towards the meeting-house; where, in compliance with a custom thus early established, and ever since observed, the Reverend Mr. Dimmesdale was to deliver an Election Sermon.

Soon the head of the procession showed itself, with a slow and stately march, turning a corner, and making its way across the market-place. First came the music. It comprised a variety of instruments, perhaps imperfectly adapted to one another, and played with no great skill, but yet attaining the great object for which the harmony of drum and clarion addresses itself to the multitude, — that of imparting a higher and more heroic air to the scene of life that passes before the eye. Little Pearl at first clapped her hands, but then lost, for an instant, the restless agitation that had kept her in a continual effervescence throughout the morning; she gazed silently, and seemed to be borne upward, like a floating sea-bird, on the long heaves and swells of sound. But she was brought back to her former mood by the shimmer of the sunshine on the weapons and bright armour of the military company, which followed after the music, and formed the honorary escort of the procession. This body of soldiery — which still sustains a corporate existence, and marches down from past ages with an ancient and honorable fame — was composed of no mercenary materials. Its ranks were filled with gentlemen, who felt the stirrings of martial impulse, and sought to establish a kind of College of Arms, where, as in an association of Knights Templars, they might learn the science, and, so far as peaceful exercise would teach them, the practices of war. The high estimation then placed upon the military character might be seen in the lofty port of each individual member of the company. Some of them, indeed, by their services in the Low Countries and on other fields of European warfare, had fairly won their title to assume the name and pomp of soldiership. The entire array, moreover, clad in burnished steel, and with plumage nodding over their bright morions, had a brilliancy of effect which no modern display can aspire to equal.

And yet the men of civil eminence, who came immediately behind the military escort, were better worth a thoughtful observer's eye. Even in outward demeanour they showed a stamp of majesty that made the warrior's haughty stride look vulgar, if not absurd. It was an age when what we call talent had far less consideration than now, but the massive materials which produce stability and dignity of character a great deal more. The people possessed, by hereditary right, the quality of reverence; which, in their descendants, if it survive at all, exists in smaller proportion, and with a vastly diminished force in the selection and estimate of public men. The change may be for good or ill, and is partly, perhaps, for both. In that old day, the English settler on these rude shores, — having left king, nobles, and all degrees of awful rank behind, while still the faculty and necessity of reverence were strong in him, — bestowed it on the white hair and venerable brow of age; on long-tried integrity; on solid wisdom and sad-colored experience; on endowments of that grave and weighty order, which gives the idea of permanence, and comes under the general definition of respectability. These primitive statesmen, therefore, — Bradstreet, Endicott, Dudley,[19] Bellingham, and their compeers, — who were elevated to power by the early choice of the people, seem to have been not often brilliant, but distinguished by a ponderous sobriety, rather than activity of intellect. They had fortitude and self-reliance, and, in time of difficulty or peril, stood up for the welfare of the state like a line of cliffs against a tempestuous tide. The traits of character here indicated were well represented in the square cast of countenance and large physical development of the new colonial magistrates. So far as a demeanour of natural authority was concerned, the mother country need not have been ashamed to see these foremost men of an actual democracy adopted into the House of Peers, or made the Privy Council of the sovereign.

Next in order to the magistrates came the young and eminently distinguished divine, from whose lips the religious discourse of the anniversary was expected. His was the profession, at that era, in which intellectual ability displayed itself far more than in political life; for — leaving a higher motive out of the question — it offered inducements powerful enough, in the almost worshipping respect of the community, to win the

[19] Simon Bradstreet (1603–1697), John Endicott (1588–1665), and Thomas Dudley (1576–1653) all served as governor of the New England colonies.

most aspiring ambition into its service. Even political power — as in the case of Increase Mather[20] — was within the grasp of a successful priest.

It was the observation of those who beheld him now, that never, since Mr. Dimmesdale first set his foot on the New England shore, had he exhibited such energy as was seen in the gait and air with which he kept his pace in the procession. There was no feebleness of step, as at other times; his frame was not bent; nor did his hand rest ominously upon his heart. Yet, if the clergyman were rightly viewed, his strength seemed not of the body. It might be spiritual, and imparted to him by angelic ministrations. It might be the exhilaration of that potent cordial, which is distilled only in the furnace-glow of earnest and long-continued thought. Or, perchance, his sensitive temperament was invigorated by the loud and piercing music, that swelled heavenward, and uplifted him on its ascending wave. Nevertheless, so abstracted was his look, it might be questioned whether Mr. Dimmesdale even heard the music. There was his body, moving onward, and with an unaccustomed force. But where was his mind? Far and deep in its own region, busying itself, with preternatural activity, to marshal a procession of stately thoughts that were soon to issue thence; and so he saw nothing, heard nothing, knew nothing, of what was around him; but the spiritual element took up the feeble frame, and carried it along, unconscious of the burden, and converting it to spirit like itself. Men of uncommon intellect, who have grown morbid, possess this occasional power of mighty effort, into which they throw the life of many days, and then are lifeless for as many more.

Hester Prynne, gazing stedfastly at the clergyman, felt a dreary influence come over her, but wherefore or whence she knew not; unless that he seemed so remote from her own sphere, and utterly beyond her reach. One glance of recognition, she had imagined, must needs pass between them. She thought of the dim forest, with its little dell of solitude, and love, and anguish, and the mossy tree-trunk, where, sitting hand in hand, they had mingled their sad and passionate talk with the melancholy murmur of the brook. How deeply had they known each other then! And was this the man? She hardly knew him now! He, moving proudly past, enveloped, as it were, in the rich music, with the procession of majestic and venerable fathers; he, so unattainable in his worldly position, and still more so in that far vista of his unsympathizing thoughts, through which she now beheld him! Her spirit sank with

[20] The leader of the Puritans, Increase Mather (1639–1723), was involved in the infamous Salem witchcraft trials.

the idea that all must have been a delusion, and that, vividly as she had dreamed it, there could be no real bond betwixt the clergyman and herself. And thus much of woman was there in Hester, that she could scarcely forgive him, — least of all now, when the heavy footstep of their approaching Fate might be heard, nearer, nearer, nearer! — for being able so completely to withdraw himself from their mutual world; while she groped darkly, and stretched forth her cold hands, and found him not.

Pearl either saw and responded to her mother's feelings, or herself felt the remoteness and intangibility that had fallen around the minister. While the procession passed, the child was uneasy, fluttering up and down, like a bird on the point of taking flight. When the whole had gone by, she looked up into Hester's face.

"Mother," said she, "was that the same minister who kissed me by the brook?"

"Hold thy peace, dear little Pearl!" whispered her mother. "We must not always talk in the market-place of what happens to us in the forest."

"I could not be sure that it was he; so strange he looked," continued the child. "Else I would have run to him, and bid him kiss me now, before all the people; even as he did yonder among the dark old trees. What would the minister have said, mother? Would he have clapped his hand over his heart, and scowled on me, and bid me begone?"

"What should he say, Pearl," answered Hester, "save that it was no time to kiss, and that kisses are not to be given in the market-place? Well for thee, foolish child, that thou didst not speak to him!"

Another shade of the same sentiment, in reference to Mr. Dimmesdale, was expressed by a person whose eccentricities — or insanity, as we should term it — led her to do what few of the townspeople would have ventured on; to begin a conversation with the wearer of the scarlet letter, in public. It was Mistress Hibbins, who, arrayed in great magnificence, with a triple ruff, a broidered stomacher, a gown of rich velvet, and a gold-headed cane, had come forth to see the procession. As this ancient lady had the renown (which subsequently cost her no less a price than her life) of being a principal actor in all the works of necromancy that were continually going forward, the crowd gave way before her, and seemed to fear the touch of her garment, as if it carried the plague among its gorgeous folds. Seen in conjunction with Hester Prynne, — kindly as so many now felt towards the latter, — the dread inspired by Mistress Hibbins was doubled, and caused a general movement from that part of the market-place in which the two women stood.

"Now, what mortal imagination could conceive it!" whispered the old lady confidentially to Hester. "Yonder divine man! That saint on earth, as the people uphold him to be, and as — I must needs say — he really looks! Who, now, that saw him pass in the procession, would think how little while it is since he went forth out of his study, — chewing a Hebrew text of Scripture in his mouth, I warrant, — to take an airing in the forest! Aha! we know what that means, Hester Prynne! But, truly, forsooth, I find it hard to believe him the same man. Many a church-member saw I, walking behind the music, that has danced in the same measure with me, when Somebody was fiddler, and, it might be, an Indian powwow or a Lapland wizard changing hands with us! That is but a trifle, when a woman knows the world. But this minister! Couldst thou surely tell, Hester, whether he was the same man that encountered thee on the forest-path!"

"Madam, I know not of what you speak," answered Hester Prynne, feeling Mistress Hibbins to be of infirm mind; yet strangely startled and awe-stricken by the confidence with which she affirmed a personal connection between so many persons (herself among them) and the Evil One. "It is not for me to talk lightly of a learned and pious minister of the Word, like the Reverend Mr. Dimmesdale!"

"Fie, woman, fie!" cried the old lady, shaking her finger at Hester. "Dost thou think I have been to the forest so many times, and have yet no skill to judge who else has been there? Yea; though no leaf of the wild garlands, which they wore while they danced, be left in their hair! I know thee, Hester; for I behold the token. We may all see it in the sunshine; and it glows like a red flame in the dark. Thou wearest it openly; so there need be no question about that. But this minister! Let me tell thee in thine ear! When the Black Man sees one of his own servants, signed and sealed, so shy of owning to the bond as is the Reverend Mr. Dimmesdale, he hath a way of ordering matters so that the mark shall be disclosed in open daylight to the eyes of all the world! What is it that the minister seeks to hide, with his hand always over his heart? Ha, Hester Prynne!"

"What is it, good Mistress Hibbins?" eagerly asked little Pearl. "Hast thou seen it?"

"No matter, darling!" responded Mistress Hibbins, making Pearl a profound reverence. "Thou thyself wilt see it, one time or another. They say, child, thou art of the lineage of the Prince of the Air! Wilt thou ride with me, some fine night, to see thy father? Then thou shalt know wherefore the minister keeps his hand over his heart!"

Laughing so shrilly that all the market-place could hear her, the weird old gentlewoman took her departure.

By this time the preliminary prayer had been offered in the meeting-house, and the accents of the Reverend Mr. Dimmesdale were heard commencing his discourse. An irresistible feeling kept Hester near the spot. As the sacred edifice was too much thronged to admit another auditor, she took up her position close beside the scaffold of the pillory. It was in sufficient proximity to bring the whole sermon to her ears, in the shape of an indistinct, but varied, murmur and flow of the minister's very peculiar voice.

This vocal organ was in itself a rich endowment; insomuch that a listener, comprehending nothing of the language in which the preacher spoke, might still have been swayed to and fro by the mere tone and cadence. Like all other music, it breathed passion and pathos, and emotions high or tender, in a tongue native to the human heart, wherever educated. Muffled as the sound was by its passage through the church-walls, Hester Prynne listened with such intentness, and sympathized so intimately, that the sermon had throughout a meaning for her, entirely apart from its indistinguishable words. These, perhaps, if more distinctly heard, might have been only a grosser medium, and have clogged the spiritual sense. Now she caught the low undertone, as of the wind sinking down to repose itself; then ascended with it, as it rose through progressive gradations of sweetness and power, until its volume seemed to envelop her with an atmosphere of awe and solemn grandeur. And yet, majestic as the voice sometimes became, there was for ever in it an essential character of plaintiveness. A loud or low expression of anguish, — the whisper, or the shriek, as it might be conceived, of suffering humanity, that touched a sensibility in every bosom! At times this deep strain of pathos was all that could be heard, and scarcely heard, sighing amid a desolate silence. But even when the minister's voice grew high and commanding, — when it gushed irrepressibly upward, — when it assumed its utmost breadth and power, so overfilling the church as to burst its way through the solid walls, and diffuse itself in the open air, — still, if the auditor listened intently, and for the purpose, he could detect the same cry of pain. What was it? The complaint of a human heart, sorrow-laden, perchance guilty, telling its secret, whether of guilt or sorrow, to the great heart of mankind; beseeching its sympathy or forgiveness, — at every moment, — in each accent, — and never in vain! It was this profound and continual undertone that gave the clergyman his most appropriate power.

During all this time Hester stood, statue-like, at the foot of the scaffold. If the minister's voice had not kept her there, there would nevertheless have been an inevitable magnetism in that spot, whence she dated the first hour of her life of ignominy. There was a sense within her, — too ill-defined to be made a thought, but weighing heavily on her mind, — that her whole orb of life, both before and after, was connected with this spot, as with the one point that gave it unity.

Little Pearl, meanwhile, had quitted her mother's side, and was playing at her own will about the market-place. She made the sombre crowd cheerful by her erratic and glistening ray; even as a bird of bright plumage illuminates a whole tree of dusky foliage by darting to and fro, half seen and half concealed, amid the twilight of the clustering leaves. She had an undulating, but, oftentimes, a sharp and irregular movement. It indicated the restless vivacity of her spirit, which to-day was doubly indefatigable in its tiptoe dance, because it was played upon and vibrated with her mother's disquietude. Whenever Pearl saw any thing to excite her ever active and wandering curiosity, she flew thitherward, and, as we might say, seized upon that man or thing as her own property, so far as she desired it; but without yielding the minutest degree of control over her motions in requital. The Puritans looked on, and, if they smiled, were none the less inclined to pronounce the child a demon offspring, from the indescribable charm of beauty and eccentricity that shone through her little figure, and sparkled with its activity. She ran and looked the wild Indian in the face; and he grew conscious of a nature wilder than his own. Thence, with native audacity, but still with a reserve as characteristic, she flew into the midst of a group of mariners, the swarthy-cheeked wild men of the ocean, as the Indians were of the land; and they gazed wonderingly and admiringly at Pearl, as if a flake of the sea-foam had taken the shape of a little maid, and were gifted with a soul of the sea-fire, that flashes beneath the prow in the night-time.

One of these seafaring men — the shipmaster, indeed, who had spoken to Hester Prynne — was so smitten with Pearl's aspect, that he attempted to lay hands upon her, with purpose to snatch a kiss. Finding it as impossible to touch her as to catch a humming-bird in the air, he took from his hat the gold chain that was twisted about it, and threw it to the child. Pearl immediately twined it around her neck and waist, with such happy skill, that, once seen there, it became a part of her, and it was difficult to imagine her without it.

"Thy mother is yonder woman with the scarlet letter," said the seaman. "Wilt thou carry her a message from me?"

"If the message pleases me I will," answered Pearl.

"Then tell her," rejoined he, "that I spake again with the black-a-visaged, hump-shouldered old doctor, and he engages to bring his friend, the gentleman she wots of, aboard with him. So let thy mother take no thought, save for herself and thee. Wilt thou tell her this, thou witch-baby?"

"Mistress Hibbins says my father is the Prince of the Air!" cried Pearl, with her naughty smile. "If thou callest me that ill name, I shall tell him of thee; and he will chase thy ship with a tempest!"

Pursuing a zigzag course across the market-place, the child returned to her mother, and communicated what the mariner had said. Hester's strong, calm, stedfastly enduring spirit almost sank, at last, on beholding this dark and grim countenance of an inevitable doom, which — at the moment when a passage seemed to open for the minister and herself out of their labyrinth of misery — showed itself, with an unrelenting smile, right in the midst of their path.

With her mind harassed by the terrible perplexity in which the shipmaster's intelligence involved her, she was also subjected to another trial. There were many people present, from the country roundabout, who had often heard of the scarlet letter, and to whom it had been made terrific by a hundred false or exaggerated rumors, but who had never beheld it with their own bodily eyes. These, after exhausting other modes of amusement, now thronged about Hester Prynne with rude and boorish intrusiveness. Unscrupulous as it was, however, it could not bring them nearer than a circuit of several yards. At that distance they accordingly stood, fixed there by the centrifugal force of the repugnance which the mystic symbol inspired. The whole gang of sailors, likewise, observing the press of spectators, and learning the purport of the scarlet letter, came and thrust their sunburnt and desperado-looking faces into the ring. Even the Indians were affected by a sort of cold shadow of the white man's curiosity, and, gliding through the crowd, fastened their snake-like black eyes on Hester's bosom; conceiving, perhaps, that the wearer of this brilliantly embroidered badge must needs be a personage of high dignity among her people. Lastly, the inhabitants of the town (their own interest in this worn-out subject languidly reviving itself, by sympathy with what they saw others feel) lounged idly to the same quarter, and tormented Hester Prynne, perhaps more than all the rest, with their cool, well-acquainted gaze at her familiar shame. Hester saw and recognized the self-same faces of that group of matrons, who had awaited her forthcoming from the prison-door, seven years ago; all save one, the youngest and only compassionate among them, whose burial-robe she had since made. At the final hour, when she was so soon to fling aside the burning letter, it had strangely become the centre of more remark and excitement, and was thus made to sear her breast more painfully, than at any time since the first day she put it on.

While Hester stood in that magic circle of ignominy, where the cunning cruelty of her sentence seemed to have fixed her for ever, the admirable preacher was looking down from the sacred pulpit upon an audience, whose very inmost spirits had yielded to his control. The sainted minister in the church! The woman of the scarlet letter in the market-place! What imagination would have been irreverent enough to surmise that the same scorching stigma was on them both?

XXIII. The Revelation of the Scarlet Letter

The eloquent voice, on which the souls of the listening audience had been borne aloft, as on the swelling waves of the sea, at length came to a pause. There was a momentary silence, profound as what should follow the utterance of oracles. Then ensued a murmur and half-hushed tumult; as if the auditors, released from the high spell that had transported them into the region of another's mind, were returning into themselves, with all their awe and wonder still heavy on them. In a moment more, the crowd began to gush forth from the doors of the church. Now that there was an end, they needed other breath, more fit to support the gross and earthly life into which they relapsed, than that atmosphere which the preacher had converted into words of flame, and had burdened with the rich fragrance of his thought.

In the open air their rapture broke into speech. The street and the market-place absolutely babbled, from side to side, with applauses of the minister. His hearers could not rest until they had told one another of what each knew better than he could tell or hear. According to their united testimony, never had man spoken in so wise, so high, and so holy a spirit, as he that spake this day; nor had inspiration ever breathed through mortal lips more evidently than it did through his. Its influence could be seen, as it were, descending upon him, and possessing him, and continually lifting him out of the written discourse that lay before him, and filling him with ideas that must have been as marvellous to himself as to his audience. His subject, it appeared, had been the relation between the Deity and the communities of mankind, with a special reference to the New England which they were here planting in the wilderness. And, as he drew towards the close, a spirit as of prophecy had come upon him, constraining him to its purpose as mightily as the old prophets of Israel were constrained; only with this difference, that, whereas the Jewish seers had denounced judgments and ruin on their country, it was his mission to foretell a high and glorious destiny for the newly gathered people of the Lord. But, throughout it all, and through the whole discourse, there had been a certain deep, sad undertone of pathos, which could not be interpreted otherwise than as the natural regret of one soon to pass away. Yes; their minister whom they so loved — and who so loved them all, that he could not depart heavenward without a sigh — had the foreboding of untimely death upon him, and would soon leave them in their tears! This idea of his transitory stay on earth gave the last emphasis to the effect which the preacher had produced; it was as if an angel, in his passage to the skies, had shaken his bright wings over the people for an instant, — at once a shadow and a splendor, — and had shed down a shower of golden truths upon them.

Thus, there had come to the Reverend Mr. Dimmesdale — as to most men, in their various spheres, though seldom recognized until they see it far behind them — an epoch of life more brilliant and full of triumph than any previous one, or than any which could hereafter be. He stood, at this moment, on the very proudest eminence of superiority, to which the gifts of intellect, rich lore, prevailing eloquence, and a reputation of whitest sanctity, could exalt a clergyman in New England's earliest days, when the professional character was of itself a lofty pedestal. Such was the position which the minister occupied, as he bowed his head forward on the cushions of the pulpit, at the close of his Election Sermon. Meanwhile, Hester Prynne was standing beside the scaffold of the pillory, with the scarlet letter still burning on her breast!

Now was heard again the clangor of the music, and the measured tramp of the military escort, issuing from the church-door. The procession was to be marshalled thence to the town-hall, where a solemn banquet would complete the ceremonies of the day.

Once more, therefore, the train of venerable and majestic fathers was seen moving through a broad pathway of the people, who drew back reverently, on either side, as the Governor and magistrates, the old and wise men, the holy ministers, and all that were eminent and renowned, advanced into the midst of them. When they were fairly in the market-place, their presence was greeted by a shout. This — though doubtless it might acquire additional force and volume from the childlike loyalty which the age awarded to its rulers — was felt to be an irrepressible outburst of the enthusiasm kindled in the auditors by that high strain of eloquence which was yet reverberating in their ears. Each felt the impulse in himself, and, in the same breath, caught it from his neighbour. Within the church, it had hardly been kept down; beneath the sky, it pealed upward to the zenith. There were human beings enough, and enough of highly wrought and symphonious feeling, to produce that more impressive sound than the organ-tones of the blast, or the thunder, or the roar of the sea; even that mighty swell of many voices, blended into one great voice by the universal impulse which makes likewise one vast heart out of the many. Never, from the soil of New England, had gone up such a shout! Never, on New England soil, had stood the man so honored by his mortal brethren as the preacher!

How fared it with him then? Were there not the brilliant particles of a halo in the air about his head? So etherealized by spirit as he was, and so apotheosized by worshipping admirers, did his footsteps in the procession really tread upon the dust of earth?

As the ranks of military men and civil fathers moved onward, all eyes were turned towards the point where the minister was seen to approach among them. The shout died into a murmur, as one portion of the crowd after another obtained a glimpse of him. How feeble and pale he looked amid all his triumph! The energy — or say, rather, the inspiration which had held him up, until he should have delivered the sacred message that brought its own strength along with it from heaven — was withdrawn, now that it had so faithfully performed its office. The glow, which they had just before beheld burning on his cheek, was extinguished, like a flame that sinks down hopelessly among the late-decaying embers. It seemed hardly the face of a man alive, with such a deathlike hue; it was hardly a man with life in him, that tottered on his path so nervelessly, yet tottered, and did not fall!

One of his clerical brethren, — it was the venerable John Wilson, — observing the state in which Mr. Dimmesdale was left by the retiring wave of intellect and sensibility, stepped forward hastily to offer his support. The minister tremulously, but decidedly, repelled the old man's arm. He still walked onward, if that movement could be so described, which rather resembled the wavering effort of an infant, with its mother's arms in view, outstretched to tempt him forward. And now, almost imperceptible as were the latter steps of his progress, he had come opposite the well-remembered and weather-darkened scaffold, where, long since, with all that dreary lapse of time between, Hester Prynne had encountered the world's ignominious stare. There stood Hester, holding little Pearl by the hand! And there was the scarlet letter on her breast! The minister here made a pause; although the music still played the stately and rejoicing march to which the procession moved. It summoned him onward, — onward to the festival! — but here he made a pause.

Bellingham, for the last few moments, had kept an anxious eye upon him. He now left his own place in the procession, and advanced to give assistance; judging from Mr. Dimmesdale's aspect that he must otherwise inevitably fall. But there was something in the latter's expression that warned back the magistrate, although a man not readily obeying the vague intimations that pass from one spirit to another. The crowd, meanwhile, looked on with awe and wonder. This earthly faintness was, in their view, only another phase of the minister's celestial strength; nor would it have seemed a miracle too high to be wrought for one so holy, had he ascended before their eyes, waxing dimmer and brighter, and fading at last into the light of heaven!

He turned towards the scaffold, and stretched forth his arms.

"Hester," said he, "come hither! Come, my little Pearl!"

It was a ghastly look with which he regarded them; but there was something at once tender and strangely triumphant in it. The child, with the bird-like motion which was one of her characteristics, flew to him, and clasped her arms about his knees. Hester Prynne — slowly, as if impelled by inevitable fate, and against her strongest will — likewise drew near, but paused before she reached him. At this instant old Roger Chillingworth thrust himself through the crowd, — or, perhaps, so dark, disturbed, and evil was his look, he rose up out of some nether region, — to snatch back his victim from what he sought to do! Be that as it might, the old man rushed forward and caught the minister by the arm.

"Madman, hold! What is your purpose?" whispered he. "Wave back that woman! Cast off this child! All shall be well! Do not blacken your fame, and perish in dishonor! I can yet save you! Would you bring infamy on your sacred profession?"

"Ha, tempter! Methinks thou art too late!" answered the minister, encountering his eye, fearfully, but firmly. "Thy power is not what it was! With God's help, I shall escape thee now!"

He again extended his hand to the woman of the scarlet letter.

"Hester Prynne," cried he, with a piercing earnestness, "in the name of Him, so terrible and so merciful, who gives me grace, at this last moment, to do what — for my own heavy sin and miserable agony — I withheld myself from doing seven years ago, come hither now, and twine thy strength about me! Thy strength, Hester; but let it be guided by the will which God hath granted me! This wretched and wronged old man is opposing it with all his might! — with all his own might and the fiend's! Come, Hester, come! Support me up yonder scaffold!"

The crowd was in a tumult. The men of rank and dignity, who stood more immediately around the clergyman, were so taken by surprise, and so perplexed as to the purport of what they saw, — unable to receive the explanation which most readily presented itself, or to imagine any other, — that they remained silent and inactive spectators of the judgment which Providence seemed about to work. They beheld the minister, leaning on Hester's shoulder and supported by her arm around him, approach the scaffold, and ascend its steps; while still the little hand of the sin-born child was clasped in his. Old Roger Chillingworth followed, as one intimately connected with the drama of guilt and sorrow in which they had all been actors, and well entitled, therefore, to be present at its closing scene.

"Hadst thou sought the whole earth over," said he, looking darkly at the clergyman, "there was no one place so secret, — no high place nor lowly place, where thou couldst have escaped me, — save on this very scaffold!"

"Thanks be to Him who hath led me hither!" answered the minister.

Yet he trembled, and turned to Hester with an expression of doubt and anxiety in his eyes, not the less evidently betrayed, that there was a feeble smile upon his lips.

"Is not this better," murmured he, "than what we dreamed of in the forest?"

"I know not! I know not!" she hurriedly replied. "Better? Yea; so we may both die, and little Pearl die with us!"

"For thee and Pearl, be it as God shall order," said the minister; "and God is merciful! Let me now do the will which he hath made plain before my sight. For, Hester, I am a dying man. So let me make haste to take my shame upon me."

Partly supported by Hester Prynne, and holding one hand of little Pearl's, the Reverend Mr. Dimmesdale turned to the dignified and venerable rulers; to the holy ministers, who were his brethren; to the people, whose great heart was thoroughly appalled, yet overflowing with tearful sympathy, as knowing that some deep life-matter — which, if full of sin, was full of anguish and repentance likewise — was now to be laid open to them. The sun, but little past its meridian, shone down upon the clergyman, and gave a distinctness to his figure, as he stood out from all the earth to put in his plea of guilty at the bar of Eternal Justice.

"People of New England!" cried he, with a voice that rose over them, high, solemn, and majestic, — yet had always a tremor through it, and sometimes a shriek, struggling up out of a fathomless depth of remorse and woe, — "ye, that have loved me! — ye, that have deemed me holy! — behold me here, the one sinner of the world! At last! — at last! — I stand upon the spot where, seven years since, I should have stood; here, with this woman, whose arm, more than the little strength wherewith I have crept hitherward, sustains me, at this dreadful moment, from grovelling down upon my face! Lo, the scarlet letter which Hester wears! Ye have all shuddered at it! Wherever her walk hath been, — wherever, so miserably burdened, she may have hoped to find repose, — it hath cast a lurid gleam of awe and horrible repugnance roundabout her. But there stood one in the midst of you, at whose brand of sin and infamy ye have not shuddered!"

It seemed, at this point, as if the minister must leave the remainder of his secret undisclosed. But he fought back the bodily weakness, — and, still more, the faintness of heart, — that was striving for the mastery with him. He threw off all assistance, and stepped passionately forward a pace before the woman and the child.

"It was on him!" he continued, with a kind of fierceness; so determined was he to speak out the whole. "God's eye beheld it! The angels were for ever pointing at it! The Devil knew it well, and fretted it continually with the touch of his burning finger! But he hid it cunningly from men, and walked among you with the mien of a spirit, mournful, because so pure in a sinful world! — and sad, because he missed his heavenly kindred! Now, at the death-hour, he stands up before you! He bids you look again at Hester's scarlet letter! He tells you, that, with all its mysterious horror, it is but the shadow of what he bears on his own breast, and that even this, his own red stigma, is no more than the type of what has seared his inmost heart! Stand any here that question God's judgment on a sinner? Behold! Behold a dreadful witness of it!"

With a convulsive motion he tore away the ministerial band from before his breast. It was revealed! But it were irreverent to describe that revelation. For an instant the gaze of the horror-stricken multitude was concentred on the ghastly miracle; while the minister stood with a flush of triumph in his face, as one who, in the crisis of acutest pain, had won a victory. Then, down he sank upon the scaffold! Hester partly raised him, and supported his head against her bosom. Old Roger Chillingworth knelt down beside him, with a blank, dull countenance, out of which the life seemed to have departed.

"Thou hast escaped me!" he repeated more than once. "Thou hast escaped me!"

"May God forgive thee!" said the minister. "Thou, too, hast deeply sinned!"

He withdrew his dying eyes from the old man, and fixed them on the woman and the child.

"My little Pearl," said he feebly, — and there was a sweet and gentle smile over his face, as of a spirit sinking into deep repose; nay, now that the burden was removed, it seemed almost as if he would be sportive with the child, — "dear little Pearl, wilt thou kiss me now? Thou wouldst not yonder, in the forest! But now thou wilt?"

Pearl kissed his lips. A spell was broken. The great scene of grief, in which the wild infant bore a part, had developed all her sympathies; and as her tears fell upon her father's cheek, they were the pledge that she would grow up amid human joy and sorrow, nor for ever do battle with the world, but be a woman in it. Towards her mother, too, Pearl's errand as a messenger of anguish was all fulfilled.

"Hester," said the clergyman, "farewell!"

"Shall we not meet again?" whispered she, bending her face down close to his. "Shall we not spend our immortal life together? Surely, surely, we have ransomed one another, with all this woe! Thou lookest far into eternity, with those bright dying eyes! Then tell me what thou seest?"

"Hush, Hester, hush!" said he, with tremulous solemnity. "The law we broke! — the sin here so awfully revealed! — let these alone be in thy thoughts! I fear! I fear! It may be, that, when we forgot our God, — when we violated our reverence each for the other's soul, — it was thenceforth vain to hope that we could meet hereafter, in an everlasting and pure reunion. God knows; and He is merciful! He hath proved his mercy, most of all, in my afflictions. By giving me this burning torture to bear upon my breast! By sending yonder dark and terrible old man, to keep the torture always at red-heat! By bringing me hither, to die this death of triumphant ignominy before the people! Had either of these agonies been wanting, I had been lost for ever! Praised be his name! His will be done! Farewell!"

That final word came forth with the minister's expiring breath. The multitude, silent till then, broke out in a strange, deep voice of awe and wonder, which could not as yet find utterance, save in this murmur that rolled so heavily after the departed spirit.

XXIV. Conclusion

After many days, when time sufficed for the people to arrange their thoughts in reference to the foregoing scene, there was more than one account of what had been witnessed on the scaffold.

Most of the spectators testified to having seen, on the breast of the unhappy minister, a SCARLET LETTER — the very semblance of that worn by Hester Prynne — imprinted in the flesh. As regarded its origin, there were various explanations, all of which must necessarily have been conjectural. Some affirmed that the Reverend Mr. Dimmesdale, on the very day when Hester Prynne first wore her ignominious badge, had begun a course of penance, — which he afterwards, in so many futile methods, followed out, — by inflicting a hideous torture on himself. Others contended that the stigma had not been produced until a long time subsequent, when old Roger Chillingworth, being a potent necromancer, had caused it to appear, through the agency of magic and poisonous drugs. Others, again, — and those best able to appreciate the minister's peculiar sensibility, and the wonderful operation of his spirit upon the body, — whispered their belief, that the awful symbol was the effect of the ever active tooth of remorse, gnawing from the inmost heart outwardly, and at last manifesting Heaven's dreadful judgment by the visible presence of the letter. The reader may choose among these theories. We have thrown all the light we could acquire upon the portent, and would gladly, now that it has done its office, erase its deep print out of our own brain; where long meditation has fixed it in very undesirable distinctness.

It is singular, nevertheless, that certain persons, who were spectators of the whole scene, and professed never once to have removed their eyes from the Reverend Mr. Dimmesdale, denied that there was any mark whatever on his breast, more than on a new-born infant's. Neither, by their report, had his dying words acknowledged, nor even remotely implied, any, the slightest connection, on his part, with the guilt for which Hester Prynne had so long worn the scarlet letter. According to these highly respectable witnesses, the minister, conscious that he was dying, — conscious, also, that the reverence of the multitude placed him already among saints and angels, — had desired, by yielding up his breath in the arms of that fallen woman, to express to the world how utterly nugatory is the choicest of man's own righteousness. After exhausting life in his efforts for mankind's spiritual good, he had made the manner of his death a parable, in order to impress on his admirers the mighty and mournful lesson, that, in the view of Infinite Purity, we are sinners all alike. It was to teach them, that the holiest among us has but attained so far above his fellows as to discern more clearly the Mercy which looks down, and repudiate more utterly the phantom of human merit, which would look aspiringly upward. Without disputing a truth so momentous, we must be allowed to consider this version of Mr. Dimmesdale's story as only an instance of that stubborn fidelity with which a man's friends — and especially a clergyman's — will sometimes uphold his character; when proofs, clear as the mid-day sunshine on the scarlet letter, establish him a false and sin-stained creature of the dust.

The authority which we have chiefly followed — a manuscript of old date, drawn up from the verbal testimony of individuals, some of whom had known Hester Prynne, while others had heard the tale from contemporary witnesses — fully confirms the view taken in the foregoing pages. Among many morals which press upon us from the poor minister's miserable experience, we put only this into a sentence: — "Be true! Be true! Be true! Show freely to the world, if not your worst, yet some trait whereby the worst may be inferred!"

Nothing was more remarkable than the change which took place, almost immediately after Mr. Dimmesdale's death, in the appearance and demeanour of the old man known as Roger Chillingworth. All his strength and energy — all his vital and intellectual force — seemed at once to desert him; insomuch that he positively withered up, shrivelled away, and almost vanished from mortal sight, like an uprooted weed that lies wilting in the sun. This unhappy man had made the very principle of his life to consist in the pursuit and systematic exercise of revenge; and when, by its completest triumph and consummation, that evil principle was left with no further material to support it, — when, in short, there was no more devil's work on earth for him to do, it only remained for the unhumanized mortal to betake himself whither his Master would find him tasks enough, and pay him his wages duly. But, to all these shadowy beings, so long our near acquaintances, — as well Roger Chillingworth as his companions, — we would fain be merciful. It is a curious subject of observation and inquiry, whether hatred and love be not the same thing at bottom. Each, in its utmost development, supposes a high degree of intimacy and heart-knowledge; each renders one individual dependent for the food of his affections and spiritual life upon another; each leaves the passionate lover, or the no less passionate hater, forlorn and desolate by the withdrawal of his object. Philosophically considered, therefore, the two passions seem essentially the same, except that one happens to be seen in a celestial radiance, and the other in a dusky and lurid glow. In the spiritual world, the old physician and the minister — mutual victims as they have been — may, unawares, have found their earthly stock of hatred and antipathy transmuted into golden love.

Leaving this discussion apart, we have a matter of business to communicate to the reader. At old Roger Chillingworth's decease (which took place within the year), and by his last will and testament, of which

Governor Bellingham and the Reverend Mr. Wilson were executors, he bequeathed a very considerable amount of property, both here and in England, to little Pearl, the daughter of Hester Prynne.

So Pearl — the elf-child, — the demon offspring, as some people, up to that epoch, persisted in considering her — became the richest heiress of her day, in the New World. Not improbably, this circumstance wrought a very material change in the public estimation; and, had the mother and child remained here, little Pearl, at a marriageable period of life, might have mingled her wild blood with the lineage of the devoutest Puritan among them all. But, in no long time after the physician's death, the wearer of the scarlet letter disappeared, and Pearl along with her. For many years, though a vague report would now and then find its way across the sea, — like a shapeless piece of driftwood tost ashore, with the initials of a name upon it, — yet no tidings of them unquestionably authentic were received. The story of the scarlet letter grew into a legend. Its spell, however, was still potent, and kept the scaffold awful where the poor minister had died, and likewise the cottage by the sea-shore, where Hester Prynne had dwelt. Near this latter spot, one afternoon, some children were at play, when they beheld a tall woman, in a gray robe, approach the cottage-door. In all those years it had never once been opened; but either she unlocked it, or the decaying wood and iron yielded to her hand, or she glided shadow-like through these impediments, — and, at all events, went in.

On the threshold she paused, — turned partly round, — for, perchance, the idea of entering, all alone, and all so changed, the home of so intense a former life, was more dreary and desolate than even she could bear. But her hesitation was only for an instant, though long enough to display a scarlet letter on her breast.

And Hester Prynne had returned, and taken up her long-forsaken shame. But where was little Pearl? If still alive, she must now have been in the flush and bloom of early womanhood. None knew — nor ever learned, with the fulness of perfect certainty — whether the elf-child had gone thus untimely to a maiden grave; or whether her wild, rich nature had been softened and subdued, and made capable of a woman's gentle happiness. But, through the remainder of Hester's life, there were indications that the recluse of the scarlet letter was the object of love and interest with some inhabitant of another land. Letters came, with armorial seals upon them, though of bearings unknown to English heraldry. In the cottage there were articles of comfort and luxury, such as Hester never cared to use, but which only wealth could have purchased, and affection have imagined for her. There were trifles, too, little ornaments, beautiful tokens of a continual remembrance, that must have been wrought by delicate fingers, at the impulse of a fond heart. And, once, Hester was seen embroidering a baby-garment, with such a lavish richness of golden fancy as would have raised a public tumult, had any infant, thus apparelled, been shown to our sombre-hued community.

In fine, the gossips of that day believed, — and Mr. Surveyor Pue, who made investigations a century later, believed, — and one of his recent successors in office, moreover, faithfully believes, — that Pearl was not only alive, but married, and happy, and mindful of her mother; and that she would most joyfully have entertained that sad and lonely mother at her fireside.

But there was a more real life for Hester Prynne, here, in New England, than in that unknown region where Pearl had found a home. Here had been her sin; here, her sorrow; and here was yet to be her penitence. She had returned, therefore, and resumed, — of her own free will, for not the sternest magistrate of that iron period would have imposed it, — resumed the symbol of which we have related so dark a tale. Never afterwards did it quit her bosom. But, in the lapse of the toilsome, thoughtful, and self-devoted years that made up Hester's life, the scarlet letter ceased to be a stigma which attracted the world's scorn and bitterness, and became a type of something to be sorrowed over, and looked upon with awe, yet with reverence too. And, as Hester Prynne had no selfish ends, nor lived in any measure for her own profit and enjoyment, people brought all their sorrows and perplexities, and besought her counsel, as one who had herself gone through a mighty trouble. Women, more especially, — in the continually recurring trials of wounded, wasted, wronged, misplaced, or erring and sinful passion, — or with the dreary burden of a heart unyielded, because unvalued and unsought, — came to Hester's cottage, demanding why they were so wretched, and what the remedy! Hester comforted and counselled them, as best she might. She assured them, too, of her firm belief, that, at some brighter period, when the world should have grown ripe for it, in Heaven's own time, a new truth would be revealed, in order to establish the whole relation between man and woman on a surer ground of mutual happiness. Earlier in life, Hester had vainly imagined that she herself might be the destined prophetess, but had long since recognized the impossibility that any mission of divine and mysterious truth should be confided to a woman stained with sin, bowed down with shame, or even burdened with a life-long sorrow. The angel and apostle of the coming revelation must be a woman, indeed, but lofty, pure, and beautiful; and wise, moreover, not through dusky grief, but the ethereal medium of joy; and showing how sacred love should make us happy, by the truest test of a life successful to such an end!

So said Hester Prynne, and glanced her sad eyes downward at the scarlet letter. And, after many, many years, a new grave was delved, near an old and sunken one, in that burial-ground beside which King's Chapel has since been built. It was near that old and sunken grave, yet with a space between, as if the dust of the two sleepers had no right to mingle. Yet one tombstone served for both. All around, there were monuments carved with armorial bearings; and on this simple slab of slate — as the curious investigator may still discern, and perplex himself with the purport — there appeared the semblance of an engraved escutcheon. It bore a device, a herald's wording of which might serve for a motto and brief description of our now concluded legend; so sombre is it, and relieved only by one ever-glowing point of light gloomier than the shadow: —

"ON A FIELD, SABLE, THE LETTER A, GULES."°

THE END.

gules: Red.

Contextual Documents and Illustrations

Supryia M. Ray

This selection of contextual documents and illustrations is designed to help readers understand two time periods central to *The Scarlet Letter:* the mid-seventeenth century, during which Nathaniel Hawthorne set the novel, and the mid-nineteenth century, which is when he wrote it. Like any author writing about a time far removed from his own, Hawthorne relied on numerous sources, including Caleb Snow's *A History of Boston,* first published in 1825, in describing the Puritan culture and community in which Hester Prynne lived, and he was doubtless influenced by the events, attitudes, and culture of his own day. The documents and illustrations included here are divided into seven sections: Personal Contexts, Puritan Contexts, Indians, Adultery, The Status and Role of Women, The Education and Custody of Children, and The Publication of *The Scarlet Letter.*

Personal Contexts

The first section highlights a few aspects of Nathaniel Hawthorne's life, including his courtship of Sophia Peabody and his experiences with Brook Farm and the Salem Custom House, both of which made a deep (and decidedly negative) impression on him. Portraits of Hawthorne and Sophia are followed by excerpts from two letters that Hawthorne wrote during their courtship. In the first, dated July 24–25, 1839, Hawthorne, referring to himself and Sophia as already married, proposes marriage and requests that Sophia keep the news secret because "the world might, as yet, misjudge us." In the second, dated August 8, 1839, Hawthorne expresses his joy at Sophia's acceptance of his proposal and writes of her beneficial spiritual influence on him. The couple was married at the Peabody home nearly three years later, on July 9, 1842, after a lengthy, secret engagement.

Next come two documentary excerpts regarding Brook Farm, a utopian community in which Hawthorne invested and lived for about six months, from April to October 1841. The first excerpt, from a letter written on November 9, 1840, by Brook Farm cofounder and Unitarian minister George Ripley to Ralph Waldo Emerson, the famous transcendentalist and essayist, sets forth Ripley's general vision for the community. (Hawthorne, who was much disappointed in the venture, ended up suing Ripley for the return of his investment and, though he won a partial judgment in his favor, was never able to collect on it. In referring to the community in "The Custom-House," he speaks of "my fellowship of toil and impracticable schemes, with the dreamy brethren of Brook Farm" [p. 38 in this volume]). The second excerpt, from the autobiography of Georgiana Bruce Kirby, a Brook Farm resident for four years, focuses on Kirby's impressions of Hawthorne.

The last two items in this section are both illustrations related to the Salem Custom House. The first is a photograph of the Custom House itself. The second is a political cartoon about the 1848 election, in which Whig candidate Zachary Taylor ultimately defeated Democratic candidate Lewis Cass. The cartoon, which was probably published before the Whig national convention, depicts Cass and incumbent Democratic president James Polk as executioners of those who have displeased them. In Hawthorne's own life, the "execution" involved a reversal of parties, as Hawthorne, a Democrat, lost his position as Surveyor at the hands of the Whigs. As Hawthorne wrote in "The Custom-House," "Keeping up the metaphor of the political guillotine, the whole may be considered as the POSTHUMOUS PAPERS OF A DECAPITATED SURVEYOR; and the sketch which I am now bringing to a close, if too autobiographical for a modest person to publish in his lifetime, will readily be excused in a gentleman who writes from beyond the grave" (p. 52).

Nathaniel Hawthorne at Forty-six. Oil Portrait by Cephas Giovanni Thompson (1850). This portrait depicts Hawthorne as he looked when *The Scarlet Letter* was published.

The Grolier Club of New York. Gift of Stephen A. Wakeman, 1913.

Sophia Peabody. Etching by S. A. Schoff.

Photograph Courtesy Peabody Essex Museum.

NATHANIEL HAWTHORNE

From Letter to Sophia Peabody (July 24 and 25, 1839)

Mine own,

I am tired this evening, as usual, with my long day's toil; and my head wants its pillow — and my soul yearns for the friend whom God has given it — whose soul He has married to my soul. Oh, my dearest, how that thought thrills me! We *are* married! I felt it long ago; and sometimes, when I was seeking for some fondest word, it has been on my lips to call you — "Wife"! I hardly know what restrained me from speaking it — unless a dread (for *that* would have been an infinite pang to me) of feeling you shrink back from my bosom, and thereby discovering that there was yet a deep place in your soul which did not know me. Mine own Dove, need I fear it now? Are we not married? God knows we are. Often, while holding you in my arms, I have silently given myself to you, and received you for my portion of human love and happiness, and have prayed Him to consecrate and bless the union. And any one of our innocent embraces — even when our lips did but touch for a moment, and then were withdrawn — dearest, was it not the symbol of a bond between our Souls, infinitely stronger than any external rite could twine around us? Yes — we are married; and as God himself has joined us, we may trust never to be separated, neither in Heaven nor on Earth. We will wait patiently and quietly, and He will lead us onward hand in hand (as He has done all along) like little children, and will guide us to our perfect happiness — and will teach us when our union is to be revealed to the world. My beloved, why should we be silent to one another — why should our lips be silent — any longer on this subject? The world might, as yet, misjudge us; and therefore we will not speak to the world; but when I hold you in my arms, why should we not commune together about all our hopes of earthly and external, as well as our faith of inward and eternal union? Farewell for to-night, my dearest — my soul's bride!

From Nathaniel Hawthorne, *The Letters 1813–1843*, ed. Thomas Woodson, L. Neal Smith, and Norman Holmes Pearson (Columbus: Ohio State UP, 1984), 329–30. Volume 15 of *The Centenary Edition of the Works of Nathaniel Hawthorne.*

. . . Perchance — but do not be frightened, dearest — the soul would wither and die within me, leaving nothing but the busy machine, no germ for immortality, nothing that could taste of heaven, if it were not for the consciousness of your deep, deep love, which is renewed to me with every letter. Oh, my Dove, I have really thought sometimes, that God gave you to me to be the salvation of my soul.

NATHANIEL HAWTHORNE

From **Letter to Sophia Peabody (August 8, 1839)**

True it is, that I never look heavenward without thinking of you, and I doubt whether it would much surprise me to catch a glimpse of you among those upper regions. Then would all that is spiritual within me yearn so towards you, that I should leave my earthly incumbrances behind, and float upward and embrace you in the heavenly sunshine. Yet methinks I shall be more content to spend a lifetime of earthly and heavenly happiness intermixed. So human am I, my beloved, that I would not give up the hope of loving and cherishing you by a fireside of our own, not for any unimaginable bliss of higher spheres. Your influence shall purify me and fit me for a better world — but it shall be by means of our happiness here below. . . .

Oh, how happy you make me by calling me your husband — by subscribing yourself my Wife. I kiss that word when I meet it in your letters; and I repeat over and over to myself, "she is my Wife — I am her Husband." Dearest, I could almost think that the institution of marriage was ordained, first of all, for you and me, and for you and me alone; it seems so fresh and new — so unlike anything that the people around us enjoy or are acquainted with. Nobody ever had a wife but me — nobody a husband, save my Dove. Would that the husband were worthier of his wife; but she loves him — and her wise and prophetic heart could never do so if he were utterly unworthy.

From *The Letters, 1813–1843* (Columbus: Ohio State UP, 1984), 333–34.

GEORGE RIPLEY

From Letter to Ralph Waldo Emerson (November 9, 1840)

My Dear Sir, — Our conversation in Concord was of such a general nature, that I do not feel as if you were in complete possession of the idea of the Association which I wish to see established. As we have now a prospect of carrying it into effect at an early period, I wish to submit the plan more distinctly to your judgment, that you may decide whether it is one that can have the benefit of your aid and cooperation.

Our objects, as you know, are to insure a more natural union between intellectual and manual labor than now exists; to combine the thinker and the worker, as far as possible, in the same individual; to guarantee the highest mental freedom, by providing all with labor, adapted to their tastes and talents, and securing to them the fruits of their industry; to do away the necessity of menial services, by opening the benefits of education and the profits of labor to all; and thus to prepare a society of liberal, intelligent, and cultivated persons, whose relations with each other would permit a more simple and wholesome life, than can be led amidst the pressure of our competitive institutions.

To accomplish these objects, we propose to take a small tract of land, which, under skillful husbandry, uniting the garden and the farm, will be adequate to the subsistence of the families; and to connect with this a school or college, in which the most complete instruction shall be given, from the first rudiments to the highest culture. Our farm would be a place for improving the race of men that lived on it; thought would preside over the operations of labor, and labor would contribute to the expansion of thought; we should have industry without drudgery, and true equality without its vulgarity.

From *History Matters,* January 2005 <http://historymatters.gmu.edu/d/6592>.

GEORGIANA BRUCE KIRBY

From Years of Experience: An Autobiographical Narrative (1887)

Hawthorne, after spending a year at the community, had now left. No one could have been more out-of-place than he, in a mixed company, no matter how cultivated, worthy, and individualized each member of it might be. He was morbidly shy and reserved, needing to be shielded from his fellows, and obtaining the fruits of observation at second-hand. He was therefore not amenable to the democratic influences at the community, which enriched the others and made them declare in after years that the years or months spent there had been the most valuable ones in their whole lives.

The mischievous Ora G. (the first syllable of her given name had been clipped off as not according with her speaking eyes) would now and then draw him out of himself by her daring badinage, and I am sure he must have been grateful for her doings, but the brisk encounter over, he shrank back into his shell and was again the cold looker-on. In the Blithedale Romance, Hawthorne adapted various characters to suit his purpose in the tale. There was at the Farm a pretty black-eyed girl who, before coming there, had been used as a clairvoyante for examining the patients of a certain physician in Boston. Young in knowledge, as in years, she yet gave the result of her clear-seeing in scientific terms. I never knew whether her powers gave out, or whether her confessor (for she was a Catholic) forbade her to pursue her profession. I think it was she who suggested "Priscilla" to Hawthorne.

From "Transcendental Ideas: Social Reform," *American Transcendentalism Web,* Virginia Commonwealth University, January 2005 <http://www.vcu.edu/engweb/transcendentalism/ideas/brkirby.html>.

The Custom-House, Salem, MA.

Political Guillotine, Lithograph (1848).
Library of Congress/LC-USZ62-69613.

Puritan Contexts

The second section of this selection of contextual documents and illustrations includes a variety of excerpts and illustrations to give the reader both a visual and documentary vantage point on the Puritan setting of *The Scarlet Letter.* First come two maps of New England and the Boston area for 1630–49, a period in which John Winthrop predominated as governor of the Massachusetts Bay Colony and in the last seven years of which Hawthorne set *The Scarlet Letter.* Next is a 1722 map of Boston, with the locations of major buildings such as the governor's house, that Hawthorne would have seen when he read Snow's *History.*

Also included in this section are excerpts and illustrations regarding the Puritans' vision and conception of themselves, their treatment of dissenters and those suspected of witchcraft, their views on punishment, and, finally, an Election Day sermon from the mid-eighteenth century discussing the relation of the individual to the republic. Perhaps the most famous document showing how the Puritans saw themselves is Winthrop's speech, "A Modell of Christian Charity," written and delivered during the Atlantic crossing from England to Massachusetts in 1630, in which he spoke of the colony as "a Citty upon a hill," an image and motif that endures in the American national consciousness to this day. In the excerpt included here, Winthrop speaks of the colonists' covenant with God, urges them always to consider their mission and community, and admonishes them to remember that "the eies of all people are uppon us." Paired with this excerpt is a portrait of Winthrop himself and an illustration of Boston from Snow's *History* that literally looks like a "Citty upon a hill."

The Puritans' response to dissent within the colony is illustrated through the famous case of Anne Hutchinson, a central figure in the Antinomian controversy of 1636–38 who was banished from the Massachusetts Bay Colony and excommunicated from the Church of Boston. Some basic background about Hutchinson and the controversy in which she became embroiled is provided through an excerpt from Peleg Chandler's 1844 account of her case; Chandler's account, which was published in Boston in 1844, would presumably have been available to Hawthorne and provides a mid-nineteenth-century perspective on Puritan treatment of religious dissenters.

The next two excerpts present cases of prosecutions for witchcraft conducted by Puritans in the 1600s. Excerpted first is an account of the Ann Hibbins case, which Hawthorne would have read about in Snow's

History — and which he altered to suit his purposes in writing *The Scarlet Letter.* Notably, after Hibbins's execution, there were no more executions for witchcraft for many years. As Chandler, who included an account of witchcraft trials in his book, wrote: "Notwithstanding the frequent instances of supposed witchcraft in Massachusetts, no person had suffered death there on that account, for nearly thirty years after the execution of Anne Hibbins. The sentence of this woman was disapproved of by many influential men, and her fate probably prevented further prosecutions."[1] Also included in this section is Nathaniel Cary's account of his wife's examination for witchcraft in Salem, Massachusetts, in May 1692, as reported by Boston merchant Robert Calef. Hawthorne's great-grandfather John Hathorne played a leading role in numerous witchcraft examinations, including that of Mrs. Cary. That Hawthorne disavowed Hathorne's actions in the Salem trials (as well as his great-great-grandfather William Hathorne's actions toward Quakers) is evident not only from "The Custom-House," where he characterizes both men as persecutors (p. 27), but also from his decision to add a *w* to his last name, thereby distancing himself from his family's past.

The last items in the Puritan Contexts section are an illustration and an excerpt from an Election Day sermon. In the illustration, a broadside depicting punishment in Puritan society, one Seth Hudson is punished in 1762 in Boston by use of the pillory, whipping, and public confession. The sermon, delivered by Universalist minister E. H. Chapin in 1844, presents something of a contrast with Puritan values as traditionally understood in its elevation of individuality as a public good, essential to the well-being of the republic — even as the event was grounded in a classically Puritan tradition: the delivery of a sermon before public officials on Election Day.

[1] Peleg W. Chandler, *American Criminal Trials,* vol. 1 (Boston: Timothy H. Carter and Company, 1844), 75.

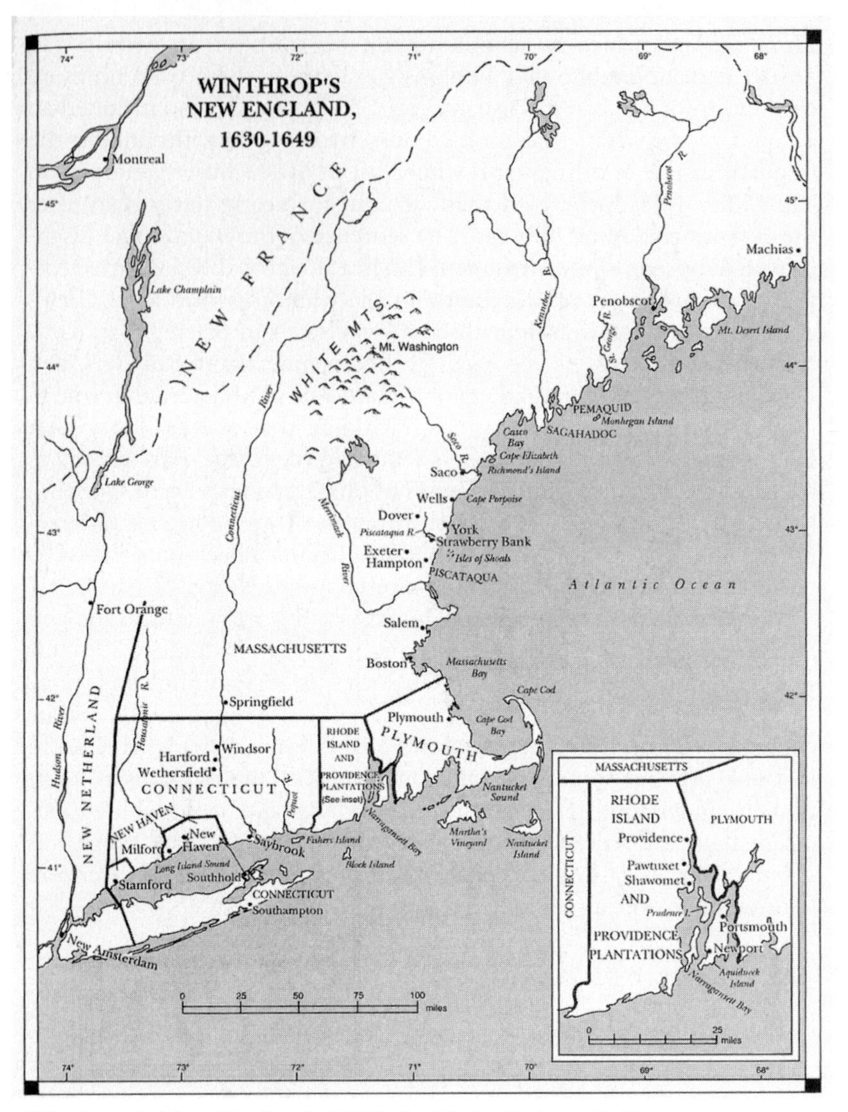

Winthrop's New England, 1630–1649, by Robert C. Forget.
From *The Journal of John Winthrop, 1630–1649*. Used by permission of Richard S. Dunn.

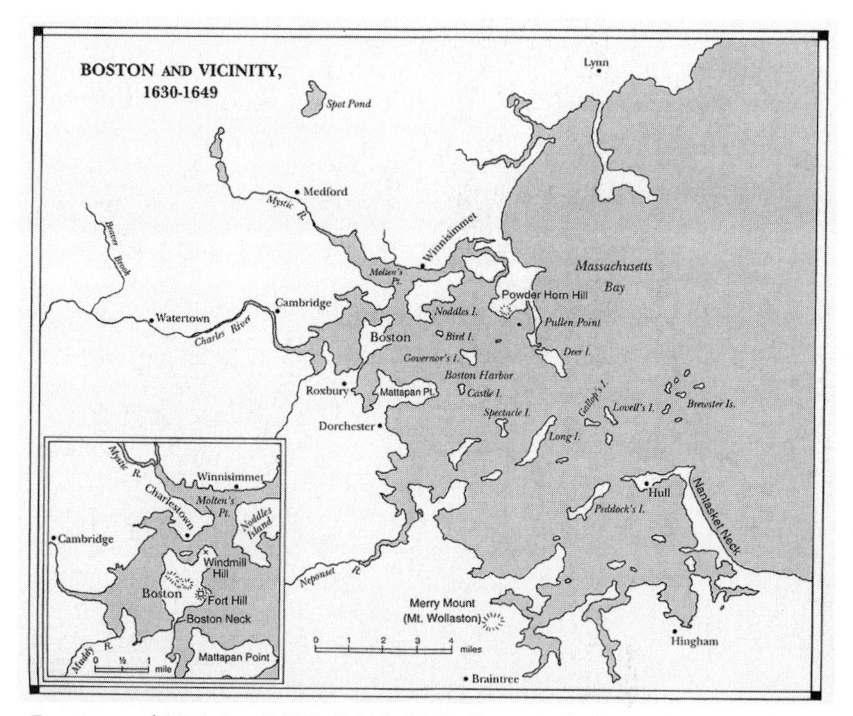

Boston and Vicinity, 1630–1649, by Robert C. Forget.

From *The Journal of John Winthrop, 1630–1649.* Used by permission of Richard S. Dunn.

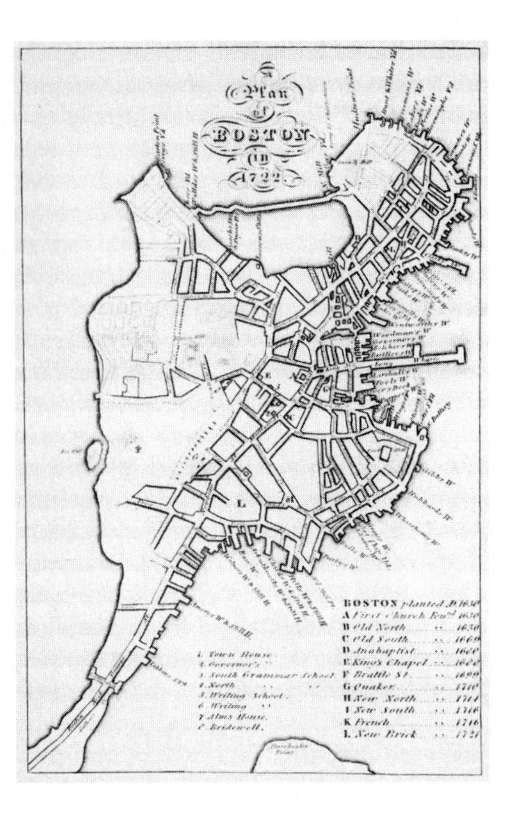

Plan of Boston in 1722, by A. Bowen.
Courtesy of the Massachusetts Historical Society.

JOHN WINTHROP

From A Modell of Christian Charity (1630)

Thus stands the cause betweene God and us, wee are entered into Covenant with him for this worke, wee have taken out a Commission, the Lord hath given us leave to drawe our owne Articles wee have professed to enterprise these Accions upon these and these ends, wee have hereupon besought him of favour and blessing: Now if the Lord shall please to heare us, and bring us in peace to the place wee desire, then hath hee ratified this Covenant and sealed our Commission, [and] will expect a strickt performance of the Articles contained in it, but if wee shall neglect the observacion of these Articles which are the ends wee

From *Colonial Religious Toleration,* which reprints Winthrop's speech from *Winthrop Papers* (Boston: Massachusetts Historical Society, 1929), 2:282–84.

John Winthrop.
Oil on canvas by Charles Osgood, 1834, after a portrait by Van Dyck. Courtesy of the Massachusetts Historical Society.

have propounded, and dissembling with our God, shall fall to embrace this present world and prosecute our carnall intencions, seeking greate things for our selves and our posterity, the Lord will surely breake out in wrathe against us be revenged of such a periured people and make us knowe the price of the breache of such a Covenant.

Now the onely way to avoyde this shipwracke and to provide for our posterity is to followe the Counsell of Micah, to doe Justly, to love mercy, to walke humbly with our God, for this end, wee must be knitt together in this worke as one man, wee must entertaine each other in brotherly Afeccion, wee must be willing to abridge our selves of our superfluities, for the supply of others necessities, wee must uphold a familiar Commerce together in all meekness, gentlenes, patience and liberallity, wee must delight in eache other, make others Condicions our owne rejoice together, mourne together, labour, and suffer together, allwayes having before our eyes our Commission and Community in the worke, our Community as members of the same body, soe shall wee keepe the unitie of the spirit in the bond of peace, the Lord will be our God and delight to dwell among us, as his owne people and will commaund a blessing upon us in all our wayes, soe that wee shall see much more of his wisdome power goodness and truthe then formerly wee have beene acquainted with, wee shall finde that the God of Israell is among us, when tenn of us shall be able to resist a thousand of our enemies, when hee shall make us a prayse and glory, that men shall say of succeeding plantacions; the lord make it like that of New England: for wee must Consider that wee shall be as a Citty upon a Hill, the eies of all people are uppon us; soe that if we shall deale falsely with our God in this worke wee have undertaken and soe cause him to withdrawe his present help from us, wee shall be made a story and a byword through the world, wee shall open the mouthes of enemies to speake evill of the wayes of god and all professours for Gods sake; wee shall shame the faces of many of Gods worthy servants, and cause theire prayers to be turned in Cursses upon us till wee be consumed out of the good land whither we are goeing.

PELEG W. CHANDLER

From Trial of Anne Hutchinson (1844)

A short time before the election of Henry Vane as governor of Massachusetts, in 1636, there came over from Alford, in the neighborhood of Boston, England, William Hutchinson and his wife Anne Hutchinson, who settled in Boston, Massachusetts, and "joined the church." They were well connected, of good estate and reputation, and received much attention in the colony. Mr. Hutchinson was chosen several times a representative of Boston in the general court. It was the fate of his wife to exert an influence in the infant commonwealth, wholly unexampled in one of her sex, and to kindle a strife, which has rendered her the heroine of a passage in its history, as singular, interesting, and tragical, as any it contains. The apparently trifling origin of the difficulties, in which she found herself involved soon after her arrival, is not the least

From Peleg W. Chandler, *American Criminal Trials,* vol. 1 (Boston: Timothy H. Carter and Company, 1844), 3–5, 23, 28–29.

South East View of Boston, by A. Bowen.
Courtesy of the Massachusetts Historical Society.

remarkable part of her story; and the mistake of magnifying and punishing that as heresy, which was simple impropriety, or, at most, harmless fanaticism, is not the least instructive portion of the history of her trial and condemnation.

By a long established custom in Boston, besides the meetings for worship on the Lord's day, and occasional lectures as in other towns, there were frequent private meetings of the brethren of the churches for religious exercises. Mrs. Hutchinson, "a woman of a haughty and fierce carriage, and a very voluble tongue," submitted with impatience to the regulation by which women, at these meetings, were debarred from the privilege of joining in the debates. She therefore set up a meeting of the sisters also, where she repeated the sermons, preached the Lord's day before, adding her own remarks and expositions. The idea was novel. . . .

At first, these meetings met the entire approbation of the clergy; but that powerful and somewhat selfish class soon began to look upon them with disapprobation. They became jealous of the influence of a custom, which brought a power to bear on the religious feelings and views of the female portion of their people, dangerous to their own authority, and wholly out of their control. They discovered, also, or thought they discovered alarming heresies in the doctrines which Mrs. Hutchinson promulgated.

* * *

The sentence was then recorded: "Mrs. Hutchinson, the wife of William Hutchinson, being convented for traducing the ministers and their ministry in the country, she declared voluntarily her revelations, and that she should be delivered and the court ruined with their posterity; and thereupon was banished; and in the meanwhile was committed to Mr. Joseph Welde, of Roxbury, until the court shall dispose of her."

* * *

Such was the fate of Anne Hutchinson; a woman of extraordinary energy, comprehension, and sagacity; in many of her religious views far beyond the age in which she lived; in intellectual ability, superior to her sex. It was probably her misfortune to be craftily made use of for political purposes, to sustain the power and authority of Henry Vane, and to draw the affections of the people from those who were their leaders in the wilderness; and her religious zeal became mixed up with political strife. The effect upon her mind of the encouragement she received from those in authority was not favorable. The admiration, which was expressed for the depth and vigor of her reasoning powers seems to have elevated in her apprehension the gifts of intellect above the graces of character; and she ventured upon extremes of doctrinal theology and fantastic theories, with a zeal and enthusiasm worthy of objects more fitting for her sex.

The merits of her case can scarcely be fairly judged of at the present day. The accounts transmitted to us are obscured by contemporary prejudice and passion; but it is impossible to doubt that she was one of the most remarkable women of that or any other age. Her understanding was bold, vigorous, and strong; her perceptions were keen; and her character, energetic and masculine, was not deficient in the graces which adorn the female sex. Her influence upon the colonists, in the apprehension of the fathers of the commonwealth, was dangerous in the extreme; and they "saw an inevitable necessity to rid her away, except they would be guilty not onely of their own ruine but also of the gospel." Of their right to banish her they entertained no doubt; and it was a right they had frequently exercised on other occasions. The pretence, that it was a mere civil proceeding for the preservation of the authority of the magistrates and the suppression of sedition, without any reference to religious doctrine, personal ill-will, or professional jealousy, will not bear a moment's examination. But it would be most unjust to pronounce judgment upon it by the lights of the present age;

or to visit it with a severity of condemnation, which would show an ignorance of the difficulties, spiritual and natural, with which the fathers of New England had to contend.

CALEB SNOW

From A History of Boston (1825)

The most remarkable occurrence in the colony in the year 1655 was the trial and condemnation of Mrs. Ann Hibbins of Boston for witchcraft. Her husband, who died July 23, 1654, was an agent for the colony in England, several years one of the assistants, and a merchant of note in the town; but losses in the latter part of his life had reduced his estate, and increased the natural crabbedness of his wife's temper, which made her turbulent and quarrelsome, and brought her under church censures, and at length rendered her so odious to her neighbours as to cause some of them to acuse her of witchcraft. The jury brought her in guilty, but the magistrates refused to accept the verdict; so the cause came to the general court, where the popular clamour prevailed against her, and the miserable old lady was condemned and executed in June 1656. Search was made upon her body for tetts,° and in her chests and boxes for puppets or images, but there is no record of any thing of that sort being found. Mr. Beach, a minister of Jamaica, in a letter to Dr. Increase Mather, says, "You may remember what I have sometimes told you your famous Mr. Norton once said at his own table, before Mr. Wilson the pastor, elder Penn and myself and wife, and others, who had the honour to be his guests: — That one of your magistrates' wives, as I remember, was hanged for a witch only for having more wit than her neighbours. It was his very expression; she having, as he explained it, unhappily guessed that two of her persecutors, whom she saw talking in the street, were talking of her, which proving true, cost her her life, notwithstanding all he could do to the contrary, as he himself told us."

This was the third instance of execution for witchcraft in New England.

tetts: Markings.

From Caleb H. Snow, *A History of Boston, the Metropolis of Massachusetts, from Its Origin to the Present Period; With Some Account of the Environs* (Boston: Abel Bowen, 1825), 140–41.

ROBERT CALEF AND NATHANIEL CARY

From Account of Mrs. Cary's Examination for Witchcraft

May 24. Mrs. Cary of Charlestown, was Examined and Committed. Her Husband, Mr. Nathaniel Cary has given account thereof, as also of her Escape, to this Effect,

I having heard some days, that my Wife was accused of Witchcraft, being much disturbed at it, by advice, we went to Salem-Village, to see if the afflicted did know her; we arrived there, 24 May, it happened to be a day appointed for Examination; accordingly soon after our arrival, Mr. Hathorn and Mr. Curwin, etc., went to the Meeting-house, which was the place appointed for that Work; the Minister began with Prayer, and having taken care to get a convenient place, I observed, that the afflicted were two Girls of about Ten Years old, and about two or three other, of about eighteen; one of the Girls talked most, and could discern more than the rest. The Prisoners were called in one by one, and as they came in were cried out of, etc. The Prisoner was placed about 7 or 8 foot from the Justices, and the Accusers between the Justices and them; the Prisoner was ordered to stand right before the Justices, with an Officer appointed to hold each hand, lest they should therewith afflict them; and the Prisoners Eyes must be constantly on the Justices; for if they look'd on the afflicted, they would either fall into Fits, or cry out of being hurt by them; after Examination of the Prisoners, who it was afflicted these Girls, etc., they were put upon saying the Lords Prayer, as a tryal of their guilt; after the afflicted seem'd to be out of their Fits, they would look steadfastly on some one person, and frequently not speak; and then the Justices said they were struck dumb, and after a little time would speak again; then the Justices said to the Accusers, "which of you will go and touch the Prisoner at the Bar?" then the most couragious would adventure, but before they had made three steps would ordinarily fall down as in a Fit; the Justices ordered that they should be taken up and carried to the Prisoner, that she might

From Robert Calef, *More Wonders of the Invisible World* (1700), reprinted in George Lincoln Burr, ed., *Narratives of the Witchcraft Cases, 1648–1706* (New York: Scribner's, 1914). Part of a series entitled *Original Narratives of Early American History.* A similar account can be found in Peleg W. Chandler, *American Criminal Trials,* vol. 1 (Boston: Timothy H. Carter and Company, 1844), 83–87. Chandler cites Calef as his source for Cary's account.

touch them; and as soon as they were touched by the accused, the Justices would say, they are well, before I could discern any alteration; by which I observed that the Justices understood the manner of it. Thus far I was only as a Spectator, my Wife also was there part of the time, but no notice taken of her by the afflicted, except once or twice they came to her and asked her name.

But I having an opportunity to Discourse Mr. Hale (with whom I had formerly acquaintance) I took his advice, what I had best to do, and desired of him that I might have an opportunity to speak with her that accused my Wife; which he promised should be, I acquainting him that I reposed my trust in him.

Accordingly he came to me after the Examination was over and told me I had now an opportunity to speak with the said Accuser, *viz.* Abigail Williams, a Girl of 11 or 12 Years old; but that we could not be in private at Mr. Parris's House, as he had promised me; we went therefore into the Alehouse, where an Indian Man attended us, who it seems was one of the afflicted; to him we gave some Cyder; he shewed several Scars, that seemed as if they had been long there, and shewed them as done by Witchcraft, and acquainted us that his Wife, who also was a Slave, was imprison'd for Witchcraft. And now instead of one Accuser, they all came in, who began to tumble down like Swine; and then three Women were called in to attend them. We in the Room were all at a stand, to see who they would cry out of; but in a short time they cried out, Cary; and immediately after a Warrant was sent from the Justices to bring my Wife before them, who were sitting in a Chamber near by, waiting for this.

Being brought before the Justices, her chief accusers were two Girls; my Wife declared to the Justices, that she never had any knowledge of them before that day; she was forced to stand with her Arms stretched out. I did request that I might hold one of her hands, but it was denied me; then she desired me to wipe the Tears from her Eyes, and the Sweat from her Face, which I did; then she desired she might lean her self on me, saying, she should faint.

Justice Hathorn replied, she had strength enough to torment those persons, and she should have strength enough to stand. I speaking something against their cruel proceedings, they commanded me to be silent, or else I should be turned out of the Room. The Indian before mentioned, was also brought in, to be one of her Accusers: being come in, he now (when before the Justices) fell down and tumbled about like a Hog, but said nothing. The Justices asked the Girls, who afflicted the Indian? they answered she (meaning my Wife) and now lay upon him;

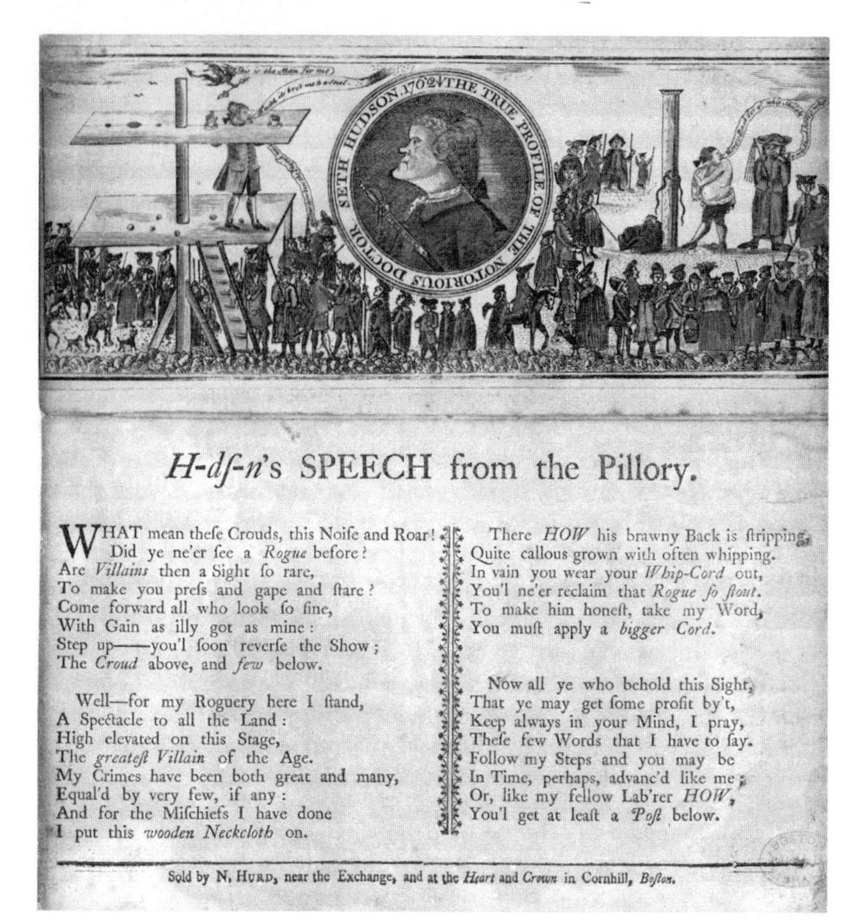

SETH HUDSON 1762 THE TRUE PROFILE OF THE NOTORIOUS DOCTOR

H-dſ-n's SPEECH from the Pillory.

WHAT mean theſe Crouds, this Noiſe and Roar!
Did ye ne'er ſee a *Rogue* before?
Are *Villains* then a Sight ſo rare,
To make you preſs and gape and ſtare?
Come forward all who look ſo fine,
With Gain as illy got as mine:
Step up——you'l ſoon reverſe the Show;
The *Croud* above, and *few* below.

Well—for my Roguery here I ſtand,
A Spectacle to all the Land:
High elevated on this Stage,
The *greateſt Villain* of the Age.
My Crimes have been both great and many,
Equal'd by very few, if any:
And for the Miſchiefs I have done
I put this *wooden Neckcloth* on.

There *HOW* his brawny Back is ſtripping,
Quite callous grown with often whipping.
In vain you wear your *Whip-Cord* out,
You'l ne'er reclaim that *Rogue ſo ſtout.*
To make him honeſt, take my Word,
You muſt apply a *bigger Cord.*

Now all ye who behold this Sight,
That ye may get ſome profit by't,
Keep always in your Mind, I pray,
Theſe few Words that I have to ſay.
Follow my Steps and you may be
In Time, perhaps, advanc'd like me;
Or, like my fellow Lab'rer *HOW*,
You'l get at leaſt a *Poſt* below.

Sold by N. HURD, near the Exchange, and at the *Heart* and *Crown* in Cornhill, *Boſton.*

Broadside Showing the Punishment of Seth Hudson in Boston (1762).
Boston Public Library/Rare Books Department—Courtesy of the Trustees.

the Justices ordered her to touch him, in order to his cure, but her head must be turned another way, least instead of curing, she should make him worse, by her looking on him, her hand being guided to take hold of his; but the Indian took hold on her hand, and pulled her down on the Floor in a barbarous manner; then his hand was taken off, and her hand put on his, and the cure quickly wrought. I being extreamly troubled at their Inhumane dealings, uttered a hasty speech (That God would take vengeance on them, and desired that God would deliver us out of the hands of unmerciful men.). Then her Mittimus° was writ. I did with difficulty and charge obtain the liberty of a Room, but no Beds in it; if there had, could have taken but little rest that Night. She was committed to Boston Prison.

Mittimus: Prison warrant.

E. H. CHAPIN

From The Relation of the Individual to the Republic (1844)

I trust that our assembling here to-day is not a mere form; but that devoutly recognizing the reason for which our fathers instituted this service, we cherish not only their custom but their sentiment. Next to the abolition of all religious ordinances, there is nothing so ominous as a hollow and weary observation of them. . . .

* * *

. . . *The importance of the individual in the republic, and the mutual obligations which rest upon him and upon the State,* form the essential ideas of the discourse to which I now invite your attention. . . .

* * *

But the indissoluble connection between the republic and the individual, presents itself in a two-fold aspect. Not only is every man solemnly obligated to the State, but the converse of this is also true.

* * *

. . . [L]et me specify one or two modes by which a State may affect the moral development of individuals, without encroaching upon private rights.

And first, *by cherishing the interests of education.* In no way can the wealth which has been rendered into the public treasury, be so appropriately distributed for each and for all, as by the establishment of public schools. . . .

* * *

From E. H. Chapin, *The Relation of the Individual to the Republic* (Boston: Dutton and Wentworth, 1844), 5–8, 10–11, 13–14, 16, 18–19, 21–23, 32.

. . . I devoutly thank God, that in Massachusetts the spirit which threw up free schools in the first clearings of the forest, continues to this day, planting those institutions side by side with our churches, and providing with careful vigilance and wise liberality for their efficient operation. Wherever New England influence is felt — and where is New England influence not felt? — they extend a blessing. . . .

* * *

. . . There is another method by which the State may secure the moral culture of the individual, without undue interference with any private right. And that is, *through its criminal legislation.* Society, as a general thing, is too prone to act upon the principle of retaliation. . . . Without interfering with private rights, there is here a direct opportunity to exert moral influence, by making the very punishment that so justly restrains the individual, also the means of his reformation. . . . And when you endeavor to accomplish anything beyond mere *restraint* — when you seek to *reform* men — you can only secure your end by moral power, by which I mean not persuasion merely, but appeals to the conscience, the reason, the heart. Such appeals I call moral power, in contradistinction from the whip, the pillory, the gallows. . . .

. . . But if we act, in our legislation, from the dictates of true republicanism — nay, if we act from the spirit of Christianity, of which republicanism is a specific form — we will seek the reformation of that criminal. . . .

* * *

But we are too prone to consider the State merely as a government, an armed police, a legal functionary that prescribes certain rules of action, regulates our political economy, declares war or makes peace. This idea may suffice for old Europe, but if there is aught that distinguishes our doctrine of civil society from that which lies at the foundation of its feudal dynasties, it is this, — that the republic, the state, is a BROTHERHOOD, consolidated by the sacred interests and bound by the solemn obligations of that relationship. . . .

* * *

But there is an exalted and permanent condition of society, — I call it the highest condition, — which is perfectly accordant with distinct and complete individualism. It is where the *whole man* is developed, and the higher powers of his nature exercise their lawful supremacy. In this case, he acts not like the barbarian from his *passions* and his *will,* but from *reason* and *conscience*. The one refuting the idea that men are held together merely by a gregarious instinct, shows him the true foundation of social union in those broad principles of human brotherhood revealed by Christianity. The other declares his eternal obligations to the right. He preserves his individualism in accordance with the State, because he is himself a state. He has learned self-government, and he knows both how to rule and to obey. In his own soul is a wide dominion perfectly controlled, perfectly free. There are the sanctions of duty, and the oracle of justice, and the law of love. From thence the institutions of society are projected. In maintaining them, he at the same time maintains his individuality. And this constitution of society is republicanism, the essence of which is not state power vested in an abstract authority, but intellectual and moral power developed in an individual. . . .

Have I not rightly concluded, then, that the obligations of the individual to the republic may be condensed into these simple words — that he must be true to his individuality, his *whole* individuality, under all the circumstances? Whatever he may do, let him hold fast his loyalty to reason and conscience, and he is, he must be, loyal to the State. There can be no prosperity, nor virtue, nor glory in the aggregate, when the individual is false to the higher dictates within him. . . .

* * *

. . . Let him feel that the best distinction is honest manhood, and that the proudest title the State can bestow is that of CITIZEN.

INDIANS

This third set of contextual documents and illustrations, the title of which is an antiquated (and, of course, inaccurate) term used both by the Puritans and in Hawthorne's time to refer to Native Americans, focuses primarily on the relationship between Indians and Puritans. Leading off this section is a reprint of the seal of the Massachusetts Bay Colony; the seal, which depicts a Native American with bow and arrow and includes the motto "Come over and help us," illustrates the colonists' view of the natives and their commitment to "civilizing" them. Next is a portrait of John Eliot, an Englishman who came to be known as "the Apostle to the Indians" for his missionary work amongst Native Americans in New England — and the man whom Arthur Dimmesdale visits "among his Indian converts" prior to meeting Hester in the forest in Chapter XVI (p. 146). Eliot, who came to the Massachusetts Bay Colony in 1631, began preaching to Indians in 1646 and later translated the Bible into Algonquian, the language of the natives with whom he was working; a page from Eliot's "Indian Bible," the first Bible printed in North America, is included here. The next set of illustrations are from John Josselyn's *New-Englands Rarities Discovered.* Josselyn, an Englishman who made two trips to Massachusetts, first in 1638 for 15 months and second in 1663 for 8 years, took it upon himself to catalog a variety of plants, animals, and native remedies in his herbal. Notably, it is such native remedies to which Chillingworth attributes much of his medical skill: "My old studies in alchemy . . . and my sojourn, for above a year past, among a people well versed in the kindly properties of simples, have made a better physician of me than many that claim the medical degree. . . . I know not Lethe or Nepenthe, . . . but I have learned many new secrets in the wilderness, and here is one of them, — a recipe that an Indian taught me, in requital of some lessons of my own, that were as old as Paracelsus. Drink it!" (pp. 70–71).

The next two illustrations and both of the excerpts that follow relate to the Puritan experience of Indian captivity, which Hawthorne represented in *The Scarlet Letter* through Chillingworth. As we learn in Chapter III, Chillingworth has "been long held in bonds among the heathen-folk, to the southward; and am now brought hither by this Indian, to be redeemed out of my captivity" (p. 63). In Puritan times — indeed, well into the nineteenth century — being captured by Indians was a serious threat. Captives were taken for a variety of reasons, including revenge, ransom, and adoption, especially as the Native American population dwindled due to war and disease. As captives returned, some began to publish their stories, and the Indian captivity narrative, the first indigenous American literary form, was born. The first captivity illustration included in this section depicts Indians dancing around one captive and poised to shoot another with an arrow. The second illustration, the title page of the most famous captivity narrative, that of Mrs. Mary Rowlandson, accompanies an excerpt from her story. Rowlandson, a minister's wife, was taken captive as a civilian during King Philip's War (1675–76), a conflict between the Indians and the colonists, and was ransomed out of captivity for the (then) princely sum of £20. Her best-selling narrative, which was published in 1682 in both Cambridge, Massachusetts, and London, England, bore two different titles. In America, it was published as *The Soveraignty and Goodness of God, Together, With the Faithfulness of His Promises Displayed; Being a Narrative of the Captivity and Restauration of Mrs. Mary Rowlandson,* emphasizing the religious lessons of her story. In England it was merely called *A True History of the Captivity and Restoration of Mrs. Mary Rowlandson, A Minister's Wife in New-England.*

That Hawthorne was interested in captivity narratives is evidenced by his sketch of an Indian raid on the Duston family home on March 15, 1697, and the ensuing captivity of Mrs. Hannah Duston, the basic facts of which he drew from Cotton Mather's account in *Magnalia Christi Americana.* (Both Cotton Mather and his father, Increase Mather, were leading clergymen in Boston with an interest in Indian captivity stories; Increase Mather played a key role in the publication of Mary Rowlandson's narrative.) The Dustons were famous in their time — Hannah for slaughtering her Indian captors and her husband for rescuing seven of their children during the raid. While Cotton Mather praised Hannah's murderous act, regarding her escape from captivity as nothing less than a miracle, Hawthorne saw things differently. Included here in its entirety is his account of the Duston story, as published in *The American Magazine of Useful and Entertaining Knowledge,* which he edited for six months in 1836.

In *The Scarlet Letter,* it is by being ransomed out of captivity, rather than by murder and escape, that Chillingworth returns to "civilization," but he must have left those who ransomed him wondering whether a complete return was possible. Chillingworth is initially described as "a white man, clad in a strange disarray of civilized and savage costume," standing "[b]y the Indian's side, and evidently sustaining a companionship with him" (p. 62), and he openly attributes his knowledge of "medicinal herbs and roots that grew in the forest" to the "savage people" (p. 69). We are also told that "[t]wo or three individuals hinted, that the man of skill, during his Indian captivity, had enlarged his medical attainments by joining in the incantations of the savage priests; who were universally acknowledged to be powerful enchanters, often performing seemingly miraculous cures by their skill in the black art" (p. 108).

The last item in this section is an excerpt from the writings of Henry Schoolcraft, a nineteenth-century explorer, ethnologist, and Indian agent who wrote extensively on Native Americans and their culture. In this excerpt, Schoolcraft recounts his "earliest impressions of the Indian race" — impressions widely held by the American public in the nineteenth century.

Seal of the Massachusetts Bay Colony.
Courtesy of the Massachusetts Historical Society.

John Eliot ("the Apostle").
Courtesy of The New York Public Library.

Kesteoun muttaok Chap. i. *nequtta tashikquinnu.*

NEGONNE OOSUKKUHWHONK *MOSES,*

Ne asoweetamuk

GENESIS.

CHAP. I.

Weske kutchisik *a* ayum God Kesuk kah Ohke.

2 Kah Ohke mô matta kuhkenauunneunkquttinnoo kah monteagunninno, kah pohkenum woskeche moonôi, kah Nashauanit popomshau woskeche nippekontu.

3 Onk noowau God *b* wequaiaj, kah mô wequai.

4 Kah wunnaumun God wequai ne en wunnegen: Kah wutchadchaabe-ponumun God noeu wequai kah noeu pohkenum.

5 Kah wutussowetamun God wequai Kesukod, kah pohkenum wutussoweetamun Nukon: kah mô wunnonkoowok kah mo mohtompog negonne kesuk.

6 Kah noowau God *c* sepakehtamoudj nôeu nippekontu, kah chadchapemoudj nashauweit nippe wutch nippekontu.

7 Kah ayimup God sepakehtamóonk, kah wutchadchabeponumunnap nashaueu nippe agwu, uttiyeu agwu sepakehtamóonk, kah nashaueu nippekontu uttiyeu ongkouwe sepakehtamóonk, kah mónkô n nih.

8 Kah wuttissoweetamun God *d* sepakehtamóonk Kesukquash, kah mô wunnonkoowok, kah mo mohtompog nahohtôeu kesukok.

9 Kah noowau God moemooidj *e* nippe ut agwu kesukquash kah pasukqunnu, kah pahkemoidj nanabpeu, kah mónkô n nih.

10 Kah wuttissoweetamun God nanabpi ohke, kah mo emoo nippe wuttissowetamun Kehtoh, & wunnaumun God ne en wunnegen.

11 Kah noowau God dtanuekej ohke moskeht, moskeht ikannémunúok ikannémunash, & meechummue mahtugquash meechummúok meechummuonk nish noh pasuk neane wuttinnuhuonk, ubbuhkumminaok et woskeche ohke, kah mônko n nih.

12 Kah ohke dtanaegenup moskeht, kah moskeht ikannemunúok ikannemunash, nish noh pasuk neane wuttinnuhuonk, kah mahtug meechummúok, ubbuhkumminaook wuhhogkut nish noh pasuk neane wattinnuhuonk, kah wunnaumun God ne en wunnegen.

13 Kah mo wunnonkoowok, kah mo mohtompog shwekesukod.

14 Kah noowau God, *f* Wequanantéganúohettich ut wussepakehtamoonganit kesukquash, & pohshachettich ut nashauwe kesukod, kah ut nashauwe nukkonut, kah kukkineasuonganúhhettich, kah uttoocheyeuhettich, kah kesukodtuwwuhhettich, kah kodtummooowuhhettich.

15 Kah n nag wequanantéganuóhettich ut sepakehtamoowonganit wequasumóhettich ohke, onk mô n nih.

16 Kah ayum God neesunash missiyeuash wequanantéganash, wequananteg mohtag nanánumoomoo kesukod, wequananteg peasik nananumoomoo nukon, kah anogqsog.

17 Kah uppónuh God wussepakehtamoonganit kesukquash, woh wequohsumwog ohke.

18 Onk woh *g* wunnananumunneau kesukod kah nukon, kah pohshemoo nashaueu wequai, kah nashaueu pohkénum, kah wunnaumun God ne en wunnegen.

19 Kah mô wunnonkoowok kah mo mohtompog yaou quinukok.

20 Kah noowau God, moonahettich nippekóntu pomomutcheg pomantamwae, kah puppinshaúussog pumunahettich ongkouwe ohket woskeche wussépahkehtamoonganit kesukquash.

21 Kah kezheau God matikkenunutcheh Potabpoh, kah nish noh pomantamoe ôaas noh pompámayit uttiyeug moonacheg nippekontu, nish noh pasuk neane wuttinnuhuonk, kah nish noh pasuk puppinshaash, nish noh pasuk neane wuttinnuhuonk, kah wunnaumun God ne en wunnegen.

22 Kah conanumoh nahhog God noowau, Mishéneetuónittegk, *b* kah muttaanoook, kah numwapegk nippe ut kehtohhannit, kah puppinshaog muttaanhettich ohket.

23 Kah mo wunnonk oo ok kah mo mohtompog napanna audtahshikqui sukok.

24 Kah noowau God, Pasuk [illegible] o'hke ôaas pomantamwieu, nish noh pasuk neane wuttinnu [illegible] kah

A

Margin notes (left): *a* Psal. 33.6. & 136. 5. Act. 14. 15. & 17. 24. Hebr. 11.3. *b* 2 Cor. 4.6. *c* Psal. 136.5. Jer. 10. 12. & 51.15. *d* Jer. 51.15. *e* Psal. 33.7. & 136. 5. Job 38. 8.

Margin notes (right): *f* Deut. 4.19. Psal. 136. 7. *g* Jer. 31.35. *b* Gen. 8.17. & 9. 1.

Handwritten annotation: anogqsok v. Eliot Grammar

A Page from John Eliot's Indian Bible.

Courtesy of the Massachusetts Historical Society.

New-Englands
RARITIES
Discovered:
IN
Birds, Beasts, Fishes, Serpents, and *Plants* of that Country.

Together with
The *Physical* and *Chyrurgical* REMEDIES wherewith the *Natives* constantly use to Cure their DISTEMPERS, WOUNDS, and SORES.

ALSO
A perfect *Description* of an *Indian SQUA,* in all her Bravery; with a POEM not improperly conferr'd upon her.

LASTLY
A CHRONOLOGICAL TABLE of the most remarkable Passages in that Country amongst the ENGLISH.

Illustrated with CUTS.

By *JOHN JOSSELYN,* Gent.

London, Printed for *G. Widdowes* at the *Green Dragon* in St. *Pauls* Church-yard, 1672.

42 New-Englands Rarities.

To procure Love.

I once took notice of a wanton Womans compounding the solid Roots of this Plant with Wine, for an Amorous Cup; which wrought the desired effect.

Watercresses.

Red Lillies grow all over the Country innumerably amongst the small Bushes, and flower in *June.*

Wild Sorrel.

Alders Tongue comes not up till *June*; I have found it upon dry hilly grounds, in places where the water hath stood all Winter, in *August*, and did then make Oyntment of the Herb new gathered; the fairest Leaves grow amongst short *Hawthorn* Bushes, that are plentifully growing in such hollow places.

One Blade.

Lilly Convallie, with the yellow Flowers, grows upon rocky banks by the Sea.

Water Plantane, here called *Water-suck-leaves.*

For Burns and Scalds, and to draw Water out of swell'd Legs.

It is much used for Burns and Scalds, and to draw water out of swell'd Legs. *Bears* feed much upon this Plant, so do the *Moose* Deer.

Sea

New-Englands Rarities. 43

Sea Plantane, three kinds.

Small-water. Archer.

Autumn Bell Flower.

White Hellibore, which is the first Plant that springs up in this Country, and the first that withers; it grows in deep black Mould and Wet, in such abundance, that you may in a small compass gather whole Cart-loads of it.

Wounds and Aches Cured by the Indians.

For the Tooth-ach. For Herpes milliares.

The *Indians* Cure their Wounds with it, annointing the Wound first with Raccoons greese, or Wild-Cats greese, and strewing upon it the powder of the Roots; and for Aches they scarifie the grieved part, and annoint it with one of the foresaid Oyls, then strew upon it the powder: The powder of the Root put into a hollow Tooth, is good for the Tooth-ach: The Root sliced thin and boyled in Vineager, is very good against *Herpes Milliaris.*

Arsmart, both kinds.

Spurge Time, it grows upon dry sandy Sea Banks, and is very like to *Rupterwort*, it is full of Milk.

Rupter-wort, with the white flower.

Jagged *Rose-penny-wort.*

D *Soda*

New-Englands Rarities Discovered (1672). Title Page and Two Pages of Text.
Courtesy of the Massachusetts Historical Society.

Early Colonial Captivity Scene.
Courtesy of the Massachusetts Historical Society.

MARY ROWLANDSON

From A Narrative of the Captivity and Restauration of Mrs. Mary Rowlandson (1682)

On the tenth of February 1675, came the Indians with great numbers upon Lancaster: Their first coming was about sun-rising; hearing the noise of some guns, we looked out; several houses were burning, and

From Gordon M. Sayre, ed., *American Captivity Narratives: Selected Narratives with Introduction / Olaudah Equiano, Mary Rowlandson, and Others* (Boston: Houghton, 2000), ch. 4.

the smoke ascending to heaven. There were five persons taken in one house, the father, and the mother and a sucking child, they knocked on the head; the other two they took and carried away alive. . . . Thus these murderous wretches went on, burning, and destroying before them.

At length they came and beset our own house, and quickly it was the dolefullest day that ever mine eyes saw. The house stood upon the edge of a hill; some of the Indians got behind the hill, others in the barn, and others behind any thing that could shelter them; from all which places they shot against the house, so that the bullets seemed to fly like hail; and quickly they wounded one man among us, then another, and then a third. About two hours (according to my observation, in that amazing time) they had been about the house before they prevailed to fire it. . . . Now is the dreadful hour come, that I have often heard of (in time of war, as it was the case of others) but now mine eyes see it. Some in our house were fighting for their lives, others wallowing in their blood, the house on fire over our heads, and the bloody heathen ready to knock us on the head, if we stirred out. Now might we hear mothers and children crying out for themselves, and one another, Lord, What shall we do? . . . No sooner were we out of the house, but my brother-in-law (being before wounded, in defending the house, in or near the throat) fell down dead whereat the Indians scornfully shouted, and holloed, and were presently upon him, stripping off his clothes, the bullets flying thick, one went through my side, and the same (as would seem) through the bowels and hand of my dear child in my arms. . . . [T]he Indians laid hold of us, pulling me one way, and the Children another, and said, Come go along with us; I told them they would kill me: they answered, If I were willing to go along with them, they would not hurt me.

. . . Of thirty-seven persons who were in this one house, none escaped either present death, or a bitter captivity, save only one, who might say as he, Job 1.15, *And I only am escaped alone to tell the news.* There were twelve killed, some shot, some stabbed with their spears, some knocked down with their hatchets. . . . [Y]et the Lord by his almighty power preserved a number of us from death, for there were twenty-four of us taken alive and carried captive.

. . . I shall particularly speak of the several removes we had up and down the wilderness.

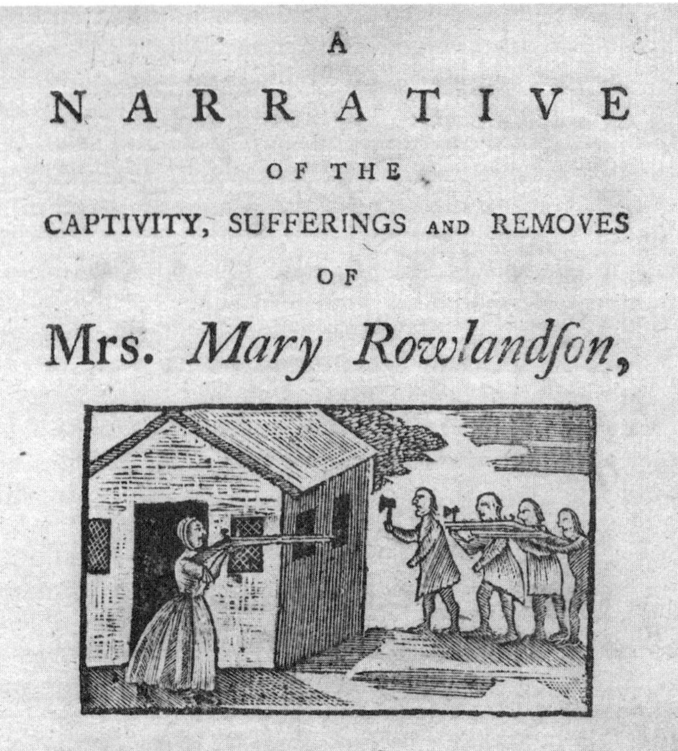

A

NARRATIVE

OF THE

CAPTIVITY, SUFFERINGS AND REMOVES

OF

Mrs. *Mary Rowlandſon*,

Who was taken Priſoner by the INDIANS with ſeveral others, and treated in the moſt barbarous and cruel Manner by thoſe vile Savages: With many other remarkable Events during her TRAVELS.

Written by her own Hand, for her private Uſe, and now made public at the earneſt Deſire of ſome Friends, and for the Benefit of the afflicted.

BOSTON:

Printed and Sold at JOHN BOYLE's Printing-Office, next Door to the *Three Doves* in Marlborough-Street. 1773.

Title Page of *A True History of the Captivity & Restoration of Mrs. Mary Rowlandson.* Version printed in London, England, 1682.

Courtesy of the Massachusetts Historical Society.

The Second Remove

But now, the next morning, I must turn my back upon the town, and travel with them into the vast and desolate wilderness, I knew not whither. It is not my tongue, or pen can express the sorrows of my heart, and bitterness of my spirit, that I had at this departure: but God was with me, in a wonderful manner, carrying me along, and bearing up my spirit, that it did not quite fail. One of the Indians carried my poor wounded babe upon a horse, it went moaning all along, I shall die, I shall die. I went on foot after it, with sorrow that cannot be expressed. . . .

After this it quickly began to snow, and when night came on, they stopped: and now down I must sit in the snow, by a little fire, and a few boughs behind me, with my sick child in my lap; and calling much for water, being now (through the wound) fallen into a violent fever.

The Nineteenth Remove

They said, when we went out, that we must travel to Wachusett this day. But a bitter weary day I had of it, travelling now three days together, without resting any day between. . . .

My master had three squaws, living sometimes with one, and sometimes with another one, this old squaw, at whose wigwam I was, and with whom my master had been those three weeks. Another was Weetamoo, with whom I had lived and served all this while: a severe and proud dame she was. . . . I understood that Weetamoo thought, that if she should let me go and serve with the old squaw, she would be in danger to lose, not only my service, but the redemption pay also. And I was not a little glad to hear this; being by it raised in my hopes, that in God's due time there would be an end of this sorrowful hour. Then in came an Indian, and asked me to knit him three pair of stockings, for which I had a hat, and a silk handkerchief. Then another asked me to make her a shift, for which she gave me an apron.

Then came Tom and Peter, with the second letter from the Council, about the captives. Though they were Indians, I got them by the hand, and burst out into tears; my heart was so full that I could not speak to them; but recovering myself, I asked them how my husband did, and all my friends and acquaintance: They said, They are all very well, but melancholy. They brought me two biscuits, and a pound of tobacco. The tobacco I quickly gave away; when it was all gone, one asked me to give him a pipe of tobacco, I told him it was all gone; then began he to rant and threaten. I told him when my husband came I would give him some: Hang him rogue (says he) I will knock out his brains, if he comes here. And then again, in the same breath they would say, That if there should come an hundred without guns, they would do them no hurt. So unstable and like madmen they were. So that fearing the worst, I durst not send to my husband, though there were some thoughts of his coming to redeem and fetch me, not knowing what might follow. For there was little more trust to them than to the master they served. When the letter was come, the sagamores met to consult about the captives, and called me to them to inquire how much my husband would give to redeem me. When I came I sat down among them, as I was wont to do, as their manner is: then they bade me stand up, and said, they were the General Court. They bid me speak what I thought he would give. Not knowing that all we had was destroyed by the Indians, I was in a great strait: I thought if I should speak of but a little, it would be slighted, and hinder the matter; if of a great sum, I knew not where it would be procured: yet at a venture, I said twenty pounds, yet desired them to take less; but they would not hear of that, but sent that message to Boston, that for twenty pounds I should be redeemed. It was a Praying Indian that wrote their letter for them. . . .

The Twentieth Remove

. . . The twenty pounds the price of my redemption was raised by some Boston gentlemen, and Mrs. Usher, whose bounty and religious charity, I would not forget to make mention of. . . . We were now in the midst of love, yet not without much and frequent heaviness of heart for our poor children, and other relations, who were still in affliction. The week following, after my coming in, the governor and Council sent forth to the Indians again; and that not without success; for they brought in my sister, and goodwife Kettle: their not knowing where our children were, was a sore trial to us still, and yet we were not without secret hopes that we should see them again.

NATHANIEL HAWTHORNE

The Duston Family (May 1836)

We must not forget Mrs. Duston, in her distress. Scarcely had her husband fled from the house, ere the chamber was thronged with the horrible visages of the wild Indians, bedaubed with paint and besmeared with blood, brandishing their tomahawks in her face, and threatening to add her scalp to those that were already hanging at their girdles. It was, however, their interest to save her alive, if the thing might be, in order to exact a ransom. . . . Seeing that there was no help for it, Mrs. Duston rose, and she and the widow Neff, with the infant in her arms, followed their captors out of doors. As they crossed the threshold, the poor babe set up a feeble wail; it was its death cry. In an instant, an Indian seized it by the heels, swung it in the air, dashed out its brains against the trunk of the nearest tree, and threw the little corpse at the mother's feet. Perhaps it was the remembrance of that moment, that hardened Hannah Duston's heart, when her time of vengeance came. . . .

. . . Mrs. Duston, the widow Neff, and an English lad, fell to the lot of a family, consisting of two stout warriours, three squaws, and seven children. These Indians, like most with whom the French had held intercourse, were Catholics; and Cotton Mather affirms, on Mrs. Duston's authority, that they prayed at morning, noon, and night, nor ever partook of food without a prayer; nor suffered their children to sleep, till they had prayed to the Christian's God. Mather, like an old hard-hearted, pedantic bigot, as he was, seems trebly to exult in the destruction of these poor wretches, on account of their Popish superstitions. Yet what can be more touching than to think of these wild Indians, in their loneliness and their wanderings, wherever they went among the dark, mysterious woods, still keeping up domestic worship, with all the regularity of a household at its peaceful fireside.

* * *

Uprose Mrs. Duston, holding her own breath, to listen to the long, deep breathing of her captors. Then she stirred the widow Neff, whose place was by her own, and likewise the English lad. . . . The next instant, each of the three captives held a tomahawk. Hark! that low moan,

From Nathaniel Hawthorne, "The Duston Family," *The American Magazine of Useful and Entertaining Knowledge* 2 (May 1836): 395–97. Reprinted in James Levernier and Hennig Cohen, eds., *The Indians and Their Captives* (Westport, CT: Greenwood, 1977), 228–30.

as of one in a troubled dream — it told a warriour's death pang! Another! — Another! . . . Of all that family, only one woman escaped, dreadfully wounded, and fled shrieking into the wilderness! and a boy, whom, it is said, Mrs. Duston had meant to save alive. But he did well to flee from the raging tigress! There was little safety for a red skin, when Hannah Duston's blood was up.

The work being finished, Mrs. Duston laid hold of the long black hair of the warriours, and the women, and the children, and took all their ten scalps, and left the island, which bears her name to this very day. According to our notion, it should be held accursed, for her sake. Would that the bloody old hag had been drowned in crossing Contocook river. . . ! But, on the contrary, she and her companions came home safe, and received the bounty on the dead Indians, besides liberal presents from private gentlemen, and fifty pounds from the Governour of Maryland. In her old age, being sunk into decayed circumstances, she claimed, and, we believe, received a pension, as a further price of blood.

Excerpt from the Writings of Henry Schoolcraft

My earliest impressions of the Indian race, were drawn from the fireside rehearsals of incidents which had happened during the perilous times of the American revolution; in which my father was a zealous actor, and were all inseparably connected with the fearful ideas of the Indian yell, the tomahawk, the scalping knife, and the firebrand. In these recitals, the Indian was depicted as the very impersonation of evil — a sort of wild demon, who delighted in nothing so much as blood and murder. Whether he had mind, was governed by any reasons, or even had any soul, nobody inquired, and nobody cared. It was always represented as a meritorious act in old revolutionary reminiscences, to have killed one of them in the border wars, and thus aided in ridding the land of a cruel and unnatural race, in whom all feelings of pity, justice, and mercy, were supposed to be obliterated. These early ideas were sustained by printed narratives of captivity and hair-breadth escapes of men and women from their clutches, which, from time to time, fell into my hands, so that long before I was ten years old, I had a most definite and terrific idea impressed on my imagination of what was sometimes called in my native precincts, "the bow and arrow race."

From Gary L. Ebersole, *Captured by Texts: Puritan to Postmodern Images of Indian Captivity* (Charlottesville: UP of Virginia, 1995), 1.

ADULTERY

Reprinted in this section are laws from the Massachusetts Bay and New Plymouth colonies regarding adultery as well as two excerpts discussing the crime. Contrary to the punishment Hester Prynne receives in *The Scarlet Letter,* the Massachusetts Bay Colony did not call for the wearing of any letter, much less a scarlet *A,* as punishment for adultery; rather, it was a capital crime. Moreover, lawmakers in the colony revisited the subject several times — each time making death the punishment. Nevertheless, whipping and banishment, rather than death, was the punishment imposed on some occasions, including for three persons in 1637 or 1638 whose sentence is included along with the series of laws making adultery a capital crime. Hawthorne may have gotten the idea of the scarlet letter from the laws of another New World colony — that of New Plymouth, where convicts were whipped and required to wear the letters *A D* sewn onto the clothes on their arm or back. The text of this law is also included, as well as the text of a 1647 law from the Massachusetts Bay Colony intended to address the problem of sexual misconduct by persons with spouses in England, a situation quite apropos to Hester's.

The two excerpts come from Winthrop's *The History of New England from 1630 to 1649* and William Cobbett's *Advice to Young Men.* Winthrop recounts the proceedings for adultery in 1645 against a married woman whose husband was in England and the (apparently single) man to whose care she was committed. It may be such cases that led to the 1647 law referenced above. Cobbett advises men that the most important quality to look for in a wife is chastity and goes to great lengths to justify the double standard that made adultery a greater crime for women than for men. Notably, Cobbett's view was reflected even in the colonial laws discussed above, as both the Massachusetts Bay and New Plymouth colonies specified that their adultery laws applied to adultery committed with a married, espoused, or betrothed woman. Adultery involving a single woman was apparently punished under fornication statutes instead. A Massachusetts Bay Colony fornication law is included here to illustrate the difference between the punishments under the adultery and fornication laws.

Laws Addressing Adultery, Massachusetts Bay Colony

Adultery Law (October 18, 1631)[2]

26–(12) It is ordered, that if any man shall have carnall copulacon with another mans wife, they both shalbee punished by death. This was confirmed the first month, 1637 or 1638.

Sentence for Three Adulterers and Adultery Law (March 12, 1637 or 1638)

It is ordered, that the 3 adulterers, John Hathaway, Rob^r^t Allen, & Margaret Seale, shalbee severely whiped, & banished, never to returne againe, vpon pain of deathe.
378– The law against adultery made by the pticuler Court in October, 1631, is confirmed, that whosoever lyeth wth another mans wife, both shalbee punished by death; and this is to bee pmulgated.

Adultery Law (October 7, 1640)

451– The first law against adultery, made by the Courte of Assistants in 1631, is declared to bee abrogated; but the other, made the first mo. 1637 or 1638, by the Generall Court, to stand in force.

Law Relating to Persons with Spouses in England (November 11, 1647)

694– Whereas div^r^s married psons, both men & weomen, living w^th^in y^s^ iurisdiction, whose wifes and husbands are in England or elsw^r^, by meanes w^r^of they live und^r^ great temptations, & some of y^m^ comit lewdnes and filthines here amongst us, & oth^rs^ make love to weomen, & attempt marriage, & have attained it, some of y^m^ live und^r^ suspition of uncleannes, & all of y^m^ great dishono^r^ to God, reproach to religion,

[2] This excerpt and the next three come from Nathaniel B. Shurtleff, ed., *Records of the Governor and Company of the Massachusetts Bay in New England* (Boston: Press of William White, 1853). As follows: 1631 law, 1: 92; 1637 or 1638 sentence and law, 1: 225; 1640 law, 1: 301; 1648 law, 2: 211–12. Both volumes of records were printed by order of the Massachusetts Legislature; vol. 1 covers 1628–41, vol. 2 1642–49 (the period during which *The Scarlet Letter* is set).

comon wealth, & churches, it is y^{r}fore ord^{r}ed, by y^{s} Co^{r}te, & ye authority y^{r}of, (for pvention of all such future evills,) y^{t} all such married psons as aforesaid shall repair to their relations, by ye first oportunity of shiping, upon ye paine or pœnalty of 20^{t}, except they can shew iust cause to ye contrary to ye next County Co^{r}te, or Co^{r}te of Assistants, to be holden at Boston, aft^{r} they are sumoned by ye cunstable y^{r} to appeare, who are hereby required to do so, upon paine of 20^{s} for his neglect; pvided, y^{t} y^{s} ord^{r} do not extend to such as are come ov^{r} to make way for their families, & are here in a transient way onely, for trafique or marchandize, for some small time.

Adultery Law (1648)[3]

9 If any person commit ADULTERIE with a married, or espoused wife; the Adulterer and Adulteresse shal surely be put to death. *Lev.* 20. 19. & 18. 20. *Deu.* 22. 23. 27.

Adultery Law, Colony of New Plymouth (1636)[4]

It is enacted by the Court and the Authoritie therof that whosoever shall comitt Adultery shalbee severely punished by whiping two severall times; viz. one whiles the Court is in being att which they are convicted of the fact, and the 2^{cond} time as the Court shal order; and likewise to weare two Capitall letters viz. A D. cut out in cloth and sowed on theire uper most Garments, on theire arme or backe; and if att any time they shalbee taken without the said letters whiles they are . . . to bee forth with taken and publickly whipt.

[3] "Adultery Law" from *The Book of the General Lawes and Libertyes of Massachusetts* (1648). Reprinted as *The Laws and Liberties of Massachusetts* (Cambridge: Harvard UP, 1929).

[4] "Adultery Law, Colony of New Plymouth" reprinted in *Compact with the Charter and Laws of the Colony of New Plymouth,* Part II (Boston: Dutton and Wentworth, 1836), 245–46. The law, with the added specification that "Adultery" involves "a Married Woman or one Betrothed to another Man," plus slight variation in spelling and wording, appears in pt. III, ch. III ("Criminals"), which contains general revised laws adopted in 1671.

Fornication Law, Massachusetts Bay Colony[5] (June 14, 1642)

519– If any man shall comit fornication wth any single woman, they shalbee punished, either by enioyning to marriage, or fine, or corporall punishm^{t}, or all or any of these, as the iudges shall appoint, most agreeablie to the word; and this order to continue till further order bee taken in it.

[5] "Fornication Law" from Nathaniel B. Shurtleff, ed., *Records of the Governor and Company of the Massachusetts Bay in New England,* vol. 2. (Boston: Press of William White, 1853), 21–22. This law was confirmed in *The Book of the General Lawes and Libertyes of Massachusetts* (1648) 23. Reprinted as *The Laws and Liberties of Massachusetts* (Cambridge: Harvard UP, 1929), with only slight and insignificant variation in the wording.

JOHN WINTHROP

From The History of New England from 1630 to 1649

A sad business fell out this year [1645] in Boston. One of the brethren of the church there, being in England in the parliamentary service about two years, had committed the care of his family and business to another of the same church, (a young man of good esteem for piety and sincerity, but his wife was in England,) who in time grew over familiar with his master's wife, (a young woman no member of the church,) so as she would be with him oft in his chamber &c. and one night two of the servants, being up, perceived him to go up into their dame's chamber, which coming to the magistrates' knowledge, they were both sent for and examined, (but it was not discovered till about a quarter of a year after, her husband being then come home,) and confessed not only that he was in the chamber with her in such a suspicious manner, but also that he was in bed with her, but both denied any carnal knowledge; and being tried by a jury upon their lives by our law, which makes adultery death, the jury acquitted them of the adultery, but found them guilty of adulterous behaviour. This was much against the minds of many, both of the magistrates and elders, who judged

From John Winthrop, *The History of New England from 1630 to 1649,* vol. 2 (Salem, NH: Ayer Company, 1992), 249–50. Reprint of James Savage's two-volume edition of Winthrop's *History* (Boston: Phelps and Farnham, 1825).

them worthy of death; but the jury attending what was spoken by others of the magistrates, 1. that seeing the main evidence against them was their own confession of being in bed together, their whole confession must be taken, and not a part of it; 2. the law requires two witnesses, but here was no witness at all, although circumstances may amount to a testimony against the person, where the fact is evident, yet it is otherwise where no fact is apparent; 3. all that the evidence could evince was but suspicion of adultery, but neither God's law nor ours doth make suspicion of adultery (though never so strong) to be death; whereupon the case seeming doubtful to the jury, they judged it safest in case of life to find as they did. So the court adjudged them to stand upon the ladder at the place of execution with halters about their necks one hour, and then to be whipped, or each of them to pay 20 pounds. The husband (although he condemned his wife's immodest behaviour, yet) was so confident of her innocency in point of adultery, as he would have paid 20 pounds rather than she should have been whipped; but their estate being but mean, she chose rather to submit to the rest of her punishment than that her husband should suffer so much for her folly. So he received her again, and they lived lovingly together. All that she had to say for herself upon her trial was the same which she had revealed to her husband as soon as he came home, before the matter had been discovered, viz. that he did indeed come into bed to her, which so soon as she perceived, she used the best arguments she could to dissuade him from so foul a sin, so as he lay still, and did not touch her, but went away again as he came; and the reason why she did not cry out, was because he had been very faithful and helpful to her in her husband's absence, which made her very unwilling to bring him to punishment or disgrace.

This punishment of standing upon the gallows was not so well approved by some of the magistrates; because the law of God appoints in case of whipping, that they should not exceed forty stripes, and the reason given is, lest thy brother should seem despised in thine eyes, and why this reason should not hold in all cases and punishments not capital doth not appear.

WILLIAM COBBETT

From Advice to Young Men (1831)

89. The things which you ought to desire in a wife are, 1. Chastity; 2. sobriety; 3. industry; 4. frugality; 5. cleanliness; 6. knowledge of domestic affairs; 7. good temper; 8. beauty.

90. I. CHASTITY, perfect modesty, in word, deed, and even thought, is so essential that, without it, no female is fit to be a wife. It is not enough that a young woman abstain from every thing approaching towards indecorum in her behaviour towards men; it is, with me, not enough that she cast down her eyes, or turn aside her head with a smile, when she hears an indelicate allusion: she ought to appear *not to understand* it, and to receive from it no more impression than if she were a post. A loose woman is a disagreeable *acquaintance:* what must she be, then, as a *wife?*

* * *

199. But, bad as is conjugal infidelity in the *husband,* it is much worse in the *wife:* a proposition that it is necessary to maintain by the force of reason, because *the women,* as a sisterhood, are prone to deny the truth of it. They say that *adultery* is *adultery,* in men as well as in them; and that, therefore, the offence is *as great* in the one case as in the other. As a crime, abstractedly considered, it certainly is; but, as to the *consequences,* there is a wide difference. In both cases, there is the breach of a solemn vow, but, there is this great distinction, that the husband, by his breach of that vow, only brings *shame* upon his wife and family; whereas the wife, by a breach of her vow, may bring the husband a spurious offspring to maintain, and may bring that spurious offspring to rob of their fortunes, and in some cases of their bread, her legitimate children. So that here is a great and evident wrong done to numerous parties, besides the deeper disgrace inflicted in this case than in the other.

200. And why is the disgrace *deeper?* Because here is a total want of *delicacy;* here is, in fact, *prostitution;* here is grossness and filthiness of mind; here is every thing that argues baseness of character. Women should be, and they are, except in few instances, far more reserved

From William Cobbett, *Advice to Young Men, and (Incidentally) to Young Women, in the Middle and Higher Ranks of Life* (New York: John Doyle, 1831). Paragraphs 89–90 come from the letter "To a Lover," p. 79; paragraphs 199–201 come from the letter "To a Husband," pp. 156–57.

and more delicate than men; nature bids them be such; the habits and manners of the world confirm this precept of nature; and therefore, when they commit this offence, they excite loathing, as well as call for reprobation. . . .

201. For these plain and forcible reasons it is that this species of offence is far more heinous in the wife than in the husband; and the people of all civilized countries act upon this settled distinction. Men who have been guilty of the offence are not cut off from society, but women who have been guilty of it are; for, as we all know well, no woman, married or single, of *fair reputation,* will risk that reputation by being ever seen, if she can avoid it, with a woman who has ever, at any time, committed this offence, which contains in itself, and by universal award, a sentence of social excommunication for life.

THE STATUS AND ROLE OF WOMEN

The fifth section in this representative sampling of contextual documents and illustrations, The Status and Role of Women, includes four documentary excerpts chosen to give the reader insight into both the legal status of women in and prior to Hawthorne's time and the special "sphere of influence" to which they were confined by social and cultural norms. The first excerpt comes from William Blackstone's *Commentaries on the Laws of England,* widely viewed as the most significant legal treatise ever written in English and one that "played a unique role in the development of the fledgling American legal system."[6] Once married, with few exceptions a woman had no legally recognized existence apart from her husband. The second excerpt, from Frenchman Alexis de Tocqueville's famous work *Democracy in America,* contains de Tocqueville's observations on equality of the sexes in America. The third excerpt, from Catherine Beecher's popular guide to housekeeping, *A Treatise on Domesticity,* defends the social order that placed women in an inferior position. Beecher, who expressly approved de Tocqueville's observations, equated the principles of democracy with those of Christianity, accepting the "cult of domesticity," under which woman was ordained, by nature and God alike, to serve in the domestic arena as wife, mother, and keeper of home and hearth.

[6] From Stanley Katz's "Introduction to Book I" of the University of Chicago Press's 1979 facsimile reprint of William Blackstone's 4-volume first edition of *Commentaries of the Laws of England.*

The final excerpt in this section, from the resolutions adopted at the 1848 Woman's Rights Convention at Seneca Falls, New York, highlights the practical impact on women in nineteenth-century America of the law and associated notions of the proper sphere for women. Relying on Blackstone, of all people, for the precept that "man shall pursue his own true and substantial happiness," the resolutions adopted at the convention condemned all laws that conflicted with women's pursuit of happiness or placed women in a position contrary to their conscience or inferior to men. Such laws included, as enumerated in the "Declaration of Sentiments" also adopted at the convention, denial of the right to vote, deprivation of earnings if married, exclusion from most professions, exclusion from colleges, and the state of coverture, which made married women "civilly dead."[7]

[7] From *Stanton and Anthony Papers Project Online*, "Texts of the Declaration of Sentiments and the Resolutions adopted by the Woman's Rights Convention, Held at Seneca Falls, New York, 19–20 July 1848." <http://ecssba.rutgers.edu/docs/seneca.html>.

WILLIAM BLACKSTONE

From Of Husband and Wife (1765)

By marriage, the husband and wife are one person in law: that is, the very being or legal existence of the woman is suspended during the marriage, or at least is incorporated and consolidated into that of the husband: under whose wing, protection, and *cover,* she performs every thing; and is therefore called in our law-french a *feme-covert;* is said to be *covert-baron,* or under the protection and influence of her husband, her *baron,* or lord; and her condition during her marriage is called her *coverture.* Upon this principle, of an union of person in husband and wife, depend almost all the legal rights, duties, and disabilities, that either of them acquire by the marriage. I speak not at present of the rights of property, but of such as are merely *personal.* For this reason, a man cannot grant any thing to his wife, or enter into covenant with her: for the grant would be to suppose her separate existence; and to covenant with her, would only be to covenant with himself. . . . The hus-

From William Blackstone, *Commentaries on the Laws of England,* vol. 1 (*Of the Rights of Persons*) (1765), 430–33. The excerpt is taken from a facsimile reprint of Blackstone's 4-volume first edition of 1765–69 by the University of Chicago Press, Chicago, 1979. The modern form of the lowercase *s* has been substituted here for the long *s* (*ƒ*) Blackstone used.

band is bound to provide his wife with necessaries by law, as much as himself; and if she contracts debts for them, he is obliged to pay them: but for any thing besides necessaries, he is not chargeable. Also if a wife elopes, and lives with another man, the husband is not chargeable even for necessaries. . . .

* * *

The husband also (by the old law) might give his wife moderate correction. For, as he is to answer for her misbehaviour, the law thought it reasonable to intrust him with this power of restraining her, by domestic chastisement, in the same moderation that a man is allowed to correct his servants or children; for whom the master or parent is also liable in some cases to answer. But this power of correction was confined within reasonable bounds. . . . But, with us, in the politer reign of Charles the second, this power of correction began to be doubted: and a wife may now have security of peace against her husband; or, in return, a husband against his wife. Yet the lower rank of people, who were always fond of the old common law, still claim and exert their antient privilege: and the courts of law will still permit a husband to restrain a wife of her liberty, in case of any gross misbehaviour.

These are the chief legal effects of marriage during the coverture; upon which we may observe, that even the disabilities, which the wife lies under, are for the most part intended for her protection and benefit. So great a favourite is the female sex of the laws of England.

ALEXIS DE TOCQUEVILLE

From How the Americans Understand the Equality of the Sexes (1835)

There are people in Europe who, confounding together the different characteristics of the sexes, would make of man and woman beings not only equal but alike. . . .

It is not thus that the Americans understand that species of democratic equality which may be established between the sexes. They admit, that as nature has appointed such wide differences between the physical and moral constitution of man and woman, her manifest design was to

From Alexis de Tocqueville, *Democracy in America,* vol. IV, trans. Henry Reeve, Esq. (1835; London: Saunders and Otley, 1840), 100.

give a distinct employment to their various faculties; and they hold that improvement does not consist in making beings so dissimilar do pretty nearly the same things, but in getting each of them to fulfil their respective tasks in the best possible manner. The Americans have applied to the sexes the great principle of political œconomy which governs the manufactures of our age, by carefully dividing the duties of man from those of woman, in order that the great work of society be the better carried on.

. . . American women never manage the outward concerns of the family, or conduct a business, or take a part in political life; nor are they, on the other hand, ever compelled to perform the rough labour of the fields, or to make any of those laborious exertions which demand the exertion of physical strength. No families are so poor as to form an exception to this rule. If on the one hand an American woman cannot escape from the quiet circle of domestic employments, on the other hand she is never forced to go beyond it. . . .

* * *

. . . I never observed that the women of America consider conjugal authority as a fortunate usurpation of their rights, not that they thought themselves degraded by submitting to it. It appeared to me, on the contrary, that they attach a sort of pride to the voluntary surrender of their own will, and make it their boast to bend themselves to the yoke, not to shake it off. Such at least is the feeling expressed by the most virtuous of their sex; the others are silent. . . .

* * *

Thus the Americans do not think that man and woman have either the duty or the right to perform the same offices, but they show an equal regard for both their respective parts; and though their lot is different, they consider both of them as beings of equal value. . . . Thus, then, whilst they have allowed the social inferiority of woman to subsist, they have done all they could to raise her morally and intellectually to the level of man; and in this respect they appear to me to have excellently understood the true principle of democratic improvement.

CATHARINE BEECHER

From The Peculiar Responsibilities of American Women (1846)

The tendencies of democratic institutions, in reference to the rights and interests of the female sex, have been fully developed in the United States; and it is in this aspect, that the subject is one of peculiar interest to American women. In this Country, it is established, both by opinion and by practice, that women have an equal interest in all social and civil concerns; and that no domestic, civil, or political, institution, is right, which sacrifices her interest to promote that of the other sex. But in order to secure her the more firmly in all these privileges, it is decided, that, in the domestic relation, she take a subordinate station, and that, in civil and political concerns, her interests be intrusted to the other sex, without her taking any part in voting, or in making and administering laws. The result of this order of things has been fairly tested, and is thus portrayed by M. De Tocqueville, a writer, who, for intelligence, fidelity, and ability, ranks second to none.

* * *

It appears then, that it is in America, alone, that women are raised to an equality with the other sex; and that, both in theory and practice, their interests are regarded as of equal value. They are made subordinate in station, only where a regard to their best interests demands it, while, as if in compensation for this, by custom and courtesy, they are always treated as superiors. Universally, in this Country, through every class of society, precedence is given to woman, in all the comforts, conveniences, and courtesies, of life.

* * *

If those who are bewailing themselves over the fancied wrongs and injuries of women in this Nation, could only see things as they are, they would know, that, whatever remnants of a barbarous or aristocratic age may remain in our civil institutions, in reference to the interests of women, it is only because they are ignorant of them, or do not use their influence to have them rectified; for it is very certain that there is

From Catharine Beecher, *A Treatise on Domestic Economy,* rev. ed. (New York: Harper, 1846), 27–28, 33–34.

nothing reasonable, which American women would unite in asking, that would not readily be bestowed.

The preceding remarks, then, illustrate the position, that the democratic institutions of this Country are in reality no other than the principles of Christianity carried into operation, and that they tend to place woman in her true position in society, as having equal rights with the other sex; and that, in fact, they have secured to American women a lofty and fortunate position, which, as yet, has been attained by the women of no other nation.

Woman's Rights Convention, Seneca Falls Resolutions (July 19, 1848)

Whereas, the great precept of nature is conceded to be, "that man shall pursue his own true and substantial happiness," Blackstone, in his Commentaries, remarks, that this law of Nature being coeval with mankind, and dictated by God himself, is of course superior in obligation to any other. It is binding over all the globe, in all countries, and at all times; no human laws are of any validity if contrary to this, and such of them as are valid, derive all their force, and all their validity, and all their authority, mediately and immediately, from this original; Therefore,

Resolved, That such laws as conflict, in any way, with the true and substantial happiness of woman, are contrary to the great precept of nature, and of no validity; for this is "superior in obligation to any other."

Resolved, That all laws which prevent woman from occupying such a station in society as her conscience shall dictate, or which place her in a position inferior to that of man, are contrary to the great precept of nature, and therefore of no force or authority.

Resolved, That woman is man's equal — was intended to be so by the Creator, and the highest good of the race demands that she should be recognized as such.

From *Stanton and Anthony Papers Project Online,* "Texts of the Declaration of Sentiments and the Resolutions adopted by the Woman's Rights Convention, Held at Seneca Falls, New York, 19–20 July 1848." January 2005, <http://ecssba.rutgers.edu/docs/seneca.html>.

Resolved, That the women of this country ought to be enlightened in regard to the laws under which they live, that they may no longer publish their degradation, by declaring themselves satisfied with their present position, nor their ignorance, by asserting that they have all the rights they want.

* * *

Resolved, That woman has too long rested satisfied in the circumscribed limits which corrupt customs and a perverted application of the Scriptures have marked out for her, and that it is time she should move in the enlarged sphere which her great Creator has assigned her.

The Education and Custody of Children

The sixth section includes excerpts from three sources bearing on Puritan and mid-nineteenth-century attitudes toward child rearing. The first excerpt, a law passed in 1642 in the Massachusetts Bay Colony regarding education, vested power in a select group of men to ensure that children were properly trained, giving them the power to test "ability to read and understand the principles of religion & the capitall lawes of this country," impose fines, and even (with judicial consent) apprentice to others any children lacking proper training. Readers may want to consider this law particularly in connection with Chapters VII and VIII of *The Scarlet Letter*, which focus on Hester's concern that Pearl might be taken away and Mr. Wilson's examination of Pearl on religious principles at Governor Bellingham's mansion. The second series of excerpts relate to proceedings in the d'Hauteville case, a custody battle between husband and wife in 1840 over their infant son that ended in a landmark decision granting custody to the wife even though she lacked grounds for divorce. Given that custody of children was then deemed a husband's right, Ellen Sears Grand d'Hauteville relied primarily on, and the court accepted, arguments as to the importance of maternal care. As the Court reasoned in granting custody to Ellen, "every instinct of humanity unerringly proclaims that *no* substitute can supply the place of HER." The third and final excerpt in this section comes from Beecher's *Treatise*, from a chapter titled "On the Management of Children," in which she discusses the importance of submission, self-denial, and religious instruction to the happiness of children.

Education Law, Massachusetts Bay Colony (June 14, 1642)

497– This Co[r]t, taking into consideration the great neglect of many parents & masters in training up their children in learning, & labo[r], and other implyments which may be proffitable to the common wealth, do hereupon order & decree, that in euery towne y[e] chosen men appointed for managing the prudentiall affajres of the same shall henceforth stand charged with the care of the redresse of this evill, so as they shalbee sufficiently punished by fines for the neglect thereof, upon presentment of the grand iury, or other information or complaint in any Court within this iurisdiction; and for this end they, or the greater numbe[r] of them, shall have powe[r] to take account from time to time of all parents and masters, and of their children, concerning their calling and implyment of their children, especially of their ability to read & understand the principles of religion & the capitall lawes of this country, and to impose fines upon such as shall refuse to render such accounts to them when they shall be required; and they shall have power, with consent of any Court or the magistrate, to put forth apprentices the children of such as they shall [find] not to be able & fitt to imploy and bring them up.

Reprinted in Nathaniel B. Shurtleff, ed., *Records of the Governor and Company of the Massachusetts Bay in New England*, vol. II (Boston: Press of William White, 1853), 6–7.

From Proceedings in the d'Hauteville Case (1840)

Return of Ellen Sears Grand d'Hauteville to the Petition for *Habeas Corpus*

That the said Frederic Sears is her son, and only child. . . . That from his birth to the present day, he has never been separated from her.

From Samuel Miller, Jr., ed., *Report of the d'Hauteville Case: The Commonwealth of Pennsylvania, at the Suggestion of Paul Daniel Gonsalve Grand d'Hauteville, versus Davis Sears, Miriam C. Sears, and Ellen Sears Grand d'Hauteville, Habeas Corpus for the Custody of an Infant Child* (Philadelphia: William S. Martien, 1840). All four excerpts here come from proceedings in the Court of General Sessions for the City and County of Philadelphia during the July Term, 1840, as reported by Miller. Excerpted pages are as follows: Return, p. 9; Relator's Suggestion, p. 15; Opening for Relator, p. 193; Opinion of the Court, pp. 288–89, 292–94.

That she is his guardian by nature and for nurture, and that her care of him is indispensably necessary for his present and future welfare. That he is now in her custody for the proper and necessary purposes of such care and guardianship, and for no other purpose, and in no other manner; and is in no respect restrained of his liberty or detained illegally. . . . That the present age of her said child does not admit of his separation from her, without the greatest danger to his health, which requires care, and even to his life, which has been more than once seriously threatened by attacks of illness. He needs, and for some years to come will need, a mother's nursing care, which no one else can supply.

Relator's Suggestion

That as to so much of the said return as avers that the said child is in no respect "detained illegally," he says, that the custody and guardianship of said child, at any age, belonging of right, and, as he is advised, according to the laws of the land, to his father, in being withheld from said custody and guardianship by its mother, it is "detained illegally." By the laws of this and every christian land, the wife is bound to adhere to her husband, to remain with him, to make his home her home, and his country her country; and if a wife, causelessly, (as your petitioner avers is the case here) abandons her husband and refuses to live with him, she forfeits all those privileges which the law so largely bestows on a faithful wife. She ceases to be exclusive guardian of the children even for nurture, and has no reason to complain of the hardness of a separation, which she has the ready means of removing, by herself returning to her duty.

Opening for Relator, by Attorney Reed (September 4, 1840)

It is unnecessary to speak of the importance of this case: in your Honours' wide jurisdiction you can hardly meet with one more worthy of your time and careful attention. It is a case on which momentous results depend; the influence of which on society no one can appreciate. The deep interest that the parties feel, and its issue as to them, are of comparatively little moment. Bereavements more hopeless and agonizing than any which can occur here, take place every day, but leave no mark, except upon the recollection of relatives and friends. This question involves the whole law of parental controul and conjugal relations: your Honours are to decide what that law is — to decide whether a wife and mother may, without any cause known to the laws of God or man — none such is pretended here — desert her husband, and deprive him of his only child.

The question thus presented is not only great and important, but also quite new, at least in Pennsylvania. In every case where, in this state, an infant child has been awarded to the mother, there has been some insuperable obstacle to her living with the father; either a divorce, or legal grounds for it. Such is not the present case. Mrs. d'Hauteville has never sought a divorce, and certainly could not obtain one.

Opinion of the Court (November 14, 1840)

On the part of the relator, it is contended that the custody of the child is the vested and absolute right of the father — one of which he cannot be deprived, excepting where it becomes forfeited either by his unfitness to take charge of its morals and interests, or by such misconduct as would afford good ground for a divorce *a vinculo matrimonii.*

We cannot subscribe to the correctness of this doctrine. . . . [W]e have been unable to convince ourselves of the justice of what is thus contended for, or to become possessed of any decision, English or American, by which it is supported. If it be the law either of nature or of the land, then have those courts most grievously erred. . . .

* * *

Having thus arrived at the conclusion that the right of the father is not absolute, and that the custody of the infant is exclusively referable to sound judicial discretion, I proceed to inquire in what manner the circumstances of this case and the interests of the child demand that that discretion shall be exercised. I take pleasure in saying, that whatever may be the faults of temper which the conduct of the relator to his wife and to her mother has developed, not the shadow of stain can be found upon his moral reputation. Apart from his somewhat Asiatic notions of a husband's rights and a wife's duties, and his conjugal misunderstandings and unprovoked treatment of Mrs. Sears, no evidence has been adduced or attempted which affixes the slightest reproach to his conduct or character as a good citizen; on the contrary, he has been shown to be habitually observant of all the proprieties of life, temperate and domestic in his habits, and apparently attached to the requirements of religion. . . .

. . . The reputation of a father may be stainless as crystal; he may not be afflicted with the slightest mental, moral, or physical disqualification from superintending the general welfare of the infant; the mother may have separated from him without the shadow of a pretence of justification; and yet the interests of the child may imperatively demand the denial of the father's right, and its continuance with the mother. . . .

* * *

The tender age and precarious state of its health, make the vigilance of the mother indispensable to its proper care; for, not doubting that paternal anxiety would seek for and obtain the best *substitute* which could be procured, every instinct of humanity unerringly proclaims that *no* substitute can supply the place of HER, whose watchfulness over the sleeping cradle or waking moments of her offspring, is prompted by deeper and holier feelings than the most liberal allowance of a nurse's wages could possibly stimulate. Not yet two years of age when the writ of habeas corpus was issued, this child has already been the subject of several distressing maladies, and has been apparently threatened with others of not inferior aggravation. . . .

. . . Doctor Warren adds, "the child is decidedly not of an age to be separated from its mother." Doctor Meigs, who was called in to consult with Doctor Chapman, and who has seen the child since the institution of this proceeding, gives his opinion, as a medical man, that "the chances of rearing the child would be diminished by removing it from its mother." . . .

* * *

. . . Our decision can properly only refer to *the present custody* of the child, and it is that he be remanded to the custody of his mother.

CATHARINE BEECHER

From On the Management of Young Children (1846)

But children can be very early taught, that their happiness, both now and hereafter, depends on the formation of *habits of submission, self-denial,* and *benevolence.* And all the discipline of the nursery can be conducted by the parents, not only with this general aim in their own

From Catharine Beecher, *A Treatise on Domestic Economy,* rev. ed. (New York: Harper, 1846), 224–26.

minds, but also with the same object daily set before the minds of the children. Whenever their wishes are crossed, or their wills subdued, they can be taught, that all this is done, not merely to please the parent, or to secure some good to themselves or to others; but as a part of that merciful training, which is designed to form such a character, and such habits, that they can hereafter find their chief happiness in giving up their will to God, and in living to do good to others, instead of merely living to please themselves.

It can be pointed out to them, that they must always submit their will to the will of God, or else be continually miserable. . . .

Parents have learned, by experience, that children can be constrained, by authority and penalties, to exercise self-denial, for *their own* good, till a habit is formed, which makes the duty comparatively easy. . . .

But it has not been so readily discerned, that the same method is needful, in order to form a habit of self-denial, in doing good to others. . . .

* * *

Religious influence should be brought to bear directly upon this point. In the very beginning of religious instruction, Jesus Christ should be presented to the child, as that great and good Being, who came into this world to teach children how to be happy, both here and hereafter. He, who made it His meat and drink to do the will of His Heavenly Father; who, in the humblest station, and most destitute condition, denied Himself, daily, and went about doing good; should constantly be presented as the object of their imitation. And as nothing so strongly influences the minds of children, as the sympathy and example of a *present* friend, all those, who believe Him to be an *ever-present Saviour,* should avail themselves of this powerful aid. Under such training, Jesus Christ should be constantly presented to them, as their ever-watchful, tender, and sympathizing friend.

THE PUBLICATION OF *THE SCARLET LETTER*

The seventh section includes excerpts and illustrations related to the writing and publication of *The Scarlet Letter* — and to public reaction to Hawthorne's novel. The section opens with excerpts from three letters written by Hawthorne: the first two to his publisher, James Fields, of Ticknor and Fields, and the third to his friend Horatio Bridge. Next come three illustrations: first a reprint of the title page to the first edition, in which Hawthorne's suggestion that the title appear in red ink was indeed taken, then two illustrations by nineteenth-century painter and illustrator George H. Broughton for a 1908 reprint of the second edition commissioned by The Grolier Club, which describes itself as "America's oldest and largest society for bibliophiles and enthusiasts in the graphic arts."[8] The first of these illustrations accompanied Chapter VIII, "The Elf-Child and the Minister," and the second, Chapter XII, "The Minister's Vigil." The section closes with four reviews of *The Scarlet Letter* by Hawthorne's contemporaries, all of which discuss, to a greater or lesser extent, the novel's morality: the propriety of the subject matter, the presentation of Christian doctrine, the effect of Hawthorne's tenure at Brook Farm,[9] the proper sphere and rights of women, and so forth.

[8] The Grolier Club, January 2005 <http://www.grolierclub.org/>.

[9] George Ripley, the man who cofounded Brook Farm and was sued by Hawthorne, praised the novel, calling it "the greatest production of the author, beautifully displaying the traits we have briefly hinted at, and sustained with a more vigorous reach of imagination, a more subtle instinct of humanity, and a more imposing splendor of portraiture, than any of his most successful previous works." *New York Tribune Supplement* IX (Apr. 1, 1850): 2. Reprinted in Brian Harding, ed., *Nathaniel Hawthorne: Critical Assessments,* vol. 1 (East Sussex, UK: Helm Information, 1995), 235.

NATHANIEL HAWTHORNE

Letter to James Fields (January 15, 1850)

"The Scarlet Letter" is rather a delicate subject to write upon, but in the way in which I have treated it, it appears to me there can be no objections on that score. The article entitled "Custom House" is introductory to the volume, so please read it first. In the process of writing, all political and official turmoil has subsided within me, so that I have not felt inclined to execute justice on any of my enemies.

From Nathaniel Hawthorne, *The Letters, 1843–1853,* ed. Thomas Woodson, L. Neal Smith, and Norman Holmes Pearson (Ohio State UP, 1985), 305, 307–08. Volume 16 of *The Centenary Edition of the Works of Nathaniel Hawthorne.*

THE

SCARLET LETTER,

A ROMANCE.

BY

NATHANIEL HAWTHORNE.

BOSTON:

TICKNOR, REED, AND FIELDS.

M DCCC L.

Title Page, First Edition of *The Scarlet Letter* (1850).
Courtesy of the Massachusetts Historical Society

Hester Prynne and Pearl at Governor Bellingham's Mansion with the Governor, John Wilson, Arthur Dimmesdale, and Roger Chillingworth. Illustration by George H. Boughton (1908).

George Boughton illustration for the 1908 edition of *The Scarlet Letter.* Courtesy of the Grolier Club of New York.

Hester Prynne, Arthur Dimmesdale, and Pearl on the Scaffold at Night, with Roger Chillingworth Below. Illustration by George H. Boughton (1908).

George Boughton illustration for the 1908 edition of *The Scarlet Letter.* Courtesy of the Grolier Club of New York.

NATHANIEL HAWTHORNE

Letter to James Fields (January 20, 1850)

I am truly glad that you like the introduction; for I was rather afraid that it might appear absurd and impertinent to be talking about myself, when nobody, that I know of, has requested any information on that subject.

As regards the size of the book, I have been thinking a good deal about it. . . . [I]f the book is made up entirely of "The Scarlet Letter," it will be too somber. I found it impossible to relieve the shadows of the story with so much light as I would gladly have thrown in. Keeping so close to its point as the tale does, and diversified no otherwise than by turning different sides of the same dark idea to the reader's eye, it will weary very many people, and disgust some. Is it safe, then, to stake the fate of the book entirely on this one chance?

* * *

In this latter event, it appears to me that the only proper title for the book would be "The Scarlet Letter"; for "The Custom House" is merely introductory — an entrance-hall to the magnificent edifice which I throw open to my guests. It would be funny, if, seeing the further passages so dark and dismal, they should all choose to stop there!

If "The Scarlet Letter" is to be the title, would it not be well to print it on the title-page in red ink? I am not quite sure about the good taste of so doing; but it would certainly be piquant and appropriate — and, I think, attractive to the great gull whom we are endeavoring to circumvent.

From *The Letters, 1843–1853* (Ohio State UP, 1985), 307–08.

NATHANIEL HAWTHORNE

Letter to Horatio Bridge (February 4, 1850)

My book, the publisher tells me, will not be out before April. He speaks of it in tremendous terms of approbation; so does Mrs. Hawthorne, to whom I read the conclusion, last night. It broke her

From *The Letters, 1843–1853* (Ohio State UP, 1985), 311–12.

heart and sent her to bed with a grievous headache — which I look upon as a triumphant success! Judging from its effect on her and the publisher, I may calculate on what bowlers call a "ten-strike." Yet I do not make any such calculation. Some portions of the book are powerfully written; but my writings do not, nor ever will, appeal to the broadest class of sympathies, and therefore will not attain a very wide popularity. Some like them very much; others care nothing for them, and see nothing in them. There is an introduction to this book — giving a sketch of my Custom-House life, with an imaginative touch here and there — which perhaps may be more widely attractive than the main narrative. The latter lacks sunshine. To tell you the truth it is — (I hope Mrs. Bridge is not present) — it is positively a h–ll-fired story, into which I found it almost impossible to throw any cheering light.

E. A. DUYCKINCK

From The Scarlet Letter: A Romance (March 30, 1850)

Mr. Hawthorne introduces his new story to the public, the longest of all that he has yet published, and most worthy in this way to be called a romance, with one of those pleasant personal descriptions which are the most charming of his compositions. . . .

The Scarlet Letter is a psychological romance. The hardiest Mrs. Malaprop would never venture to call it a novel. It is a tale of remorse, a study of character in which the human heart is anatomized, carefully, elaborately, and with striking poetic and dramatic power. Its incidents are simply these. A woman in the early days of Boston becomes the subject of the discipline of the court of those times, and is condemned to stand in the pillory and wear henceforth, in token of her shame, the scarlet letter A attached to her bosom. She carries her child with her to the pillory. Its other parent is unknown. At this opening scene her husband from whom she had been separated in Europe, preceding him by ship across the Atlantic, reappears from the forest, whither he had been thrown by shipwreck on his arrival. He was a man of cold intellectual temperament, and devotes his life thereafter to search for his wife's

From *The Literary World* VI. 165 (Mar. 30, 1850): 323–25. Reprinted in Brian Harding, ed., *Nathaniel Hawthorne: Critical Assessments,* vol. 1 (East Sussex, UK: Helm Information, 1995), 231–33.

guilty partner and a fiendish revenge. The young clergyman of the town, a man of devout sensibility and warmth of heart, is the victim, as this Mephistophilean old physician fixes himself by his side to watch over him and protect his health, an object of great solicitude to his parishioners, and, in reality, to detect his suspected secret and gloat over his tortures. This slow, cool, devilish purpose, like the concoction of some sublimated hell broth, is perfected gradually and inevitably. The wayward, elfish child, a concentration of guilt and passion, binds the interests of the parties together, but throws little sunshine over the scene. These are all the characters, with some casual introductions of the grim personages and manners of the period, unless we add the scarlet letter, which, in Hawthorne's hands, skilled to these allegorical, typical semblances, becomes vitalized as the rest. It is the hero of the volume. . . .

Mr. Hawthorne has, in fine, shown extraordinary power in this volume, great feeling and discrimination, a subtle knowledge of character in its secret springs and outer manifestations. He blends, too, a delicate fancy with this metaphysical insight. We would instance the chapter towards the close, entitled "The Minister in a Maze," where the effects of a diabolic temptation are curiously depicted, or "The Minister's Vigil," the night scene in the pillory. The atmosphere of the piece also is perfect. It was the mystic element, the weird forest influences of the old Puritan discipline and era. Yet there is no affrightment which belongs purely to history, which has not its echo even in the unlike and perversely commonplace custom-house of Salem. Then for the moral. Though severe, it is wholesome, and is a sounder bit of Puritan divinity than we have been of late accustomed to hear from the degenerate successors of Cotton Mather. We hardly know another writer who has lived so much among the new school who would have handled this delicate subject without an infusion of George Sand.[10] The spirit of his old Puritan ancestors, to whom he refers in the preface, lives in Nathaniel Hawthorne.

[10] George Sand (1804–1876) was a French novelist known for works that exalted passion and stressed the need for individuals to follow the dictates of their hearts, not moral conventions.

ANNE ABBOTT

From Review of *The Scarlet Letter* (July 1850)

. . . [W]e confess that, to our individual taste, this naughty chapter is more piquant than any thing in the book; the style is racy and pungent, not elaborately witty, but stimulating the reader's attention agreeably by original turns of expression, and unhackneyed combinations of words, falling naturally in their places, as if of their own accord. . . .

* * *

We know of no writer who better understands and combines the elements of the picturesque in writing than Mr. Hawthorne. . . . There is a naturalness and a continuous flow of expression in Mr. Hawthorne's books, that makes them delightful to read, especially in this our day, when the fear of triteness drives some writers, (even those who might otherwise avoid that reproach,) to adopt an abrupt and dislocated style, administering to our jaded attention frequent thumps and twitches, by means of outlandish idioms and forced inversions. . . . One cannot but wonder, by the way, that the master of such a wizard power over language as Mr. Hawthorne manifests should not choose a less revolting subject than this of *The Scarlet Letter,* to which fine writing seems as inappropriate as fine embroidery. The ugliness of pollution and vice is no more relieved by it than the gloom of the prison is by the rose tree at its door. There are some palliative expressions used, which cannot, even as a matter of taste, be approved.

* * *

With this portrait, we close our remarks on the book, which we should not have criticized at so great length, had we admired it less.

From *North American Review* LXII (July 1850): 135–48. Reprinted in Brian Harding, ed., *Nathaniel Hawthorne: Critical Assessments,* vol. 1 (East Sussex, UK: Helm Information, 1995), 243, 249–51.

ORESTES BROWNSON

From Review of *The Scarlet Letter* (October 1850)

The Christian who reads *The Scarlet Letter* cannot fail to perceive that the author is wholly ignorant of Christian asceticism, and that the highest principle of action he recognizes is pride. . . . Mr. Hawthorne seems never to have learned that pride is not only sin, but the root of all sin, and that humility is not only a virtue, but the root of all virtue. . . . All true remorse, all genuine repentance, springs from humility, and is sorrow for having offended God, not sorrow for having offended ourselves.

Mr. Hawthorne also mistakes entirely the effect of Christian pardon upon the interior state of the sinner. He seems entirely ignorant of the religion that can restore peace to the sinner, — true, inward peace, we mean. . . .

Again Mr. Hawthorne mistakes the character of confession. He does well to recognize and insist on its necessity; but he is wrong in supposing that its office is simply to disburden the mind by communicating its secrets to another, to restore the sinner to his self-complacency, and to relieve him from the charge of cowardice and hypocrisy. Confession is a duty we owe to God, and a means, not of restoring our self-complacency, but of restoring us to the favor of God, and reëstablishing us in his friendship. The work before us is full of mistakes of this sort, in those portions where the author really means to speak like a Christian, and therefore we are obliged to condemn it, where we acquit him of all unchristian intention.

As a picture of the old Puritans, taken from the position of a moderate transcendentalist and liberal of the modern school, the work has its merits; but as little as we sympathize with those stern old Popery-haters, we do not regard the picture as at all just. We should commend where the author condemns, and condemn where he commends. Their treatment of the adulteress was far more Christian than his ridicule of it. But enough of fault-finding, and as we have no praise, except what we have given, to offer, we here close this brief notice.

From *Brownson's Quarterly Review* IV (New Series) (October 1850): 528–32. Reprinted in Brian Harding, ed., *Nathaniel Hawthorne: Critical Assessments*, vol. 1 (East Sussex, UK: Helm Information, 1995), 268–70.

ARTHUR C. COXE

From The Writings of Hawthorne (January 4, 1851)

And this brings inquiry to its point. Why has our author selected such a theme? Why, amid all the suggestive incidents of life in a wilderness; of a retreat from civilization to which, in every individual case, a thousand circumstances must have concurred to reconcile human nature with estrangement from home and country; or amid the historical connections of our history with Jesuit adventure, savage invasion, regicide outlawry, and French aggression, should the taste of Mr. Hawthorne have preferred as the proper material for romance, the nauseous amour of a Puritan pastor, with a frail creature of his charge, whose mind is represented as far more debauched than her body? Is it, in short, because a running undertide of filth has become as requisite to a romance, as death in the fifth act to a tragedy? Is the French era actually begun in our literature? And is the flesh, as well as the world and the devil, to be henceforth dished up in fashionable novels, and discussed at parties, by spinsters and their beaux, with as unconcealed a relish as they give to the vanilla in their ice cream? We would be slow to believe it, and we hope our author would not willingly have it so, yet we honestly believe that *The Scarlet Letter* has already done not a little to degrade our literature, and to encourage social licentiousness. . . .

We shall entirely mislead our reader if we give him to suppose that *The Scarlet Letter* is coarse in its details, or indecent in its phraseology. This very article of our own, is far less suited to polite ears, than any page of the romance before us; and the reason is, we call things by their right names, while the romance never hints the shocking words that belong to its things, but, like Mephistopheles, insinuates that the archfiend himself is a very tolerable sort of person, if nobody would call him Mr. Devil. . . . The language of our author, like patent blacking, "would not soil the whitest linen," and yet the composition itself, would suffice, if well laid on, to Ethiopize° the snowiest conscience that ever sat like a swan upon that mirror of heaven, a Christian maiden's

Ethiopize: Blacken.

From *The Church Review* III (Jan. 4, 1851): 489–511. Reprinted in Brian Harding, ed., *Nathaniel Hawthorne: Critical Assessments,* vol. 1 (East Sussex, UK: Helm Information, 1995), 285–86, 288–89.

imagination. We are not sure we speak quite strong enough, when we say, that we would much rather listen to the coarsest scene of Goldsmith's *Vicar,*[11] read aloud by a sister or daughter, than to hear from such lips, the perfectly chaste language of a scene in *The Scarlet Letter,* in which a married wife and her reverend paramour, with their unfortunate offspring, are introduced as the actors, and in which the whole tendency of the conversation is to suggest a sympathy for their sin, and an anxiety that they may be able to accomplish a successful escape beyond the seas, to some country where their shameful commerce may be perpetuated. . . . The *Vicar of Wakefield* is sometimes coarsely virtuous, but *The Scarlet Letter* is delicately immoral.

* * *

. . . [T]he whole moral of the tale is given in the words — "Be true — be true," as if sincerity in sin were virtue, and as if "Be clean — be clean," were not the more fitting conclusion. . . .

We suppose this sort of sentiment must be charged to the doctrines enforced at "Brook-farm," although "Brook-farm" itself could never have been Mr. Hawthorne's home, had not other influences prepared him for such a Bedlam. At all events, this is no mere slip of the pen; it is the essential morality of the work. . . .

. . . The late Convention of females at Boston, to assert the "rights of woman," may show us that there are already some, who think the world is even now *ripe for it,* and safe as we may suppose our own fair relatives to be above such a low contagion, we must remember that to a woman, the very suggestion of a mode of life for her, as preferable to that which the Gospel has made the glorious sphere of her duties and her joys, is an insult and a degradation to which no one that loves her would allow her to be exposed.

We assure Mr. Hawthorne, in conclusion, that nothing less than an earnest wish that his future career may redeem this misstep, and prove a blessing to his country, has tempted us to enter upon a criticism so little suited to our tastes, as that of his late production.

[11] Oliver Goldsmith's novel *The Vicar of Wakefield* (1766).

PART TWO

The Scarlet Letter: A Case Study in Contemporary Criticism

A Critical History of *The Scarlet Letter*

EARLY RECEPTION

In a letter written to a friend just after the publication of *The Scarlet Letter,* Hawthorne began to write the history of the novel's critical reception. First, he sums up the response of his wife to its concluding chapter: "It broke her heart and sent her to bed with a grievous headache — which I look upon as a triumphant success! Judging from its effect on her and the publisher, I may calculate on what bowlers call a ten-strike. Yet," Hawthorne goes on to say, "I do not make any such calculation. My writings do not, nor ever will, appeal to the broadest class of sympathies." He proceeds by predicting that if anything the introduction to his novel, "The Custom-House," which has "an imaginative touch here and there . . . may be more widely attractive than the main narrative." *The Scarlet Letter,* he admits, not only "lacks sunshine" but is a "positively h–ll fired story, into which I found it almost impossible to throw any cheering light" (qtd. in Crowley 151).

Hawthorne's predictions proved prophetic, in the sense that many of those who reviewed the volume in the year following its publication *were* pleased by the imaginative touches of "The Custom-House" and *did* find the novel that followed it considerably less "attractive." George Ripley, writing in the *New York Tribune Supplement,* praised "The Custom-House" for its "unrivalled force of graphic delineation" and predicted it "will furnish an agreeable amusement to those who are so far from the scene of action as to feel no wound in their personal relations" (qtd. in Crowley 155, 159). "We confess," Anne W. Abbott wrote in the *North American Review,* "that to our individual taste, this naughty [Custom-House] chapter is more piquant than anything in the book. . . . We like the preface better than the tale" (qtd. in Crowley 164–65). As for "the tale," contemporary reviewers saw *The Scarlet Letter* as evidence of national moral decay as well as of the decline of the novel. "Our interest" in Hester Prynne, Abbott claims, "only continues while we have hope for her soul"; once Hester's "humility catches a new tint, and we find it pride, . . . she disappoints us. . . . We were looking to behold a Christian." As for Arthur Dimmesdale, "we are told repeatedly, that the Christian element yet pervades his character and guides its efforts; but it seems strangely wanting" (165–66).

A self-described Christian, Abbott was nonetheless not writing in a Christian forum; those reviewers who did were even more severe. In the *Church Review,* Arthur Cleveland Coxe declares himself "astonished" that Hawthorne would choose adultery for his subject. Such incidents may have been common even in Puritan times, he admits, but "good taste might be pardoned for not giving them prominence in fiction." Summarizing the story as the "nauseous amour" of a Puritan pastor and a woman whose mind is even more "debauched" than her body, Coxe goes on to ask whether "filth" is now requisite to romance and whether "the French era" has "actually begun in our literature" (182).

To be sure, some of these early reviewers did *not* see *The Scarlet Letter* as either a danger to morals or a precursor to a "French" (that is, amoral or immoral) era in American literature. George Bailey Loring, for instance, writing in the *Massachusetts Quarterly Review,* went so far as to say that the novel was a "vehicle of religion and ethics" because it "properly exposed the inhumanity of Puritanism, which repressed the sensuous element in human nature" (qtd. in Crowley 169). But most of those who assessed the morality of *The Scarlet Letter* positively did so by claiming that the novel was actually a morally instructive, even puritanical, work that warned against the pitfalls of sensuality in general and adulterous misdeeds in particular. E. A. Duyckinck took that tack in *The Literary World.* As for "the moral," he writes, "though severe, it is wholesome, and is a sounder bit of Puritan divinity than we have been of late accustomed to hear from the degenerate successors of Cotton Mather. . . . The spirit of his old Puritan ancestors, to whom he refers in the preface, lives in Nathaniel Hawthorne" (qtd. in Crowley 156–57).

E. P. Whipple agreed, stating in *Graham's Magazine* that the "moral purpose of the book" is so "definite" that "the most abandoned libertine could not read the volume without being thrilled into something like virtuous resolution." In Whipple's view, no novel could be more *un*-French: "To those who have theories of seduction and adultery modeled after the French school of novelists," he says,

> the volume may afford matter for very instructive and edifying contemplation; for, in truth, Hawthorne, in *The Scarlet Letter*, has utterly undermined the whole philosophy on which the French novel rests. . . . He has made his guilty parties end, not as his own fancy or his own benevolent sympathies might dictate, but as the spiritual laws, lying back of all persons, dictated to him. (qtd. in Crowley 156, 157, 161–62)

In addition to finding sound moral teaching in the book, both Whipple and Duyckinck detected philosophy and artfulness. Duyckinck referred to the novel as "a drama in which thoughts are acts," while describing as "perfect" the "atmosphere of the piece." Whipple called *The Scarlet Letter* a "beautiful and touching romance" with "a profound philosophy underlying the story"; Hawthorne's regular readers, he predicted, "will hardly be prepared for a novel of so much tragic interest and tragic power, so deep in thought and so condensed in style." The only fault he finds in the book, "if fault it have, is the almost morbid intensity with which the characters are realized, and the consequent lack of sufficient geniality in the delineation" (qtd. in Crowley 160–61).

In the century following the appearance of these early reviews, *The Scarlet Letter* was of course often discussed. But because literary criticism had not yet developed into the intellectual discipline that it has become since the 1940s, Hawthorne's novel was not written about — certainly it was not carefully and systematically analyzed — with the frequency that it has been in the past fifty years. Nonetheless, a few interesting studies were published between the last of the contemporary reviews and the advent of modern Hawthorne criticism, two of them by eminent novelists. In 1879, a book was published simply entitled *Hawthorne*, written by the American novelist Henry James. Praising the novel as "the finest piece of imaginative writing yet put forth in this country" and as "something" that could be "sent to Europe as exquisite in quality as anything that had been received" (110–11), James nonetheless had much that was critical to say as well. Like his predecessors, and like Hawthorne himself, he found the story somewhat too painful, too somber: "It is densely dark," he writes, "with a single spot of vivid colour in it; and will probably long remain the most consistently gloomy of English novels of the first order" (109). Also like the first reviewers, he viewed the novel as a novel of ideas. But whereas E. A Duyckinck had approved of the novel for being one in which "thoughts are acts," James objected to the fact that even "characters," when examined closely, turn out to be "representatives of a single state of mind" (114). He felt that the philosophical abstractness of the novel made it somewhat frigid; as for the "symbolism" contributing to that abstractness, "there is," James writes, "I think, too much." Especially excessive, in James's view, is Hawthorne's placement of the letter *A* in the sky toward the end of the novel. Here, James politely suggests, "we feel that he goes too far" (114, 117, 118).

On the question of the book's ethical content (or lack thereof), James sides squarely with that minority who had found the book highly moral in character. In fact, he refuses even to say that the book is *about* adultery, which, he points out, has been committed long before the story begins. "To Hawthorne's imagination," James argues, "the fact that these two persons had loved each other too well was of an interest comparatively vulgar; what appealed to him was the idea of their moral situation in the long years that were to follow" (112). Because the plot turns on that situation, it is, in James's view, "full of the moral presence of the race that invented Hester's penance":

> Puritanism, in a word is there, not only objectively, as Hawthorne tried to place it there, but subjectively as well. Not, I mean in his judgment of his characters, in any harshness of prejudice, or in the obtrusion of a moral lesson; but in the very quality of his own vision, in a certain coldness and exclusiveness of treatment. (112–14)

It is hard not to recall, while reading James's words, those written by Duyckinck some thirty years earlier: "The spirit of his old Puritan ancestors, to whom he refers in the preface, lives in Nathaniel Hawthorne." The difference between Duyckinck and James is that the former approved of what the latter found "cold," or a weakness in an otherwise great artistic sensibility.

In 1923, just over forty years after James had published his evaluation, *The Scarlet Letter* was once again being debated by an influential writer. This time, it was D. H. Lawrence, author of *Sons and Lovers* and *Lady Chatterley's Lover,* who was refocusing critical attention on the novel. Lawrence, who devoted the seventh chapter of his *Studies in*

Classic American Literature (1923) to "Hawthorne and *The Scarlet Letter*," in many ways brings to culmination the views of his critical predecessors while at the same time writing a highly idiosyncratic and provocative account of Hawthorne's novel meant to justify his own agnostic and sensual worldview.

Lawrence agreed with James that the story was not a romance, calling the book "a sort of parable, an earthly story with a hellish meaning" (121). Like James and a few of the early reviewers, he finds the book *too* dark, painful, and hellish; like them, he sees the spirit of the book as essentially moral and didactic and the author of the book as essentially Puritan in spirit. But he goes further, attacking the book as a deeply destructive myth that teaches hypocrisy and the sinfulness of the sensual and instinctive life. *The Scarlet Letter*, in Lawrence's view, is a particularly American reworking of the biblical story of the Fall containing the following message: one should either deny the body and die, as Dimmesdale does, or deny the sensual through self-sacrifice, by becoming a sister of mercy, as does Hester. Finally, one should keep up appearances, as do both Hester and Dimmesdale.

In a sense, Lawrence weaves together two long-divergent strands of argument about *The Scarlet Letter*. Along with some of his precursors, he finds the novel to be puritanical and moral, but he doesn't believe the novel to be great in *spite* of that fact. Like the pious reviewers for Christian journals, he regards the novel as "hellish[ly]" dangerous and destructive. But to Lawrence, its danger resides not in any approval of the life of the flesh, but rather in what he sees as the novel's "devilish" parable: "*Be good! Be good!* warbles Nathaniel. *Be good, and never sin! Be sure your sins will find you out*" (123).

MODERNIST PERSPECTIVES: THE NEW CRITICISM

In the 1940s, when academic criticism began to flourish as a discipline, it was the artistry of *The Scarlet Letter* — not its moral or mythical content — that critics such as F. O. Matthiessen, Hyatt Waggoner, and Richard Harter Fogle tended to stress. These critics and others of their generation, the so-called New Critics, were far more prone to follow James by discussing the symbolism of *The Scarlet Letter* than to expand on Lawrence's perception of the novel as a destructive revision of the myth of the Fall as worked out by an American moralist with a Puritan bent.

The New Criticism, or formalism as it is now usually called, was a modernist reaction against the tendency to read the literary work as a product of its author's personal experience and historical context. One proponent, William K. Wimsatt, warned against trying to determine or discern an author's purpose in writing a work (Wimsatt and Monroe C. Beardsley referred to this as the "Intentional Fallacy"). Our time as readers is better spent, the formalists suggested, in describing the way the parts of a work relate to form a beautiful artistic unity. They avoided talking about the effects that works of literature might have on readers (or on the national morality), believing the critic's job to be that of identifying the form and meaning of a work, not describing the responses of readers to it or, indeed, any factors extrinsic to it.

When F. O. Matthiessen discussed *The Scarlet Letter* in *American Renaissance: Art and Expression in the Age of Emerson and Whitman* (1941), he stressed the artfulness of the novel, developing an idea first advanced in 1902 by a scholar named George Edward Woodberry, namely, that *The Scarlet Letter* is intrinsically theatrical. Matthiessen argues that in this novel Hawthorne

> developed his most coherent plot. Its symmetrical design is built around the three scenes on the scaffold or the pillory. There Hester endures her public shaming in the opening chapter. There, midway through the book, the minister . . . ascends one midnight for self-torture, and is joined by Hester. . . . There also, at the end, . . . the exhausted and death-stricken Dimmesdale totters to confess his sin . . . and to die in Hester's arms. (275)

Matthiessen's stress on the "coherence" and "symmetrical[ity]" provided by the twice-repeated scaffold setting is typical of formalist criticism.

In *Hawthorne: A Critical Study* (1955), Hyatt Waggoner exposed a different kind of coherent pattern in *The Scarlet Letter*, one involving imagery. He shows how a given image, like that of flowers or weeds, "is established as a motif" and how, once established, it is able to function symbolically (127). Hawthorne typically begins by presenting a "pure sensory image" (the prison is described as dark), then "expands it into a mixed image, exploring its connotations" (Chillingworth's "face darkened with some powerful emotion"), repeating the process until the image, "enriched by the relations," is "drained" of its original status as a sensory descriptor and becomes part of "a work of symbolism" (119–29 passim). Thus, by the time "Governor Bellingham says that Pearl is 'in the dark' concerning her soul, the expression means far more to the reader than that she is not . . . properly instructed: it calls up the whole range of colors, and the moral and other values attached to them, which the reader has absorbed by this time" (127).

Richard Harter Fogle was another New Critic who analyzed motifs involving color, light, and darkness in *The Scarlet Letter;* indeed, his most influential critical study, published in 1952, was entitled *Hawthorne's Fiction: The Light and the Dark.* In addition to showing how the interconnected imagery of darkness, of the "waxing and waning of sunlight," and of "the . . . hell-fire which occurs throughout *The Scarlet Letter*" come to serve as indices of the emotional or spiritual states of characters, Fogle discusses another kind of unity: that provided by the book's "sustained and rigorous dramatic irony" resulting from its repetition of scenes in which one character is aware of something known to some, but not all, of the characters present in the scene. For instance, when Dimmesdale tries to persuade Hester to confess publicly the name of her partner in adultery, "his words have a double meaning — one to the onlookers, another far different to Hester and the speaker himself" (*Hawthorne's Fiction* 111, 114–15).

Fogle argues that these dramatic ironies not only help advance the theme of tragic concealment, but also provide the basis for the novel's climax, in which Chillingworth arrives at "a moment of terrible self-knowledge." The old man's sudden realization that the ultimate result of his long-concealed purpose is the destruction not so much of Dimmesdale as of himself provides not only the book's final dramatic irony but also "an Aristotelian reversal, where a conscious and deep-laid purpose brings about totally unforeseen and opposite results" (*Hawthorne's Fiction* 112). (Fogle's use of Aristotle, though not forbidden by the formalistic tenets of the New Criticism, nonetheless takes us beyond Hawthorne's text and its intrinsic relationships — and causes us to see *The Scarlet Letter* in the light of a wider context, that of literary history.)

Darrel Abel was another critic writing during the 1950s who combined a formalist attention to artistic structure with an interest in literary antecedents. In writing about Arthur Dimmesdale, he adheres closely to the text, developing Matthiessen's argument about the structural importance of the three scaffold scenes by showing that these scenes prove that Dimmesdale, not Hester Prynne, is the novel's main character. In his study, *The Moral Picturesque: Studies in Hawthorne's Fiction* (1988), Abel outlines the scenes as follows: at the beginning of the book, Dimmesdale is not on the scaffold with Hester but knows he should be; in the middle, he ascends the scaffold alone, at night; at the end he does so in public, to confess his sin. The plot of the novel, in Abel's view, "exhibits the protracted struggle between influences seeking to prevent the minister from ascending this emblematic scaffold . . . and influences seeking to induce him to do so" (227). But when Abel turns his attention from this character whose "role is the structural and thematic center of the romance" (225) to other characters, he widens the angle of his vision to encompass not just the form of one novel but also the backdrop of literary history. Through Pearl, according to Abel, Hawthorne argued with a specific Romantic poet, Wordsworth, and showed that the Wordsworthian child of nature is not necessarily a pure and moral child, because humanity, not nature, is the source of the morality.

The debate about whether Hester or Dimmesdale lies at the novel's center was, to some extent, finessed by Roy R. Male in his book *Hawthorne's Tragic Vision* (1957). Male argues that the first third of *The Scarlet Letter* describes Hester's "limited ascension," as she "recognizes her guilt" and "reaches the peak of her moral development"; that the second third of the novel is concerned with the shifting of the burden of guilt, represented by Chillingworth, from Hester to Dimmesdale; and that "the final third (Chapters XVII to XXIV) deals with Dimmesdale's ascension. . . . Where Hester's ascension was limited," Male explains, Dimmesdale's "is complete" (97–98). Male's reading turns the novel into something like a Christian tragedy: Christian in that it is about the burden of original sin (symbolized for Male by the act of adultery committed before the opening of the novel); tragic in that, "like *Oedipus Tyrannus* and *King Lear*, [it] is about ways of seeing" (recognition, discovery, insight, self-recognition) and, finally, about cathartic revelations (101 passim).

BEYOND THE NEW CRITICISM: *THE SCARLET LETTER* CONTEXTUALIZED

With the advantage of hindsight, we can see that formalism was in flux by 1957, the year Male published his study depicting *The Scarlet Letter* as a kind of Christian tragedy and Richard Chase published his even more influential book, *The American Novel and Its Tradition.* Chase not only sought to define Hawthorne's novel in light of literary tradition (his chapter on *The Scarlet Letter* was entitled "Hawthorne and the Limits of Romance"), but also politely attacked the formalist New Critics. "The New Criticism," Chase wrote, "has been interested primarily in poetry and when it has turned to the novel it has too often assumed that the techniques of criticism which are suitable to poetry are sufficient for the novel." Specifically, Chase identifies as inappropriate the New Critics' intense interest in novelistic "metaphor and symbol" (70). That the novel in general and *The Scarlet Letter* in particular were becoming subject to new and hybrid critical approaches became even clearer a year later, in 1958, when Harry Levin published *The Power of Blackness.* In that important study, works by Hawthorne, Poe, and Melville are seen (re)expressing timeless parables or fables that survive the centuries and "pass from one environment to another," each being "an irreducible unit of what [Carl] Jung," a contemporary of Sigmund Freud's who proposed an alternative psychoanalytic theory, "would call the collective unconscious" (9–10).

The fable Levin discovers concerns what Melville called "the power of blackness," a blackness "from whose visitations, in some shape or other, no deeply thinking mind is always and wholly free." Citing D. H. Lawrence's description of "the Pilgrim Fathers" as "'black, masterful men' who had crossed a 'black sea' in 'black revulsion' from Europe," Levin finds in the fable what Lawrence had found in it: something particularly American. And yet, he hastens to remind us, the "obsession" with the awful power of blackness "takes us back to the very beginning of things, the primal darkness, the void that God shaped by creating light and dividing night from day." The world's religions "all . . . seem to posit some dichotomy [between darkness and light], such as the Yin and Yang" (26, 29). Whereas Hawthorne's images of black flowers and black weeds had interested formalist critics because such images provided unity within *The Scarlet Letter,* these same images captivate post-formalists like Levin because they exemplify an ancient mythology of blackness and thus a unity within human consciousness.

Levin was not the first critic to read *The Scarlet Letter* in light of a persistent fable or mythology. As early as 1953, when formalism was still the dominant critical approach, William Bysshe Stein viewed Hawthorne's novel as a relatively recent version of the ancient Faust myth in his *Hawthorne's Faust: A Study of the Devil Archetype.* (Faust, of course, was the scholar-magician who sold his soul to the devil in exchange for secret or forbidden knowledge.) Stein points out that Chillingworth, like Faust, pays a terrible price for the knowledge he seeks:

> After Hester refuses to reveal the identity of her lover, [Chillingworth] extorts a pledge of silence from her on the legal state of their relations. But something in his cruel smile causes her to

> regret her promise, and she inquires in fear: "Art thou like the Black Man that haunts the forest round about us? Hast thou enticed me into a bond that will prove the ruin of my soul?" His answer is sardonically elusive: "Not thy soul! No, not thine!" (109)

Having yielded to the temptation to exchange his own soul for knowledge, Chillingworth, like Faust, becomes a tempter himself. And Hester, by entering into a pact with her husband not to tell anyone that she is his wife, becomes a secondary Faust figure. She is Faustian in her suffering; Faustian insofar as she becomes an intellectual rebel in whose mind, the novel tells us, "the world's law was not law"; and Faustian, too, because she also becomes a tempter. (Dimmesdale, whom she tempts in the forest to run away with her, wonders "[A]m I given over utterly to the fiend? Did I make a contract with him in the forest, and sign it with my blood?" [p. 172 in this volume].) Stein's study of "the devil archetype" in Hawthorne was one of the earliest examples of a kind of criticism that came to be known as archetypal or "myth criticism." Now usually associated with Northrop Frye, this emerging type of criticism taught the importance of uncovering not only the larger cultural myths (of the Fall, of Faust, or of the Power of Blackness) that underlie individual literary works but also the personal mythology of an individual writer, part of which is expressed in each work.

One of the first critics since the advent of the formalist New Criticism to (re)turn scholarly attention to the author was Charles Feidelson Jr. Feidelson, who in 1953 had published a typically formalist analysis of "Hawthorne the Symbolist," revisited *The Scarlet Letter* in a 1964 essay published in *Hawthorne Centenary Essays.* Drawing on biography, which only a little while ago had been out of bounds to formalists, and "The Custom-House," which had proved of little interest except insofar as it helped "frame" the novel proper, Feidelson argues that an isolated and lonely Hawthorne forged a link with the human community through his writing of *The Scarlet Letter.* (Interestingly, in making the case, Feidelson may have committed what Wimsatt and Beardsley had called "the Intentional Fallacy.") Hawthorne may seem to have gone about his business in an odd or even paradoxical way, that is, by writing about a woman who was herself alienated from a community that was itself a community of exiles. But, in fact, Feidelson suggests, Hester is able to accomplish in the novel exactly what Hawthorne needed to accomplish in life, for she comes to transform her enforced life apart from others into a positive individuality: "She converts disinheritance into freedom, isolation into individuality, excommunication into a personal presence that is actual and communicable" (35).

PSYCHOANALYTIC, FEMINIST, AND NEW HISTORICIST VIEWS: THE EMERGENCE OF CONTEMPORARY APPROACHES

Feidelson's reading of *The Scarlet Letter* could almost be called a psychoanalytic interpretation, because it views the novel as the product of an author's struggle with a complex personal problem. What this interpretation lacks — namely, the explicit application of psychoanalytic theory — was not long in coming. In *The Sins of the Fathers: Hawthorne's Psychological Themes* (1966), Frederick C. Crews was to reread the novel in light of terms and concepts developed by psychoanalytic theorist Sigmund Freud: such as the libido, or sex drive, and the ego, that part of the mind that typically censors, or sublimates, forbidden desires into more socially acceptable alternatives. As a result of his Freudian applications, Crews came up with a reading of *The Scarlet Letter* quite different from all preceding ones, and very different, indeed, from formalist and quasiformalist accounts. Taking seriously Hawthorne's own description of the novel as a "h–ll-fired story, into which I found it almost impossible to throw any cheering light," Crews dismisses as particularly wrongheaded interpretations (by Male, specifically, but presumably by Fogle as well) representing *The Scarlet Letter* as culminating in self-recognition, revelation, and redemption. In Crews's view, the novel is a dark piece of psychological realism throughout. It explores libidinous desire, the ego's repression of such desire, and the variety of ways in which desire may be gratified after it has been disguised or sublimated.

Central to Crews's analysis of the novel is the passage where Hawthorne speaks of the psyche or "soul" as "a ruined wall" continually "watched and guarded," lest the "enemy . . . force his way" through again or circumvent the "breach" via "some other avenue" (p. 159). The enemy, according to Crews, would be a forbidden impulse (and the guilt that accompanies it); the guardian of the wall would, in Freudian terms, be the repressive or censoring ego. But the ego is a less than effective sentry; disguised or sublimated, the forbidden impulse may be readmitted and entertained via other avenues. In scourging himself, Crews suggests, Dimmesdale reindulges libidinous desire in a disguised and twisted form; similarly, in rewriting and delivering the impassioned Election Day sermon, the minister draws on and sublimates the same sexual energies that once drove him to break the law of this society. "Dimmesdale's penance," according to Crews, continually "fail[s] to purify him because it . . . has incorporated and embodied the very urge it has been punishing" (141).

Archetypal and psychoanalytical criticism afford two examples of contemporary critical approaches whose practitioners are skeptical of New Critical, or formalist, analysis. Feminist and new historicist criticism provide two other, more recent examples. Nina Baym begins a 1981 feminist study of Hawthorne with the reminder that, just "prior to" the advent of formalism or "the New Criticism," the novel "was widely agreed to be a glorification of Hester." Then, New Critics like Abel had come along, arguing that "Dimmesdale was the novelist's true protagonist" and that "Hawthorne portrayed Hester as woefully inadequate." But "to minimize Hester's significance . . . it is necessary to minimize or ignore the plot which points so unequivocally to her importance," Baym protests (49–59). Thus, even "from a structural point of view, this position is untenable. Of the romance's twenty-four chapters, thirteen are 'about' Hester, three are 'about' Hester and Dimmesdale both, and eight are 'about' Dimmesdale" (51). Baym continues: "I have asked myself over and over why it is that critics of the 1950s were almost unanimously concerned to deny Hester her place as protagonist of *The Scarlet Letter*." One answer she comes up with is that Hester is associated with "passion, freedom, and individualism," whereas the New Critics valued form and order. "Beyond this," Baym writes,

> I have come to the regretful conclusion that some of the unwillingness, perhaps much of it, to recognize Hester as the protagonist came from a more covert aspect of the New Critical social ideology, its strong sense of appropriate male/female roles and its consequent conviction that it would be improper for a woman character to be the protagonist in what might well be the greatest American book. (51–52)

As evidence that formalists were straining to "diminish the significance of Hester," Baym points to the fact that, in order to accomplish their end, they had to associate her with "romantic individualism," whereas "almost nothing that she does in *The Scarlet Letter* can be labeled as an example of romantic individualism" (53).

Several of the critics who have analyzed *The Scarlet Letter* from a new historicist perspective have focused on the historical period during which *The Scarlet Letter* was produced, suggesting that the novel — though set in seventeenth-century America — in fact reflects the concerns and biases of the author's nineteenth-century American culture. The Puritan past in which the novel is set is thus a kind of disguise, or screen, that hides the novel's true agenda. And, according to Jonathan Arac's essay "The Politics of *The Scarlet Letter*" (1986), that agenda is to warn against the dangers of the abolitionist movement. "Abolitionism," after all, "made the young Henry Adams feel that Boston in 1850 was once again revolutionary," and Hawthorne, cautioning against revolutionary activity, told the tale of an alienated revolutionary thinker, Hester, who gradually comes to see that acceptance plus patient, sympathetic work accomplish more than rebellious thoughts or actions (248). "Students judge *The Scarlet Letter* an intransitive 'work of art,'" Arac writes, "unlike, say, *Uncle Tom's Cabin*, which is 'propaganda' rather than 'art,' for it aims to change your life. If recent revaluation has shown that *Uncle Tom's Cabin* is also art, may it not be equally important to show that *The Scarlet Letter* is also propaganda — not to change your life?" (251).

Arac — who adapts the theories of Marx, Benjamin, and Foucault — was not the first of the new historicists to discuss the conservative subtext of Hawthorne's text. That subject had been first broached in 1985 by Larry J. Reynolds, in his groundbreaking essay "*The Scarlet Letter* and Revolutions Abroad." Beginning with the observation that the novel was written "in the wake of the revolutions [in France, Austria, and what is now Italy] in 1849," Reynolds argued that Hawthorne, unlike his wife and fellow New England writers, had been less than supportive of European revolutionary activity. Furthermore, he had worried that radical movements in Europe might be imminent or already under way in America. In "The Custom-House," which he at one point refers to as the "Posthumous Papers of a Decapitated Surveyor" (52), Hawthorne implicitly compares the victory of the Whigs over the Democrats to revolution gone wrong in France. Even the setting of the novel, remote though it seems from mid-nineteenth-century Europe, has a revolutionary context. "The opening scenes of the novel take place in May 1642 and the closing ones in May 1649. These dates coincide almost exactly with those of the English Civil War fought between King Charles I and his Puritan Parliament," Reynolds pointed out.

> When Hester Prynne is led from the prison by the beadle who cries, "Make way, good people, make way, in the King's name," less than a month has passed since Charles' Puritan Parliament had

> sent him what amounted to a declaration of war. . . . By the final scenes of the novel, when Arthur is deciding to die as a martyr, Charles I has just been beheaded. (52–53)

Arguing that "a strong reactionary spirit underlies the work," Reynolds maintained that *The Scarlet Letter* is an antirevolutionary text: "when Hester or Arthur battle to maintain or regain their rightful place in the social or spiritual order, the narrator sympathizes with them; when they become revolutionary instead and attempt to overthrow an established order, he becomes unsympathetic" (48, 58).

Of the various new historicist approaches to *The Scarlet Letter*, the most influential has been Sacvan Bercovitch's 1988 essay "Hawthorne's A-Morality of Compromise." (Bercovitch describes himself as an "ideological critic," but his layered historical analysis provides exactly the sort of "thick description" — a phrase coined by anthropologist Clifford Geertz — that is the goal of the new historicist perspective.) Like Arac, Bercovitch sees the novel as a subtle piece of nineteenth-century propaganda — "thick propaganda," as he puts it — as well as a work of art (9). He extends significantly Arac's argument that Hawthorne was writing against the abolitionists and their radical demands for an immediate end to slavery. He also develops the seminal ideas of Reynolds, arguing that *The Scarlet Letter* is a nineteenth-century American cultural artifact that contains among its subtexts a warning against the fruitless dangers of European-style radicalism. By describing Hester as emerging from a "moral wilderness" in which she looked at "whatever priests or legislators had established" with "hardly more reverence than the Indian would feel" (157), Hawthorne also pictures her emergence from the "spirit" of speculative radicalism, "then common enough on the other side of the Atlantic," into a spirit of community and compromise (133). Like Reynolds, Bercovitch recognizes that Hawthorne saw in the Whig victory over the Democrats — the victory that had swept Hawthorne from office, turned him into a "decapitated Surveyor," and *returned* him to his writing desk — a sign that revolutionary activity might be spreading to his own country. But Bercovitch goes beyond Reynolds (and Arac) by suggesting that Hawthorne saw another such sign. That omen was none other than the women's rights movement, a movement that "social commentators" of the day had, as Bercovitch demonstrates, viewed as symptomatic of a "red plague of European revolutions on these shores" (Stanton 805).

Three years after publishing "Hawthorne's A-Morality of Compromise," Bercovitch published a book-length study of Hawthorne entitled *The Office of The Scarlet Letter* (1991), in which he significantly expanded the scope of his original essay to discuss related and supporting aspects of Hawthorne's novel: its roots in works by writers such as Alexis de Tocqueville and Ralph Waldo Emerson; its tendency to universalize crime as sin; and its way of preparing the reader *not* to be surprised by Hester's eventual return to Boston. In doing so, he produced a body of work that, perhaps more than any other scholarly enterprise of its era, created far-reaching ripples and countercurrents, especially in historically oriented Hawthorne scholarship published after 1988.

One scholar who used and wrestled with Bercovitch's ideas is Charles Swann, who in *Nathaniel Hawthorne, Tradition and Revolution* (1991) argues that, like the scarlet letter Hawthorne claims he found in the Salem Custom House, *The Scarlet Letter* makes sense only in light of history. (In fact, Swann points out, "if the Democrats had won the Presidential Election of 1848 and if we are to believe Hawthorne, *The Scarlet Letter* would most likely not have been written" [76].) But history, Swann goes on to suggest, makes sense only in light of the imagination. When Hawthorne claims that the old needlework *A* is "the groundwork of a tale," he hardly opposes tale and historical artifact, because "groundwork" turns out to be a term needlework artists used to refer to the plain cloth foundation through which they wove the brighter, externally visible threads. Thus, the implication is clear: even the historical grounds of fiction are, themselves, weavings of sorts; for Swann, as for other new historicists, these would be the complexly interspersed discourses without which historical artifacts or works of historical fiction would make no sense — or even be identifiable as having historical significance.

Like many critics practicing the new historicist perspective, Swann is interested in the discourses underlying and emanating from public ceremonies, and particularly in those symbolic elements that both reveal and "reinforce the power and structure of society" (87). He pays close attention to Hawthorne's description of the clothing worn by "men assuming the reins of power," noting that the "deep ruffs, painfully wrought bands, and gorgeously embroidered gloves" that Hawthorne tells us "were readily allowed to individuals dignified by rank and wealth" but "forb[idden] to the plebeian order" were in fact, produced by powerless individuals at the bottom of the social order — poor laborers and even social outcasts such as Hester. Class, for Swann, turns out to be one of the embroidered fictions via which society defends the status quo and fends off change.

In discussing class, Swann avails himself of Marxist thought, drawing upon Christopher Hill's *The World Turned Upside Down* (1972), in part to take issue with Bercovitch and, in particular, with Bercovitch's characterization of Hawthorne and *The Scarlet Letter* as agents of moderation and compromise. "I fail to see how a desire for — expressed as a prediction of — a transformation of the relationships between men and women can be called 'reconciliation' or 'compromise,'" Swann writes with apparent urgency:

> To argue that Hawthorne speaks from and celebrates an ideology of liberal consensus seems entirely wrong. A man recently fired for his political views is hardly likely to think that political consensus exists in his own political culture, and — as he quite gratuitously chooses to identify himself in "The Custom House" however ironically as the Loco-foco Surveyor, that is, as a radical, an egalitarian Democrat — he is hardly trying to assimilate himself to a consensus position. (94)

Whereas Swann's study blends the new historicist approach with the Marxist approach, Elizabeth Perry Hodge's "The Letter of the Law: Reading Hawthorne and the Law of Adultery" (1996) blends the new historicist perspective with the so-called law and literature movement, a contemporary approach to literature that looks at the political history it expresses from a legal angle. Hodges begins by reminding us that *The Scarlet Letter* is about Massachusetts Bay Colony settlers living in a rough-hewn environment in a new land, people who "brought with them a rigid legal and moral code based on Mosaic Law" (137). Due to this code, or covenant, the community tended to unite itself through the "humiliation, banishment, or death" of "any wayward member" (138). The transgression committed by the one ***known*** wayward member at the heart of Hawthorne's novel is of course adultery, which over centuries of Western European history had gone from being a private crime subject to personal or familial acts of revenge to a moral wrong punishable by the whole community and, ultimately, the state itself. *The Scarlet Letter* thus "stands on a precarious line between primitive law, where private wrongs are righted by an individual act of revenge, and modern state law, where the state takes over the job of punishing the wrong" (146). Hodges explains that, in Massachusetts, adultery was a capital offense from 1641 until 1694, when the penalty requiring adulterers to wear letters was introduced, partly to recognize that letter-wearing had been the usual punishment for decades. "Although death was the legal punishment for adultery," Hodges writes, "courts hesitated to act with such harshness." Besides, "the letter penalty related not only to the general tradition of public humiliation but to such intimate forms of bodily punishment as branding, stigmatizing, and mutilation which were common in the . . . period" (148).

NEW AMERICANIST, NEW FEMINIST, AND GENDER APPROACHES: COMBINING CRITICAL PERSPECTIVES

In "Sacvan Bercovitch, Stanley Cavell, and the Romance Theory of American Fiction" (1992), Emily Budick returns to the view, prevalent in the 1950s and 1960s, that *The Scarlet Letter* — like much of classic American fiction — is more properly described as "romance." She associates this theory with the isolationist tendencies of the New Critics, who she says "sought to disengage the United States from ideology" — fascist ideology having drawn the country into a worldwide conflict of unprecedented proportions (79). Making this association allows her not only to discuss but also to contextualize Bercovitch's important essay. She views its argument — that *The Scarlet Letter* is *not* a romance of resistance and rebellion but, rather, a novel that (in her words) "socializes the reader to the dominant American ideology it incorporates" — as one of a number of critiques of the romance theory of American fiction mounted during the 1980s by new historicists, feminists, and African American scholars that Budick refers to as "new Americanists" (81).

In spite of the critique developed by Bercovitch, elaborated by later scholars, and summarized by Budick, the tendency to view *The Scarlet Letter* as a romance has persisted and, perhaps *because* of the critique, evolved since 1990. For instance, in *Practicing Romance: Narrative Form and Cultural Engagement in Hawthorne's Fiction* (1992), Richard Millington reverts to the more traditional generic classification of *The Scarlet Letter.* However, instead of characterizing it as a romance subversively affirming resistance and rebellion, he sees it as promoting a complex and balanced view of cultural constraint and individual freedom. For instance, he argues that, by the story's end, the inescapable public punishment outwardly imposed on Hester has conferred on her enough inner freedom to become a critic of the Puritan community. According to Millington, to achieve true freedom of mind is, for Hawthorne, to understand that "the meaning of one's own life . . . belongs to the community, but to refuse nevertheless to accede to the coercive patterns of mind that the community attempts to enforce" (100).

Whereas both "romance theory" and the "new Americanist" critique of that theory have persisted into the twenty-first century, they have competed with other approaches to *The Scarlet Letter* — perhaps especially with new modalities of feminist criticism and of its more recent offshoot, gender criticism (the latter of which is sometimes focused on sexual orientation and referred to as *queer theory*). In "Rereading Women: Hester Prynne-ism and the Scarlet Mob of Scribblers" (1997), contemporary feminist critic Jamie Barlowe argues that generations of male commentators have admired Hester Prynne's strength and even suggested approvingly that her creator, Nathaniel Hawthorne, was a feminist. Yet despite their own "professed radicalism," Barlowe asserts, "these critics of *The Scarlet Letter* have remained conservative in their relationship to women." This conservatism comes out both in the masculinist way they read Hester — as a sexual transgressor who is therefore titillatingly desirable but also politically radical — and in the way they have shown an "almost total disregard of women's scholarship on *The Scarlet Letter*" (198). But other female feminist Hawthorne scholars have subsequently taken issue with Barlowe; Budick, for instance, has argued that the reductive approach of separating critics into "two groups — male and female" — and of "oversimplify[ing]" their "multiple and competing critical approaches" promotes the same tendency toward Othering that Barlowe so opposes ("We Damned-If-You-Do" 233).

One of the earliest examples of the gender approach was Robert K. Martin's "Hester Prynne, *C'est Moi:* Nathaniel Hawthorne and the Anxieties of Gender" (1990), an essay that analyzes "Hawthorne's anxieties about his own masculinity." These anxieties, Martin suggests, were "as much about his intrusion, as a man, into a female world [i.e., that of fiction writing] as about women's intrusions into his male world" (122). In "The Custom-House," according to Martin, we hear about the kind of "place where Hawthorne feels he *ought* to be" (125), a place far away from (in Hawthorne's own words) "the dreamy brethren of Brook Farm" and the "fastidious[ness]" and "refinement" of New England literary culture. But this realm of what Hawthorne calls the "man of business" (p. 37) is hardly where his heart is. He no more fits in with nineteenth-century patriarchs such as the Inspector than he would have been understood by his seventeenth-century Puritan ancestors, forefathers he imagines wondering scornfully how their lineage has beget "a writer of story-books!" (p. 27).

Thus, according to Martin, male progenitors and coworkers come to serve in "The Custom House" as "the framework for a story that is just the opposite, a story of a mother and a daughter" (126) — a story, furthermore, in which the author identifies more deeply with that mother, his heroine, than with any male character. From the moment, described in "The Custom-House," in which he places the dusty old scarlet *A* "on my breast" to the last words of *The Scarlet Letter*, Hawthorne is (in Martin's words) "wearing her clothes and speaking in her voice" (128). In part this is because he "clearly sees Hester as an artist, if in a different medium" and empowers her to "speak . . . clearly for the kind of freedom that Hawthorne would not allow her *or* himself" (129). With regard to male characters in *The Scarlet Letter*, Martin argues that Hawthorne explores a relationship between men that is anything but boundary-driven and, at points, bizarrely transgressive. To quote from a long passage in which Martin cites phrases of Hawthorne's:

> Chillingworth's "care" for Dimmesdale brings the two men into "a kind of intimacy" that permits the physician to dig "into the poor clergyman's heart, like a miner searching for gold." The apparent affection of the older man is but a trap, his motives concealed and intrusive, as he accomplishes by his medicines and his surveillance of Dimmesdale's body an act of penetration he cannot perform on Hester. The "prying" and "probing" of Dimmesdale's "bosom" reaches a climax in Chillingworth's exposure of the male breast, as he "thrusts aside the vestment that, hitherto, had always covered it even from the professional eye." In this extraordinarily erotic moment, Dimmesdale "shuddered, and slightly stirred" while Chillingworth displays a "wild look of wonder, joy, and horror!" (132–33)

Martin stops short of using the word *homosexual* in describing this "erotic" moment involving men who, having been intimate with the same woman, end up living with one another, but he does go on to characterize the Chillingworth-Hester-Dimmesdale relationship as a "triangular" one, "replete with suggestions of vicarious sexual fulfillment and possession" (132).

Scott S. Derrick goes further in his essay "'A Curious Subject of Observation': Homoeroticism, the Body, and Authorship in Hawthorne's *The Scarlet Letter*" (1995), arguing that the novel "contains the kind of erotic triangle that [gender theorist] Eve Kosofsky Sedgwick has argued can function as a disguise of, and conduit for, desire between men." Derrick goes on to maintain that, through its representation of the Dimmesdale-Chillingworh relationship, Hawthorne's novel "helps to show" that "both homosexuality and homophobia have clear prehistories" (309). He finds the seeds of homophobia in the minister's reaction to the doctor's deformed, misshapen physique (he looked "fearfully," in Hawthorne's words, with "horror" and "antipathy" [p. 117]), and Derrick even finds telling the still-common scholarly habit of using the word "rape" to characterize Chillingworth's admittedly perverse efforts to know the secret of Dimmesdale's body. "With a slight adjustment of vision," he points out, "we might just as easily argue that Dimmesdale's unconsciousness in the [so-called rape] scene represents a desire to have some sort of erotic contact with the older man and yet to escape any responsibility for enacting such a prohibited desire" (311).

By referring to Dimmesdale's "unconsciousness" and its repressed "desire to have" a "prohibited," or taboo, experience, Derrick — though primarily taking the gender approach — shows the influence of recent Hawthorne critics who have again made *The Scarlet Letter* the subject of psychoanalytical interpretation. (These contemporary psychoanalytic critics often ground their work in a variety of sources, both within and outside of psychoanalytic theory, thereby making interpretive forays into the text that in many ways go beyond the basic Freudian approach taken by Frederick C. Crews in the 1960s.) In *Using Lacan, Reading Fiction* (1991), James M. Mellard uses the psychoanalytic theories of Jacques Lacan in approaching *The Scarlet Letter*, arguing that Chillingworth, though himself a psychotic, is more like a psychoanalyst than a physician, because "his aims are to uncover material from within the mind of his patient, rather than to heal physical infirmities" (94). Mellard also maintains that, in Hawthorne's representation of Pearl, we may follow a human being's "passage from . . . the *infant's* stage of the child-without-speech . . . through the moment of the mirror stage [when she sees herself, her mother, and Dimmesdale reflected in a brook]" (71). At this point, Pearl begins to come to terms with her "suspicions" that she is indebted "not to one, but to two, not merely to Mother, but also to Father" (74). This, in turn, leads "to the assumption of gender" and "the resolution of the Oedipus complex," the result being that Pearl "comes at last under the authority of her father as the representative of Law" (71). (Lacan, whose theory and terminology is explained at greater length in the essay "What Is Psychoanalytic Criticism?" [see p. 297], used the term *Law* to refer, among other things, to the whole patriarchal system of names, naming, and kinship determination that forms the basis not only of a human being's self-conception but also, more generally, of social institutions such as paternity law and property law.)

Allison Easton, another critic taking a contemporary psychoanalytic approach to *The Scarlet Letter,* suggests in her book *The Making of the Hawthorne Subject* (1996) that the twin "catalysts" of the novel were Hawthorne's "controversial dismissal from the Custom House in June [1849] and his mother's death in July" (189). Easton maintains that, through the resulting work's three main characters, Hawthorne provides a compelling portrait of human "subjectivity," which Easton defines as the "mental space" where "consciousness struggles" with the "gap[s] between the various positions assigned in the social order and those aspects of the self neither accepted nor represented there" (208). In "Guardian of the 'Inmost Me': Hawthorne and Shame" (1999), Joseph Adamson similarly relates *The Scarlet Letter* to the mental state of its author, drawing a relationship between Hawthorne's expressed fear of revealing his inmost self to his reader or audience and a recurring theme in his fiction, namely, "the shameless intrusion by one person into the innermost sanctum of another self" (61).

But the two most interesting psychoanalytic studies to appear since Bercovitch seemed to make Hawthorne studies and the new historicism perspective synonymous are Joanne Feit Diehl's "Re-Reading *The Letter:* Hawthorne, the Fetish, and the (Family) Romance (1988, rev. 1991) — which follows this essay on "The Critical Background" on page 314 in this volume — and John Dolis's *The Style of Hawthorne's Gaze: Regarding Subjectivity* (1993). Dolis effectively combines the Lacanian, psychoanalytic approach with new historicist interests, arguing that the advent of daguerreotype photography in the nineteenth century led to a limiting psychological tendency to perceive the world through definite and definable frames — and to assume that what is framed within the line of vision is objectively, scientifically knowable. Citing Marshall McLuhan's claim that "the function of the artist" is "correcting the unconscious bias of perception in any given culture," Dolis maintains that Hawthorne resisted the "daguerrean" worldview of his day by seeking constantly, through his fiction, to reopen recently closed doors of perception (43). For example, Hawthorne employs various types of mirrors, not to make the world seem coherent and comprehensible in the light of logical reflection but, rather, to reveal fragmented and highly subjective realities, as well as to suggest that subjective reflections can reveal truths deeper than those derived from more objectively verifiable analyses. (As one example, Dolis cites the scene in which Hester is looking at her own image as reflected in her daughter's eyes: "suddenly, . . . she fancied that she beheld, not her own miniature portrait, but another face in the small black mirror of

Pearl's eye. It was a face, fiend-like, full of smiling malice, yet bearing the semblance of features that she had known full well, though seldom with a smile, and never with malice, in them" [p. 87])

What makes Dolis's essay stand out among contemporary psychoanalytic approaches is its author's use of a mixed approach combining several contemporary critical perspectives, in this case Lacanian theory and the new historicist perspective. Like several of the contemporary essays summarized above — and like the mixed-approach essay provided in the final section of this book entitled "Combining Perspectives on *The Scarlet Letter*"— it shows how supposedly diverse critical assumptions and traditions can be used simultaneously and even to support one another, unlocking doors of understanding toward which no single approach could lead.

WORKS CITED

Abel, Darrel. *The Moral Picturesque: Studies in Hawthorne's Fiction.* West Lafayette: Purdue UP, 1988. This is a collection of essays first printed in various journals in the 1950s.

Adamson, Joseph. "Guardian of the 'Inmost Me': Hawthorne and Shame." *Scenes of Shame: Psychoanalysis, Shame, and Writing* (electronic book). Ed. Joseph Adamson and Hilary Clark. Albany: State U of New York P, 1999.

Arac, Jonathan. "The Politics of *The Scarlet Letter.*" *Ideology and Classic American Literature.* Ed. Sacvan Bercovitch and Myra Jehlen. Cambridge: Harvard UP, 1986.

Barlowe, Jamie. "Rereading Women: Hester Prynne-ism and the Scarlet Mob of Scribblers." *American Literary History* 9 (1997): 197–225.

Baym, Nina. "The Significance of Plot in Hawthorne's Romances." *Ruined Eden of the Present: Hawthorne, Melville, and Poe.* Ed. G. R. Thompson and Virgil L. Lokke. West Lafayette: Purdue UP, 1981.

Bercovitch, Sacvan. "Hawthorne's A-Morality of Compromise." *Representations* 24 (1988): 1–28.

———. *The Office of "The Scarlet Letter."* Baltimore: Johns Hopkins UP, 1991.

Budick, Emily. "Sacvan Bercovitch, Stanley Cavell, and the Romance Theory of American Fiction." *PMLA* 107 (1992): 78–91.

———. "We Damned-If-You-Do, Damned-If-You-Don't Mob of Scribbling Scholars." *American Literary History* 9 (1997): 233–37.

Chase, Richard. *The American Novel and Its Tradition.* Garden City: Doubleday, 1957.

Crews, Frederick C. *The Sins of the Fathers: Hawthorne's Psychological Themes.* New York: Oxford UP, 1966.

Crowley, J. Donald, ed. *Hawthorne: The Critical Heritage.* New York: Barnes, 1971. Contains all the early reviews quoted in the preceding essay.

Derrick, Scott S. "'A Curious Subject of Observation': Homoeroticism, The Body, and Authorship in Hawthorne's *The Scarlet Letter.*" *Novel: A Forum on Fiction* 28 (1995): 308–26.

Dolis, John. *The Style of Hawthorne's Gaze: Regarding Subjectivity* (electronic book). Tuscaloosa: U of Alabama P, 1993.

Easton, Allison. *The Making of the Hawthorne Subject.* Columbia: U of Missouri P, 1996.

Feidelson, Charles, Jr. *"The Scarlet Letter." Hawthorne Centenary Essays.* Ed. Roy Harvey Pearce. Columbus: Ohio State UP, 1964.

Fogle, Richard Harter. *Hawthorne's Fiction: The Light and the Dark.* Norman: U of Oklahoma P, 1952.

———. *Hawthorne's Imagery.* Norman: U of Oklahoma P, 1969.

Hodge, Elizabeth Perry. "The Letter of the Law: Reading Hawthorne and the Law of Adultery." *Law and Literature Perspectives.* Ed. Bruce L. Rockwood. New York: Peter Lang, 1996.

James, Henry. *Hawthorne.* 1879. New York: AMS, 1968.

Lawrence, D. H. *Studies in Classic American Literature.* New York: Seltzer, 1923.

Levin, Harry. *The Power of Blackness.* New York: Knopf, 1958.

Male, Roy R. *Hawthorne's Tragic Vision.* New York: Norton, 1957.

Martin, Robert K. "Hester Prynne, *C'est Moi:* Nathaniel Hawthorne and the Anxieties of Gender." *Engendering Men.* Ed. Joseph Boone and Michael Cadden. London: Routledge, 1990.

Matthiessen, F. O. *American Renaissance: Art and Expression in the Age of Emerson and Whitman.* New York: Oxford UP, 1941.

Mellard, James M. *Using Lacan: Reading Fiction.* Urbana: U of Illinois P, 1991.

Millington, Richard. *Practicing Romance: Narrative Form and Cultural Engagement in Hawthorne's Fiction.* Princeton UP, 1992.

Reynolds, Larry J. "*The Scarlet Letter* and Revolutions Abroad." *American Literature* 57 (1985): 44–67.

Stanton, Elizabeth Cady, Susan B. Anthony, and Matilda Joslyn Gage, eds. *History of Woman Suffrage*. Vol. 1. New York: Arno, 1969. 6 vols.

Stein, William Bysshe. *Hawthorne's Faust: A Study of the Devil Archetype*. Gainesville: U of Florida P, 1953.

Swann, Charles. *Nathaniel Hawthorne, Tradition and Revolution*. Cambridge: Cambridge UP, 1991.

Waggoner, Hyatt H. *Hawthorne: A Critical Study*. Cambridge: Belknap-Harvard UP, 1955.

Psychoanalytic Criticism and *The Scarlet Letter*

WHAT IS PSYCHOANALYTIC CRITICISM?

It seems natural to think about novels in terms of dreams. Like dreams, literary works are fictions, inventions of the mind that, although based on reality, are by definition not literally true. Like a literary work, a dream may have some truth to tell, but, like a literary work, it may need to be interpreted before that truth can be grasped. We can live vicariously through romantic fictions, much as we can through daydreams. Terrifying novels and nightmares affect us in much the same way, plunging us into an atmosphere that continues to cling, even after the last chapter has been read — or the alarm clock has sounded.

The notion that dreams allow such psychic explorations, of course, like the analogy between literary works and dreams, owes a great deal to the thinking of Sigmund Freud, the famous Austrian psychoanalyst who in 1900 published a seminal essay, *The Interpretation of Dreams.* But is the reader who feels that Emily Brontë's *Wuthering Heights* is dreamlike — who feels that Mary Shelley's *Frankenstein* is nightmarish — necessarily a Freudian literary critic? To some extent the answer has to be yes. We are all Freudians, really, whether or not we have read a single work by Freud. At one time or another, most of us have referred to ego, libido, complexes, unconscious desires, and sexual repression. The premises of Freud's thought have changed the way the

Western world thinks about itself. Psychoanalytic criticism has influenced the teachers our teachers studied with, the works of scholarship and criticism they read, and the critical and creative writers *we* read as well.

What Freud did was develop a language that described, a model that explained, a theory that encompassed human psychology. Many of the elements of psychology he sought to describe and explain are present in the literary works of various ages and cultures, from Sophocles' *Oedipus Rex* to Shakespeare's *Hamlet* to works being written in our own day. When the great novel of the twenty-first century is written, many of these same elements of psychology will probably inform its discourse as well. If, by understanding human psychology according to Freud, we can appreciate literature on a new level, then we should acquaint ourselves with his insights.

Freud's theories are either directly or indirectly concerned with the nature of the unconscious mind. Freud didn't invent the notion of the unconscious; others before him had suggested that even the supposedly "sane" human mind was conscious and rational only at times, and even then at possibly only one level. But Freud went further, suggesting that the powers motivating men and women are *mainly* and *normally* unconscious.

Freud, then, powerfully developed an old idea: that the human mind is essentially dual in nature. He called the predominantly passional, irrational, unknown, and unconscious part of the psyche the *id*, or "it." The *ego*, or "I," was his term for the predominantly rational, logical, orderly, conscious part. Another aspect of the psyche, which he called the *superego*, is really a projection of the ego. The superego almost seems to be outside of the self, making moral judgments, telling us to make sacrifices for good causes even though self-sacrifice may not be quite logical or rational. And, in a sense, the superego *is* "outside," since much of what it tells us to do or think we have learned from our parents, our schools, or our religious institutions.

What the ego and superego tell us *not* to do or think is repressed, forced into the unconscious mind. One of Freud's most important contributions to the study of the psyche, the theory of repression, goes something like this: much of what lies in the unconscious mind has been put there by consciousness, which acts as a censor, driving underground unconscious or conscious thoughts or instincts that it deems unacceptable. Censored materials often involve infantile sexual desires, Freud postulated. Repressed to an unconscious state, they emerge only in disguised forms: in dreams, in language (so-called Freudian slips), in creative activity that may produce art (including literature), and in neurotic behavior.

According to Freud, all of us have repressed wishes and fears; we all have dreams in which repressed feelings and memories emerge disguised, and thus we are all potential candidates for dream analysis. One of the unconscious desires most commonly repressed is the childhood wish to displace the parent of our own sex and take his or her place in the affections of the parent of the opposite sex. This desire really involves a number of different but related wishes and fears. (A boy — and it should be remarked in passing that Freud here concerns himself mainly with the male — may fear that his father will castrate him, and he may wish that his mother would return to nursing him.) Freud referred to the whole complex of feelings by the word *oedipal*, naming the complex after the Greek tragic hero Oedipus, who unwittingly killed his father and married his mother.

Why are oedipal wishes and fears repressed by the conscious side of the mind? And what happens to them after they have been censored? As Roy P. Basler puts it in *Sex, Symbolism, and Psychology in Literature* (1975), "from the beginning of recorded history such wishes have been restrained by the most powerful religious and social taboos, and as a result have come to be regarded as 'unnatural,'" even though "Freud found that such wishes are more or less characteristic of normal human development":

> In dreams, particularly, Freud found ample evidence that such wishes persisted. . . . Hence he conceived that natural urges, when identified as "wrong," may be repressed but not obliterated. . . . In the unconscious, these urges take on symbolic garb, regarded as nonsense by the waking mind that does not recognize their significance. (14)

Freud's belief in the significance of dreams, of course, was no more original than his belief that there is an unconscious side to the psyche. Again, it was the extent to which he developed a theory of how dreams work — and the extent to which that theory helped him, by analogy, to understand far more than just dreams — that made him unusual, important, and influential beyond the perimeters of medical schools and psychiatrists' offices.

The psychoanalytic approach to literature not only rests on the theories of Freud; it may even be said to have *begun* with Freud, who was interested in writers, especially those who relied heavily on symbols. Such writers regularly cloak or mystify ideas in figures that make sense only when interpreted, much as the unconscious mind of a neurotic disguises secret thoughts in dream stories or bizarre actions that need to be interpreted by an analyst. Freud's interest in literary artists led him to make some unfortunate generalizations about creativity; for example, in the twenty-third lecture in *Introductory Lectures on Psycho-Analysis* (1922), he defined the artist as "one urged on by instinctive needs that are too clamorous" (314). But it also led him to write creative literary criticism of his own, including an influential essay on "The Relation of a Poet to Daydreaming" (1908) and "The Uncanny" (1919), a provocative psychoanalytic reading of E. T. A. Hoffman's supernatural tale "The Sandman."

Freud's application of psychoanalytic theory to literature quickly caught on. In 1909, only a year after Freud had published "The Relation of a Poet to Daydreaming," the psychoanalyst Otto Rank published *The Myth of the Birth of the Hero.* In that work, Rank subscribes to the notion that the artist turns a powerful, secret wish into a literary fantasy, and he uses Freud's notion about the "oedipal" complex to explain why the popular stories of so many heroes in literature are so similar. A year after Rank had published his psychoanalytic account of heroic texts, Ernest Jones, Freud's student and eventual biographer, turned his attention to a tragic text: Shakespeare's *Hamlet.* In an essay first published in the *American Journal of Psychology,* Jones, like Rank, makes use of the oedipal concept: he suggests that Hamlet is a victim of strong feelings toward his mother, the queen.

Between 1909 and 1949, numerous other critics decided that psychological and psychoanalytic theory could assist in the understanding of literature. I. A. Richards, Kenneth Burke, and Edmund Wilson were among the most influential to become interested in the new approach. Not all of the early critics were committed to the approach; neither were all of them Freudians. Some followed Alfred Adler, who believed that writers wrote out of inferiority complexes, and others applied the ideas of Carl Gustav Jung, who had broken with Freud over Freud's emphasis on sex and who had developed a theory of the *collective* unconscious. According to Jungian theory, a great work of literature is not a disguised expression of its author's personal, repressed wishes; rather, it is a manifestation of desires once held by the whole human race but now repressed because of the advent of civilization.

It is important to point out that among those who relied on Freud's models were a number of critics who were poets and novelists as well.

Conrad Aiken wrote a Freudian study of American literature, and poets such as Robert Graves and W. H. Auden applied Freudian insights when writing critical prose. William Faulkner, Henry James, James Joyce, D. H. Lawrence, Marcel Proust, and Toni Morrison are only a few of the novelists who have either written criticism influenced by Freud or who have written novels that conceive of character, conflict, and creative writing itself in Freudian terms. The poet H. D. (Hilda Doolittle) was actually a patient of Freud's and provided an account of her analysis in her book *Tribute to Freud* (1944). By giving Freudian theory credibility among students of literature that only they could bestow, such writers helped to endow earlier psychoanalytic criticism with a largely Freudian orientation that has begun to be challenged only in the last two decades.

The willingness, even eagerness, of writers to use Freudian models in producing literature and criticism of their own consummated a relationship that, to Freud and other pioneering psychoanalytic theorists, had seemed fated from the beginning; after all, therapy involves the close analysis of language. René Wellek and Austin Warren included "psychological" criticism as one of the five "extrinsic" approaches to literature described in their influential book *Theory of Literature* (1942). Psychological criticism, they suggest, typically attempts to do at least one of the following: provide a psychological study of an individual writer; explore the nature of the creative process; generalize about "types and laws present within works of literature"; or theorize about the psychological "effects of literature upon its readers" (81). Entire books on psychoanalytic criticism began to appear, such as Frederick J. Hoffman's *Freudianism and the Literary Mind* (1945).

Probably because of Freud's characterization of the creative mind as "clamorous" if not ill, psychoanalytic criticism written before 1950 tended to psychoanalyze the individual author. Poems were read as fantasies that allowed authors to indulge repressed wishes, to protect themselves from deep-seated anxieties, or both. A perfect example of author analysis would be Marie Bonaparte's 1933 study of Edgar Allan Poe. Bonaparte found Poe to be so fixated on his mother that his repressed longing emerges in his stories in images such as the white spot on a black cat's breast, said to represent mother's milk.

A later generation of psychoanalytic critics often paused to analyze the characters in novels and plays before proceeding to their authors. But not for long, since characters, both evil and good, tended to be seen by these critics as the author's potential selves, or projections of various repressed aspects of his or her psyche. For instance, in *A Psychoanalytic*

Study of the Double in Literature (1970), Robert Rogers begins with the view that human beings are double or multiple in nature. Using this assumption, along with the psychoanalytic concept of "dissociation" (best known by its result, the dual or multiple personality), Rogers concludes that writers reveal instinctual or repressed selves in their books, often without realizing that they have done so.

In the view of critics attempting to arrive at more psychological insights into an author than biographical materials can provide, a work of literature is a fantasy or a dream — or at least so analogous to daydream or dream that Freudian analysis can help explain the nature of the mind that produced it. The author's purpose in writing is to gratify secretly some forbidden wish, in particular an infantile wish or desire that has been repressed into the unconscious mind. To discover what the wish is, the psychoanalytic critic employs many of the terms and procedures developed by Freud to analyze dreams.

The literal surface of a work is sometimes spoken of as its "manifest content" and treated as a "manifest dream" or "dream story" would be treated by a Freudian analyst. Just as the analyst tries to figure out the "dream thought" behind the dream story — that is, the latent or hidden content of the manifest dream — so the psychoanalytic literary critic tries to expose the latent, underlying content of a work. Freud used the words *condensation* and *displacement* to explain two of the mental processes whereby the mind disguises its wishes and fears in dream stories. In condensation, several thoughts or persons may be condensed into a single manifestation or image in a dream story; in displacement, an anxiety, a wish, or a person may be displaced onto the image of another, with which or whom it is loosely connected through a string of associations that only an analyst can untangle. Psychoanalytic critics treat metaphors as if they were dream condensations; they treat metonyms — figures of speech based on extremely loose, arbitrary associations — as if they were dream displacements. Thus figurative literary language in general is treated as something that evolves as the writer's conscious mind resists what the unconscious tells it to picture or describe. A symbol is, in Daniel Weiss's words, "a meaningful concealment of truth as the truth promises to emerge as some frightening or forbidden idea" (20).

In a 1970 article entitled "The 'Unconscious' of Literature," Norman Holland, a literary critic trained in psychoanalysis, succinctly sums up the attitudes held by critics who would psychoanalyze authors, but without quite saying that it is the *author* that is being analyzed by the psychoanalytic critic. "When one looks at a poem psychoanalytically," he writes, "one considers it as though it were a dream or as though some ideal patient [were speaking] from the couch in iambic pentameter." One "looks for the general level or levels of fantasy associated with the language. By level I mean the familiar stages of childhood development — oral [when desires for nourishment and infantile sexual desires overlap], anal [when infants receive their primary pleasure from defecation], urethral [when urinary functions are the locus of sexual pleasure], phallic [when the penis or, in girls, some penis substitute is of primary interest], oedipal." Holland continues by analyzing not Robert Frost but Frost's poem "Mending Wall" as a specifically oral fantasy that is not unique to its author. "Mending Wall" is "about breaking down the wall which marks the separated or individuated self so as to return to a state of closeness to some Other" — including and perhaps essentially the nursing mother ("'Unconscious'" 136, 139).

While not denying the idea that the unconscious plays a role in creativity, psychoanalytic critics such as Holland began to focus more on the ways in which authors create works that appeal to *our* repressed wishes and fantasies. Consequently, they shifted their focus away from the psyche of the author and toward the psychology of the reader and the text. Holland's theories, which have concerned themselves more with the reader than with the text, have helped to establish another school of critical theory: reader-response criticism. Elizabeth Wright explains Holland's brand of modern psychoanalytic criticism in this way: "What draws us as readers to a text is the secret expression of what we desire to hear, much as we protest we do not. The disguise must be good enough to fool the censor into thinking that the text is respectable, but bad enough to allow the unconscious to glimpse the unrespectable" (117).

Holland is one of dozens of critics who have revised Freud significantly in the process of revitalizing psychoanalytic criticism. Another such critic is R. D. Laing, whose controversial and often poetical writings about personality, repression, masks, and the double or "schizoid" self have (re)blurred the boundary between creative writing and psychoanalytic discourse. Yet another is D. W. Winnicott, an "object relations" theorist who has had a significant impact on literary criticism. Critics influenced by Winnicott and his school have questioned the tendency to see reader/text as an either/or construct; instead, they have seen reader and text (or audience and play) in terms of a *relationship* taking place in what Winnicott calls a "transitional" or "potential" space — space in which binary terms such as *real* and *illusory, objective* and *subjective,* have little or no meaning.

Psychoanalytic theorists influenced by Winnicott see the transitional or potential reader/text (or audience/play) space as being *like* the space entered into by psychoanalyst and patient. More important, they also see it as being similar to the space between mother and infant: a space characterized by trust in which categorizing terms such as *knowing* and *feeling* mix and merge and have little meaning apart from one another.

Whereas Freud saw the mother-son relationship in terms of the son and his repressed oedipal complex (and saw the analyst-patient relationship in terms of the patient and the repressed "truth" that the analyst could scientifically extract), object-relations analysts see both relationships as *dyadic* — that is, as being dynamic in both directions. Consequently, they don't depersonalize analysis or their analyses. It is hardly surprising, therefore, that contemporary literary critics who apply object-relations theory to the texts they discuss don't depersonalize critics or categorize their interpretations as "truthful," at least not in any objective or scientific sense. In the view of such critics, interpretations are made of language — itself a transitional object — and are themselves the mediating terms or transitional objects of a relationship.

Like critics of the Winnicottian school, the French structuralist theorist Jacques Lacan focused on language and language-related issues. He treated the unconscious *as* a language and, consequently, viewed the dream not as Freud did (that is, as a form and symptom of repression) but rather as a form of discourse. Thus we may study dreams psychoanalytically to learn about literature, even as we may study literature to learn more about the unconscious. In Lacan's seminar on Poe's "The Purloined Letter," a pattern of repetition like that used by psychoanalysts in their analyses is used to arrive at a reading of the story. According to Wright, "the new psychoanalytic structural approach to literature" employs "analogies from psychoanalysis . . . to explain the workings of the text as distinct from the workings of a particular author's, character's, or even reader's mind" (125).

Lacan, however, did far more than extend Freud's theory of dreams, literature, and the interpretation of both. More significantly, he took Freud's whole theory of psyche and gender and added to it a crucial third term — that of language. In the process, he both used and significantly developed Freud's ideas about the oedipal stage and complex.

Lacan pointed out that the pre-oedipal stage, in which the child at first does not even recognize its independence from its mother, is also a pre*verbal* stage, one in which the child communicates without the medium of language, or — if we insist on calling the child's communications a language — in a language that can only be called *literal.* ("Coos," certainly, cannot be said to be figurative or symbolic.) Then, while still in the pre-oedipal stage, the child enters the *mirror* stage.

During the mirror period, the child comes to view itself and its mother, later other people as well, *as* independent selves. This is the stage in which the child is first able to fear the aggressions of another, to desire what is recognizably beyond the self (initially the mother), and, finally, to want to compete with another for the same desired object. This is also the stage at which the child first becomes able to feel sympathy with another being who is being hurt by a third, to cry when another cries. All of these developments, of course, involve projecting beyond the self and, by extension, constructing one's own self (or "ego" or "I") as others view one — that is, as *another.* Such constructions, according to Lacan, are just that: constructs, products, artifacts — fictions of coherence that in fact hide what Lacan called the "absence" or "lack" of being.

The mirror stage, which Lacan also referred to as the *imaginary* stage, is fairly quickly succeeded by the oedipal stage. As in Freud, this stage begins when the child, having come to view itself as self and the father and mother as separate selves, perceives gender and gender differences between its parents and between itself and one of its parents. For boys, gender awareness involves another, more powerful recognition, for the recognition of the father's phallus as the mark of his difference from the mother involves, at the same time, the recognition that his older and more powerful father is also his rival. That, in turn, leads to the understanding that what once seemed wholly his and even indistinguishable from himself is in fact someone else's: something properly desired only at a distance and in the form of socially acceptable *substitutes.*

The fact that the oedipal stage roughly coincides with the entry of the child into language is extremely important for Lacan. For the linguistic order is essentially a figurative or "Symbolic" order; words are not the things they stand for but are, rather, stand-ins or substitutes for those things. Hence boys, who in the most critical period of their development have had to submit to what Lacan called the "Law of the Father" — a law that prohibits direct desire for and communicative intimacy with what has been the boy's whole world — enter more easily into the realm of language and the Symbolic order than do girls, who have never really had to renounce that which once seemed continuous with the self: the mother. The gap that has been opened up for boys, which includes the gap between signs and what they substitute — the gap marked by the phallus and encoded with the boy's sense of his maleness — has not opened up for girls, or has not opened up in the same way, to the same degree.

For Lacan, the father need not be present to trigger the oedipal stage; nor does his phallus have to be seen to catalyze the boy's (easier) transition into the Symbolic order. Rather, Lacan argued, a child's recognition of its gender is intricately tied up with a growing recognition of the system of names and naming, part of the larger system of substitutions we call language. A child has little doubt about who its mother is, but who is its father, and how would one know? The father's claim rests on the mother's *word* that he is in fact the father; the father's relationship to the child is thus established through language and a system of marriage and kinship — names — that in turn is basic to rules of everything from property to law. The name of the father (*nom du père*, which in French sounds like *non du père*) involves, in a sense, nothing of the father — nothing, that is, except his word or name.

Lacan's development of Freud has had several important results. First, his sexist-seeming association of maleness with the Symbolic order, together with his claim that women cannot therefore enter easily into the order, has prompted feminists not to reject his theory out of hand but, rather, to look more closely at the relation between language and gender, language and women's inequality. Some feminists have gone so far as to suggest that the social and political relationships between male and female will not be fundamentally altered until language itself has been radically changed. (That change might begin dialectically, with the development of some kind of "feminine language" grounded in the presymbolic, literal-to-imaginary communication between mother and child.)

Second, Lacan's theory has proved of interest to deconstructors and other poststructuralists, in part because it holds that the ego (which in Freud's view is as necessary as it is natural) is a product or construct. The ego-artifact, produced during the mirror stage, *seems* at once unified, consistent, and organized around a determinate center. But the unified self, or ego, is a fiction, according to Lacan. The yoking together of fragments and destructively dissimilar elements takes its psychic toll, and it is the job of the Lacanian psychoanalyst to "deconstruct," as it were, the ego, to show its continuities to be contradictions as well.

Joanne Feit Diehl, whose essay begins on page 314, is far from being the first critic to use Freudian concepts in coming to terms with *The Scarlet Letter.* Joseph Levi published a groundbreaking study in *American Imago* in 1953, and slightly more than a decade later Frederick C. Crews published his classic Freudian reading of the novel in his book *The Sins of the Fathers: Hawthorne's Psychological Themes* (1966). (A summary of Crews's argument may be found in the preceding "A Critical History of *The Scarlet Letter.*") Other psychoanalytic readings of the novel, most of them Freudian but some of them based on the theories of Lacan and others, have been published since 1966.

Whereas Crews had focused on Arthur Dimmesdale's libidinous (and forbidden) desire for Hester Prynne, and on how that desire, because it has been suppressed, must be fulfilled through other disguised means (scourging, writing, etc.), most of the more recent Freudian readings have developed Levi's somewhat older idea that the novel is grounded in the author's oedipal feelings. As Clay Daniel puts it in "*The Scarlet Letter:* Hawthorne, Freud, and the Transcendentalists" (1986), "Hawthorne's masterwork in part is the product of the author's attempt to resolve his Oedipal complex, which was reactivated immediately prior to his writing the story by the death of his mother" (23). Psychoanalytic critics who have interpreted the novel since Daniel have similarly assumed that Hawthorne expresses his disguised oedipal desire through his portrayal of Dimmesdale's relationship with Hester. Hester, after all, *is* a mother, and the reason Dimmesdale can't have her is that she already has a husband.

In "Re-Reading *The Letter:* Hawthorne, the Fetish, and the (Family) Romance," Diehl follows the lead of predecessors such as Daniel in reading the novel as an expression of its author's oedipal feelings. Using Freud's discussion of the guilt felt by sons on the death of their fathers, she discusses Hawthorne's particular biographical situation of being left, as a young child, by a father he practically never saw, to be raised by a mother whose eventual death he found emotionally overwhelming. And, making use of the text of *The Scarlet Letter,* she discusses scenes in which Hester is figured as a distant, unattainable, even dead mother and in which Dimmesdale, through language, tries to reach and regain the woman he has lost.

But Diehl's focus is neither just on the Dimmesdale-Hester relationship nor on Hawthorne's feelings toward his mother. Rather, Diehl concentrates on the scarlet letter itself, which she maintains is, in

Freud's terms, a fetishistic object. According to Freud, certain things replace and stand for other things that are desired but taboo (a foot fetish isn't really a desire for feet, for example). The *A* in *The Scarlet Letter,* Diehl maintains, "functions in several ways that parallel Freud's concept of the fetish, which by its very presence recalls the conflict between desire and its necessary repression" (p. 315 in this volume). Along with other characters, Dimmesdale is fascinated by the letter, which seems to signify adultery but, in fact, suggests something else to the beholder's unconscious. Thus the *A,* like all fetishistic objects, conceals what it ultimately signifies and "represents what cannot be spoken, the inviolate truth of what is most desired and what must be repressed, predominantly, the longing for the mother" (p. 323).

Diehl goes beyond her precursors by focusing on the letter and by showing how it functions fetishistically for characters other than Dimmesdale. She also breaks new ground by showing how *The Scarlet Letter* (like the scarlet letter) engages the psychology of the reader, thus implicating the reader in the novel's "family romance." One of the most difficult passages in Diehl's essay is also one that is worth pondering:

> [F]or just as Dimmesdale depends on the Puritan community's misinterpretation of narrative events (the appearance of the lost glove on the scaffold and the revelation of the *A* shining in the night sky) to protect his guilt and not to expose it, so the narrative establishes a pattern of substitutive identifications that play equally on the community of its readers to *fail* to recognize the sublimated incestuous wishes covered by the text. (p. 320)

We too, in other words, are drawn to *The Letter* both because we don't know what it signifies and because, at some level, we do.

Ross C Murfin

PSYCHOANALYTIC CRITICISM: A SELECTED BIBLIOGRAPHY

Some Short Introductions to Psychological and Psychoanalytic Theory

Holland, Norman. "The 'Unconscious' of Literature: The Psychoanalytic Approach." *Contemporary Criticism.* Ed. Malcolm Bradbury and David Palmer. Stratford-Upon-Avon Studies 12, 1970. Reprinted. New York: St. Martin's, 1971. 131–53.

Natoli, Joseph, and Frederik L. Rusch, comps. *Psychocriticism: An Annotated Bibliography.* Westport: Greenwood, 1984.

Scott, Wilbur. *Five Approaches to Literary Criticism.* London: Collier-Macmillan, 1962. See the essays by Burke and Gorer as well as Scott's introduction to the section "The Psychological Approach: Literature in the Light of Psychological Theory."

Wellek, René, and Austin Warren. *Theory of Literature.* New York: Harcourt, 1942. See the chapter "Literature and Psychology" in pt. 3, "The Extrinsic Approach to the Study of Literature."

Wright, Elizabeth. "Modern Psychoanalytic Criticism." *Modern Literary Theory: A Comparative Introduction.* Ed. Ann Jefferson and David Robey. Totowa: Barnes, 1982. 113–33.

Freud, Lacan, and Their Influence

Althusser, Louis. *Writings on Psychoanalysis: Freud and Lacan.* Ed. Olivier Corpet and François Matheron. Trans. Jeffrey Mehlman. New York: Columbia UP, 1996.

Basler, Roy P. *Sex, Symbolism, and Psychology in Literature.* New York: Octagon, 1975. See especially 13–19.

Clement, Catherine. *The Lives and Legends of Jacques Lacan.* Trans. Arthur Goldhammer. New York: Columbia UP, 1983.

Copjec, Joan. *Read My Desire: Lacan Against the Historicists.* Cambridge: MIT P, 1994.

Feldstein, Richard, Bruce Fink, and Maire Jaanus, eds. *Reading Seminar XI: Lacan's Four Fundamental Concepts of Psychoanalysis.* Albany: State U of New York P, 1995.

Fink, Bruce. *The Lacanian Subject: Between Language and Jouissance.* Princeton: Princeton UP, 1995.

Freud, Sigmund. *The Interpretation of Dreams.* Trans. James Strachey. New York: Avon, 1965.

———. *Introductory Lectures on Psycho-Analysis.* Trans. Joan Riviere. London: Allen, 1922.

H. D. (Hilda Doolittle). *Tribute to Freud.* Boston: G. R. Godine, 1974.

Hill, Philip. *Lacan for Beginners.* New York: Writers and Readers, 1997.

Hoffman, Frederick J. *Freudianism and the Literary Mind.* 2nd ed. Baton Rouge: Louisiana State UP, 1957. First edition published in 1945.

Lacan, Jacques. *Écrits: A Selection.* Trans. Alan Sheridan. New York: Norton, 1977.

———. *The Ego in Freud's Theory and in the Technique of Psychoanalysis 1954–1955.* Ed. Jacques-Alain Miller. Trans. Sylvana Tomaselli. The Seminar of Jacques Lacan Book II. New York: Norton, 1988.

———. *The Ethics of Psychoanalysis: 1959–1960.* Ed. Jacques-Alain Miller. Trans. Dennis Porter. The Seminar of Jacques Lacan Book VII. New York: Norton, 1992.

———. *Feminine Sexuality: Lacan and the ecole freudienne.* Ed. Juliet Mitchell and Jacqueline Rose. Trans. Rose. New York: Norton, 1982.

———. *The Four Fundamental Concepts of Psychoanalysis.* Trans. Alan Sheridan. London: Penguin, 1980.

———. *Freud's Papers on Technique 1953–1954.* Ed. Jacques-Alain Miller. Trans. John Forrester. The Seminar of Jacques Lacan Book I. New York: Norton, 1988.

———. *On Feminine Sexuality: The Limits of Love and Knowledge.* Ed. Jacques-Alain Miller. Trans. Bruce Fink. The Seminar of Jacques Lacan Book XX: Encore 1972–1973. New York: Norton, 1998.

Lee, Jonathan Scott. *Jacques Lacan.* Boston: Twayne, 1990.

Ragland-Sullivan, Ellie. *Essays on the Pleasures of Death: From Freud to Lacan.* New York: Routledge, 1995.

Rank, Otto. *The Myth of the Birth of the Hero: A Psychological Exploration of Myth.* Trans. Gregory C. Richter and E. James Lieberman. Intro. Robert A. Segal. Baltimore: Johns Hopkins UP, 2004.

Roudinesco, Elisabeth. *Jacques Lacan.* Trans. Barbara Bray. New York: Columbia UP, 1997.

Schneiderman, Stuart. *Jacques Lacan: The Death of an Intellectual Hero.* Cambridge: Harvard UP, 1983.

Zizek, Slavoj. *Enjoy Your Symptom: Jacques Lacan in Hollywood and Out.* New York: Routledge, 1992.

———. *The Metastases of Enjoyment: Six Essays on Woman and Causality.* New York: Verso, 1994.

———. *The Sublime Object of Ideology.* New York: Verso, 1989.

Psychoanalysis, Feminism, and Literature

Barr, Marleen S., and Richard Feldstein. *Discontented Discourses: Feminism/Textual Intervention/Psychoanalysis.* Urbana: U of Illinois P, 1989.

Benjamin, Jessica. *The Bonds of Love: Psychoanalysis, Feminism and the Problem of Domination.* New York: Pantheon, 1988.

Bernheimer, Charles, and Claire Kahane, eds. *In Dora's Case: Freud-Hysteria-Feminism.* New York: Columbia UP, 1985.

de Lauretis, Teresa. *The Practice of Love: Lesbian Sexuality and Perverse Desire*. Bloomington: Indiana UP, 1994.

Elliott, Patricia. *From Mastery to Analysis: Theories of Gender in Psychoanalytic Criticism*. Ithaca: Cornell UP, 1991.

Felman, Shoshana. *What Does a Woman Want? Reading and Sexual Difference*. Baltimore: Johns Hopkins UP, 1993.

Gallop, Jane. *The Daughter's Seduction: Feminism and Psychoanalysis*. Ithaca: Cornell UP, 1982.

———. *Thinking Through the Body*. New York: Columbia UP, 1988.

Garner, Shirley Nelson, Claire Kahane, and Madelon Sprengnether. *The (M)other Tongue: Essays in Feminist Psychoanalytic Interpretation*. Ithaca: Cornell UP, 1985.

Grosz, Elizabeth. *Jacques Lacan: A Feminist Introduction*. New York: Routledge, 1990.

Irigaray, Luce. *This Sex Which Is Not One*. Trans. Catherine Porter. Ithaca: Cornell UP, 1985.

———. *Speculum of the Other Woman*. Trans. Gillian C. Gill. Ithaca: Cornell UP, 1985.

Jacobus, Mary. "Is There a Woman in This Text?" *New Literary History* 14 (1982): 117–41.

Kristeva, Julia. *The Kristeva Reader*. Ed. Toril Moi. New York: Columbia UP, 1986. See especially the selection from *Revolution in Poetic Language* 89–136.

MacCannell, Juliet Flower. *The Regime of the Brother: After the Patriarchy*. New York: Routledge, 1991.

Mitchell, Juliet. *Psychoanalysis and Feminism*. New York: Random, 1974.

Mitchell, Juliet, and Jacqueline Rose, Introduction I and Introduction II. Lacan, *Feminine Sexuality: Jacques Lacan and the école freudienne* 1–26, 27–57.

Rose, Jacqueline. *Sexuality in the Field of Vision*. New York: Verso, 1986.

Sprengnether, Madelon. *The Spectral Mother: Freud, Feminism, and Psychoanalysis*. Ithaca: Cornell UP, 1990.

Psychological and Psychoanalytic Studies of Literature, Culture, and the Arts

Apollon, Willy, and Richard Feldstein, eds. *Lacan. Politics, Aesthetics*. Albany: State U of New York P, 1996.

Bersani, Leo. *Baudelaire and Freud.* Berkeley: U of California P, 1977.

———. *The Freudian Body: Psychoanalysis and Art.* New York: Columbia UP, 1986.

Bettelheim, Bruno. *The Uses of Enchantment: The Meaning and Importance of Fairy Tales.* New York: Knopf, 1976.

Bracher, Mark. *Lacan, Discourse, and Social Change: A Psychoanalytic Cultural Criticism.* Ithaca: Cornell UP, 1993.

Grosz, Elizabeth. *Space, Time, and Perversion: Essays on the Politics of Bodies.* New York: Routledge, 1995.

Hartman, Geoffrey, ed. *Psychoanalysis and the Question of the Text.* Baltimore: Johns Hopkins UP, 1978.

Hertz, Neil. *The End of the Line: Essays on Psychoanalysis and the Sublime.* New York: Columbia UP, 1985.

Jacobus, Mary. *First Things: The Maternal Imaginary in Literature, Art, and Psychoanalysis.* New York: Routledge, 1995.

Krauss, Rosalind. *The Optical Unconscious.* Cambridge: MIT P, 1994.

Poizat, Michel. *The Angel's Cry: Beyond the Pleasure Principle in Opera.* Trans. Arthur Denner. Ithaca: Cornell UP, 1992.

Rogers, Robert. *A Psychoanalytic Study of the Double in Literature.* Detroit: Wayne State UP, 1970.

Salecl, Renata, and Slavoj Zizek, eds. *Gaze and Voice as Love Objects.* Durham: Duke UP, 1996.

Silverman, Kaja. *The Threshold of the Visible World.* New York: Routledge, 1996.

Weiss, Daniel. *The Critic Agonistes: Psychology, Myth, and the Art of Fiction.* Posthumously published lectures and papers. Ed. Eric Solomon and Stephen Arkin. Seattle: U of Washington P, 1985.

Lacanian Psychoanalytic Studies of Literature

Booker, M. Keith. "Notes Toward a Lacanian Reading of Wallace Stevens." *Journal of Modern Literature* 16 (1990): 493–509.

Davis, Robert Con, ed. *The Fictional Father: Lacanian Readings of the Text.* Amherst: U of Massachusetts P, 1981.

———. *Lacan and Narration: The Psychoanalytic Difference in Narrative Theory.* Baltimore: Johns Hopkins UP, 1984.

Devlin, Kim. "Castration and Its Discontents: A Lacanian Approach to *Ulysses.*" *James Joyce Quarterly* 29 (1991): 117–44.

Felman, Shoshana, ed. *Literature and Psychoanalysis: The Question of Reading: Otherwise.* Baltimore: Johns Hopkins UP, 1982. Includes Lacan's seminar on Shakespeare's *Hamlet.*

Homans, Margaret. *Bearing the Word: Language and Female Experience in Nineteenth-Century Women's Writing*. Chicago: U of Chicago P, 1986.

Lacan, Jacques. "The Essence of Tragedy: A Commentary on Sophocles's *Antigone*." Lacan, *The Ethics of Psychoanalysis* 243–87.

Mellard, James M. *Using Lacan, Reading Fiction*. Urbana: U of Illinois P, 1991.

Miller, David Lee. "Writing the Specular Son: Jonson, Freud, Lacan, and the (K)not of Masculinity." *Desire in the Renaissance: Psychoanalysis and Literature*. Ed. Valeria Finucci and Regina Schwartz. Princeton: Princeton UP, 1994. 233–60.

Muller, John P., and William J. Richardson, eds. *The Purloined Poe: Lacan, Derrida. and Psychoanalytic Reading*. Baltimore: Johns Hopkins UP, 1988. Includes Lacan's seminar on Poe's "The Purloined Letter."

Netto, Jeffrey A. "Dickens with Kant and Sade." *Style* 29 (1995): 441–58.

Rapaport, Herman. *Between the Sign & the Gaze*. Ithaca: Cornell UP, 1994.

Schad, John. "'No One Dreams': Hopkins, Lacan, and the Unconscious." *Victorian Poetry* 32 (1994): 141–56.

Other Psychoanalytic Approaches to Hawthorne

Adamson, Joseph. "Guardian of the 'Inmost Me': Hawthorne and Shame." *Scenes of Shame: Psychoanalysis, Shame, and Writing* (electronic book). Ed. Joseph Adamson and Hilary Clark. Albany: State U of New York P, 1999.

Crews, Frederick C. *The Sins of the Fathers: Hawthorne's Psychological Themes*. New York: Oxford UP, 1966.

Daniel, Clay. "*The Scarlet Letter:* Hawthorne, Freud, and the Transcendentalists." *American Transcendental Quarterly* 61 (1986): 23–35.

Dolis, John. *The Style of Hawthorne's Gaze: Regarding Subjectivity* (electronic book). Tuscaloosa: U of Alabama P, 1993.

Easton, Allison. *The Making of the Hawthorne Subject*. Columbia: U of Missouri P, 1996.

Hilgers, Thomas L. "The Psychology of Conflict Resolution in *The Scarlet Letter:* A Non-Freudian Perspective." *American Transcendental Quarterly* 43 (1979): 211–13.

Irwin, John T. *American Hieroglyphics: The Symbol of Egyptian Hieroglyphics in the American Renaissance.* New Haven: Yale UP, 1980. See Part Three, "Hawthorne and Melville."

Levi, Joseph. "Hawthorne's *The Scarlet Letter:* (A Psychoanalytic Interpretation)." *American Imago* 10 (1953): 291–305.

Mellard, James. *Using Lacan: Reading Fiction.* Urbana: U of Illinois P, 1991.

A PSYCHOANALYTIC PERSPECTIVE

JOANNE FEIT DIEHL

Re-Reading *The Letter:* Hawthorne, the Fetish, and the (Family) Romance

> The text is a fetish object, and *this fetish desires me.* The text chooses me, by a whole disposition of invisible screens, selective baffles: vocabulary, references, readability, etc.; and, lost in the midst of a text (not *behind* it, like a *deus ex machina*) there is always the other, the author.
>
> — ROLAND BARTHES, *The Pleasure of the Text*

> "Your father — where is your father? Your mother — is she living? have you been much with her? and has she been much with you?"
>
> — WALT WHITMAN

Almost halfway through *The Scarlet Letter,* in a nightmarish inversion of the moonlit-room description of the conditions necessary for the writing of romance, Arthur Dimmesdale ends a night of vigilant introspection by gazing into the mirror, viewing his face in a looking glass, by the most powerful light which he could throw upon it. "He thus typified," Hawthorne writes, "the constant introspection wherewith he tortured, but could not purify, himself. In these lengthened vigils, his brain often reeled, and visions seemed to flit before him; . . . Now came the dead friends of his youth, and his white-bearded father, with a saint-like frown, and his mother, turning her face away as she passed by. Ghost of a mother, — thinnest fantasy of a mother, — methinks she might yet have thrown a pitying glance towards her son!" (p. 121 in this volume). Other images come and go without comment; the rejecting mother alone receives a direct appeal, voiced not in the third person that speaks throughout the passage, but in the first. The dispassionate objectivity that hitherto separated the authorial voice from his description dissolves with the "methinks," which, in its very immediacy, breaks through the fabric of reserve and seems to speak straight from the heart.

This search for the redemptive mother's pitying glance echoes throughout *The Scarlet Letter*, for, although Hawthorne narratively conceptualizes the work of his romance as the enactment of a desire to reestablish relations with those patriarchal forebears who would so severely judge him, although competition with the father is everywhere on the surface of the text, *The Scarlet Letter* nevertheless harbors a subtext that links the motives for writing to a search for the lost mother, whom the novel envisions as having rejected her only son. Nina Baym has recently argued for the centrality of the maternal in *The Scarlet Letter;* however, my discussion differs from hers in that I am interested in examining what I understand to be a much more ambivalent relationship between the authorial self and the lost mother as it functions in the narrative. Furthermore, I would question her assertion that "the consciously articulated intentions of *The Scarlet Letter*, one might say, are to rescue its heroine from the oblivion of death and to rectify the injustices that were done to her in life" (Baym 21). In my estimation, the romance's "intentions" have less to do with rescuing the heroine/mother from death than they do with returning the son to his mother's presence and exposing a deep authorial conflict toward Hester as the lover/mother.

Consequently, rather than following any single line of interpretation based on character, my discussion will focus on the letter *A* and its matrix of energies, for it is within the sign's history that the conflicts engendered from repressed authorial desires are most compellingly and intricately articulated. It is, furthermore, in the figure of the letter *A* itself that the conflict between desire for the mother and the guilt associated with this desire finds its boldest articulation. Specifically, what I want to suggest is that the *A* functions in several ways that parallel Freud's concept of the fetish, which by its very presence recalls the conflict between desire and its necessary repression. The desire for the mother and the censoring power of custom conjoin in Hawthorne's "A," both in its geometric patterning and in its scarlet threads.

Before expanding on the ways that I understand the *A* to function as a fetishistic object, however, I want briefly to recall the specific biographical circumstances that would have led Hawthorne to this complex and deeply ambivalent sign. Writing on "Mourning and Melancholia," Freud asserts that the son's guilt at the death of the father is associated with his wish to vanquish him, to destroy the father in order to clear the way to sleep with the mother. The greater the intensity of the previously unresolved oedipal feelings, the more severe the guilt following a parent's death. In the case of the father's death, the son experiences the guilt of harboring a death wish for him that has now come true. In the case of the death of the mother, the guilt is complicated by resentment, by the feeling that she has deprived him both of a means of fulfilling his oedipal fantasy and of finding forgiveness for it; her death, then, becomes a kind of double deprivation. Incest, as fantasy and as taboo, lies at the center of his multiple guilt. How great a factor such guilt would have been in Hawthorne's own psychosexual development must be left to surmise; however, pertinent to an interpretation of *The Scarlet Letter* is an understanding of the narrative's treatment of issues related to early conflicts from Hawthorne's own history. Nathaniel's father, a sea captain, was mostly absent during the first three years of his son's life. That the absence of the father would have intensified the boys feelings toward the mother there is little doubt. Moreover, the conversion of the father's absence into permanent separation through his death when Nathaniel was four years old — unmarked by any visible event at home — would have offered the young boy no sign to substantiate his father's disappearance in actuality, thus enhancing its importance to him on the level of fantasy.

In regard to the mother, Hawthorne's experience reveals an aspect of the Family Romance that is equally intense. Once again, the particular circumstances of the early life are crucial: one recalls Nathaniel's mother's rejection by her husband's family and the later difficulties the mother found in making an independent home for her children. Such early trauma may lie at the origins of the extraordinary burst of energy Hawthorne experienced following what his wife Sophia called his "brain fever," suffered immediately after his mother's death, an energy related to the reawakening of early repressed drives associated with ambivalent feelings toward his mother and as-yet-unresolved guilt over his father's failure to return.

In two descriptions that mark endings, one physical, the other literary, Hawthorne recounts his attempt and failure to achieve control over a flood of feeling. Here is Hawthorne on his last moments with his mother:

> At about five o'clock, I went to my mother's chamber, and was shocked to see such an alteration since my last visit, the day before yesterday. I love my mother; but there has been, ever since my boyhood, a sort of coldness of intercourse between us, such as is apt to come between persons of strong feelings, if they are not managed rightly. I did not expect to be much moved at the time — that is to say, to feel any overpowering emotion struggling, just then — though I knew that I should deeply remember and regret. . . . Mrs. Dike left the chamber, and then I found the tears slowly gathering in my eyes. I tried to keep them down; but it would not be — I kept filling up, till, for a few moments, I shook with sobs. For a long time, I knelt there, holding her hand; and surely it is the darkest hour I ever lived. (*American Notebooks* 428–29)

Hawthorne confesses to a similar struggle to attain control in only one other instance — when he read the closing pages of *The Scarlet Letter* to his wife: ". . . my emotions when I read the last scene . . . to my wife, just after writing it, — tried to read it, rather, for my voice swelled and heaved, as if I were tossed up and down on an ocean as it subsides after a storm" (*English Notebooks* 95). Once again Hawthorne is surprised by the power of the emotions that overwhelm him. And as in the earlier description, he employs rhythms of ebb and flow to characterize the conflict between attempts to stifle tears and their reemergence against his will. This struggle for control and the necessity to express his longing for his mother are the precipitating psychological occasions for the composition of Hawthorne's romance. For in its gestures of intermittent withdrawal and return, in its provisional endings, in its associative images of oceanic rhythms and vast tracts of land, *The Scarlet Letter* continually reenacts an unfulfilled or thwarted desire: the desire to traverse a distance that becomes more specifically an authorial search for a discourse that can carry Hawthorne back not simply into an amorphous time past, but, more precisely, into the lost mother's presence. Such yearnings are, however, everywhere restricted as enclosure dominates the characters' movements; jail, scaffold, governor's mansion, even the clandestine forest contribute to a claustrophobic intensity in which the human glance at times seems the only possible form of action.

On a narrative level, the antithetical significance of the *A* manifests itself as a tension between stricture and flight that determines the very texture of the romance. In a crucial conjunction between motive and image, for example, Hawthorne describes the moment when Dimmesdale, returning from the forest reunion with Hester where he has agreed to flee with her (the most extreme attempt to break away found in the book), sits down to write, or rather to rewrite, the Election Day sermon. Dimmesdale associates the power of inspired composition with a voyage over time and space as the text enacts the only journey of which Dimmesdale will prove capable, a distance traversed by language: "Thus the night fled away, as if it were a winged steed, and he careering on it; . . . There he was, with the pen still between his fingers, and a vast, immeasurable tract of written space behind him!" (p. 176). The scene of writing has become the space over which Dimmesdale travels, a ground he traverses to attain his goal; and although Hawthorne does not dwell on the implications of his description, the reader surmises, given the power of language, that the "word" might just possibly transport its author (as narratively it will carry Dimmesdale) past life itself.

That such verbal power should be tied to violation of order is not surprising; that it should be accompanied by a fear of perversion, by an aura of unreality, suggests the extent to which "inspiration" incurs psychic risk. The knowledge Dimmesdale gains in the forest is the self-knowledge that results from his having chosen to flee Boston with Hester. What he learns about himself enforces a sense of doubleness that, although valuable in terms of self-consciousness, tortures his soul:

> The wretched minister! . . . Tempted by a dream of happiness, he had yielded himself with deliberate choice, as he had never done before, to what he knew was deadly sin. And the infectious poison of that sin had been thus rapidly diffused throughout his moral system. It had stupefied all blessed impulses, and awakened into vivid life the whole brotherhood of bad ones. Scorn, bitterness, unprovoked malignity, gratuitous desire of ill, ridicule of whatever was good and holy, all awoke, to tempt, even while they frightened him. (pp. 173–74)

Such pervasive self-alienation comes from an uncensored desire rising to the surface and articulating its demands. Despite the cloud of wickedness in which Dimmesdale perceives himself to be wandering, that release of unchecked desire serves on another level to free his imagination so that he can write the most powerful sermon of his career. His flight into the forest and subsequent self-knowledge allow access to previously unconscious powers associated with the repressed self.

When Dimmesdale delivers the sermon he composed in his newly released fires of thought, the narrative again associates the language of travel with the power of words. Articulated speech now assumes less importance than the power of the voice itself as the reader listens to the sermon as Hester Prynne does, the words obliterated by the distance between herself and the minister. Despite their socially determined positions, Dimmesdale in the church at the center of his congregation and Hester near the scaffold beyond the church walls, the minister's voice nonetheless speaks straight to *her* heart. Communication thus escapes the confines of articulated speech as Hester experiences the sermon's power without recourse to language; voice triumphs over word. "Muffled as the sound was by its passage through the church-walls," the cry of pain reaches out to Hester and "[t]he complaint of a human heart, sorrow-laden, perchance guilty, telling its secret, whether of guilt or sorrow, to the great heart of mankind; beseeching its sympathy or forgiveness, — at every moment, — in each accent, — and never in vain!" (p. 188).

Hawthorne follows this description of oracular power with a vision of Hester immobile, almost lifeless, listening attentively to the muffled strains of Dimmesdale's voice:

> During all this time Hester stood, statue-like, at the foot of the scaffold. If the minister's voice had not kept her there, there would nevertheless have been an inevitable magnetism in that spot, whence she dated the first hour of her life of ignominy. (p. 188)

She is transfixed by history (*his story*), objectified by the passion of the past. The sinful minister reaches out to the mute woman through his voice; but by the close of the afternoon, he will have fallen into her arms in an ultimate appeal for disclosure and reunification.

Before observing this climactic moment, however, the reader should note how Hawthorne's language prepares his audience to imagine this public reunion between Dimmesdale and Hester not simply as the meeting of two formerly clandestine lovers, but as a reunion of mother and son as well. The dynamics of family interaction (specifically, between infant and mother) and the anxiety over language's capacity to carry the self into the presence of what it most desires dominate the descriptions that precede Dimmesdale and Hester's final meeting. Throughout the Election Day scene, Hawthorne employs images that associate Dimmesdale with the rejected, ever-apprehensive son who longs to journey back to the sexually tainted, yet longed-for mother. Within the description of communal activities of Election Day, Hawthorne sketches the drama of the toddler, reaching out to an immobile, statue-like woman who welcomes him only when he collapses, on the verge of death, in her arms. Stasis and movement acquire great poignancy, as the extreme efforts of a dying man evoke his earliest beginnings. Furthermore, Hawthorne partly builds his sustained narrative of filial return on his characterizations of Hester as an image of death. Her face, he writes, resembled "a mask; or rather . . . the frozen calmness of a dead woman's features; owing this dreary resemblance to the fact that Hester was actually dead, in respect to any claim of sympathy, and had departed out of the world with which she still seemed to mingle" (p. 176).

This portrayal of Hester as death mask and statue reinforces the prohibition associated with the son's incestuous fantasy and through its very lifelessness serves to protect the perceiver from his own desires. The scarlet letter alone shines out from the grayness of maternal death, at once preserving the sign of desire and barring the possibility of its fulfillment. The simultaneity of the *A*'s function as both signifier and denier of desire opens the letter to ever-recurrent *mis*interpretation, for just as Dimmesdale depends on the Puritan community's misinterpretation of narrative events (the appearance of the lost glove on the scaffold and the revelation of the *A* shining in the night sky) to protect his guilt and not to expose it, so the narrative establishes a pattern of substitutive identifications that play equally on the community of its readers to *fail* to recognize the sublimated incestuous wishes covered by the text. This tension between disclosure and concealment is the narrative corollary to the fetish's function: to mask desire while naming it. Both depend on the intersubjectivity of author, narrator, and reader — an affiliative community that for the readers of *The Scarlet Letter* provokes a certain anxiety.

Therefore, what Dimmesdale witnesses is a mask of deception and a sign that discloses, for Hester's frozen calmness belies her passionate conviction that she and Dimmesdale should leave Boston and flee to Europe. As instigator of this plot and in a maternal assumption of responsibility, Hester attempts to direct their mutual future as lovers. That Dimmesdale subverts Hester's intentions by succumbing to his own death speaks to the deeply violative cast of her double role as mother and lover — as well as to the son's desperate psychic need to suppress the incestuous wish and to keep his already violated mother intact. But, although the death mask presages the defeat of Hester's "solution" on one level of the narrative, the *A* nevertheless holds before Dimmesdale the sign that the worst has already happened; it is the ever-present sign of transgression kept firmly before his and our eyes.

When Dimmesdale, exhausted from having delivered his sermon, moves from the altar and joins the procession of church fathers, he begins his regressive journey back to the maternal, statue-like form:

"He still walked onward," Hawthorne writes, "if that movement could be so described, which rather resembled the wavering effort of an infant, with its mother's arms in view, outstretched to tempt him forward" (p. 193). By rejecting the hand of the "venerable John Wilson," Dimmesdale turns away from the powerful fathers and totters toward his greater need, reunion with the long-denied mother. As Dimmesdale finally reaches his literal family and reunites with them, it is with all the weakness of the child in need of support, yet with the moral righteousness of the savior; he is at once the infant Jesus and a sacrificial Christ:

> "Hester Prynne," cried he, with a piercing earnestness, "in the name of Him, so terrible and so merciful, who gives me grace, at this last moment, to do what — for my own heavy sin and miserable agony — I withheld myself from doing seven years ago, come hither now, and twine thy strength about me!" (p. 194)

Hester lends him her physical support as the crowd next beholds "the minister, leaning on Hester's shoulder and supported by her arm around him, approach the scaffold, and ascend its steps; while still the little hand of the sin-born child was clasped in his" (pp. 194–95). It is only when Dimmesdale confesses that he achieves true union with the tainted mother; the comfort of the breast, the reunion with the mother/lover, robs Chillingworth, the vengeful father, of life, as Dimmesdale turns his eyes from his adversary toward the source of maternal comfort. "He withdrew his dying eyes from the old man, and fixed them on the woman and the child" (p. 196). In his last moments, Dimmesdale, drained by the extraordinary effort his last sermon has cost him, achieves reunion with Hester and fixes his eyes on the double origins of both his pain and his desire. Yet the kiss he gives Pearl, while freeing her to enter the human community, only further ensures his certain death because it reawakens the knowledge that the chain of desire cannot be broken, that the violative incestuous feelings from which he is barred are awakened in the kiss that the father bestows on his daughter. For Dimmesdale, unable to resolve the terrifying involutions of such a Family Romance, death remains the sole escape.

Must a surrender of health, power, and maturity precede the return to the forbidden woman, and must the return lead to death? This question, shadowed as it is by guilt and longing, speaks not solely of Dimmesdale's predicament but, as I have been suggesting, of deep authorial anxieties as well. If the novel takes as one of its concerns the exploration of the extent of language's power, then the recurrent gestures of appeal and failure within the text signal a disturbing and potentially self-defeating judgment on Hawthorne's capacity as author to attain his desires and survive them, a premonitory warning about the nature of fiction writing that may have contributed to his difficulties in completing the novels — and, by the close of his life, his repeated abandonment of them. *The Scarlet Letter,* that most apparently "complete" of Hawthorne's fictions, challenges language to reach beyond the grave, to test the powers of the word in order to discover whether language can carry the writer over the ground of human loss.

In the opening pages of the novel, the prefatory "Custom-House" section, Hawthorne repeatedly plays on this theme of departure, on the need to quit Salem. Invoking the revolutionary image of the guillotine, he ruefully adopts a proleptic, postmortem self that not only escapes the press of the familiar but, with his beheading, the enactment of vulnerability as well. The narrator writes from "beyond the grave"; the "future editor" of *The Scarlet Letter,* at the start of his work, consigns himself to the "realm of quiet" (p. 52). Elaborating on the metaphor of the political guillotine, the narrator assures us that the whole may be considered as the "POSTHUMOUS PAPERS OF A DECAPITATED SURVEYOR" (p. 52). The beheading acts not only as a device for distancing both text and speaker, but also serves (albeit futilely) as an attempt to dissociate "Hawthorne the editor" from the sexual desires that are the origins of the story he is about to relate. Indeed, as John Irwin has suggested in his *American Hieroglyphics* (1980), the image of the beheading itself may be seen as a symbolic castration. By presencing an absence, the allusion to beheading functions much as does the letter inscribed on Hester's breast, simultaneously marking her incriminating sexuality and gesturing toward its status as forbidden object. However, in the first instance of figural beheading the effect is to displace the fear of castration while preserving the affective charge of punishment; in the second instance, the addition of the sign, of the *A,* symbolically marks Hester as the object of a desire that must be denied.

In a description that echoes neither the theme of rejection nor a longing for death, Hawthorne recounts the discovery of the cloth letter itself:

> But the object that most drew my attention, in the mysterious package, was a certain affair of fine red cloth, much worn and faded. . . . It had been wrought, as was easy to perceive, with wonderful skill of needlework; and the stitch (as I am assured by ladies conversant with such mysteries) gives evidence of a now forgotten art, not to be recovered even by the process of picking out the threads. (p. 43)

No amount of disentanglement can retrieve the letter's lost secret of composition, and thus Hawthorne makes clear that the *A* cannot be reconstituted through analysis:

> This rag of scarlet cloth, — for time, and wear, and a sacrilegious moth, had reduced it to little other than a rag, — on careful examination, assumed the shape of a letter. . . . My eyes fastened themselves upon the old scarlet letter, and would not be turned aside. Certainly, there was some deep meaning in it, most worthy of interpretation, and which, as it were, streamed forth from the mystic symbol, subtly communicating itself to my sensibilities, but evading the analysis of my mind. (p. 43)

By obscuring the *A*'s origins while intensifying its power, Hawthorne protects the object from scrutiny as he prepares the way for its special status in the text, *its function as a fetishistic object.* Surveyor Hawthorne must uncover in himself the reasons for such an identification/fixation, and this need for self-mastery through understanding becomes the occasion for the story's retelling. Just as Dimmesdale's Election Day sermon affects Hester in the absence of any articulated speech, so the power of the *A* depends not on linguistic prowess, but on the direct impact of all that cannot be articulated, the power of those unconscious forces that resist our ability either to adumbrate or to censor them.

Consequently, the *A* acquires power because among its many meanings it represents what cannot be spoken, the inviolate truth of what is most desired and what must be repressed, predominantly, the longing for the mother. Hawthorne's narrative achieves the identification of the mother's power with the *A* through its treatment of Hester, who demonstrates woman's ability to revise transgression in order to lead a socially constructive, if psychically restricted, life at the same time that she marks, with the wearing of the letter, the barrier against future temptation, or (given her sociocultural milieu) against "sin." Hester's identifying *A* not only lends her freedom by separating her from the community; it also leads her, in the narrator's view, dangerously close to chaos. For all its apparent freedoms, Hester's marginalization subdues her even as it becomes the source of her strength; even as it bestows compassion on others, motherhood blocks Hester's full intellectual development. In Hester, Hawthorne thus combines a vision of motherhood rendered inviolate with a portrait of the dangerous woman deprived of her full capacity to threaten either the community or contemporary standards of femininity. By making Hester Dimmesdale's contemporary, Hawthorne relaxes the oedipal connection, severing the male from the generational drama of separation anxiety that occurs instead between two females (Hester and *her* daughter, Pearl). Furthermore, by imposing both biological and communal constraints on Hester, Hawthorne reveals her power while he maintains authorial control over her actions and over his own suppressed, unresolved affect toward his biological mother. Narrative displacement serves the authorial "ego" by protecting it from the full force of its unconscious, yet-to-be-resolved conflicts.

When Hester hovers on the edge of a full-blown prophecy, her words are seized from her and an authorial apology is made to stand in their stead: "A tendency to speculation, though it may keep woman quiet," the narrator avers,

> as it does man, yet makes her sad. She discerns, it may be, such a hopeless task before her. As a first step, the whole system of society is to be torn down, and built up anew. Then, the very nature of the opposite sex, or its long hereditary habit, which has become *like* nature, is to be essentially modified, before woman can be allowed to assume what seems a fair and suitable position. (p. 135; emphasis added)

Here one recognizes an equivocation that more generally characterizes Hawthorne's attitude toward Hester, for by describing the "very nature of the opposite sex" as something that may be culturally derived, "which has become *like* nature," Hawthorne introduces a textual mark of his own ambivalence. If it is culture that has determined woman's essential character, then indeed he may, however gently, be calling for a release of woman's nature from her "his-tory"; whereas if biology is destiny, she would perhaps be wise to accept her fate. By such verbal equivocations, Hawthorne marks, though he does not resolve, the conflict that characterizes his problematic understanding of Hester. Is he on her side or is he not? As father and as son, how can he afford to acknowledge her power without violating his own sense of authority, the masculine aspect of the self? By sympathizing with the enormity of the woman's task of transforming society, the narrator has rendered her beyond speech. Not only does all society act as an obstruction to woman's full expression, but also her public character mitigates against any speculative freedom that might culminate in action. So, to efface the discourse of woman while longing for her presence is to assign her a role that could not be equaled were she admitted to the community of social and verbal intercourse. By stripping her of her capacity to act,

Hawthorne thus renders her safe: by converting her into myth, he condemns her to silence.

Placing such severe personal and historical restrictions on Hester — curtailing her power while granting Dimmesdale, in the midst of his duplicity, the freedom of speech — Hawthorne, as author, withstands being submerged by female presence. Among the rhetorical attempts to control female power, the most audacious is the metaphorical process whereby Hester Prynne, lover and mother, herself becomes orphaned, isolated, and homeless. Venturing too far in her speculative ruminations, she is lost, wandering "without a clew in the dark labyrinth of mind; now turned aside by an insurmountable precipice; now starting back from a deep chasm. There was wild and ghastly scenery all around her, and a home and comfort nowhere" (p. 135).

Despite the narrative containment of Hester's threatening power, the *A* will not relinquish its tenacious hold over the narrator's imagination. Discussing the motive that generally informs Hawthorne's narratives, Frederick Crews remarks, "Relief, indeed, is the desired endpoint of each romance; not a solution to its thematic issues but oblivion to them" (17). What are the sources of the *A*'s residual power and why will it not fade with the story constructed to release its power? If the *A* functions as a hieroglyph within the context of the romance, if its meanings accrue through various points of view, then it may be immune (as Hawthorne had stated in the "Preface") to unraveling and hence to analysis. The clue to its power, Hawthorne reveals, is contact with the wearer and the ability of the *A* to draw all eyes toward it, to *fix* the viewer's gaze. By escaping the boundaries of story, the *A* achieves status as a sign that draws us back to the origins of Hawthorne's romance, and, as I have argued, back to the scene of the mother's death. Desire for the lost mother and the censoring power of the Custom-House merge in the scarlet *A*. And it is to a discussion of the *A* as fetish that I now turn.

According to Freud, the origins of the fetish can be traced to its function as a "substitute for the woman's (the mother's) penis that the little boy once believed in and — for reasons familiar to us — does not want to give up." Freud continues: "What happened, therefore, was that the boy refused to take cognizance of the fact of his having perceived that a woman does not possess a penis," and that "if a woman had been castrated, then his (the boy's) own possession of a penis was in danger" (21: 152–53ff.). As a sign of the history of this fear and longing, which Hawthorne can face only in the disguised form of fictive displacement, the *A* functions in the narrative both to focus and to dispel such authorial tensions. Whether or not the fetish serves as a textual "symptom" is not really my concern; of interpretive interest here is the way the scarlet letter operates as a narrative means for resolving an otherwise unresolvable conflict within the fiction; in other words, the text functions therapeutically to provide a means for treating material otherwise closed off from literary production.

The *A* would therefore represent among its meanings the desired Other whose presence in the fiction can only be acknowledged through its absence, the penis displaced by a vagina that becomes a sign of the female genitalia of the mother forever barred from her son. Indeed, the *A* articulates through its linear geometry the illustration of forbidden desire. Its divergent verticals suggest a schematic drawing of the vagina, viewed at once frontally and from below, and the horizontal bar of the letter signifies the intact hymeneal membrane, the sign that no violation has occurred. Thus the *A* signifies a double denial: no marriage and no consummation. Scarlet recalls both the blood of the torn hymen (presenting what is in the same symbol denied — that the mother has [not] been violated) and the color of sexual passion. Moreover, in its artful complexity, the embroidered letter converts this potentially threatening vision of blood and pubic hair, the Medusan coils of active sexuality, into a refined and highly elaborated pattern. Constructed by that most domestic of crafts, the female art of needlework, the letter again operates as a fetish by recalling the forbidden sight even as it protects the gazer from the object's symbolic identity.

The relationship between the scarlet letter and its viewers is not, however, restricted to that of a fetishist and his fetish; for there is no *single* character who defines herself or himself solely in these terms. Instead, the scarlet letter becomes a focus that attracts the kinds of sexual ambivalence and tensions that characterize the text in its entirety and that defines itself in relation to each of the primary characters. For Dimmesdale, the *A* serves as a mirror of the physical torment he suffers — the outward, external elaboration of the stigmatizing desire for the other disguised as a desire for remorse. Consequently, the flagellation he pursues, the simultaneous stimulation and punishment of the self, is a practice that discloses his libidinal energies as it releases them. For Chillingworth, the *A* functions as the mark of his home; it is what keeps him on the edges of a civilization therefore negatively defined, and what, through his direct and active intervention, reifies his revenge against Dimmesdale, the transgressor, the son. Hester as the mother who is everywhere present but unattainable, who is given a free imagination yet kept from action, who undergoes "rehabilitation" in terms of society yet must suffer the constant torture of shame, receives the kind of ambivalent treatment from the author that Freud would also ascribe to the fetishist. When Dimmesdale, in his dying moments, abjures any hope for Hester's soul, we may sense the anger behind the rhetorical orthodoxy of his rejection of the possibility that her soul, too, might be saved. And the wearer of the fetish herself participates in ambivalence toward the object when she attempts to cast it off, to deny its historicity and return instead to her lover. Out of this matrix of identities, the *A* emerges not simply as a mark of the forbidden phallic mother, but also as a sign of the complex interdependencies that are at the center of all human relationships.

Furthermore, it is not without significance that Hester wears the *A* on her breast and that she should first be seen leaving that dark prison with the infant Pearl at her bosom, for the sign of the forbidden transmuted into art — the craft of embroidery — is, throughout the romance, associated with female fecundity. The power of the mother as nurturing artist, albeit severely restricted by the innately conservative narrator's control, stands clear before the reader. Trapped by societal expectations, Dimmesdale, unlike Hester, wins verbal power but is denied all earthly freedom. Oppressed and outwardly punished as she may be, it is the woman who, by the very fact of becoming an outcast, discovers her more "modest" freedom on the margins of community.

This radical, transforming power thus depends on Hester's marginalization; what keeps her from a more austere radicalism are the presence of Pearl and the narrator's convictions concerning the inherently passive nature of woman. However, to the extent that Hester, no matter how tentatively, turns the *A* into a symbol of compassion, she wins the potential for transmuting guilt into strength. Dimmesdale, unable to do so until his dying hour (itself troubling in its sadistic orthodoxy), spends his postlapsarian years apparently enduring a festering wound that becomes a masochistic sign of the destructive, if supremely eloquent, artist. This somatization of guilt has a double origin in Chillingworth and the minister, as one feeds on the other in a relationship that grotesquely caricatures that of the nursing mother and her infant Pearl.

If, in conclusion, we accept the scarlet letter's resemblance to the fetish, then Hester, rather than Dimmesdale, embodies an alternative prevision to Freudian theories of the fetish. By drawing our eyes to the woman's breast and the art inscribed thereon, Hawthorne not only ensures visibility for the letter, but he also reinforces Hester's roles of nurturer and artist as synonymous and mutually dependent functions.

Rather than signifying the fetish as a denial of an unwished-for absence (the way the letter functions for Dimmesdale), for Hester the letter serves to transform the double negative association of the absence of male genitalia and thwarted desire into a sign that represents the combined powers of nursing mother and creative woman. That Pearl is such a difficult child, that through her milk Hester transmits turbulence as well as nourishment, only further underscores the difficulties inherent in the relationship between sexuality and art — an ambivalence toward maternal origins which, in Hawthorne's works, neither man nor woman can evade.

Free to bury, dismiss, or redeem his characters, Hawthorne, at the close of the novel, performs all three gestures, but it is the paradoxical triumph of the *A*'s imaginative life that it will not fade with time, but evades closure to shine with all the initial fervor of the burning desire with which the story began. Vivid as the letter within the narrator's imagination, it shines out past the final moments of the text, but with a telling difference: what we see when we read "'ON A FIELD, SABLE, THE LETTER A, GULES'" (p. 202) is a verbal substitution for the engraving that is inscribed on a tombstone. The sign is doubly displaced, first by the descriptive sentence that contains the sign and second by the heraldic device that represents, or stands in for, the words bearing the message that identifies the letter. Thus, the fetishistic object undergoes a further distancing as it is associated directly both with death and with the two lovers resting, albeit with a space between them, side by side. Despite the narrator's claim that the inscription serves as a motto for the story that precedes it, the heraldic device, when translated into words, does not so much explain or "sum up" the story as it insists upon the *A*'s abiding presence. In this final description's act of double distancing, Hawthorne reiterates the resilience of what the *A* symbolizes: the desire for contact and reunion with the forbidden, which must be approached through a language that will protect the very distance the author seeks to traverse.

Theorizing on the character of desire and its relation to denial, Leo Bersani has commented that

> a sense both of the forbidden nature of certain desires and of the incompatibility of reality with our desiring imagination makes the negation of desire inevitable. But to deny desire is not to eliminate it; in fact, such denials multiply the appearances of each desire in the self's history. In denying a desire, we condemn ourselves to finding it everywhere. (6)

In narrative terms, this would suggest that the *A*, rather than diminishing in force, gathers its own momentum, just as writing provides access to the origins of the scene of repression but cannot, of course, restore the scene with the incestuous wish intact. Although in the opening pages of "The Custom-House," the narrator had announced his desire to depart Salem and escape the "press of the familiar," the romance's close reveals instead a desire to return to the motherland and to speak with a voice that will reach the dead. Like the archives of the unconscious that, as Derrida maintains, "are *always* already transcriptions," so the worn yet still powerfully evocative A-shaped piece of cloth Surveyor Hawthorne discovers *already* represents the transcription of his author's unconscious transgressive desire for the dead mother. As a sign that bars itself, the *A* operates for Dimmesdale within *The Scarlet Letter* as does the fetish, both to presence the forbidden desire and to keep that forbidden incestuous wish from being brought to consciousness. That the *A*, on the other hand, empowers rather than defeats Hester, that the experience of mothering affords her the capacity to transmute the stigma of shame into a badge of commitment and charity, suggests the regenerative power of the woman — a fact that she is nevertheless prohibited from displaying in verbal discourse, forbidden as she is from becoming the prophet of a new and more enlightened age. In my judgment, that she is so deprived speaks to the Hawthornian insistence on silencing the mother and thereby of further identifying the deeply troubled but verbally empowered fetishist with the father and the son.

Shadowing the text and shining beyond it, the scarlet *A* therefore signifies at once the articulated oedipal anxieties and the covert incestuous desires expressed in the fetishistic silence. Yet the *A* also signifies a breaking of that silence, for it represents a conflict between the desiring authorial son and the yearnings of the phallic mother, the mother who would free herself from his fetishizing imagination to achieve the authority tested, but finally denied her, in *The Scarlet Letter* — the power of the woman's voice. Imprisoned in her maternal identity while protected by it, Hester cannot escape its stigmatization as Pearl can, because the mother is drawn back to the scene of the "crime," as much victimized by the altruism that converts her *A* into "Angel" as by the adultery for which it ostensibly stands. Similarly, Dimmesdale, the transgressing son, can acknowledge his paternity only at the moment of his death: punishment for the violation that has always already occurred is the price of adulthood. That maternity and paternity are psychically illicit from the point of view of the child only underscores the significance of the primal scene. Finally, when we, as readers, gaze at the scarlet letter, we might imagine the unconscious text Hawthorne recollects in his narrative, witnessing along with him the scar of primal desire, the bleeding yet inviolate wound, the cultural script, or, as Chillingworth would have it, the "dark necessity" that implicates us all in the novel's fatal Family Romance.

WORKS CITED

Baym, Nina. "Nathaniel Hawthorne and His Mother: A Biographical Speculation." *American Literature* 54 (1982): 1–27.

Bersani, Leo. *A Future for Astyanax.* Boston: Little, 1976.

Crews, Frederick C. *The Sins of the Fathers: Hawthorne's Psychological Themes.* New York: Oxford UP, 1966.

Freud, Sigmund. *The Standard Edition of the Complete Psychological Works of Sigmund Freud.* Ed. James Strachey. Vol. 2. London: Hogarth, 1953–74.

Hawthorne, Nathaniel. *The American Notebooks.* Ed. Claude M. Simpson. Columbus: Ohio State UP, 1972.

———. *The English Notebooks.* Ed. Randall Stewart. New York: Russell, 1962.

Irwin, John. *American Hieroglyphics: The Symbol of the Egyptian Hieroglyphics in the American Renaissance.* New Haven: Yale UP, 1980.

Reader-Response Criticism and *The Scarlet Letter*

WHAT IS READER-RESPONSE CRITICISM?

Students are routinely asked in English courses for their reactions to texts they are reading. Sometimes there are so many different reactions that we may wonder whether everyone has read the same text. And some students respond so idiosyncratically to what they read that we say their responses are "totally off the wall." This variety of response interests reader-response critics, who raise theoretical questions about whether our responses to a work are the same as its meanings, whether a work can have as many meanings as we have responses to it, and whether some responses are more valid than others. They ask what determines what is and what isn't "off the wall." What, in other words, is the wall, and what standards help us to define it?

In addition to posing provocative questions, reader-response criticism provides us with models that aid our understanding of texts and the reading process. Adena Rosmarin has suggested that a literary text may be likened to an incomplete work of sculpture: to see it fully, we must complete it imaginatively, taking care to do so in a way that responsibly takes into account what exists. Other reader-response critics have suggested other models, for reader-response criticism is not a monolithic school of thought but, rather, an umbrella term covering a variety of approaches to literature.

Nonetheless, as Steven Mailloux has shown, reader-response critics *do* share not only questions but also goals and strategies. Two of the basic goals are to show that a work gives readers something to do and to describe what the reader does by way of response. To achieve those goals, the critic may make any of a number of what Mailloux calls "moves." For instance, a reader-response critic might typically (1) cite direct references to reading in the text being analyzed, in order to justify the focus on reading and show that the world of the text is continuous with the one in which the reader reads; (2) show how other nonreading situations in the text nonetheless mirror the situation the reader is in ("Fish shows how in *Paradise Lost* Michael's teaching of Adam in Book XI resembles Milton's teaching of the reader throughout the poem"); and (3) show, therefore, that the reader's response is, or is analogous to, the story's action or conflict. For instance, Stephen Booth calls *Hamlet* the tragic story of "an audience that cannot make up its mind" (Mailloux, "Learning" 103).

Although reader-response criticism is often said to have emerged in the United States in the 1970s, it is in one respect as old as the foundations of Western culture. The ancient Greeks and Romans tended to view literature as rhetoric, a means of making an audience react in a certain way. Although their focus was more on rhetorical strategies and devices than on the reader's (or listener's) response to those methods, the ancients by no means left the audience out of the literary equation. Aristotle thought, for instance, that the greatness of tragedy lay in its "cathartic" power to cleanse or purify the emotions of audience members. Plato, by contrast, worried about the effects of artistic productions, so much so that he advocated evicting poets from the Republic on the grounds that their words "feed and water" the passions!

In our own century, long before 1970, there were critics whose concerns and attitudes anticipated those of reader-response critics. One of these, I. A. Richards, is usually associated with formalism, a supposedly objective, text-centered approach to literature that reader-response critics of the 1970s roundly attacked. And yet in 1929 Richards managed to sound surprisingly *like* a 1970s-vintage reader-response critic, writing in *Practical Criticism* that "the personal situation of the reader inevitably (and within limits rightly) affects his reading, and many more are drawn to poetry in quest of some reflection of their latest emotional crisis than would admit it" (575). Rather than deploring this fact, as many of his formalist contemporaries would have done, Richards argued that the reader's feelings and experiences provide a kind of reality check, a way of testing the authenticity of emotions and events represented in literary works.

Approximately a decade after Richards wrote *Practical Criticism,* an American named Louise M. Rosenblatt published *Literature as Exploration* (1938). In that seminal book, now in its fourth edition (1983), Rosenblatt began developing a theory of reading that blurs the boundary between reader and text, subject and object. In a 1969 article entitled "Towards a Transactional Theory of Reading," she sums up her position by writing that "a poem is what the reader lives through under the guidance of the text and experiences as relevant to the text" (127). Rosenblatt knew her definition would be difficult for many to accept: "The idea that a *poem* presupposes a *reader* actively involved with a text," she wrote, "is particularly shocking to those seeking to emphasize the objectivity of their interpretations" ("Transactional" 127).

Rosenblatt implicitly and generally refers to formalists (also called the "New Critics") when she speaks of supposedly objective interpreters shocked by the notion that a "poem" is something cooperatively produced by a "reader" and a "text." Formalists spoke of "the poem itself," the "concrete work of art," the "real poem." They had no interest in what a work of literature makes a reader "live through." In fact, in *The Verbal Icon* (1954), William K. Wimsatt and Monroe C. Beardsley defined as fallacious the very notion that a reader's response is relevant to the meaning of a literary work:

> The Affective Fallacy is a confusion between the poem and its *results* (what it *is* and what it *does*). . . . It begins by trying to derive the standards of criticism from the psychological effects of a poem and ends in impressionism and relativism. The outcome . . . is that the poem itself, as an object of specifically critical judgment, tends to disappear. (21)

Reader-response critics have taken issue with their formalist predecessors. Particularly influential has been Stanley Fish, whose early work is seen by some as marking the true beginning of contemporary reader-response criticism. In "Literature in the Reader: Affective Stylistics" (1970), Fish took on the formalist hegemony, the New Critical establishment, by arguing that any school of criticism that would see a work of literature as an object, claiming to describe what it *is* and never what it *does,* is guilty of misconstruing the very essence of literature and reading. Literature exists when it is read, Fish suggests, and its force is an affective force. Furthermore, reading is a temporal process. Formalists assume it is a spatial one as they step back and survey the literary work as if it were an object spread out before them. They may find elegant patterns in the texts they examine and reexamine, but they fail to take into account that the work is quite different to a reader who is turning the pages and being moved, or affected, by lines that appear and disappear as the reader reads.

In discussing the effect that a sentence penned by the seventeenth-century physician Thomas Browne has on a reader reading, Fish pauses to say this about his analysis and also, by extension, about his critical strategy: "Whatever is persuasive and illuminating about [it] is the result of my substituting for one question — what does this sentence mean? — another, more operational question — what does this sentence do?" He then quotes a line from John Milton's *Paradise Lost,* a line that refers to Satan and the other fallen angels: "Nor did they not perceive their evil plight." Whereas more traditional critics might say that the "meaning" of the line is "They did perceive their evil plight," Fish relates the uncertain movement of the reader's mind *to* that half-satisfying interpretation. Furthermore, he declares that "the reader's inability to tell whether or not 'they' do perceive and his involuntary question . . . are part of the line's *meaning,* even though they take place in the mind, not on the page" (*Text* 26).

This stress on what pages *do* to minds (and what minds do in response) pervades the writings of most, if not all, reader-response critics. Stephen Booth, whose book *An Essay on Shakespeare's Sonnets* (1969) greatly influenced Fish, sets out to describe the "reading experience that results" from a "multiplicity of organizations" in a sonnet by Shakespeare (*Essay* ix). Sometimes these organizations don't make complete sense, Booth points out, and sometimes they even seem curiously contradictory. But that is precisely what interests reader-response critics, who, unlike formalists, are at least as interested in fragmentary, inconclusive, and even unfinished texts as in polished, unified works. For it is the reader's struggle to *make sense* of a challenging work that reader-response critics seek to describe.

The German critic Wolfgang Iser has described that sense-making struggle in his books *The Implied Reader* (1974) and *The Act of Reading: A Theory of Aesthetic Response* (1978). Iser argues that texts are full of "gaps" (or "blanks," as he sometimes calls them). These gaps powerfully affect the reader, who is forced to explain them, to connect what they separate, to create in his or her mind aspects of a poem or novel or play that aren't *in* the text but that the text incites. As Iser puts it in *The Implied Reader,* the "unwritten aspects" of a story "draw the reader into the action" and "lead him to shade in the many outlines suggested by the given situations, so that these take on a reality of their own." These "outlines" that "the reader's imagination animates" in turn "influence" the way in which "the written part of the text" is subsequently read (276).

In *Self-Consuming Artifacts: The Experience of Seventeenth-Century Literature* (1972), Fish reveals his preference for literature that makes readers work at making meaning. He contrasts two kinds of literary presentation. By the phrase "rhetorical presentation," he describes literature that reflects and reinforces opinions that readers already hold; by "dialectical presentation," he refers to works that prod and provoke. A dialectical text, rather than presenting an opinion as if it were truth, challenges readers to discover truths on their own. Such a text may not even have the kind of symmetry that formalist critics seek. Instead of offering a "single, sustained argument," a dialectical text, or self-consuming artifact, may be "so arranged that to enter into the spirit and assumptions of any one of [its] . . . units is implicitly to reject the spirit and assumptions of the unit immediately preceding" (*Artifacts* 9). Whereas a critic of another school might try to force an explanation as to why the units are fundamentally coherent, the reader-response critic proceeds by describing how the reader deals with the sudden twists and turns that characterize the dialectical text, returning to earlier passages and seeing them in an entirely new light.

"The value of such a procedure," Fish has written, "is predicated on the idea of meaning as *an event*," not as something "located (presumed to be embedded) *in* the utterance" or "verbal object as a thing in itself" (*Text* 28). By redefining meaning as an event rather than as something inherent in the text, the reader-response critic once again locates meaning in time: the reader's time. A text exists and signifies while it is being read, and what it signifies or means will depend, to no small extent, on *when* it is read. (*Paradise Lost* had some meanings for a seventeenth-century Puritan that it would not have had for a twentieth-century atheist.)

With the redefinition of literature as something that only exists meaningfully in the mind of the reader, with the redefinition of the literary work as a catalyst of mental events, comes a concurrent redefinition of the reader. No longer is the reader the passive recipient of those ideas that an author has planted in a text. "The reader is *active*," Rosenblatt insists ("Transactional" 123). Fish begins "Literature in the Reader" with a similar observation: "If at this moment someone were to ask, 'what are you doing,' you might reply, 'I am reading,' and thereby acknowledge that reading is . . . something *you do*" (*Text* 22). Iser, in focusing critical interest on the gaps in texts, on what is not expressed, similarly redefines the reader as an active maker.

Amid all this talk of "the reader," it is tempting and natural to ask, "Just who *is* the reader?" (Or, to place the emphasis differently, "Just who is *the* reader?") Are reader-response critics simply sharing their own idiosyncratic responses when they describe what a line from *Paradise Lost* does in and to the reader's mind? "What about my responses?" you may want to ask. "What if they're different? Would reader-response critics be willing to say that my responses are equally valid?"

Fish defines "the reader" in this way: "*the* reader is the *informed* reader." The informed reader (whom Fish sometimes calls "the *intended* reader") is someone who is "sufficiently experienced as a reader to have internalized the properties of literary discourses, including everything from the most local of devices (figures of speech, etc.) to whole genres." And, of course, the informed reader is in full possession of the "semantic knowledge" (knowledge of idioms, for instance) assumed by the text (*Artifacts* 406).

Other reader-response critics define "*the* reader" differently. Wayne C. Booth, in *A Rhetoric of Irony* (1974), uses the phrase "the implied reader" to mean the reader "made by the work itself" [228]. (Only "by agreeing to play the role of this created audience," Susan Suleiman explains, "can an actual reader correctly understand and appreciate the work" [8].) Gerard Genette and Gerald Prince prefer to speak of "the narratee, . . . the necessary counterpart of a given narrator, that is, the person or figure who receives a narrative" (Suleiman 13). Like Booth, Iser employs the term "the implied reader," but he also uses "the educated reader" when he refers to what Fish calls the "informed" reader.

Jonathan Culler, who in 1981 criticized Fish for his sketchy definition of the informed reader, set out in *Structuralist Poetics* (1975) to describe the educated or "competent" reader's education by elaborating those reading conventions that make possible the understanding of poems and novels. In retrospect, however, Culler's definitions seem sketchy as well. By "competent reader," Culler meant competent reader of "literature." By "literature," he meant what schools and colleges mean when they speak of literature as being part of the curriculum. Culler, like his contemporaries, was not concerned with the fact that curricular content is politically and economically motivated. And "he did not," in Mailloux's words, "emphasize how the literary competence he described was embedded within larger formations and traversed by political ideologies extending beyond the academy" ("Turns" 49). It remained for a later generation of reader-oriented critics to do those things.

The fact that Fish, following Rosenblatt's lead, defined reader-response criticism in terms of its difference from and opposition to the New Criticism or formalism should not obscure the fact that the formalism of the 1950s and early 1960s had a great deal in common with the reader-response criticism of the late 1960s and early 1970s. This has become increasingly obvious with the rise of subsequent critical approaches whose practitioners have proved less interested in the close reading of texts than in the way literature represents, reproduces, and/or resists prevailing ideologies concerning gender, class, and race. In a retrospective essay entitled "The Turns of Reader-Response Criticism" (1990), Mailloux has suggested that, from the perspective of hindsight, the "close reading" of formalists and "Fish's early 'affective stylistics'" seem surprisingly similar. Indeed, Mailloux argues, the early "reader talk of . . . Iser and Fish enabled the continuation of the formalist practice of close reading. Through a vocabulary focused on a text's manipulation of readers, Fish was especially effective in extending and diversifying the formalist practices that continued business as usual within literary criticism" (48).

Since the mid-1970s, however, reader-response criticism (once commonly referred to as the "School of Fish") has diversified and taken on a variety of new forms, some of which truly *are* incommensurate with formalism, with its considerable respect for the integrity and power of the text. For instance, "subjectivists" like David Bleich, Norman Holland, and Robert Crosman have assumed what Mailloux calls the "absolute priority of individual selves as creators of texts" (*Conventions* 31). In other words, these critics do not see the reader's response as one "guided" by the text but rather as one motivated by deep-seated, personal, psychological needs. What they find in texts is, in Holland's phrase, their own "identity theme." Holland has argued that as readers we use "the literal work to symbolize and finally to replicate ourselves. We work out through the text our own characteristic patterns of desire" ("UNITY" 816). Subjective critics, as you may already have guessed, often find themselves confronted with the following question: If all interpretation is a function of private, psychological identity, then why have so many readers interpreted, say, Shakespeare's *Hamlet* in the same way? Different subjective critics have answered the question differently. Holland simply has said that common identity themes exist, such as that involving an oedipal fantasy.

Meanwhile, Fish, who in the late 1970s moved away from reader-response criticism as he had initially helped define it, came up with a different answer to the question of why different readers tend to read the same works the same way. His answer, rather than involving common individual identity themes, involved common *cultural* identity. In "Interpreting the *Variorum*" (1976), he argues that the "stability of interpretation among readers" is a function of shared "interpretive strategies." These strategies, which "exist prior to the act of reading and therefore determine the shape of what is read," are held in common by "interpretive communities" such as the one constituted by American college students reading a novel as a class assignment (*Text* 167, 171). In developing the model of interpretive communities, Fish truly has made the break with formalist or New Critical predecessors, becoming in the process something of a social, structuralist, reader-response critic. Recently, he has been engaged in studying reading communities and their interpretive conventions in order to understand the conditions that give rise to a work's intelligibility.

Fish's shift in focus is in many ways typical of changes that have taken place within the field of reader-response criticism — a field that, because of those changes, is increasingly being referred to as "reader-*oriented*" criticism. Less and less common are critical analyses examining the transactional interface between the text and its individual reader. Increasingly, reader-oriented critics are investigating reading communities, as the reader-oriented cultural critic Janice A. Radway has done in her study of female readers of romance paperbacks (*Reading the Romance,* 1984). They are also studying the changing reception of literary works across time; see, for example, Mailloux in his "pragmatic readings" of American literature in *Interpretive Conventions* (1982) and *Rhetorical Power* (1989).

An important catalyst of this gradual change was the work of Hans Robert Jauss, a colleague of Iser's whose historically oriented reception theory (unlike Iser's theory of the implied reader) was not available in English book form until the early 1980s. Rather than focusing on the implied, informed, or intended reader, Jauss examined actual past readers. In *Toward an Aesthetics of Reception* (1982), he argued that the reception of a work or author tends to depend upon the reading public's "horizons of expectations." He noted that, in the morally conservative climate of mid-nineteenth-century France, *Madame Bovary* was literally put on trial, its author Flaubert accused of glorifying adultery in passages representing the protagonist's fevered delirium via free indirect discourse, a mode of narration in which a third-person narrator tells us in an unfiltered way what a character is thinking and feeling.

As readers have become more sophisticated and tolerant, the popularity and reputation of *Madame Bovary* have soared. Sometimes, of course, changes in a reading public's horizons of expectations cause a work to be *less* well received over time. As American reception theorists influenced by Jauss have shown, Mark Twain's *Adventures of Huckleberry Finn* has elicited an increasingly ambivalent reaction from a reading public increasingly sensitive to demeaning racial stereotypes and racist language. The rise of feminism has prompted a downward revaluation of everything from Andrew Marvell's "To His Coy Mistress" to D. H. Lawrence's *Women in Love.*

Some reader-oriented feminists, such as Judith Fetterley, Patrocinio Schweickart, and Monique Wittig, have challenged the reader to become what Fetterley calls "the resisting reader." Arguing that literature written by men tends, in Schweickart's terms, to "immasculate" women, they have advocated strategies of reading that involve substituting masculine for feminine pronouns and male for female characters in order to expose the sexism inscribed in patriarchal texts. Other feminists, such as Nancy K. Miller in *Subject to Change* (1988), have suggested that there may be essential differences between the way women and men read and write.

That suggestion, however, has prompted considerable disagreement. A number of gender critics whose work is oriented toward readers and reading have admitted that there is such a thing as "reading like a woman" (or man), but they have also tended to agree with Peggy Kamuf that such forms of reading, like gender itself, are cultural rather than natural constructs. Gay and lesbian critics, arguing that sexualities have been similarly constructed within and by social discourse, have argued that there is a homosexual way of reading; Wayne Koestenbaum has defined "the (male twentieth-century first world) gay reader" as one who "reads resistantly for inscriptions of his condition, for texts that will confirm a social and private identity founded on a desire for other men. . . . Reading becomes a hunt for histories that deliberately foreknow or unwittingly trace a desire felt not by author but by reader, who is most acute when searching for signs of himself" (176–77).

Given this kind of renewed interest in the reader and reading, some students of contemporary critical practice have been tempted to conclude that reader-oriented theory has been taken over by feminist, gender, gay, and lesbian theory. Others, like Elizabeth Freund, have suggested that it is deconstruction with which the reader-oriented approach has mixed and merged. Certainly, all of these approaches have informed and been informed by reader-response or reader-oriented theory. The case can be made, however, that there is in fact still a distinct reader-oriented approach to literature, one whose points of tangency are neither with deconstruction nor with feminist, gender, and so-called queer theory but, rather, with the new historicism and cultural criticism.

This relatively distinct form of reader theory is practiced by a number of critics, but is perhaps best exemplified by the work of scholars like Mailloux and Peter J. Rabinowitz. In *Before Reading: Narrative Conventions and the Politics of Interpretation* (1987), Rabinowitz sets forth four conventions or rules of reading, which he calls the rules of "notice," "signification," "configuration," and "coherence" — rules telling us which parts of a narrative are important, which details have a reliable secondary or special meaning, which fit into which familiar patterns, and how stories fit together as a whole. He then proceeds to analyze the misreadings and misjudgments of critics and to show that politics governs the way in which those rules are applied and broken ("The strategies employed by critics when they read [Raymond Chandler's] *The Big Sleep,*" Rabinowitz writes, "can teach us something about the structure of misogyny, not the misogyny of the novel itself, but the misogyny of the world outside it" [195]). In subsequent critical essays, Rabinowitz proceeds similarly, showing how a society's ideological assumptions about gender, race, and class determine the way in which artistic works are perceived and evaluated.

Mailloux, who calls his approach "rhetorical reception theory" or "rhetorical hermeneutics," takes a similar tack, insofar as he describes the political contexts of (mis)interpretation. In a recent essay, "Misreading as a Historical Act" (1993), he shows that a mid-nineteenth-century review of Frederick Douglass's *Narrative* by proto-feminist Margaret Fuller seems to be a misreading until we situate it "within the cultural conversation of the 'Bible politics' of 1845" (Machor 9). Woven through Mailloux's essay on Douglass and Fuller are philosophical pauses in which we are reminded, in various subtle ways, that all reading (including Mailloux's and our own) is culturally situated and likely to seem like *mis*reading someday. One such reflective pause, however, accomplishes more; in it, Mailloux reads the map of where reader-oriented criticism is today, affords a rationale for its being there, and plots its likely future direction. "However we have arrived at our present juncture," Mailloux writes,

> the current talk about historical acts of reading provides a welcome opportunity for more explicit consideration of how reading is historically contingent, politically situated, institutionally embedded, and materially conditioned; of how reading any text, literary or nonliterary, relates to a larger cultural politics that goes well beyond some hypothetical private interaction between an autonomous reader and an independent text; and of how our particular views of reading relate to the liberatory potential of literacy and the transformative power of education. (5)

In the essay that follows, entitled "The Address of *The Scarlet Letter,*" Stephen Railton extends the work of critics interested in readers, interpretive communities, and reception theory by focusing on Hawthorne's *audience,* a term he uses to refer to Hawthorne's original audience. In Railton's view, the audience for which a given author wrote should be of primary interest to his or her scholars and critics. "As reader-response criticism shows," he writes, "any reader's ideological allegiances as a member of a particular community play a crucial role in determining the way that reader produces meaning from a work of literature. But only 'the audience,' as I am suggesting we define it, can play a role in the creation of the work itself" (p. 348 in this volume).

To Walter J. Ong's suggestion that a writer's sense of audience is an imaginative abstraction, even a "fiction," Railton responds by saying that it is one grounded in a very real sense of real readers — in Hawthorne's case the nineteenth-century American reading public. "The contemporary audience for *The Scarlet Letter* was there, both sociologically and psychologically, before Hawthorne sat down to write his novel: it was 'there' in America in 1850 as the actual reading public available to him as a professional writer and 'there' in [his] mind as his internalized construct of the people he hoped would buy, read, and understand his novel" (pp. 348–49). What interests Railton about readers of *our* day is that "it is almost impossible for us to imagine how [Hawthorne's first] readers would have initially reacted. . . . We cannot help but bring to the novel a very different set of preconceptions — about someone like Hester, about adultery, about Christianity" (p. 350). Railton in no way denies the validity of *our* way of reading *The Scarlet Letter:* "[e]very reader's responses," he writes, "are relevant to any attempt to determine the ultimate significance of the text." But he does believe that we "can . . . gain a lot by trying to reconstruct the way Hawthorne wrote it for his contemporary audience, by trying to understand how it was meant to speak to and work on the readers of his day" (p. 350).

Just as other reader-response critics have shown how certain authors represent the reader in the text, thereby figuring (or "reading") the act of reading, Railton argues that Hawthorne figuratively represents his audience in the Puritan populace of Boston. (This is the group, after all, "for whom the scarlet letter is first 'published' " as Hester steps out of the prison wearing it on her person [p. 351].) And a "terrible audience" they turn out to be, Railton reminds us: "[t]heir responses, and the assumptions behind them, are wholly inadequate to either the moral or the interpretive demands of his story." Railton points out that, in its "opening scene," the novel "explicitly condemns [the Puritans] for their failure" to "sympath[ize]" with Hester and that, at its "climax, which depicts another publication of the scarlet letter while again [the Puritan multitudes] stand around the scaffold as a literal audience," their "failure as 'readers' of the story is brought home" (p. 354). (Whereas "they expect to see Dimmesdale ascend in glory to heaven," he instead ascends the scaffold in shame.) According to Railton, "Hawthorne put this surrogate audience into the text to guide his own audience's responses" — not by setting positive interpretive examples but, rather, by showing "how not to read *The Scarlet Letter*" (p. 354).

Referring to a passage in "The Custom-House" where Hawthorne speaks of standing in a "true relation" with his "audience," then to a letter in which he speaks of the "plan of" his novel, Railton posits that Hawthorne's "plan" is ultimately to forge a relationship between himself and his audience that is, more precisely, a "fellowship of seekers for the truth of the heart, united by a knowledge of their mutual human frailties" (p. 356). "What he felt standing between him and the achievement of that plan were just the kind of moral and psychological simplifications that the book's Puritans accept as true" (p. 355). Sexual frailty is, of course, among the vulnerabilities shared by the human fellowship, and hypocrisy with regard to sexuality was among the repressive "simplifications" practiced by Hawthorne's Puritan Bostonians and mid-nineteenth-century audience alike. Among the "most devout pieties" of Hawthorne's culture was "the idea of true womanhood, which insisted on the segregation of heroines from sin, especially from sinful sexuality. Thus, Hawthorne knew, his audience was likely to put almost as much distance as the Puritans do between themselves and Hester as a convicted adulteress" (p. 358).

Through specific narrative practices that Railton defines and examines, Hawthorne resists his nineteenth-century audience's puritanical tendencies via strategies ranging from "emphasizing the uncertainty" regarding matters assumed to be "factual" to raising questions but then "postponing answers" (p. 360). He counters their faultiest assumptions (e.g., Dimmesdale is too pious, read "good," to be Scarlet Hester's unnamed lover), ultimately creating a more sympathetic relation with his heroine than Victorian-era mores would otherwise have permitted. As he does so, he allows the group through which he figures his audience, i.e., Boston's sternly hypocritical Puritans, to soften as well, treating them more sympathetically and more as individuals as they, too, come to associate multiple, complex, even contradictory meanings with Hester and her scarlet *A*.

Many aspects of Railton's essay defy summary here, such as his "reconsideration of Sophia Hawthorne's response" to *The Scarlet Letter* (it sent Hawthorne's wife "to bed with a grievous headache") and his demonstration of the parallels between Hawthorne and Harriet Beecher Stowe's efforts to take their audiences into account (p. 364). (Stowe's *Uncle Tom's Cabin* was published a year after *The Scarlet Letter.*) Finally, it is tempting but not necessary to discuss Railton's account of how his own insights might look through the eyes of other "post-deconstructionist" critics (p. 367). As a student using this edition, you are well prepared to decide on your own how Railton's views differ from or complement the "feminist readings of the novel" (p. 368) about which he hypothesizes.

Ross C Murfin

READER-RESPONSE CRITICISM: A SELECTED BIBLIOGRAPHY

Some Introductions to Reader-Response Criticism

Beach, Richard. *A Teacher's Introduction to Reader-Response Theories.* Urbana: NCTE, 1993.

Fish, Stanley E. "Literature in the Reader: Affective Stylistics." *New Literary History* 2 (1970): 123–61. Rpt. in Fish *Text* 21–67, and in Primeau 154–79.

Freund, Elizabeth. *The Return of the Reader: Reader-Response Criticism.* London: Methuen, 1987.

Holub, Robert C. *Reception Theory: A Critical Introduction.* New York: Methuen, 1984.

Leitch, Vincent B. *American Literary Criticism from the Thirties to the Eighties.* New York: Columbia UP, 1988.

Mailloux, Steven. "Learning to Read: Interpretation and Reader-Response Criticism." *Studies in the Literary Imagination* 12 (1979): 93–108.

———. "Reader-Response Criticism?" *Genre* 10 (1977): 413–31.

———. "The Turns of Reader-Response Criticism." *Conversations: Contemporary Critical Theory and the Teaching of Literature.* Ed. Charles Moran and Elizabeth F. Penfield. Urbana: NCTE, 1990. 38–54.

Rabinowitz, Peter J. "Whirl Without End: Audience-Oriented Criticism." *Contemporary Literary Theory.* Ed. G. Douglas Atkins and Laura Morrow. Amherst: U of Massachusetts P, 1989. 81–100.

Rosenblatt, Louise M. "Towards a Transactional Theory of Reading." *Journal of Reading Behavior* 1 (1969): 31–47. Rpt. in Primeau 121–46.

Suleiman, Susan R. "Introduction: Varieties of Audience-Oriented Criticism." Suleiman and Crosman 3–45.

Tompkins, Jane P. "An Introduction to Reader-Response Criticism." Tompkins ix–xxiv.

Reader-Response Criticism in Anthologies and Collections

Flynn, Elizabeth A., and Patrocinio P. Schweickart, eds. *Gender and Reading: Essays on Readers, Texts, and Contexts.* Baltimore: Johns Hopkins UP, 1986.

Garvin, Harry R., ed. *Theories of Reading, Looking, and Listening.* Lewisburg: Bucknell UP, 1981. Essays by Cain and Rosenblatt.

Machor, James L., ed. *Readers in History: Nineteenth-Century American Literature and the Contexts of Response.* Baltimore: Johns Hopkins UP, 1993. Contains Mailloux essay "Misreading as a Historical Act: Cultural Rhetoric, Bible Politics, and Fuller's 1845 Review of Douglass's *Narrative.*"

Primeau, Ronald, ed. *Influx: Essays on Literary Influence.* Port Washington: Kennikat, 1977. Essays by Fish, Holland, and Rosenblatt.

Suleiman, Susan R., and Inge Crosman, eds. *The Reader in the Text: Essays on Audience and Interpretation.* Princeton: Princeton UP, 1980. See especially the essays by Culler, Iser, and Todorov.

Tompkins, Jane P., ed. *Reader-Response Criticism: From Formalism to Post-Structuralism.* Baltimore: Johns Hopkins UP, 1980. See especially the essays by Bleich, Fish, Holland, Prince, and Tompkins.

Reader-Response Criticism: Some Major Works

Bleich, David. *Subjective Criticism.* Baltimore: Johns Hopkins UP, 1978.

Booth, Stephen. *An Essay on Shakespeare's Sonnets.* New Haven: Yale UP, 1969.

Booth, Wayne C. *A Rhetoric of Irony.* Chicago: U of Chicago P, 1974.

Crosman, Robert. *Reading "Paradise Lost."* Bloomington: Indiana UP, 1980.

Crosman, Robert. "Do Readers Make Meaning?: The Issue of Subjectivity in Criticism." Ed. S. R. Suleiman and R. Crosman. *The Reader in the Text.* Princeton: Princeton UP, 1980.

Eco, Umberto. *The Role of the Reader: Explorations in the Semiotics of Texts.* Bloomington: Indiana UP, 1979.

Fish, Stanley Eugene. *Doing What Comes Naturally: Change, Rhetoric, and the Practice of Theory in Literary and Legal Studies.* Durham: Duke UP, 1989.

———. *Is There a Text in This Class? The Authority of Interpretive Communities.* Cambridge: Harvard UP, 1980. This volume contains most of Fish's most influential essays, including "Literature in the Reader: Affective Stylistics," "What It's Like to Read *L'Allegro* and *Il Penseroso*," "Interpreting the *Variorum*," "How to Recognize a Poem When You See One," "Is There a Text in This Class?" and "What Makes an Interpretation Acceptable?"

———. *Self-Consuming Artifacts: The Experience of Seventeenth-Century Literature.* Berkeley: U of California P, 1972.

———. *Surprised by Sin: The Reader in Paradise Lost.* 2nd ed. Berkeley: U of California P, 1971.

Holland, Norman N. *5 Readers Reading.* New Haven: Yale UP, 1975.

———. "UNITY IDENTITY TEXT SELF." *PMLA* 90 (1975): 813–22.

Iser, Wolfgang. *The Act of Reading: A Theory of Aesthetic Response.* Baltimore: Johns Hopkins UP, 1978.

———. *The Implied Reader: Patterns of Communication in Prose Fiction from Bunyan to Beckett.* Baltimore: Johns Hopkins UP, 1974.

Jauss, Hans Robert. *Toward an Aesthetics of Reception*. Trans. Timothy Bahti. Intro. Paul de Man. Brighton, UK: Harvester, 1982.

Mailloux, Steven. *Interpretive Conventions: The Reader in the Study of American Fiction*. Ithaca: Cornell UP, 1982.

———. *Rhetorical Power.* Ithaca: Cornell UP, 1989.

Messent, Peter. *New Readings of the American Novel: Narrative Theory and Its Application*. New York: Macmillan, 1991.

Prince, Gerald. *Narratology*. New York: Mouton, 1982.

Rabinowitz, Peter. *Before Reading: Narrative Conventions and the Politics of Interpretation*. Ithaca: Cornell UP, 1987.

Radway, Janice A. *Reading the Romance: Women, Patriarchy, and Popular Literature*. Chapel Hill: U of North Carolina P, 1984.

Rosenblatt, Louise M. *Literature as Exploration*. 1938. 4th ed. New York: MLA, 1983.

———. *The Reader, the Text, the Poem: The Transactional Theory of the Literary Work*. Carbondale: Southern Illinois UP, 1978.

Slatoff, Walter J. *With Respect to Readers: Dimensions of Literary Response*. Ithaca: Cornell UP, 1970.

Steig, Michael. *Stories of Reading: Subjectivity and Literary Understanding*. Baltimore: Johns Hopkins UP, 1989.

Exemplary Short Readings of Major Texts

Anderson, Howard. "*Tristram Shandy* and the Reader's Imagination." *PMLA* 86 (1971): 966–73.

Berger, Carole. "The Rake and the Reader in Jane Austen's Novels." *Studies in English Literature, 1500–1900* 15 (1975): 531–44.

Booth, Stephen. "On the Value of *Hamlet*." *Reinterpretations of English Drama: Selected Papers from the English Institute*. Ed. Norman Rabkin. New York: Columbia UP, 1969. 137–76.

Easson, Robert R. "William Blake and His Reader in *Jerusalem*." *Blake's Sublime Allegory*. Ed. Stuart Curran and Joseph A. Wittreich. Madison: U of Wisconsin P, 1973. 309–28.

Kirk, Carey H. "*Moby-Dick:* The Challenge of Response." *Papers on Language and Literature* 13 (1977): 383–90.

Leverenz, David. "Mrs. Hawthorne's Headache: Reading *The Scarlet Letter*." *Nathaniel Hawthorne, "The Scarlet Letter*." Ed. Ross C Murfin. Case Studies in Contemporary Criticism Series. Boston: Bedford, 1991. 263–74.

Lowe-Evans, Mary. "Reading with a 'Nicer-Eye': Responding to *Frankenstein*." *Mary Shelley, "Frankenstein."* Ed. Johanna M. Smith. Case Studies in Contemporary Criticism Series. Boston: Bedford, 1992. 215–29.

Rabinowitz, Peter J. "'A Symbol of Something': Interpretive Vertigo in 'The Dead.'" *James Joyce, "The Dead."* Ed. Daniel R. Schwarz. Case Studies in Contemporary Criticism. Boston: Bedford, 1994. 137–49.

Other Works Referred to in "What Is Reader-Response Criticism?"

Culler, Jonathan. *Structuralist Poetics: Structuralism, Linguistics, and the Study of Literature.* Ithaca: Cornell UP, 1975.

Koestenbaum, Wayne. "Wilde's Hard Labor and the Birth of Gay Reading." *Engendering Men: The Question of Male Feminist Criticism.* Ed. Joseph A. Boone and Michael Cadden. New York: Routledge, 1990.

Miller, Nancy K. *Subject to Change: Reading Feminist Writing.* New York: Columbia UP, 1988.

Richards, I. A. *Practical Criticism.* New York: Harcourt, 1929. Rpt. in *Criticism: The Major Texts.* Ed. Walter Jackson Bate. Rev. ed. New York: Harcourt, 1970. 575.

Wimsatt, William K., and Monroe C. Beardsley. *The Verbal Icon.* Lexington: U of Kentucky P, 1954. See especially the discussion of "The Affective Fallacy," with which reader-response critics have so sharply disagreed.

Other Reader-Oriented Approaches to Hawthorne

Brodhead, Richard H. *Hawthorne, Melville, and the Novel.* Chicago: U of Chicago P, 1973.

Dauber, Kenneth. *Rediscovering Hawthorne.* Princeton: Princeton UP, 1977.

Leverenz, David. "Mrs. Hawthorne's Headache: Reading *The Scarlet Letter.*" *Nineteenth-Century Fiction* 37 (1983): 552–75.

A READER-RESPONSE PERSPECTIVE

STEPHEN RAILTON

The Address of *The Scarlet Letter*[1]

Reader-response critics often use "reader" and "audience" as synonymous terms, but it is worthwhile preserving a distinction between them. We could use the term "reader" for anyone who at any time opens a book and begins processing a text. "Audience," on the other hand, could be reserved to designate the specific group, the contemporary reading public, to whom an author originally addresses the text. All readers, of course, can be identified with larger groups, which Stanley Fish has taught us to call "interpretive communities."[2] But as an author writes a text, there is one particular group for whom he or she is writing; let us call that group the author's "audience." Thus, the readers of *The Scarlet Letter* have all come into existence after the novel was written. The novel's audience, though, was there before Hawthorne sat down to write it. As reader-response criticism shows, any reader's ideological allegiances as a member of a particular community play a crucial role in determining the way that reader produces meaning from a work of literature. But only the "audience," as I am suggesting we define it, can play a role in the creation of the work itself. The reader responds to the text, but first, in the very act of literary conception, there is the response of the text to its audience: the way the text is shaped by the author's ambitions and anxieties about performing for a particular group.

Because the role that this audience plays in the text is a subjective one, we have to make further distinctions. The contemporary audience for *The Scarlet Letter* was there, both sociologically and psychologically, before Hawthorne sat down to write his novel: it was "there" in America in 1850 as the actual reading public available to him as a professional writer and "there" in Hawthorne's mind as his internalized construct of

[1]Parts of this essay are derived from my chapter on Hawthorne and *The Scarlet Letter* in *Authorship and Audience: Literary Performance and the American Renaissance* (Princeton: Princeton UP, 1991).

[2]See Stanley Fish, "Interpreting the *Variorum*," *Critical Inquiry* 2 (1976): 465–85; also Fish, *Is There a Text in This Class? The Authority of Interpretive Communities* (Cambridge: Harvard UP, 1980).

the people he hoped would buy, read, and understand his novel. As Walter J. Ong has pointed out, any writer's sense of audience is an imaginative abstraction, a "fiction."[3] But Ong's emphasis needs to be qualified and historicized. For Hawthorne, or for any writer who hopes to perform successfully for his or her audience, this "fiction" is dialectically constructed by inescapable cultural facts. How Hawthorne conceptualized his audience had to start with his sense of the readers, real rather than ideal, who constituted the reading public in mid-nineteenth-century America.[4] Thus, it was this historically given audience, as I shall try to show in the first half of my essay, that inhabited his imagination and that presided over the fiction that he wrote as *The Scarlet Letter.*

In the second part of this essay, I will focus on the difference between the way a text originally responds to its audience and the way readers subsequently respond to a text. Because a text's audience and its readers are constructed in historically different ways, there is necessarily a distance between their potentialities as responders.[5] Secure in our chronological place as the latest arrivals on the literary historical scene, we are likely to think that we are better equipped to understand or appreciate a text than its original audience, that we know better. This seems especially true of our attitude toward the Victorian Americans for whom Hawthorne wrote. As readers, after all, we have rescued *Moby-Dick, Walden,* and *Leaves of Grass* from their benighted failure as an audience. It is certainly true that we know differently. *The Scarlet Letter* was the first novel to use a woman's sexuality to explore and challenge

[3]Walter J. Ong, "The Writer's Audience Is Always a Fiction," *PMLA* 90 (1975): 21.

[4]More than one kind of reading public was available to Hawthorne. Henry Nash Smith has suggested distinguishing the readers of the early 1850s by "brow levels" — i.e., high-, middle-, and lowbrow audiences (*Democracy and the Novel* [New York: Oxford UP, 1978] 6–10). And David S. Reynolds's *Beneath the American Renaissance* (New York: Knopf, 1988) shows us how the literary expectations and appetites of the type of audience that Smith would call "lowbrow" differed from the values we associate with the genteel culture. I am assuming that Hawthorne wrote *The Scarlet Letter* for the same kind of audience that had read his tales and sketches for twenty-five years in such "middlebrow" publications as *Godey's;* in "The Custom-House," for instance, when he describes the place where his imagination works, the environment is that of an unmistakably genteel parlor.

[5]See Hans Robert Jauss, "Literary History as a Challenge to Literary Theory," in *Toward an Aesthetic of Reception,* trans. Timothy Bahti (Minneapolis: U Minnesota P, 1982). Jauss's great contribution is to remind us that at any given literary-historical moment, readers approach a new text from within a certain "horizon of expectations," which will determine their response to a work of art; once read, a text can in turn begin to reshape or expand that horizon, so that at subsequent literary-historical moments it can be read in previously unthought of ways (see 21–25).

the structures of society; in the hundred and forty years since, many other writers have followed Hawthorne's lead. We could say that we have the benefit of this additional experience, but we should also acknowledge what we have lost. Just as it is apparently impossible for anyone these days to read Hawthorne's book without already knowing that Dimmesdale had been Hester's lover — a fact that even the most perceptive contemporary reader could not have suspected until the book's third chapter,[6] and would not know for sure until the middle — so it is almost impossible for us to imagine how those contemporary readers would have initially reacted to Hester Prynne. We know otherwise than the readers of 1850. We cannot help but bring to the novel a very different set of preconceptions — about someone like Hester, about adultery, about Christianity.

And we should admit that we often know less. At Petroglyph Point in Mesa Verde National Park is a rock covered with signs scratched by the Anasazi who lived there 700 years ago. No one now can interpret them. They communicated without ambiguity to the people for whom they were "written" but are perfectly opaque to us. As itself a hieroglyphic emblem, *The Scarlet Letter* looks like a much more accessible sign. That it works for and speaks so powerfully to modern readers is a measure of its achievement. But Hawthorne was not writing for us or for the theoretical reader of much reader-response criticism. Every reader's responses are relevant to any attempt to determine the ultimate significance of the text. We can, however, gain a lot by trying to reconstruct the way Hawthorne wrote it for his contemporary audience, by trying to understand how it was meant to speak to and work on the readers of his day.

There is no question about the force of his concern with the

[6]Chapter 3 is called "The Recognition." Since it begins by describing Chillingworth's deformed appearance as he emerges from the forest to see Hester on the scaffold, while chapter 2 ended by describing the man Hester had married as "slightly deformed" (p. 61), the novel tempts its reader to jump to the conclusion that *this* is the recognition. For Hester and Chillingworth to see each other after two years in such a setting is a dramatic recognition, but *the* recognition occurs much later in the chapter: when Dimmesdale speaks to Hester, and Pearl somehow recognizes her father's voice: "the poor baby . . . directed its hitherto vacant gaze towards Mr. Dimmesdale, and held up its little arms, with a half pleased, half plaintive murmur" (pp. 67–68). Since the immediate question of the chapter — for Chillingworth, for the Puritans, and for the uninitiated reader — is who is Pearl's father, Hawthorne is thus very subtly rewarding readers who do not jump to interpretive conclusions, who keep open a question like "What does the recognition mean?" Of course, readers who cannot delay interpretive closure will not recognize the recognition.

response of his contemporary audience. In the letters he wrote as he was finishing the novel, the emphasis is not on whether his novel had succeeded on its own terms — he seemed to know he'd written a great book, though a "dark and dismal" one. For him the question was whether it would succeed with its audience.[7] He was urgently worried about material success: he had lost his job at the Custom House; he was broke with a family to support. He was, however, equally anxious about rhetorical success. He and his publisher arranged with Melville's friend Duyckinck to publish an excerpt from the book in *The Literary World* as a kind of promotional device. Hawthorne's one stipulation was that the excerpt come from "The Custom-House," not from *The Scarlet Letter:* "I don't think it advisable to give any thing from the story itself; because I know of no passage that would not throw too much light on the plan of the book."[8] He says "plan," not "plot," which suggests that he had organized the novel strategically to work on its contemporary audience in a specific way. Given his concern here with a kind of secrecy, we could even say that the novel's deepest "plot" was somehow against its audience. That leads to the question I want to try to answer first: how did *The Scarlet Letter* address its audience? That question in turn leads to a more theoretical one. *The Scarlet Letter* reaches us a century and a half after it was addressed. Can readers in the 1990s respond according to plan, when the plan was worked out in 1850?

I

There is in fact an aboriginal audience inscribed into the text. Before Hester appears in the marketplace, the narrative puts in place the throng of Puritan men and women for whom the scarlet letter is first "published." Putting a "crowd of spectators" (p. 59 in this volume) in place before the story itself begins is Hawthorne's acknowledgment of the point that the audience precedes the text. His preoccupation with audience response is signaled by the way he puts those Puritans at the center of his stage: both chapter 1 *and* chapter 2 begin by drawing our attention to them. How historical *The Scarlet Letter* is, how much it is "about" the Puritan culture that provides its occasion, is a question that

[7]See his letters to J. T. Fields, January 20, 1850, and to Horatio Bridge, February 4, 1850, in *Nathaniel Hawthorne: The Letters, 1843–1853,* ed. Thomas Woodson et al. (Columbus: Ohio State UP, 1985), 307–8, 311–12.

[8]*Letters, 1843–1853,* 322.

has long been debated by the commentators.[9] But the main role the "Puritans" play in the text is that of audience to its drama: they exist chiefly as an interpretive community.[10] Hawthorne regularly pauses the narrative to elaborate on how the people of Boston react to a new development in the story, how they "see" Hester and the other central characters, how they interpret the scarlet letter. And as an audience, the "Puritans" are not very historical. Although they dress like seventeenth-century colonists, their reactions, and the assumptions behind those reactions, are those of the genteel readers who formed Hawthorne's mid-nineteenth-century audience. The first step in appreciating Hawthorne's "plan" is to recognize the way he writes into the novel a version of his reading public, disguised in period costumes.

The "Puritans"' understanding of human nature is hardly Calvinist. Rather, it reflects the polarizations of the moral melodramas that were the most popular works of Hawthorne's time. *Uncle Tom's Cabin,* usually considered the best-selling book of this period, began appearing a year after *The Scarlet Letter.*[11] One characteristic Stowe's novel shares

[9]The most ingenious recent advocate for reading the novel as an examination of colonial Puritanism is Michael J. Colacurcio; see his "Footsteps of Ann Hutchinson: The Context of *The Scarlet Letter,*" *ELH* 39 (1972): 459–94, and "'The Woman's Own Choice': Sex, Metaphor, and the Puritan 'Sources' of *The Scarlet Letter,*" in *New Essays on "The Scarlet Letter,"* ed. Michael J. Colacurcio (Cambridge: Cambridge UP, 1985), 101–36.

[10]I am not so much borrowing Fish's idea of "interpretive communities" here as trying to co-opt it. Hawthorne would have liked Fish's phrase but not his relativism. For him there is a right and a wrong interpretive community. The Puritans' reading of the scarlet letter defines the wrong one. Yet his faith in the possibility of a definitive interpretation — one that finds, not makes meaning — is announced at the very start of "The Custom-House," where he says he writes for "the few who will understand him, better than most of his schoolmates and lifemates" (p. 22). The community adumbrated here eventually emerges, as we will see, within the text itself.

[11]To develop my analysis of how Hawthorne's novel addresses his audience's preoccupations, I will be comparing *The Scarlet Letter* to *Uncle Tom's Cabin.* Because my emphasis is on the way Hawthorne's vision of human nature set him outside and at odds with those preconceptions, the comparison may seem an invidious one, a mere reformulation of what Jane Tompkins refers to as a "long tradition of academic parochialism" that "assigns Hawthorne and Melville the role of heroes, the sentimental novelists the role of villains" (*Sensational Designs: The Cultural Work of American Fiction* [New York: Oxford UP, 1985], 125, 149). That is not my intention. The contempt Hawthorne could at moments feel for the contemporary audience that made "sentimental novels" the best-selling fiction of his time and place is notorious these days and certainly has to be included in our understanding of his hypostatization of his audience. But comparing Hawthorne's and Stowe's novel does not require one to assent to his frustrated vilification of "that damned mob of scribbling women." I am in complete agreement with what Tompkins says elsewhere, that "the work of the sentimental writers is complex and significant in ways *other than* those that characterize the established masterpieces" such as *The Scarlet Letter* (126). (I have registered my own appreciation for the greatness of Stowe's novel in

with the more conventional genteel best-sellers is its distribution of characters into the fixed patterns of melodramatic allegory: little Eva St. Clare is wholly angelic, Simon Legree is the incarnation of evil. These are also the patterns into which the Puritans of Hawthorne's novel keep trying to fit the central characters. To them, in that first scene, the *A* Hester wears "seemed to derive its scarlet hue from the flames of the infernal pit" (p. 68). To them Dimmesdale appears as if robed in the spotless white Eva invariably wears: "They deemed the young clergyman a miracle of holiness. . . . In their eyes, the very ground on which he trod was sanctified" (p. 119). When in the penultimate chapter they realize Dimmesdale is about to die, "it [would not] have seemed a miracle too high to be wrought for one so holy, had he ascended before their eyes, waxing dimmer and brighter, and fading at last into the light of heaven!" (p. 194). Such an image would have been inconceivable to a Calvinist. It was, however, a very familiar one to Hawthorne's contemporaries: the first staged version of *Uncle Tom's Cabin,* which opened to eager throngs of spectators in 1852, actually ended with little Eva rising up from the stage into heaven.[12] The Puritans cannot settle on an interpretation of Chillingworth — to some he has been sent miraculously by "Heaven" to cure their saintly minister's body (pp. 103–04); to others, he is either "Satan himself, or Satan's emissary," come to plot against the saintly minister's soul (p. 108) — but in either case their reading of his character relies on the type of moral dichotomies found in genteel fiction.

Why Hawthorne felt he had to plan carefully for his own audience becomes clear when we realize that the Puritans are a terrible audience.

"Mothers, Husbands and *Uncle Tom.*" *Georgia Review* 38 [1984]: 129–44.) "Conventionality" is also a term with many possible referents: if we were to focus on the politics of Hawthorne's and Stowe's novels rather than on what Hawthorne defined as his central thematic concern, the truth of the human heart, I could be comparing the radicalism of *Uncle Tom's Cabin* to the conventionality of *The Scarlet Letter* (see, for example, Sacvan Bercovitch, "The A-Politics of Ambiguity in *The Scarlet Letter,*" *New Literary History* 19 [1988]: 629–54). What my comparison does depend on, however, is the cultural-historical legitimacy of Hawthorne's belief that his conception of the human self was in conflict with the genteel self-image that Stowe's readers found reflected and confirmed in her novel. While Stowe brilliantly challenges her audience's assumptions about a social evil, Hawthorne is trying to complicate and change that audience's assumptions about themselves.

[12]The dramatization was written by George L. Aikens. The ascent into heaven was an impressive piece of stagecraft — and an impressive instance of Victorian faith, which did not require wires and a winch to make the trick believable. Even in Stowe's novel, Tom twice has a vision of Eva being directly translated, in a radiant cloud of glory, into heaven (*Uncle Tom's Cabin* [New York: Library of America, 1982], 368, and 406–7).

Their responses, and the assumptions behind them, are wholly inadequate to either the moral or the interpretive demands of his story. In that opening scene the novel explicitly condemns them for their failure of sympathy: they see Hester as an Other and cast her out of their society, even though the novel shows us that she is still essentially governed by their values: "She knew that her deed had been evil" (p. 82). In the second half, they take "Another View of Hester." Since she quietly goes about her charitable duties as "a Sister of Mercy" to the poor and sick (p. 132), they see her as "our Hester, — the town's own Hester" (p. 133). But when the chapter titled "Another View of Hester" goes on to show us still *another* view of Hester,[13] we see how profoundly estranged from the town she has become: "she cast away the fragments of a broken chain. The world's law was no law for her mind" (p. 134). The Puritans' utter failure as "readers" of the story is brought home to them dramatically at the climax, which depicts another publication of the scarlet letter while again they stand around the scaffold as a literal audience. Hawthorne, as he does throughout the novel, divides his focus in this scene between the action and their reaction. As we noted, they expect to see Dimmesdale ascend in glory to heaven. Instead, he goes up the steps of the scaffold to take his shame upon him. This not only explodes their predictions about the plot of Dimmesdale's life; it also razes the structure of assumptions by which they have understood reality. When Hester "published" her letter at the start, they stood in self-righteous certainty of their judgment on her. When Dimmesdale reveals his letter at the end, however, they are thrown into the "tumult" of interpretive chaos, "so taken by surprise, and so perplexed as to the purport of what they saw, — unable to receive the explanation which most readily presented itself, or to imagine any other, — that they remained silent and inactive spectators of the judgment which Providence seemed about to work" (p. 194).

Hawthorne put this surrogate audience into the text to guide his own audience's responses. His readers could watch them watching the story, and learn from them how not to read *The Scarlet Letter.* That explains why those Puritans are disguised Victorian Americans, for the assumptions that Hawthorne plots against are those that he identifies with his contemporary readers. He valued fiction for the truth that it could tell, but also said he wrote "to open up an intercourse with the

[13]This chapter's title is another instance of the kind of punning in which Hawthorne engages in "The Recognition"; once again, the reader who suspends closure is rewarded.

world."[14] He summed up his thematic project as a writer by referring to himself as "a person, who has been burrowing, to his utmost ability, into the depths of our common nature, for the purposes of psychological romance."[15] But inseparable from this was his rhetorical project, the "apostolic errands" he refers to obliquely in "The Custom-House" (p. 25). His "plan" for *The Scarlet Letter* was to communicate as well as to explore the depths of our common nature, the truths of the human heart. What he felt standing between him and the achievement of that plan were just the kind of moral and psychological simplifications that the book's Puritans accept as true. Their superficial judgments cut them off from the depths of our common nature.

When Dimmesdale gets back to his study after the breathtaking reunion with Hester in the woods, the narrative provides a final gloss on what has happened to him: "Another man had returned out of the forest; a wiser one; with a knowledge of hidden mysteries which the simplicity of the former never could have reached" (p. 174). This characterization links Dimmesdale with such earlier figures in Hawthorne's fiction as Young Goodman Brown and Ethan Brand, both of whom also learn the dark secrets of the heart (Brown in the forest). By their knowledge Brown and Brand are estranged from the world. In the first paragraph of "The Custom-House," however, Hawthorne announces his desire as a "speaker" to "stand in some true relation with his audience" (p. 22). It is this desire to publish the truth — about himself, about the hidden mysteries his own experience has taught him — that carries Dimmesdale at the end up the scaffold's steps. There he becomes, at last, a true preacher, trying to stand in a true relation with *his* audience, and his text (like Hawthorne's) is "The Revelation of the Scarlet Letter." But Dimmesdale's revelation falls on blind eyes as his audience proves unwilling to abandon the "simplicities" of their former interpretation. To sum up the Puritans' failure even in this scene, we can invoke the novel's tersest paragraph: "The scarlet letter had not done its office" (p. 135). As a sign of the truth of the human heart, the letter remains

[14]Hawthorne, Preface to the 1851 edition of *Twice-Told Tales,* ed. Roy Harvey Pearce et al. (Columbus: Ohio State UP, 1974), 6. That Hawthorne felt fiction had to tell the truth is an idea that appears in many places throughout his work. In the preface to *The House of the Seven Gables,* for instance, he writes that even fiction that claims the "latitude" of Romance "sins unpardonably" if it "swerve[s] aside from the truth of the human heart" (*The House of the Seven Gables,* ed. William Charvat et al. [Columbus: Ohio State UP, 1965], 1).

[15]Hawthorne, Preface, *The Snow-Image* (1852), in *The Snow-Image and Uncollected Tales,* ed. Roy Harvey Pearce et al. (Columbus: Ohio State UP, 1974), 4.

opaque to its aboriginal audience. By letting his audience see this other audience's blindness, however, Hawthorne is looking for a way to enable the scarlet letter to perform its office as a letter: to communicate.

For we are meant to consider the reason for the Puritans' failure. It is not simply their lack of sympathy for Hester as a sinner; that is but the symptom of a deeper cause: their failure to be honest with themselves and each other about the truths of their own nature. By means of the "sympathetic knowledge of the hidden sin in other hearts" that Hester's letter gives her, we see the people of Boston in much the same light that reveals Salem to Goodman Brown in the wilderness, as a brotherhood of shame and guilt: "if truth were everywhere to be shown, a scarlet letter would blaze forth on many a bosom besides Hester Prynne's" (p. 80). Like Brown, however, the Puritans self-righteously reject this community: he exiles himself from society; they project their hidden sinfulness onto Hester and then, as a kind of repression, banish her and her *A* from their knowledge of themselves. In this unwillingness to "Be true" (p. 199) to the truth of their common nature lies the source of their inadequacies as "spectators." They see the world in the simplistic terms on which the repression of self-knowledge depends. Their reading of Dimmesdale's character is the obverse side of their repression of Hester. Onto the minister they project their image of the pure, angelic self, the self-gratulatory image that is fostered by their denial of the sinful self. Their misreading of Dimmesdale is as egregious as their inability to sympathize or identify with Hester, and it is treated even more explicitly as their failure as an audience. The minister achieves "a brilliant popularity in his sacred office," but "the people knew not the power that moved them thus." On the other hand, we're told exactly what that power consists of — the burden of guilty self-knowledge: "this very burden it was, that gave him sympathies so intimate with the sinful brotherhood of mankind; so that his heart vibrated in unison with theirs, and received their pain into itself, and sent its own throb of pain through a thousand other hearts, in gushes of sad, persuasive eloquence" (p. 119).

What Hawthorne is describing here is the basis of the "true relation" in which, as the "speaker" of *The Scarlet Letter*, he hopes to "stand with his audience": a fellowship of seekers for the truth of the heart, united by a knowledge of their mutual human frailties.[16] It is this

[16]Hawthorne repeats this passage at the end, when he describes the source of Dimmesdale's oratorical power in the Election Day sermon: "if the auditor listened intently, and for the purpose, he could detect the same cry of pain. What was it? The

way of "reading" the scarlet letter that he models for every reader in "The Custom-House," when he depicts himself taking up the *A* and placing it on his own breast (p. 43). This is exactly the opposite of what the Puritans do, when they condemn an Other to wear the letter as their scapegoat. This, though, is what Dimmesdale himself will finally do, when he reveals his letter to them. And this is the lesson Hester ultimately learns from Dimmesdale, when at the very end she voluntarily puts the *A* back on. It is, we learn in "The Custom-House," and learn authoritatively, the true way to interpret the novel: we must not merely pick up *The Scarlet Letter* — we must wear it, must admit the truth it tells us about ourselves. In terms of Hawthorne's "plan," this means he must lead his audience beyond the psychological "simplicities" reflected in their conventional, melodramatic moral categories. In this sense, the whole rhetorical problem of the novel is summed up, anxiously, in the last three sentences of chapter 22, the chapter that precedes "The Revelation of the Scarlet Letter": "The sainted minister in the church! The woman of the scarlet letter in the market-place! What imagination would have been irreverent enough to surmise that the same scorching stigma was on them both?" (pp. 190–91). The answer, of course, is Hawthorne's imagination. But that answer only locates the point from which, as a Victorian American author, he felt he had to begin. The end toward which he worked depended upon his audience's willingness to accept the terms of his imagination. Given the pieties of his genteel audience, "irreverent" is a good term for those terms. He wants to unite those aspects of human nature which his culture kept asunder — the most saintly and the most debased, the best and worst.

---

complaint of a human heart, sorrow-laden, perchance guilty, telling its secret, whether of guilt or sorrow, to the great heart of mankind; beseeching its sympathy or forgiveness,— at every moment,— in each accent,— and never in vain! It was this profound and continual undertone that gave the clergyman his most appropriate power" (p. 188). Hawthorne's repetition of this idea, not to mention the evident earnestness of the passage itself, indicates how crucial to him was the ideal of sympathy for mutual human frailty as the basis of the bond between author and audience. I do not have space in this essay to contrast this with the basis on which Emerson put the relation between himself as speaker and his American audience; suffice it to say that it was diametrically opposed. To Emerson, every heart vibrates, not to human frailty, but to godlike self-reliance; the power of the Emersonian orator flows from the way he addresses himself to "the better part" of every auditor, not the worst. I point this out just to indicate that if one draws a wider circle around Hawthorne's available audience than I limit myself to — if one were to include the people who listened so enthusiastically to Emerson in 1850 as well as those who read genteel fiction — one would still be staring at the problem Hawthorne knew he was up against: that his truths of the human heart were at odds with the popular assumptions of his culture.

Among the culture's most devout pieties was the idea of true womanhood, which insisted on the segregation of heroines from sin, especially from sinful sexuality.[17] Thus, Hawthorne knew, his audience was likely to put almost as much distance as the Puritans do between themselves and Hester as a convicted adulteress. The literary type to which contemporary readers would have referred her was not the one that probably comes first to the modern reader's mind — the feminist protagonist, whom they had never met — but rather the Dark Heroine, a figure familiar from other books. Victorian American preconceptions about such a figure define the second step in Hawthorne's rhetorical plan: to create sympathy for Hester. The first eight chapters of the novel are largely devoted to this task. When Hester enters the story through the prison door, before describing her, before describing the *A* to which all the Puritans' eyes are drawn, Hawthorne describes the baby in her arms. His audience meets her first as "the mother of this child" (p. 57). Stowe, who had her own rhetorical design on the same reading public, and knew as much as Hawthorne about how to achieve it, relies on exactly the same strategy. To that audience, a male black slave was as much an Other as a convicted adulteress. To close the gap between her hero and her readers, Stowe lets them meet for the first time in Tom's cabin, where he is meekly learning how to write from the master's child while his wife cooks in the foreground and his children play in the background. As if these domestic emanations weren't enough, Stowe allows only a few pages to pass before Tom too has a baby in his arms.[18] Both Hester's and Tom's babies are intended as passports to admit their bearers into the region where genteel readers and their sympathies were already at home.

By continually referring to Hester as a "mother" — as sacred a category to contemporary readers as minister was to the Puritans — and by developing in detail her struggles both to make her way as a woman in the wider world and to raise a daughter (the focus of chapters 5 and 6), Hawthorne seeks to complicate his readers' response to "this poor victim of her own frailty, and man's hard law" (p. 81). This strategy culminates in chapters 7 and 8, the most dramatic episode of the novel's first half. Hester, "a lonely woman, backed by the sympathies of nature" (p. 90), goes to the Governor's Hall to argue "a mother's rights" (p. 98) before the men who intend to take Pearl from her. This scene

[17]See Barbara Welter, "The Cult of True Womanhood: 1820–1860," *American Quarterly* 18 (1966): 151–74.

[18]See *Uncle Tom's Cabin,* ch. 4, "An Evening in Uncle Tom's Cabin," 32–44.

goes after the sympathies of contemporary readers as directly and as shrewdly as Stowe does in her novel, where the forced separation of mothers and children is restaged again and again as the surest way to get white women readers to identify with the sufferings of slaves. The brilliantly plotted intention of this episode in which Hester fights "the public" (p. 89) to keep her child is once and for all to split Hawthorne's audience's responses from the Puritans' admonitory attitude: Victorian readers can only take Hester's side *against* the Puritans, and thus have been compelled to identify with her. Thematically, this means that they have been forced to include the Dark Heroine inside their sense of what it is to be human, even to be a mother.

Hawthorne works toward the same end in other ways. A major component of his plan could be called his strategy of narrative delay. Perhaps the most remarkable trait of the book's opening is the way it stalls and stutters before allowing the story proper to begin. We have already seen how chapter 2 restates the opening of chapter 1, by redescribing the audience before the prison door. Then chapter 2 goes on for about 300 words to wonder what this waiting throng "might be" assembled to see (p. 55). Who is about to emerge from the prison? The narrative actually offers eight different answers to this question, none of which is accurate. It then keeps its audience waiting eight paragraphs more before Hester herself appears. This pattern of asking questions but delaying the answers recurs in many different contexts. Hawthorne leaves open such trivial questions as whether Hester cut her hair off, or just confined it under her cap (p. 133), and such crucial questions as "where was [Dimmesdale's] mind" as he marches forward to give the Election Sermon after having agreed to run away with Hester (p. 185). In a sense this pattern organizes the whole novel. In the opening scene, both Chillingworth privately and the Puritans publicly ask who is the father of Hester's infant (pp. 64, 67–8); the answer to this question is withheld — from Chillingworth (and the reader) until the middle, from the Puritans until the end.

Much more is at stake here than narrative suspense. One part of the reputation Puritanism had in the nineteenth century was its intolerance. Hawthorne's concern, as I have said, was with his contemporaries' assumptions, but as a means of addressing his concern he exploits the association of Puritanism with intolerance for all it is worth to him as a writer trying to complicate and enlarge those assumptions. At the heart of the Puritans' failure as interpreters of the scarlet letter is their inability to tolerate any kind of ambiguity. They cannot profit from the delay the narrative provides at the start: they "know" who is coming out of jail and how they should respond to her. When they see her — pointedly, they see only the letter she wears — Hester's appearance simply reconfirms their preconceptions. On the other hand, what Hawthorne's own audience is meant to learn from the narrative's habit of postponing answers to the questions it raises is how to suspend judgment — how, for example, to take another view of Hester. Hawthorne models this too in "The Custom-House," when he recounts how, after finding the *A*, he tried many different ways to solve the "riddle" of what it might mean (see p. 43).

Closely allied to this pattern of narrative delay are the novel's stylistic or syntactic habits. In the book's second paragraph we are told that "it may safely be assumed that" the Puritans picked a site for their prison early in Boston's history (p. 53). Such a point, we might think, could easily have been determined; his use of this construction (I mean the syntactic one, not the jail) indicates again how much more interested he is in his contemporary audience than in New England history. Indeed, the syntactic construction stands in opposition to the jail: it opens up rather than locks in possibility. By emphasizing the uncertainty of even so factual a matter as a date, Hawthorne is calling attention to the problematic relationship between "assumption" and truth. Just as his narrative delays answers, his style withholds certainties. "We shall not take it upon us to determine," he writes in the last paragraph of chapter 1, "whether" the rose beside the prison door is merely natural, "or whether, as there is fair authority for believing," it supernaturally symbolizes Ann Hutchinson's antinomianism (p. 54). In the first paragraph of chapter 2, he has no sooner suggested that "some noted culprit" might be about to emerge from the prison than he qualifies himself: "An inference of this kind could not so indubitably be drawn" (p. 55). Instances of this stylistic indefiniteness could be multiplied almost indefinitely. Very little in *The Scarlet Letter* is stated as unequivocal fact. "It may be," "it might be," "perchance," "perhaps," "it seemed," "according to some," "it was reported" — these or similar locutions appear in almost every paragraph. While the Puritans cannot tolerate ambiguity, Hawthorne requires his audience to live with it. What "may safely be assumed" or what "kind of inference" should be drawn remains much of the time an explicitly open question, which is how this stylistic trait echoes the narrative one we looked at. The audience, forced in this way to abandon any privileged position as mere spectators, must become an active part of Hawthorne's interpretive community. Hawthorne separates his audience from the "simplicity" of the Puritans' responses and from the black-and-white terms of contemporary moral melodrama, and initiates them instead into the problematic realm of the "hidden mysteries" that is his subject.

"Simplicity" versus "hidden mysteries" — these are the antitheses he uses to measure the difference between the assumptions Dimmesdale takes into the woods and the knowledge which, after meeting Hester, he brings back. In terms of his "plan," the great scene between the lovers is the one for which Hawthorne has been carefully preparing his audience all along. Structurally, it occupies the same position in the novel's second half that Hester's confrontation in the Governor's Hall occupies in the first; thematically, it completes the project that he began by enabling the audience to sympathize, and thus identify, with Hester. Now he is ready dramatically to expose them to what meeting Hester in the wilderness can reveal about the truths of their own hearts.

Like the scene in which Hester fights to keep her child, her meeting with Dimmesdale in the forest evokes a paradigm readers would have met frequently in the period's best-selling melodramas. According to the biblical archetypes on which those stories relied, it is a temptation in the wilderness. *Uncle Tom's Cabin* offers a parallel scene at Simon Legree's, when Cassie, Stowe's version of the Dark Heroine and Hester's sister in passion and despair, exhorts Tom to choose a better life. With "a wild and peculiar glare" in her "large, black eyes," with "a flash of sudden energy," Cassie urges him to murder Legree and be free.[19] When Hester uses "her own energy" to exhort Dimmesdale to break with "these iron men" who "have kept thy better part in bondage too long already," she too "fix[es] her deep eyes on the minister's, and instinctively exercis[es] a magnetic power over [his] spirit" (pp. 156–57). "Any life is better than this," cries Cassie; Hester exclaims, "Do any thing, save to lie down and die!" (p. 157).

There is, of course, an apparently crucial difference between these two exhortations. Cassie, full of hate, tempts Tom to murder, but Hester's voice, which sounds so full of love, seems to summon Dimmesdale toward a "new life" of "human affection and sympathy" (p. 159). It might seem beside any point Hawthorne had in mind to note that the Decalogue equally forbids killing and committing adultery. Yet Hawthorne's novel goes on to show decisively, in its own terms, which are psychological rather than Mosaic, that the passions Hester arouses in the woods are just as destructive as Cassie's murderous rage at Legree's. Hawthorne takes his audience into the woods with Hester, but he brings them back out with Dimmesdale. Chapter 20, "The Minister in

[19] *Uncle Tom's Cabin,* 461–63.

a Maze," follows him homeward, which allows Hawthorne carefully to explore the "revolution in the sphere of [his] thought and feeling" that breaks loose after he yields his "will" to "Hester's will" (p. 170). Chapter 20 also forces a sudden change in the text's representation of the Puritans. Hawthorne abruptly individualizes them. Instead of an aggregate, admonitory audience or an iron-visaged, repressive society, they are converted into men and women, as Dimmesdale meets an aged, venerable deacon, a "poor, widowed, lonely" old mother, and a maiden "fair and pure" (pp. 171–72). In the woods Hester rejects society as scornfully as it originally exiled her, but when Dimmesdale comes out of the woods society is portrayed as individuals with sympathetically human faces. And in each encounter with these members of his congregation, Dimmesdale feels "incited to do some strange, wild, wicked thing or other" (p. 170) — not premeditated murder, certainly, but something equally destructive of "human affection and sympathy." Dimmesdale, horrified to discover the anarchic violence of his own desires, wonders if he has somehow sold his soul to Satan in the woods. In the passage that follows, Hawthorne offers his own interpretive gloss on the meeting with Hester and states conclusively that indeed it was a temptation in the wilderness:

> The wretched minister! He had made a bargain very like it! Tempted by a dream of happiness, he had yielded himself with deliberate choice, as he had never done before, to what he knew was deadly sin. And the infectious poison of that sin had been thus rapidly diffused throughout his moral system. It had stupefied all blessed impulses, and awakened into vivid life the whole brotherhood of bad ones. Scorn, bitterness, unprovoked malignity, gratuitous desire of ill, ridicule of whatever was good and holy, all awoke, to tempt, even while they frightened him. (pp. 173–74)

We have yet to note the real distinction between Stowe's and Hawthorne's versions of this temptation scene. If there is not finally much difference in the kind of lawless, selfish, violent energies that fuel Cassie's and Hester's exhortations, there is nonetheless a vast difference in the larger role that meeting the Dark Heroine plays in the novels' thematic economies. Despite Cassie's attractiveness, Tom is never really tempted, nor is Stowe's audience. When she comes with her murderous scheme and Tom hastily replies, "Don't sell your precious soul to the devil, that way!" Stowe's audience is reminded of what evil is; when a few seconds later Tom asks God to "help us follow in His steps, and love our enemies," Stowe's audience is reminded what good is. At no point during Tom's temptation in Legree's wilderness does the narrative challenge that audience's preconceptions. Hawthorne, though, in keeping with his pattern of openness and delay, withholds his definitive interpretation of what transpired in the woods until three chapters after Hester seduces Dimmesdale with that "dream of happiness." Because Dimmesdale at first succumbs to the temptation, he is forced to realize firsthand the "hidden mysteries" of his own heart: that is the maze he gets lost in, and at the center of it is "a profounder self" (p. 170) than he had previously suspected.

Within this pattern — and we had better be explicit about this — Hawthorne allows Hester to seduce the audience as well. Probably every reader's hopes for her and Dimmesdale's happiness, and something fiercer and profounder too, are aroused when she lets down her magnificent hair in the woods. By letting desire loose inside the narrative, Hawthorne attempts a radical challenge to the Victorian audience's self-image. At the very start of the scene he quietly insinuates what meeting Hester in the woods should mean: "The soul beheld its features in the mirror of the passing moment" (p. 151). By withholding his authoritative reading of the scene for twenty pages, he gives his audience an opportunity to follow Dimmesdale through the maze; for when he realizes what has been let loose *in himself*, "the Reverend Mr. Dimmesdale thus communed with himself" (p. 173), and it is by thus communing with his self, with his own previously hidden impulses, that Dimmesdale discovers his "profounder self" and becomes "another man," and "a wiser one." The conventional temptation-in-the-wilderness scene of popular fiction, by signaling itself as such, allowed readers to shield themselves against any disturbing response. In Stowe's novel, the true way depends on rejecting the Dark Heroine — and so remaining safe from any self-knowledge her character might reveal. Evil remains an abstraction to be resisted; Cassie is allowed to learn from Tom, but not to teach him anything. In Hawthorne's novel, though, the truth depends on communing first with Hester and then with oneself. The encounter in the woods is ultimately a *self*-recognition scene. The way it works on its audience makes lawless desire a fact of human nature that, as a fact of human nature, cannot be denied. In place of the straight lines and neat polarities of moral melodrama, Hawthorne has led his audience deep into the maze of their own hearts.[20]

[20]Chillingworth is vouchsafed such a chance as well. Just before she seeks out Dimmesdale in the woods, Hester goes to talk with Chillingworth at the seashore. Here, too, meeting Hester represents an opportunity to see one's self: "The unfortunate

II

We know who the first "reader" of *The Scarlet Letter* was, and as it happens, we also know a bit about her response. The day Hawthorne finished writing the manuscript, he finished reading it aloud to his wife. "It broke her heart," he wrote a friend, "and sent her to bed with a grievous headache — which I look upon as triumphant success!"[21] Signs of her distress are still evident in a letter she wrote to a friend a week later: "I do not know what you will think of the Romance. It is most powerful, & contains a moral as terrific & stunning as a thunderbolt. It shows that the Law cannot be broken."[22] As modern readers we may be tempted to smile here and congratulate ourselves on our increased sophistication. Despite Sophia Hawthorne's credentials — both as an intimate of the author, and as a reader herself (Melville, for example, was very impressed with her response to *Moby-Dick*)[23] — we are likely to dismiss her reading as naive. Her insistence on "the Law" sounds too much like the narrow-minded reading the "Puritans" try to impose on the story. And we have outgrown her quaint Victorian reductiveness, which values a work of art for the "moral" it supplies — as if literature, Ezra Pound wrote contemptuously in 1918, were merely "the ox-cart and post-chaise for transmitting thoughts poetic or otherwise."[24]

I want to end this essay by considering the gap between the way *The Scarlet Letter* addressed its contemporary audience and the way it seems to speak to us at the end of the twentieth century. Let me start with a reconsideration of Sophia Hawthorne's response. Behind her assertion of "the Law" is nothing like the Puritans' self-righteous smugness. They take the law for granted, but it is clear from her reactions — the grief, the headache, the mixed emotions she betrays even a week later with words like "terrific" and "stunning" — that as a reader she has been fully open to the experience of the text. As far as the Law goes, she

physician . . . lifted his hands with a look of horror, as if he had beheld some frightful shape, which he could not recognize, usurping the place of his own image in a glass. It was one of those moments — which sometimes occur only at the interval of years — when a man's moral aspect is faithfully revealed to his mind's eye. Not improbably, he had never before viewed himself as he did now" (p. 139). Hawthorne's emphases here underscore the centrality of this kind of self-recognition scene to his project in the novel.

[21] Hawthorne to Horatio Bridge, February 4, 1850 (*Letters 1843–1853,* 311).

[22] Sophia Hawthorne to Mary Mann, February 12, 1850, ibid. 313.

[23] See Melville's letter to Sophia Hawthorne, January 8, 1852, *The Letters of Herman Melville,* ed. M. R. Davis and W. H. Gilman (New Haven: Yale UP, 1960), 145–47.

[24] Ezra Pound, "A Retrospect," rpt. in *Literary Essays of Ezra Pound,* ed. T. S. Eliot (New York: New Directions, 1968), 11.

is clearly right about the values Hawthorne's novel ultimately privileges. It was post-Victorian writers like Henry James and Pound who taught us to look for the meaning of form in works of literature; when we approach *The Scarlet Letter* from that perspective, it seems even more inexorably, less ambiguously to affirm the Law. At the start, in the absolute middle, and again at the end the novel returns to the scaffold that represents the Law. From a strictly formal point of view, we should never have been tempted in the wilderness; the structural placement of that scene, given the logic of returning to the scaffold that the narrative has already established, is enough to indicate that in the "wild, heathen Nature of the forest" (p. 161), we have gone astray. Of course, it is by vicariously going astray with Hester in "the mystery of the primeval forest" (p. 147) that readers can discover the truth of their hearts — but it is from Dimmesdale, whose attempt to come home from the woods leads him too to return to the scaffold, that Hawthorne expects his audience to learn how to live with that knowledge. Even Hester eventually agrees, as we can tell from her decision to resume the letter that Dimmesdale has taught her must be revealed.

One reason to value Sophia's response is that it registers Hawthorne's radical achievement even as an apostle of the moral law. The law must be obeyed — this, in one form or another, is the moral of every genteel fiction of his time. But Hawthorne's exploration of this truth in *The Scarlet Letter* more closely resembles (and anticipates) the severe wisdom of Freud's *Civilization and Its Discontents:* the law must be obeyed, and therein lies the tragedy of our instinctual lives. Sophia's broken heart indicates that she too was seduced by Hester's "dream of happiness" in the woods. The novel's deepest power flows from the way it enacts, not simply moralizes on, its theme. When the anarchic desires that the forest represents get let loose in the novel, we want to live there. To the palpable promise of erotic fulfillment that Hester's lawless energy summons up in us we are prepared to sacrifice everything — even, to take the human fact with which the narrative immediately daunts the lovers in the woods, to sacrifice Pearl. Amidst the imperious claims of their re-aroused passion, Hester and Dimmesdale, and probably even the Victorian audience, forgot about this child. But if in the first half Hawthorne uses Pearl's presence to encourage his audience to sympathize with Hester, here he uses her absence to keep a kind of moral distance from Hester's exhortation. When Pearl comes back into view, which happens even before the lovers leave the woods, she points the way that Dimmesdale later realizes he must take. When he climbs up to the scaffold, he sacrifices his own desires to the claims of his relationships as an adult to other people: to Pearl as her father, to his parishioners as their minister, even to Hester as her partner in shame. But embracing the Law instead of Hester is hard, even tragic, as *The Scarlet Letter* almost alone among the period's fictions acknowledges. Like most best-selling novels, including *Uncle Tom's Cabin,* it ends with a recovered family: on the scaffold at the end are Dimmesdale, Hester, Pearl, and Chillingworth, finally united in public. But unlike all those other endings, Hawthorne's fully reckons the cost, in terms of an individual's instinctual desires, by which a family is achieved and maintained.

The law must be obeyed, but this is a terrific truth, not a conventional truism: Mrs. Hawthorne's reading seems both critically and emotionally sound. Yet because the terms it relies on — a moral, the Law — seem so distant from those that modern readers bring to a text, such terms also establish the cultural gap across which the novel speaks to us. For example, published modern readings of it often regret or more often simply ignore the moral that Hawthorne himself provides. We know he was pleased with his wife's reaction as an audience. We cannot say exactly how he felt about her conclusions as a critic. Presumably he knew literature could not do police work, could not lay down or enforce laws. But we also know that he wanted his work to explore and express truths. The moral he offers his audience exhorts them to the same project: "Be true! Be true! Be true! Show freely to the world, if not your worst, yet some trait whereby the worst may be inferred" (p. 199). It is true that he offers this as only one among the "many morals" that may be drawn from the tale he has told, but this is one of those points in the text where he abandons his technique of narrative and stylistic ambiguity. Instead of offering us a number of morals to choose from, he insists, with all the unequivocality of the imperative mood, on this one. This moral does bring toward a conclusion the rhetorical project that governs Hawthorne's intentions throughout the book: to initiate contemporary readers into the truths about themselves that their culture has repressed. But in our time there remains our distrust, not to say positive distaste, for a moral. Do readers have the right of re-vision? Can we ignore or reject the author's own reading, offered inside the text itself?

Well, we could say that this enjoinment is not addressed to "us." Given the way our century began, for instance, with Freud's revelations about the truths of the human psyche, we do not approach Hawthorne's "drama of guilt and sorrow" (p. 195) with anything like the self-image of his Victorian American readers. Since we do not share their pieties, we cannot easily appreciate the "irreverence" of the burden he puts on his imagination by tasking it to show that the scarlet woman and the saintly minister both wear the "same scorching stigma." It is analogous to the way that every modern reader already knows that Dimmesdale is Hester's lover: the "hidden mysteries" into which Hawthorne felt obliged to guide his audience so carefully are not hidden for us. The "profounder self" that Dimmesdale is amazed to discover, and that Hawthorne's contemporaries did not consciously recognize either, is a fact of human nature that our culture largely takes for granted. Or think how differently a Victorian and a modern reader are apt to react to Hester in that first scene. In both cases the reflexes are conditioned by cultural experience. But whereas Hawthorne's culture had conditioned his audience, as they valued the image of themselves that the genteel culture sanctioned, to reject any identification with so dark a heroine, our own cultural experience, including the high ideological status accorded the dissatisfied wife, leads today's readers to prejudge Hester, so passionate a victim of a bad marriage and a repressive society, almost antithetically.

We need not judge such differences as either for better or for worse. But we should take account of them. Americans going to Latin America have to be warned not to use their thumb and forefinger to signal "OK" — because in Mexico or Brazil that friendly sign stands for something very different. Similarly, the gestures Hawthorne uses to communicate his vision to his contemporaries speak to postmodern readers in ways he could not have anticipated. The context in which he wrote was defined by his audience's mid-nineteenth-century faiths; for our part, we cannot help but read from within the context of late-twentieth-century doubts. Thus to post-deconstructionist critics, the various maneuvers by which Hawthorne sought to recondition the responses of Victorian readers — delay, withholding, equivocation, ambiguity — may look definitive. What for Hawthorne was a means — a strategy to change his audience's preconceptions — now seems, given our preconceptions, to be an end. Within the past ten years, as could have been expected, have appeared critical readings that argue the "indeterminacy," the "illegibility," the "pervasive ambiguity" of the novel.[25] That ambiguity

[25]These epithets are from, respectively, Millicent Bell's "The Obliquity of Signs: *The Scarlet Letter*," *Massachusetts Review* 23 (1982): 9–26; Norman Brysons "Hawthorne's Illegible Letter," in *Teaching the Text*, ed. Susanne Kappeler and Norman Bryson (London: Routledge, 1983), 92–108, rpt. in *Nathaniel Hawthorne's "The Scarlet Letter,"* ed. Harold Bloom (New York: Chelsea, 1986), 81–95; and Evan Carton's *The Rhetoric of American Romance* (Baltimore: Johns Hopkins UP, 1985), 191–227.

was a means for Hawthorne seems clear from the care he takes eventually to provide interpretive closure, as in that sequence we examined where, twenty pages after Hester's urging instinctual fulfillment in the wilderness has had a chance to work on Dimmesdale (and on us), the narrator tells us unambiguously that Dimmesdale (and we) have been seduced by our own profoundest self. But such authoritative passages, though written in the language that spoke most authoritatively to his contemporaries, fall deafly on our modern ears. Satanic bargain, deadly sin, whatever was good and holy — post-deconstructionist readers can ignore such locutions or dismiss them as inauthentic. It is an irony of literary history that Hawthorne begins by acknowledging the problem of trying to speak the truth to a culture of euphemism, which means there are many words he cannot use without "startl[ing]" his "present day" readers (p. 56). He manages to solve that problem brilliantly, writing one of the nineteenth century's most mature explorations of adult sexuality so tactfully that only a few extremists were upset. But he could not have anticipated the problem of trying to define the truth for a culture of doubt, and so the novel cannot defend itself from the postmodern emptiness of the words it ultimately relies on to make its truths persuasive to its audience.

Feminist readings of the novel are also likely to confuse Hawthorne's means with ends. The strategic care he takes in the first third to nurture his Victorian audience's sympathy for Hester can similarly seem definitive, so that the passions she arouses in the forest can seem exemplary, the novel's ultimate act of visionary witness. Modern readers, unlike Victorian ones, are prepared to go as deep into the wilderness as Hester can take them, but are often simply unwilling to follow Dimmesdale back from the woods to the scaffold, although that is the ground, the ground of moral duty, that Victorian readers were most familiar with.[26] Never mind that the narrative decisively defines the "dream of happiness" in the woods as a "temptation"; to such recent readers, Dimmesdale's decision to stand with Hester in "shame" rather than live with her in "joy," his decision to "reveal" the scarlet letter, does not look like moral heroism, but rather psychological cowardice or emotional betrayal. When Hawthorne makes Dimmesdale Christ-like

[26]Recent critics who find the book's imaginative center with Hester in the woods or who reject Dimmesdale's revelation on the scaffold include Nina Baym, *The Shape of Hawthorne's Career* (Ithaca: Cornell UP, 1976), 123–51; and David Leverenz, "Mrs. Hawthorne's Headache: Reading *The Scarlet Letter*," *Nineteenth-Century Fiction* 37 (1983): 552–75.

in this scene of "triumphant ignominy before the people" (p. 197) — he submits to "the will which God hath granted [him]"; he forgives his enemy; he stands (in fact, we are told explicitly that though he tottered on the way to the scaffold, he "did not fall!") "as one who, in the crisis of acutest pain, had won a victory" (pp. 193, 194, 196) — the novel again relies on the most definitive terms available at the time to convince a contemporary audience. Uncle Tom dies a similarly Christ-like death when he wins his "victory" at the end of Stowe's novel. But the Christian scaffolding with which Hawthorne props up Dimmesdale's actions no longer resonates with us. For many modern readers, Dimmesdale dies — and publishes the truth — in vain.

Certainly for most readers, in Hawthorne's time and ours, the tragic waste of Hester's powers and passions is what resonates most deeply as we close the tale. Doubtless it was this that broke Mrs. Hawthorne's heart. The novel redeems this loss, however, in two ways. Neither is the redemption that contemporary readers may have been looking for. When Sambo and Quimbo witness Tom's martyrdom at Legree's, we are told explicitly that by this means their souls are saved.[27] Yet we are not told about the eternal fate of Hester's soul. (Indeed, Hawthorne leaves out this detail so conspicuously that we seem warranted in thinking that his use of Christian iconography at Dimmesdale's death is largely a means too: his means of giving Dimmesdale's act of "being true" the highest possible stature in his audience's eyes.) Rather, the most immediate event that redeems Hester's, Dimmesdale's, and our anguish at being on the scaffold instead of in the woods is the earthly fate of Pearl's self. By living up to his responsibilities as her father, Dimmesdale frees her from her "errand as a messenger of anguish" to "grow up amid human joy and sorrow" (p. 197). This is probably the one place where the novel backs down from its commitment to tell the truth, however tragic — for the notion that parents, by doing the right thing, can somehow spare their children from the tragedies of their own lives is hopelessly naive, however attractive. The happy ending permitted Pearl is another place where the novel would have spoken more convincingly to Victorian than to modern readers.

The novel, though, does not quite end with the prospect of Pearl as "married, and happy, and mindful of her mother" (p. 201). It goes on to describe Hester's earthly fate as well. Having learned from Dimmesdale how to "be true," Hester settles permanently in Boston and puts on the letter "of her own free will" (p. 201). To modern readers who

[27] Stowe, *Uncle Tom's Cabin*, 481–82.

see the letter as "illegible" or as only the badge of Hester's "victimization by patriarchy,"[28] this ending must seem absurd or grotesque. But in terms of the novel's rhetorical project, the most redemptive thing that happens when Hester resumes the *A* is the growth of a new interpretive community around it. As we noted, Dimmesdale's revelation of the scarlet letter confounds rather than communicates to the Puritans who make up the novel's internal audience. At the very end, however, another group of viewers emerges to see the *A* in a wholly new way: "the scarlet letter ceased to be a stigma which attracted the world's scorn and bitterness, and became a type of something to be sorrowed over, and looked upon with awe, yet with reverence too" (p. 201).

Like the first time we see someone seeing the letter — when Hawthorne puts it on his own breast in "The Custom-House" — this last time is exemplary. This is how to read the scarlet letter: with sorrow for human frailty, awe at the hidden mysteries of the heart, reverence for another soul as equally human. By interpreting the letter in this spirit, the community that gathers around Hester at the end forms a third term to mediate between the repressive injustices of society and the lawless desires of the wilderness. The bases for this community's interpretation are sympathy and self-knowledge, and in their sensitivity as interpreters we see the basis for the belief that Hester prophetically embodies at the end: that "a new truth would be revealed, in order to establish the whole relation between man and woman on a surer ground of mutual happiness" (p. 201). Is not this "new truth" the truth that Hawthorne has tried to express in *The Scarlet Letter*? If the profounder self he reveals in the wilderness had been recognized and rightly understood, the Puritans never would have banished Hester. In fact, if we think about it, is it not likely that if the needs and desires of that profounder self had been acknowledged, Hester and Chillingworth never would have married? Hester, we have to remember, had to repress the truth about herself and her own desires to marry Chillingworth in the first place, and in a sense it is from that first act of repression that the tragedy of her life follows.

But if the novel reaches interpretive closure at the end, in this sympathetic community's reading of the *A*, it does not reach stasis. Restoring the status quo is not the end of Hawthorne's rhetorical project. For just as the ultimate interpretive community in the novel has been

[28]This is the feminist reading offered by Cynthia S. Jordan, *Second Stories: The Politics of Language, Form, And Gender in Early American Fictions* (Chapel Hill: U of North Carolina P, 1989), 152–72.

brought into existence by the experience of the tale itself, so Hawthorne hopes to change his audience by the "new truth" he has revealed and carefully enabled them to experience by reading the tale. The novel's very last line leaves his readers staring at the *A*. It leaves them, that is, with a project of their own: to join the community that sees the letter as the sign that speaks to all of us about our own profounder self. What Mrs. Hawthorne read in the novel — that life is tragic, but redeemed by moral significance — would qualify her, I think, for membership in that community. Self-knowledge and sympathy are not outdated virtues, but it is legitimate to ask whether many modern readers are interested in belonging to the particular interpretive community into which Hawthorne sought to turn his contemporary audience. He addresses himself to their nineteenth-century assumptions and leads them to the new truths revealed at the end, in the woods and on the scaffold. We start with different assumptions. His novel is bound to lead us to other, different ends.

Feminist and Gender Criticism and *The Scarlet Letter*

WHAT ARE FEMINIST AND GENDER CRITICISM?

Among the most exciting and influential developments in the field of literary studies, feminist and gender criticism participate in a broad philosophical discourse that extends far beyond literature, far beyond the arts in general. The critical *practices* of those who explore the representation of women and men in works by male or female, heterosexual or homosexual, writers inevitably grow out of and contribute to a larger and more generally applicable *theoretical* discussion of how gender and sexuality are constantly shaped by and shaping institutional structures and attitudes, artifacts, and behaviors,

Feminist criticism was accorded academic legitimacy in American universities "around 1981," Jane Gallop claims in her book *Around 1981: Academic Feminist Literary Theory* (1992). With Gallop's title and approximation in mind, Naomi Schor has since estimated that "around 1985, feminism began to give way to what has come to be called gender studies" (275). Some would argue that feminist criticism became academically legitimate well before 1981. Others would take issue with the notion that feminist criticism and women's studies have been giving way to gender criticism and gender studies, and with the either/or distinction that such a claim implies. Taken together, however, Gallop and

Schor provide us with a useful fact — that of feminist criticism's historical precedence — and a chronological focus on the early to mid-1980s, a period during which the feminist approach was unquestionably influential and during which new interests emerged, not all of which were woman centered.

During the early 1980s, three discrete strains of feminist theory and practice — commonly categorized as French, North American, and British — seemed to be developing. French feminists tended to focus their attention on language. Drawing on the ideas of the psychoanalytic philosopher Jacques Lacan, they argued that language as we commonly think of it — as public discourse — is decidedly phallocentric, privileging what is valued by the patriarchal culture. They also spoke of the possibility of an alternative, feminine language and of *l'écriture féminine:* women's writing. Julia Kristeva, who is generally seen as a pioneer of French feminist thought, even though she dislikes the feminist label, suggested that feminine language is associated with the maternal and derived from the pre-oedipal fusion between mother and child. Like Kristeva, Hélène Cixous and Luce Irigaray associated feminine writing with the female body. Both drew an analogy between women's writing and women's sexual pleasure, Irigaray arguing that just as a woman's *"jouissance"* is more diffuse and complex than a man's unitary phallic pleasure ("woman has sex organs just about everywhere"), so "feminine" language is more diffuse and less obviously coherent than its "masculine" counterpart (*This Sex* 101–03).

Kristeva, who helped develop the concept of *l'écriture féminine,* nonetheless urged caution in its use and advocacy. Feminine or feminist writing that resists or refuses participation in "masculine" discourse, she warned, risks political marginalization, relegation to the outskirts (pun intended) of what is considered socially and politically significant. Kristeva's concerns were not unfounded: the concept of *l'écriture féminine* did prove controversial, eliciting different kinds of criticism from different kinds of feminist and gender critics. To some, the concept appears to give writing a biological basis, thereby suggesting that there is an *essential* femininity, and/or that women are *essentially* different from men. To others, it seems to suggest that men can write as women, so long as they abdicate authority, sense, and logic in favor of diffusiveness, playfulness, even nonsense.

While French feminists of the 1970s and early 1980s focused on language and writing from a psychoanalytic perspective, North American critics generally practiced a different sort of criticism. Characterized by close textual reading and historical scholarship, it generally took one of two forms. Critics like Kate Millett, Carolyn Heilbrun, and Judith Fetterley developed what Elaine Showalter called the "feminist critique" of "male constructed literary history" by closely examining canonical works by male writers, exposing the patriarchal ideology implicit in such works, and arguing that traditions of systematic masculine dominance are indelibly inscribed in our literary tradition. Fetterley urged women to become "resisting readers" — to notice how biased most of the classic texts by male authors are in their language, subjects, and attitudes and to actively reject that bias as they read, thereby making reading a different, less "immasculating" experience. Meanwhile, another group of North American feminists, including Showalter, Sandra Gilbert, Susan Gubar, and Patricia Meyer Spacks, developed a different feminist critical model — one that Showalter referred to as "gynocriticism." These critics analyzed great books by women from a feminist perspective, discovered neglected or forgotten women writers, and attempted to recover women's culture and history, especially the history of women's communities that nurtured female creativity.

The North American endeavor to recover women's history — for example, by emphasizing that women developed their own strategies to gain power within their sphere — was seen by British feminists like Judith Newton and Deborah Rosenfelt as an endeavor that "mystifies" male oppression, disguising it as something that has created a special world of opportunities for women. More important from the British standpoint, the universalizing and "essentializing" tendencies of French theory and a great deal of North American practice disguised women's oppression by highlighting sexual difference, thereby seeming to suggest that the dominant system may be impervious to change. As for the North American critique of male stereotypes that denigrate women, British feminists maintained that it led to counterstereotypes of female virtue that ignore real differences of race, class, and culture among women.

By now, the French, North American, and British approaches have so thoroughly critiqued, influenced, and assimilated one another that the work of most Western practitioners is no longer easily identifiable along national boundary lines. Instead, it tends to be characterized according to whether the category of *woman* is the major focus in the exploration of gender and gender oppression or, alternatively, whether the interest in sexual difference encompasses an interest in other differences that also define identity. The latter paradigm encompasses the work of feminists of color, Third World (preferably called postcolonial) feminists, and lesbian feminists, many of whom have asked whether the universal category of woman constructed by certain French and North American predecessors is appropriate to describe women in minority groups or non-Western cultures.

These feminists stress that, while all women are female, they are something else as well (such as African American, lesbian, Muslim Pakistani). This "something else" is precisely what makes them — including their problems and their goals — different from other women. As Armit Wilson has pointed out, Asian women living in Great Britain are expected by their families and communities to preserve Asian cultural traditions; thus, the expression of personal identity through clothing involves a much more serious infraction of cultural rules than it does for a Western woman. Gloria Anzaldúa has spoken personally and eloquently about the experience of many women on the margins of Eurocentric North American culture. "I am a border woman," she writes in *Borderlands: La Frontera = The New Mestiza* (1987). "I grew up between two cultures, the Mexican (with a heavy Indian influence) and the Anglo. . . . Living on the borders and in margins, keeping intact one's shifting and multiple identity and integrity is like trying to swim in a new element, an 'alien' element" (i).

Instead of being divisive and isolating, this evolution of feminism into femin*isms* fostered a more inclusive, global perspective. The era of recovering women's texts, especially texts by white Western women, has been succeeded by a new era in which the goal is to recover entire cultures of women. Two important figures of this new era are Trinh T. Minh-ha and Gayatri Spivak. Spivak, in works such as *In Other Worlds: Essays in Cultural Politics* (1987) and *Outside in the Teaching Machine* (1993), has shown how political independence (generally looked upon by metropolitan Westerners as a simple and beneficial historical and political reversal) has complex implications for "subaltern" or subproletarian women.

The understanding of woman not as a single, deterministic category but rather as the nexus of diverse experiences has led some white, Western, "majority" feminists like Jane Tompkins and Nancy K. Miller to advocate and practice "personal" or "autobiographical" criticism. Once reluctant to reveal themselves in their analyses for fear of being labeled idiosyncratic, impressionistic, and subjective by men, some feminists are now openly skeptical of the claims to reason, logic, and objectivity that male critics have made in the past. With the advent of more personal feminist critical styles has come a powerful new interest in women's autobiographical writings, manifested in essays such as "Authorizing the Autobiographical" by Shari Benstock, which first appeared in her influential collection *The Private Self: Theory and Practice of Women's Autobiographical Writings* (1988).

Traditional autobiography, some feminists have argued, is a gendered, "masculinist" genre; its established conventions call for a life-plot that turns on action, triumph through conflict, intellectual self-discovery, and often public renown. The body, reproduction, children, and intimate interpersonal relationships are generally well in the background and often absent. Arguing that the lived experiences of women and men differ — women's lives, for instance, are often characterized by interruption and deferral — Leigh Gilmore has developed a theory of women's self-representation in her book *Autobiographics: A Feminist Theory of Self-Representation.*

Autobiographics was published in 1994, well after the chronological divide that, according to Schor, separates the heyday of feminist criticism and the rise of gender studies. Does that mean that Gilmore's book is a feminist throwback? Is she practicing gender criticism instead, the use of the word "feminist" in her book's subtitle notwithstanding? Or are both of these questions overly reductive? As implied earlier, many knowledgeable commentators on the contemporary critical scene are skeptical of the feminist/gender distinction, arguing that feminist criticism is by definition gender criticism and pointing out that one critic whose work *everyone* associates with feminism (Julia Kristeva) has problems with the feminist label while another critic whose name is continually linked with the gender approach (Teresa de Lauretis) continues to refer to herself and her work as feminist.

Certainly, feminist and gender criticism are not polar opposites but, rather, exist along a continuum of attitudes toward sex and sexism, sexuality and gender, language and the literary canon. There are, however, a few distinctions to be made between those critics whose writings are inevitably identified as being toward one end of the continuum or the other.

One distinction is based on focus: as the word implies, "feminists" have concentrated their efforts on the study of women and women's issues. Gender criticism, by contrast, has not been woman centered. It has tended to view the male and female sexes — and the masculine and feminine genders — in terms of a complicated continuum, much as we are viewing feminist and gender criticism. Critics like Diane K. Lewis have raised the possibility that black women may be more like white men in terms of familial and economic roles, like black men in terms of their relationships with whites, and like white women in terms of their relationships with men. Lesbian gender critics have asked whether lesbian women are really more like straight women than they are like gay (or for that matter straight) men. That we refer to gay and lesbian studies as gender studies has led some to suggest that gender studies is a misnomer; after all, homosexuality is not a gender. This objection may easily be answered once we realize that one purpose of gender criticism is to criticize gender as we commonly conceive of it, to expose its insufficiency and inadequacy as a category.

Another distinction between feminist and gender criticism is based on the terms "gender" and "sex." As de Lauretis suggests in *Technologies of Gender* (1987), feminists of the 1970s tended to equate gender with sex, gender difference with sexual difference. But that equation doesn't help us explain "the differences among women, . . . the differences *within women*." After positing that "we need a notion of gender that is not so bound up with sexual difference," de Lauretis provides just such a notion by arguing that "gender is not a property of bodies or something originally existent in human beings"; rather, it is "the product of various social technologies, such as cinema" (2). Gender is, in other words, a construct, an effect of language, culture, and its institutions. It is gender, not sex, that causes a weak old man to open a door for an athletic young woman. And it is gender, not sex, that may cause one young woman to expect old men to behave in this way, another to view this kind of behavior as chauvinistic and insulting, and still another to have mixed feelings (hence de Lauretis's phrase "differences *within women*") about "gentlemanly gallantry."

Still another related distinction between feminist and gender criticism is based on the *essentialist* views of many feminist critics and the *constructionist* views of many gender critics (both those who would call themselves feminists and those who would not). Stated simply and perhaps too reductively, the term *essentialist* refers to the view that women are essentially different from men. *Constructionist,* by contrast, refers to the view that most of those differences are characteristics not of the male and female sex (nature) but, rather, of the masculine and feminine genders (nurture). Because of its essentialist tendencies, "radical feminism," according to the influential gender critic Eve Kosofsky Sedgwick, "tends to deny that the meaning of gender or sexuality has ever significantly changed; and more damagingly, it can make future change appear impossible" (*Between Men* 13).

Most obviously essentialist would be those feminists who emphasize the female body, its difference, and the manifold implications of that difference. The equation made by some avant-garde French feminists between the female body and the *maternal* body has proved especially troubling to some gender critics, who worry that it may paradoxically play into the hands of extreme conservatives and fundamentalists seeking to reestablish patriarchal family values. In her book *The Reproduction of Mothering* (1978), Nancy Chodorow, a sociologist of gender, admits that what we call "mothering" — not having or nursing babies but mothering more broadly conceived — is commonly associated not just with the feminine gender but also with the female sex, often considered nurturing by nature. But she critically interrogates the common assumption that it is in women's nature or biological destiny to "mother" in this broader sense, arguing that the separation of home and workplace brought about by the development of capitalism and the ensuing industrial revolution made mothering *appear* to be essentially a woman's job in modern Western society.

If sex turns out to be gender where mothering is concerned, what differences *are* grounded in sex — that is, nature? *Are* there *essential* differences between men and women — other than those that are purely anatomical and anatomically determined (for example, a man can exclusively take on the job of feeding an infant milk, but he may not do so from his own breast)? A growing number of gender critics would answer the question in the negative. Sometimes referred to as "extreme constructionists" and "postfeminists," these critics have adopted the viewpoint of philosopher Judith Butler, who in her book *Gender Trouble* (1990) predicts that "sex, by definition, will be shown to have been gender all along" (8). As Naomi Schor explains their position, "there is nothing outside or before culture, no nature that is not always and already enculturated" (278).

Whereas a number of feminists celebrate women's difference, postfeminist gender critics would agree with Chodorow's statement that men have an "investment in difference that women do not have" (Eisenstein and Jardine 14). They see difference as a symptom of oppression, not a cause for celebration, and would abolish it by dismantling gender categories and, ultimately, destroying gender itself. Since gender categories and distinctions are embedded in and perpetuated through language, gender critics like Monique Wittig have called for the wholesale transformation of language into a nonsexist, and nonheterosexist, medium.

Language has proved the site of important debates between feminist and gender critics, essentialists and constructionists. Gender critics have taken issue with those French feminists who have spoken of a feminine language and writing and who have grounded differences in language and writing in the female body.[1] For much the same reason they have disagreed with those French-influenced Anglo-American critics who, like Toril Moi and Nancy K. Miller, have posited an essential relationship between sexuality and textuality. (In an essentialist sense, such critics have suggested that when women write, they tend to break the rules of plausibility and verisimilitude that men have created to evaluate fiction.) Gender critics like Peggy Kamuf posit a relationship only between *gender* and textuality, between what most men and women *become* after they are born and the way in which they write. They are therefore less interested in the author's sexual "signature"— in whether the author was a woman writing — than in whether the author was (to borrow from Kamuf) "Writing like a Woman."

Feminists like Miller have suggested that no man could write the "female anger, desire, and selfhood" that Emily Brontë, for instance, inscribed in her poetry and in *Wuthering Heights* (*Subject* 72). In the view of gender critics, it is and has been possible for a man to write like a woman, a woman to write like a man. Shari Benstock, a noted feminist critic whose investigations into psychoanalytic and poststructuralist theory have led her increasingly to adopt the gender approach, poses the following question to herself in *Textualizing the Feminine* (1991): "Isn't it precisely 'the feminine' in Joyce's writings and Derrida's that carries me along?" (45). In an essay entitled "Unsexing Language: Pronomial Protest in Emily Dickinson's 'Lay this Laurel,'" Anna Shannon Elfenbein has argued that "like Walt Whitman, Emily Dickinson crossed the gender barrier in some remarkable poems," such as "We learned to like the Fire / By playing Glaciers — when a Boy —" (Berg 215).

It is also possible, in the view of most gender critics, for women to read as men, men as women. The view that women can, and indeed have been forced to, read as men has been fairly noncontroversial. Everyone agrees that the literary canon is largely "androcentric" and that writings by men have tended to "immasculate" women, forcing them to see the world from a masculine viewpoint. But the question of whether men can read as women has proved to be yet another issue

[1]Because feminist/gender studies, not unlike sex/gender, should be thought of as existing along a continuum of attitudes and not in terms of simple opposition, attempts to highlight the difference between feminist and gender criticism are inevitably prone to reductive overgeneralization and occasional distortion. Here, for instance, French feminism is made out to be more monolithic than it actually is. Hélène Cixous has said that a few men (such as Jean Genet) have produced "feminine writing," although she suggests that these are exceptional men who have acknowledged their own bisexuality.

dividing feminist and gender critics. Some feminists suggest that men and women have some essentially different reading strategies and outcomes, while gender critics maintain that such differences arise entirely out of social training and cultural norms. One interesting outcome of recent attention to gender and reading is Elizabeth A. Flynn's argument that women in fact make the best interpreters of imaginative literature. Based on a study of how male and female students read works of fiction, she concludes that women come up with more imaginative, open-ended readings of stories. Quite possibly the imputed hedging and tentativeness of women's speech, often seen by men as disadvantages, are transformed into useful interpretive strategies — receptivity combined with critical assessment of the text — in the act of reading (Flynn and Schweickart 286).

In singling out a catalyst of the gender approach, many historians of criticism have pointed to Michel Foucault. In his *History of Sexuality* (1976, r. 1978), Foucault distinguished sexuality (that is, sexual behavior or practice) from sex, calling the former a "technology of sex." De Lauretis, who has deliberately developed her theory of gender "along the lines of . . . Foucault's theory of sexuality," explains his use of "technology" this way: "Sexuality, commonly thought to be a natural as well as a private matter, is in fact completely constructed in culture according to the political aims of the society's dominant class" (*Technologies* 2, 12). Foucault suggests that homosexuality as we now think of it was to a great extent an invention of the nineteenth century. In earlier periods there had been "acts of sodomy" and individuals who committed them, but the "sodomite" was, according to Foucault, "a temporary aberration," not the "species" he became with the advent of the modern concept of homosexuality (42–43). By historicizing sexuality, Foucault made it possible for his successors to consider the possibility that all of the categories and assumptions that currently come to mind when we think about sex, sexual difference, gender, and sexuality are social artifacts, the products of cultural discourses.

In explaining her reason for saying that feminism began to give way to gender studies "around 1985," Schor says that she chose that date "in part because it marks the publication of *Between Men*," a seminal book in which Eve Kosofsky Sedgwick "articulates the insights of feminist criticism onto those of gay-male studies, which had up to then pursued often parallel but separate courses (affirming the existence of a homosexual or female imagination, recovering lost traditions, decoding the cryptic discourse of works already in the canon by homosexual or feminist authors)" (276). Today, gay and lesbian criticism is so much a part of gender criticism that some people equate it with the gender approach, while others have begun to prefer the phrase "sexualities criticism" to "gender criticism."

Following Foucault's lead, some gay and lesbian gender critics have argued that the heterosexual/homosexual distinction is as much a cultural construct as is the masculine/feminine dichotomy. Arguing that sexuality is a continuum, not a fixed and static set of binary oppositions, a number of gay and lesbian critics have critiqued heterosexuality as a norm, arguing that it has been an enforced corollary and consequence of what Gayle Rubin has referred to as the "sex/gender system." (Those subscribing to this system assume that persons of the male sex should be masculine, that masculine men are attracted to women, and therefore that it is natural for masculine men to be attracted to women and unnatural for them to be attracted to men.) Lesbian gender critics have also taken issue with their feminist counterparts on the grounds that they proceed from fundamentally heterosexual and even heterosexist assumptions. Particularly offensive to lesbians like the poet-critic Adrienne Rich have been those feminists who, following Doris Lessing, have implied that to make the lesbian choice is to make a statement, to act out feminist hostility against men. Rich has called heterosexuality "a beachhead of male dominance" that, "like motherhood, needs to be recognized and studied as a political institution" ("Compulsory Heterosexuality" 143, 145).

If there is such a thing as reading like a woman and such a thing as reading like a man, how then do lesbians read? Are there gay and lesbian ways of reading? Many would say that there are. Rich, by reading Emily Dickinson's poetry as a lesbian — by not assuming that "heterosexual romance is the key to a woman's life and work" — has introduced us to a poet somewhat different from the one heterosexual critics have made familiar (*Lies* 158). As for gay reading, Wayne Koestenbaum has defined "the (male twentieth-century first world) gay reader" as one who "reads resistantly for inscriptions of his condition, for texts that will confirm a social and private identity founded on a desire for other men. . . . Reading becomes a hunt for histories that deliberately foreknow or unwittingly trace a desire felt not by author but by reader, who is most acute when searching for signs of himself" (Boone and Cadden 176–77).

Lesbian critics have produced a number of compelling reinterpretations, or inscriptions, of works by authors as diverse as Emily Dickinson, Virginia Woolf, and Toni Morrison. As a result of these provocative readings, significant disagreements have arisen between straight and lesbian critics and among lesbian critics as well. Perhaps the most famous and interesting example of this kind of interpretive controversy involves the claim by Barbara Smith and Adrienne Rich that Morrison's novel *Sula* can be read as a lesbian text — and author Toni Morrison's counterclaim that it cannot.

Gay male critics have produced a body of readings no less revisionist and controversial, focusing on writers as staidly classic as Henry James and Wallace Stevens. In Melville's *Billy Budd* and *Moby-Dick,* Robert K. Martin suggests, a triangle of homosexual desire exists. In the latter novel, the hero must choose between a captain who represents "the imposition of the male on the female" and a "Dark Stranger" (Queequeg) who "offers the possibility of an alternate sexuality, one that is less dependent upon performance and conquest" (*Hero* 5).

Masculinity as a complex construct producing and reproducing a constellation of behaviors and goals, many of them destructive (like performance and conquest) and most of them injurious to women, has become the object of an unprecedented number of gender studies. A 1983 issue of *Feminist Review* contained an essay entitled "Anti-Porn: Soft Issue, Hard World," in which B. Ruby Rich suggested that the "legions of feminist men" who examine and deplore the effects of pornography on women might better "undertake the analysis that can tell us why men like porn (not, piously, why this or that exceptional man does *not*)" (Berg 185). The advent of gender criticism makes precisely that kind of analysis possible. Stephen H. Clark, who alludes to Ruby Rich's challenge, reads T. S. Eliot "as a man." Responding to "Eliot's implicit appeal to a specifically masculine audience — 'You! hypocrite lecteur! — mon semblable, — mon *frère!*'" — Clark concludes that poems like "Sweeney Among the Nightingales" and "Gerontion," rather than offering what they are usually said to offer — "a social critique into which a misogynistic language accidentally seeps" — instead articulate a masculine "psychology of sexual fear and desired retaliation" (Berg 173).

Some gender critics focusing on masculinity have analyzed "the anthropology of boyhood," a phrase coined by Mark Seltzer in an article in which he comparatively reads, among other things, Stephen Crane's *Red Badge of Courage,* Jack London's *White Fang,* and the first *Boy Scouts of America* handbook (Boone and Cadden 150). Others have examined the fear men have that artistry is unmasculine, a guilty worry that surfaces perhaps most obviously in "The Custom-House," Hawthorne's lengthy preface to *The Scarlet Letter.* Still others have studied the representation in literature of subtly erotic disciple-patron relationships, relationships like the ones between Nick Carraway and Jay Gatsby, Charlie Marlow and Lord Jim, Doctor Watson and Sherlock Holmes, and any number of characters in Henry James's stories. Not all of these studies have focused on literary texts. Because the movies have played a primary role in gender construction during our lifetimes, gender critics have analyzed the dynamics of masculinity (vis-à-vis femininity and androgyny) in films from *Rebel Without a Cause* to *Tootsie* to last year's Best Picture. One of the "social technologies" most influential in (re)constructing gender, film is one of the media in which today's sexual politics is most evident.

Necessary as it is, in an introduction such as this one, to define the difference between feminist and gender criticism, it is equally necessary to conclude by unmaking the distinction, at least partially. The two topics just discussed (film theory and so-called queer theory) give us grounds for undertaking that necessary deconstruction. The alliance I have been creating between gay and lesbian criticism on one hand and gender criticism on the other is complicated greatly by the fact that not all gay and lesbian critics are constructionists. Indeed, a number of them (Robert K. Martin included) share with many feminists the *essentialist* point of view; that is to say, they believe homosexuals and heterosexuals to be essentially different, different by nature, just as a number of feminists believe men and women to be different.

In film theory and criticism, feminist and gender critics have so influenced one another that their differences would be difficult to define based on any available criteria, including the ones outlined above. Cinema has been of special interest to contemporary feminists like Minh-ha (herself a filmmaker) and Spivak (whose critical eye has focused on movies including *My Beautiful Laundrette* and *Sammie and Rosie Get Laid*). Teresa de Lauretis, whose *Technologies of Gender* (1987) has proved influential in the area of gender studies, continues to publish film criticism consistent with earlier, unambiguously feminist works in which she argued that "the representation of woman as spectacle — body to be looked at, place of sexuality, and object of desire — so pervasive in our culture, finds in narrative cinema its most complex expression and widest circulation" (*Alice* 4).

Feminist film theory has developed alongside a feminist performance theory grounded in Joan Riviere's recently rediscovered essay "Womanliness as a Masquerade" (1929), in which the author argues that there is no femininity that is *not* masquerade. Marjorie Garber, a contemporary cultural critic with an interest in gender, has analyzed the constructed nature of femininity by focusing on men who have apparently achieved it — through the transvestism, transsexualism, and other forms of "cross-dressing" evident in cultural productions from Shakespeare to Elvis, from "Little Red Riding Hood" to *La Cage aux Folles.* The future of feminist and gender criticism, it would seem, is not one of further bifurcation but one involving a refocusing on femininity, masculinity, and related sexualities, not only as represented in poems, novels, and films but also as manifested and developed in video, on television, and along the almost infinite number of waystations rapidly being developed on the information highways running through an exponentially expanding cyberspace.

In 1982, Nina Baym reviewed the history of American feminist criticism at the beginning of an essay on Nathaniel Hawthorne. "The initial works of feminist criticism," Baym wrote, "analyzed the writings of important male authors . . . in an attempt to uncover the . . . destructive attitudes toward women that they contained." Because Hawthorne's works "presented many problems to the critics who wished to define him as an orthodox espouser of patriarchal attitudes," she went on to argue, American feminists "ultimately abandoned him for other writers more suited to their aims" ("Thwarted Nature" 58). In short time, however, Hawthorne's works once again attracted the interest of feminist (and gender) critics.

In 1976 Judith Fryer published *The Faces of Eve: Women in the Nineteenth-Century American Novel.* Writing at the end of the era in which feminists critiqued the work of male authors, Fryer revealed patriarchal attitudes in Hawthorne while recognizing other, conflicting ones — those that, in Baym's words, had always "presented problems" for early feminists. Using "The Custom-House" to show that Hawthorne believed his own artistic nature "unmanly," Fryer went on to argue that "Hawthorne's ambiguity about Hester" is "an attempt to work out his ambiguity toward himself," both as "an artist" and as "a man." Fryer recognized something "feminine," and sympathetic with the feminine in Hawthorne, while, at the same time, being skeptical of "twentieth-century readers who would see . . . Hawthorne as a writer with 'feminist sympathies'" (74). Fryer points out that Hester's dark broodings on "the whole race of womanhood" are clearly "bothersome to Hawthorne" (78); they are succeeded by the narrator's observation that "[a] woman never overcomes these problems by any exercise of thought" (p. 135 in this volume). Indeed, in life Hawthorne "married a pale maiden" as conventionally feminine as Hester is unconventional (Fryer 78).

Since Baym started a return-to-Hawthorne movement in 1982, feminists who have written on *The Scarlet Letter* have been much influenced by her — but by Fryer as well. In her book *Women, Ethnics, and Exotics* (1983), Kristin Herzog has perpetuated Fryer's image of Hester as a darkly sensual type of Eve. Arguing that Hester's "'lawless passion' . . . turns her into a kind of white Indian," Herzog concludes her discussion by calling Hawthorne's most memorable heroine "an example of a new American Eve" (15–16).

Other modern American feminists interested in Hawthorne have further analyzed the "ambiguity" or ambivalence detected and discussed by both Fryer and Baym. In *Gender and the Writer's Imagination* (1987), Mary Suzanne Schriber points out that Hester is herself ambivalent, or self-divided. "Assertive, rather than submissive," Hester is nonetheless "conventional" and even "lady-like" (48–49), so much so that "the community eventually comes around, attributing to Hester's A the meaning of 'Angel' and 'Able' rather than adulteress" (50). Regarding the novel's ambivalent attitude toward Hester, Schriber suggests that it results from inconsistencies in the mind of the less-than-reliable narrator, as well from differences between the narrator's views and those of the "implied author" (56).

In his *Aesthetic Headaches: Women and a Masculine Poetics in Poe, Melville, and Hawthorne* (1988), a male feminist, Leland S. Person, argues that the "phallic" power to control or "master" women is a favorite subject of Hawthorne's (recall Dimmesdale's temptation to "blight" a young girl's innocence with "but a word" [p. 172]) and one of Hawthorne's own measures of artistic success. Person reminds us that Hawthorne considered *The Scarlet Letter* "'a triumphant success,' a 'ten-strike'" because it "had such an effect on [his wife] Sophia that it 'broke her heart and sent her to bed with a grievous headache'" (122).

The phallic power to control and master women is very much what the following essay is about. In it, Shari Benstock explains how a patriarchal Puritan society attempts to master one woman, Hester Prynne, in part by marking her with a letter that reduces her to a single, rather simple identity — that of a sinner.

Benstock also shows how Hester subverts such attempts from the moment she steps forth from the prison door and, instead of trying to hide what is meant to stand for her sin, openly reveals the letter on her breast. Through that and other, consequent actions, she identifies herself not as a sinner but as a sexual woman — and more. For, as Benstock points out, Hester proceeds by artfully altering both the letter and other symbols constructed by the Puritan society. Slowly, carefully, sometimes luxuriously, she makes them stand for things unintended by the patriarchs who, by controlling language, have controlled women as well. In fact, Hester ends up by opening "an inexhaustible chain of substitutions," making the scarlet *A* stand for "angel, able, adored"— and, finally, "Authority over her own identity" (p. 397).

As Benstock realizes, Hawthorne begins to raise the issue of gender in his introduction to the novel, "The Custom-House." There he associates embroidery, femininity, and storytelling, reinforcing the kind of connections that are part of our culture's masculine-dominated "logic" and forming the kind of connections that Toril Moi refers to as "sexual/textual" in her book *Sexual/Textual Politics: Feminist Literary Theory* (1985). Ultimately, *The Scarlet Letter* critiques those same kinds of associations — femininity and falsity, truth and masculinity. Like Hester, the novel teaches us to distrust easy, traditional, patriarchal modes of interpretation that would tell us that *A* (or woman) does *not* mean "Able." Moreover, by demonstrating the multiple meanings of a letter and by occasionally dissociating meaning from gender, the novel even manages to undermine or challenge the *idea* of absolute sexual difference.

Benstock's reading of *The Scarlet Letter* has obviously been influenced by French as well as American feminist theory. The French influence shows in local details, such as references to Kristeva's theory. But it is also evident in Benstock's general focus on women and patriarchal or phallocentric language, which associates the feminine with certain words and ideas, the masculine with others. Returning to the Greeks, Benstock explains that early myths linked the earth with the female body, the plow with the penis, and, by extension, with masculinity. Furthermore, she suggests that since civilization has been equated with dominion over the earth, it has also come to imply the domination of women by men. Equally French is Benstock's allusion to a primary bond between Hester and Pearl that precedes language and, therefore, culture.

Benstock's essay, however, does more than critique the logic of binary oppositions (male/female, plow/earth, dominant/passive) and associations (male/plow/dominant, female/earth/passive) inherent in masculine-dominated language; it also shows Hawthorne engaged in the same enterprise. As Benstock points out, Hawthorne portrays a New England earth from which wild rosebushes grow but that resists patriarchal, civilizing law; it seems that neither plans nor plows can help the Puritans raise up an ornamental garden from such hard soil. In doing so, Benstock again demonstrates what American feminists like Baym and Fryer have long known, namely, that Hawthorne himself is not easily categorized. At once backward- and forward-looking, he is as patriarchal as he is prototypically feminist, as much a part of the answer to "the dark question" concerning "the whole race of womanhood" as he has been part of the problem.

Benstock's essay, though solidly feminist due to its focus on a woman — and women — in patriarchal society, nonetheless is informed by any number of other, theory-based approaches to literature — so many, in fact, that it could almost be placed in the "Combining Perspectives" section of this critical edition! It draws on deconstruction (defined in the "Glossary of Critical and Theoretical Terms" at the end of this book) insofar as it shows how a text both subverts the logic of binary oppositions and undermines the notion of determinate, determinable meanings (by opening up a "profusion of possible meanings" for the single symbol, *A*). Additionally, it is informed by psychoanalytic criticism; Benstock not only cites the work of Nicholas Abraham and Maria Torak but also draws on Jacques Lacan's psychoanalytic theory in her discussion of Pearl as a person for whom there is no identifying "name-of-the-Father."

But of all the approaches, beyond feminism, that influence Benstock's analysis, the type of gender criticism that has emerged from feminism is far and away the most predominant, as can be seen in her explicit and implicit arguments that gender is a social construct. (She discusses the attempted construction of a woman, Hester, as a sinner by the Puritan patriarchs in *The Scarlet Letter*, and she shows how Hester responds by *re*constructing symbols and discourses to make herself — and woman — mean other things.) Benstock also shows the influence of gender criticism when she shows how Hawthorne's text "expose[s] the fictional nature" both of "absolute sexual difference" and of traditional "sexual-textual" associations (p. 398) — for instance, the association between feminine writing and fanciful storytelling that held sway in Hawthorne's own day and that left its marks in his writings, particularly in "The Custom-House." (In deconstructing these fictions, she implicitly admits that, though she is indebted to early French feminists, she disagrees with their essentialist positions on sexual difference, on "writing [and reading] like a woman," etc., siding instead with the constructionist views of other feminists and of gender theorists.) Finally, in her discussion of the attempt by Puritan society "to regulate female sexuality" via "religious, legal, and economic" discourses (p. 398), she implicitly alludes to the work of Michel Foucault, whose influence over gender theory, gender criticism, has been far-reaching and profound.

Ross C Murfin

FEMINIST AND GENDER CRITICISM: A SELECTED BIBLIOGRAPHY

French Feminist Theory

Cixous, Hélène. "The Laugh of the Medusa." Trans. Keith Cohen and Paula Cohen. *Signs* 1 (1976): 875–93.

Cixous, Hélène, and Catherine Clément. *The Newly Born Woman.* Trans. Betsy Wing. Minneapolis: U of Minnesota P, 1986.

Irigaray, Luce. *An Ethics of Sexual Difference.* Trans. Carolyn Burke and Gillian C. Gill. Ithaca: Cornell UP, 1993.

———. *This Sex Which Is Not One.* Trans. Catherine Porter. Ithaca: Cornell UP, 1985.

Jones, Ann Rosalind. "Inscribing Femininity: French Theories of the Feminine." *Making a Difference: Feminist Literary Criticism.* Ed. Gayle Green and Coppélia Kahn. London: Methuen, 1985. 80–112.

———. "Writing the Body: Toward an Understanding of *L'Écriture féminine.*" Showalter, *The New Feminist Criticism* 361–77.

Kristeva, Julia. *Desire in Language: A Semiotic Approach to Literature and Art.* Ed. Leon S. Roudiez. Trans. Thomas Gora, Alice Jardine, and Roudiez. New York: Columbia UP, 1980.

Marks, Elaine, and Isabelle de Courtivron, eds. *New French Feminisms: An Anthology.* Amherst: U of Massachusetts P, 1980.

Moi, Toril, ed. *French Feminist Thought: A Reader.* Oxford: Basil Blackwell, 1987.

Feminist Theory: Classic Texts, General Approaches, Collections

Abel, Elizabeth, and Emily K. Abel, eds. *The "Signs" Reader: Women, Gender, and Scholarship.* Chicago: U of Chicago P, 1983.

Barrett, Michèle, and Anne Phillips. *Destabilizing Theory: Contemporary Feminist Debates.* Stanford: Stanford U, 1992.

Beauvoir, Simone de. *The Second Sex.* 1953. Trans. and ed. H. M. Parshley. New York: Bantam, 1961.

Benstock, Shari. *Textualizing the Feminine: Essays on the Limits of Genre.* Norman: U of Oklahoma P, 1991.

Butler, Judith. *Gender Trouble: Feminism and the Subversion of Identity.* New York: Routledge, 1990.

de Lauretis, Teresa, ed. *Feminist Studies/Critical Studies.* Bloomington: Indiana UP, 1986.

Felman, Shoshana. "Women and Madness: The Critical Phallacy." *Diacritics* 5 (1975): 2–10.

Fetterley, Judith. *The Resisting Reader: A Feminist Approach to American Fiction.* Bloomington: Indiana UP, 1978.

Fuss, Diana. *Essentially Speaking: Feminist Nature and Difference.* New York: Routledge, 1989.

Gallop, Jane. *Around 1981: Academic Feminist Literary Theory.* New York: Routledge, 1992.

———. *The Daughter's Seduction: Feminism and Psychoanalysis.* Ithaca: Cornell UP, 1982.

Heilburn, Carolyn. *Toward a Recognition of Androgyny.* New York: Harper Colophon, 1973.

hooks, bell. *Feminist Theory: From Margin to Center.* Boston: South End, 1984.

Kolodny, Annette. "Dancing Through the Minefield: Some Observations on the Theory, Practice, and Politics of a Feminist Literary Criticism." Showalter, *The New Feminist Criticism* 144–67.

———. "Some Notes on Defining a 'Feminist Literary Criticism.'" *Critical Inquiry* 2 (1975): 78.

Lovell, Terry, ed. *British Feminist Thought: A Reader.* Oxford: Basil Blackwell, 1990.

Meese, Elizabeth, and Alice Parker, eds. *The Difference Within: Feminism and Critical Theory.* Philadelphia: John Benjamins, 1989.

Miller, Nancy K., ed. *The Poetics of Gender.* New York: Columbia UP, 1986.

Millett, Kate. *Sexual Politics.* Garden City: Doubleday, 1970.

Moi, Toril. *Sexual/Textual Politics: Feminist Literary Theory.* New York: Methuen, 1985.

Rich, Adrienne. *On Lies, Secrets, and Silence: Selected Prose, 1966–1979.* New York: Norton, 1979.

Showalter, Elaine. "Toward a Feminist Poetics." Showalter, *The New Feminist Criticism* 125–43.

———, ed. *The New Feminist Criticism: Essays on Women, Literature, and Theory.* New York: Pantheon, 1985.

Stimpson, Catherine R. "Feminist Criticism." *Redrawing the Boundaries: The Transformation of English and American Literary Studies.* Ed. Stephen Greenblatt and Giles Gunn. New York: MLA, 1992. 251–70.

Tompkins, Jane. *Sensational Designs: The Cultural Work of American Fiction.* 1790–1860. Oxford: Oxford UP, 1985.

Warhol, Robyn, and Diane Price Herndl, eds. *Feminisms: An Anthology of Literary Theory and Criticism.* New Brunswick: Rutgers UP, 1991.

Weed, Elizabeth, ed. *Coming to Terms: Feminism, Theory, Politics.* New York: Routledge, 1989.

Woolf, Virginia. *A Room of One's Own.* New York: Harcourt, 1929.

Women's Writing and Creativity

Abel, Elizabeth, ed. *Writing and Sexual Difference.* Chicago: U of Chicago P, 1982.

Berg, Temma F., ed. *Engendering the Word: Feminist Essays in Psychosexual Poetics.* Co-ed. Anna Shannon Elfenbein, Jeanne Larsen, and Elisa Kay Sparks. Urbana: U of Illinois P, 1989.

DuPlessis, Rachel Blau. *The Pink Guitar: Writing as Feminist Practice.* New York Routledge, 1990.

Finke, Laurie. *Feminist Theory, Women's Writing.* Ithaca: Cornell UP, 1992.

Gilbert, Sandra M., and Susan Gubar. *The Madwoman in the Attic: The Woman Writer and the Nineteenth-Century Literary Imagination.* New Haven: Yale UP, 1979.

Homans, Margaret. *Bearing the Word: Language and Female Experience in Nineteenth-Century Women's Writing.* Chicago: U of Chicago P, 1986.

Jacobus, Mary, ed. *Women Writing and Writing about Women.* New York: Barnes, 1979.

Miller, Nancy K. *Subject to Change: Reading Feminist Writing.* New York: Columbia UP, 1988.

Newton, Judith Lowder. *Women, Power and Subversion: Social Strategies in British Fiction, 1778–1860.* Athens: U of Georgia P, 1981.

Poovey, Mary. *The Proper Lady and the Woman Writer: Ideology as Style in the Works of Mary Wollstonecraft, Mary Shelley, and Jane Austen.* Chicago: U of Chicago P, 1984.

Showalter, Elaine. *A Literature of Their Own: British Women Novelists from Brontë to Lessing*. Princeton: Princeton UP, 1977.

Spacks, Patricia Meyer. *The Female Imagination*. New York: Knopf, 1975.

Feminism, Race, Class, and Nationality

Anzaldúa, Gloria. *Borderlands: La Frontera = The New Mestiza*. San Francisco: Spinsters/Aunt Lute, 1987.

Christian, Barbara. *Black Feminist Criticism: Perspectives on Black Women Writers*. New York: Pergamon, 1985.

hooks, bell. *Ain't I a Woman?: Black Women and Feminism*. Boston: South End, 1981.

———. *Black Looks: Race and Representation*. Boston: South End, 1992.

Kaplan, Cora. *Sea Changes: Essays on Culture and Feminism*. London: Verso, 1986.

Moraga, Cherrie, and Gloria Anzaldúa. *This Bridge Called My Back: Writings by Radical Women of Color*. New York: Kitchen Table, 1981.

Newton, Judith, and Deborah Rosenfelt, eds. *Feminist Criticism and Social Change: Sex, Class, and Race in Literature and Culture*. New York: Methuen, 1985.

Pryse, Marjorie, and Hortense Spillers, eds. *Conjuring: Black Women, Fiction, and Literary Tradition*. Bloomington: Indiana UP, 1985.

Robinson, Lillian S. *Sex, Class, and Culture*. 1978. New York: Methuen, 1986.

Smith, Barbara. "Towards a Black Feminist Criticism." Showalter, *The New Feminist Criticism* 168–85.

Feminism and Postcoloniality

Emberley, Julia. *Thresholds of Difference: Feminist Critique, Native Women's Writings, Postcolonial Theory*. Toronto: U of Toronto P, 1993.

Mohanty, Chandra Talpade, Ann Russo, and Lourdes Torres, eds. *Third World Women and the Politics of Feminism*. Bloomington: Indiana UP, 1991.

Schipper, Mineke, ed. *Unheard Words: Women and Literature in Africa, the Arab World, Asia, the Caribbean, and Latin America*. London: Allison, 1985.

Spivak, Gayatri Chakravorty. *In Other Worlds: Essays in Cultural Politics.* New York: Methuen, 1987.

———. *Outside in the Teaching Machine.* New York: Routledge, 1993.

Trinh T. Minh-ha. *Woman, Native, Other: Writing, Postcoloniality and Feminism.* Bloomington: Indiana UP, 1989.

Wilson, Armit. *Finding a Voice: Asian Women in Britain.* 1979. London: Virago, 1980.

Women's Self-Representation and Personal Criticism

Benstock, Shari, ed. *The Private Self: Theory and Practice of Women's Autobiographical Writings.* Chapel Hill: U of North Carolina P, 1988.

Gilmore, Leigh. *Autobiographics: A Feminist Theory of Self-Representation.* Ithaca: Cornell UP, 1994.

Miller, Nancy K. *Getting Personal: Feminist Occasions and Other Autobiographical Acts.* New York: Routledge, 1991.

Smith, Sidonie. *A Poetics of Women's Autobiography: Marginality and the Fictions of Self-Representation.* Bloomington: Indiana UP, 1988.

Feminist Film Theory

de Lauretis, Teresa. *Alice Doesn't: Feminism, Semiotics, Cinema.* Bloomington: Indiana UP, 1986.

Doane, Mary Ann. *Re-vision: Essays in Feminist Film Criticism.* Frederick: U Publications of America, 1984.

Modleski, Tania. *Feminism without Women: Culture and Criticism in a "Postfeminist" Age.* New York: Routledge, 1991.

Mulvey, Laura. *Visual and Other Pleasures.* Bloomington Indiana UP, 1989.

Penley, Constance, ed. *Feminism and Film Theory.* New York: Routledge, 1988.

Studies of Gender and Sexuality

Boone, Joseph A., and Michael Cadden, eds. *Engendering Men: The Question of Male Feminist Criticism.* New York: Routledge, 1990.

Butler, Judith. *Gender Trouble: Feminism and the Subversion of Identity.* New York: Routledge, 1990.

Chodorow, Nancy. *The Reproduction of Mothering: Psychoanalysis and the Sociology of Gender.* Berkeley: U of California P, 1978.

Claridge, Laura, and Elizabeth Langland, eds. *Out of Bounds: Male Writing and Gender(ed) Criticism.* Amherst: U of Massachusetts P, 1980.

de Lauretis, Teresa. *Technologies of Gender: Essays on Theory, Film, and Fiction.* Bloomington: Indiana UP, 1987.

Doane, Mary Ann. "Masquerade Reconsidered: Further Thoughts on the Female Spectator." *Discourse* 11 (1988–89): 42–54.

Eisenstein, Hester, and Alise Jardine, eds. *The Future of Difference.* Boston: G. K. Hall, 1980.

Flynn, Elizabeth A., and Patrocinio P. Schweickart, eds. *Gender and Reading: Essays on Readers, Texts, and Contexts.* Baltimore: Johns Hopkins UP, 1986.

Foucault, Michel. *The History of Sexuality: Volume I: An Introduction.* Trans. Robert Hurley. New York: Pantheon, 1978.

Kamuf, Peggy. "Writing Like a Woman." *Women and Language in Literature and Society.* New York: Praeger, 1980. 284–99.

Laqueur, Thomas. *Making Sex: Body and Gender from the Greeks to Freud.* Cambridge: Harvard UP, 1990.

Riviere, Joan. "Womanliness as a Masquerade." 1929. Rpt. in *Formations of Fantasy.* Ed. Victor Burgin, James Donald, and Cora Kaplan. London: Methuen, 1986. 35–44.

Rubin, Gayle. "Thinking Sex: Notes for a Radical Theory of the Politics of Sexuality." Abelove et al., *The Lesbian and Gay Reader* 3–44.

———. "The Traffic in Women: Notes on the 'Political Economy' of Sex." *Toward an Anthropology of Women.* Ed. Rayna R. Reiter. New York: Monthly Review, 1975. 157–210.

Schor, Naomi. "Feminist and Gender Studies." *Introduction to Scholarship in Modern Languages and Literatures.* Ed. Joseph Gibaldi. New York: MLA, 1992. 262–87.

Sedgwick, Eve Kosofsky. *Between Men: English Literature and Male Homosocial Desire.* New York: Columbia UP, 1988.

———. "Gender Criticism." *Redrawing the Boundaries: The Transformation of English and American Literary Studies.* Ed. Stephen Greenblatt and Giles Gunn. New York: MLA, 1992. 271–302.

Lesbian and Gay Criticism

Abelove, Henry, Michèle Aina Barale, and David Halperin, eds. *The Lesbian and Gay Studies Reader.* New York: Routledge, 1993.

Butters, Ronald, John M. Clum, and Michael Moon, eds. *Displacing Homophobia: Gay Male Perspectives in Literature and Culture.* Durham: Duke UP, 1989.

Craft, Christopher. *Another Kind of Love: Male Homosexual Desire in English Discourse, 1850–1920.* Berkeley: U of California P, 1994.

de Lauretis, Teresa. *The Practice of Love: Lesbian Sexuality and Perverse Desire.* Bloomington: Indiana UP, 1994.

Dollimore, Jonathan. *Sexual Dissidence: Augustine to Wilde, Freud to Foucault.* Oxford: Clarendon, 1991.

Fuss, Diana, ed. *Inside/Out: Lesbian Theories, Gay Theories.* New York: Routledge, 1991.

Garber, Marjorie. *Vested Interests: Cross-Dressing and Cultural Anxiety.* New York: Routledge, 1992.

Halperin, David M. *One Hundred Years of Homosexuality and Other Essays on Greek Love.* New York: Routledge, 1990.

Koestenbaum, Wayne. "Wilde's Hard Labor and the Birth of Gay Reading." *Engendering Men: The Question of Male Feminist Criticism.* Ed. Joseph A. Boone and Michael Cadden. New York: Routledge, 1990.

The Lesbian Issue. Special issue, *Signs* 9 (1984).

Martin, Robert K. *Hero, Captain, and Stranger: Male Friendship, Social Critique, and Literary Form in the Sea Novels of Herman Melville.* Chapel Hill: U of North Carolina P, 1986.

Munt, Sally, ed. *New Lesbian Criticism: Literary and Cultural Readings.* New York: Harvester Wheatsheaf, 1992.

Rich, Adrienne. "Compulsory Heterosexuality and Lesbian Existence." Ed. Elizabeth Abel and Emily K. Abel, *The "Signs" Reader* 139–68.

Stimpson, Catherine R. "Zero Degree Deviancy: The Lesbian Novel in English." *Critical Inquiry* 8 (1981): 363–79.

Weeks, Jeffrey. *Sexuality and Its Discontents: Meanings, Myths, and Modern Sexualities.* London: Routledge, 1985.

Wittig, Monique. "The Mark of Gender." Miller, *The Poetics of Gender* 63–73.

———. "One Is Not Born a Woman." *Feminist Issues* 1.2 (1981): 47–54.

———. *The Straight Mind and Other Essays.* Boston: Beacon, 1992.

Queer Theory

Butler, Judith. *Bodies That Matter: On the Discursive Limits of "Sex."* New York: Routledge, 1993.

Cohen, Ed. *Talk on the Wilde Side: Towards a Genealogy of Discourse on Male Sexualities.* New York: Routledge, 1993.

de Lauretis, Teresa, ed. Issue on Queer Theory, *differences* 3.2 (1991).

Sedgwick, Eve Kosofsky. *Epistemology of the Closet.* Berkeley: U of California P, 1991.

———. *Tendencies.* Durham: Duke UP, 1993.

Sinfield, Alan. *Cultural Politics — Queer Reading.* Philadelphia: U of Pennsylvania P, 1994.

———. *The Wilde Century: Effeminacy, Oscar Wilde, and the Queer Moment.* New York: Columbia UP, 1994.

Warner, Michael, ed. *Fear of a Queer Planet: Queer Politics and Social Theory.* Minneapolis: U of Minnesota P, 1993.

Other Feminist and Gender Approaches to Hawthorne and *The Scarlet Letter*

Barlowe, Jamie. "Rereading Women: Hester Prynne-sism and the Scarlet Mob of Scribblers. *American Literary History* 9 (1997): 197–225.

Baym, Nina. "The Significance of Plot in Hawthorne's Romances." *Ruined Eden of the Present: Hawthorne, Melville, and Poe.* Ed. G. R. Thompson and Virgil Lokke. West Lafayette: Purdue UP, 1981. 49–70.

———. "Thwarted Nature: Nathaniel Hawthorne as Feminist." *American Novelists Revisited: Essays in Feminist Criticism.* Ed. Fritz Fleischmann. Boston: Hall, 1982. 58–77.

Budick, Emily. "We Damned-If-You-Do, Damned-If-You-Don't Mob of Scribbling Scholars." *American Literary History* 9 (1997): 233–37.

Derrick, Scott S. "'A Curious Subject of Observation': Homoeroticism, The Body, and Authorship in Hawthorne's *The Scarlet Letter.*" *Novel: A Forum on Fiction* 28 (1995): 308–26.

Fryer, Judith. *The Faces of Eve: Women in the Nineteenth-Century American Novel.* New York: Oxford UP, 1976.

Herzog, Kristin. *Women, Ethics, and Exotics: Images of Power in Mid-Nineteenth-Century Fiction.* Knoxville: U of Tennessee P, 1983.

Kamuf, Peggy. "Hawthorne's Genres: The Letter of the Law *Appliquée. After Strange Texts: The Role of Theory in the Study of Literature.* Ed. Gregory S. Jay and David L. Miller. Tuscaloosa: U of Alabama P, 1985. 69–84.

Martin, Robert K. "Hester Prynne, *C'est Moi:* Nathaniel Hawthorne and the Anxieties of Gender." Boone and Cadden, *Engendering Men.*

Person, Leland S. *Aesthetic Headaches: Women and a Masculine Poetics in Poe, Melville, and Hawthorne.* Athens: U of Georgia P, 1988.

Schriber, Mary Suzanne. *Gender and the Writer's Imagination: From Cooper to Wharton.* Lexington: UP of Kentucky, 1987.

FEMINIST AND GENDER PERSPECTIVES

SHARI BENSTOCK

The Scarlet Letter (a)dorée, or the Female Body Embroidered

> The word is understood only as an extension of the body which is there in the process of speaking. . . . To the extent that it does not know repression, femininity is the downfall of interpretation.
>
> – MICHELE MONTRELAY, "Inquiry into Femininity"

> As women our relationship to the past has been problematical. We have been every culture's core obsession (and repression).
>
> – ADRIENNE RICH, *Of Woman Born*

When the jail door is "flung open from within" and Hester Prynne "step[s] into the open air, as if by her own free-will," she stands, we are told, "fully revealed before the crowd" (p. 57 in this volume). She denies an initial impulse to cover the token of her shame, the scarlet letter from which the text takes its title, with the body of her infant daughter. Instead, Hester parades her sin, exhibiting baby and letter before the collective gaze of the Puritan community:

> she took the baby on her arm, and, with a burning blush, and yet a haughty smile, and a glance that would not be abashed, looked around at her townspeople and neighbours. On the breast of her gown, in fine red cloth, surrounded with an elaborate embroidery and fantastic flourishes of gold thread, appeared the letter A. (p. 57)

This gesture of revelation, like the exquisitely wrought letter itself, masks self-representation. Offering herself as an object of scrutiny to the crowd, Hester remains obscured to the degree that "her beauty shone out, and made a halo of the misfortune and ignominy in which she was enveloped" (p. 58). As Peggy Kamuf (79) has suggested, the *A* "so fantastically embroidered and illuminated upon her bosom" (p. 58) opens an inexhaustible chain of substitutions (adulteress, angel, able, adored, etc.) that includes Authority over her own identity, an authority that the letter protects.

The opening scene of *The Scarlet Letter* parades before the reader and the assembled Boston public the body of sin, or more accurately, woman's body as (emblem of) sin. The female body is both an agent of human reproduction and a field of representation, emblematized first by the scarlet letter on Hester's slate-gray gown and again at the story's end by the slate tombstone bearing the heraldic legend "ON A FIELD, SABLE, THE LETTER A, GULES" (p. 202). *The Scarlet Letter* exposes a relation between babies and words, between biological reproduction and symbolic representations. Puritan theocracy would suppress one element of this relation, symbolizing the baby as the sign of God's will in the universe ordered by patriarchal religious and civil law. Woman's body serves as the space where social, religious, and cultural values are inscribed (quite literally in Hester's case); moreover, it produces the very terms of that inscription: Pearl *is* the scarlet letter in human form (p. 90).

Hester Prynne, however, subverts the Puritan-patriarchal laws of meaning in two ways. First, she embroiders and embellishes the community's representational codes, thereby confusing them. The letter *A*, which is to stand as the sign of sexual fall, escapes by way of Hester's needle the interpretive code it would enforce, opening itself to a wholly other logic. It makes a spectacle of femininity, of female sexuality, of all that Puritan law hopes to repress. Second, Hester refuses to name her child's father, thereby placing Pearl — material sign of the mother's sin — outside the bo(u)nds of Puritan ideology. By her birth, which is represented textually as a form of mysterious regeneration, Pearl cannot circulate within the terms of symbolic, communal social-sexual exchange. Missing a father, the guiding term of paternal authority, she remains her "mother's child" (p. 96). Despite all efforts by the Puritan community to bring mother and daughter under the authority of God and man, Hester and Pearl remain resolutely outside patriarchal conventions.

Issues of gender, then, are at the very heart of the story told by *The Scarlet Letter:* the history of the letter, supposedly discovered by Hawthorne in the Custom-House, bears importantly on the questions the tale poses about narrative sources and symbolic powers as well as about the mystery of paternal origins that the story seeks to solve. The scarlet letter is passed from generation to generation by men, and Hawthorne feels burdened by "filial duty" to his "official ancestor," Jonathan Pue, to present again the tale of the letter. "Mr. Surveyor Pue" is the Custom-House official who "authorized and authenticated" the historical events on which the story is based (p. 44).

The tale itself, however, focuses attention on representations of *womanhood,* with special emphasis on Puritan efforts to regulate female sexuality within religious, legal, and economic structures. Puritan thought assigns the powers of naming, owning, and ordering to a paternal theological order, derived linearly (and literally) from the Word of God-the-Father. Divinity transcends biology; God-the-Father is Alpha and Omega, origin of life and its final meaning; the human body is corporeal matter to be transcended. As agents of human reproduction, women are subsumed by this symbolic order, which assigns weight and value to women's work.

Repeating a particularly misogynistic version of paternal ordering, *The Scarlet Letter* draws a relation between mere storytelling and the domestic art of embroidery. In "The Custom-House," the autobiographical introduction to the text, Hawthorne reveals his fear of losing his "imaginative faculty," or "fancy" (pp. 46, 47). The text that follows, which he claims to have found and "dress[ed] up" as a romance (p. 44), fashions a tale around the "fantastic" artistry of Hester Prynne's needlework skills (p. 58). By various means, then, Hawthorne suggests that literary genres are marked by gender, displaying forms of sexual-textual difference not only in their subject matter but also in their structures and narrative methods. *The Scarlet Letter* prompts us to ask: does the feminine bear the same relation to storytelling as it does to embroidery or the female body to sin? Following recent developments in feminist theory, I will argue that the feminine, so powerfully at work in Hawthorne's tale, works not to exploit oppositional structures of sexual-textual difference but rather to expose the fictional nature of these modes, revealing absolute sexual difference as a fantasy of patriarchal oppositional and hierarchical logic. I refer to this figure as the "textual feminine," since it reveals itself in language, where it both supports traditional notions of femininity and subverts these powerful representations of woman-in-the-feminine. Fantasies of the feminine undergird classic Western models of narrative, which the textual feminine — represented in Hawthorne's text by the gilded letter *A* — elaborates, ornaments, embellishes, and seeks to undermine.

The patriarchal construction of femininity, based on masculine fantasies of the female body, is the sign under which sexual difference parades itself in our culture. This spectacle of womanhood, the female body dressed as icon or effigy, wards off patriarchal fears of female sexuality. The Puritan community means to make Hester play such a role, but its efforts fail because she — like all women — embodies an "other" femininity that cannot be fully controlled within the terms of phallic law. As Jacqueline Rose explains, this other feminine, which is not visible to the eye of man, is the place where representation is obscured and where interpretation fails. Refusing to expose itself to public view or to mouth the words it has been culturally assigned, this "other" femininity unsettles orders of patriarchal logic, rendering as nonsense the stories by which culture explains itself to itself. The age-old stories of men's adventures at war and on the high seas (narratives Hawthorne overheard while a customs inspector) and the tales men invent of women — adored as virgins, feared as witches, despised as spinsters, or exploited and abused as wives and prostitutes — assume new meanings according to these "other" terms. The sexual-textual feminine confounds the structures of traditional narratives and circumscribes their limits.

The scarlet letter itself reveals how this double logic works. As Alpha, first letter of the alphabet, it challenges the conventions of meaning and origins of words. For example, if the letter is to mean "Adulteress," all other words beginning with the letter *A* must be repressed: for the *A* to signify, it must serve as a sign of *absolute difference*. By not assigning the *A* to a single word that would inscribe a transcendent meaning, *The Scarlet Letter* opens itself to a profusion of possible meanings that the author and seamstress elaborate. By their silence, Hawthorne and Hester undo traditional methods of interpretation: he refuses to assign the letter to a word (as she refuses to name her baby's father); she embellishes the letter, making it an item of adornment, representation of an extravagant, excessive femininity. Because the letter refuses to call out its name and thereby submit to the law by which meaning (like paternity) can be assigned, the letter comes to signify the fantasy of sexual difference. Some members of the Puritan community interpret it to mean "able" or "angel"; a contemporary feminist might see in its fertile and "gorgeous luxuriance of fancy" (p. 57) an emblem of the female sexual organ itself, a perverse revision of seventeenth-century sexual-textual optics. To the degree that *The Scarlet Letter* is marked by the textual feminine, it makes a fiction of patriarchal, not to say Puritan, modes of interpretation: it is the ador(n)ed emblem of their downfall.

OF GARDENS, GOLD, AND LITTLE GIRLS

> At some future day, it may be, I shall remember a few scattered fragments and broken paragraphs, and write them down, and find the letters turn to gold upon the page.
>
> – NATHANIEL HAWTHORNE (p. 48)

By the same rhetorical gestures that *The Scarlet Letter* exposes the effects of secret (sexual) sin to the light of noonday sun, it also hides the cultural assumptions that have historically undergirded representations of women. Feminist criticism demonstrates that these assumptions are not "natural" or God-given, as cultures and religions would have us believe, but are socially and economically constructed to further the ends of patriarchy. Patriarchy defines social gender roles for women and men from biological sex functions, thus keeping women within the confines of domesticity and under the husband's power as familial patriarch. Because reproduction of the species takes place through the woman's body, she is seen as closer to "nature," while man is the agent of society and culture, which he creates through symbolic representations of the natural environment. The power of symbols and signs to enforce social order is manifest in Puritan thought, where the spiritual and immaterial is figured by signs and portents and where all natural occurrences (lightning, thunder) take on symbolic meaning. Woman's body, whose sexual organs are hidden internally and whose reproductive operations remain mysterious, becomes a vessel to be filled with symbolic meaning: virgin/adulteress, madonna/mother, whore/witch. Gabriele Schwab suggests that witchcraft was a male invention, born of the fear of sexually powerful or independent women who represented natural forces that needed to be "tamed."

These dichotomous and oppressive representations of woman are the product of the binary structure of Western thought, the earliest forms being those from fifth-century Greek culture, which rewrote earlier agricultural myths. In the most ancient myths, both the land and the female body were inherently fertile, giving birth to seeds and babies by spontaneous generation. The triangular shape of the letter *A*, for instance, reproduces the sign for the Nile River Delta, an ancient pre-Christian symbol of female fertility and rebirth of the land. Early myths of reproduction linked woman's body to the earth: regeneration of field and family were seen as similar activities associated with female fertility. Later Platonic versions of reproduction, however, imaged the female body as a field in need of ploughing and planting. In these myths, regenerative power was transferred to the male. Penis and plow were instruments of insemination with which man cultivated woman's empty furrow. According to Page DuBois, this later metaphor of woman's body as empty field and open furrow underwrites Western notions of sexual difference enforced through cultural symbols, ritual practices, and agricultural methods. Cultivation of the land is equated with civilization, man's dominion over the earth inscribed by field and furrow.

The shift in Greek thought can be accounted for by the social reorganization of the city-states, especially the move away from religious superstitions associated with the ancient gods of earth and environment toward the new written laws of the community, inscripted and enacted by male citizens. The Calvinist religion as examined by *The Scarlet Letter* invokes this world of archaic myth, which gives symbolic power to natural (and inexplicable) occurrences, and also enforces a *communitas* supported by rationality and civility governed by the Puritan selectmen. Ancient notions of female fertility and sexual power provide the (repressed) grounds on which Puritan law constrains sexuality within the bonds of marriage, thereby protecting paternity rights and keeping the "feminine" within the domestic. The question of paternity that the community seeks to answer encompasses both the natural world of forest wilderness and the civilized world of the community. The drama of *The Scarlet Letter* takes place across a dividing line between forest, where the sexual act took place and which shelters the secret of the child's paternity, and village, where the material effects of the sexual union are exposed to communal speculation.

The "untamed forest" of the New World represents a "moral wilderness," a space of sexual and ethnic otherness where Indians roam and the "witch" Mistress Hibbins meets the Black Man. It is a "wild, free atmosphere of an unredeemed, unchristianized, lawless region" (p. 160), a space to be colonized and cultivated by Puritan *communitas*, with its basis in patriarchal and capitalist ideologies. Even within the village limits, however, the landscape resists all but the most primitive efforts at cultivation. Governor Bellingham fails to reproduce in the hard soil his "native English taste for ornamental gardening" (p. 94). Cabbages grow in plain sight of his garden-walk, and a pumpkin vine rooted outside the garden proper "had run across the intervening space, and deposited one of its gigantic products directly beneath the hall-window" (p. 94). A number of symbolic associations attach to this rude image of reproductive excess. Vegetation that overruns its boundaries emblematizes unrestrained female sexuality, which is believed to know no limits or boundaries. In this instance, the cabbages and pumpkin invoke folk mythology of human origins, where babies are found under cabbage leaves. The gigantic pumpkin in the Governor's garden represents not only reproductive excess but capitalist productivity, the ability of gold to reproduce itself: "this great lump of vegetable gold was as rich an ornament as New England earth would offer him" (p. 94). This is one of many places in the text in which capitalist-patriarchal gains are figured as ornament and sumptuary excess. Within the value systems of the story, Hester Prynne's needlework elaborates a gendered relation of economic (re)production to ornament in Puritan society: lacking financial support from her husband or from the father of her child, she produces by her womanly art the gold necessary to support herself and Pearl.

The failure of civilization to bring nature under its control is even more dramatically symbolized by the wild rosebush that blooms in the overgrown grass-plot in front of the prison from which Hester emerges. The rosebush gives rise to various stories about its origins, including speculation that "it had sprung up under the footsteps of the sainted Ann Hutchinson, as she entered the prison-door" (p. 54). Ann Hutchinson, founder of the antinomian sect (which means, literally, "against the law"), figures an alternate history for Hester Prynne, a lost story of female independence and resistance to patriarchal law. Hester's daughter, in response to Pastor Wilson's catechism ("Canst thou tell me, my child, who made thee?" [p. 97]), traces her origins to this rosebush. Rather than attributing her origins to God the father, as church doctrine decrees, Pearl returns to an archaic, preliterate story, substituting roses for cabbages: "the child finally announced that she had not been made at all, but had been plucked by her mother off the bush of wild roses, that grew by the prison-door" (p. 97). In this schema, Pearl is not her mother's daughter but rather a symbolic descendant of Ann Hutchinson.

Pearl is certainly a rarer, more exotic fruit than anything the Governor's garden can produce, and her radiant beauty is intensified by the mystery of her origins: a "lovely and immortal flower," she "had sprung . . . out of the rank luxuriance of a guilty passion" (p. 81). If in the hermeneutics of Hawthorne's romance Hester's gold embroidery signifies spiritual adornment, the "application of a design" on "the fabric of experience" as Evan Carton claims (197–98), then Pearl represents the material sign of Hester's sin, the human matter that invites Puritan speculation. The community imbues her physical features and infant gestures with meaning, but Pearl's beauty (which is described through sets of opposites: pale/radiant, shadow/light, crimson/gold, etc.) and her quixotic personality baffle the citizenry. The name Pearl itself seems inappropriate to a child of ruby or red rose complexion (p. 96). The profound duality that the community imparts to Pearl's character — angel/devil — leads to the scene in the governor's hall when Hester is forced to call on Arthur Dimmesdale in support of her efforts to retain custody of her child. The circumstances of this confrontation between Hester and the community elders bear close scrutiny.

The news of the Boston community's interest in Pearl's relationship to her mother reaches Hester by word of mouth, that is, by gossip: "It had reached her ears, that there was a design on the part of some of the leading inhabitants, cherishing the more rigid order of principles in religion and government, to deprive her of her child" (p. 89). Public attention is drawn to the child by her fantastic dress, the product of Hester's needle, and her untamed and impulsive behavior. The reasons offered for the intervention of civic and religious authorities into a domestic scene, however, are contradictory and constitute a failure of the hermeneutic project that would attach a single meaning to Pearl's presence in Hester's life:

> On the supposition that Pearl, as already hinted, was of demon origin, these good people not unreasonably argued that a Christian interest in *the mother's soul* required them to remove such a stumbling-block from her path. If the child, on the other hand, were really capable of moral and religious growth, and possessed the elements of ultimate salvation, then, surely, it would enjoy all the fairer prospect of these advantages by being transferred to *wiser and better guardianship* than Hester Prynne's. (p. 89; emphasis added)

Without evidence of the child's origin, the community cannot judge her capacity for moral growth. Following the oppositional structure of Puritan thought, the absent paternal signifier can mean one of two things: either Pearl's father is the devil, the "Black Man" who it is rumored impregnated Hester in the woods, or God the Father, in which case her soul is "capable of moral and religious growth" (p. 89). If Pearl belongs to the devil, then it is her *mother's* soul that is in danger; if the daughter belongs to God, then the mother's sinful presence in her life is a stumbling block. That there is no clear material sign of Pearl's spiritual state (or biological paternity), no name-of-the-father to identify her lineage, leaves the community without the means of interpretation.

Pleading before the magistrate and church fathers, Hester claims that Pearl plays a double role in her life: "She is my happiness!— she is my torture, none the less! Pearl keeps me here in life! Pearl punishes me too!" (p. 98). When she asks Dimmesdale to support her cause, she asks him to speak from his knowledge of her soul, bringing to bear his pastoral and spiritual authority. In this moment, the double aspect of Pearl's beauty — which is described as both "pale" and "wild" — is divided between the parents, visible evidence of the contrast between Hester and Dimmesdale: she is "provoked . . . to little less than madness" while he is "pale . . . holding his hand over his heart" (p. 98). The child's opposed nature might be reconciled into a single sign had the authorities the means by which to interpret it, knowledge of the paternal signifier. Roger Chillingworth calls on philosophy to answer the question: "It is easy to see the mother's part in her. Would it be beyond a philosopher's research, think ye, gentlemen, to analyze that child's nature, and, from its make and mould, to give a shrewd guess at the father?" (p. 100). The Church fathers reject "profane philosophy," elevating the question to the higher authority of divinity: "leave the mystery as we find it, unless Providence reveal it of its own accord." This gesture does not resolve the mystery but lifts it, unresolved, to higher paternal authority, an authority that gives a "title" to "every good Christian man . . . to show a father's kindness towards the poor, deserted babe" (p. 100).

The scene in the governor's hall reveals a gendered relation between spirit and matter. First, the question of paternity is taken out of the provenance of law (represented by Governor Bellingham) or of philosophy and medicine (Roger Chillingworth) and left to religious authority, which removes it to yet a higher authority. At first glance this decision seems to benefit Hester's rights to custody of her child, returning the question of paternity to the realm of the spiritual, which makes a legal fiction of it. Hester aids the process by remaining silent about her relationship with Dimmesdale, a relationship she claims before the authorities to be solely spiritual. The reasons for her silence are wholly mysterious and never resolved within the text; by keeping silent, however, she exposes herself and her child to possible economic hardship and allows Dimmesdale to ignore the material reality of her situation. Indeed, Dimmesdale never fully recognizes the material existence of Pearl. The riches Pearl later inherits are at the bequest of Roger Chillingworth, Hester's wronged husband. These riches, of course, account for the "very material change in the public estimation" (p. 200) of little Pearl, providing evidentiary proof of her value in God's eyes. That proof comes not through the mother, although Hester is finally deemed by the community an admirable mother, but through an (absent, dead) paternal line, from the man who should have fathered Hester's children but could not. The phallic power that Chillingworth lacked in life, its failure ascribed to the intellectual and ascetic life he led, is transformed in death through the legacy of his properties in England and the New World. Dimmesdale's unacknowledged and illicit legacy is Pearl herself.

MOTHER AS MATTER

> We live in a civilization in which the *consecrated* (religious or secular) representation of femininity is subsumed under maternity. Under close examination, however, this maternity turns out to be an adult (male and female) fantasy of a lost continent.
>
> – JULIA KRISTEVA, "Stabat Mater"

Before the authorities in the governor's hall, Hester declares that Dimmesdale has sympathies that other men lack, ascribing to him knowledge of maternal matters: "thou knowest what is in my heart, and what are a mother's rights, and how much the stronger they are, when that mother has but her child and the scarlet letter" (p. 98). Her claim is that maternal ties and mother rights are stronger in the absence of the father, and she charges Dimmesdale to "look to it," that is, to see to it that she not lose her child. Although Dimmesdale's physical weakness feminizes him (he seems hardly able to support the secret phallic signifier he is supposed to bear), he argues forcefully for her in his "sweet, tremulous, but powerful" voice (p. 98). Hester's strength, drawn in no small measure from her maternal role, overshadows her aging husband and her weakened lover, leading many critics (D. H. Lawrence foremost among them) to conclude that she is a witch figure who saps the phallic power invested in these men, unsexing herself in the process. The Puritan code demands that she relinquish her femininity as the price of survival; she assumes a serenity and calm that appear as "marble coldness" (p. 134). The scarlet letter, whose rich embroidery in other circumstances might be read as a sign of feminine adornment, is here the sign that Hester has forfeited her place in the normal exchange of women among men, where fathers hand daughters to husbands. The letter is Hester's "passport into regions where other women dared not tread" (p. 158).

Hester's "lost" sexual nature is transferred to her daughter, whose passionate temperament apparently knows no repression. Indeed, Pearl appears to harbor secret knowledge associated with the scarlet letter, knowledge that Hester both fears and tries to discover in her daughter's regard. Gabriele Schwab argues that the mother makes the child mirror her own fears. Hester tries through her needlework "to create an analogy between the object of her affection [Pearl], and the emblem of her guilt and torture [the letter]" (p. 90). Mother and daughter reflect each other and read each other as signs: Hester searches for evidence of an "original sin," the sin that the mother confers on the daughter through the circumstances of her conception; Pearl searches for the meaning of the scarlet letter, which she sees as the key to her mother's identity and the source of her own origins. In response to Pearl's insistent questions, Hester claims that she wears the scarlet letter "for the sake of its gold thread" (p. 145). This enigmatic response, which the child does not accept, hints that the *A* is worn for adornment and that the gold embroidery, not the letter, carries meaning. When Hester flings the letter aside in the scene by the brook, Pearl cannot recognize her *as mother* and refuses her insistent demands for recognition. By this time the effects of the scarlet letter are already lodged within the daughter's heart. Hester has succeeded in turning her daughter into a symbol, an image of the mother's (suppressed) sexual nature, by dressing her in the crimson and gold colors of the letter.

If phallic authority and power are handed from father to son along a patriarchal chain of entitlement, mothers hand on to daughters a divided feminine sexuality scored by repressive social and cultural prescriptions. The myth of an unrestrained feminine libido that operates *independently* of cultural codes is a male fantasy-fear whose counterpart is the feminist dream of an idealized primary bond between mother and infant that exists prior to and outside of the social-cultural frame. Society charges fathers with bringing their children — sons and daughters — to conscious awareness of power structures under patriarchal law: boys must learn to uphold the (phallic) law; girls must learn to submit to it. According to psychoanalysts Nicholas Abraham and Maria Torok, the mother's gift (and burden) to her children is the repressed maternal unconscious; although communicated in silence, it becomes part of the child's language and the core to which the child's own repressions will be added. This maternal unconscious becomes the center of the daughter's psychosexual identity, whereas for sons it represents the feminine that the phallic must overcome.

Hawthorne's text dramatizes this psychological passage by way of the scarlet letter, the sign by which Hester passes on to Pearl the patriarchy's double message about sin and seduction. Feminist analysis would see the letter as agent of a *gendered* psychosexual identity. Under its auspices Hester must relinquish her individuality (as woman) to become a generalized symbol of "woman's frailty and sinful passion" (p. 75) — Woman. In a passage that describes Hester's transformation from person to pedagogical tool for Puritan ideology, we learn by oblique reference that the baby we see her holding on the scaffold is a girl: "Thus the young and pure would be taught to look at her, with the scarlet letter flaming on her breast, — at her, the child of honorable parents, — at her, the mother of a babe, that *would hereafter be a woman,* — at her, who had once been innocent, — as *the figure, the body, the reality of sin*" (p. 75; emphasis added). The baby is not yet a woman (womanhood in Western culture is attained only through sexual maturity), but the ways in which she will *become* woman make gender an issue in which the community has an interest. By the circumstance of her birth and the stigma of the scarlet letter, Pearl already inhabits a sexual-textual body: the body that gave birth to her and nurtures her, the mother who will instruct her in the ways of womanhood, figure the body and reality of sin.

The relationship of mother to child in *The Scarlet Letter* has been overlooked by traditional critics whose interpretations of the text center on the absent figure of the father and the question of paternity. However, early in the text this relationship is invoked in reference to the most powerful myth of maternity in the West, the Virgin and child, a myth with pagan roots that replaced earlier metaphors of the female body as the spontaneously regenerating earth. The image of virgin mother and holy child that dominates religious iconography is alluded to in the opening scene of *The Scarlet Letter.* At one stroke Hawthorne overlays the Christian myth on its pagan antecedents and supplants Catholic belief with Puritan revisions and purification of Papist excess. A Papist, we are told, might see in the spectacle of Hester and her baby on the scaffold "the image of Divine Maternity" (p. 60). Hester's baby has not yet been assigned gender by the text, but the infant that the Madonna cradles is a male, the son of God.

There is more than mere irony at work in this textual reference to Mary and Jesus, to the circumstances of Immaculate Conception through the Word of the Holy Ghost. All that the child represents in the images of Divine Maternity depends on an invisible, spiritual relationship to

God, mankind's origin and final end. The image of maternity that dominates our religious-cultural history is this image of mother and son, repeated in the Pietà. The spiritual transference of power takes place across Mary's body; she is the mat(t)er through which the spirit of God passes into humankind. God's word is the agent of the Immaculate Conception, and, as Julia Kristeva argues, this method of impregnation escapes not only the biological, human condition that Christ must transcend but also avoids the inevitable equation of sex with death (Kristeva 103). Hester and her baby represent a corrupted version of the Virgin Mary–Holy Child icon, of course, but the differences between these sacred and profane visions of motherhood are drawn textually through similar images. The Virgin's halo signifies her special place among women ("alone of all her sex"), while Hester's beauty "made a halo of the misfortune and ignominy in which she was enveloped" (p. 58). Commenting on Hester, a Puritan "goodwife" declares, "This woman has brought shame upon us all, and ought to die" (p. 56). Dressed in blue and white, the Virgin displays the colors of holiness and purity, while Hester is draped in somber gray, appropriate to her status as sinner. Kristeva comments that representations of the virginal body reduce female sexuality to "a mere implication," exposing only "the ear, the tears, and the breasts" (108). Hester reveals even less of herself, her entire body shrouded in gray, her hair covered by a tightfitting cap, her breasts shielded by the scarlet letter. Hester Prynne stands before the crowd not "fully revealed" (p. 57) as the text claims, but fully concealed, her sexual body hidden by the cultural text that inscripts her. Only when she unclasps the scarlet letter from her bosom and removes the cap that confines her hair is the sexual power of her body revealed synecdochically — that is, by mere implication.

These images of maternity inscribe sexual difference around the veiled figure of the mother's body. Daughters read the mother's body as sexual text differently than do sons. Sons, including the Son of God, pass by way of the mother's body into the world of the fathers, whose work they carry on in culture and society. For the son, the mother's body inscribes the myth of sexual difference and the space of an originary otherness: it textualizes alienation and desire. For the daughter, however, the mother's body emblematizes her biological-cultural fate, her place in the reproductive chain. The female body is also the locus of patriarchal fears and sexual longing, its fertile dark continent bound and cloaked. It is a space of shame, of castration. For the daughter, the maternal body maps both her past and future; it is a space of repetition.

Pearl enters this space, however, only to escape seemingly unscathed her own fate as the living emblem of sinful, shameful passion. She slips through the umbilical knot that ties representation to repetition. Made heir to Chillingworth's wealth, she comes to stand in the place of the son, one paternal figure standing in for another, the absent (and unacknowledged) father. The sign of Pearl's altered status is her material wealth, which rewrites the maternal script: she grows up to become "the richest heiress of her day" (pp. 199–200), a circumstance that brings about "a very material change in the public estimation" of her. Material riches controvert notions of Pearl as an "elf-child" or "demon offspring" and open the possibility of her full participation in Puritan life: "had the mother and child remained here, little Pearl, at a marriageable period of life, might have mingled her wild blood with the lineage of the devoutest Puritan among them all" (p. 200). Pearl's future and final end remain matters of speculation among Salem gossips, however. Pearl leaves the Puritan community, and her mother — who returns in old age, still wearing the scarlet letter — remains silent about the circumstances of her daughter's life.

If Pearl insists that the scarlet letter remain with the mother and refuses its message for herself, Hester hands the scarlet letter on to Hawthorne, for whom the "frayed and defaced" cloth calls forth his own repressed sexual anxieties and the feared loss of his storytelling skills. The faded symbol, which Hawthorne finds to hold "some deep meaning . . . most worthy of interpretation" (p. 43), communicates to his "sensibilities" a subtle, subliminal message. The message is never directly stated but remains bound to the "forgotten art" of Hester's cross-stitch that embellishes the letter. Hawthorne, who has felt his imaginative abilities fading the longer he toils in the Custom-House for "Uncle Sam's gold" (which he refers to as "the Devil's wages," p. 48), finds himself haunted by the "rag of scarlet cloth" (p. 43). Hester's story becomes the subject of his meditations as he paces "to and fro across my room, or traversing, with a hundredfold repetition, the long extent . . . of the Custom-House" (p. 45). Hawthorne's steps retrace the golden cross-stitch that frames the letter.

"The Custom-House" records Hawthorne's hope to transcribe the stories he heard daily there, tales of the sea told by inspectors and sea captains who sat before the fire. Although he muses that "at some future day" these "scattered fragments and broken paragraphs" may "turn to gold upon the page" (p. 48), he rejects the men's stories, claiming that their style and coloring outdistance his weakened faculties

(p. 47). These tales of adventures, whose roots extend to the classical epic, defeat Hawthorne's narrative powers. They are a sign that work in the Custom-House threatens to unman him (p. 48). To take up the woman's story, however, would require quite different storytelling skills and carry certain risks that Hawthorne only dimly perceives in the "tarnished mirror" of his imagination (p. 45). Sexual-textual risk for Hawthorne is always associated with financial gain, with the effort to turn words into gold. His rage against the hoard of "female scribblers" who wrote novels was in no small measure due to their financial success. Thus he transcribes Surveyor Pue's authorized version of Hester's story within the frame of romance, a genre entirely separate from the novel of daily life and a form that elevates the ordinary and domestic nearer to the "imaginative" and mysterious (p. 46). Hawthorne is able to write under the auspices of the textual feminine while carefully distancing himself from the material realities of sexual difference. From the perspective of his Puritan forefathers (William and John Hathorne, for example, who were famous for persecuting witches and heretics), "storytelling" is a "worthless" even "disgraceful" occupation (p. 27). Announcing himself as "editor, or very little more" of Hester's story (p. 23), Hawthorne nonetheless attaches his signature to the text, thus turning her gold embroidery to his financial gain while paying his filial debt to Surveyor Pue and rewriting his relationship to his Puritan forebears. Within the curves and flourishes of that signature, the fantasy of sexual-textual difference is both repeated and reversed, erasing the grounds on which interpretation might stake its claim to any final authority.

WORKS CITED

Abraham, Nicholas, and Maria Torok. *L'ecorce et le noyau*. 2nd ed. Paris: Flammarion, 1987.

Benstock, Shari. *Textualizing the Feminine: Essays on the Limits of Genre*. Norman: U of Oklahoma P, 1991.

Carton, Evan. *The Rhetoric of American Romance*. Baltimore: Johns Hopkins UP, 1985.

DuBois, Page. *Sowing the Body: Psychoanalysis and Ancient Representations of Women*. Chicago: U of Chicago P, 1988.

Kamuf, Peggy. "Hawthorne's Genres: The Letter of the Law *Appliquée*." *After Strange Texts: The Role of Theory in the Study of*

Literature. Ed. Gregory S. Jay and David L. Miller. University: U of Alabama P, 1985. 69–84.

Kristeva, Julia. "Stabat Mater." *Tales of Love*. Trans. Leon S. Roudiez. New York: Columbia UP, 1987. 234–63.

Montrelay, Michele. "Inquiry into Femininity." *m/f* 1 (1978): 82–91.

Rich, Adrienne. *Of Woman Born*. New York: Norton, 1986.

Rose, Jacqueline. *Sexuality in the Field of Vision*. London: Verso, 1986.

Schwab, Gabriele. "Seduced by Witches: Nathaniel Hawthorne's *The Scarlet Letter* in the Context of New England Witchcraft Fictions." *Seduction and Theory: Readings of Gender, Representation, and Rhetoric*. Ed. Dianne Hunter. Champaign-Urbana: U of Illinois P, 1989. 170–91.

The New Historicism and *The Scarlet Letter*

WHAT IS THE NEW HISTORICISM?

The title of Brook Thomas's *The New Historicism and Other Old-Fashioned Topics* (1991) is telling. Whenever an emergent theory, movement, method, approach, or group gets labeled with the adjective "new," trouble is bound to ensue, for what is new today is either established, old, or forgotten tomorrow. Few of you will have heard of the band called "The New Kids on the Block." New Age bookshops and jewelry may seem "old hat" by the time this introduction is published. The New Criticism, or formalism, is just about the oldest approach to literature and literary study currently being practiced. The new historicism, by contrast, is *not* as old-fashioned as formalism, but it is hardly new, either. The term "new" eventually and inevitably requires some explanation. In the case of the new historicism, the best explanation is historical.

Although a number of influential critics working between 1920 and 1950 wrote about literature from a psychoanalytic perspective, the majority took what might generally be referred to as the historical approach. With the advent of the New Criticism, however, historically oriented critics almost seemed to disappear from the face of the earth. The dominant New Critics, or formalists, tended to treat literary works as if they were self-contained, self-referential objects. Rather than basing their interpretations on parallels between the text and historical contexts (such as the author's life or stated intentions in writing the work), these critics concentrated on the relationships *within* the text that give it its form and meaning. During the heyday of the New Criticism, concern about the interplay between literature and history virtually disappeared from literary discourse. In its place was a concern about intratextual repetition, particularly of images or symbols but also of rhythms and sound effects.

About 1970 the New Criticism came under attack by reader-response critics (who believe that the meaning of a work is not inherent in its internal form but rather is cooperatively produced by the reader and the text) and poststructuralists (who, following the philosophy of Jacques Derrida, argue that texts are inevitably self-contradictory and that we can find form in them only by ignoring or suppressing conflicting details or elements). In retrospect it is clear that, their outspoken opposition to the New Criticism notwithstanding, the reader-response critics and poststructuralists of the 1970s were very much *like* their formalist predecessors in two important respects: for the most part, they ignored the world beyond the text and its reader, and, for the most part, they ignored the historical contexts within which literary works are written and read.

Jerome McGann first articulated this retrospective insight in 1985, writing that "a text-only approach has been so vigorously promoted during the last thirty-five years that most historical critics have been driven from the field, and have raised the flag of their surrender by yielding the title 'critic,' and accepting the title 'scholar' for themselves" (*Inflections* 17). Most, but not all. The American Marxist Fredric Jameson had begun his 1981 book *The Political Unconscious* with the following two-word challenge: "Always historicize!" (9). Beginning about 1980, a form of historical criticism practiced by Louis Montrose and Stephen Greenblatt had transformed the field of Renaissance studies and begun to influence the study of American and English Romantic literature as well. And by the mid-1980s, Brook Thomas was working on an essay in which he suggests that classroom discussions of Keats's "Ode on a Grecian Urn" might begin with questions such as the following: Where would Keats have seen such an urn? How did a Grecian urn end up in a museum in England? Some very important historical and political realities, Thomas suggests, lie behind and inform Keats's definitions of art, truth, beauty, the past, and timelessness.

When McGann lamented the surrender of "most historical critics," he no doubt realized what is now clear to everyone involved in the study of literature. Those who had *not* yet surrendered — had not yet "yield[ed] the title 'critic'" to the formalist, reader-response, and post-structuralist "victors" (*Inflections* 17) — were armed with powerful new arguments and intent on winning back long-lost ground. Indeed, at about the same time that McGann was deploring the near-complete dominance of critics advocating the text-only approach, Herbert Lindenberger was sounding a more hopeful note: "It comes as something of a surprise," he wrote in 1984, "to find that history is making a powerful comeback" ("New History" 16).

We now know that history was indeed making a powerful comeback in the 1980s, although the word is misleading if it causes us to imagine that the historical criticism being practiced in the 1980s by Greenblatt and Montrose, McGann and Thomas, was the same as the historical criticism that had been practiced in the 1930s and 1940s. Indeed, if the word *new* still serves any useful purpose in defining the historical criticism of today, it is in distinguishing it from the old historicism. The new historicism is informed by the poststructuralist and reader-response theory of the 1970s, plus the thinking of feminist, cultural, and Marxist critics whose work was also "new" in the 1980s. New historicist critics are less fact- and event-oriented than historical critics used to be, perhaps because they have come to wonder whether the truth about what really happened can ever be purely and objectively known. They are less likely to see history as linear and progressive, as something developing toward the present or the future ("teleological"), and they are also less likely to think of it in terms of specific eras, each with a definite, persistent, and consistent *Zeitgeist* ("spirit of the times"). Consequently, they are unlikely to suggest that a literary text has a single or easily identifiable historical context.

New historicist critics also tend to define the discipline of history more broadly than it was defined before the advent of formalism. They view history as a social science and the social sciences as being properly historical. In *Historical Studies and Literary Criticism* (1985), McGann speaks of the need to make "sociohistorical" subjects and methods central to literary studies; in *The Beauty of Inflections: Literary Investigations in Historical Method and Theory* (1985), he links sociology and the future of historical criticism. "A sociological poetics," he writes, "must be recognized not only as relevant to the analysis of poetry, but in fact as central to the analysis" (62). Lindenberger cites anthropology as particularly useful in the new historical analysis of literature, especially anthropology as practiced by Victor Turner and Clifford Geertz.

Geertz, who has related theatrical traditions in nineteenth-century Bali to forms of political organization that developed during the same period, has influenced some of the most important critics writing the new kind of historical criticism. Due in large part to Geertz's anthropological influence, new historicists such as Greenblatt have asserted that literature is not a sphere apart or distinct from the history that is relevant to it. That is what the old criticism tended to do: present the background information you needed to know before you could fully appreciate the separate world of art. The new historicists have used what Geertz would call "thick description" to blur distinctions, not only between history and the other social sciences but also between background and foreground, historical and literary materials, political and poetical events. They have erased the old boundary line dividing historical and literary materials, showing that the production of one of Shakespeare's historical plays was a political act and historical event, while at the same time showing that the coronation of Elizabeth I was carried out with the same care for staging and symbol lavished on works of dramatic art.

In addition to breaking down barriers that separate literature and history, history and the social sciences, new historicists have reminded us that it is treacherously difficult to reconstruct the past as it really was, rather than as we have been conditioned by our own place and time to believe that it was. And they know that the job is utterly impossible for those who are unaware of that difficulty and insensitive to the bent or bias of their own historical vantage point. Historical criticism must be "conscious of its status as interpretation," Greenblatt has written (*Renaissance* 4). McGann obviously concurs, writing that "historical criticism can no longer make any part of [its] sweeping picture unselfconsciously, or treat any of its details in an untheorized way" (*Studies* 11).

Unselfconsciously and *untheorized* are the key words in McGann's statement. When new historicist critics of literature describe a historical change, they are highly conscious of, and even likely to discuss, the *theory* of historical change that informs their account. They know that the changes they happen to see and describe are the ones that their theory of change allows or helps them to see and describe. And they know, too, that their theory of change is historically determined. They seek to minimize the distortion inherent in their perceptions and representations by admitting that they see through preconceived notions; in other words, they learn to reveal the color of the lenses in the glasses that they wear.

Nearly everyone who wrote on the new historicism during the 1980s cited the importance of the late Michel Foucault. A French philosophical historian who liked to think of himself as an archaeologist of human knowledge, Foucault brought together incidents and phenomena from areas of inquiry and orders of life that we normally regard as being unconnected. As much as anyone, he encouraged the new historicist critic of literature to redefine the boundaries of historical inquiry.

Foucault's views of history were influenced by the philosopher Friedrich Nietzsche's concept of a *wirkliche* ("real" or "true") history that is neither melioristic (that is, "getting better all the time") nor metaphysical. Like Nietzsche, Foucault didn't see history in terms of a continuous development toward the present. Neither did he view it as an abstraction, idea, or ideal, as something that began "In the beginning" and that will come to THE END, a moment of definite closure, a Day of Judgment. In his own words, Foucault "abandoned [the old history's] attempts to understand events in terms of . . . some great evolutionary process" (*Discipline and Punish* 129). He warned a new generation of historians to be aware of the fact that investigators are themselves "situated." It is difficult, he reminded them, to see present cultural practices critically from within them, and because of the same cultural practices, it is extremely difficult to enter bygone ages. In *Discipline and Punish: The Birth of the Prison* (1975), Foucault admitted that his own interest in the past was fueled by a passion to write the history of the present.

Like Marx, Foucault saw history in terms of power, but his view of power probably owed more to Nietzsche than to Marx. Foucault seldom viewed power as a repressive force. He certainly did not view it as a tool of conspiracy used by one specific individual or institution against another. Rather, power represents a whole web or complex of forces; it is that which produces what happens. Not even a tyrannical aristocrat simply wields power, for the aristocrat is himself formed and empowered by a network of discourses and practices that constitute power. Viewed by Foucault, power is "positive and productive," not "repressive" and "prohibitive" (Smart 63). Furthermore, no historical event, according to Foucault, has a single cause; rather, it is intricately connected with a vast web of economic, social, and political factors.

A brief sketch of one of Foucault's major works may help clarify some of his ideas. *Discipline and Punish* begins with a shocking but accurate description of the public drawing and quartering of a Frenchman who had botched his attempt to assassinate King Louis XV in 1757. Foucault proceeds by describing rules governing the daily life of modern Parisian felons. What happened to torture, to punishment as public spectacle? he asks. What complex network of forces made it disappear? In working toward a picture of this "power," Foucault turns up many interesting puzzle pieces, such as the fact that in the early years of the nineteenth century, crowds would sometimes identify with the prisoner and treat the executioner as if *he* were the guilty party. But Foucault sets forth a related reason for keeping prisoners alive, moving punishment indoors, and changing discipline from physical torture into mental rehabilitation: colonization. In this historical period, people were needed to establish colonies and trade, and prisoners could be used for that purpose. Also, because these were politically unsettled times, governments needed infiltrators and informers. Who better to fill those roles than prisoners pardoned or released early for showing a willingness to be rehabilitated? As for rehabilitation itself, Foucault compares it to the old form of punishment, which began with a torturer extracting a confession. In more modern, "reasonable" times, psychologists probe the minds of prisoners with a scientific rigor that Foucault sees as a different kind of torture, a kind that our modern perspective does not allow us to see as such.

Thus, a change took place, but perhaps not as great a change as we generally assume. It may have been for the better or for the worse; the point is that agents of power didn't make the change because mankind is evolving and, therefore, more prone to perform good-hearted deeds. Rather, different objectives arose, including those of a new class of doctors and scientists bent on studying aberrant examples of the human mind. And where do we stand vis-à-vis the history Foucault tells? We are implicated by it, for the evolution of discipline as punishment into the study of the human mind includes the evolution of the "disciplines" as we now understand that word, including the discipline of history, the discipline of literary study, and now a discipline that is neither and both, a form of historical criticism that from the vantage point of the 1980s looked "new."

Foucault's type of analysis has been practiced by a number of literary critics at the vanguard of the back-to-history movement. One of them is Greenblatt, who along with Montrose was to a great extent responsible for transforming Renaissance studies in the early 1980s and revitalizing historical criticism in the process. Greenblatt follows Foucault's lead in interpreting literary devices as if they were continuous with all other representational devices in a culture; he therefore turns to scholars in other fields in order to better understand the workings of literature. "We wall off literary symbolism from the symbolic structures operative elsewhere," he writes, "as if art alone were a human creation, as if humans themselves were not, in Clifford Geertz's phrase, cultural artifacts" (*Renaissance* 4).

Greenblatt's name, more than anyone else's, is synonymous with the new historicism; his essay entitled "Invisible Bullets" (1981) has been said by Patrick Brantlinger to be "perhaps the most frequently cited example of New Historicist work" ("Cultural Studies" 45). An English professor at the University of California, Berkeley — the early academic home of the new historicism — Greenblatt was a founding editor of *Representations*, a journal published by the University of California Press that is still considered today to be *the* mouthpiece of the new historicism.

In *Learning to Curse* (1990), Greenblatt cites as central to his own intellectual development his decision to interrupt his literary education at Yale University by accepting a Fulbright fellowship to study in England at Cambridge University. There he came under the influence of the great Marxist cultural critic Raymond Williams, who made Greenblatt realize how much — and what — was missing from his Yale education. "In Williams' lectures," Greenblatt writes, "all that had been carefully excluded from the literary criticism in which I had been trained — who controlled access to the printing press, who owned the land and the factories, whose voices were being repressed as well as represented in literary texts, what social strategies were being served by the aesthetic values we constructed — came pressing back in upon the act of interpretation" (2).

Greenblatt returned to the United States determined not to exclude such matters from his own literary investigations. Blending what he had learned from Williams with poststructuralist thought about the indeterminacy or "undecidability" of meaning, he eventually developed a critical method that he now calls "cultural poetics." More tentative and less overtly political than cultural criticism, it involves what Thomas calls "the technique of montage. Starting with the analysis of a particular historical event, it cuts to the analysis of a particular literary text. The point is not to show that the literary text reflects the historical event but to create a field of energy between the two so that we come to see the event as a social text and the literary text as a social event" ("New Literary Historicism" 490). Alluding to deconstructor Jacques Derrida's assertion that "there is nothing outside the text," Montrose explains that the goal of this new historicist criticism is to show the "historicity of texts and the textuality of history" (Veeser 20).

The relationship between the cultural poetics practiced by a number of new historicists and the cultural criticism associated with Marxism is important, not only because of the proximity of the two approaches but also because one must recognize the difference between the two to understand the new historicism. Still very much a part of the contemporary critical scene, cultural criticism (sometimes called "cultural studies" or "cultural critique") nonetheless involves several tendencies more compatible with the old historicism than with the thinking of new historicists such as Greenblatt. These include the tendency to believe that history is driven by economics; that it is determinable even as it determines the lives of individuals; and that it is progressive, its dialectic one that will bring about justice and equality.

Greenblatt does not privilege economics in his analyses and views individuals as agents possessing considerable productive power. (He says that "the work of art is the product of a negotiation between a creator or class of creators . . . and the institutions and practices of a society" [*Learning* 158]: he also acknowledges that artistic productions are "intensely marked by the private obsessions of individuals," however much they may result from "collective negotiation and exchange" [*Negotiations* vii].) His optimism about the individual, however, should not be confused with optimism about either history's direction or any historian's capacity to foretell it. Like a work of art, a work of history is the negotiated product of a private creator and the public practices of a given society.

This does not mean that Greenblatt does not discern historical change, or that he is uninterested in describing it. Indeed, in works from *Renaissance Self-Fashioning from More to Shakespeare* (1980) to *Shakespearean Negotiations* (1988), he has written about Renaissance changes in the development of both literary characters and real people. But his view of change — like his view of the individual — is more Foucauldian than Marxist. That is to say, it is not melioristic or teleological. And, like Foucault, Greenblatt is careful to point out that any one change is connected with a host of others, no one of which may simply be identified as cause or effect, progressive or regressive, repressive or enabling.

Not all of the critics trying to lead students of literature back to history are as Foucauldian as Greenblatt. Some even owe more to Marx than to Foucault. Others, like Thomas, have clearly been more influenced by Walter Benjamin, best known for essays such as "The Work of Art in the Age of Mechanical Reproduction" (1936) and "Theses on the Philosophy of History" (1950). Still others — McGann, for example — have followed the lead of Soviet critic M. M. Bakhtin, who viewed literary works in terms of discourses and dialogues between the official, legitimate voices of a society and other, more challenging or critical voices echoing popular or traditional culture. In the "polyphonic" writings of Rabelais, for instance, Bakhtin found that the profane language of Carnival and other popular festivals offsets and parodies the "legitimate" discourses representing the outlook of the king, church, and socially powerful intellectuals of the day.

Moreover, there are other reasons not to consider Foucault the single or even central influence on the new historicism. First, he critiqued the old-style historicism to such an extent that he ended up being antihistorical, or at least ahistorical, in the view of a number of new historicists. Second, his commitment to a radical remapping of the relations of power and influence, cause and effect, may have led him to adopt too cavalier an attitude toward chronology and facts. Finally, the very act of identifying and labeling *any* primary influence goes against the grain of the new historicism. Its practitioners have sought to "decenter" the study of literature, not only by overlapping it with historical studies (broadly defined to include anthropology and sociology) but also by struggling to see history from a decentered perspective. That struggle has involved recognizing (1) that the historian's cultural and historical position may not afford the best purview of a given set of events and (2) that events seldom have any single or central cause. In keeping with these principles, it may be appropriate to acknowledge Foucault as just one of several powerful, interactive intellectual forces rather than to declare him the single, master influence.

Throughout the 1980s it seemed to many that the ongoing debates about the sources of the new historicist movement, the importance of Marx or Foucault, Walter Benjamin or Mikhail Bakhtin, and the exact locations of all the complex boundaries between the new historicism and other "isms" (Marxism and poststructuralism, to name only two) were historically contingent functions of the new historicism's *newness*. In the initial stages of their development, new intellectual movements are difficult to outline clearly because, like partially developed photographic images, they are themselves fuzzy and lacking in definition. They respond to disparate influences and include thinkers who represent a wide range of backgrounds; like movements that are disintegrating, they inevitably include a broad spectrum of opinions and positions.

From the vantage point of the later decades, however, it seems the inchoate quality of the new historicism is characteristic rather than a function of newness. The boundaries around the new historicism remain fuzzy, not because it hasn't reached its full maturity but because, if it is to live up to its name, it must always be subject to revision and redefinition as historical circumstances change. The fact that so many critics we label new historicist are working right at the border of Marxist, poststructuralist, cultural, postcolonial, feminist, and now even a new form of reader-response (or at least reader-oriented) criticism is evidence of the new historicism's multiple interests and motivations, rather than of its embryonic state.

New historicists themselves advocate and even stress the need to perpetually redefine categories and boundaries — whether they be disciplinary, generic, national, or racial — not because definitions are unimportant but because they are historically constructed and thus subject to revision. If new historicists like Thomas and reader-oriented critics like Steven Mailloux and Peter Rabinowitz seem to spend most of their time talking over the low wall separating their respective fields, then maybe the wall is in the wrong place. As Catherine Gallagher has suggested, the boundary between new historicists and feminists studying "people and phenomena that once seemed insignificant, indeed outside of history: women, criminals, the insane" often turns out to be shifting or even nonexistent (Veeser 43).

If the fact that new historicists all seem to be working on the border of another school should not be viewed as a symptom of the new historicism's newness (or disintegration), neither should it be viewed as evidence that new historicists are intellectual loners or divisive outriders who enjoy talking over walls to people in other fields but who share no common views among themselves. Greenblatt, McGann, and Thomas all started with the assumption that works of literature are simultaneously influenced by and influencing reality, broadly defined. Whatever their disagreements, they share a belief in referentiality — a belief that literature refers to and is referred to by things outside itself — stronger than that found in the works of formalist, poststructuralist, and even reader-response critics. They believe with Greenblatt that the "central concerns" of criticism "should prevent it from permanently sealing off one type of discourse from another or decisively separating works of art from the minds and lives of their creators and their audiences" (*Renaissance* 5).

McGann, in his introduction to *Historical Studies and Literary Criticism,* turns referentiality into a rallying cry:

> What will not be found in these essays . . . is the assumption, so common in text-centered studies of every type, that literary works are self-enclosed verbal constructs, or looped intertextual fields of autonomous signifiers and signifieds. In these essays, the question of referentiality is once again brought to the fore. (3)

In "Keats and the Historical Method in Literary Criticism," he suggests a set of basic, scholarly procedures to be followed by those who have rallied to the cry. These procedures, which he claims are "practical derivatives of the Bakhtin school," assume that historicist critics will study a literary work's "point of origin" by studying biography and bibliography. The critic must then consider the expressed intentions of the author, because, if printed, these intentions have also modified the developing history of the work. Next, the new historicist must learn the history of the work's reception, as that body of opinion has become part of the platform on which we are situated when we study the work at our own particular "point of reception." Finally, McGann urges the new historicist critic to point toward the future, toward his or her *own* audience, defining for its members the aims and limits of the critical project and injecting the analysis with a degree of self-consciousness that alone can give it credibility (*Inflections* 62).

In his introduction to a collection of new historical writings on *The New Historicism* (1989), H. Aram Veeser stresses the unity among new historicists, not by focusing on common critical procedures but, rather, by outlining five "key assumptions" that "continually reappear and bind together the avowed practitioners and even some of their critics":

> 1. that every expressive act is embedded in a network of material practices;
> 2. that every act of unmasking, critique, and opposition uses the tools it condemns and risks falling prey to the practice it exposes;
> 3. that literary and non-literary texts circulate inseparably;
> 4. that no discourse, imaginative or archival, gives access to unchanging truths nor expresses inalterable human nature;
> 5. finally, . . . that a critical method and a language adequate to describe culture under capitalism participate in the economy they describe. (xi)

These same assumptions are shared by a group of historians practicing what is now commonly referred to as "the new cultural history." Influenced by *Annales*-school historians in France, post-Althusserian Marxists, and Foucault, these historians share with their new historicist counterparts not only many of the same influences and assumptions but also the following: an interest in anthropological and sociological subjects and methods; a creative way of weaving stories and anecdotes about the past into revealing thick descriptions; a tendency to focus on nontraditional, noncanonical subjects and relations (historian Thomas Laqueur is best known for *Making Sex: Body and Gender from the Greeks to Freud* [1990]); and some of the same journals and projects.

Thus, in addition to being significantly unified by their own interests, assumptions, and procedures, new historicist literary critics have participated in a broader, interdisciplinary movement toward unification virtually unprecedented within and across academic disciplines. Their tendency to work along disciplinary borderlines, far from being evidence of their factious or fractious tendencies, has been precisely what has allowed them to engage historians in a conversation certain to revolutionize the way in which we understand the past, present, and future.

In the essay that follows, Brook Thomas points out that when Hawthorne deems the "scaffold" an agent of "good citizenship" in 1642 Boston, his use of both terms is anachronistic. Good citizenship is for the most part a nineteenth-century — not seventeenth-century — concept. "Scaffolds" *is* evocative of earlier epochs, but it suggests seventeenth-century England and eighteenth-century France, not Puritan New England, where the term *citizen* typically would have been used to denote a city-dweller whose "political status" was that of a king's "subject."

Having made this point, Thomas proceeds to acknowledge that "it was precisely in June 1642 that civil war broke out in England," leading to a king's decapitation (p. 433 in this volume). And he quotes J. G. A. Pocock's statement that, during the years of this Puritan revolution, "the Englishman could develop a civic consciousness, an awareness of himself as a political actor in a public realm" (p. 433). This consciousness, this awareness, would later make possible, in the nineteenth century, the full development of "good citizenship" as an idea and ideal.

Thomas proceeds to point out an even more interesting feature of Hawthorne's technical anachronism, namely, that "[w]hen Hawthorne inserts the nineteenth-century term *good citizenship* into a seventeenth-century setting he subtly participates in a persistent national myth" (p. 433). According to that myth, U.S. citizenship is "an outgrowth of citizenship developed in colonial New England." But, Thomas insists, Hawthorne "participat[es]" in the myth by "challenging its standard version," which holds that "conditions for democratic citizenship flourished the moment colonists made the journey to the 'New World'" (p. 433). Stating that "much of Hawthorne's notorious irony is directed against the idealization of [our] New England ancestors" by nineteenth-century historians like George Bancroft, Thomas goes on to maintain that, in *The Scarlet Letter,* it is only at the novel's "romance" level — where "Hawthorne employs little or no irony" — that good citizenship modeled (p. 435).

And by whom? By Hester Prynne, who, having "no selfish ends" and not living "in any measure for her own profit and enjoyment," helps those with "sorrows and perplexities" (p. 201). Thomas identifies this understanding that the "good citizen" leads a life of commitment to community as a *nonstandard* but emerging myth of American citizenship. It is this new "civic myth" that Hawthorne "helps shape" through the writing of *The Scarlet Letter,* a novel that, according to Thomas, doesn't really "advocate" the kind of "obedience" to the "state" recommended in its "political plot."

It is, rather, through what Thomas calls the novel's "love plot" that *The Scarlet Letter* reshapes America's sense of what it means to be a good citizen in a civil society. "To understand *The Scarlet Letter* as civic myth," Thomas argues, "we need to understand why, after marshaling all of his rhetorical force to make us sympathize with his lovers [in the forest scene], Hawthorne does not allow them a new beginning" (p. 440). Citing Puritan "John Winthrop's distinction between natural and civil liberty" (p. 440), Thomas points out that, for a seventeenth-century Puritan, Dimmesdale's proclamation that his adulterous relationship with Hester "had a consecration of its own" would have been sinful. To Hawthorne's mind, it may not have been sinful, but it certainly would have reflected an argument for natural, not civil, liberty, whereas "*The Scarlet Letter* is a civic myth about the importance of civil society, not about the glories of natural man or woman" (p. 441).

From Winthrop's Puritan point of view, the relationship between a "subject" and governing magistrates was analogous to a woman's subjection in marriage to her husband. From that same point of view, "citizen" still referred to subjects and, more specifically, to residents of cities. From Hawthorne's later perspective, these terms and relationships had changed. Insisting that "[t]his distinction between subjects and citizens is not just a quibble over terms," Thomas reminds us that, "[a]s a political category, not simply a resident of a city, *citizen* implies the capacity to rule as well as to be ruled" (p. 442). The independence of citizens as Hawthorne understood them would have flown in the face of "Winthrop's analogy between the wife in a marriage under coverture and the subjects of a commonwealth" (p. 442). Thus, while generally concurring with Puritan concerns regarding the "potential dangers of natural liberty," Hawthorne would have distrusted the competence of Puritan patriarchs to judge Hester. "Assuming the moral position of God," Thomas explains, "the magistrates lack what Hester develops over the course of the book: the 'power to sympathize'" that "flourish[es] best in Hawthorne's world in the space of civil society not directly under state supervision" (pp. 442–43).

From Hawthorne's treatment of Hester and the Puritan patriarchs, Thomas turns his attention to the novelist's take on Roger Chillingworth, which, he notes, "starkly contrasts with the sympathetic treatment" afforded to wronged husbands in much "popular literature" and "some courts" during the 1840s (p. 443). Reversing legal and literary conventions — which in their most extreme versions dealt sympathetically even with "cuckolded husbands taking revenge into their own hands" (p. 444) — Hawthorne makes Chillingworth despicable insofar as he seeks "justice outside the law" (thereby "illustrat[ing] natural liberty's potential for evil as well as for good" [p. 444]) and insofar as he, too, acts in denial of his marriage vows. (In prison, Hester asks her husband why he will not "announce [himself] openly, and cast [her] off at once." He replies, "It may be . . . because I will not encounter the dishonor that besmirches the husband of a faithless woman" [p. 445])

Under the prevailing laws of coverture, Chillingworth not only has husbandly rights to Hester but also paternal rights to her child (no matter the identity of its natural, or biological, father). Thus, Thomas argues, "the same man who knows his legal rights of possession as a husband refuses to take on his legal responsibilities as a father" (p. 445) when he says to his wife, "Speak; and give your child a father" (p. 68). It might seem, Thomas goes on to suggest, that "this book's emphasis on failed fathers raises the possibility that Hester will earn her claim to good citizenship through her role as a mother" (p. 446) — and through the claims she makes to her rights as a mother. In fact, however, the maternal rights Hester lays claim to before the magistrates turns out to be yet another anachronism. It wasn't until "just before Hawthorne began writing *The Scarlet Letter,*" Thomas explains, that a few mothers won custody from bad fathers (p. 447). This legal shift reflected the growing belief that the "education of children as citizens was best accomplished by . . . the nurturing role of the mother" and that maternal "quality of sympathy" intrinsic to good citizenship" (p. 447).

After making these and other observations relevant to the question and qualities of citizenship, Thomas eventually concludes that it is *not* through Hester's version of good motherhood that she becomes Hawthorne's model of the good citizen. Rather, it is through the decision she makes, "with her lover and husband dead and her child apparently married and in another country," to return to Boston "as a woman . . . devoted . . . not to individual fulfillment but to the interpersonal relations of a civil society (p. 449). "Through her return," Thomas writes,

> Hester acknowledges the civil law in a way that she did not in her rebellious earlier days. Nonetheless, she does not, as Dimmesdale does, submit totally to the state. On the contrary, she receives the Puritan magistrates' toleration of— and even admiration of— actions that are not directly under their supervision. Concerned with counseling and comforting those who feel marginalized by official Puritan society, . . . [she concerns herself with] affairs of the heart that no affairs of state seem capable of remedying. (p. 450)

A pioneer of the new historicism, Thomas distinguishes himself from two other historically inclined critics of *The Scarlet Letter,* Sacvan Bercovich and Lauren Berlant, who in his words turn "a nineteenth-century liberal democracy into a secular version of the Puritans' seventeenth-century theocracy" (p. 451). By contrast, Thomas contrasts Puritan society as represented by Hawthorne and the liberal democracy Hester foreshadows within the theocracy to which she voluntarily resubmits herself.

Thomas, who views himself as part of the emerging "law and literature movement," nonetheless typifies the new historicist approach by viewing *The Scarlet Letter* in light of the novelist's historical moment, the seventeenth-century Puritan era as represented by Hawthorne, and that same period understood from our present-day vantage point. (It is there that, as mentioned above, he places himself alongside other new historicist critics who take a different view of the Puritan past.) Equally typical of the new historicism are: (a) his treatment of the Puritans in *The Scarlet Letter* as *representations* of seventeenth-century Puritans, and (b) his interest in sociohistorical *discourses* such as the developing concept of "good citizenship." In any case, the following essay by Thomas truly provides what Clifford Geertz has called a "thick description" of a literary work and its relationship to changing definitions of power (in the Foucauldian sense), definitions that lead from the relation of king over subject to the relationship of magistrates to unmarried women to the unsubjected, informal power forged within a democracy by a concerned, committed *citizen.*

Ross C Murfin

THE NEW HISTORICISM: A SELECTED BIBLIOGRAPHY

The New Historicism: Further Reading

Brantlinger, Patrick. "Cultural Studies vs. the New Historicism." *English Studies/Cultural Studies: Institutionalizing Dissent.* Ed. Isaiah Smithson and Nancy Ruff. Urbana: U of Illinois P, 1994. 43–58.

Cox, Jeffrey N., and Larry J. Reynolds, eds. *New Historical Literary Study.* Princeton: Princeton UP, 1993.

Dimock, Wai-Chee. "Feminism, New Historicism, and the Reader." *American Literature* 63 (1991): 601–22.

Howard, Jean. "The New Historicism in Renaissance Studies." *English Literary Renaissance* 16 (1986): 13–43.

Lindenberger, Herbert. *The History in Literature: On Value, Genre, Institutions.* New York: Columbia UP, 1990.

———. "Toward a New History in Literary Study." *Profession: Selected Articles from the Bulletins of the Association of Departments of English and the Association of the Departments of Foreign Languages.* New York: MLA, 1984. 16–23.

Liu, Alan. "The Power of Formalism: The New Historicism." *English Literary History* 56 (1989): 721–71.

McGann, Jerome. *The Beauty of Inflections: Literary Investigations in Historical Method and Theory.* Oxford: Clarendon–Oxford UP, 1985.

———. *Historical Studies and Literary Criticism.* Madison: U of Wisconsin P, 1985. See especially the introduction and the essays in the following sections: "Historical Methods and Literary Interpretations" and "Biographical Contexts and the Critical Object."

Montrose, Louis Adrian. "Renaissance Literary Studies and the Subject of History." *English Literary Renaissance* 16 (1986): 5–12.

Morris, Wesley. *Toward a New Historicism.* Princeton: Princeton UP, 1972.

New Literary History 21 (1990). "History and . . ." (special issue). See especially the essays by Carolyn Porter, Rena Fraden, Clifford Geertz, and Renato Rosaldo.

Representations. This quarterly journal, printed by the University of California Press, regularly publishes new historicist studies and cultural criticism.

Thomas, Brook. "The Historical Necessity for — and Difficulties with — New Historical Analysis in Introductory Courses." *College English* 49 (1987): 509–22.

———. *The New Historicism and Other Old-Fashioned Topics.* Princeton: Princeton UP, 1991.

———. "The New Literary Historicism." *A Companion to American Thought.* Ed. Richard Wightman Fox and James T. Klappenberg. New York: Basil Blackwell, 1995.

———. "Walter Benn Michaels and the New Historicism: Where's the Difference?" *Boundary 2* 18 (1991): 118–59.

Veeser, H. Aram, ed. *The New Historicism.* New York: Routledge, 1989. See especially Veeser's introduction, Louis Montrose's "Professing the Renaissance," Catherine Gallagher's "Marxism and the New Historicism," and Frank Lentricchia's "Foucault's Legacy: A New Historicism?"

Wayne, Don E. "Power, Politics and the Shakespearean Text: Recent Criticism in England and the United States." *Shakespeare Reproduced: The Text in History and Ideology.* Ed. Jean Howard and Marion O'Connor. New York: Methuen, 1987. 47–67.

Winn, James A. "An Old Historian Looks at the New Historicism." *Comparative Studies in Society and History* 35 (1993): 859–70.

The New Historicism: Influential Examples

The new historicism has taken its present form less through the elaboration of basic theoretical postulates and more through certain influential examples. The works listed represent some of the most important contributions guiding research in this area.

Bercovitch, Sacvan. *The Rites of Assent: Transformations in the Symbolic Construction of America.* New York: Routledge, 1993.

Brown, Gillian. *Domestic Individualism: Imagining Self in Nineteenth-Century America.* Berkeley: U of California P, 1990.

Dollimore, Jonathan. *Radical Tragedy: Religion, Ideology and Power in the Drama of Shakespeare and His Contemporaries.* Brighton, UK: Harvester, 1984.

Dollimore, Jonathan, and Alan Sinfield, eds. *Political Shakespeare: New Essays in Cultural Materialism*. Manchester, UK: Manchester UP, 1985. This volume occupies the borderline between new historicist and cultural criticism. See especially the essays by Dollimore, Greenblatt, and Tennenhouse.

Gallagher, Catherine. *The Industrial Reformation of English Fiction*. Chicago: U of Chicago P, 1985.

Goldberg, Jonathan. *James I and the Politics of Literature*. Baltimore: Johns Hopkins UP, 1983.

Greenblatt, Stephen J. *Learning to Curse: Essays in Early Modern Culture*. New York: Routledge, 1990.

———. *Marvelous Possessions: The Wonder of the New World*. Chicago: U of Chicago P, 1991.

———. *Renaissance Self-Fashioning from More to Shakespeare*. Chicago: U of Chicago P, 1980. See chapter 1 and the chapter on *Othello* titled "The Improvisation of Power."

———. *Shakespearean Negotiations: The Circulation of Social Energy in Renaissance England*. Berkeley: U of California P, 1988. See especially "The Circulation of Social Energy" and "Invisible Bullets."

Liu, Alan. *Wordsworth, the Sense of History*. Stanford: Stanford UP, 1989.

Marcus, Leah. *Puzzling Shakespeare: Local Reading and Its Discontents*. Berkeley: U of California P, 1988.

McGann, Jerome. *The Romantic Ideology*. Chicago: U of Chicago P, 1983.

Michaels, Walter Benn. *The Gold Standard and the Logic of Naturalism: American Literature at the Turn of the Century*. Berkeley: U of California P, 1987.

Montrose, Louis Adrian. "'Shaping Fantasies': Figurations of Gender and Power in Elizabethan Culture." *Representations* 2 (1983): 61–94. One of the most influential early new historicist essays.

Mullaney, Steven. *The Place of the Stage: License, Play, and Power in Renaissance England*. Chicago: U of Chicago P, 1987.

Orgel, Stephen. *The Illusion of Power: Political Theater in the English Renaissance*. Berkeley: U of California P, 1975.

Sinfield, Alan. *Literature, Politics and Culture in Postwar Britain*. Berkeley: U of California P, 1989.

Tennenhouse, Leonard. *Power on Display: The Politics of Shakespeare's Genres*. New York: Methuen, 1986.

Foucault and His Influence

As I point out in the introduction to the new historicism, some new historicists would question the "privileging" of Foucault implicit in this section heading ("Foucault and His Influence") and the following one ("Other Writers and Works"). They might cite the greater importance of one of those other writers or point out that to cite a central influence or a definitive cause runs against the very spirit of the movement.

Dreyfus, Hubert L., and Paul Rabinow. *Michel Foucault: Beyond Structuralism and Hermeneutics.* Chicago: U of Chicago P, 1983.

Foucault, Michel. *The Archaeology of Knowledge.* Trans. A. M. Sheridan Smith. New York: Harper, 1972.

———. *Discipline and Punish: The Birth of the Prison.* 1975. Trans. Alan Sheridan. New York: Pantheon, 1978.

———. *The History of Sexuality.* Trans. Robert Hurley. Vol. 1. New York: Pantheon, 1978.

———. *Language, Counter-Memory, Practice.* Ed. Donald F. Bouchard. Trans. Donald F. Bouchard and Sherry Simon. Ithaca: Cornell UP, 1977.

———. *The Order of Things: An Archaeology of the Human Sciences.* New York: Vintage, 1973.

———. *Politics, Philosophy, Culture.* Ed. Lawrence D. Kritzman. Trans. Alan Sheridan et al. New York: Routledge, 1988.

———. *Power/Knowledge.* Ed. Colin Gordon. Trans. Colin Gordon et al. New York: Pantheon, 1980.

———. *Technologies of the Self.* Ed. Luther H. Marin, Huck Gutman, and Patrick H. Hutton. Amherst: U of Massachusetts P, 1988.

Sheridan, Alan. *Michel Foucault: The Will to Truth.* New York: Tavistock, 1980.

Smart, Barry. *Michel Foucault.* New York: Ellis Horwood and Tavistock, 1985.

Other Writers and Works of Interest to New Historicist Critics

Bakhtin, M. M. *The Dialogic Imagination: Four Essays.* Ed. Michael Holquist. Trans. Caryl Emerson. Austin: U of Texas P, 1981. Bakhtin wrote many influential studies on subjects as varied as Dostoyevsky, Rabelais, and formalist criticism. But this book, in part due to Holquist's helpful introduction, is probably the best place to begin reading Bakhtin.

Benjamin, Walter. "The Work of Art in the Age of Mechanical Reproduction." 1936. *Illuminations.* Ed. Hannah Arendt. Trans. Harry Zohn. New York: Harcourt, 1968.

Fried, Michael. *Absorption and Theatricality: Painting and Beholder in the Works of Diderot.* Berkeley: U of California P, 1980.

Geertz, Clifford. *The Interpretation of Cultures.* New York: Basic, 1973.

———. *Negara: The Theatre State in Nineteenth-Century Bali.* Princeton: Princeton UP, 1980.

Goffman, Erving. *Frame Analysis.* New York: Harper, 1974.

Jameson, Fredric. *The Political Unconscious.* Ithaca: Cornell UP, 1981.

Koselleck, Reinhart. *Futures Past.* Trans. Keith Tribe. Cambridge: MIT P, 1985.

Laqueur, Thomas Walter. *Making Sex: Body and Gender from the Greeks to Freud.* Cambridge: Harvard UP, 1990.

Said, Edward. *Orientalism.* New York: Columbia UP, 1978.

Turner, Victor. *The Ritual Process: Structure and Anti-Structure.* Chicago: Aldine, 1969.

Young, Robert. *White Mythologies: Writing History and the West.* New York: Routledge, 1990.

Other New Historicist (and Related) Approaches to *The Scarlet Letter*

Arac, Jonathan. "The Politics of *The Scarlet Letter.*" Bercovitch and Jehlen 247–66.

Bercovitch, Sacvan. *The Office of The Scarlet Letter.* Baltimore: Johns Hopkins UP, 1991.

Bercovitch, Sacvan, and Myra Jehlen, eds. *Ideology and Classic American Literature.* Cambridge: Harvard UP, 1986.

Berlant, Lauren. *The Scarlet Letter: The Anatomy of National Fantasy: Hawthorne, Utopia, and Everyday Life.* Chicago: U of Chicago P, 1991.

Colacurcio, Michael, ed. *New Essays on The Scarlet Letter.* Cambridge: Cambridge UP, 1985. See especially Colacurcio's own essay, "'The Woman's Own Choice': Sex, Metaphor, and the Puritan Sources of *The Scarlet Letter.*"

Hodge, Elizabeth Perry. "The Letter of the Law: Reading Hawthorne and the Law of Adultery." *Law and Literature Perspectives.* Ed. Bruce L. Rockwood. New York: Peter Lang, 1996. An example of the "Law and Literature" approach, this essay nonetheless hews close to the assumptions of the new historicism.

Millington, Richard. *Practicing Romance: Narrative Form and Cultural Engagement.* Princeton: Princeton UP, 1992.

Pease, Donald E. *Visionary Compacts: American Renaissance Writings in Cultural Contexts.* Madison: U of Wisconsin P, 1987. See especially chapter 2, "Hawthorne's Discovery of a Pre-Revolutionary Past."

Reynolds, Larry J. "*The Scarlet Letter* and Revolutions Abroad." *American Literature* 57 (1985): 44–67.

A NEW HISTORICIST PERSPECTIVE

BROOK THOMAS

Citizen Hester: *The Scarlet Letter* as Civic Myth

Early in *The Scarlet Letter* (1850), as Hester Prynne faces public discipline, the narrator halts to comment, "In fact, this scaffold constituted a portion of a penal machine, which now, for two or three generations past, has been merely historical and traditionary among us, but was held, in the old time, to be as effectual an agent in the promotion of good citizenship, as ever was the guillotine among the terrorists of France" (p. 59 in this volume). In a subtle reading of this passage Larry Reynolds notes the anachronistic use of "scaffold" — the normal instruments of punishment in the Massachusetts Bay Colony were the whipping post, the stocks, and the pillory — to argue that Nathaniel Hawthorne self-consciously alludes to public beheadings, especially the regicidal revolutions in seventeenth-century England and eighteenth-century France. But none of Hawthorne's many critics has noted the anachronistic use of *good citizenship*, a phrase that suggests the rich historical layering of Hawthorne's nineteenth-century romance about seventeenth-century New England Puritans.

Of course, *citizen* existed in English in the seventeenth century, but it was used primarily to designate an inhabitant of a city, as Hawthorne does when he mentions "an aged handicraftsman . . . who had been a citizen of London at the period of Sir Thomas Overbury's murder, now some thirty years agone" (p. 108). The official political status of residents of Boston in June 1642 was not that of citizens, but subjects of the King, a status suggested when Hester leaves the prison and the

Beadle cries, "Make way, good people, make way, in the King's name" (p. 58). Historically resonant itself, this cry reminds us that it was precisely in June 1642 that civil war broke out in England (Ryskamp, Newberry). In fact, the book's action unfolds over the seven years in which the relation between the people and their sovereign was in doubt, the years generally acknowledged as the time when "the Englishman could develop a civic consciousness, an awareness of himself as a political actor in a public realm" (Pocock 335); that is, as a citizen as those in the nineteenth century would have understood the term.[1] Even so, it was not until after the French and American Revolutions that *good citizenship* came into common use.

When Hawthorne inserts the nineteenth-century term *good citizenship* into a seventeenth-century setting he subtly participates in a persistent national myth that sees U.S. citizenship as an outgrowth of citizenship developed in colonial New England. Hawthorne's participation in this myth is important to note because much of his labor is devoted to challenging its standard version. According to the standard version, conditions for democratic citizenship flourished the moment colonists made the journey to the "New World." If the people in the 13 colonies were officially subjects of the king, the seeds of good citizenship were carried across the Atlantic, especially by freedom-loving Pilgrims, who found a more fertile soil for civic participation than in England. A recent example of this version of the story comes in the work of the noted historian Edmund S. Morgan. Describing "the first constitution of Massachusetts" in 1630 when the assistants of the Massachusetts Bay Company were "transformed from an executive council to a legislative body," Morgan writes, "the term 'freeman' was transformed from a designation for members of a commercial company, exercising legislative and judicial control over that company and its

[1]Thomas Hobbes in *De Cive,* published in Latin in 1642 and translated into English in 1651, did use *citizen* to designate membership in a commonwealth. But he did not use it as Aristotle did to designate a member of a republic who has the capacity to both rule and be ruled. Instead, like the French absolutist Jean Bodin, he distinguished citizens, who had specific benefits, from other subjects, like denizens, who did not have all or any of them. In *Leviathan* (1651) Hobbes uses *citizen* more in the sense of a city dweller. For instance, he writes of a man: "Let him therefore consider with himself, when taking a journey, he armes himselfe, and seeks to go well accompanied; when going to sleep, he locks his dores; when even in his house he locks his chests; and this when he knows there bee Lawes, and publike Officers, armed to revenge all injuries shall be done him; what opinion he has of his fellow subjects, when he rides armed; of his fellow Citizens, when he locks his dores; and his children, and servants, when he locks his chests" (186–187). "Fellow Citizens" are clearly those "fellow subjects" who dwell in close proximity to the man.

property, into a designation for the citizens of a state, with the right to vote and hold office. . . . This change presaged the admission to freemanship of a large proportion of settlers, men who could contribute to the joint stock nothing but godliness and good citizenship (*Puritan Dilemma* 91)."[2] When Morgan designates freemen *citizens,* he projects onto Puritan New England his awareness of political changes still to come just as most studies of colonial American literature project the country's present political boundaries backward and treat only the 13 colonies that eventually became the U.S.

This tendency to read the Puritan past teleologically is a product of the antebellum period. For instance, in his multivolume *History of the United States,* which found its way into nearly a third of New England homes (Nye, *George* 102), George Bancroft attributed the "political education" of people in Connecticut "to the happy organization of towns, which here, as indeed throughout all New England, constituted each separate settlement as a little democracy in itself. It was the natural reproduction of the system, which the instinct of humanity had imperfectly revealed to our Anglo-Saxon ancestors. In the ancient republics, citizenship had been an hereditary privilege. In Connecticut, citizenship was acquired by inhabitancy, was lost by removal. Each town-meeting was a little legislature, and all inhabitants, the affluent and the more needy, the wise and the foolish, were members with equal franchises." Quoting this passage, an anonymous reviewer for the *American Jurist and Law Magazine* enthusiastically adds that in colonial New England's "institutions lies the germ of all that distinguishes our government from others, which are more or less founded in individual freedom" (230).

Clearly, the "mild" and "humane" laws of Bancroft's Puritans are not those of Hawthorne's (229). Indeed, much of Hawthorne's notorious irony is directed against the idealization of New England ancestors by Bancroft and others.[3] For instance, if Bancroft celebrates New England as the breeding ground of democratic citizenship because of the people's civic participation in town hall meetings and the like, Hawthorne's image of the scaffold reminds us that good citizenship requires obedience. If Bancroft stresses the freedom entailed in good citizenship, Hawthorne reminds us of the repressions required to pro-

[2]Morgan also uses the term *good citizen* when he acknowledges that the Puritans' phrase would have been a "civil man" (*Puritan Family* 1).

[3]For an excellent summary of speeches by people like Daniel Webster, Joseph Story, and Edward Everett that share Bancroft's view of the Puritans' republican institutions, see John P. McWilliams, 25–36. On Bancroft, see Levin.

duce good citizens. Hawthorne's irony reaches a peak late in the book when he calls Chillingworth, the book's villain, a "reputable" "citizen" (p. 181). Truly good citizens, it seems, cannot be distinguished from those who simply appear respectable.

In different ways some of Hawthorne's best historically minded critics have noted his challenge to the standard version of the Puritan origins of U.S. citizenship. But for all of their brilliance, none have noted Hawthorne's anachronistic use of the term *citizen*. On the contrary, like Hawthorne, some of these same critics refer to Puritans in seventeenth-century Boston as citizens in the political sense of the term (Berlant; Colacurcio, "Woman's Own Choice"; and Pease), just as does the allegedly ahistorical Frederick Crews (149). In doing so they unconsciously participate in the very myth they think they are demystifying, a participation that makes it impossible for them to recognize Hawthorne's important contribution to it.[4]

We can start to identify that contribution by noting that Hawthorne employs little or no irony at the end of his romance when Hester returns to Boston and devotes herself to serving the unfortunate. Having "no selfish ends," not living "in any measure for her own profit and enjoyment," counseling those bringing to her "their sorrows and perplexities" (p. 201), Hester in her unselfish commitment to her community has by most measures earned the label *good citizen*. By most, but not by all. For instance, Judith Shklar identifies the two most important attributes of U.S. citizenship as the right to vote and the right to earn a living. Although Hester earlier earned her keep with her needlework, economic self-sufficiency is not a defining aspect of her citizenship. Nor is the right to vote. Indeed, as a woman, Hester in the seventeenth (even in the early nineteenth) century could not fit definitions of *good citizenship* in either the economic or the political spheres.

[4]In noting that many of Hawthorne's critics remain as much within the myth of the Puritan origins of U.S. citizenship as he does, I am not implying that I somehow can stand outside of and above myth to expose it as an ideological distortion. Whereas I fully recognize that *The Scarlet Letter,* as a work of fiction, does not give us a historically accurate account of seventeenth-century Puritan society and political thought, to dismiss it as mere ideology does not get us very far. On the contrary, since according to today's critical commonplace we are always within ideology, it is not enough to expose persistent national myths as ideological, which is how the present generation of critics of American literature has generally distinguished itself from the myth and symbol school. What we need to do as well is to evaluate the effect of various myths in terms of what Kenneth Burke called "equipment for living." Such work on/with myth might help to generate a revitalized political criticism that once again, like Aristotle, sees politics as the art of the possible.

Even so, rather than abandon the concept of *good citizenship*, Hawthorne through Hester expands our notion of what it can entail by stressing the importance of actions within what political scientists call *civil society*, "a sphere of social interaction between economy and the state, composed of the intimate sphere (especially the family), the sphere of associations (especially voluntary associations), social movements, and forms of public communication" (Cohen and Arato ix).[5] Acutely aware that the stress on civic participation could obscure important interior matters of the heart and spirit, Hawthorne does not, as many critics argue he does, retreat from public to private concerns, but instead tells the tale of how a "fallen woman" finds redemption by helping to generate within a repressive Puritan community the beginnings of an independent civil society. In telling that tale Hawthorne provides more than a civics lesson. He participates in and helps to shape the contours of a powerful civic myth.[6]

1. WORKING ON/WITH MYTH

But what is a civic myth? The term comes from *Civic Ideals: Conflicting Visions of Citizenship in U.S. History* (1997), Rogers Smith's exhaustive study of how the law both reflects and helps to produce attitudes toward citizenship in the U.S. In Smith's complex account, U.S. citizenship has been determined not only by liberal civic ideals, but also by civic myths, which he defines as "compelling stories" that explain "why persons form a people, usually indicating how a political community originated, who is eligible for membership, who is not and why, and what the community's values and aims are" (33).

[5]Informed by events in the former Soviet bloc in 1989, where the economic sphere was controlled by the state, this and other current definitions do not include the economic in civil society, as did Adam Smith, Adam Ferguson, and Hegel.

[6]My point is not that Hawthorne set out to write a story arguing for the importance of an independent civil society in the way that a political economist might. His goal was to write the most compelling story that he could. Nonetheless, in its reception, especially the role it has played in education in the U.S., *The Scarlet Letter*, with its representation of people's desires and how those desires can best be fulfilled, imparts certain attitudes, values, and structures of feeling that coincide with the attitudes, values, and structures of feeling associated with civil society arguments. Furthermore, even if Hawthorne did not self-consciously set out to make an argument for an independent civil society, he would have known about such arguments through the Scottish Enlightenment figures of Adam Smith and Ferguson.

Literature's potential to generate civic myths was the topic of an 1834 speech called "The Importance of Illustrating New England History by a Series of Romances Like the Waverley Novels," which was given in Hawthorne's home town of Salem by the Whig lawyer Rufus Choate. Alluding to the Scottish nationalist Andrew Fletcher's often-quoted statement that "I know a very wise man . . . [who] believed if a man were permitted to make all the ballads, he need not care who should make the laws of the nation" (108), Choate argues that a proper literary treatment of the past would mold and fix "that final, grand, complex result — the national character."[7] In doing so it would make the country forget its "recent and overrated diversities of interest" and "reassemble, as it were, the people of America in one vast congregation." "Reminded of our fathers," he argues, "we should remember that we are brethren" (1: 344).

Choate understands how works of literature can serve as civic myths, but he also reveals why Smith worries about the effects of civic myths and their "fictional embroidery" (33). The stories Choate advocates would not, he admits, be a full disclosure of the past. A literary artist should remember that "it is an heroic age to whose contemplation he would turn us back; and as no man is a hero to his servant, so no age is heroic of which the whole truth is recorded. He tells the truth, to be sure, but he does not tell the whole truth, for that would be sometimes misplaced and discordant" (1: 340).[8] Aware that "much of what history relates . . . chills, shames and disgusts us," producing "discordant and contradictory emotions," Choate, therefore, counsels writers to leave out accounts of the "persecution of the Quakers, the controversies with Roger Williams and Mrs. Hutchinson" (1: 339). Literature as civic myth would seem to allow authors to avoid altogether those embarrassing national events that historians should not ignore, even if there is, as Herman Melville puts it, "a considerate way of historically treating them" (55).

[7]The quotation comes from *An Account of a Conversation Concerning a Right Regulation of Governments for the Common Good of Mankind in a Letter to the Marquis of Montrose, the Earls of Rothes, Roxburg and Haddington* (1703). It might seem ironic that in making a plea for the U.S. to unite and to forget regional differences Choate quotes a Scottish nationalist. At the same time, Fletcher advocated a federal union of Scotland and England, so he could be said to have anticipated the federal system of the U.S.

[8]Choate is echoed by Will Kymlicka, the contemporary theorist of multicultural citizenship, who argues that finding a shared national identity in history "often requires a very selective, even manipulative retelling of that history" (189).

But the Hawthorne that Melville so admired presents a more complicated case.[9] He had, for instance, already written about precisely the topics that Choate says should be avoided, evidence of a critical attitude toward the past that has caused so many critics to focus on his ironic demystifications. But, as we have seen, Hawthorne does more than demystify prevailing myths. As George Dekker shrewdly puts it, Hawthorne's "best hope for both short- and long-term success was to make the great American myths his own" (148). Hawthorne is neither solely a mythmaker nor a critical demystifier. Instead, to use Hans Blumenberg's phrase, he "works on/with myth." Effectively working on/with the myth of the nation's relation to its Puritan past, *The Scarlet Letter* as civic myth does not advocate obedience to the state or even primary loyalty to the nation.[10] Instead, it illustrates how important it is for liberal democracies to maintain the space of an independent civil society in which alternative obediences and loyalties are allowed a chance to flourish. It should come as no surprise then that the novel's power comes more through its love story than through its politics, or perhaps better put, its politics reminds us of the importance love stories have for most citizens' lives.

Of course, most readers of *The Scarlet Letter* do not need to be reminded that its mythopoetic power lies in its love story. All the more noteworthy, therefore, that recent political readings of the novel have tended to divert our attention from the love story or downplay its sig-

[9]On Hawthorne and a national literature see Doubleday. See also Arac, "Narrative Forms," who argues that *The Scarlet Letter* is an aesthetic narrative, not a national narrative, and that it became representative of the nation only through a retrospective process of canonization that devalued national narratives. Arac's provocative argument reminds us that literature can do many more things than give us compelling stories about national membership and values. Indeed, many works do not even have the potential to become civic myths. Nonetheless, *The Scarlet Letter*'s engagement with the myth of Puritan origins does give it that potential. More important, Arac focuses on a work's form and content, but form and content alone do not make a narrative national; its reception plays a role as well. Whereas a study of *The Scarlet Letter*'s reception is beyond the scope of this essay (see Brodhead), the important question for me is why Arac's "aesthetic narratives," like *The Scarlet Letter* and *Adventures of Huckleberry Finn* (1884), become civic myths while more explicitly national or patriotic narratives have lost favor over time. Simply to raise that question is to suggest that literature's relation to nationalist ideologies is a complicated one. Answering it might also demonstrate, as I try to do in this essay, that those ideologies are themselves more complicated than the ones that many recent literary critics are so intent on demystifying.

[10]Some of the most provocative — if conflicting — accounts of Hawthorne's relation to the Puritans are Baym; Bell; Bercovitch; Colacurcio, "Footsteps" and "Woman's Own Choice"; and Pease.

nificance.[11] What those readings fail to acknowledge is that the love plot is a vital part of Hawthorne's civic vision because it is in the love plot that he explores the possibilities of life in civil society. He does so by working on/with the great exceptionalist myth that America offers the hope for a radical break with the past and the promise of a new start.

2. BEGIN ALL ANEW

Hawthorne's romance is an extended account of various efforts to begin anew. It starts with reflections on the Puritans' attempt to establish a fresh start in the New World and the narrator's whimsical comment that "[t]he founders of a new colony, whatever Utopia of human virtue and happiness they might originally project, have invariably recognized it among their earliest practical necessities to allot a portion of

[11]Almost three decades ago Colacurcio began turning critics' attention away from the novel's love story to examine the chapter "Another View of Hester" and Hester's final return. Nonetheless, he pointedly remarks on the danger of turning "away from the richness and particularity of Hester's own love story" ("Footsteps" 461). In contrast, Berlant sees the love story as a retreat from the book's more important political concerns: "Now the tale of Hester and Dimmesdale, a political scandal, is reduced to a mere love plot" (154). According to Bercovitch the dramatic reunion of Hester and Dimmesdale in the forest "is a lovers' reunion, a pledge of mutual dependence, and no doubt readers have sometimes responded in these terms, if only by association with other texts. But in *this* text the focus of our response is the individual, not the couple (or the family)" (122). In contrast, see Millington's claim that Bercovitch's "erasure of the book's emotional investments" is "characteristic of the present moment in the history of Americanist criticism" (6, 2).

Millington's observation helps me to address what might seem to be a contradiction in my argument. If, as I claim in note 9, a work's status as civic myth depends in large part on its reception, do not all readings contribute to that status? And if they do, how can I claim that some readings are misreadings? There is no easy answer to those questions, but I can at least suggest the direction that an answer might take. First, it is partially true that the entire reception of a work — including its misreadings — helps to give a work the status of civic myth, since without a widespread reception the book could not serve as myth. Nonetheless, the fact should not keep us from recognizing that very often popular readings tend to perpetuate commonplace myths and miss how a novel or story also works on those myths. Take, for instance, the recent Demi Moore film of *The Scarlet Letter.* By completely sympathizing with the lovers against a harsh Puritan society it misreads the novel as much as many undergraduates do. If the book were indeed that simple-minded, it would not have had a very long reception history. Even so, by responding to this emotional aspect of the book, such misreadings do give us a sense of the book's popular power that critical dismissals of the love plot miss. A novel or story that simply works on myth without working with it will have little chance of having a popular reception. My reading of *The Scarlet Letter* as civic myth tries to account for both its long and its popular reception.

the virgin soil as a cemetery, and another portion as the site of a prison" (p. 53). It then opens the second half with "Another View of Hester" and Hester's realization that the radical reforms she imagines would require "the whole system of society . . . to be torn down, and built up anew" (p. 135). Hester's radical speculations are in turn linked to the book's emotional climax in the forest scene when Hester pleads to Dimmesdale, "Leave this wreck and ruin here where it hath happened! Meddle no more with it! Begin all anew!" (p. 157).

Even though each of these efforts is frustrated, much of the story's emotional tension has to do with readers' hopes — secret or not — that one or the other — or all — will succeed. Of all the attempts, however, that of Hester and Dimmesdale has awakened most readers' hopes. Confronted with a book of memorable scenes, readers past and present have found the forest meeting between Dimmesdale and Hester the most memorable.[12] It is so powerful that, as anyone who has taught the book knows, students have to be carefully guided to those passages in which the narrator in fact condemns the lovers' sentiments. To understand *The Scarlet Letter* as civic myth, we need to understand why, after marshaling all of his rhetorical force to make us sympathize with his lovers, Hawthorne does not allow them a new beginning.

Puritan authorities might have answered that question by relying on John Winthrop's distinction between natural and civil liberty. "The first is common to man with beasts and other creatures. By this, man, as he stands in relation to man simply, hath liberty to do what he lists; it is a liberty to evil as well as to good." In contrast, civil liberty has to do with the "covenant between God and man, in the moral law, and the politic covenants and constitutions, amongst men themselves. This liberty is the proper end and object of authority, and cannot subsist without it; and it is a liberty to that only which is good, just, and honest" (83–84). Significant for a novel about adultery, Winthrop's analogy for political covenants is marriage. Assuming the common law doctrine of coverture in which husband and wife become one corporate body with the husband granted sole legal authority, Winthrop compares a woman's willing subjection in marriage to an individual's subjection to the magistrates who govern the political covenant to which he consents. "The woman's own choice makes such a man her husband; yet

[12]Of this moment, when the two "recognize that, in spite of all their open and secret misery, they are still lovers, and capable of claiming for the very body of their sin a species of justification," William Dean Howells writes, "there is greatness in this scene unmatched, I think, in the book, and I was almost ready to say, out of it" (105, 108).

being so chosen, he is her lord, and she is to be subject to him, yet in a way of liberty, not of bondage; and a true wife accounts her subjection her honor and her freedom. . . . Even so brethren, it will be between you and your magistrates" (238–39). In turn, both marriage and political covenants are analogous to "the covenant between God and man, in the moral law" in which a Christian can achieve true liberty only through total submission to Christ. For the Puritans, the political institutions of civil society and the civil ceremony of marriage are governed by the moral law because they have God's sanction. A political covenant is not simply a contract among men; like the marriage contract between a man and woman, it needs God's witness.

To apply this doctrine of covenant theology to *The Scarlet Letter* is to see that for the Puritans Hester's greatest sin would not have been her adultery, whose visible evidence they see in the birth of Pearl, but a remark that Dimmesdale alone hears her make: her defiant cry that what the two lovers did "had a consecration of its own" (p. 155). Resonating with so many readers, this proclamation is in fact sinful because it implies that Hester's and Dimmesdale's love is a self-contained act, not one in need of God's sanction. As such their love exists in the realm of natural, not civil, liberty and must be contained.

The nineteenth-century version of Winthrop's distinction between natural and civil liberty is the distinction often made in political oratory between license and liberty. *The Scarlet Letter* is a civic myth about the importance of civil society, not about the glories of natural man or woman, because Hawthorne, despite the sympathy that he creates for his lovers, recognizes with Winthrop the dangers of natural liberty. But if Hawthorne shares Winthrop's distrust of natural liberty, he does not share the Puritan's belief that the only way for political subjects to achieve civil liberty is through absolute submission to civil authority.

Because Winthrop speaks of a political subject's participation in a covenant rather than of his relation to a monarch and because of Hawthorne's own reference to *good citizenship,* critics who evoke Winthrop while writing on *The Scarlet Letter* have assumed that he is describing the situation of citizens, not subjects.[13] But he is not. Winthrop's subjects are still subjects, and citizens for him remain residents of a city, as is the case for John Cotton, who in 1645 declared that the best way to unite or combine people together into "one visible

[13]See Colacurcio, "Woman's Own Choice," and his student Berlant, who asserts that for Winthrop the citizen is a woman. Citizens, we need to remember, are subjects, but not all subjects are citizens.

body" was a "mutual covenant" between "husband and wife in the family, Magistrates and subjects in the Commonwealth, fellow Citizens in the same citie" (qtd. in Norton 13). This distinction between subjects and citizens is not just a quibble over terms. As a political category, not simply a resident of a city, *citizen* implies the capacity to rule as well as be ruled. The relative independence of citizens would, therefore, undercut Winthrop's analogy between the wife in a marriage under coverture and the subjects of a commonwealth. For instance, as Linda Kerber has shown, covenant theology's strict analogy between marriage and political covenants broke down in the Revolutionary era. On the one hand, independence generated an ideological disjunction. Founded on the principle that the terms of political obligation of British subjects could be renegotiated to create U.S. citizens, the nation was ruled, nonetheless, by men who for the most part wanted to retain a family structure in which a wife owed her husband eternal obedience (13). On the other hand, the rhetoric of citizenship generated a new republican model of marriage that challenged the doctrine of coverture. As Merril Smith puts it, "Tyranny was not to be considered in public or private life, and marriage was now to be considered a republican contract between wives and husbands, a contract based on mutual affection" (51).

Hawthorne's challenge to Winthrop's belief in the absolute authority of magistrates is thus as important a part of *The Scarlet Letter*'s function as civic myth as is their shared distrust of the potential dangers of natural liberty. Winthrop claims absolute authority because he lives in a theocracy in which, as Hawthorne puts it, "forms of authority were felt to possess the sacredness of divine institutions" (p. 65). Distrustful of granting civil authority divine sanction, Hawthorne questions the capacity of the Puritan magistrates to judge Hester. Their problem is not that they are evil men. "They were, doubtless, good men, just and sage" (p. 65). Their problem is that "out of the whole human family, it would not have been easy to select the same number of wise and virtuous persons, who should be less capable of sitting in judgment on an erring woman's heart, and disentangling its mesh of good and evil" (p. 65). Assuming the moral position of God, the magistrates lack what Hester develops over the course of the book: the "power to sympathize" (p. 132).[14] That power causes a political dilemma. If on the one hand Hawthorne appeals to sympathy to temper the rigid and authoritarian rule of a system in which "religion and law were almost identical"

[14]The best discussion of sympathy in the novel is Hutner.

(50), on the other he warns of the dangers of having that sympathy lapse into a sentimental embrace of natural liberty with all of its potential dangers.

That dilemma is, of course, precisely the dilemma Hawthorne's readers confront when they sympathize with his two lovers in the forest. Hawthorne's answer to it is not, as critics too often assume, to advocate absolute submission to the existing civil authority. It is instead to imagine alternative possibilities for human relations within the civil order by drawing on the power to sympathize. Both that capacity of the imagination and the power to sympathize flourish best in Hawthorne's world in the space of civil society not directly under state supervision, a space prohibited in the Puritan theocracy at the beginning of Hawthorne's novel.

Hester will help generate that space, but she first has to acknowledge the importance of civil society by recognizing her sin. For Hawthorne that sin is not so much — as it would have been for Winthrop — a sin against God's law as it is a sin against the intersubjective agreements that human beings make with one another. Indeed, her adultery is another example of a premature effort to begin anew. After all, Hester's adultery with Dimmesdale takes place with her assuming, before the fact, that her husband is dead. When Chillingworth appears, therefore, he appears not only as a vengeful, cuckolded husband but also as a figure from a not-yet-buried past prepared to block Hester and Dimmesdale from achieving her dream of starting anew. To expand our understanding of why Hawthorne does not allow that new beginning, we need to look again at that "reputable" "citizen" (p. 181), Hester's husband.

3. ANOTHER VIEW OF MR. PRYNNE

Hawthorne may elicit our sympathy for Hester and Dimmesdale while condemning their adultery, but he generates little sympathy for Hester's husband. From Chaucer's January to various figures in Shakespeare to Charles Bovary to Leopold Bloom, the cuckolded husband has been treated with varying amounts of humor, pathos, sympathy, and contempt. Few, however, are as villainous as Roger Chillingworth. Hawthorne's treatment of him starkly contrasts with the sympathetic treatment some courts gave to cuckolded husbands in the 1840s, when various states began applying the so-called unwritten law by which a husband who killed his wife's lover in the act of adultery was acquitted.

Arguments for those acquittals portrayed avenging husbands as "involuntary agents of God." In contrast, lovers were condemned as "children of Satan," "serpents," and "noxious reptiles" with supernatural power allowing them to invade the "paradise of blissful marriages" (Ireland, "Libertine" 32).[15]

In *The Scarlet Letter* this imagery is reversed. It is the avenging husband who stalks his wife's lover with "other senses than [those ministers and magistrates] possess" and who is associated with "Satan himself, or Satan's emissary" (p. 108). In the meantime, we imagine Arthur, Hester, and Pearl as a possible family (Herbert 201). The narrator so writes off Chillingworth as Hester's legal husband that he refers to him as her "former husband" (p. 136), causing Michael T. Gilmore to follow suit (93) and D. H. Lawrence to designate Mr. Prynne Hester's "first" husband. A legal scholar writing on adultery goes so far as to call Hester an "unwed mother" (Weinstein 225).

By reversing the sympathy that courts gave to cuckolded husbands taking revenge into their own hands, Hawthorne draws attention to the importance of seeking justice within the confines of the written law. Dramatizing the dangers of achieving justice outside the law, Chillingworth illustrates natural liberty's potential for evil as well as for good. On the one hand, it prompts Hester to question the law in the name of a more equitable social order. On the other, it can allow Chillingworth to take the law into his own hands for personal revenge. If Hester's desire to create the world "anew" suggests utopian possibilities, Chillingworth's revenge, driven by "new interests" and "a new purpose" (p. 102), suggests the potential for a reign of terror. Hawthorne links these two seeming opposites through the secret pact that Hester and her husband forge on his return. Their secret bond in turn parallels the secret bond of natural lovers that Hester and Dimmesdale contemplate in their meeting in the forest. The two bonds even have structural similarities. For instance, just as Hester's new bond with her husband can be maintained only because he has taken on a new name, so Hester counsels her lover, "Give up this name of Arthur Dimmesdale, and make thyself another" (p. 157). More importantly, the secrecy in which both bonds are made isolates everyone involved from the human community. As such, both are in stark contrast to the bond created by the civil ceremony of marriage whose public witness links husband and wife to the community.

[15]For more on cases involving the "unwritten law," see Ireland, "Insanity"; Hartog; and Ganz.

Much has been made of Hester's adulterous violation of her marriage vows. Not much attention, however, has been paid to her husband's violation of his vows, even though the narrator comments on it. For instance, in prison Hester asks her husband why he will "not announce thyself openly, and cast me off at once?" His reply: "It may be . . . because I will not encounter the dishonor that besmirches the husband of a faithless woman. It may be for other reasons. Enough, it is to my purpose to live and die unknown" (p. 73). In legal terms, Chillingworth's fear of dishonor makes no sense inasmuch as he has committed no crime. But if some antebellum courts displayed great sympathy to cuckolded husbands through the unwritten law, there was a long tradition — still powerful in the seventeenth century — of popular and bawdy rituals mocking cuckolded husbands (Ramsey 202–07). No matter what other motives Chillingworth might have, the narrator makes clear that the man "whose connection with the fallen woman had been the most intimate and sacred of them all" resolves "not to be pilloried beside her on her pedestal of shame" (p. 101). That resolve explains "why — since the choice was with himself —" he does not "come forward to vindicate his claim to an inheritance so little desirable" (p. 101).

According to coverture, that undesirable inheritance was not only Hester, but also her child. Fully aware of his husbandly rights, Chillingworth tells his wife, "Thou and thine, Hester Prynne, belong to me" (p. 73). Nonetheless, he refuses to acknowledge his inheritance, telling Hester in the same scene, "The child is yours, — she is none of mine, — neither will she recognize my voice or aspect as a father's" (p. 70). The doctrine of coverture was clearly a patriarchal institution; nonetheless, it was not solely to the advantage of the husband. It was also a means to hold him responsible for the well-being of his wife and children. Chillingworth might not be Pearl's biological father, but he was her father in the eyes of the law. That legal status adds another dimension to the recognition scene that occurs when Chillingworth walks out of the forest and finds his wife on public display for having committed adultery. "Speak, woman!" he "coldly and sternly" cries from the crowd. "Speak; and give your child a father!" (p. 68). Commanding his wife to reveal the name of her lover, the wronged husband also inadvertently reminds us that at any moment Hester could have given Pearl a legal father by identifying him. Even more important, Chillingworth could have identified himself. But the same man who knows his legal rights of possession as a husband refuses to take on his legal responsibilities as a father.

Pearl, in other words, has not one but two fathers who refuse to accept their responsibilities. Having lost his own father as a young boy and doubting his ability financially to support his children on losing his job at the Custom House, Hawthorne was acutely aware of the need for fathers to live up to their name. In fact, by the end of the novel he ensures Pearl's future by having her two fathers finally accept their responsibilities. At his death Dimmesdale publicly acknowledges his paternity, eliciting from Pearl a "pledge that she would grow up amid human joy and sorrow, nor for ever do battle with the world" (p. 197). At his death Chillingworth bequeaths to his once-rejected inheritance "a very considerable amount of property, both here and in England" (p. 199). Even so, the book's emphasis on failed fathers raises the possibility that Hester will earn her claim to good citizenship through her role as a mother.

4. A MOTHER'S RIGHTS

The Scarlet Letter, according to Tony Tanner, is a major exception to the "curiously little interest" the novel of adultery pays to the child of an illicit liaison, "even on the part of the mother (or especially on part of the mother)" (98). Indeed, Hester's relation to Pearl is a major part of Hawthorne's story. Accompanying her mother in almost every scene in which Hester appears, Pearl embodies a major paradox: although there is perhaps no better symbol of the hope for a new beginning than the birth of a child, Hester's daughter continually reminds her mother of her sinful past. Like the scarlet letter to which she is frequently compared, Pearl serves therefore as an agent of her mother's socialization. Part of Hester's socialization is in turn to socialize her daughter. Worried that Pearl is of demon origin or that her mother is not doing a proper job of raising her, some of the "leading inhabitants" are rumored to be campaigning to transfer Pearl "to wiser and better guardianship than Hester Prynne's" (p. 89). In response Hester concocts an excuse to go to the governor's hall, only to find Governor Bellingham and Reverend Wilson convinced of their plan when Pearl impiously responds to their interrogations. Desperately turning to Dimmesdale, Hester implores: "I will not lose the child! Speak for me! Thou knowest, — for thou hast sympathies which these men lack! — thou knowest what is in my heart, and what are a mother's rights" (p. 98).

As much an anachronism as Hawthorne's evocation of the concept of good citizenship, Hester's appeal to a mother's rights helps to locate

Hawthorne's attitude toward motherhood. In the seventeenth century no mother threatened with losing custody of her child could have successfully evoked the idea of a mother's rights. On the contrary, as we have seen, under the doctrine of coverture the child belonged legally to the father. In fact, in custody disputes between husband and wife a common law court did not grant custody to the mother until 1774. Even in this landmark case Chief Justice Lord Mansfield acknowledged the "father's natural right" while ruling that "the public right to superintend the education of its citizens" had more weight (qtd. in Grossberg 52). Mansfield's seemingly revolutionary ruling, in other words, would have confirmed the Puritan elders' sense that for her own good and that of the commonwealth Pearl, who had no father willing to claim her, could be taken from her mother. It was not until the courts were convinced that the education of children as citizens was best accomplished by their mothers that the idea of a mother's right to her child could gain force.

That process began in a few highly publicized cases in the U.S. just before Hawthorne began writing *The Scarlet Letter.* These cases in which a mother won custody from a father coincided with a challenge to coverture posed by the rise of republican rhetoric that opposed coverture's image of marriage as a corporate body presided over by the husband with the image of marriage as a contractual relation, with husband and wife bringing to the union complementary, if not identical, duties and obligations. Not yet willing to grant women an active role in the political sphere of the new republic, this rhetoric still gave them an important role to play, that of raising children as citizens in service of the nation. Emphasizing the nurturing role of the mother, this cult of republican motherhood bolstered a wife's claim to gain custody of her child, especially one of "tender" years. Indeed, in the D'Hauteville case, one of the most publicized custody battles, the wife's lawyers contrasted the increasingly progressive republican nature of marriage in the U.S. to the outmoded feudal concept of coverture maintained by her Swiss husband (Grossberg).

In her plea for a mother's rights Hester echoes the antebellum rhetoric of republican motherhood, which, like Hester's appeal to Dimmesdale, emphasized the capacity for sympathy. A product of "paternal" and "maternal" qualities, a proper republican citizen was not simply the obedient subject produced under the paternal regime of both coverture and seventeenth-century Puritanism. Instead, a good citizen should also have the moral quality of sympathy nurtured through a mother's love. Hawthorne dramatizes the marriage of these two qualities in the final scaffold scene when Dimmesdale, the biological father, elicits Pearl's pledge of obedience, a pledge that comes in the form of tears produced because the scene has "developed all her sympathies" (p. 197).

It would, nonetheless, be a mistake to assume that Hester becomes a model citizen by the end of *The Scarlet Letter* through her role as a mother. If republican mothers were supposed to raise citizens for the nation, Pearl does not become a "citizen" of Boston. Whereas, in typical Hawthornian fashion, we are not completely certain where Pearl ends up, circumstantial evidence indicates that she has successfully married and lives somewhere in Europe, most likely on the continent, not even in England. Measured by the most important standard of success for a republican mother, therefore, Hester fails. Rather than raise a child inculcated in proper values to serve the nation/commonwealth, Hester raises a child who finds "a home and comfort" in an "unknown region" (pp. 135, 201), just as Hawthorne ends "The Custom-House" imagining himself a "citizen of somewhere else" (p. 53).

To the patriotically minded, Hester's failure to produce a representative of the new generation bound by loyalty to the nation would seem to disqualify her as a model citizen. The primary goal is not necessarily to produce citizens who display loyalty to the state as representative of "the people" bound together as a nation. The goal instead is to produce independent citizens capable of choosing where they can best develop their capacities. To be sure, this goal is in part conditioned by the ideology of liberal democracies, like the U.S., which values freedom of choice. In the U.S. of Hawthorne's day that freedom was officially endorsed through the government's support of a citizen's right to expatriation, whereas British subjects owed perpetual allegiance to their sovereign (Tsiang; James).[16] The power of *The Scarlet Letter* as civic myth has to do with its dramatization of the difference that a preference for freedom of choice can make and how important the existence of an independent civil society is for its cultivation. That difference is most poignantly dramatized in Hester's decision to return to Boston at the end of the book.

[16]Hawthorne's celebration in "The Custom-House" of the renewing powers of "frequent transplantation" indirectly lends support to arguments for the right to expatriation (p. 26). Although he describes what, "in lack of a better phrase," he must call "affection" for his "native place" of Salem (p. 26), he also insists, "Human nature will not flourish, any more than a potato, if it be planted and replanted, for too long a series of generations, in the same worn-out soil. My children have had other birthplaces, and so far as their fortunes may be within my control, shall strike their roots into unaccustomed earth" (p. 28).

That decision is freely chosen in the sense that no one forces Hester to make it, but it is certainly not a decision made without pressure from many complicated historical and psychological factors, just as one's decision as to where to maintain or seek citizenship is not simply a rational choice about possibilities for political or economic freedom but one conditioned by numerous factors that one cannot control, such as where one was born and where one's intimate ties are located. In this regard Hester's return is especially important because she returns no longer primarily defined by relations of status that so governed the women of her time; that is, the status of lover, mother, or wife. On the contrary, with her lover and husband dead and her child apparently married and in another country, she returns as a woman, a woman devoted, nonetheless, not to individual fulfillment but to the interpersonal relations of civil society. It is in this space, which incorporates "many of the associations and identities that we value outside of, prior to, or in the shadow of state and citizenship" (Walzer, Introduction 1), that Hester provides us paradoxically with a model of good citizenship that no liberal democracy can afford to do without.

5. HESTER'S UNEXCEPTIONAL RETURN

At the start of the novel the scarlet letter has "the effect of a spell" on Hester, "taking her out of the ordinary relations with humanity, and inclosing her in a sphere by herself" (p. 58). As the novel goes on, however, it assumes the scaffold's role of promoting good citizenship. With Hester's return and her willing resumption of the letter — "for not the sternest magistrate of that iron period would have imposed it" (p. 201) — the scarlet letter has, as Sacvan Bercovitch has argued, finally done its office. But just as Hester's actions change the meaning that people give to the scarlet A, so too they alter the sense of good citizenship with which the book begins.

The book begins with an image of good citizenship as the sort of absolute obedience that Winthrop wanted his subjects to give to their magistrates. The distance Hawthorne moves away from that image can be measured by a comparison between Dimmesdale and Hester. Tempted in the forest to break completely with the dictates of civil authority, Dimmesdale goes back on his resolve and instead seeks salvation by submitting totally to the existing civil order through participation in the civic activities of the election-day ceremonies. His submission culminates in his sermon that teleologically projects a utopian vision of a cohesive — and, it is important to emphasize, closed — Puritan community into the future. Dimmesdale, in other words, becomes the obedient subject that Winthrop desires. He is joined during these public ceremonies by almost the entire Puritan crowd, which submits "with child-like loyalty" to its rulers (p. 192). Hester, however, is not among that crowd. Her good citizenship comes because of, rather than despite of, her failure to submit so loyally.

Through her return Hester acknowledges the civil law in a way that she did not in her rebellious earlier days. Nonetheless, she does not, as Dimmesdale does, submit totally to the state. On the contrary, she receives the Puritan magistrates' toleration of — and even admiration of — actions that are not directly under their supervision. Concerned with counseling and comforting those who feel marginalized by official Puritan society, especially women whose attempts at intimacy had failed, those activities extend the parameters of good citizenship to an interpersonal realm concerned with affairs of the heart that no affairs of state seem capable of remedying. If Dimmesdale simply channels his capacity for sympathy into total service to the state, Hester dramatizes how important it is for the state to promote spaces in which the capacity for sympathy can be cultivated while simultaneously guarding against the dangers of natural liberty. Thus, even though Hester has no place within the civic sphere, she, unlike Dimmesdale, helps to bring about a possible structural realignment of Puritan society by having it include what we can call the nascent formation of an independent civil society.

Stressing the importance of the civil order, the Puritans, as represented by Hawthorne, had no place for an independent civil society because they felt the need to control all aspects of life. As the narrator notes regarding the concern over Pearl's upbringing, "[M]atters of even slighter public interest, and of far less intrinsic weight than the welfare of Hester and her child, were strangely mixed up with the deliberations of legislators and acts of state" (p. 89). Indeed, the relative independence granted to Hester at the end of the book markedly contrasts with an earlier description of her cottage which she could possess only "by the license of the magistrates, who still kept an inquisitorial watch over her" (p. 76).[17]

[17]Pease makes a number of interesting points about *The Scarlet Letter* in relation to civic duty, but he neglects the crucial role of civil society and confines himself to a discussion of the "reciprocity between the public and private worlds" (82). His sense of community also depends upon Rousseau's "general will," which Pease equates with an American notion of a "public will" (24). But an independent civil society is important

If the Puritan theocracy, like all absolutist forms of government, has no room for an independent civil society, such a society is an essential feature of liberal democracies. In Michael Walzer's words, "It is very risky for a democratic government when the state takes up all the available room and there are no alternative associations, no protected social space, where people can seek relief from politics, nurse wounds, find comfort, build strength for future encounters" (Introduction 1). It is so risky that one of the functions of the state in liberal democracies is to ensure that alternative associations and protected spaces exist. In dramatizing the importance of their existence, Hester's activities on her return to Boston indicate the kinds of nonpolitical transformations that for Hawthorne were necessary for democratic rule to emerge from the Puritans' authoritarian rule.

By emphasizing the Puritans' authoritarianism rather than their democracy, Hawthorne works on/with the antebellum myth of the Puritan origins of American democracy. That myth has been perpetuated by both supporters of the country's claim to foster democratic rule and critics of it, such as Bercovitch and Lauren Berlant, the two best recent readers of Hawthorne's politics. Like most recent critics, including myself, both Bercovitch and Berlant read *The Scarlet Letter*'s seventeenth-century moment of representation as a comment on its antebellum moment of production.[18] But, unlike me, they do so by turning a nineteenth-century liberal democracy into a secular version of the Puritans' seventeenth-century theocracy.[19] Fitting *The Scarlet Letter* into the project he has conducted throughout his distinguished career, Bercovitch plots a complicated narrative of secularization in which the New

because it allows for associations that resist potentially tyrannical conformity enforced in the name of an abstract "general will," the most obvious example being the "reign of terror." It is no accident that Pease champions Hawthorne's Puritans, finding in them a positive "unrealized vision of community" (53).

[18]According to Colacurcio, "If the plot leaves Hester Prynne suspended between the repressive but obsolescent world of Ann Hutchinson and the dangerous new freedoms of the world of Margaret Fuller, the theme of the romance takes us very surely from the high noon of the Puritan theocracy to the dawn of the Romantic Protest in the nineteenth century" (*Province* 32). Both Gilmore and Herbert argue that *The Scarlet Letter*'s world may be Puritan New England but that its major characters have a nineteenth-century moral outlook. Both follow Baym, who claims that Hawthorne "has created an authoritarian [Puritan] state with a Victorian moral outlook" (215). Baym's comment is extremely important since it reminds us of the extent to which Hawthorne's representation of the Puritans is work on/with myth, not an accurate representation.

[19]Bercovitch's narrative of secularization necessarily minimizes important developments in the eighteenth century, such as the structural transformation of the public sphere and its relation to the rise of a relatively independent civil society (Habermas).

England Way becomes the American Way, while Berlant without elaboration simply posits the continuities of the "Puritan/American project" (158).

Bercovitch is acutely aware of how resistance to the state can serve the ideology of liberal democracies. Nonetheless, his need to see the U.S. nineteenth-century democracy as a secularized version of the Puritans' seventeenth-century theocracy betrays his otherwise magnificent reading of Hawthorne's novel in two important ways. First, since the great crisis for Puritanism was the antinomian controversy, Bercovitch needs to assert that "the only plausible modes of American dissent are those that center on the self" and then to read *The Scarlet Letter* as a book about Hester's individualism (31). But Hester, I hope I have established, is defined much more by her commitment to interpersonal relations than by her individualism, which is not to say that Hawthorne does not value the independence that she displays in contrast to the "childlike loyalty" of other Puritan subjects. But that independence for Hawthorne is not a product of a naturally self-sufficient self; it is instead bred and cultivated in the associational activities of an independent civil society.[20]

Bercovitch's second misreading has to do with Hawthorne's attitude toward the nation. Certainly many Americans see the U.S. as fulfilling a divine mission, just as the Puritans saw themselves as the chosen people. But Hawthorne's work on/with that exceptionalist myth is too powerful to be confined by Bercovitch's narrative of secularization, however subtle and complicated that narrative is. On the contrary, Hawthorne's well-documented skepticism about revolutionary reformers questions the sacred mission they grant to themselves. For instance, both the Puritan Revolution in England and the French Revolution toppled sovereigns claiming divine authority, and yet Cromwell's mission in England was to establish a New Jerusalem while the revolutionaries of France transferred the king's claim to absolute authority to the nation and, with religious zeal, condemned to death anyone opposed

[20]"Rather than revealing that . . . 'the only plausible modes of American dissent are those that center on the self,' *The Scarlet Letter* seems to demonstrate that the only form of selfhood worth having is generated by reciprocal connection to others — and that one may choose constraints because there are no meanings without them. Hester's deepest yearning, this is to say, is not for freedom but for a reimagined social life (the very thing that in Bercovitch's account, consensus ideology removes from view), for a lover, and for a community able to accommodate the forms of connection she envisions for them" (Millington 6). To which I add: the relative freedom from state supervision provided by an independent civil society enhances the possibility of imagining and working toward that different social life.

to its new principles. From a Hawthornian perspective, the danger is not that America will stray from its divine mission, but that it will follow the path of other revolutions and believe too fervently that it has such an exceptional destiny.

That ever-present danger means that, although there is a structural difference between an antebellum democracy and a seventeenth-century theocracy, perpetual work is required to guard against a patriotism that "loses all sense of the distinction between State, nation, and government" (Bourne 357). Hawthorne accomplishes that work in his introductory sketch of "The Custom-House" as well as in his novel. Hawthorne, Stephen Nissenbaum has documented, was heavily involved in local partisan politics and fought extremely hard to retain his civil service post in the Custom House. Nonetheless, his fictional version of his dismissal tells a different story. If, as Gordon Hutner puts it, Hawthorne "introduces his novel about the public history of private lives with his private history of public lives" (20), in both the novel and the sketch he ends by locating his protagonists in the space of civil society between the public and private. And just as the novel looks ironically at various ideals of good citizenship, so does the sketch. For instance, Hawthorne's portrayal of the ex-military men working at the Custom House undercuts the ideal of the citizen-soldier, an ideal that contributed to the election of military hero Zachary Taylor as president and thus indirectly led to Hawthorne's dismissal. Taylor's election is a perfect example of the failure of a second ideal: people displaying and cultivating their virtue through participation in the political process. Far from a realm in which citizens sacrifice their own interests for the good of the nation, politics in "The Custom-House" has degenerated into a battle of self-interest. Its debilitating effects are most prominently displayed in the spoils system, which, especially in Hawthorne's hands, puts a lie to a third ideal: the good citizen as devoted civil servant.

Presided over by a flag that marks it as "a civil, and not a military post of Uncle Sam's government" (p. 23), the Custom House is occupied by people who fail to heed the fierce look of the American eagle over its entrance that warns "all citizens, careful of their safety, against intruding on the premises which she overshadows with her wings" (p. 24). Instead, they seek "to shelter themselves under the wing of the federal eagle" (p. 24), not so much to serve the country as to be guaranteed a comfortable livelihood. The expectation that the federal eagle's "bosom has all the softness and snugness of an eider-down pillow" (p. 24) is the mirror-image of the childlike loyalty that causes the

Puritan crowd uncritically to submit to its magistrates' rule. Choosing neither the nation's maternal protection nor its paternal authority, Hawthorne weaves a fiction in which he best serves the country not as a civil servant paid by the state but as a nonpartisan writer located in an independent civil society. Thus he portrays himself as happily leaving the Custom House so that he could once again take up his pen. The novel that he subsequently wrote, which more than any other work has become part of the "general incorporation of literature into education" and thus part of the "channel through which the [national] ethos is disseminated and . . . the means by which outsiders are brought inside it," gives substance to the cliché that democracy is a way of life as well as a political system (Brodhead 61, 60).

6. CONCLUSION

If *The Scarlet Letter* suggests that political institutions alone cannot make a democracy, its emphasis on good citizenship in the civil as well as in the civic sphere is by no means a solution to all of the country's problems. The issue of race, for instance, marks an important limit to that emphasis. Conflicted between loyalties to an individual state and to the federal union, Hawthorne searched for a reason to fight the Civil War.[21] Writing to his friend Horatio Bridge, he identified the issue of slavery. "If we are fighting for the annihilation of slavery . . . it might be a wise object, and offers a tangible result, and the only one which is consistent with a future Union between North and South. A continuance of the war would soon make this plain to us; and we should see the expediency of preparing our black brethren for future citizenship by allowing them to fight for their own liberties, and educating them through heroic influences" (*Letters* 381). Whereas the annihilation of slavery was indeed the basis for restoring the Union, a truly equitable

[21]In an essay that caused some to question his patriotism Hawthorne wrote: "The anomaly of two allegiances (of which that of the State comes nearest home to a man's feelings, and includes the altar and the hearth, while the General Government claims his devotion only to an airy mode of law, and has no symbol but a flag)" means that "[t]here never existed any other government, against which treason was so easy, and could defend itself by such plausible arguments" ("Chiefly" 416). He added: "In the vast extent of our country — too vast, by far, to be taken into one small human heart — we inevitably limit to our own State, or, at farthest, to our own Section, that sentiment of physical love for the soil which renders an Englishman, for example, so intensely sensitive to the dignity and well-being of his little island" ("Chiefly" 416–17).

citizenship for blacks was, as we know, derailed by the reconciliation of white North and South.

Even though he died in 1864, Hawthorne unintentionally anticipates a reason for those derailed efforts in his metaphoric descriptions of the scarlet letter. The letter is called variously a mark, a brand, a badge of shame, and a stigma. What Hawthorne could not have known was that a few years after *The Scarlet Letter* appeared, Justice Taney in the *Dred Scott* case would use similar metaphors to deny citizenship to anyone of African descent — free or slave. Taney argued that, since in a republic there is only one class of citizens, and because slavery had so degraded and stigmatized blacks, they should be excluded from the sovereign body constituting the nation. In an effort to undo the damage done by Dred Scott, the Supreme Court after the Civil War ruled that the Thirteenth Amendment forbade not only slavery but also all "badges and incidents" of slavery. The difference between a badge and a stigma is significant. A badge can be removed; a stigma, coming from the Greek word for a brand, is implanted for a lifetime — and for Taney could be passed from generation to generation (Thomas).

The Scarlet Letter ends by giving Hester a choice of whether to wear her "badge of shame" (p. 132). She willingly chooses to wear it, in part because through her own agency the letter has "ceased to be a stigma" (p. 201). In contrast, the possibility of achieving the status of model citizen through individual effort was denied African Americans because their race meant that, as a group, they inherited a badge of slavery, whose stigma persisted. The civil society argument about "uncoerced human associations" by itself is not adequate to deal with that problem (Walzer, "Concept" 7). Instead a much more traditional argument about active citizen participation in the political sphere would seem to be called for.

Clearly, a danger of an exclusive emphasis on good citizenship in civil society is political quietism of the sort that Hawthorne succumbed to in the 1850s when he argued that slavery would wither and die of its own accord. As regrettable as Hawthorne's quietism was, however, that biographical fact should not be, as some critics make it, the final word on "the politics" of his most famous novel (Cheyfitz; Arac, "Politics"). *The Scarlet Letter* does not so much reject civic notions of good citizenship as question empty platitudes about them while expanding our sense of what they can entail. That expanded sense of good citizenship is by no means sufficient to solve issues of racial inequality — as if any one course of action is — but it may be an important component of any solution. Indeed, it is not simply an accident that the movement agitating for first-class citizenship for African Americans was called the *civil* rights movement. To be sure, civil rights by definition are guaranteed by the state, and to be effective they have to be enforced by the state. Nonetheless, agitation for civil rights reminds us that one of the most important goals of political activism is the creation of a space where the voluntary associations located in civil society exist according to principles of equity and fairness. As Walzer puts it, "Only a democratic state can create a democratic civil society; only a democratic civil society can sustain a democratic state. The civility that makes democratic politics possible can only be learned in the associational networks; the roughly equal and widely dispersed capabilities that sustain the networks have to be fostered by the democratic state" ("Concept" 24).[22]

What Walzer does not do, however, is give us a concrete sense of what a democratic civil society looks like. Thus his helpful, but too balanced, formulation needs to be supplemented by the observation that a major debate within democratic politics is how to define a democratic civil society. *The Scarlet Letter* does not provide that definition, but it does contribute to democratic politics by implying an answer to another question raised by Walzer's formulation: which comes first, democratic state or democratic civil society? Challenging the standard account that locates the seeds of a later democracy in the political institutions of seventeenth-century New England, *The Scarlet Letter* implies that the nascent formation of an independent civil society precedes and helps to generate a democratic state. If that implied narrative has limits — and like all narratives it does — it has also served as a powerful and enabling civic myth for many, like those whom Hester counsels, whose failed efforts at sympathy make them feel marginalized by the existing — not so — civil order.[23]

[22]Walzer continues, "The state can never be what it appears to be in liberal theory, a mere framework for civil society. It is also the instrument of the struggle, used to give particular shape to the common life." Nonetheless, he adds that it is not necessary to find "in politics, as Rousseau urged, the greater part of our happiness. Most of us will be happier elsewhere, involved only sometimes in affairs of state. But we must leave the state open to our sometime involvement" ("Concept" 24).

[23]I am grateful for the comments provided by Jayne Lewis, Robert Milder, Frederick Newberry, Steven Mailloux, and audiences at the University of Oregon, the University of Washington, and the Kennedy Institute for North American Studies in Berlin.

WORKS CITED

Althusser, Louis. "Ideology and Ideological State Apparatuses (Notes Toward an Investigation)." *Lenin and Philosophy, and Other Essays.* Trans. Ben Brewster. New York: Monthly Review Press, 1971. 127–86.

Anon. "Bancroft's History of the United States." *American Jurist and Law Magazine* 2 (1838): 229–31.

Arac, Jonathan. "Narrative Forms." *The Cambridge History of American Literature.* Ed. Sacvan Bercovitch. Vol. 2. New York: Cambridge UP, 1995. 605–777.

———. "The Politics of *The Scarlet Letter.*" *Ideology and Classic American Literature.* Ed. Sacvan Bercovitch and Myra Jehlen. New York: Cambridge UP, 1986. 247–66.

Baym, Nina. "Passion and Authority in *The Scarlet Letter.*" *New England Quarterly* 43 (1970): 209–30.

Bell, Michael Davitt. *Hawthorne and the Historical Romance of New England.* Princeton: Princeton UP, 1971.

Bercovitch, Sacvan. *The Office of "The Scarlet Letter."* Baltimore: Johns Hopkins UP, 1991.

Berlant, Lauren. *The Anatomy of National Fantasy: Hawthorne, Utopia, and Everyday Life.* Chicago: U of Chicago P, 1991.

Blumenberg, Hans. *Work on Myth.* Cambridge: MIT P, 1985.

Bourne, Randolph. *The Radical Will: Selected Writings, 1911–1918.* Ed. Olaf Hansen. New York: Urizen, 1977.

Brodhead, Richard. *The School of Hawthorne.* New York: Oxford UP, 1986.

Burke, Kenneth. "Literature as Equipment for Living." *The Philosophy of Literary Form.* Baton Rouge: Louisiana State UP, 1941. 293–304.

Cheyfitz, Eric. "The Irresistibleness of Great Literature: Reconstructing Hawthorne's Politics." *American Literary History* 6 (1994): 539–58.

Choate, Rufus. "The Importance of Illustrating New England History by a Series of Romances Like the Waverley Novels." *The Works of Rufus Choate with a Memoir of His Life.* Ed. Samuel Gilman Brown. 2 vols. Boston: Brown, 1862. 1: 319–46.

Cohen, Jean, and Andrew Arato. *Civil Society and Political Theory.* Cambridge: MIT P, 1992.

Colacurcio, Michael J. "Footsteps of Ann Hutchinson: The Context of *The Scarlet Letter.*" *ELH* 39 (1972): 459–94.

———. *The Province of Piety: Moral History in Hawthorne's Early Tales.* Cambridge: Harvard UP, 1984.

———. "'The Woman's Own Choice': Sex, Metaphor, and the Puritan 'Sources' of *The Scarlet Letter.*" *Doctrine and Difference.* New York: Routledge, 1997. 205–28.

Crews, Frederick C. *The Sins of the Fathers: Hawthorne's Psychological Themes.* New York: Oxford UP, 1966.

Dayton, Cornelia. *Women Before the Bar: Gender, Law, and Society in Connecticut, 1639–1789.* Chapel Hill: U of North Carolina P, 1995.

Dekker, George. *The American Historical Romance.* New York: Cambridge UP, 1987.

Doubleday, Neal Frank. "Hawthorne and Literary Nationalism," *American Literature* 12 (1942): 447–53.

Dred Scott v. Sandford. 19 Howard 393 (1857).

Fletcher, Andrew. *Andrew Fletcher of Saltoun: Selected Political Writings.* Ed. David Daiches. Edinburgh: Scottish Academic Press, 1979.

Ganz, Melissa J. "Wicked Women and Veiled Ladies: Gendered Narratives of the McFarland-Richardson Tragedy." *Yale Journal of Law and Feminism* 9 (1997): 255–303.

Gilmore, Michael T. "Hawthorne and the Making of the Middle Class." *Discovering Difference.* Ed. Christoph K. Lohman. Bloomington: Indiana UP, 1993. 88–104.

Grossberg, Michael. *A Judgment for Solomon: The D'Hauteville Case and Legal Experience in Antebellum America.* New York: Cambridge UP, 1996.

Habermas, Jürgen. *The Structural Transformation of the Public Sphere.* Cambridge: MIT P, 1989.

Hartog, Hendrik. "Lawyering Husbands' Rights, and 'the Unwritten Law' in Nineteenth-Century America." *Journal of American History* 84 (1997): 67–96.

Hawthorne, Nathaniel. "Chiefly about War Matters. By a Peaceable Man." *Miscellaneous Prose.* Centenary Edition. Vol. 23. Columbus: Ohio State UP, 1994. 403–42.

———. *The Letters, 1857–1864.* Centenary Edition. Vol. 18. Columbus: Ohio State UP, 1987.

Herbert, T. Walter. *Dearest Beloved: The Hawthornes and the Making of the Middle-Class Family.* Berkeley: U of California P, 1993.

Hobbes, Thomas. *On the Citizen.* 1642. Trans. Richard Tuck and Michael Silverthorne. Cambridge: Cambridge UP, 1998.

———. *Leviathan.* 1651. New York: Penguin, 1986.

Holmes, Oliver Wendell, Jr. *The Common Law.* Cambridge: Belknap P of Harvard UP, 1963.

Howells, William Dean. "Hawthorne's Hester Prynne." *The Critical Response to Nathaniel Hawthorne's* The Scarlet Letter. Ed. Gary Scharnhorst. Westport, CT: Greenwood Press, 1992. 101–09.

Hull, N. E. H. *Female Felons: Women and Serious Crime in Colonial Massachusetts.* Urbana: U of Illinois P, 1989.

Hutner, Gordon. *Secrets and Sympathy: Forms of Disclosure in Hawthorne's Novels.* Athens: U of Georgia P, 1988.

Ireland, Robert M. "The Libertine Must Die: Sexual Dishonour and the Unwritten Law in the Nineteenth-Century United States." *Journal of Social History* 23 (1989): 27–44.

———. "Insanity and the Unwritten Law." *American Journal of Legal History* 32 (1988): 157–72.

James, Alan G. "Expatriation in the United States: Precept and Practice Today and Yesterday." *San Diego Law Review* 27 (1990): 853–905.

Kerber, Linda K. *No Constitutional Right 'to Be Ladies': Women and the Obligations of Citizenship.* New York: Hill and Wang, 1998.

Koehler, Lyle. *A Search for Power: The "Weaker Sex" in Seventeenth-Century New England.* Urbana: U of Illinois P, 1980.

Korobkin, Laura Hanft. *Criminal Conversations: Sentimentality and Nineteenth-Century Legal Stories of Adultery.* New York: Columbia UP, 1998.

Kymlicka, Will. *Multicultural Citizenship.* Oxford: Clarendon, 1995.

Lawrence, D. H. *Studies in Classic American Literature.* Garden City, NY: Doubleday, 1951.

Levin, David. *History as Romantic Art.* Stanford: Stanford UP, 1959.

Maine, Sir Henry Sumner. *Ancient Law: Its Connection with the Early History of Society and Its Relation to Modern Ideas.* 1861. New York: Dorset, 1986.

McWilliams, John P., Jr. *Hawthorne, Melville, and the American Character. A Looking-Glass Business.* New York: Cambridge UP, 1984.

McWilliams, W. Carey. *The Idea of Fraternity in America.* Berkeley: U of California P, 1973.

Melville, Herman. *Billy Budd, Sailor (An Inside Narrative).* Ed. Harrison Hayford and Merton M. Sealts, Jr. Chicago: U of Chicago P, 1962.

Millington, Richard. "*The Office of 'The Scarlet Letter'*: An 'Inside Narrative'?" *Nathaniel Hawthorne Review* 22 (1996): 1–8.

Morgan, Edmund S. *The Puritan Dilemma: The Story of John Winthrop*. Boston: Little, Brown, 1958.

———. *Puritan Family*. New York: Harper, 1966.

Newberry, Frederick. *Hawthorne's Divided Loyalties: England and America in His Work*. Rutherford: Fairleigh Dickinson UP, 1987.

Nissenbaum, Stephen, ed. Introduction. *The Scarlet Letter and Selected Writings of Nathaniel Hawthorne*. New York: The Modern Library, 1984. vii–xiv.

Norton, Mary Beth. *Founding Mothers and Fathers: General Power and the Forming of American Society*. New York: Knopf, 1996.

Nye, R. B. *George Bancroft*. New York: Knopf, 1945.

———. Introduction. *History of the United States* (abridged). By George Bancroft. Chicago: U of Chicago P, 1966.

Pateman, Carole. *The Sexual Contract*. Stanford: Stanford UP, 1988.

Pease, Donald E. *Visionary Compacts: American Renaissance Writings in Cultural Context*. Madison: U of Wisconsin P, 1987.

Pocock, J. G. A. *The Machiavellian Moment: Florentine Political Thought and the Atlantic Republican Tradition*. Princeton: Princeton UP, 1975.

Ramsey, Carolyn B. "Sex and Social Order: The Selective Enforcement of Colonial American Adultery Laws in the English Context." *Yale Journal of Law & the Humanities* 10 (1998): 191–228.

Reynolds, Larry J. *European Revolutions and the American Literary Renaissance*. New Haven: Yale UP, 1988.

Ryskamp, Charles. "The New England Sources of *The Scarlet Letter*." *American Literature* 31 (1960): 237–72.

Shklar, Judith. *American Citizenship: The Quest for Inclusion*. Cambridge: Harvard UP, 1991.

Smith, Merril D. *Breaking the Bonds: Marital Discord in Pennsylvania, 1730–1830*. New York: New York UP, 1991.

Smith, Rogers. *Civic Ideals: Conflicting Visions of Citizenship in U.S. History*. New Haven: Yale UP, 1997.

Tanner, Tony. *Adultery in the Novel: Contract and Transgression*. Baltimore: Johns Hopkins UP, 1979.

Thomas, Brook. "Stigmas, Badges, and Brands: Discriminating Marks in Legal History." *History, Memory, and the Law*. Ed. Austin Sarat and Tomas R. Kearns. Ann Arbor: U of Michigan P, 1999. 249–82.

Tsiang, I-Mien. *The Question of Expatriation in America Prior to 1907.* Baltimore: Johns Hopkins UP, 1942.

Walzer, Michael. "The Concept of Civil Society." *Toward a Global Civil Society.* Ed. Michael Walzer. Providence: Berghahn, 1995. 7–27.

———. Introduction. *Toward a Global Civil Society.* Ed. Michael Walzer. Providence: Berghahn, 1995. 1–4.

Weinstein, Jeremy D. "Adultery, Law, and the State: A History." *Hastings Law Journal* 38 (1986): 195–238.

Winthrop, John. *Winthrop's Journal: "History of New England."* Ed. J. K. Hosmer. Vol. 2. New York: Scribners, 1908.

Combining Perspectives on *The Scarlet Letter*

So far, this volume's emphasis has been on defining four different critical approaches to literature — and on exemplifying them with essays that, though informed by other perspectives, can be shown to exhibit the salient features of a single approach. In presenting this final essay, the emphasis is reversed; the intention is to demonstrate and even emphasize the permeability of critical approaches, to show how diverse critical assumptions and traditions can mix, merge, and metamorphose.

Put more plainly, the purpose is to show how a critic can draw on the insights of *several* approaches, combining perspectives not in equal measure, necessarily, but with the clear intent of presenting a view of a text that would be unavailable from a single critical vantage point. In the exemplary, mixed-approach essay that follows, Lora Romero combines critical perspectives that you have been introduced to already with others that will be described briefly here — and that you can learn still more about by consulting the "Glossary of Critical and Theoretical Terms" at the back of this volume.

In the opening paragraph of "Homosocial Romance: Nathaniel Hawthorne," Romero cites Eve Kosofsky Sedgwick's assertion that certain late-eighteenth- and early-nineteenth-century British gothic novels involve a "paranoid plot" in which a male character "not only is persecuted by, but considers himself transparent to and often under the compulsion of, another male" (p. 466 in this volume). *The Scarlet Letter,*

Romero asserts, is an American variation on this version of the gothic, as it "describes precisely such an instance of one man's subjection to another male's gaze and will" (p. 466). Indeed, Hawthorne's "narrator describes Chillingworth's assault on Dimmesdale as if it were a rape: the doctor 'probes,' 'burrows,' 'violates.'" (p. 467).

Stating that her argument "poses no threat to Hawthorne's staunchly heterosexual reputation," Romero nonetheless sees a relationship between the "erotic ambiguity" of *The Scarlet Letter* and the "political and literary difference" between "male mid-century" writers like Hawthorne and "their female contemporaries" (p. 469). The difference is grounded in what Sedgwick has termed "homosocial" relationships: those male-male bonds that, on one hand, seem to exist along some blurred boundary between heterosexuality and homosexuality and that, on the other, "function . . . strategically" to "ensur[e] . . . male entitlement" and "secure male hegemony" (p. 470).

Developing the theme of homosocial relationships, Romero tells of a trip Hawthorne took in the summer of 1837, when he was a thirty-three-year-old bachelor, to Augusta, Maine. There, for five weeks, he lived — in his own words — "as queer a life as any body leads" (p. 473) with his old college friend Horatio Bridge (who would later become his patron) and M. Schaeffer, a French boarder. Romero, who describes this idyll as a "paradise of bachelors," is quick to point out that "at the time 'queer' did not have the sexual connotation" it has today. Still, she convincingly asserts that Hawthorne's use of the term *does* imply that the men were living a life of "escape from the manners" and "mores . . . of what Huck Finn would later call 'sivilization,'" an existence that "at the time could only be conceived of as a parody of proper heterosexual domesticity" (pp. 473–74).

This homosocial existence involved intense scrutiny, by Hawthorne, of the other men ("The little Frenchman impresses me very strongly . . . so lonely as he is here, struggling against the world, with bitter feelings in his breast . . . enjoying here what little domestic comfort and confidence there is for him" [p. 473]) *and* intense self-scrutiny (Hawthorne came to refer to himself as a "queer character"). This experience of the homosocial other and, relatedly, of oneself as a stranger lies, in Romero's view, at the heart of Hawthorne's "gothic" aesthetic, which turns on moments of defamiliarization so intense that nothing — not even the self — is as it once seemed. Examples of these radical "perspectival shifts" at the core of Hawthorne's aesthetic that are manifested in *The Scarlet Letter* include, not surprisingly, the scene from *The Scarlet Letter* in which Hester and Arthur take a nighttime stand on the gallows with Pearl, while meteors cast heretofore familiar sights in an unfamiliar light.

Romero cites Robert K. Martin's assertions that Hawthorne's aesthetics are grounded in an "estrangement" that "was foreclosed to most American women of Hawthorne's time, who were increasingly bound to the familiar limitations of the domestic" (p. 476). She also reminds us that, in *The Scarlet Letter,* women are more or less "presen[t] . . . by their absence." Of course, by "women" Romero doesn't mean Hester Prynne; rather, she means women like "most American women of Hawthorne's time"— women like Hawthorne's wife Sophia, who encouraged her husband to stand aloof from the "wear & tear" of domestic life while reassuring him that she herself did "not need to stand apart from our daily life to see how fair & blest is our lot, because it is the mother's vocation to be in the midst of little cares & great blisses" (p. 476).

Hester Prynne, by contrast, is unlike most women of Hawthorne's day, living anything but the life of little cares and great blisses. She is estranged from her former identity and her former life, for the letter she wears has what the narrator calls "the effect of a spell, taking her out of the ordinary relations with humanity, and inclosing her in a sphere by herself" (p. 58). Once outside, she is able to "look . . . from [an] estranged point of view at human institutions, . . . criticizing all with hardly more reverence than the Indian would feel for the clerical band, the judicial robe, the pillory, the gallows, the fireside, or the church" (p. 158). In her estrangement and self-estrangement, Hester represents Hawthorne's nineteenth-century version of a "male subjectivity" and aesthetic. (The narrator even comments that one of the "effect[s] of the symbol" she wears is that "[s]ome attribute . . . departed from her, the permanence of which had been essential to keep her a woman" [p. 133].)

As the novel ends, Romero points out, Hester is "reassimilated into the 'feminine' realm of everyday life" (p. 479), becoming what the narrator calls a "voluntary nurse" who heals others by giving "advice in all matters, especially those of the heart" (p. 44). At that point, fully reinscribed in the realm of the feminine/domestic, she becomes more like the female writers Hawthorne referred to in a letter as "scribbling women" than she is like the Hawthorne living among men in a custom house, looking at previously familiar objects by firelight and moonlight, and "finding" there the *A* that would serve as agent for a story about defamiliarization.

In addressing the issue of Hawthorne's aesthetic, Romero uses the insights of the feminist approach. For instance, she addresses the separate spheres inhabited by men and women, with particular emphasis on the "feminine" sphere of domesticity that served as a quasi-prison for middle-class women (including women writers) of Hawthorne's day. But Romero augments the insights of feminism with those arising from gender theory, that later but in some senses broader gender-based approach that is as interested in the social construction "masculine" as it is in "feminine." (Eve Kosofsky Sedgwick, whose work Romero begins by quoting, is a feminist critic who pioneered gender criticism.) Within this field of a gender-based criticism, she cites the work of Robert K. Martin, a gender critic associated with so-called queer theory, a sexuality-based development within gender criticism that takes a particular interest in explicit or sublimated representations of homosexual desire. (For further information about queer theory, see the "Glossary of Critical and Theoretical Terms" at the back of this volume.)

But Romero reaches far beyond feminist, gender, and queer theory in her search for ways of approaching the complex issues she addresses. For one thing, without Freud and psychoanalytic theory and criticism, it is hard to imagine how a critic like Romero could conceptualize "erotic ambiguity" in a text and find the language of rape beneath the surface of a language describing intellectual "probings." Nor is it likely that the whole subject of "homosocial bonding" could be apprehended and discussed, depending as it surely does on the psychoanalytic notion that taboo desires are often sublimated in self-perpetuating, culturally acceptable forms.

Along with the relatively old psychoanalytical approach to literary texts, Romero avails herself of the new historicism in carrying out her gender-based analysis. Her use of letters and other primary materials demonstrating the cult of domesticity is theorized: that is to say, her analysis is cognizant of the fact that Hester Prynne's life outside the domestic, feminine paradigm has little to do with paradigms operative during the seventeenth-century Puritan period in which the novel is set, but a great deal to do with ones operative during the nineteenth-century period in which Hawthorne wrote "about" the Puritan past. This concept that, when we write about the past, we reflect into history the values of the present even extends to Romero's own analysis. For she is implicitly if not explicitly cognizant of how her insights into Hawthorne's period depend upon current and contemporary movements (e.g., "queer" discourse) that Hawthorne himself would presumably have rejected in a state of shock and denial. In other words, she is as fully aware as any reader-reception critic that Hawthorne's audience was far different from the one comprised of twentieth-century university students — and would have responded far differently to the text of *The Scarlet Letter.*

Ross C Murfin

COMBINING PERSPECTIVES

LORA ROMERO

Homosocial Romance: Nathaniel Hawthorne

> The very inmost soul of [Dimmesdale] seemed to be brought out before [Chillingworth's] eyes, so that he could see and comprehend its every movement. He became . . . not a spectator only, but a chief actor, in the poor minister's interior world. He could play upon him as he chose.
>
> – NATHANIEL HAWTHORNE, *The Scarlet Letter*

Critics have long associated the gothic with all that is considered "decadent," including homosexuality. More recently, Eve Kosofsky Sedgwick has specified the terms of this association by identifying a group of late-eighteenth- and early-nineteenth-century British gothic novels that share a paranoid plot. In them a male character "not only is persecuted by, but considers himself transparent to and often under the compulsion of, another male."[1]

Hawthorne's *The Scarlet Letter* describes precisely such an instance of one man's subjection to another male's gaze and will. The Dimmesdale-Chillingworth plot grows in part out of an 1839 notebook entry in which Hawthorne records his interest in the psychic state which we would now call "paranoia." The entry reads: "The strange sensation of a person who feels himself an object of deep interest, and close observa-

[1]Eve Kosofsky Sedgwick, *Between Men: English Literature and Male Homosocial Desire* (New York: Columbia UP, 1985), 91.

tion, and various construction of all his actions, by another person."[2] Under Chillingworth's reign of terror, Dimmesdale becomes so paranoid that he is unable to recognize his real enemy, even though that man has moved into his home. "Mr. Dimmesdale," explains the narrator, "would perhaps have seen this individual's character more perfectly, if a certain morbidness, to which sick hearts are liable, had not rendered him suspicious of all mankind. Trusting no man as his friend, he could not recognize his enemy. . . ." (p. 110 in this volume).

In the psychodynamics of the erotic triangle underwriting the plot of Hawthorne's text, Hester Prynne (the feminine term) serves as little more than a pretext for an affective exchange between men. Robert Penn Warren remarked that "the two men are more important to each other than Hester is to either" and that "theirs is the truest marriage."[3] Sedgwick proposes (drawing from Rene Girard) that often "the bonds of 'rivalry' and 'love,' differently as they are experienced, are equally powerful and in many senses equivalent."[4] Hawthorne's narrator encourages a similar line of inquiry into the rivalry between his male characters, asking "whether hatred and love be not the same thing at bottom":

> Each, in its utmost development, supposes a high degree of intimacy and heart-knowledge; each renders one individual dependent for the food of his affections and spiritual life upon another; each leaves the passionate lover, or the no less passionate hater, forlorn and desolate by the withdrawal of his object. (p. 199)

The Scarlet Letter provokes interpretation of "passion" in sexual terms. The narrator describes Chillingworth's assault on Dimmesdale as if it were rape: the doctor "probes," "burrows," "violates." Chillingworth's mysterious demise at the end of the story adheres to this sexual trajectory by conjuring up an image of detumescence. Having finally achieved the "completest triumph and consummation" of his plot

[2]Nathaniel Hawthorne, *The American Notebooks,* vol. VIII of *The Centenary Edition of the Works of Nathaniel Hawthorne* (Columbus: Ohio State UP, 1972), 183. Subsequent quotations from Hawthorne's notebooks will be taken from this edition and cited parenthetically.

[3]Robert Penn Warren, "Hawthorne Revisited: Some Remarks on Hellfiredness," *The Sewanee Review* 81 (Jan.–Mar. 1973): 107. Scott S. Derrick offered a very persuasive reading of Hawthorne's Chillingworth-Dimmesdale plot within the context of Sedgwick's homosocial/homoerotic triangle in his paper, "Homophobia, Homosociality, and Authorship in *The Scarlet Letter*" (presented at the American Literature Association's Annual Conference on American Literature, Baltimore, Md., 28 May 1993).

[4]Sedgwick, 21.

against the minister, the physician's "strength and energy . . . seemed at once to desert him," and he "positively withered up" and "shrivelled away" (p. 199). One wonders, *pace* Ernest Sandeen, if *The Scarlet Letter* isn't a love story after all.[5]

The scarcity of commentary on *The Scarlet Letter*'s homoerotic subtext is striking, particularly in light of the wealth of criticism addressing sexual equivocality in the works of the other canonical writers of Hawthorne's time (Melville, Cooper, Whitman).[6] Perhaps the relative visibility of traditional heterosexual relations in Hawthorne's biography explains the reticence. Because of the publication of his love letters to his wife Sophia Peabody Hawthorne and his notebook entries recording the behavior and growth of his three children, Hawthorne's artistic genius has been cast in solidly heterosexual terms.[7] Henry James, for example, believed that Hawthorne "lived primarily in his domestic affections, which were of the tenderest kind."[8] A more contemporary critic pronounces Hawthorne "the most perfectly domestic of all [the male canonical] American writers, the one most devoted to the family as the scene of fulfilling relation."[9]

[5]In "*The Scarlet Letter* as a Love Story" (*PMLA* 4 [Sept. 1962]: 425–35), Ernest Sandeen describes Hawthorne's work as "the typical love story of our Western tradition" inasmuch as the plot is based on an erotic triangle.

[6]One exception is critic Monika Elbert, who argues at some length for the homoerotic nature of the relationship between Chillingworth and Dimmesdale. Elbert, noting as I have, that "there is something sexual in Chillingworth's search for mastery over Dimmesdale," contends that Dimmesdale reciprocates the passion. See Elbert's "Hester on the Scaffold, Dimmesdale in the Closet: Hawthorne's Seven-Year Itch," *Essays in Literature* 16 (fall 1989): 234–55. Also see Robert K. Martin "Hester Prynne *C'est Moi:* Nathaniel Hawthorne and the Anxieties of Gender," in *Engendering Men,* ed. Joseph Boone and Michael Cadden (New York: Routledge, 1990), 122–39. For a compelling rationale for *not* reading the Chillingworth-Dimmesdale plot in homoerotic terms, see Christopher Newfield, "The Politics of Male Suffering: Masochism and Hegemony in the American Renaissance," *differences* 1, no. 3 (1989): 79, n. 8.

[7]Biographer Edwin Haviland Miller upsets this image of Hawthorne somewhat by emphasizing the intensity of Hawthorne's friendships with men. For Miller, Melville's apparent infatuation with Hawthorne was just one in a series of equivocal male friendships punctuating Hawthorne's adult life. See Miller, *Salem Is My Dwelling Place: A Life of Nathaniel Hawthorne* (Iowa City: U of Iowa P, 1991), 70–1; 192–95; 217–22; 299–318.

[8]Henry James, "Hawthorne," in *The Shock of Recognition,* ed. Edmund Wilson (1879; reprint New York: Modern Library, 1943), 565.

[9]Richard H. Brodhead, *The School of Hawthorne* (New York: Oxford UP, 1986), 48. In his study of Hawthorne's relation to domesticity, *Dearest Beloved: The Hawthornes and the Making of the Middle-Class Family* (Berkeley and Los Angeles: U of California P, 1993), T. Walter Herbert describes the tensions in the Hawthorne family that such images of their domestic felicity conceal.

The argument of this essay poses no threat to Hawthorne's staunchly heterosexual reputation. Nor will it attempt to relocate *The Scarlet Letter* in the expanding list of "classic American" gay crypto-texts. I begin with the question of the erotic ambiguity because ambiguity so often serves as a critical touchstone, marking the political and literary difference between the work of male mid-century canonical writers and their female contemporaries. This analysis will show that reading the ties between linguistic ambiguity and erotic ambiguity in Hawthorne's homosocial plot is the first step in removing the touchstone, which I argue is also a stumbling block for understanding the politics of women's domestic fiction.

MODERNISM AND THE "AMERICAN RENAISSANCE"

The Chillingworth-Dimmesdale plot does not bespeak its author's or its male characters' repressed or manifest sexuality so much as the structural conditions of male-male relationships in the homophobic culture which we share with Hawthorne.[10] Sedgwick describes an underlying but occasionally visible "continuum between homosocial and homosexual" exercising influence over these relationships. There exists, she writes, a "tendency toward important correspondences and similarities between the most sanctioned forms of male-homosocial bonding, and the most reprobated expressions of male homosexual sociality." This is because "paths of male entitlement in Euro-American societies [require] certain intense male bonds": "male friendship, mentorship, admiring identification, bureaucratic subordination, and heterosexual rivalry." The minimal articulation of difference between homosocial and homosexual fosters the instability characteristic of representations of male-male relationships:

> the fact that what goes on at football games, in fraternities, at the Bohemian Grove, and at climactic moments in war novels can look, with only a slight shift of optic, quite startlingly "homosexual," is not most importantly an expression of the psychic origin of these institutions in a repressed or sublimated homosexual genitality. Instead, it is the coming to visibility of the normally implicit

[10] I admit that, in the end, it is impossible to distinguish between "personal" sexual preferences and "social" conditions for interpersonal relationships. I make the distinction between sexual and social here only to differentiate my project from a more traditional biographical interpretation that would read the Dimmesdale-Chillingworth plot as symptomatic of Hawthorne's own repressed homosexuality.

> terms of a coercive double bind. . . . For a man to be a man's man is separated only by an invisible, carefully blurred, always-already-crossed line from being "interested in men."

Sedgwick's double bind represents more than a paradox; it functions strategically, ensuring that homosocial paths of male entitlement simultaneously secure male hegemony and leave men (homosexual or otherwise) open to policing and self-policing through "the leverage of homophobia."[11] Even if it were possible, out-ing Hawthorne would merely satisfy the logic of minimal difference upon which our culture manufactures the all-important but ever-unstable difference between homosocial and homosexual.

Of course, critics have commented at length upon *The Scarlet Letter*'s perspectival shifts — but not typically in relation to the text's sexual and gender politics. In particular, the meteor scene in "The Minister's Vigil" has provoked a great deal of commentary. In that chapter, Dimmesdale mounts the scaffold where years earlier Hester had stood at mid-day. Making her way home from the governor's sickbed with Pearl, Hester happens upon Dimmesdale. After the family is reunited on the scaffold, a meteor illuminates the midnight sky. The meteor, writes Hawthorne,

> showed the familiar scene of the street, with the distinctness of mid-day, but also with the awfulness that is always imparted to familiar objects by an unaccustomed light. The wooden houses, with their jutting stories and quaint gable-peaks; the doorsteps and thresholds, with the early grass springing up about them; the garden-plots, black with freshly turned earth; the wheel-track, little worn, and, even in the market-place, margined with green on either side; — all were visible, but with a singularity of aspect that seemed to give another moral interpretation to the things of this world than they had ever borne before. (p. 127)

Several critics have located the politics of Hawthorne's aesthetics in such shifts of optics. For example, Evan Carton proposes that "*The Scarlet Letter* and the meteor are subversive in the same subtle way: each produces an illumination that unsettles the objectivity of objects by revealing the act of perception that figures their constitution." Describing a position taken by other critics, Carton writes that, by exposing reality "as multiply and irresolvably interpreted," Hawthorne "challenges a fundamentalist understanding of perception, morality,

[11]Sedgwick, 1, 89.

and language [and] frustrates the attempt to validate them by reference to a reality that exists prior to and independent of their operations."[12]

Moreover, critics have based claims for Hawthorne's modernism or premodernism on his optic shifts and the self-reflexivity they are said to indicate. In David Leverenz's view, Hawthorne and other American Renaissance authors "help[ed] to inaugurate the modernist tradition of alienated mind play" and threw one of the first punches in the "modernist sparring match between avant-garde writers and bourgeois readers."[13] Another critic asserts that "the theory of the Romance," developed in large part in response to Hawthorne's work, "allowed America's nineteenth-century novelists to be seen as prototypes of alienated modern artists."[14]

These critical statements suggest a way of reframing my initial reading of the Chillingworth-Dimmesdale plot within the critical parameters of modernist aesthetics; however, such a reframing neither contains nor diminishes the relevance of the sexual and gender protocols to Hawthorne's optic shifts. After all, the canon of the premodernist American Renaissance has been steadfastly homosocial. Furthermore, as Nina Baym suggests, its homosociality is constitutional; it is impossible to insert women writers into a canon whose coherence depends upon their serving as its other.[15] One cannot, for example, include women writers in Leverenz's American Renaissance because he articulates self-reflexivity along the antimonies of gender (however historicized) when he asserts that the "feminization" of the profession of letters meant that male writers felt out of place in an occupation where women writers could feel at home. "Male writers developed premodernist styles to explore and exalt their sense of being deviant from male norms" while women writers felt no alienation and therefore clung to the familiar realist style. "Unlike the women writers" of the antebellum period, "classic male writers" satisfy the expectations of contemporary critics by "[destabilizing] their narrations" and creating texts with "false bottoms."[16]

[12]Evan Carton, *The Rhetoric of American Romance: Dialectic and Identity in Emerson, Dickinson, Poe, and Hawthorne* (Baltimore, Md.: Johns Hopkins UP, 1985), 207, 209.

[13]David Leverenz, *Manhood and the American Renaissance* (Ithaca, N.Y.: Cornell UP, 1989), 2, 16.

[14]John McWilliams, "The Rationale for 'The American Romance,'" *boundary* 2 17 (1990): 72.

[15]See Nina Baym, "Melodramas of Beset Manhood: How Theories of American Literature Exclude Women," in her *Feminism & American Literary History: Essays* (New Brunswick, N.J.: Rutgers UP, 1992), 3–18.

[16]Leverenz, 17–18.

Even a feminist-identified critic like Leverenz reconstructs the American Renaissance along male homosocial lines because, as Leverenz's thesis indicates, definitions of literary modernism remain steadfastly homosocial, dependent upon a gendered schematics in which men have an imagined special access to alienation and self-alienation.[17] Thus, reframing Hawthorne's optic shifts within critical accounts of the modernism of the mid-century classic in no way disposes of sexuality and gender as relevant analytic categories. To the contrary, as I will argue over the course of this chapter, contemporary critical understanding of the self-reflexivity of Hawthorne's premodernist novel is entirely obligated to the sex/gender system Hawthorne figures through his perspectival shifts.[18]

HAWTHORNE'S HOMOSOCIAL IDYLL

My conviction in the necessity of juxtaposing *The Scarlet Letter*'s erotic ambiguities with the critical discussion of self-reflexive texts grows out of interpretation of several of Hawthorne's early works representing relationships between men. *The Scarlet Letter*'s perspectival disruptions constitute one link in a chain of associations extending across Hawthorne's earlier fictional and nonfictional writing and wedding his premodernist aesthetics to male homosociality.

The chain begins in the summer of 1837 when Hawthorne took up residence for five weeks in Augusta, Maine, at the home of Horatio Bridge (a college chum who would become Hawthorne's lifelong patron and, ultimately, his biographer).[19] Hawthorne's notebook entries from this period depict a paradise of bachelors worthy of Melville himself. According to *The American Notebooks,* Hawthorne, Bridge, and a French boarder by the name of M. Schaeffer lived together at Bridge's house "in great harmony and brotherhood" (46). Like other

[17] Leverenz mentions his intellectual debt to feminist criticism and theory on p. 2.

[18] In "The Traffic in Women," Gayle Rubin defines a "sex/gender system" as a "set of arrangements by which a society transforms biological sexuality into products of human activity." Rubin's article appears in *Toward an Anthropology of Woman,* ed. Reyna R. Reiter (New York: Monthly Review Press, 1975), 159. Also see Rubin's further commentary on the term in her "Thinking Sex: Notes Towards a Radical Theory of the Politics of Sexuality," in *Pleasure and Danger: Exploring Female Sexuality,* ed. Carole S. Vance (Boston: Routledge and Kegan Paul, 1984), 307ff.

[19] Miller provides a thorough account of the friendship between Hawthorne and Horatio Bridge. See pages 100–1 for his description of Hawthorne's visit. Also see Bridge's recollections of the summer in Augusta in his *Personal Recollections of Nathaniel Hawthorne* (New York: Harper and Brothers Publishers, 1893), 63–7.

nineteenth-century male homosocial idylls, Hawthorne's figures as an escape from the manners, mores, and morals of what Huck Finn would later call "sivilization." Comments Hawthorne in one entry from this period, "I think I should soon become strongly attached to our way of life — so independent, and untroubled by the forms of restrictions of society" (34).[20]

In the notebook entries male homosocial relations are more than just one thematic locale ripe for perspectival disruptions. The minimal difference between homosocial and homosexual (along with the heightened scrutiny and self-scrutiny minimal difference entails in an all-male setting) guaranteed that relations among the three men would be particularly productive of perspectival shifts. Initially, Hawthorne found M. Schaeffer slightly repulsive and dismissed him as "a queer little Frenchman" (32); however, over the course of his residence, Hawthorne came to admire Schaeffer's intelligence and to identify with his "queerness." One comment suggests that Hawthorne saw Schaeffer in a role that he would increasingly claim for himself, alien(ated) intellectual trying to make his living off a dullard bourgeoisie:

> The little Frenchman impresses me very strongly . . . so lonely as he is here, struggling against the world, with bitter feelings in his breast . . . enjoying here what little domestic comfort and confidence there is for him; and then going about all the live-long day, teaching French to blockheads who sneer at him. (33)

Bridge's recollections make it clear that the bond that developed between the three men grew out of a shared sense of economic failure, for which lack of domestic comfort in the form of a wife and family became the sign.[21] Soon Hawthorne began referring to himself as "a queer character" (34). And before his stay at Bridge's bachelor establishment had ended, he wrote that all three of its residents were "as queer a set as may be found anywhere," living "as queer a life as any body leads" (46).

[20] I believe it is important to resist the heterosexual developmental narrative that might tempt us to dismiss the significance of Hawthorne's living arrangements by reference to his sexual "immaturity." Furthermore, the fact that Hawthorne presents his paradise of bachelors as a temporary interlude does not make his residence in Augusta any less sexually equivocal. As Jeff Nunokawa explains in "'All the Sad Young Men': AIDS and the Work of Mourning," when men who love other men can be represented at all, it is often in the elegiac mode appropriate to the heterosexual developmental narrative which makes homosexuality into an immature sexual phase. Nunokawa's essay appears in *Inside/Out: Lesbian Theories, Gay Theories,* ed. Diana Fuss (New York: Routledge, 1991), 311–23.

[21] See Bridge, 63, 66.

Of course, at the time "queer" did not have the sexual connotation that today may very well constitute its primary meaning. But contemporary usage is not entirely beside the point. Although Hawthorne never clarifies what it is exactly that makes him and his roommates so queer, in context the word seems to refer primarily to the trio's deviance from antebellum norms of male heterosexual subjectivity. All three men were bachelors, and (like Queequeg and Ishmael in bed at the beginning of *Moby Dick*) they composed what at the time could only be conceived of as a parody of proper heterosexual domesticity. Hawthorne was thirty-three years old, and his romantic experiences had (in the words of Edwin Haviland Miller) been limited to "voyeurism" and "fantasies."[22] According to *The American Notebooks,* Bridge had "almost . . . made up his mind never to be married" (33), and Schaeffer "had never yet sinned with woman" (46).

Augusta, then, was an atmosphere ripe for sexual equivocality. "Queer" records this equivocality, and it also suggests the connection in homophobic cultures between male homosociality and the sensation of perspectival shift. Hawthorne's feeling of liberation from social constraints ensued from his sense that he was (to borrow the language of "The Minister's Vigil") seeing familiar things in an unaccustomed light. In his paradise of bachelors, the heightened vigilance elicited by Schaeffer (*"He's queer!"*) fomented parallel estrangements (*"I guess if I didn't know Bridge as well as I do, I'd think he was queer too . . ."*), culminating in the defamiliarization of what is most familiar, the self (*"Come to think of it, I guess I'm pretty queer myself!"*).

Consciously or unconsciously Hawthorne continued to associate such moments of self-reflection with homosocial interaction. What purports to be the translator's preface to his tale "Rappaccini's Daughter" (1844) perhaps best exemplifies the self-reflexive quality of Hawthorne's later imaginative writing. The preface is self-reflexive in the most literal sense. In it, Hawthorne scrutinizes himself, but does so as if he were another man — a stranger, an alien, one M. de l'Aubepine. In this supremely ironic assessment of his own literary reputation, Hawthorne, significantly, attributes his tale to the fictitious Aubepine, the "Frenchification" of "Hawthorne" that the queer M. Schaeffer had affectionately bestowed upon him during his residence in Augusta.[23]

[22] Miller, 100.

[23] Hawthorne credits Schaeffer with the name's invention on page 46 of *The American Notebooks.*

That detail, along with the fact that "Rappaccini's Daughter" records a quasi-gothic struggle of will between two men (Giovanni and Rappaccini), suggests a symbolic circuit in Hawthorne's mind between looking at other men and looking at himself. Hence the resemblance between the 1838 notebook entry describing intensive scrutiny of another man ("the strange sensation of a person who feels himself an object of deep interest, and close observation, and various construction of all his actions, by another person") and an entry made one year earlier describing intensive scrutiny of oneself as if one were another man:

> A perception, for a moment, of one's eventual and moral self, as if it were another person, — the observant faculty being separated, and looking intently at the qualities of the character. There is a surprise when this happens, — this getting out of oneself, — and then the observer sees how queer a fellow he is. (178)

The Scarlet Letter's Dimmesdale-Chillingworth plot brings the two notebook entries together by coupling the "homo-" with the "auto-." Chillingworth's ambiguous ontological status (Is he a gothic persecutor or a projection of Dimmesdale's troubled conscience?) supports Sedgwick's attempt to trace a literary historical genealogy connecting the paranoid gothic to high male modernism. The gothic novel's representation of "two potent male figures locked in an epistemologically indissoluble clench of will and desire," she insists, was evacuated of its sexual contents and refigured as the man at war with himself, the theme of modern man's divided consciousness.[24] Although *The Scarlet Letter* lends itself to this psychological interpretation, it does not erase the sexual anxiety suffusing its homosocial plot; nor do Hawthorne's early notebook entries describing the sensation of looking at himself ever entirely disown their kinship to the experience of being looked at by another man — and being revealed as "a queer fellow" in the process.

MEN LOOKING AT THEMSELVES

Historicizing Hawthorne's "revolutionary" aesthetics also requires attention to the structural presence women have by virtue of their absence from *The Scarlet Letter*'s homosocial plot. Robert K. Martin writes that Hawthorne's subversive aesthetics originate in estrangement

[24] Eve Kosofsky Sedgwick, *Epistemology of the Closet* (Berkeley and Los Angeles: U of California P, 1990), 187, 131–80.

and that "estrangement . . . was foreclosed to most American women of Hawthorne's time, who were increasingly bound to the familiar limitations of the domestic."[25] The next two sections of this essay propose that critics have not been able to detach their estimations of Hawthorne's literary value from their figurations of a feminized realm of domestic familiarity because Hawthorne himself labored so hard to make them appear indissoluble.

Even after Hawthorne entered into a traditional heterosexual relationship by marrying Sophia Peabody, he persisted in thematizing his estrangement from the domestic in his correspondence and his notebooks. Not until shortly before his death would Hawthorne declare that he was, finally, "beginning to take root . . . and feel myself, for the first time in my life, really at home."[26] Despite frequent references to his domestic felicity, Hawthorne was strangely predisposed to see himself partaking in that joy from a distance. In a comment that links him to the voyeuristic Miles Coverdale in *The Blithedale Romance,* Hawthorne tells of the regret he feels when he retires to bed at night, leaving the parlor with its evidence of family life behind: "after closing the sitting-room door, I re-open it, again and again, to peep back at the warm, cheerful, solemn repose . . ." (284).

Once, while temporarily separated from Sophia and their children, he voiced a wish that his wife too could "now and then stand apart from thy lot, in the same manner, and behold how fair" their life was. "I think we are very happy," he mused, "— a truth that is not always so evident to me, until I step aside from our daily life." Sophia responded that, although her husband should protect himself from "the wear & tear" of domestic life, she herself did "not need to stand apart from our daily life to see how fair & blest is our lot, because it is the mother's vocation to be in the midst of little cares & great blisses."[27] Catharine Beecher, who insisted that a successful housekeeper must stand above the "minutiae of domestic arrangements" which would otherwise absorb all her attention, would have read Sophia Hawthorne's embrace of the "wear & tear" of daily domestic life as a recipe for weakmindedness.[28]

Robert K. Martin's generalizations about domesticity have little relevance to Beecher's *Treatise on Domestic Economy,* which advocates its

[25] Martin, 130.

[26] Quoted in Herbert, 4.

[27] Ibid., 174–5.

[28] Catharine E. Beecher, *Treatise on Domestic Economy* (1841; reprint New York: Schocken Books, 1977), 144–8.

own ethos of defamiliarization. Instead Martin's view of domestic womanhood and the homosocial constitution of the canon he supports it with subsume Hawthorne's own construction of women. Despite the momentary wavering in his letter to his wife, Nathaniel seems ultimately to have shared Sophia's perspective on women's obligation to live in the quotidian. *The Scarlet Letter* represents the ability to stand apart from daily life as a distinctly male prerogative. Hawthorne introduces Hester Prynne — or rather, the scarlet letter she is condemned to wear — as an agent of defamiliarization. As Lauren Berlant writes, "the juridical spectacle . . . situates the novel, from its very origins, in an overcoming of daily life."[29] When Hester emerges from the prison and stands before the crowd gathered in the marketplace to witness her shame,

> the point which drew all eyes, and, as it were, transfigured the wearer, — so that both men and women, who had been familiarly acquainted with Hester Prynne, were now impressed as if they beheld her for the first time, — was that SCARLET LETTER, so fantastically embroidered and illuminated upon her bosom. It had the effect of a spell, taking her out of the ordinary relations with humanity, and inclosing her in a sphere by herself. (p. 58)

Hawthorne uses the letter to demarcate an opposition between "the state's theatrical and symbolic domination of the public sphere" and something "much harder to represent, the mental and physical practices of . . . personal life."[30] Hence, in chapter 5, when Hester returns home after being displayed in the marketplace as the public symbol of sin, she retreats back into privacy, into "daily custom" and the "ordinary resources of her nature," which will sustain her during more quotidian trials "[t]omorrow," "the next day," and "the next" (p. 74).

Although outwardly Hester's life proceeds uneventfully, inwardly the letter continues to disrupt daily custom and ordinary relations. "Made into a stranger, she gains the stranger's ability to see the arbitrariness of signs,"[31] an ability contemporary criticism identifies as the ground of all struggle against the status quo. Hester's dedication to a revolutionary ethos ("the world's law was no law for her mind" [p. 134]) ensues from her exile from the ordinary. At her most radical, her

> intellect and heart had their home, as it were, in desert places, where she roamed as freely as the wild Indian in his woods. . . .

[29] Lauren Berlant, *The Anatomy of National Fantasy: Hawthorne, Utopia, and Everyday Life* (Chicago: U of Chicago P, 1991), 191.

[30] Ibid., 192.

[31] Martin, 130.

> [S]he . . . looked from this estranged point of view at human institutions, and whatever priests or legislators had established; criticizing all with hardly more reverence than the Indian would feel for the clerical band, the judicial robe, the pillory, the gallows, the fireside, or the church. (p. 158)

The "as it were" qualifying "home" suggests that for Hawthorne social critique demands disengagement from the familiar. Hester views society from the estranged perspective Hawthorne attributes to the "wild Indian," that is, the person who has no home and roams about at will. "There was wild and ghastly scenery all around her, and a home . . . nowhere." This "ghastly scenery" is *unheimlich* both in the sense of "unhomelike" and "uncanny." Its landscape is that of gothic romance rather than the realist novel: "Hester Prynne . . . wandered without a clew in the dark labyrinth of mind; now turned aside by an insurmountable precipice; now starting back from a deep chasm" (p. 135).

Home is such a powerful symbol in Hawthorne's imaginative writings, notebooks, and letters because he associates it with that which is most familiar: the self. Hester's situation recalls that of Wakefield, the antihero in Hawthorne's tale of the same name, who for twenty years lives a block away from his house, contemplating the events that occur there in his absence. In both "Wakefield" (1837) and *The Scarlet Letter* home is the symbol of everyday life. Only after they have disengaged themselves from the domestic can Hawthorne's characters study it, or "awaken" to it. Like the narrator of the preface to "Rappaccini's Daughter," Wakefield is the figure of the man trying to look at himself, to see himself from the outside, to witness his own queerness.

For Hawthorne, self-estrangement constitutes male subjectivity. It also signifies a fundamental violation of female subjectivity. "Wakefield" presents its alienated and self-alienated male protagonist as "foolish" and perhaps even "mad."[32] *The Scarlet Letter,* on the other hand, suggests that the woman with access to this estranged perspective is unsexed by it. One of the "effect[s] of the symbol" that Hester wears on her breast is that "[s]ome attribute . . . departed from her, the permanence of which had been essential to keep her a woman" (p. 133). Radical Hester resembles the female suicide whose body Hawthorne once witnessed a team of men pull from a river. "I suppose one friend would have saved her," Hawthorne reflected on the suicide in his notebooks,

[32]Nathaniel Hawthorne, "Wakefield," in *Twice-Told Tales,* vol. ix of *The Centenary Edition of the Works of Nathaniel Hawthorne* (Columbus: Ohio State UP, 1974), 133, 138.

"but she died for want of sympathy — a severe penalty for having cultivated and refined herself out of the sphere of her natural connections."[33]

Introduced to the reader as an object of melodramatic spectacle, Hester Prynne is gradually reassimilated into the "feminine" realm of everyday life. The aura of the letter fades, and Hester becomes "a kind of voluntary nurse" in the community, "doing whatever miscellaneous good she might; taking upon herself, likewise, to give advice in all matters, especially those of the heart" (p. 44). Unlike Hawthorne's principal male characters, Hester not only survives her sorrows but is said to be residing just outside of Salem long after the events of the narrative have transpired — as though she had some existence independent of her textual one. Hawthorne creates the effect of realism through the illusion of self-sufficiency. Ultimately, Hawthorne refamiliarizes Hester, bringing her back within the codes of novelistic probability and back within the "miscellaneous" realm of domestic concerns ("matters of the heart").

TROUBLE IN CRITICISM'S PARADISE OF BACHELORS

Regarding his acceptance of the position of Surveyor of Salem's Custom House, Hawthorne wrote:

> It is a good lesson — though it may often be a hard one — for a man who has dreamed of literary fame, and of making for himself a rank among the world's dignitaries by such means, to step aside out of the narrow circle in which his claims are recognized, and to find how utterly devoid of significance, beyond that circle, is all that he achieves, and all that he aims at. (p. 39)

This passage expresses more than simply Hawthorne's sense of dislocation in the Custom House. It also relocates within a proper, male subject (that is, Hawthorne himself) the radical Hester's ability to "step aside out of the narrow circle" of the familiar and indulge contrary opinions and values. Hawthorne further appropriates the political significance of Hester's temporary estrangement in *The Scarlet Letter* by disavowing any partisan loyalty despite his status as a Democratic Party appointee in Boston's Custom House. Thus the preface appears doubly tendentious when read in light of Hester's reinscription within the "narrow circle" of realist codes: it defines distance from the familiar as a

[33]The drowning is, of course, thought to be the model for Zenobia's death in *The Blithedale Romance*.

male prerogative and recaptures for the author himself the freedom from institutions and conventions gained through Hester's defamiliarized perspective.

By the time Hawthorne wrote *The Scarlet Letter*, the familiar was increasingly associated with women, home, and realism. George Dekker writes that as early as the 1820s there was "a polar opposition" (at least in the minds of the writers of the period) "between [the novel or] a kind [of prose fiction] that faithfully mirrors familiar and contemporary experience and [the romance or a kind of prose fiction] that in various ways . . . defies or departs from the norm."[34] Moreover, by mid-century, writers, reviewers, and publishers insisted upon the difference between homey or domestic narratives and sublime art.[35]

But categories of prose narrative (like all categories founded upon a binary opposition) have no discrete existence; they possess meaning only in relation to each other. "The Custom-House" conveys the codependence of the domestic and the sublime when it depicts home as the scene of writing romance. Pressure on the language of the familiar and the strange in the discussion of romance in "The Custom-House" reveals that Hawthorne's apparent fondness for domestic scenes is in fact part of a strategy for differentiating between the "homelike" and his own aesthetic. "The Custom-House" aligns romance with the defamiliarizing effect of the aura. In a passage whose imagery and syntax anticipate that of the meteor scene, Hawthorne describes how a "dim coal-fire," partially illuminating the parlor in which he writes, transforms "the floor of our familiar room" into the "neutral territory" of romance by defamiliarizing the everyday life represented by the contents of the room. The fire "throws its unobtrusive tinge throughout the room, with a faint ruddiness upon the walls and ceiling, and a reflected gleam from the polish of the furniture." This aura represents a literary method explicitly divorced from the familiar and instead associated with "dream[ing] *strange* things, and mak[ing] them look like truth" (pp. 46–47; my italics).

As in the meteor scene, the order of the *heimlich* in this passage is designated by the hypotactic, by the details that go into conveying the effect of realism. A list of familiar/familial objects follows Hawthorne's

[34]George Dekker, "Once More: Hawthorne and the Genealogy of American Romance," *ESQ* 35 (1989): 71. Dekker cites an entry in the 1828 edition of Webster's *An American Dictionary of the English Language*. "Romance," it reads, "differs from the novel, as it treats great actions and extraordinary adventures, that is, . . . it vaults or soars beyond the limits of fact and real life, and often of probability."

[35]Brodhead, 3–47.

declaration that "moonlight, in a familiar room . . . is a medium the most suitable for a romance-writer": "There is the little domestic scenery of the well-known apartment; the chairs, with each its separate individuality; the centre-table, sustaining a work-basket, a volume or two, and an extinguished lamp; the sofa; the book-case; the picture on the wall . . ." These "details" are "completely seen" but "are so spiritualized by the unusual light, that they seem to lose their actual substance, and become things of intellect":

> Nothing is too small or too trifling to undergo this change, and acquire dignity thereby. A child's shoe; the doll, seated in her little wicker carriage; the hobby-horse; — whatever, in a word, has been used or played with, during the day, is now invested with a quality of strangeness and remoteness, though still almost as vividly present as by daylight. (p. 46)[36]

The enumerated objects in this passage (like the ones in the meteor scene) represent what Naomi Schor calls the *"detail as negativity":* "the *everyday,* whose 'prosiness' is rooted in the domestic sphere of social life presided over by women."[37] To define his aesthetic in opposition to the feminine order, Hawthorne must enumerate domestic details and familiar scenes. *The Scarlet Letter* must fashion the home and its aesthetic in order to disavow them.

In Hawthorne's aesthetics of defamiliarization we see the beginnings of what Andreas Huyssen calls the "repudiation of *Trivialliteratur* that has always been one of the constitutive features of a modernist aesthetic intent on distancing itself and its products from the trivialities and banalities of everyday life."[38] The terms of repudiation are Hawthorne's own imaginary labors — not self-evident truths on which critics can base their estimates of literary value. Hawthorne manufactures the familiar and scenarios of defamiliarization in order to designate the literary value of his own writing. Explaining in the preface to *The Scarlet Letter* why he did not compose a book out of his experiences in the Custom House, Hawthorne asserts that he was unable to find "the true and indestructible value that lay hidden in the petty and wearisome

[36]This section of "The Custom-House" is, evidently, based on an entry appearing on pages 283–4 of *The American Notebooks.* Hawthorne's description of himself "peeping" (quoted above) concludes his description of the room in the notebook version.

[37]Naomi Schor, *Reading in Detail: Aesthetics and the Feminine* (New York: Routledge, 1987), 4.

[38]Andreas Huyssen, *After the Great Divide: Modernism, Mass Culture, Postmodernism* (Bloomington and Indianapolis: Indiana UP, 1986), 47.

incidents, and ordinary characters, with which [he] was . . . conversant" while employed there. Perhaps at some point in the future, he speculates, he may put his now too-familiar experiences on paper and suddenly see them defamiliarized, "turn[ed] to gold upon the page" (p. 48) — a formulation recalling his speculation that, "[i]n the spiritual world, the old physician and the minister . . . may, unawares, have found their earthly stock of hatred and antipathy transmuted into golden love" (p. 199).

The realist quotidian represented by the author's experience in the Custom House, repudiated at some future point, will yield literary value ("gold"). Hawthorne's repudiation of realist language takes a variety of forms in his work, but at some level they all express Hawthorne's attempt to create professional currency for himself by defining literary value against a feminine realm, which he associates with Hester Prynne's quotidian afterlife, the domestic scenes from which he stages his early exclusion and later detachment, and finally the realist language he interprets as "feminine."

Hawthorne imagined that the women writers of his day lacked the capacity to overcome the petty and wearisome realm of the domestic. In a letter to his publisher William Ticknor (who also published the work of several prominent women writers), Hawthorne complained that the poetry of Julia Ward Howe "let out a whole history of domestic unhappiness" (presumably, the history of Howe's own troubled marriage).[39] Another letter states that Howe has "no genius or talent, except for making public what she ought to keep to herself."[40] Even when Hawthorne spoke well of his female competitors, he referred to their work as though it were an unmediated transcription of their private lives. According to him, the strength of Fanny Fern's semi-autobiographical *Ruth Hall* lay in its author's willingness to "throw off the restraints of decency, and come before the public stark naked, as it were."[41]

Whereas Hawthorne imagined that women's texts were scandalously underdressed records of personal experience, throughout his career he insisted upon the distance between his creative work and his private life. Hawthorne's vision of himself as a writer "disinclined to

[39] Letter to William D. Ticknor (17 Feb. 1854), printed in *The Letters, 1853–56*, vol. XVII of *The Centenary Edition of the Works of Nathaniel Hawthorne* (Columbus: Ohio State UP, 1987), 177.

[40] Letter to Ticknor (24 April 1857), printed in *Letters of Hawthorne to William D. Ticknor: 1851–1864* (Washington, D.C.: NCR/Microcard Editions, 1972), 50.

[41] Letter to Ticknor (5 February 1855), printed in *The Letters, 1853–56*, 308.

talk overmuch of [him]self and [his] affairs at the fireside" (p. 22) contrasts markedly with his image of women writers unable to leave the fireside or themselves. "These things hide the man, instead of displaying him," reads the preface to *The Snow-Image*.[42] "So far as I am a man of really individual attributes," he states in the preface to *Mosses from an Old Manse*, "I veil my face."[43] A letter he wrote to his wife suggests that his estranging veil represents a claim to universality for his art. There Hawthorne refers to an "involuntary reserve" on his part, which gives "objectivity" to his writing: "when people think that I am pouring myself out in a tale or essay, I am merely telling what is most common to human nature, not what is peculiar to myself."[44]

The nakedness of women writers symbolizes their inability to get away from what is peculiar to themselves. Their lack of proper attire leaves them house-bound, unsuitable for any function except the private one of sexual reproduction. Doomed to live in the domestic, they can never step back, see things "objectively," or undergo the estrangements of perspective Hawthorne demarcates as a male prerogative. Like the scenes of the defamiliarized domestic in *The Scarlet Letter*, Hawthorne's veil shields him from women's inevitable self-identity.

Yet being veiled is not exactly the opposite of being naked; male privilege comes with its own restrictions. As an image the veil has its own sexual connotations, expressed in a desire to uncover, to reveal, and to know. In the preface to *The Scarlet Letter*, Hawthorne refers to "the inmost Me behind its veil" (p. 23), but the veil does not hide Hawthorne without also rendering him (like Dimmesdale) an object of sexualized investigation. Hawthorne's sign of male privilege comes with its own regulatory power. And Hawthorne's repudiation of homey novels does not liberate his literary imagination from compulsory heterosexuality; it leads him to author a homosocial plot expressing and provoking male sexual panic, fear of exposure, and terror in self-disclosure.

The Scarlet Letter stages the scenarios of defamiliarization by which critics recognize the text as ideologically subversive, universally significant, historically transcendent — as, in short, a modernist text. A great

[42]Hawthorne, preface to *The Snow-Image*, in *The Snow-Image and Uncollected Tales*, vol. XI of *The Centenary Edition of the Works of Nathaniel Hawthorne* (Columbus: Ohio State UP, 1974), 4.

[43]Hawthorne, "The Old Manse," in *Mosses from an Old Manse*, vol. X of *The Centenary Edition of the Works of Nathaniel Hawthorne* (Columbus: Ohio State UP, 1974), 33.

[44]Quoted in Gordon Hutner, *Secrets and Sympathy: Forms of Disclosure in Hawthorne's Novels* (Athens: U of Georgia P, 1988), 7.

deal rides on the association of Hawthorne's defamiliarizing aesthetics with modernist self-reflexivity. The alliance helped transform the literature of the nineteenth-century United States into a legitimate field for academic study. "Preference for self-reflexive (romance and symbolistic) form," notes one critic, "is stressed in twentieth-century accounts of the American Renaissance."[45] As Gerald Graff points out, since World War I literary critics have "tended to believe that the project of cultural politics is to undermine all 'bourgeois' perceptual, artistic, and philosophical categories, which allegedly prop up authoritarianism." This has resulted in the widespread conviction "that formalist art and self-reflexive writing are more fundamentally subversive than critical realisms." Graff concludes that the "highest expression [of self-reflexivity] defines for many critics the classic American literary tradition," and he includes in this generalization even very contemporary critics who have rewritten "the Americanness of American literature" in the "deconstructionist register [of] reflexive awareness of the problematic of writing itself."[46]

Through his scenes of defamiliarization Hawthorne relived the paradise of bachelors at Augusta. The homosocial canon of the American Renaissance represents another means of reliving a fantasy of freedom from society. But, like Hawthorne's paradise, this premodernist canon *is* troubled by "restrictions of society," against which it is defined. Critics will not discern the trouble in paradise until they begin to read the antebellum figures of self-identical womanhood and alienated manhood as textual productions.

Hawthorne in fact expended a great deal of creative effort in making estrangement a male province, a symbol of radicalism, and the basis of literary hierarchy: strange things which now look like truth. Critical celebrations of the modernism of mid-century "classics" ignore Hawthorne's labor, presenting his optic shifts as the truth — rather than a trope — of demystification, a trope which embeds its figures of familiarity and transcendence within protocols of gender and sexuality.

[45] Deborah Masden, "The Romance of the New World," *Journal of American Studies* 24 (1990): 104.

[46] Gerald Graff, "American Criticism Left and Right," in *Ideology and Classic American Literature,* ed. Sacvan Bercovitch and Myra Jehlen (New York: Cambridge UP, 1986), 112–3. For a more sustained consideration of the politics of self-reflexive art in contemporary criticism, see my article, "'When Something Goes Queer': Familiarity, Formalism, and Minority Intellectuals in the 1980s," *Yale Journal of Criticism* 6 (spring 1993): 121–41.

Glossary of Critical and Theoretical Terms

ABSENCE The idea, advanced by French theorist Jacques Derrida, that authors are not present in texts and that meaning arises in the absence of any authority guaranteeing the correctness of any one interpretation.

See **Presence and Absence** for a more complete discussion of the concepts of presence and absence.

AFFECTIVE FALLACY *See* **New Criticism, the; Reader-Response Criticism.**

BASE *See* **Marxist Criticism.**

CANON A term used since the fourth century to refer to those books of the Bible that the Christian church accepts as being Holy Scripture — that is, divinely inspired. Books outside the canon (noncanonical books) are referred to as *apocryphal*. *Canon* has also been used to refer to the Saints Canon, the group of people officially recognized by the Catholic Church as saints. More recently, it has been employed to refer to the body of works generally attributed by scholars to a particular author (for example, the Shakespearean canon is currently believed to consist of thirty-seven plays that scholars feel can be definitively attributed to him). Works sometimes attributed to an author, but whose authorship is disputed or otherwise uncertain, are called apocryphal. *Canon* may also refer more generally to those literary works that are "privileged," or given special status, by a culture. Works we tend to think of as classics or

Note: The definitions in this glossary are adapted and/or abridged versions of ones found in *The Bedford Glossary of Critical and Literary Terms,* Second Edition, by Ross Murfin and Supryia M. Ray (© Bedford Books 2003).

as "Great Books"— texts that are repeatedly reprinted in anthologies of literature — may be said to constitute the canon.

Contemporary **Marxist** and **feminist** critics, as well as scholars of **postcolonial literature and postcolonial theory**, have argued that, for political reasons, many excellent works never enter the canon. Canonized works, they claim, are those that reflect — and respect — the culture's dominant ideology or perform some socially acceptable or even necessary form of "cultural work." Attempts have been made to broaden or redefine the canon by discovering valuable texts, or versions of texts, that were repressed or ignored for political reasons. These have been published both in traditional and in nontraditional anthologies. The most outspoken critics of the canon, especially certain critics practicing **cultural criticism**, have called into question the whole concept of canon or "canonicity." Privileging no form of artistic expression, these critics treat cartoons, comics, and soap operas with the same cogency and respect they accord novels, poems, and plays.

CULTURAL CRITICISM, CULTURAL STUDIES Critical approaches with roots in the British cultural studies movement of the 1960s. A movement that reflected and contributed to the unrest of that decade, it both fueled and was fueled by the challenges to tradition and authority apparent in everything from the anti-war movement to the emergence of "hard rock" music. Birmingham University's Centre for Contemporary Cultural Studies, founded by Stuart Hall and Richard Hoggart in 1964, quickly became the locus of the movement, which both critiqued elitist definitions of culture and drew upon a wide variety of disciplines and perspectives.

In Great Britain, the terms *cultural criticism* and *cultural studies* have been used more or less interchangeably, and, to add to the confusion, both terms have been used to refer to two different things. On one hand, they have been used to refer to the analysis of literature (including popular literature) and other art forms in their social, political, or economic contexts; on the other hand, they have been used to refer to the much broader interdisciplinary study of the interrelationships between a variety of cultural **discourses** and practices (such as advertising, gift-giving, and racial categorization). In North America, the term *cultural studies* is usually reserved for this broader type of analysis, whereas *cultural criticism* typically refers to work with a predominantly literary or artistic focus.

Cultural critics examine how literature emerges from, influences, and competes with other forms of discourse (such as religion, science, or advertising) within a given culture. They analyze the social contexts in which a given text was written, and under what conditions it was — and is — produced, disseminated, and read. Like practitioners of cultural studies, they oppose the view that culture refers exclusively to high culture, culture with a capital *C*, seeking to make the term refer to popular, folk, urban, and mass (mass-produced, disseminated, mediated, and consumed) culture, as well as to that culture we associate with so-called "great literature." In other words, cultural critics argue that what we refer to as a culture is in fact a set of interactive *cultures*, alive and changing, rather than static or monolithic. They favor analyzing literary works not as aesthetic objects complete in themselves but as works to be seen in terms of their relationships to other works, to economic conditions, or to broad social discourses (about childbirth, women's education, rural decay, etc.). Cultural critics have emphasized what Michel de Certeau, a French theorist, has called "the practice of everyday life," approaching literature more as an anthropologist than as a traditional "elitist" literary critic.

Several thinkers influenced by **Marxist** theory have powerfully affected the development of cultural criticism and cultural studies. The French philosophical historian Michel Foucault has perhaps had the strongest influence on cultural criticism and **the new historicism**, a type of literary criticism whose evolution has often paralleled that of North American cultural criticism. In works such as *Discipline and Punish* (1975) and *The History of Sexuality* (1976), Foucault studies cultures in terms of power relationships, a focus typical of Marxist thought. Unlike Marxists, however, Foucault did not see power as something exerted by a dominant class over a subservient one. For Foucault, power was more than repressive power: it was a complex of forces generated by the confluence — or conflict — of discourses; it was that which produces what happens. British critic Raymond Williams, best known for his book *Culture and Society: 1780–1950* (1958), influenced the development of cultural studies by arguing that culture is living and evolving rather than fixed and finished, further stating in *The Long Revolution* (1961) that "art and culture are ordinary." Although Williams did not define himself as a Marxist throughout his entire career, he always followed the Marxist practice of viewing culture in relation to **ideologies**, which he defined as the "residual," "dominant," or "emerging" ways in which individuals or social classes view the world.

Recent practitioners of cultural criticism and cultural studies have focused on issues of nationality, race, gender, and sexuality, in addition to those of power, ideology, and class. As a result, there is a significant overlap between cultural criticism and **feminist criticism**, and between cultural studies and African American studies. This overlap can be seen in the work of contemporary feminists such as Gayatri Chakravorty Spivak, Trinh T. Minh-ha, and Gloria Anzaldúa, who stress that although all women are female, they are something else as well (working-class, lesbian, Native American), a facet that must be considered in analyzing their writings. It can also be seen in the writings of Henry Louis Gates, who has shown how black American writers, to avoid being culturally marginalized, have produced texts that fuse the language and traditions of the white Western **canon** with a black vernacular and tradition derived from African and Caribbean cultures.

Interest in race and ethnicity has accompanied a new, interdisciplinary focus on colonial and postcolonial societies, in which issues of race, class, and ethnicity loom large. Scholars of **postcolonial literature and postcolonial theory**, branches of cultural studies inaugurated by Edward Said's book *Orientalism* (1978), have, according to Homi K. Bhabha, revealed the way in which certain cultures (mis)represent others in order to achieve and extend political and social domination in the modern world order. Thanks to the work of scholars like Bhabha and Said, education in general and literary study in particular is becoming more democratic, multicultural, and "decentered" (less patriarchal and Eurocentric) in its interests and emphases.

DECONSTRUCTION Deconstruction involves the close reading of **texts** in order to demonstrate that any given text has irreconcilably contradictory meanings, rather than being a unified, logical whole. As J. Hillis Miller, the preeminent American deconstructor, has explained in an essay entitled "Stevens'

Rock and Criticism as Cure" (1976), "Deconstruction is not a dismantling of the structure of a text, but a demonstration that it has already dismantled itself. Its apparently solid ground is not rock but thin air."

Deconstruction was both created and has been profoundly influenced by the French philosopher of language Jacques Derrida. Derrida, who coined the term *deconstruction,* argues that in Western culture, people tend to think and express their thoughts in terms of *binary oppositions.* Something is white but not black, masculine and therefore not feminine, a cause rather than an effect. Other common and mutually exclusive pairs include beginning/end, conscious/unconscious, **presence/absence**, and speech/writing. Derrida suggests these oppositions are hierarchies in miniature, containing one term that Western culture views as positive or superior and another considered negative or inferior, even if only slightly so. Through deconstruction, Derrida aims to erase the boundary between binary oppositions — and to do so in such a way that the hierarchy implied by the oppositions is thrown into question.

Although its ultimate aim may be to criticize Western logic, deconstruction arose as a response to **structuralism** and to **formalism**. Structuralists believed that all elements of human culture, including literature, may be understood as parts of a system of signs. Derrida did not believe that structuralists could explain the laws governing human signification and thus provide the key to understanding the form and meaning of everything from an African village to Greek myth to a literary text. He also rejected the structuralist belief that texts have identifiable "centers" of meaning, a belief structuralists shared with formalists.

Formalist critics, such as **the New Critics**, assume that a work of literature is a freestanding, self-contained object whose meaning can be found in the complex network of relations between its parts (allusions, images, rhythms, sounds, etc.). Deconstructors, by contrast, see works in terms of their *undecidability.* They reject the formalist view that a work of literary art is demonstrably unified from beginning to end, in one certain way, or that it is organized around a single center that ultimately can be identified. As a result, deconstructors see texts as more radically heterogeneous than do formalists. Formalists ultimately make sense of the ambiguities they find in a given text, arguing that every ambiguity serves a definite, meaningful — and demonstrable — literary function. Undecidability, by contrast, is never reduced, let alone mastered. Though a deconstructive reading can reveal the incompatible possibilities generated by the text, it is impossible for the reader to decide among them.

DIALECTIC Originally developed by Greek philosophers, mainly Socrates and Plato (in *The Republic* and *Phaedrus* [c. 360 BC]), a form and method of logical argumentation that typically addresses conflicting ideas or positions. When used in the plural, dialectics refers to any mode of argumentation that attempts to resolve the contradictions between opposing ideas.

The German philosopher G. W. F. Hegel described dialectic as a process whereby a *thesis,* when countered by an *antithesis,* leads to the *synthesis* of a new idea. Karl Marx and Friedrich Engels, adapting Hegel's idealist theory, used the phrase *dialectical materialism* to discuss the way in which a revolutionary class war might lead to the synthesis of a new socioeconomic order.

In literary criticism, *dialectic* typically refers to the oppositional ideas and/or mediatory reasoning that pervade and unify a given work or group of works. Critics may thus speak of the dialectic of head and heart (reason and passion) in William Shakespeare's plays. The American **Marxist critic** Fredric Jameson has coined the phrase "dialectical criticism" to refer to a Marxist critical approach that synthesizes **structuralist** and **poststructuralist** methodologies.

DIALOGIC *See* **Discourse**.

DISCOURSE Used specifically, (1) the thoughts, statements, or dialogue of individuals, especially of characters in a literary work; (2) the words in, or text of, a **narrative** as opposed to its story line; or (3) a "strand" within a given narrative that argues a certain point or defends a given value system. Discourse of the first type is sometimes categorized as *direct* or *indirect*. Direct discourse relates the thoughts and utterances of individuals and literary characters to the reader unfiltered by a third-person narrator. ("Take me home this instant!" she insisted.) Indirect discourse (also referred to as free indirect discourse) is more impersonal, involving the reportage of thoughts, statements, or dialogue by a third-person narrator. (She told him to take her home immediately.)

More generally, *discourse* refers to the language in which a subject or area of knowledge is discussed or a certain kind of business is transacted. Human knowledge is collected and structured in discourses. Theology and medicine are defined by their discourses, as are politics, sexuality, and literary criticism.

Contemporary literary critics have maintained that society is generally made up of a number of different discourses or *discourse communities,* one or more of which may be dominant or serve the dominant ideology. Each discourse has its own vocabulary, concepts, and rules — knowledge of which constitutes power. The psychoanalyst and **psychoanalytic critic** Jacques Lacan has treated the unconscious as a form of discourse, the patterns of which are repeated in literature. **Cultural critics**, following Soviet critic Mikhail Bakhtin, use the word *dialogic* to discuss the dialogue between discourses that takes place within language or, more specifically, a literary text. Some **poststructuralists** have used *discourse* in lieu of ***text*** to refer to any verbal structure, whether literary or not.

FEMINIST CRITICISM *See* "What Are Feminist and Gender Criticism?" pp. 372–88.

FIGURE, FIGURE OF SPEECH *See* **Trope**.

FORMALISM A general term covering several similar types of literary criticism that arose in the 1920s and 1930s, flourished during the 1940s and 1950s, and are still in evidence today. Formalists see the literary work as an object in its own right. Thus, they tend to devote their attention to its intrinsic nature, concentrating their analyses on the interplay and relationships between the text's essential verbal elements. They study the form of the work (as opposed to its content), although form to a formalist can connote anything from **genre** (for example, one may speak of "the sonnet form") to grammatical or rhetorical structure to the "emotional imperative" that engenders the work's (more mechanical) structure. No matter which connotation of form pertains, however, formalists seek to be objective in their analysis, focusing on the work itself and eschewing external considerations. They pay particular attention to literary devices used in the work and to the patterns these devices establish.

Formalism developed largely in reaction to the practice of interpreting literary **texts** by relating them to "extrinsic" issues, such as the historical circumstances and politics of the era in which the work was written, its philosophical or theological milieu, or the experiences and frame of mind of its author. Although the term *formalism* was coined by critics to disparage the movement, it is now used simply as a descriptive term.

Formalists have generally suggested that everyday language, which serves simply to communicate information, is stale and unimaginative. They argue that "literariness" has the capacity to overturn common and expected patterns (of grammar, of story line), thereby rejuvenating language. Such novel uses of language supposedly enable readers to experience not only language but also the world in an entirely new way.

A number of schools of literary criticism have adopted a formalist orientation, or at least make use of formalist concepts. **The New Criticism**, an American approach to literature that reached its height in the 1940s and 1950s, is perhaps the most famous type of formalism. But Russian formalism was the first major formalist movement; after the Stalinist regime suppressed it in the early 1930s, the Prague Linguistic Circle adopted its analytical methods. The Chicago School has also been classified as formalist insofar as the Chicago Critics examined and analyzed works on an individual basis; their interest in historical material, on the other hand, was clearly not formalist.

GAPS When used by **reader-response critics** familiar with the theories of Wolfgang Iser, the term refers to "blanks" in **texts** that must be filled in by readers. A gap may be said to exist whenever and wherever a reader perceives something to be missing between words, sentences, paragraphs, stanzas, or chapters. Readers respond to gaps actively and creatively, explaining apparent inconsistencies in point of view, accounting for jumps in chronology, speculatively supplying information missing from plots, and resolving problems or issues left ambiguous or "indeterminate" in the text.

Reader-response critics sometimes speak as if a gap actually exists in a text; a gap, of course, is to some extent a product of readers' perceptions. One reader may find a given text to be riddled with gaps while another reader may view that text as comparatively consistent and complete; different readers may find different gaps in the same text. Furthermore, they may fill in the gaps they find in different ways, which is why, a reader-response critic might argue, works are interpreted in different ways.

Although the concept of the gap has been used mainly by reader-response critics, it has also been used by critics taking other theoretical approaches. Practitioners of **deconstruction** might use *gap* when explaining that every text contains opposing and even contradictory **discourses** that cannot be reconciled. **Marxist critics** have used the term *gap* to speak of everything from the gap that opens up between economic base and cultural superstructure to two kinds of conflicts or contradictions found in literary texts. The first of these conflicts or contradictions, they would argue, results from the fact that even realistic texts reflect an **ideology**, within which there are inevitably subjects and attitudes that cannot be represented or even recognized. As a result, readers at the edge or outside of that ideology perceive that something is missing. The second kind of conflict or contradiction within a text results from the fact that works do more than reflect ideology; they are also fictions that, consciously or unconsciously, distance themselves from that ideology.

GAY AND LESBIAN CRITICISM sometimes referred to as *queer theory,* an approach to literature currently viewed as a form of **gender criticism**.

See "What Are Feminist and Gender Criticism?" pp. 372–88.

GENDER CRITICISM *See* "What Are Feminist and Gender Criticism?" pp. 372–88.

GENRE From the French *genre* for "kind" or "type," the classification of literary works on the basis of their content, form, or technique. The term also refers to individual classifications. For centuries works have been grouped and associated according to a number of classificatory schemes and distinctions, such as prose/poem/fiction/drama/lyric, and the traditional classical divisions: comedy/tragedy/lyric/pastoral/epic/satire. More recently, Northrop Frye has suggested that all literary works may be grouped with one of four sets of archetypal myths that are in turn associated with the four seasons; for Frye, the four main genre classifications are comedy (spring), romance (summer), tragedy (fall), and satire (winter). Many more specific genre categories exist as well, such as autobiography, the essay, the Gothic novel, the picaresque novel, the sentimental novel. Current usage is thus broad enough to permit varieties of a given genre (such as the Gothic novel) as well as the novel in general to be legitimately denoted by the term *genre.*

Traditional thinking about genre has been revised and even roundly criticized by contemporary critics. For example, the prose/poem dichotomy has been largely discarded in favor of a lyric/drama/fiction (or narrative) scheme. The more general idea that works of imaginative literature can be solidly and satisfactorily classified according to set, specific categories has also come under attack in recent times.

HEGEMONY Most commonly, one nation's dominance or dominant influence over another. The term was adopted (and adapted) by the Italian **Marxist critic** Antonio Gramsci to refer to the process of consensus formation and to the pervasive system of assumptions, meanings, and values — the web of **ideologies**, in other words — that shapes the way things look, what they mean, and therefore what reality is for the majority of people within a given culture. Although Gramsci viewed hegemony as being powerful and persuasive, he did not believe that extant systems were immune to change; rather, he encouraged people to resist prevailing ideologies, to form a new consensus, and thereby to alter hegemony.

Hegemony is a term commonly used by **cultural critics** as well as by Marxist critics.

IDEOLOGY A set of beliefs underlying the customs, habits, and practices common to a given social group. To members of that group, the beliefs seem obviously true, natural, and even universally applicable. They may seem just as obviously arbitrary, idiosyncratic, and even false to those who adhere to another ideology. Within a society, several ideologies may coexist; one or more of these may be dominant.

Ideologies may be forcefully imposed or willingly subscribed to. Their component beliefs may be held consciously or unconsciously. In either case, they come to form what Johanna M. Smith has called "the unexamined ground of our experience." Ideology governs our perceptions, judgments, and prejudices — our sense of what is acceptable, normal, and deviant. Ideology may cause a revolution; it may also allow discrimination and even exploitation.

Ideologies are of special interest to politically oriented critics of literature because of the way in which authors reflect or resist prevailing views in their texts. Some **Marxist critics** have argued that literary texts reflect and reproduce the ideologies that produced them; most, however, have shown how ideologies are riven with contradictions that works of literature manage to expose and widen. Other Marxist critics have focused on the way in which texts themselves are characterized by **gaps**, conflicts, and contradictions between their ideological and anti-ideological functions.

Fredric Jameson, an American Marxist critic, argues that all thought is ideological, but that ideological thought that knows itself as such stands the chance of seeing through and transcending ideology.

Not all of the politically oriented critics interested in ideology have been Marxists. Certain non-Marxist **feminist critics** have addressed the question of ideology by seeking to expose (and thereby call into question) the patriarchal ideology mirrored or inscribed in works written by men — even men who have sought to counter sexism and break down sexual stereotypes. **New historicists** have been interested in demonstrating the ideological underpinnings not only of literary representations but also of our interpretations of them.

IMAGINARY ORDER *See* **Psychological Criticism and Psychoanalytic Criticism**.

IMPLIED READER *See* **Reader-Response Criticism**.

INTENTIONAL FALLACY *See* **New Criticism, the**.

INTERTEXTUALITY The condition of interconnectedness among texts, or the concept that any text is an amalgam of others, either because it exhibits signs of influence or because its language inevitably contains common points of reference with other texts through such things as allusion, quotation, genre, stylistic features, and even revisions. The critic Julia Kristeva, who popularized and is often credited with coining this term, views any given work as part of a larger fabric of literary **discourse**, part of a continuum including the future as well as the past. Other critics have argued for an even broader use and understanding of the term *intertextuality,* maintaining that literary history per se is too narrow a context within which to read and understand a literary text. When understood this way, *intertextuality* could be used by a **new historicist** or **cultural critic** to refer to the significant interconnectedness between a literary text and contemporary, nonliterary discussions of the issues represented in the literary text. Or it could be used by a **poststructuralist** to suggest that a work of literature can only be recognized and read within a vast field of signs and **tropes** that is like a text and that makes any single text self-contradictory and **undecidable**.

MARXIST CRITICISM A type of criticism in which literary works are viewed as the product of work and whose practitioners emphasize the role of class and **ideology** as they reflect, propagate, and even challenge the prevailing social order. Rather than viewing texts as repositories for hidden meanings, Marxist critics view texts as material products to be understood in broadly historical terms. In short, literary works are viewed as a product of work (and hence of the realm of production and consumption we call economics).

Marxism began with Karl Marx, the nineteenth-century German philosopher best known for writing *Das Kapital* (*Capital*) (1867), the seminal work of the communist movement. Marx was also the first Marxist literary critic, writing critical essays in the 1830s on writers such as Johann Wolfgang von Goethe and William Shakespeare. Even after Marx met Friedrich Engels in 1843 and began collaborating on overtly political works such as *The German Ideology* (1846) and *The Communist Manifesto* (1848), he maintained a keen interest in literature. In *The German Ideology,* Marx and Engels discussed the relationship between the arts, politics, and basic economic reality in terms of a general social theory. Economics, they argued, provides the *base,* or infrastructure, of society, from which a *superstructure* consisting of law, politics, philosophy, religion, and art emerges.

The revolution anticipated by Marx and Engels did not occur in their century, let alone in their lifetime. When it did occur, in 1917, it did so in a place unimagined by either theorist: Russia, a country long ruled by despotic czars but also enlightened by the works of powerful novelists and playwrights including Anton Chekhov, Alexander Pushkin, Leo Tolstoi, and Fyodor Dostoyevsky. Russia produced revolutionaries like Vladimir Lenin, who shared not only Marx's interest in literature but also his belief in its ultimate importance. Leon Trotsky, Lenin's comrade in revolution, took a strong interest in literary matters as well, publishing a book called *Literature and Revolution* (1924) that is still viewed as a classic of Marxist literary criticism.

Of those critics active in the USSR after the expulsion of Trotsky and the triumph of Stalin, two stand out: Mikhail Bakhtin and Georg Lukács. Bakhtin viewed language — especially literary texts — in terms of **discourses** and dialogues. A novel written in a society in flux, for instance, might include an official, legitimate discourse, as well as one infiltrated by challenging comments. Lukács, a Hungarian who converted to Marxism in 1919, appreciated prerevolutionary, realistic novels that broadly reflected cultural "totalities" and were populated with characters representing human "types" of the author's place and time.

Perhaps because Lukács was the best of the Soviet communists writing Marxist criticism in the 1930s and 1940s, non-Soviet Marxists tended to develop their ideas by publicly opposing his. In Germany, dramatist and critic Bertolt Brecht criticized Lukács for his attempt to enshrine realism at the expense not only of the other "isms" but also of poetry and drama, which Lukács had largely ignored. Walter Benjamin praised new art forms ushered in by the age of mechanical reproduction, and Theodor Adorno attacked Lukács for his dogmatic rejection of nonrealist modern literature and for his elevation of content over form.

In addition to opposing Lukács and his overly constrictive **canon**, non-Soviet Marxists took advantage of insights generated by non-Marxist critical theories being developed in post–World War II Europe. Lucien Goldmann, a Romanian critic living in Paris, combined **structuralist** principles with Marx's base-superstructure model in order to show how economics determines the mental structures of social groups, which are reflected in literary texts. Goldmann rejected the idea of individual human genius, choosing instead to see works as the "collective" products of "trans-individual" mental structures. French Marxist Louis Althusser drew on the ideas of the **psychoanalytic** theorist Jacques Lacan and the Italian communist Antonio Gramsci, who discussed the relationship between ideology and **hegemony**, the pervasive system of assumptions and values that shapes the perception of reality for people in a given culture. Althusser's followers included Pierre Macherey, who in *A Theory of Literary Production* (1966) developed Althusser's concept of the relationship between literature and ideology; Terry Eagleton, who proposed an elaborate theory about how history enters texts, which in turn may alter history; and Fredric Jameson, who has argued that form is "but the working out" of content "in the realm of superstructure."

METAPHOR A figure of speech (more specifically a **trope**) that associates two unlike things; the representation of one thing by another. The image (or activity or concept) used to represent or "figure" something else is the **vehicle** of the figure of speech; the thing represented is called the **tenor**. For instance, in the sentence "That child is a mouse," the child is the *tenor,* whereas the mouse is the *vehicle.* The image of a mouse is being used to represent the child, perhaps to emphasize his or her timidity.

Metaphor should be distinguished from **simile**, another figure of speech with which it is sometimes confused. Similes compare two unlike things by using a connective word such as *like* or *as.* Metaphors use no connective word to make their comparison. Furthermore, critics ranging from Aristotle to I. A. Richards have argued that metaphors equate the vehicle with the tenor instead of simply comparing the two.

This identification of vehicle and tenor can provide much additional meaning. For instance, instead of saying, "Last night I read a book," we might say, "Last night I plowed through a book." "Plowed through" (or the activity of plowing) is the vehicle of our metaphor; "read" (or the act of reading) is the tenor, the thing being figured. (As this example shows, neither vehicle nor tenor need be a noun; metaphors may employ other parts of speech.) The increment in meaning through metaphor is fairly obvious. Our audience knows not only *that* we read but also *how* we read, because to read a book in the way that a plow rips through earth is surely to read in a relentless, unreflective way. Note that in the sentence above, a new metaphor — "rips through" — has been used to explain an old one. This serves (which is a metaphor) as an example of just how thick (another metaphor) language is with metaphors!

Metaphors may be classified as *direct* or *implied.* A direct metaphor, such as "That child is a mouse" (or "He is such a doormat!"), specifies both tenor and vehicle. An implied metaphor, by contrast, mentions only the vehicle; the tenor is implied by the context of the sentence or passage. For instance, in the sentence "Last night I plowed through a book" (or "She sliced through traffic"), the tenor — the act of reading (or driving) — can be inferred.

Traditionally, metaphor has been viewed as the principal trope. Other figures of speech include simile, **symbol**, personification, allegory, **metonymy**, synecdoche, and conceit. **Deconstructors** have questioned the distinction between metaphor and metonymy.

METONYMY A figure of speech (more specifically a **trope**), in which one thing is represented by another that is commonly and often physically associated with it. To refer to a writer's handwriting as his or her "hand" is to use a metonymic figure.

Like other figures of speech (such as **metaphor**), metonymy involves the replacement of one word or phrase by another; thus, a monarch might be referred to as "the crown." As narrowly defined by certain contemporary critics, particularly those associated with **deconstruction**, the **vehicle** of a metonym is arbitrarily, not intrinsically, associated with the **tenor**. (There is no special, intrinsic likeness between a crown and a monarch; it's just that crowns traditionally sit on monarchs' heads and not on the heads of university professors.)

More broadly, *metonym* and *metonymy* have been used by recent critics to refer to a wide range of figures. **Structuralists** such as Roman Jakobson, who emphasized the difference between metonymy and metaphor, have recently been challenged by deconstructors, who have further argued that *all* figuration is arbitrary. Deconstructors such as Paul de Man and J. Hillis Miller have questioned the "privilege" granted to metaphor and the metaphor/metonymy distinction or "opposition," suggesting instead that all metaphors are really metonyms.

MODERNISM *See* **Postmodernism**.

NARRATIVE A story or a telling of a story, or an account of a situation or events. Narratives may be fictional or true; they may be written in prose or verse. Some critics use the term even more generally; Brook Thomas, a **new historicist**, has critiqued "narratives of human history that neglect the role human labor has played."

NARRATOLOGY The analysis of the **structural** components of a **narrative**, the way in which those components interrelate, and the relationship between this complex of elements and the narrative's basic story line. Narratology incorporates techniques developed by other critics, most notably Russian **formalists** and French **structuralists**, applying in addition numerous traditional methods of analyzing narrative fiction (for instance, those methods outlined in the "Showing as Telling" chapter of Wayne Booth's *The Rhetoric of Fiction* [1961]). Narratologists treat narratives as explicitly, intentionally, and meticulously constructed systems rather than as simple or natural vehicles for an author's representation of life. They seek to analyze and explain how authors transform a chronologically organized story line into a literary plot. (Story is the raw material from which plot is selectively arranged and constructed.)

Narratologists pay particular attention to such elements as point of view; the relations among story, teller, and audience; and the levels and types of **discourse** used in narratives. Certain narratologists concentrate on the question of whether any narrative can actually be neutral (like a clear pane of glass through which some subject is objectively seen) and on how the practices of a given culture influence the shape, content, and impact of "historical" narratives. Mieke Bal's *Narratology: Introduction to the Theory of Narrative* (1980) is a standard introduction to the narratological approach.

NEW CRITICISM, THE A type of **formalist** literary criticism that reached its height during the 1940s and 1950s, and that received its name from John Crowe Ransom's 1941 book *The New Criticism*. New Critics treat a work of literary art as if it were a self-contained, self-referential object. Rather than basing their interpretations of a **text** on the reader's response, the author's stated intentions, or parallels between the text and historical contexts (such as the author's life), New Critics perform a close reading of the text, concentrating on the internal relationships that give it its own distinctive character or form. New

Critics emphasize that the structure of a work should not be divorced from meaning, viewing the two as constituting a quasi-organic unity. Special attention is paid to repetition, particularly of images or symbols, but also of sound effects and rhythms in poetry. New critics especially appreciate the use of literary devices, such as irony and paradox, to achieve a balance or reconciliation between dissimilar, even conflicting, elements in a text.

Because of the importance placed on close textual analysis and the stress on the text as a carefully crafted, orderly object containing observable formal patterns, the New Criticism has sometimes been called an "objective" approach to literature. New Critics are more likely than certain other critics to believe and say that the meaning of a text can be known objectively. For instance, **reader-response critics** see meaning as a function either of each reader's experience or of the norms that govern a particular interpretive community, and **deconstructors** argue that texts mean opposite things at the same time.

The foundations of the New Criticism were laid in books and essays written during the 1920s and 1930s by I. A. Richards (*Practical Criticism* [1929]), William Empson (*Seven Types of Ambiguity* [1930]), and T. S. Eliot ("The Function of Criticism" [1933]). The approach was significantly developed later, however, by a group of American poets and critics, including R. P. Blackmur, Cleanth Brooks, John Crowe Ransom, Allen Tate, Robert Penn Warren, and William K. Wimsatt. Although we associate the New Criticism with certain principles and terms (such as the *affective fallacy* — the notion that the reader's response is relevant to the meaning of a work — and the *intentional fallacy* — the notion that the author's intention determines the work's meaning — the New Critics were trying to make a cultural statement rather than to establish a critical dogma. Generally Southern, religious, and culturally conservative, they advocated the inherent value of literary works (particularly of literary works regarded as beautiful art objects) because they were sick of the growing ugliness of modern life and contemporary events. Some recent theorists even link the rising popularity after World War II of the New Criticism (and other types of formalist literary criticism such as the Chicago School) to American isolationism. These critics tend to view the formalist tendency to isolate literature from biography and history as symptomatic of American fatigue with wider involvements. Whatever the source of the New Criticism's popularity (or the reason for its eventual decline), its practitioners and the textbooks they wrote were so influential in American academia that the approach became standard in college and even high school curricula through the 1960s and well into the 1970s.

NEW HISTORICISM, THE *See* "What Is the New Historicism?" pp. 412–27.

POSTCOLONIAL LITERATURE AND POSTCOLONIAL THEORY *Postcolonial literature* refers to a body of literature written by authors with roots in countries that were once colonies established by European nations, whereas *postcolonial theory* refers to a field of intellectual inquiry that explores and interrogates the situation of colonized peoples both during and after colonization.

Postcolonial literature includes works by authors with cultural roots in South Asia, Africa, the Caribbean, and other places in which colonial independence movements arose and colonized peoples achieved autonomy in the past hundred years. Works by authors from so-called settler colonies with large white populations of European ancestry — such as Australia, New Zealand, Canada, and Ireland — are sometimes also included. Critical readings of postcolonial literature regularly proceed under the overt influence of *postcolonial theory*, which raises and explores historical, cultural, political, and moral issues surrounding the establishment and disintegration of colonies and the empires they fueled.

The most influential postcolonial theorists are Edward Said, Gayatri Chakravorty Spivak, and Homi K. Bhabha. Said laid the groundwork for the development of postcolonial theory in his book *Orientalism* (1978). In this study, Said, who was influenced by French philosophical historian Michel Foucault, analyzed European **discourses** concerning the exotic, arguing that stereotypes systematically projected on peoples of the East contributed to establishing European domination and exploitation through colonization. Spivak, an Indian scholar, highlighted the ways in which factors such as **gender** and class complicate our understanding of colonial and postcolonial situations. Bhabha, another Indian scholar, has shown how colonized peoples have co-opted and transformed various elements of the colonizing culture, a process he refers to as "hybridity."

POSTMODERNISM A term referring to certain radically experimental works of literature and art produced after World War II. *Postmodernism* is distinguished from *modernism*, which generally refers to the revolution in art and literature that occurred during the period 1910–1930, particularly following the disillusioning experience of World War I. The postmodern era, with its potential for mass destruction and its shocking history of genocide, has evoked a continuing disillusionment similar to that widely experienced during the modern period. Much of postmodernist writing reveals and highlights the alienation of individuals and the meaninglessness of human existence. Postmodernists frequently stress that humans desperately (and ultimately unsuccessfully) cling to illusions of security to conceal and forget the void over which their lives are perched.

Not surprisingly, postmodernists have shared with their modernist precursors the goal of breaking away from traditions (including certain modernist traditions, which, over time, had become institutionalized and conventional to some degree) through experimentation with new literary devices, forms, and styles. While preserving the spirit and even some of the themes of modernist literature (the alienation of humanity, historical discontinuity, etc.), postmodernists have rejected the order that a number of modernists attempted to instill in their work through patterns of allusion, symbol, and myth. They have also taken some of the meanings and methods found in modernist works to extremes that most modernists would have deplored. For instance, whereas modernists such as T. S. Eliot perceived the world as fragmented and represented that fragmentation through poetic language, many also viewed art as a potentially integrating, restorative force, a hedge against the cacophony and chaos that postmodernist works often imitate (or even celebrate) but do not attempt to counter or correct.

Because postmodernist works frequently combine aspects of diverse **genres**, they can be difficult to classify — at least according to traditional schemes of classification. Postmodernists, revolting against a certain modernist tendency toward elitist "high art," have also generally made a concerted effort to appeal to popular culture. Cartoons, music, "pop art," and television have thus become acceptable and even common media for postmodernist artistic expression. Postmodernist literary developments include such genres as the Absurd, the antinovel, concrete poetry, and other forms of avant-garde poetry written in free verse and challenging the **ideological** assumptions of contemporary society. What postmodernist theater, fiction, and poetry have in common is the view (explicit or implicit) that literary language is its own reality, not a means of representing reality.

Postmodernist critical schools include **deconstruction**, whose practitioners explore the undecidability of texts, and **cultural criticism**, which erases the boundary between "high" and "low" culture. The foremost theorist of postmodernism is Francois Lyotard, best known for his book *La Condition postmoderne* (The Postmodern Condition) (1979).

POSTSTRUCTURALISM The general attempt to contest and subvert **structuralism** and to formulate new theories regarding interpretation and meaning, initiated particularly by **deconstructors** but also associated with certain aspects and practitioners of **psychoanalytic**, **Marxist**, **cultural**, **feminist**, and **gender criticism**. Poststructuralism, which arose in the late 1960s, includes such a wide variety of perspectives that no unified poststructuralist theory can be identified. Rather, poststructuralists are distinguished from other contemporary critics by their opposition to structuralism and by certain concepts they embrace.

Structuralists typically believe that meaning(s) in a text, as well as the meaning of a text, can be determined with reference to the system of signification — the "codes" and conventions that governed the text's production and that operate in its reception. Poststructuralists reject the possibility of such "determinate" knowledge. They believe that signification is an interminable and intricate web of associations that continually defers a determinate assessment of meaning. The numerous possible meanings of any word lead to contradictions and ultimately to the dissemination of meaning itself. Thus, poststructuralists contend that texts contradict not only structuralist accounts of them but also themselves.

To elaborate, poststructuralists have suggested that structuralism rests on a number of distinctions — between signifier and signified, self and language (or **text**), texts and other texts, and text and world — that are overly simplistic, if not patently inaccurate, and they have made a concerted effort to discredit these oppositions. For instance, poststructuralists have viewed the self as the subject, as well as the user, of language, claiming that although we may speak through and shape language, it also shapes and speaks through us. In addition, poststructuralists have demonstrated that in the grand scheme of signification, all "signifieds" are also signifiers, for each word exists in a complex web of language and has such a variety of denotations and connotations that no one meaning can be said to be final, stable, and invulnerable to reconsideration and substitution. Signification is unstable and indeterminate, and thus so is meaning. Poststructuralists, who have generally followed their structuralist predecessors in rejecting the traditional concept of the literary "work" (as the work of an individual and purposeful author) in favor of the impersonal "text," have gone structuralists one better by treating texts as "intertexts": crisscrossed strands within the infinitely larger text called language, that weblike system of denotation, connotation, and signification in which the individual text is inscribed and read and through which its myriad possible meanings are ascribed and assigned. (Poststructuralist **psychoanalytic critic** Julia Kristeva coined the term ***intertextuality*** to refer to the fact that a text is a "mosaic" of preexisting texts whose meanings it reworks and transforms.)

Although poststructuralism has drawn from numerous critical perspectives developed in Europe and in North America, it relies most heavily on the work of French theorists, especially Jacques Derrida, Kristeva, Jacques Lacan, Michel Foucault, and Roland Barthes. Derrida's 1966 paper "Structure, Sign and Play in the Discourse of the Human Sciences" inaugurated poststructuralism as a coherent challenge to structuralism. Derrida rejected the structuralist presupposition that texts (or other structures) have self-referential centers that govern their language (or signifying system) without being in any way determined, governed, co-opted, or problematized by that language (or signifying system). Having rejected the structuralist concept of a self-referential center, Derrida also rejected its corollary: that a text's meaning is thereby rendered determinable (capable of being determined) as well as determinate (fixed and reliably correct). Lacan, Kristeva, Foucault, and Barthes have all, in diverse ways, arrived at similarly "antifoundational" conclusions, positing that no foundation or "center" exists that can ensure correct interpretation.

Poststructuralism continues to flourish today. In fact, one might reasonably say that poststructuralism serves as the overall paradigm for many of the most prominent contemporary critical perspectives. Approaches ranging from **reader-response criticism** to **the new historicism** assume the "antifoundationalist" bias of poststructuralism. Many approaches also incorporate the poststructuralist position that texts do not have clear and definite meanings, an argument pushed to the extreme by those poststructuralists identified with deconstruction. But unlike deconstructors, who argue that the process of signification itself produces irreconcilable contradictions, contemporary critics oriented toward other poststructuralist approaches (discourse analysis or Lacanian psychoanalytic theory, for instance) maintain that texts do have real meanings underlying their apparent or "manifest" meanings (which often contradict or cancel out one another). These underlying meanings have been distorted, disguised, or repressed for psychological or **ideological** reasons but can be discovered through poststructuralist ways of reading.

PRESENCE AND ABSENCE Words given a special literary application by French theorist of **deconstruction** Jacques Derrida when he used them to make a distinction between speech and writing. An individual speaking words must actually be present at the time they are heard, Derrida pointed out, whereas an individual writing words is absent at the time they are read. Derrida, who associates presence with "logos" (the creating spoken Word of a present God who "In the beginning" said "Let there be light"), argued that the Western concept of language is *logocentric*. That is, it is grounded in "the metaphysics of presence," the belief that any linguistic system has a basic foundation (what Derrida terms an "ultimate referent"), making possible an identifiable and correct meaning or meanings for any potential statement that can be made within that system. Far from supporting this common Western view of language as logocentric, however, Derrida in fact argues that presence is not an ultimate referent" and that it does not guarantee determinable (capable of being determined) — much less determinate (fixed and reliably correct) — meaning. Derrida thus calls into question the "privileging" of speech and presence over writing and absence in Western thought.

PSYCHOLOGICAL CRITICISM AND PSYCHOANALYTIC CRITICISM *See* "What Is Psychoanalytic Criticism?" pp. 297–308.

QUEER THEORY *See* **Gay and Lesbian Criticism**; "What Are Feminist and Gender Criticism?" pp. 372–388.

READER-RESPONSE CRITICISM *See* "What Is Reader-Response Criticism?" pp. 331–43.

REAL, THE *See* **Psychoanalytic Criticism and Psychological Criticism**.

SEMIOLOGY Another word for **semiotics**, created by Swiss linguist Ferdinand de Saussure in his 1915 book *Course in General Linguistics*.

See **Semiotics**.

SEMIOTICS A term coined by Charles Sanders Peirce to refer to the study of signs, sign systems, and the way meaning is derived from them. **Structuralist** anthropologists, psychoanalysts, and literary critics developed semiotics during the decades following 1950, but much of the pioneering work had been done at the turn of the century by Peirce and by the founder of modern linguistics, Ferdinand de Saussure.

To a semiotician, a sign is not simply a direct means of communication, such as a stop sign or a restaurant sign or language itself. Rather, signs encompass body language (crossed arms, slouching), ways of greeting and parting (handshakes, hugs, waves), artifacts, and even articles of clothing. A sign is anything that conveys information to others who understand it based upon a system of codes and conventions that they have consciously learned or unconsciously internalized as members of a certain culture. Semioticians have often used concepts derived specifically from linguistics, which focuses on language, to analyze all types of signs.

Although Saussure viewed linguistics as a division of semiotics (semiotics, after all, involves the study of all signs, not just linguistic ones), much semiotic theory rests on Saussure's linguistic terms, concepts, and distinctions. Semioticians subscribe to Saussure's basic concept of the linguistic sign as containing a *signifier* (a linguistic "sound image" used to represent some more abstract concept) and *signified* (the abstract concept being represented). They have also found generally useful his notion that the relationship between signifiers and signifieds is arbitrary; that is, no intrinsic or natural relationship exists between them, and meanings we derive from signifiers are grounded in the differences among signifiers themselves. Particularly useful are Saussure's concept of the *phoneme* (the smallest basic speech sound or unit of pronunciation) and his idea that phonemes exist in two kinds of relationships: diachronic and synchronic.

A phoneme has a diachronic, or "horizontal," relationship with those other phonemes that precede and follow it (as the words appear, left to right, on this page) in a particular usage, utterance, or **narrative** — what Saussure called *parole* (French for "word"). A phoneme has a synchronic, or "vertical," relationship with the entire system of language within which individual usages, utterances, or narratives have meaning — what Saussure called *langue* (French for "tongue," as in "native tongue," meaning "language"). *Up* means what it means in English because those of us who speak the language are plugged into the same system (think of it as a computer network where different individuals access the same information in the same way at a given time). A principal tenet of semiotics is that signs, like words, are not significant in themselves, but instead have meaning only in relation to other signs and the entire system of signs, or *langue*. Meaning is not inherent in the signs themselves, but is derived from the differences among signs.

Given that semiotic theory underlies structuralism, it is not surprising that many semioticians have taken a broad, structuralist approach to signs, studying a variety of phenomena ranging from rites of passage to methods of preparing and consuming food to understand the cultural codes and conventions they reveal. Because of the broad-based applicability of semiotics, furthermore, structuralist anthropologists such as Claude Lévi-Strauss, literary critics such as Roland Barthes, and **psychoanalytic theorists** such as Jacques Lacan and Julia Kristeva have made use of semiotic theories and practices. The affinity between semiotics and structuralist literary criticism derives from the emphasis placed on *langue,* or system. Structuralist critics were reacting against **formalists** and their method of focusing on individual words as if meanings did not depend on anything external to the text.

See also **Structuralism**.

SIMILE *See* **Metaphor; Trope**.

STRUCTURALISM A theory of humankind whose proponents attempted to show systematically, even scientifically, that all elements of human culture, including literature, may be understood as parts of a system of **signs**. Critic Robert Scholes has described structuralism as a reaction to "'modernist' alienation and despair."

European structuralists such as Roman Jakobson, Claude Lévi-Strauss, and Roland Barthes (before his shift toward poststructuralism) attempted to develop a **semiology**, or **semiotics** (science of signs). Barthes, among others, sought to recover literature and even language from the isolation in which they had been studied and to show that the laws that govern them govern all signs, from road signs to articles of clothing.

Structuralism was heavily influenced by linguistics, especially by the pioneering work of linguist Ferdinand de Saussure. Particularly useful to structuralists were Saussure's concept of the phoneme (the smallest basic speech sound or unit of pronunciation) and his idea that phonemes exist in two kinds of relationships: diachronic and synchronic. A phoneme has a diachronic, or "horizontal," relationship with those other phonemes that precede and follow it (as the words appear, left to right, on this page) in a particular usage, utterance, or narrative — what Saussure called *parole* (French for "word"). A phoneme has a synchronic, or "vertical," relationship with the entire system of language within which individual usages, utterances, or narratives have meaning — what Saussure called *langue* (French for "tongue," as in "native tongue," meaning language). *An* means what it means in English because those of us who speak the language are plugged into the same system (think of it as a computer network where different individuals can access the same information in the same way at a given time).

Following Saussure, Lévi-Strauss, an anthropologist, studied hundreds of myths, breaking them into their smallest meaningful units, which he called "mythemes." Removing each from its diachronic relations with other mythemes in a single myth (such as the myth of Oedipus and his mother), he vertically aligned those mythemes that he found to be homologous (structurally correspondent). He then studied the relationships within as well as between vertically aligned columns, in an attempt to understand scientifically, through ratios and proportions, those thoughts and processes that humankind has shared, both at one particular time and across time. Whether Lévi-Strauss was studying the structure of myths or the structure of villages, he looked for recurring, common elements that transcended the differences within and among cultures.

Structuralists followed Saussure in preferring to think about the overriding *langue,* or language, of myth, in which each mytheme and mytheme-constituted myth fits meaningfully, rather than about isolated individual *paroles,* or narratives. Structuralists also followed Saussure's lead in believing that sign systems must be understood in terms of **binary oppositions** (a proposition later disputed by poststructuralist Jacques Derrida). In analyzing myths and texts to find basic structures, structuralists found that opposite terms modulate until they are finally resolved or reconciled by some intermediary third term. Thus a structuralist reading of Milton's *Paradise Lost* (1667) might show that the war between God and the rebellious angels becomes a rift between God and sinful, fallen man, a rift that is healed by the Son of God, the mediating third term.

Although structuralism was largely a European phenomenon in its origin and development, it was influenced by American thinkers as well. Noam Chomsky, for instance, who powerfully influenced structuralism through works such as *Reflections on Language* (1975), identified and distinguished between "surface structures" and "deep structures" in language and linguistic literatures, including **texts**.

SYMBOL Something that, although it is of interest in its own right, stands for or suggests something larger and more complex — often an idea or a range of interrelated ideas, attitudes, and practices.

Within a given culture, some things are understood to be symbols: the flag of the United States is an obvious example, as are the five intertwined Olympic rings. More subtle cultural symbols might be the river as a symbol of time and the journey as a symbol of life and its manifold experiences. Instead of appropriating symbols generally used and understood within their culture, writers often create their own symbols by setting up a complex but identifiable web of associations in their works. As a result, one object, image, person, place, or action suggests others, and may ultimately suggest a range of ideas.

A symbol may thus be defined as a **metaphor** in which the **vehicle** — the image, activity, or concept used to represent something else — represents many related things (or **tenors**), or is broadly suggestive. The urn in John Keats's "Ode on a Grecian Urn" (1820) suggests interrelated concepts, including art, truth, beauty, and timelessness.

Symbols have been of particular interest to **formalists**, who study how meanings emerge from the complex, patterned relationships among images in a work, and **psychoanalytic critics**, who are interested in how individual authors and the larger culture both disguise and reveal unconscious fears and desires through symbols. Recently, French **feminist critics** have also focused on the symbolic, suggesting that, as wide-ranging as it seems, symbolic language is ultimately rigid and restrictive. They have favored **semiotic** language and writing — writing that neither opposes nor hierarchically ranks qualities or elements of reality nor symbolizes one thing but not another in terms of a third — contending that semiotic language is at once more fluid, rhythmic, unifying, and feminine.

SYMBOLIC ORDER *See* **Psychological Criticism and Psychoanalytic Criticism; Symbol**.

TENOR *See* **Metaphor; Metonymy; Symbol**.

TEXT From the Latin *texere,* meaning "to weave," a term that may be defined in a number of ways. Some critics restrict its use to the written word, although they may apply the term to objects ranging from a poem to the words in a book to a book itself to a Biblical passage used in a sermon to a written transcript of an oral statement or interview. Other critics include nonwritten material in the designation text, as long as that material has been isolated for analysis.

French **structuralist** critics took issue with the traditional view of literary compositions as "works" with a form intentionally imposed by the author and a meaning identifiable through analysis of the author's use of language. These critics argued that literary compositions are texts rather than works, texts being the product of a social institution they called *écriture* (writing). By identifying compositions as texts rather than works, structuralists denied them the personalized character attributed to works wrought by a particular, unique author. Structuralists believed not only that a text was essentially impersonal, the confluence of certain preexisting attributes of the social institution of writing, but that any interpretation of the text should result from an impersonal *lecture* (reading). This *lecture* included reading with an active awareness of how the linguistic system functions.

The French writer and theorist Roland Barthes, a structuralist who later turned toward **poststructuralism**, distinguished text from *work* in a different way, characterizing a text as open and a work as closed. According to Barthes, works are bounded entities, conventionally classified in the **canon**, whereas texts engage readers in an ongoing relationship of interpretation and reinterpretation. Barthes further divided texts into two categories: *lisible* (readerly) and *scriptible* (writerly). Texts that are *lisible* depend more heavily on convention, making their interpretation easier and more predictable. Texts that are *scriptible* are generally experimental, flouting or seriously modifying traditional rules. Such texts cannot be interpreted according to standard conventions.

TROPE One of the two major divisions of **figures of speech** (the other being *rhetorical figures*). Trope comes from a word that literally means "turning"; to trope (with figures of speech) is, figuratively speaking, to turn or twist some word or phrase to make it mean something else. **Metaphor**, **metonymy**, simile, personification, and synecdoche are sometimes referred to as the principal tropes.

UNDECIDABILITY *See* **Deconstruction**.

VEHICLE *See* **Metaphor; Metonymy; Symbol**.

About the Contributors

THE EDITOR

Ross C Murfin, general editor of the *Case Studies in Contemporary Criticism* and volume editor of Joseph Conrad's *Heart of Darkness* and Nathaniel Hawthorne's *The Scarlet Letter* in the series, was provost and vice president for academic affairs from 1996 until 2005 at Southern Methodist University, where he is now professor of English. He has taught at the University of Miami, Yale University, and the University of Virginia, and has published scholarly studies of Joseph Conrad, Thomas Hardy, and D. H. Lawrence.

THE CRITICS

Shari Benstock is professor of English at the University of Miami, where she has served as director of the Women's Series Program. She is editor of a series on feminist criticism, *Reading Women Writing*, published by Cornell University Press. Her books include *Women of the Left Bank: Paris, 1900–1940* (1987); *Textualizing the Feminine: On the Limits of Genre* (1991); and a biography of Edith Wharton, *No Gifts from Chance* (1994). She is coauthor of *A Handbook of Literary Feminisms* (2002).

Joanne Feit Diehl is professor of English at the University of California at Davis, where she teaches literary theory and American literature. She is author of *Dickinson and the Romantic Imagination* (1981), *Women Poets and the American Sublime* (1990), and *Elizabeth Bishop and Marianne Moore: The Psychodynamics of Creativity* (1993).

Stephen Railton is a professor of American literature at the University of Virginia and is a member of the Advisory Board of *Nineteenth-Century Literature.* He has published numerous books and articles on American literature, including *Authorship and Audience: Literary Performance in the American Renaissance* (1991). Professor Railton has also won awards for the creation of two Web-based electronic archives that use electronic technology for teaching and studying American literature: *Twain in His Times* and *Uncle Tom's Cabin & American Culture,* which won the Lincoln Prize.

The late **Lora Romero** was a professor of nineteenth- and twentieth-century American fiction and American Studies at Stanford University. Professor Romero was an active member of the American Studies Association and the recipient of numerous awards, including a Ford Foundation Postdoctoral Fellowship and the Forester Prize for the best article published in American literature in 1991. Her case study of classic American novelists, *Home Fronts: Domesticity and Its Critics in the Antebellum United States,* was published in 1997 by Duke University Press.

Brook Thomas is a professor of English and comparative literature at the University of California, Irvine, where he also serves as Chair of the Department of English. He has been a Von Humboldt Fellow and Woodrow Wilson Center Fellow. He has also authored several articles and books, including *American Literary Realism and the Failed Promise of Contract* (1997), *The New Historicism and Other Old-Fashioned Topics* (1991), and *Cross-examinations of Law and Literature: Cooper, Hawthorne, Stowe, and Melville* (1987).

(continued from p. iv)